A Tale of Origins

A Tale of Origins

Book two of The Black Throne trilogy

To those who love the villain as much as I; let their stories be
known and enjoyed, but not forgiven

Content Warning:

This trilogy is meant for mature audiences.

If you cannot handle or do not like the following: gore, blood, death, child abuse, domestic abuse, torture, implications of insanity, alcoholism, implications of suicide, near sexual assault, slavery, LGBTQ+ representation, and consensual sex, stop reading here.

Seriously. *The Black Throne* was light in comparison to what lies ahead. Consider this as your second warning.

For everyone else, enjoy.

Character Index

Rulers

Anselm Oakens—King of Oakens Region, father of Leontios, barbarian

Basia Zeldine—Queen of Zeldine's Region, followed tradition by slaying the previous ruler, orc

Caroline Boon—Queen of Jared's Region, close friend of Thorn, created and hosts the Celebration of Peace, elf

Damir 'Reap'—King of Hordes Region, husband of Shavon, father of Rohit, Lilija, and Vendetta, demon, deceased

Decimus Cain—King of Cain's Region, tenth generation of rulers, friend of Surin, human

Emil 'Reap'—King of Hordes Region, husband of Vendetta, father of Elias, Draga, Inyene, Odovacar, Sok, Rayen, and Malice, figurehead, demon

Holister Castine—King of Alucard's Region, husband of Vesh, father of Magnus and Padma, angel

Jaci Castine—King of Alucard's Region, father of Holister, grandfather of Magnus and Padma, angel, death by disease

Ko Wolfgang—King of Wolfgang's Region, eldest of four siblings, friend of Yoon Woo, wolf beastman

Shavon 'Reap'—Queen of Hordes Region, wife of Damir, mother of Rohit, Lilija, and Vendetta, demon, deceased

Surin Raelle—King of Raelle's Region, friend of Decimus, fishman

Thorn Maziar—King of Maziar's Region, close friend of Caroline, second eldest ruler, dark elf

Thusitha Cain—Former King of Cain's Region, father of Decimus, human

Valentine Ezhil—Ruler of Florence's Region, third eldest ruler, parent of Nikanor, fairy

Vendetta 'Reap'—Queen of Hordes Region, daughter of Damir and Shavon, younger sister of Rohit and Lilija, wife of Emil, mother of Elias, Draga, Inyene, Odovacar, Sok, Rayen, and Malice, demon

Violet Yeager—Queen of Yeager's Region, dwarf

Yoon Woo Braxton—King of Braxton's Region, father of one, friend of Ko, giant

Royals of Hordes Region

Alkeim Brannon—First sword to Vendetta, Knight of Hordes Region, elder brother of Felim, father of Shohre, orc

Aglaia Kumar—First sword to Sok, dwarf

Buhle—Member of Toussaint's Squad, fairy

Charikleia Tor   General of Hordes Region, friend of Alkeim, human

Duncan—Member of Toussaint's Squad, half orc half beastman

Elias 'Reap'—Commander of Hordes Region, eldest son of Vendetta and Emil, eldest brother of Draga, Inyene, Odovacar, Sok, Rayen, and Malice, demon, deceased

Eunice Baklav—First sword to Malice, wife of Helle, Knight of Hordes Region, bear beastman

Felim Brannon—First sword to Emil, Royal of Hordes Region, younger brother of Alkeim, orc

Issur Laska—Royal of Hordes Region, former Head of House Laska of Mondlesgrave, wife of Fausta, father of Zephyrus and Ester, half demon half fairy

Iqaluk—Member of Toussaint's squad, half fishman half barbarian

Jayesh—Royal of Hordes Region, member of Malice's warband, human

Nikanor—First sword to Odovacar, first sword to Malice, Knight of Hordes Region, bastard son of Valentine, fairy

Nor Leroux—Member of Ushas' squad, demon

Odovacar 'Reap'—General of Hordes Region, second eldest son of Vendetta and Emil, second eldest brother of Sok, Rayen, and Malice, younger brother of Elias, Draga, and Inyene, demon

Sonam—Member of Toussaint's Squad, Royal of Hordes Region, dwarf

Tumelo—Member of Toussaint's Squad, Royal of Hordes Region, demon

Toussaint—Leader of a Squad, Royal of Hordes Region, angel

Ushas—Leader of a Squad, Royal of Hordes Region, fishman

Xenon Lavoie—First sword to Rayen, Knight of Hordes Region, fishman

Nobles of Hordes Region

Balios—Lord of Bextierther, human

Freya Venczel—Lady of Khuomouth, appointed noble by Malice, previously sworn to Vendetta, dark elf

Hyacinthia Valor—Former noble of Ryzion, friend of Hordes, mother of Nyx, grandmother of Malice, Berhane, and Juno, demon partial human

Sophronius—Lord of Ryzion, youngest noble of Hordes Region, fairy

Thutmose—Lord of Estera, demon

Yvonne Apostolov—Lady of Mondlesgrave, younger sister of Karlisle, aunt of Malice, Berhane, and Juno, demon

Others

Annabeth—Servant of Hordes Kingdom, caretaker of Malice, human

Berhane Reap—Eldest son of Nyx and Karlisle, 'deceased'

Blodwen Pretorius—Witch doctor of Vendetta, wife of Tendai, mother of Kiran, cow beastman

Draga 'Reap'—Advisor of Vendetta, eldest daughter of Vendetta and Emil, younger sister of Elias, eldest sister of Inyene, Odovacar, Sok, Rayen, and Malice, demon

Ester Laska—Daughter of Issur and Fausta, younger sister of Zephyrus, demon partial fairy

Fausta Laska—Shipwright, wife of Issur, mother of Zephyrus and Ester, demon

Heba—Personal guard of Freya, hails from Yeager's Region, half giant half dwarf

Helle Baklav—Seamstress, wife of Eunice, human

Inyene 'Reap'—Executioner of Hordes Kingdom, second eldest daughter of Vendetta and Emil, younger sister of Elias and Draga, elder sister of Odovacar, Sok, Rayen, and Malice, demon

Juno Reap—Daughter of Nyx and Karlisle, younger sister of Berhane and Malice, demon partial human

Karlisle Apostolov—Former noble of Mondlesgrave, husband of Nyx, father of Berhane, Malice, and Juno, demon

Kiran Pretorius—Advisor and regent to Malice, elder brother of Malice, son of Tendai and Blodwen, cow and bison beastman

Lilija 'Reap'—Princess of Hordes Region, daughter of Damir and Shavon, younger sister of Rohit, elder sister of Vendetta, second in the line of succession for Hordes Region, demon, deceased

Malice Reap—King of Hordes Region, youngest son of Vendetta and Emil, youngest brother of Elias, Draga, Inyene, Odovacar, Sok, Rayen, and Kiran, grandson of Hordes and Hyacinthia, eldest son of Nyx and Karlisle, elder brother of Juno, devil

Nyx Reap—Former heir of Hordes Region, daughter of Hordes and Hyacinthia, wife of Karlisle, mother of Berhane, Malice, and Juno, demon partial human

Priscilla Wheelock—Eldest servant of Hordes Kingdom, sole elder of Hordes Kingdom, fairy partial human

Quinci Genkov—Traveler, hails from Guruhm, elf

Rayen 'Reap'—Youngest daughter of Vendetta and Emil, twin of Sok, youngest sister of Elias, Draga, Inyene, and Odovacar, elder sister of Malice, demon

Rohit 'Reap'—Prince of Hordes Region, first in the line of succession for Hordes Region, son of Damir and Shavon, eldest brother of Lilija and Vendetta, demon, deceased

Rosalina—Servant of Hordes Kingdom, lover of Kiran, human

Shevanti—Servant of Hordes Kingdom, caretaker of Malice, demon

Shohre Brannon—Daughter of Alkeim, orc

Sok 'Reap'—Second youngest son of Vendetta and Emil, younger brother of Elias, Draga, Inyene, and Odovacar, elder brother of Malice, demon

Tendai Pretorius—Doctor of Hordes Kingdom, husband of Blodwen, father of Kiran, bison beastman

Una—Midwife of Nyx, sheep beastman

Zephyrus Laska—Eldest son of Issur and Fausta, elder brother of Ester, Royal of Hordes Region, friend of Malice, demon partial fairy

Alucard's Region

Abel—Lord of Ntesal, fairy

Chestimir—Lord of Ivory's Kingdom, human

Gareth Birch—Right-hand man of Magnus and Holister, Royal Knight rank S, dark elf

Gazika—Lord of Cytor, husband of Zoja, half orc half angel

Iset—Lady of Anddulia, eldest noble of Alucard's Region, half angel half dwarf

Joan Bosch—Lord of Liotkin, barbarian

Magnus Castine—Eldest son of Holister and Vesh, elder brother of Padma, Prince of Alucard's Region, half angel half human

Padma Castine—Youngest son of Holister and Vesh, younger brother of Magnus, half angel half human

Thais Priek—Lady of the Kingdom of Phoenix, youngest noble of Alucard's Region, angel

Vesh Castine—Mother of Magnus and Padma, wife of Holister, former prostitute, human

Yeong-Suk Dahl—Elder of Alucard's Kingdom, regent of Alucard's Region, giant

Zoja—Lady of Cytor, wife of Gazika, angel

Founding Rulers

Alucard Castine—Fourth great grandfather of Magnus, lover of Hordes, gathered the founding rulers and ended the War of Species, angel, killed by Coatliris

Amori Oakens—Shared the designs of boats, devised the *Ways to Kingship*, barbarian, killed by Coatliris

Bilge Cain—Creator of the Kings Summit, human, killed by Coatliris

Dieu Maziar—Grandfather of Thorn, dark elf, killed by Coatliris

Florence Ezhil—Great grandfather of Valentine, created the *Minding the Peace* law, killed by Coatliris

Hordes Reap—Father of Nyx, friend of Hyacinthia, grandfather of Berhane, Malice, and Juno, lover of Alucard, gathered the founding rulers and ended the War of Species, demon, killed by Coatliris

Hyeon Braxton—Outlawed slavery, predecessor of Yoon Woo, giant, killed by Coatliris

Ikram Yeager—Created the law of *Independence*, predecessor of Violet, dwarf, killed by Coatliris

Jared Boon—Leader of the resistance before joining Hordes, grandfather of Caroline, elf, killed by Coatliris

Kamen Zeldine—Created the *Crime of Region* law, orc, killed by Coatliris

Lior Raelle—Created the first maps of Vinyamar, fishman, killed by Coatliris

Slava Wolfgang—Established the first trading routes of Vinyamar, predecessor of Ko, wolf beastman, killed by Coatliris

Species Index

Angel—Angels are an immortal race. It is rare for an angel to have a single set of eyes. It is also rare for an angel to be born without feathered wings or to be born wingless. Angels are descendants of archangels. One bloodline is a direct descendent of archangels: the Castine bloodline.

Barbarian—A barbarian's lifespan is one hundred twenty to one hundred fifty years of age. Barbarians are the sister race to humans. Barbarians are physically superior to humans. Tattoos hold a significant meaning to the barbarian culture.

Beastman—Beastmen are a humanoid race; beasts with human-like features, or vice versa. Beastmen are land mammals such as wolves, bears, rabbits, and so on. The human characteristics vary per person. Beastmen's lifespan is fifty to ninety years of age.

Dark Elf—Dark elves are an immortal race. The complexion of a dark elf stays on the desaturated purple to blue spectrum, unless mixed. Dark elves are the sister race to elves. Ears are shorter and pointed downward. Dark elves are descendants of high elves.

Demon—Demons are an immortal race. A demon's appearance varies per person. It is rare for a demon to be born with feathered wings. Demons can control certain aspects of their appearance, such as horns, wings, tails, and/or claws. Demons are descendants of devils. Three bloodlines are direct descendants of devils: the Reap, Valor, and Apostolov bloodlines.

Dwarf—Dwarves' lifespan is one hundred eighty to two hundred years of age. A dwarf's height will not exceed one-hundred fifty centimeters. Dwarves are descendants of Trolls. Worship toward different deities and their ruler is a significant practice in the homeland of Yeager's Region.

Elf—Elves are an immortal race. Ears are long and pointed upward. Elves are the sister race to dark elves. Elves are descendants of high elves. Elves live off and respect the land. Most villages and communities in the homeland of Jared's Region are deeply connected to one another and often come together for song and dance.

Fairy—Faires are an immortal species. Skin tone varies per person, but it is rare for them to have vibrant skin like a demon would. The majority of fairies have wings, said wings mirror that of an insect. Faires are a naturally androgynous and intersex race. Faires are descendants of Nymphs. Wearing clothes in the homeland of Florence's Region is seen as restrictive.

Fishman—Fishmen are a humanoid race; sea creatures with human-like features, or vice versa. The human characteristics vary per person. Rarely will a fishman be born without gills even if they are mixed. Fishmen's lifespan is eighty to one hundred thirty years of age.

Giant—Giant's lifespan is one hundred forty to one hundred eighty years of age. A giant's height will not exceed two-hundred fifty centimeters and will not dip below one-hundred ninety-five centimeters. Giants are descendants of Titans. Respect and tradition are significant values in the homeland of Braxton's Region.

Human—Human's lifespan is eighty to one hundred ten years of age. Humans are the sister race to Barbarians. Humans have adopted various ways of life from the other species. In the homeland of Cain's Region, hunting for game is a significant part of human culture.

Orc—Orc's lifespan is one hundred to two hundred years of age. Orc's skin tone stays within the green spectrum. The size of an orc's tusks varies per person. Orcs are descendants of Ogres. Warriors and battles hold a high significance in orc culture.

God—Gods are an immortal species. Across the world, there are a total of six gods inhabiting six continents.

Voident—Voident's are born from their god. Voidents can resurrect so long as their god is alive. Those born from Coatliris are creatures of darkness. There are three tiers of intelligence: the mindless, the masters, and the commanders. The hierarchy also determines appearance.

Goliath—Goliath's are the ancestors of Titans and Giants. Goliath's can reach the size of twenty-four meters.

Devil—Devils are the ancestors of Demons. Devils are an immortal species.

Archangel—Archangels are the ancestors of angels. Archangels are an immortal species. They were known to inhabit the Barren Circle and had built the castle at its center as a place of worship.

VINYAMAR

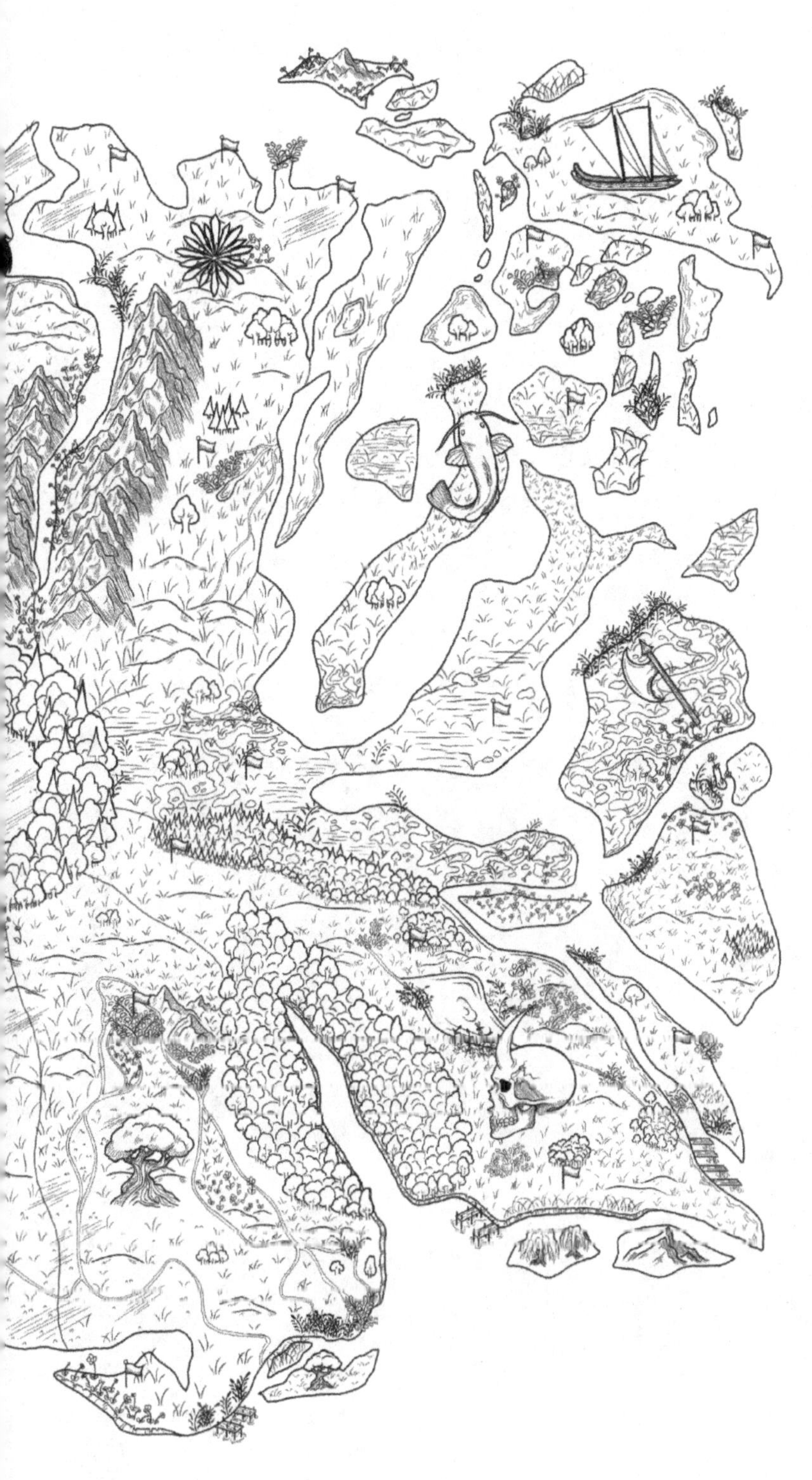

Prologue

Tears are priceless, her mother had told her.

Vendetta had sold countless vials with a single, salty droplet to those desperate enough to hold the ocean in their hands. Those desperate enough to fool themselves into thinking a tear was the sea captured. As a child, however, she had idolized the words of wisdom her mother bestowed upon her. No matter the circumstance, whether it was the death of her beloved pet or scraping her knee from a fall, she shed not a single tear. They were priceless, after all.

Yet, tears blurred her vision of the corridor, and her heart ached as if pumping blood had become far too strenuous.

She had meticulously laid out her plan like figurines on a map while discussing military tactics—of which her mother disapproved. Said it was unbefitting of a princess. There were many of her mother's views Vendetta had come to disagree with. The state of Hordes Region and Vinyamar being one of them.

The gothic castle of Hordes Kingdom—the very heart of Hordes Region—resonated the clacks of Vendetta's heels as she strode through the second floors eastern wing. The halls were dimly lit, the smell of linseed oil from torches and lamps hinting the air. It was late, the last she checked, past midnight. The corridors were void of life; all servants having already retired. In between the clacks of her shoes, the subtle plop of blood dripping onto the marble floor sounded. Her grip on the dagger gifted by her father tightened.

Third in line, Vendetta would not so much as touch the throne with the tip of her nail for centuries to come. That time would lengthen considerably if her siblings bore children. While she sat and waited dutifully for her chance, those as competent as fish in the sky would rule and continue to ruin the region.

Stopping, Vendetta faced her elder brother's bedchamber. She recalled the look of devastation on her elder sister's face as Vendetta's magic crushed every organ in her body. Pain stole the color from Lilija's complexion, robbed her of breath and coherency before death had taken her. Mother's blood was still on Vendetta's hands, underneath her nails, staining the purity of her pale lavender skin. Fathers dripped fresh from her dagger, ichor that would ruin the blade if she were to leave it.

Vendetta hadn't bothered knocking when she opened the door. Rohit jumped to a start in his bed at the room's center, crimson hair tousled, eyes squinted at the light pouring from the doorway. A wall of musk and cedar hit Vendetta as she stepped beyond the threshold. Clothes lay strewn about the ground; papers clustered the surfaces of his desk and tables. Cleanliness was never his strong suit.

"Vendetta?" Rohit said, voice soft with weariness he had not yet shaken off. "Is that you?"

"It is," she said, crossing the room to his bedside. Where there were not discarded garments, fur rugs kept the cloudy marble floor hidden, silencing her footfalls.

"Is something the matter?" Stretching, Rohit swung his legs over the edge of the mattress, his night clothes wrinkled.

"You know as well as I," Vendetta spoke, her tone as she had practiced, cold and emotionless. Her tears would not be known through her voice. "Who ought to have claim over the throne."

Rohit, with those black orbs, studied her. "I do," he said slowly.

"You will not take this personally."

His eyes finally settled on her bloodied dagger. "I will." He scowled and, as a prince might, his shoulders rolled to correct his slouched posture. "Are we not kin? Blood? Siblings, you, Lilija, and I? Need our death be a part of your reign when you could have our service if you desire the throne so badly?"

There was a point to his words, Vendetta knew, but she could not undo what she had already done. Nor would she want to. Lilija was far too naïve to see the fragile state Hordes Region was in. Economy was plummeting, agriculture was difficult to foster, trade was practically nonexistent, and peace between the other regions was palpably weak. The people wore smiles; therefore, everything was well and right. She had gotten that mindset from Mother. Meanwhile, Father and Rohit only knew how to swing their blades and feed the rulers sweet nothings.

For years, Vendetta had tried to get them to see the error in their ways. "None of you would listen. You've left me little choice." Vendetta added, "Besides, Lilija is already dead. Mother and Father as well."

Rohit stiffened, every muscle tensing as sorrow darkened his angular features. They looked much alike, Vendetta and her siblings, mirrors of one another. She had the same eyes, red hair, and those sharp attributes.

He rose to stand toe-to-toe with Vendetta. It was only then he must've seen the wetness streaming down her face. He turned away as his eyes screwed shut, and his mouth became a hard line, fists bunching at his sides.

Vendetta accepted the reason for her tears and let herself cry, for she would not do it again.

"Do not make this difficult," Vendetta said, her voice as level as it would be if she were addressing a servant. "Receive the gift it is to die by my hand. Lay your life down for the future of Hordes Region."

"For your selfish desire!" he hissed, his sclerae a stinging red.

"Power is necessary if I am to rule over this region," Vendetta countered, patience wearing thin like a frayed string. "Complacency will get us nowhere, will not allow us to advance. The rulers are breathing down our necks. They want our downfall. You and Lilija seem happy to give it to them. I am not."

"Complacency?" he echoed. "This is a time of peace. The regions have found common ground, yet you wish to rouse old feuds, is that it?"

"It is not."

"Then what is it you desire enough to kill my sister and parents, Vendetta?"

To speak as if they were not her kin as well was as if he drove the dagger in her hands into her core. She banished the hurt crawling up her throat, bound to reveal itself when she spoke, to the pits of her stomach. "I want power."

"You have it!"

"Over this small hunk of land. What of the other regions? My word means little more than a feeble request for the rulers to grant or deny."

Reeling, Rohit's expression shifted once more. Realization dawned on her brother's face. "You want an empire," he said.

"It is time the lands unite as one and I will be at the head of it," she said. "You will only be a hindrance."

They stared at one another for a time. Defiance had blazed in Lilija's eyes; the very same fire burned strongly in Rohit's gaze. Perhaps she would have her empire *and* her family. It would simply not be in this life. Which meant, with her immortality, Vendetta chose what mattered most right now and what would matter in the centuries to come.

"You will not be the death of me." Rohit's movements were swift, too fast for Vendetta to track until his hand met his sternum, red seeping through his light green shirt.

Water splashed when he released his grip, and he teetered. Vendetta caught him, guiding him to the floor, dumbfounded.

"Why?" she heard herself say, her heartbeat pounding louder and louder in her ears.

Ichor bubbled at the corners of his mouth, metal a growing stench burning her nostrils. He smiled softly, warmly, as he always had, as if he were truly pleased with himself and with Vendetta's reaction. Lifting his hand, the back of his fingers brushed her cheek.

"I pray your defeat will be most bittersweet, Vendetta," he said, voice like honey. "That your power and greed consume you."

Awe gave way to anger, a boiling rage coursing through her veins.

"I pray your death will bring unfathomable agony," he went on, red dripping down his face and neck as her dress stuck to her legs, his blood pooling beneath them. "For that, my dearest sister, is the least you deserve."

Rohit slumped in her arms. Blood continued to drain from his body. His eyes glossed over.

Trembling, Vendetta flung her brother off and stood. *How dare he! How dare he curse me!* His final breath was wasted! She stormed out of his bedchamber and marched down the corridor, no specific destination in mind. The castle was hers now. Everything from the coastline to Dun Raik belonged to her! *Her!* The crown and throne, the royals and nobles, the servants and commoners, every little thing within the borders of Hordes Region was Vendetta's to claim.

That was all that mattered.

She would *pray* Rohit's afterlife be filled with misery, pray he never rested peacefully, for that was what cowardice earned him. *That* was what *he* deserved.

They all had their chances. Vendetta tried repeatedly to get her kin to see the continent's dire situation from her vantage. To get them to understand how the people would benefit from an empire, not a fragmented monarchy, still brittle from the war of species.

Peace could thrive, but more needed to be done to ensure its continuation. She needed to make peace something she could seize as she saw fit. Return on a whim. Hand out like sweet treats at a festival.

Born of Snow

I

Nyx went into labor.

Una the midwife, a lamb beastman, prepared a tonic of various herbs to relieve pain that morning, as well as multiple salves in jars and mortars sitting on the dining room table, a basin of warmed water, and a wool blanket beside them. She had explained the importance of regular healing sessions time and time again over the past three weeks, while Karlisle advanced his skill in the craft. When Una needed to leave, he would be able to care for his wife and newborn.

Nyx, one hand on her rounded stomach, squeezed Karlisle's shoulder as he moved her legs onto the bed, pain screwing her paled expression. With her fully on the mattress, he climbed behind and helped her to her feet, then braced her back with his, their arms linked. Body tensing, her thin, barbed tail wrapped around his leg, strained groans forcing their way from her throat.

The parent will share their magical energy with their fetus. During labor, the magic will stay with the newborn and the parent's energy will be depleted. Said energy, now halved, will regenerate the damage of birth, but leave the parent extremely vulnerable and fatigued. Dread coiled in Karlisle's intestines, knotting them. He could do very little for his wife. Feeling her entire body constrict with another contraction, his heart throbbed wildly.

"Do you have her, Karlisle?" Una asked, her voice slightly accented, as she came to stand at the edge of the bed, sleeves rolled up, hands lifted and ready.

"Yes." Karlisle sucked in a breath and closed his eyes, hoping what he was about to do would not affect the babe and would relieve if only a fraction of Nyx's pain. He injected his magic into Nyx through his back into her core, a stream the width of a string, moving as sluggishly as sap down a tree.

The midwife said, "Nyx, I need you to push." She adjusted her posture, her hooves clacking on the floorboards. Karlisle, his eyes still closed, assumed her hands were underneath Nyx as she was hunched over the bed.

Arms tightening around Karlisle's, Nyx pushed, and her grunt turned into a blood-curdling scream. She gasped, inhaled, and pushed again, muscles tensing. Karlisle increased the flow of his magic, for it was all he could do to help her. That simple fact wrenched his insides out of his body and stomped on them. Sweat dampened Nyx's skin, the wetness seeping into his clothes as well. Mumbled prayers to long forgotten gods left his lips. *Let my wife be all right, let her survive this.*

When a wail and snip sounded over Nyx's haggard breathing, Una scampered to the dining room, hooves bounding. Nyx suddenly went limp. Karlisle twisted around, half catching her and half falling backward onto the bed, the frame creaking in protest. Her cardinal red skin was ashen from exertion, and perspiration gleamed in the candlelight. Her midnight blue hair stuck in clumps to her back and forehead and strands twisted around her slightly curved horns. He brushed all of it out of her face and kissed her, again and again, as he reintroduced his flow of magic, guiding the stream into her core a second time. Nyx gradually relaxed into him.

"You did so well," he whispered in her ear between kisses.

With a bundle of wool in her arms, Una walked to the bedside, a smile on her aged face. "He is healthy." She placed the babe in Nyx's arms, Karlisle's underneath to support her exhausted limbs.

They gasped.

"It is rare," Una said, smoothing her blood-stained apron, "but he is born of snow. It is nothing to be concerned about."

He had neither Nyx's red skin nor Karlisle's black. His hair was not midnight blue or charcoal grey. The babe did not have horns, a tail, or a set of wings like his mother. His skin was paler than a pearl, a pinkness coloring his cheeks from the warm water Una bathed him in, the wisps of hair atop his head as white as fresh snow.

"Are you sure he is well?" He did not mean to doubt her decades of experience, but he had never seen a babe born so pale to parents so dark.

"Of course," Una said. "I have seen this twice. Once in a set of twins. One had the coloring of her parents; the other was bone white. The second was a dwarf. All grew up well and vigorous." She smiled and clasped her hands in front of her.

Karlisle grunted softly, his gaze falling back to his son. The babe was beautiful and small, so incredibly small. He reached his hand around Nyx to caress his son's face, his skin smooth and warm.

"Berhane," Nyx muttered. "*My light*."

His name. "It is perfect," Karlisle said as Berhane opened his eyes. A breath caught in his throat. Berhane had his mother's eyes, a vibrant green like leaves in the spring.

Tears bubbled to the surface as Karlisle wrapped his arms around Nyx and Berhane, gently holding them closer, resting his head on Nyx's shoulder. Deeply, he breathed in, relief taking over him. Perhaps the gods listened just this once.

"I must tend to Nyx now," Una said solemnly and stepped toward Nyx. "The second birth will be any moment now."

When Karlisle released Nyx of his embrace, she twitched, her head turned toward Una as she reached for the babe. Her hand shot up to Una's collar, her nails now long and sharp. Una halted, a chill biting the air.

"Nyx," Karlisle breathed, a protective hand covering Berhane's head.

"You will speak of this to no one," Nyx said, her voice low and husky. "Or I will hunt you down and skin you alive."

Briefly, Karlisle stared astonished at his wife, and his jaw snapped shut. She was right. Should word spread of their having a child, it could reach the wrong ears. Karlisle lifted his gaze to the midwife. Fear oozed from the lamb's horizontal pupils, a tremor radiating through her body.

"You have my word," Una said. "I was never here."

A heartbeat later, Nyx eased, her claws retracting, and relented Berhane to Una, so Karlisle could shift out from behind Nyx. As he laid her down, she grimaced. He lingered, his thumb rubbing her cheek when he smiled at her, bent down to kiss her forehead, and turned to Una. Wasting no time, she handed Berhane to him. Nyx groaned, fists balling the sheets, when Una hurried to the table, gathered the mortar, and fed Nyx two spoonsful. Soon enough, Karlisle sitting in the rocking chair alongside the bed with Berhane coddled in his arms, the agony contorting his wife's face and keeping her muscles as rigid as stone waned.

The cottage was quiet now, the wind a low howl outside, the fire crackling in the hearth on the wall opposite the door. Nyx was fast asleep while Una cleaned the blood, changed the sheets, and propped his wife's head up with another pillow. Then she concentrated on feeding her magic into Nyx's core at the center of her being. Karlisle sensed the magical energy leaving the beastman's body and entering Nyx like a feather tickling his skin. If there was anything he was grateful for when it came to his blood, it was the Apostolov's ability to heal and regenerate, to feel other magic outside of their own, like a seer could see all energy. The complete control over one's magic, no matter the amount.

With Nyx cleaned and sleeping, Karlisle watched Una head to the kitchen to wash her supplies in the sink. Berhane was warm in his arms, the quick pace of his breathing working to relax Karlisle, but he refused to sleep until Una retired for the night. She dipped her head, then vanished within the hallway, the door to his and Nyx's room clicking shut.

Una left the next morning. Whether a letter came for her stating there was an emergency—both mother and child could die—had come, or if she simply wanted to leave, Karlisle could only assume. He did not stop her either way. So long as her lips remained sealed, Una could run wherever she wished. He could take care of his wife and son on his own.

*

After a week, Nyx wanted to walk so Karlisle helped her around the house, Berhane swaddled to his chest by a long, soft piece of cloth. Una taught him how to wrap a wooden doll to his chest and had him doing household tasks in the three weeks she was here. Nyx certainly got a kick out of it. He was awkward and rightfully so, he thought. To be carrying around a wooden doll with a face that could haunt children's nightmares made the entire process a struggle.

Flowers decorated the cottage now as well. Karlisle, while Nyx and Berhane slept, brought bouquets of wildflowers into the house, putting them in vases, or hanging them to dry. A sweet floral scent sat heavy in the air, masking the stench of filth that had accumulated from Karlisle ignoring the household chores to focus on his wife and son. There was only so much time in the day, and he only had so much energy to expend.

*

"I think we're overdue for a bath," Nyx said from the living room. She sat with her back to the wall on the bed, legs crossed out in front of her, Berhane suckling on her breast.

"Can you handle it?" Karlisle asked as he flipped a slab of ham in the skillet, the grease spitting and popping.

Karlisle did not want Nyx to overexert herself when a basin of water, soap, and a cloth worked fine. For all of them. He turned toward the center counter where two plates were and slipped the ham onto one of them, completing their meals. Dried fruits, eggs, oats, and ham with a cup of echinacea tea.

"I wouldn't have suggested it if I didn't think I could," she said. She winced and made a face down at Berhane. He must have sucked too hard or pinched her with those tiny hands of his.

Leaving his plate on the counter, Karlisle brought the other to the nightstand before he grabbed Berhane and Nyx took the plate onto her lap. As he walked to the kitchen, he patted Berhane's back, getting him to belch.

"Then tonight, that is what we will do." Karlisle glanced around the messy home, rounding the corner to stand in front of his plate. They had made this cottage a little over one hundred years ago when they settled in Hordes Region again. Beforehand, they had traversed Vinyamar. Together, they maintained the condition of the house, until

Berhane was born, of course. How quickly the mess amassed when one ignored it.

Once they were finished eating and Berhane was laid down in his crib, Karlisle knelt beside Nyx on the floor, placing his hands on her sternum—her core. It was far easier to inject magic directly into the core, allowing the magic to flow as it normally would, repairing any damage on the way.

"Do you think it is strange?" he asked, his magic steadily flowing into Nyx's body. Nyx quirked a dark eyebrow. "That Berhane appears human?"

"I was hoping to see little knubs for horns," she admitted with a smile, "but the smallest amount of human can outshine the rest."

Nyx's mother, Hyacinthia Valor, was part human, which meant she was too. He was a full-blooded demon, but he had no wings, talons, extra appendages, or tails, he had no fangs or horns either. Karlisle's skin was the black of night, his sclerae inky. The iris was also void of color, though opposite on the spectrum.

"There's a chance they will come in as he grows," Nyx said.

"Most likely." He rose, settled on the edge of the mattress, and kissed Nyx's cheek. She was beautiful like a rose, radiant like the moon, and his eyes could look nowhere else. She kissed him back, a gentle touch of their lips, when she grinned.

"I'm always right."

He chuckled. "Get some rest while I clean." They kissed again and Nyx shifted to lie flat, Karlisle bringing the covers up to her chest.

A cry reverberated through the cottage, startling Karlisle, Nyx shooting up. He raced to the nursery. Berhane yowled in his crib, his face red and sloppy with tears and snot as he wiggled and squirmed in his blankets.

Picking him up, Karlisle pressed the babe against his chest, so his heartbeat could be heard, and rocked on his feet. "It is all right," he whispered. "You are all right."

In seconds, Berhane calmed, his squirming settled, his sniffles stopped, and his eyes closed. Though, his little face was flushed red. Glad yet surprised he subsided so quickly—he'd heard babes were not so easy to soothe—Karlisle returned to the living room. Nyx stared at him, eyes wide with concern. He came to her side and placed Berhane in her arms.

"He is fine," Karlisle said softly, stroking the back of Nyx's head.

She cradled him, then moved forward to lie down. "We'll sleep together."

Karlisle smiled. Una had warned them Berhane might not want to be left without his parents for long, and that was all right. He did not mind. With Berhane on his back and Nyx on her side, the two fell asleep. Karlisle stayed there a moment longer, admiring his wife and son, a part of him wanting to lie down with them, but he knew things needed doing. Reluctantly, he rose and began his laborious list of chores.

*

Nyx stepped into the big wooden tub alone, sank, and turned, extending her arms for Berhane. Karlisle handed their son over and she cradled him with one arm, the other submerging. When the warm water from Nyx's hand touched Berhane, he wiggled, his squishy face going sour. Before long, the scowl turned into a toothless giggle. Overtop the babe's smooth head, Nyx scooped and ran the water over him. Berhane startled, a jerk of his entire body, his piercing green eyes big as he reached above him as if to catch the culprit. Laughing, Nyx continued to wet the babe down while Karlisle moved to her backside where the soap sat next to the tub.

"Tilt your head back for me," Karlisle said.

She did and Karlisle brought water up to her hair, soaking the mass of dark greyish blue snarls. He lathered her head, scrubbed her scalp as it expelled the tension in her shoulders, and rinsed her hair. With hair such as hers, he had to massage coconut oil throughout her curls.

"How about we try going outside tomorrow?" Nyx suggested, wagging her finger in Berhane's face, which made him chortle. "With Berhane?"

"If that is what you want."

Nyx was healing much faster than he anticipated, and, despite all the flowers, she had grown tired of the same four walls encompassing her. Who was he to tell her no if she felt strong enough to go outside? Berhane concerned him, but he would need to be exposed to the outside at some point.

Karlisle stepped away from the tub, got a hair pin off the shelf opposite the shower spout and twisted Nyx's hair to the top of her head, securing it. When he climbed into the tub, he took over holding Berhane, so Nyx could wash her body. There were stretch marks on her stomach now, her inner thighs and hips etched with them as if carved, all a shade or two lighter than her red skin tone. Her body was plumper, which was not surprising, seeing how much Berhane ate. Nyx had always been hungry while she was heavy with child, food lasting no longer than three days.

His eyes traced her curves and her loosely defined muscles as she stood, gaze lifting once more when he reached the water. She was exquisite. Nyx took pride in her ability to do hard labor but around six months, her stomach impeded most tasks, leaving her so frustrated she cried. He laughed and helped, but only when she wanted him to.

Nyx nodded to Karlisle. "Turn around so I can wash your hair."

Eyebrow raised, Karlisle looked in the eyes their son inherited, a flutter in his chest. She swirled her finger and Karlisle obeyed, turning his back to his wife. Nyx, once she wetted it, gently massaged soap through his hair.

"I ought to thank you for all you've done, but it's your fault in the first place," she said sarcastically, a chuckle at the tail end of her words. Karlisle could imagine the smirk on her face.

He held back his laughter and took a deep breath. "Una wanted to scold me about that, I think."

"You think?"

"I *know* she wanted to scold me," Karlisle corrected himself. "I cannot say I blame her." Pregnancy for immortals had a higher chance of mortality for both the babe and the parent. Once adulthood was reached, immortals ceased to age and everything within their body slowed in production if not completely stopped. Most became infertile. After a few centuries of bedding Nyx, Karlisle did not think it was possible to conceive.

Nyx gave a quick yank to Karlisle's hair, a hiss of pain escaping through his teeth, then continued scrubbing. He supposed he deserved that. "I'm aware of the consequences," she said. "Look at what those risks created. Look at our son and tell me they were not worth taking."

Berhane caught and squeezed Karlisle's finger hard, which surprised him. "I cannot," he sighed, any argument melting before it had the chance to develop further. "Nor do I want to."

"Good." Nyx leaned forward to kiss Karlisle's cheek and rinsed his hair out. "You would've lost any argument presented."

"I always do," he chuckled.

Born of Snow
"Informing the Queen"

Candles lit the queen's dreary study. Four elders sat across from Odovacar and his siblings, his father in an armchair behind the couch near her highness's desk. They had been discussing the punishment for five royals, who refused to complete their mission. In his mind, they had done nothing wrong, but justice had no room in this counsel.

Queen Vendetta had sent the Squad to a stronghold in the southeast of Hordes Region between Mondlesgrave and the southeastern docks. Whispers spread on the wind, eventually reaching the queen's ears: The family supposedly planned to break their oath by fleeing to another region, where his mother could not touch them. The royals refused to kill the family, to kill a child, opting to arrest them.

"They disobeyed an order!" one elder shouted, his old, wrinkled hand slamming on the arm of the couch.

"Odovacar," Mother said, her attention slicing to him. "What is your opinion on the matter? They are *your* men."

By his men, she meant another Squad he had a hand in training. To that definition, every royal in Hordes Kingdom was his to take responsibility for. Odovacar kept his gaze on the quaint table in front of him, swallowed, and opened his mouth.

"Your highness!" The doors burst open, and a royal flung himself to the floor, forehead pressed to the dark marble floor.

"How dare you interrupt this counsel!" the same elder barked, spittle flying.

A wet thud shook the table. Odovacar was suddenly staring at the head of the elder, his sagging skin spotted with brown dots, his sclerae a yellowish color. Silence descended. Blood wafted, a heavy metallic tang assaulting his nostrils. Draga, his eldest sister, made a sound of disgust and put her pipe to her lips.

"He is mine," she said, a cloud of smoke expelling from her mouth.

"Speak now or lose your head," Queen Vendetta said calmly. "Your choice."

"I come bearing news, your highness!" Draga's informant spat out, his entire body trembling like a leaf. "Nyx Reap has borne a child."

Vendetta shifted in her seat, her nails hitting the desk's surface: *tap, tap, tap.* "Karlisle is the father?"

"Yes, your highness."

"That is interesting, indeed," she drawled.

Nyx Reap was the last of the Reap bloodline, daughter of the founding ruler Hordes Reap and Hyacinthia Valor of Ryzion. Karlisle was of the Apostolov line hailing from Mondlesgrave. The child would have the three great demon bloodlines running through his veins. Odovacar knew his mother thought the same. He, simply because of lineage, could become extremely powerful if brought up in the right manner.

When Odovacar finally looked at her highness, the scars on his back itched. She smiled. His body went rigid, and he turned away, scars aching.

"Send for Alkeim and Felim," Queen Vendetta demanded.

"Of course, your highness," the informant squawked, barely stood from his knees, and raced out of the study, the door closing behind him.

Iron and smoke combined to create a foul stench in the room. Something curdled in Odovacar's gut as they waited for the Brannon brothers—first swords to his mother and father. Fear perhaps. But that was not quite it. He'd known fear. It stared at him every day, made a home within the hollow of his bones many years ago. Foreboding, he realized.

The Brannon brothers knocked, then entered. They were orcs. The older of the two, Alkeim, was broader in the shoulders and taller. The younger, Felim, was nastier looking, a scowl on his scarred face. They got down on their knees, their heads bowed.

"You know where Nyx resides, yes?" the queen asked.

"Aye," Alkeim answered, his voice gruff.

"She was with child and gave birth. I want you to retrieve the child."

Alkeim flinched. He was a father himself, his daughter only a year or so. "May I ask why, your highness?"

"No." The queen waved a dismissive hand toward the brothers. "You'll do it tonight. If Nyx and Karlisle resist, kill them."

After a moment of hesitation, the brothers said, "Yes, your highness," rose, and departed. It would take no less than three days to reach the couple's abode if the brothers pushed their horses. Seven at most.

Odovacar fought the urge to leave with them, to follow his old mentor. He was, however, firmly planted where he sat, his nails digging into his pants, his chest heavy.

"Now, where were we?"

"The royals, your highness," the second elder reminded his mother, their voice hushed, their eyes downcast, and their body stiff.

Queen Vendetta's attention settled on him like molten steel once more, ready to be molded and forged. Saving his own skin, despite how scarred and maimed it already was, Odovacar answered with what he knew she wanted to hear. "Behead them."

Mother grinned, her fingers interlocking on the desk. "Good answer."

Stolen

II

Eyes followed Nyx as she walked through Mutuwa, the biggest forest on the continent. Her father brought her here multiple times during her childhood, teaching her it was like any other forest, so long as she respected its compounds and laws. The luscious foliage hid what lay hardly ten meters in front of her, yet the trees could not dampen the sounds of nature.

She continued forward, feet bare, hair tickling her back, the humid air strangely comforting.

"You've become a disappointment," a familiar voice said from behind. Nyx whipped around. Her father stared down at her. Her heart twinged in her chest. Hordes' features were vague. A visage of ruby red, his hair of long cords was as blue as the ocean, the undertones nearly black, his clothes an array of colors and patterns. The last she saw her father was five hundred years ago, almost a century into his reign.

Nyx's gaze fled to the ground. "I did what I thought best, what I thought would bring me happiness."

"Yes," Hordes breathed, head surveying the enormous trees around them. "And look at what it has cost you and your people."

Nyx bit her lip; she was but a child again in her father's presence, small and naïve. Perhaps she would have had a good, happy life as queen. But what of freedom? What of love?

Hordes said, "You have freedom now? Dwelling on the outskirts of civilization, visiting the nearest kingdom only for necessities, cooping yourselves within a withering cabin; that is *surviving*, my poppy, not *living*."

The next words that came from Hordes' lips were not words at all, they were the muted clumps of boots on wooden planks. The hair on Nyx's nape stood on edge, a worm inching its way down her spine when her eyes flung open, and she was no longer standing amidst trees and fronds of vibrant green.

There was a low kindle in the hearth across the room, Karlisle's shoulder acting as her pillow on the couch. Burning timber and flowers scented the air, the small fire no longer enough to keep the chill of winter from seeping through the walls. Nyx, half awake, lifted her head, listening for the footsteps that wrenched her out of her slumber. Berhane had only begun to sleep on his own two weeks ago, sleep formerly a short and arbitrary experience. The only reason he was sound asleep now, she believed, was because of their adventure into Bextierther three days ago, taking a full day to arrive and return on foot.

She waited, still as stone. Shoes bounded from the nursery.

Nyx raced to the door on the right side of the hallway and yanked it open, nearly ripping it off the hinges if the creak and snap told her anything. Two men froze, heads jerking toward her, dim orange light flooding the space. Metal stars and crescent moons hung above the oak crib, her son no longer within. A rocking chair sat in the corner with a blanket thrown over the back, Karlisle's favorite spot to read Berhane the fairytales on the shelves surrounding the open window.

In the arms of the bigger man, an orc, was a swaddled, quiet babe, face peeking from the bundle of fur blankets. His cheeks and nose were rosy. Nyx bristled as the breeze howled through the room, rage warming her up again.

The smaller orc slipped his foot backward and reached for his hip. Nyx lifted her hands, magic coursing from her core to her palms like a flooded river. Darkness rushed from the floorboards. Black rose and crashed into the orcs, both raising their arms to shield themselves. Nyx slipped a tendril of darkness around Berhane. The reflectionless wave crashed into the intruders, Berhane gently coming to rest in Nyx's arms.

"Don't make this difficult!" One of them shouted through the haze of darkness.

She spun on her heels, watching Karlisle jump to his feet, dazed. "Nyx?"

"We need to go," was all she said when she stormed past him. Karlisle's feet quickly followed her.

Opening the front door, an icy boulder of air hit Nyx. Berhane shifted in her arm and started wailing, the cold far too jarring for an infant. She had no time to comfort him right now. They needed to get away.

"What is wrong?" Karlisle asked, hurrying to catch up to Nyx. "What happened?"

"The queen found us." Patches of snow and dead grass crunched beneath their footsteps. The sky was clear, the half-moon bright, their breath fogging.

Why did she want Berhane? What could a babe possibly provide for her?

The land was flat and mostly clear. North of them, where she was headed, however, brimmed with trees. In the cold, the sulfur smell of the swamps in Zeldine's Region wasn't so intense but there, nonetheless. In another region, Queen Vendetta could not reach Nyx and her family, could not touch, prosecute or search for them. They would finally be free of her. It was something they had talked about here and there. Short stints Karlisle never took seriously since he was content with their current life of *peace*. The version of her father she saw in her dreams was right. This was not living. She knew the sensation of freedom and every refreshing breath which came with it, the weightlessness consuming her every waking moment, the sheer amount of happiness she had taken for granted.

Youth entailed a certain gullibility that harmed one later in life. Her mother had taught her that and she, too, was right.

The border wasn't far. Twigs and rocks stabbed the soles of her feet. Karlisle's breathing gradually became labored. Berhane still sobbed into Nyx's collarbone, wetness soaking her shirt.

Karlisle grunted in pain and crashed, inciting another wince. Nyx halted, scanned the horizon in which they came, then bent beside him. As he reached for his ankles, dark liquid oozed, two rods of earth penetrating the tendon.

"Brace yourself," she warned and moved closer to his feet. His entire body tensed. Nyx held Berhane tighter with one arm and ripped the rods out of her husband's ankles with the other, subdued cries turned to haggard groans, a tremble raking his body. He ought to recover quickly.

"Can you stand?" she asked, eyes flitting back to their home. Two bulky figures grew nearer. Teeth grinding, she looked at Karlisle's feet, silently urging the wounds to close faster. They had to leave. They were close, so very close! "You must anyway."

He nodded frantically, attempting to gather his bearings, when another spear sank into Karlisle's side, impaling his kidney and sending him sprawling. Mentally, Nyx cursed as she rose to shield her husband, Berhane firmly pressed against her bosom.

They could not run or hide. Out of practice as she may be, she was raised by Hordes Reap. She knew how to kill. If words would not convince those two orcs to return to the queen empty handed, they would not return at all. Their corpses would rot right here, where no one treaded and no one would think to look, where only scavengers feasted.

The orcs halted meters out, while Karlisle rustled behind her.

"No more runnin'," the smaller one said. "Hand over the babe and you'll live."

"Over my dead body," she snarled.

He jerked forward and grabbed the hilt on his hip, yanking his sword free from its scabbard, the metal ringing. "Think the queen would prefer you dead than livin' anyway."

The bigger orc's arm shot out to stop the smaller, Nyx now seeing the resemblance between the two. Both wore fur cloaks, the leather beneath gleaming when exposed to the moonlight. The bigger and older, she guessed based on the amount of warrior's braids he had compared to the other, had a longer shaggier beard, small plaits throughout, tusks jutting from his bottom lip. The younger one had a rougher exterior, a single scar splicing his face in two, brows furrowed.

The elder brother glared down at the younger. "No, Felim." Then he glanced at Nyx. "We don't want to kill you."

"Yet you want my babe," she said. "You'll die before I ever give him up." Nyx hoped all this talk gave Karlisle the time he needed to regenerate, so he could take Berhane and run for the border.

"He will lead a better a life if you surrender him to the queen," he said pleadingly, hand still in front of his brother. "So will you."

Out of the corner of her eye, Karlisle sluggishly rose and swayed, turning to face Nyx with a ghastly, pain riddled expression. She shoved Berhane into his arms, followed by another shove to his shoulders. Eyes locked, stomach knotting, she mouthed, *run*. Whether she caught up or not, they would live in a realm without the constant suffrage of a queen who loathed their very existence. They would live in peace.

Hesitantly, Karlisle slid one foot backward and darted northward. Felim, cursing, made to go after him, but Nyx stamped her heel diagonally into the semi-frozen earth, sweeping the orc's legs out from beneath him. He hit the ground with a thud.

The older brother, eyes jetting between Nyx and the orc on his ass, seemed torn, face shifting from one emotion to the next. Until he pulled his sword out, crouched, and leveled the blade at Nyx, dark eyes focused and steady.

Having given birth two months ago, she needed to end this swiftly, her magical energy still depleted and weak. As her barbed tail whipped, she lowered herself defensively, nails growing into claws, her flow of magic strengthening. The tension was thick, as if vibrating the surrounding space. Adrenaline surged through her veins faster than her magic did. She could not remember the last she fought someone, nor were her father's lessons as clear as they ought to have been, as they once were.

Everything heightened. The wind like needles crashing against her bare feet, legs, and forearms. The light blinding as if the moon suddenly turned into the sun. Distant howls and hoots sounded, echoing. She counted the rise and fall of the big orc's breaths while Felim, face scrunched with anger, stood, and mirrored his brother's stance.

A single heartbeat passed. Nyx sprinted forward, expecting one or both orcs to startle. Neither did. Instead, Felim shuffled closer, hefting his sword high to meet Nyx's attack, whatever he thought it to be, head-on. She knew better. The big one would attack while she shortsightedly put all her focus on Felim. She stopped short as Felim's blade began its descent and the brother shifted his body weight, sword angling toward her midsection. Skirting around them, Nyx slammed her palms onto the damp mix of shriveled grass, mud, and snow, flipped them over and—dirt peppered her face, got in her eyes, and entered her nose. Blinded, she lost balance and fell onto her hip. She frantically ridded her eyes of debris.

It only lasted a handful of seconds. The sound of boots pounding the earth fled. Nyx snarled as she regained her footing and created a sword of black in her clenched fists. The big one remained, his own blade poised, Felim too far for her blurred vision to see.

Pain lanced her core, robbing Nyx of breath. She ignored the throb. She couldn't afford to back down.

Solemnly, the orc attacked. The strength behind it numbed Nyx's arms and shoulders, which instantly made her knees quake. Gritting her teeth, she hardly pushed herself out from under his sword, pivoted, and swung at his ribs. Parallel to his stance, darkness connected with steel, embers of ink exploding from the impact. Clearly, she was outmatched.

Abruptly, she stomped on his foot. The orc's bushy brows furrowed. Then she rammed her elbow into his core, forcing the air from his diaphragm. He dropped, cradling his midsection.

Nyx sprinted in the opposite direction of the fallen orc, only to stop dead in her tracks. Felim had caught Karlisle, and her heart crashed into her stomach. His blade rested against his throat, while a spike of earth projected from the right side of his chest. His blood was as black as Nyx's magic, tainting the tans of his clothes. Berhane, swathed in warmth, was in Felim's opposite arm. Even at this distance, Nyx saw every twitch and tremble that raked her husband's body.

"The queen simply wants to give him a better life," the orc behind her said, his tone gentle. "She can make sure he never goes a day without food or water. He'll always have a warm bed and clothes that fit. He would be surrounded by servants ready to help him with whatever he needs." He entered the corner of her sight, her eyes flitting toward him. His big hands were presented empty, his sword once again in its sheath. Wetness matted patches of his fur cloak, the bottom clumped with mud.

"Your son would be raised in the castle he was meant to have," the orc continued. "He would ascend the throne you gave up."

Nyx's blood ran cold. *Look at what it has cost you and your people.* Tears, smoldering hot, bubbled, her chin and lip quivering. How could she give up her son? Her first-born and only child? She had planned to tell Berhane of his heritage one day, let him choose his path then, as her father did for her.

"You," the orc spoke, "will have your freedom again, and he will be protected."

Shut up! She wanted to scream.

Felim brought Karlisle closer, blood wafting toward her, their shoes crunching the frosted ground. "Give us the babe," he said, voice lacking all the compassion his brother's had. "And we'll leave. Lives intact."

The blood seeping from Karlisle's chest showed no signs of slowing. Had he put up a fight, depleting his magic? Gods, please let him have put up as much of a fight as she had. Berhane was *their son*. White irises lifted to Nyx's gaze, a hollowness dimming them. Felim tucked behind Karlisle's person, she could not see Berhane, and she doubted Felim would allow her the privilege until she voiced her decision.

"On my father's name, I swear to take every life in that wretched kingdom if my son is hurt." Every breath was painful, a tearing of her heart leaving her chest cavernous; vacant and hollow.

"And I swear on my parent's graves," the older orc said, placing a hand on Nyx's shoulder. "Your son *will* be safe." Looking at him, there was kindness in this orc's dark eyes, soft lines forming around them, a certain pain hardening his mouth.

He was a father, she realized. He knew what he was doing, knew the pain he was inflicting, and did it, nevertheless. Despite every fiber of her being warring for a different answer, if they all lived, what else could she do? "Release my husband." She turned toward Felim. "Just let me see my son before you take him."

His head shifted to his brother, who nodded. Felim released Karlisle and, stepping aside, revealed the bundled babe of two months. Face pink, Berhane lay content in the arms of a thief, of which Nyx let him become.

Soon, too soon, Felim started southward, the big one joining, glancing over his shoulder once.

Nyx collapsed, defeated, stones digging into her knees, icy mud sending shivers through her body like earthquakes. Karlisle stumbled, joined her on the ground, and sobbed. Blood pulsed out of his wounds. Upon closer inspection, he *had* fought back. His clothes were tarnished, bumps welled on his arms, cuts and scrapes lines of red over his black skin. Her intestines wrung themselves. Neither of them was strong enough to fight properly.

Vendetta wanted them dead, and they practically were. She had succeeded.

The Start of Friendship
III

Four years later

Kiran had wandered too far from home. When he looked behind him, his little cottage wasn't in view anymore. Then he peeked at the forest floor where he'd been picking mushrooms and putting them into a wicker basket. There were small ones, big ones, red ones, and white ones. Mother said to collect all the ones he could find. Although she always tossed half of them. Which didn't make much sense.

It was warm, the sun a white dot in the sky that hurt Kiran's eyes if he stared at it for too long. He continued toward the stone wall protecting the grounds and the huge raven black castle. He had seen it many times and knew there were four archways opening to the courtyard. Soft grass tickling his bare feet, he ventured to the closest one.

Around the wall, covered in vines and flowers, there was a boy in the middle of the courtyard. He was picking daisies and putting them in a cluster. He looked lonely all by himself. Kiran had seen him a few times in the castle too, but he always had a servant at his side, a lady with orange hair. Eyes darting all around, she wasn't with the boy today. Odd, she was always near him.

Carefully, Kiran approached the boy—the prince, his mother had told him. Malice was his name. Kiran stopped a little ways from Malice. He was pale like the daisies in his hand, wearing a big shirt that slipped off his shoulders and was more like a dress.

"Malice," Kiran said.

The prince whipped around and dropped all the flowers. His eyes, the color of the grass surrounding them, were big and round.

"Why are you alone?" Kiran asked, stepping closer to pick up Malice's bouquet.

"Annabeth said she'd be right back," the prince answered and helped collect his flowers. "So, I've been making her a posy. She likes daisies."

"Me too." Kiran handed the blooms to Malice, who bunched them together, a few white petals fluttering to the ground. He suddenly remembered the basket he left in the forest. "Do you want to help me pick some mushrooms?" He saw some clusters on the way to the castle.

"Mushrooms?"

"I'll show you."

Offering his hand, Malice timidly took it, and they moseyed through the courtyard to the woods. A path of tall grass lay in between them, and off in the distance was a massive forest. Kiran's mother said it was dangerous, though.

In the fringes of the woods, Kiran spotted a gathering of tiny reddish-brown mushrooms and pointed. "Those," he said and squatted in front of them, Malice joining him.

"They look weird," Malice commented.

Kiran nodded. "But they taste good."

"Really?"

Kiran grunted, plucked the mushrooms from the earth, dirt crumbling away, and rose. "I have more over here. Want to see?"

Malice, saying nothing, let go of Kiran's hand and followed. He waded through stalks as tall as his knees, Malice behind him making the greenery rustle. The wicker basket was right where Kiran left it at the base of a small tree, the roots covered in spongy moss that smelled sometimes. After a quick glance over his shoulder, Kiran led Malice deeper into the forest. That was where his home was, and he wanted Malice to taste the good mushrooms. *Whichever ones those are.* Mother picked through them so swiftly, Kiran couldn't tell the difference between one and the next!

Stringy vines hung from the branches and bright pink flowers were scattered along the forest floor, their stems almost red. Soon the cottage came into view and Kiran quickened his pace, Malice keeping up. It was small; the roof covered in a thick layer of green moss— almost the color of Malice's eyes but dirtier—the chimney pouring out smoke being consumed by the fuzz. The front of the house had rounded windows, each glowing orange.

Kiran opened the wooden door with a creak, stepped in, and made room for Malice to come inside as well. Father stood in the kitchen chopping something at the center counter when his attention shifted toward them. His nose was flat, the horns coming from the sides of his head slightly curved and pointed backward. Sitting at the other end of the kitchen was Mother. She had pale blotches all over her skin and her dark brown curly hair was like Kiran's.

When the door closed, she glared at Kiran. He gripped the handle of the basket and averted his gaze. He didn't like that look.

"Where do you think you've been?" she asked and stood, crossing the room in a heartbeat. "I've called for you three times."

"Sorry," Kiran muttered, then held up the mushrooms for his mother to see. "I filled the basket." He smiled crookedly.

"And brought home the prince," his father pointed out from the kitchen, his knife clacking.

Mother sighed as she drew her hand over her face. Kiran fidgeted. He couldn't help it. Malice looked so lonely.

"Kiran." She kneeled, took the basket from Kiran's hands, and placed it on the floor beside her, so she was eye level with him and Malice. "I have to take Malice back to the castle."

"But I don't want to go back," Malice said.

Kiran glanced between Malice and his mother, scooping Malice's hand in his. "He's my friend!" he declared and puffed his chest.

"That may be, but he can't stay here," she said sadly, which made Kiran frown. He didn't understand why Malice had to go back, especially when he didn't want to return, either.

"But why?" Malice asked.

"Because Annabeth will be worried and you don't want that, do you?"

Malice's eyes widened briefly, and his head drooped a bit. "… No."

Tears sprang to Kiran's eyes as his lip quivered. Mother rose, smiled, and wiped the few that had fallen. "I'll make sure you see each other again."

Kiran nodded, yet didn't feel any better. He wanted Malice to have some mushrooms. Maybe they could have them next time. But how long would next time be? Father stepped away from the counter, catching Kiran's attention when he motioned for Kiran to come to him. Kiran did, reluctantly. Father's hands rested on his shoulders as Mother guided Malice to the door. He turned and waved goodbye, Kiran waving back. The door closed.

"Now." Suddenly, Kiran was lifted into Father's arms. Bending forward, he grabbed the basket of mushrooms and suggested, "How about we sort these?"

Kiran nodded, and they headed into the kitchen.

"Blodwen"

Doors closing behind her, the castle's foyer was as black as night until her eyes adjusted, lamps and candles giving just enough light for one not to trip over themselves. There was always a foul smell in the air that no amount of perfume could mask. It was heavy, the odor saturating Blodwen's skin as she would take it home with her. Blood.

Voices carried through the vastness of the castle, red and gold accents scattered in the ornate detail of the architecture. At this time of day, servants were busy finishing their morning duties or starting their afternoon tasks. Blodwen recognized one of them, the sleek bitterness of the queen defiling another poor soul. The second whimpered incomprehensible excuses, tone pitched with worry and fear. It was Annabeth.

Blodwen glanced down at her side, where the young prince's little fingers twirled a string from his shirt's collar. Like pearls, his skin and hair were multiple shades lighter than his stained cream garments. Blodwen climbed the stairs, holding Malice's free hand in case he needed a little extra help, her shoes echoing, his feet slapping. His grip was loose. She had noticed over the years how little he talked to anyone. Though, she would rarely catch him anywhere other than the castle's fourth floor, the servant's quarters.

Toward the western wing, Queen Vendetta stood before a servant on her hands and knees. Her highness was straight-backed, crimson hair spilling over her shoulders, her inky wells for eyes steady on Prince Malice's caretaker. She quickened her pace.

"Your highness," Blodwen said, catching the queen's attention. Annabeth flinched.

Her highness's gaze flicked to Malice, then to Blodwen. "So, you have the mutt," she said, and Blodwen's gut curdled. How she spoke of her children was vile, as if they truly were dogs who ran away or barked too loud on occasion.

Blodwen dropped to her knees alongside Annabeth, her head down. Malice stood awkwardly behind them. His bare feet twisted, and his toes wiggled. "I deeply apologize. My son convinced Malice to help him pick mushrooms in the forest," she lied, but had a hunch it was exactly what Kiran had done.

The queen grunted. "It was her fault for taking her eyes off the mutt in the first place, Blodwen." Using her second set of arms, Queen Vendetta dusted her skirt and clasped her fingers. Her upper set of arms was in a similar position, one hand resting on top of the other in front of her sternum.

"Perhaps." Blodwen couldn't argue. Annabeth should have taken Malice with her wherever she went or had another servant watch him. Children were reckless and foolish because they didn't know any better. "Still, Kiran should have left him alone."

"It matters not anymore." She waved her hand. "The mutt is returned, and your brat has his mushrooms."

Blodwen ground her teeth, suppressing every emotion her body might show, the anger and disgust like roaches scurrying and nesting inside her veins. "If I may be so bold, your highness?" Good, her voice came out level and controlled.

"Make it quick."

"I think it would benefit Malice if he were to have a friend, someone close to his age," Blodwen said. She knew how much Kiran also wished to have a playmate.

"Oh?" the queen mused, her bat-like wings placed on her lower back twitching. "And why is that?"

Blodwen finally lifted her head. Her highness's skin was a ghostly purple, touched with the faintest bit of warmth from the lamps on the walls. The shadows hallowed the curves and crevices of her face and pronounced her already sharp features.

"I believe," she strained, each word like acid on her tongue, "Malice will be easier to control if he had a friend." Blodwen knew if she did not present things in a way that benefited the queen, the likelyhood of her accepting the request was low if not zero.

"All right," the queen said and turned, her shoes clacking on the cloudy marble floor. She rounded the corner and vanished from sight.

Both Blodwen and Annabeth sighed, their bodies deflating. Annabeth sat up, shifted, and held her arms out to Malice. "I'm so sorry," she sniffled, her eyes red and puffy.

Malice walked into her embrace, silent as she squeezed him.

"Thank you, Lady Blodwen," Annabeth said, her amber eyes on Blodwen. "I don't know what would have happened if you had not showed when you had." The servant—a human—was older than Blodwen, thin lines on her forehead, in the corners of her eyes and around her mouth, her orange hair streaked with silver.

Blodwen smiled falsely. "I'm simply glad everything turned out."

"I just," Annabeth said, her cheeks flushing, "needed to relieve myself and I was in a rush. I did not think he would wander. He's never done so in the past."

"No need to justify yourself to me." Blodwen stood. "Next time, to avoid the queen's wrath, take him with you." As a mother, she understood the desire to take some time for oneself. She couldn't blame the servant. More so when motherhood had been forced upon the poor woman.

"Of course." With Malice in her arms, Annabeth got to her feet as well. "Thank you again."

Blodwen nodded and regarded Malice. "I'll bring Kiran with me more often." The prince beamed, nodding enthusiastically as she turned to leave.

As Queen Vendetta's personal doctor, she had access to the castle whenever she needed. Her husband Tendai did as well, being the castle's primary doctor. Looking over her shoulder, Annabeth and Malice climbed to the upper floors of the castle.

The outside air hit Blodwen, warming what her highness's bitter presence had cooled and inflating her lungs to their capacity. The grounds were a sharp contrast to the dreary halls of the queen's home, vibrant with life and refreshing.

With five other children, the prince was treated like dirt. Albeit even dirt was walked upon, thoughtless as the action may be. Today was the first since Queen Vendetta's orders were given that Blodwen had seen her give a smidge of attention to her youngest son. *Act as if the mutt exists not, unless told otherwise.* The queen hadn't explained herself and no one asked—who would dare question the queen?

The Start of Friendship
"A Gift of Blue"

Annabeth woke Malice with a tender shake of his shoulder.

He sat up, tossing the blankets off him, and yawned. He lazily looked around his room, the candle flames dancing on his desk and nightstands. There were no windows. Annabeth moved across the floor to the closet, plucking different articles of clothing for the day. Her own clothes never changed. A black knee-length dress with slightly puffed sleeves and a white apron around her waist, like all the other servants in the castle. Shifting to the side of his bed, Malice nodded forward, blinking rapidly to keep the floor and wall from blurring.

Annabeth knelt in front of him, pulled his oversized tunic off, and helped him dress. His shirt was black, the sleeves loose, his trousers the same color, and then a vest and topcoat the color of wine. It was all very uncomfortable. Malice's eyes refused to stay fully open when she guided him to the desk chair. A mirror leaned against the wall, a brush, a comb, and two bottles sat on the dark wooden surface. Coconut oil filled one, water the other. Annabeth used the comb to tease his curls, and fingered the oil through his hair afterward, slicking it back. He wondered if Kiran's mother had to do this with his hair, too.

"What am I dressed up for?" Malice asked as he hopped down. This was the first time he had worn anything other than a shirt. He stayed inside during winter, so he didn't need to wear anything else. Different attire was always in the closet though, only touched when Annabeth shoved them aside.

"You'll be attending the Kings Summit," Annabeth answered.

"What's that?"

She said, "The summit is where all the rulers come to meet once a year and talk."

"Why do I have to go?" He wasn't a ruler. Despite what Kiran's parents said, he wasn't a prince either. Or maybe he was. He'd never seen one, he didn't think.

For a split second, Annabeth's expression changed. "I'm sure it is because the king and queen want you to learn everything there is to know, so one day, you can rule the region confidently." Her tone was strange, like a bird screeching instead of singing.

She extended her hand for Malice to grab. He did, and they strolled their way down to the first floor.

Wearing a similar outfit to Malice, a man stood by the open doors, the brightness forcing Malice's eyes to narrow.

Annabeth bent over. "That is King Emil, your father," she whispered.

His majesty's skin was a dull blue and his short hair was the color of a plum. The thought made Malice want a plum as they stepped into the foyer. King Emil was thin, his limbs lanky and his facial features sunken in, pronouncing his low cheekbones. On top of his brow, unlike Malice, sat a crown of shadowy points. Abruptly, the king spun and walked out of the castle.

"Felim Brannon," Annabeth informed once more. "Your father's first sword." She let go of his hand, urging him toward the orc. His skin was olive green, two white tusks poking through his lips, his beard and hair both braided. He looked mean. Malice hesitated.

"Let's go," the orc said softly and waited for Malice, his dark eyes on the floor.

Eventually, he nodded and followed the orc outside, where the sun blazed and blinded Malice. Warmth embraced him, quickly making his clothes, which he'd grown used to during the trek to the first floor, uncomfortable again. A carriage of red and gold waited on the flagstone path, a servant holding the door open. Felim hefted Malice into the cabin before he settled beside him. The carriage rocked and squeaked. Emil was on the other seat, motionless, quiet, and dead-eyed. Sinking into himself, Malice swallowed and let his gaze fall to the red carpeted floor. The door closed, and they were in motion.

The quality of clacks on the ground changed after a short time. Malice moved the white curtains a tiny bit with his finger. They were in the kingdom! Lampposts were on either side of the granite paved roads, all types of people walking around. A lady with a big round belly passed a beastman with furry legs. Chatter was so loud he could hear it through the carriage walls, nothing he could make out but still! Every house and building were slightly different. Some of brown or red clay, some were rounded, some blocky. Few had over two windows, while fewer yet were completely stone. Timber framed a flower shop and a tavern. Orange terracotta made the rooftops. The scrumptious smell of baking bread penetrated the carriage, Malice's mouth suddenly watering. Then a dog, small and scraggly, darted past, a group of kids chasing it.

When someone locked eyes with Malice, he grinned and waved. They waved back, their smile soft and kind looking. Butterflies fluttered in his chest. Why wasn't he allowed to go beyond the castle's wall? He could go with Annabeth and Kiran and chase dogs until they ran out of breath, too!

*

After a week of travels, they reached a forest called Dun Raik. King Emil was the first to step out of the carriage, Felim second, and lastly, Malice, with help from the orc. Not a single ray of light broke through the foliage. It was pitch black beyond the first few trees. He stayed put and clutched the bottom of Felim's leather jacket. The big man turned.

"Don't worry," he said, "the forest's empty. Promise." He sounded strange to Malice, his accent nothing like Annabeth's or Kiran's.

Malice nodded, and Felim hoisted him into his arms. They walked toward King Emil, who stood at the edge of the forest, going past him. Shadow engulfed them. Malice shrunk into Felim's arms as the king's footsteps quieted. Peeking down, the ground morphed into moss, thicker than what he'd seen in Kiran's forest. Tree limbs, trunks, and roots were buried in it, vines hanging down to create a veil. Bugs whizzed. Birds chirped. Shrubs obscuring the bases of these massive trees rustled and jostled as if critters wrestled behind its leaves. The air was dry compared to the humidity Malice knew in Hordes Kingdom. It was nice, not so sticky and unpleasant. The darkness wasn't so bad now that they were inside the forest. Especially when glowing blue dots started appearing. They were everywhere, just like the moss. Closer to a cluster of pale blue, Malice cringed and looked away. They were mushrooms.

Finally reaching the end of Dun Raik, they stepped onto gravelly dirt, the crunch of their boots almost deafening after the silent forest floor. Felim also put Malice down, his hand remaining in the orc's huge grasp. The king was quick on his feet, his strides hard to keep up with as he headed toward the gigantic castle at the circle's center. Malice hurried alongside Felim to match his majesty's pace, gawking. Half of the castle had been reduced to rubble. The stone was white, small cracks zig-zagging and splitting from the base. Stained glass windows depicting meadows in full bloom almost glowed in the sun.

Inside, the emerald floors were dull despite the rainbow of light coming from the windows, as were the pillars on either side of the winding staircase around a marble statue. The statue looked like an angel, but there were rings of eyes sprouting from and circling its head.

Or maybe they were horns. Wings of all sizes jutted from the creature's body, the biggest folded against its back, kissing the platform it stood on. A cloth wrapped around its midsection as if the wind were tugging at it. It couldn't have been an angel. There were plenty at home, so he would know.

Through the stairs, Malice glimpsed a courtyard or something like it, and to the sides of the staircase were two sets of double doors, the handles a weathered gold against dark cherry stained wood.

Hiking up the steps, Malice admired the beautiful castle. He liked the easy, breathable colors compared to his own dark, suffocating castle of blacks, reds, and greys.

The second floor had two hallways of doors. Then, on the third floor, Malice, Felim, and King Emil walked into a great hall. In the center of the room, the long, dark oak table looked tiny next to the wall of windows. He didn't know a room *could* have that many windows. Above the table hung a metal chandelier, catching the light and creating patches of white on random surfaces. On the opposite side of the stairs, the space was a little emptier with a single couch and table at its heart. Whoever lived here must've left in a rush.

Many chairs were empty at the table when the king took his seat, putting a distance between him and the few rulers already there. Felim assumed his place behind his majesty, and guided Malice to stand at his side.

An elf sat at the head of the table talking with a dark elf, her fair hair flowing down her back. Her cream-colored dress slipped from her shoulders, leaving them bare. It reminded Malice of his over-sized shirts. She was pale, almost as pale as Malice, and her eyes were the same shade of green as his, too. She looked kind.

Two chairs down was a human, his chin, neck, and bald head covered in black swirls and twists. Lines creased his big nostrils down to his chin, surrounding his mouth, and a few wrinkles started at the corners of his eyes. He wore a cloak of light tan bird feathers that covered his wide torso.

Malice tugged at Felim's shirt, who lowered himself. "Why does he have those swirls on his skin?" he asked.

The ruler turned toward him, and the room went silent. Felim sighed. "I apologize, your majesty's," he said, turned and bowed to the table. Malice looked from him to the others, then mirrored the orc, confused.

"That's quite all right," the man with the swirls said, smiling. "They're called tattoos. All barbarians get them at some point in their lives."

"What's a barbarian?" Were they different from humans?

The ruler cackled, throwing his head back as the elf laughed in to her hand.

"Malice," Felim whispered to him, "enough questions for now."

He nodded dejectedly as the elf went back to her conversation. With an exhale, he peeked at the king and froze. King Emil smiled for a second.

Gradually, more rulers trickled in, till all the seats at the table were occupied.

"I see you've brought yet another child with you," a ruler across the table said. His tone was smooth, appealing, the type of voice Annabeth used to tell Malice stories before he slept. "Who is this one?"

"My son, Malice Reap," his majesty said.

The man's eyebrows—Holister, someone said when he first sat down—jolted, his mouth twisting into a frown. "Malice?" he repeated. Malice didn't understand. Was something wrong with his name? Holister's expression suggested there was. Kiran had never said anything though.

When Holister glanced over his shoulder, Malice looked at the boy behind him as well. He was slender, his freckled cheeks round and his eyes the color of a lilac. Unlike Holister's somewhat tanned skin, the boy's skin was dark like the bark of an oak tree, his hair brick red. Malice thought the boy was beautiful as his face and ears warmed, his gaze dropping to the table.

"Why don't our sons get to know each other, Emil?" Holister's tone changed back to what it was as he addressed the king, grinning.

Holister's son snapped toward his father, a look on his face saying he would rather not get to know Malice. Malice slouched and rubbed the fabric of his shirt between his fingers. Maybe he looked funny to Holister's son, or maybe it was his name. Neither of which he could really help.

"All right." Emil waved his hand dismissively toward Malice, telling him to leave. None of the other rulers voiced complaint. In fact, most seemed to welcome the idea as nods of approval rippled through the table.

Felim patted Malice on the head. "Behave," he said.

Malice shifted around Felim and Holister's son reluctantly met him a little way beyond the table, and they walked out of the great hall.

The sound of their shoes clacking against the emerald floors echoed as Malice, trailing behind Holister's son, trudged down the stairwell. He wore simple clothes—a white shirt with puffed sleeves tucked into dark blue trousers and a matching dark blue coat thrown over his shoulders. Malice wished Annabeth had dressed him like that instead. It appeared more comfortable.

Turning at the platform to the second floor, the boy led Malice down the corridor, stopped and opened a door, then waited for Malice to step into a lounge. Stale musk pervaded the shadowy room, making Malice's nostrils flare. Holister's son quickly lit the lamps on the walls and the candles on the two tables in the room. How? Did he have a fire starter in his pocket? But Malice heard nothing aside from his heels striking the ground. Was it magic? Annabeth said everyone had it, so maybe she was right.

Six chairs surrounded a round table, and empty shelves made up the rightmost side. To the left was a small square table with dual armchairs on either side of it. Beyond the table, spanning the wall, were multiple empty glass cabinets.

"My name is Magnus, by the way," the boy said as he bent down beside the square table, pulling out a checkered board from underneath and blowing the dust off it in a big huff. Magnus coughed, swinging his hand around to rid the dust in the air, and set it on the table.

"My name is Malice," he said and immediately felt silly since his majesty had introduced him earlier.

"Do you know how to play chess?" Magnus asked. He sat in front of the armchair as he plucked out the chess pieces and placed them on the board.

Malice shook his head, making his way closer, sitting opposite of Magnus.

"I could teach you, if you want?"

He nodded eagerly. Magnus smiled. "My father taught me how." He was still digging out pieces from under the table. "He said it would help with battle strategies later on." Shrugging, Magnus ran his thumb over the last figure.

The board was old, scratched and scuffed, black and white paint faded or chipped, revealing the light wood underneath. Magnus placed the black pieces on his side and the white on Malice's. There were six different figurines, the smallest having the most in the front row.

"I'll go first to show you how." He pushed a piece forward two squares. "This is a pawn. It can move one or two tiles for the first move but only once for the rest of the game."

Malice moved the second to last pawn on the right two spaces as well.

"However," Magnus went on, putting his horse on a spot near his pawn. "A pawn can only capture another piece diagonally." He took the pawn, stole the horse, and put it back in its place. "Now it's your turn."

Choosing a different pawn near the middle of the board, Malice moved it a single square, then it was Magnus's turn. They went back and forth, while Magnus explained what each figurine was, how they moved, and were captured. Malice listened intently, occasionally glancing up to meet Magnus's gaze. His eyes were mesmerizing, a soft yet brilliant shade of violet, the shape of a down-turned almond, eyelashes long and dark like his hair.

Magnus captured all of Malice's pieces in no time. Malice pouted.

"You know," he said, "my brother isn't very good either." A smirk rested on his lips as he reset the board, switching the colors, dimples forming divots in his freckled cheeks.

"What's his name?" Malice asked.

"Padma. He's only three, so I guess it's okay that he's bad." When the board was made up, Magnus gestured to it, allowing Malice to make the first move. "Do you have any siblings?"

"Five." Malice moved his pawn one tile. "I'm the youngest. Annabeth said the queen once had a son who died long before Draga was born, so I guess six."

Magnus gasped and reeled at the same time. "Five!" he echoed. "Whenever I see my brother, he never leaves me alone. I can't imagine how tough it is for you."

"… They don't like me all that much."

Magnus slid his knight three squares forward and one to the left. He made a face. "You must be lonely."

Malice shook his head as he moved his bishop diagonally across a few squares, stealing Magnus's knight. "Kiran said that too." Maybe it was true, but not anymore. Since spring, Kiran had visited Malice almost every day. Recently, he started sleeping in Malice's bedchamber, so Annabeth put a collection of his clothes in the closet.

"But why don't they like you?" He overtook two of Malice's pieces and grunted with satisfaction.

"I don't know. Annabeth said Sok and Rayan are jealous of my magic." Malice didn't understand how they could be jealous of something he didn't have.

"What kind of magic do you have?"

"Dark magic, I think. At least, that was what Annabeth told me." He wasn't sure, though. He'd never seen it.

Magnus's expression brightened. "Really?" he exclaimed. "Then you're just like me." Quickly abandoning the game, he rushed around the table to Malice, Malice lurching backward in surprise. "I have light magic!"

"How are they alike?"

Magnus sat back on his legs. "Well… we can do similar things…" he guessed, paused, and added, "I know we can use the four main elements!"

"But I don't have magic," Malice said. *What are the elements?*

Perking up, Magnus said, "I'll teach you, like how I taught you to play chess. Watch."

Magnus inhaled deeply, eyes closing as he put his palms

together. When he let go of his breath, he pried his hands apart. A web of thin, glowing, yellowish lines connected his palms, illuminating the surrounding space more than the candles did. Warmth tickled Malice's face, his mouth ajar as he stared at Magnus's light magic. Where the web met skin, it shone the brightest, winking brighter, as if it were in sync with his heart. The light dissipated into embers, gradually dimming until they disappeared. Magnus opened his eyes, his chest heaving a bit.

"Beautiful," Malice muttered.

Magnus smiled bashfully and demanded, "Hold your hand out."

Malice did.

"Now close your eyes."

Malice closed them.

"And focus on your hand."

What exactly was he supposed to focus on? Malice didn't know what to do, so he pictured the lines running across his palm down to his wrist. Annabeth once told him people could read the lines and tell someone's future. *You will have a very long life,* she had said to Malice, tracing one of the creases.

One deep breath after another, nothing happened for a time. Then he felt a twinge below the center of his chest. Malice opened his eyes and glanced at his chest and Magnus.

"Close your eyes!" Magnus reached out and brushed his hand over Malice's eyes, closing them again.

Malice continued to breathe the way Magnus had, thinking about the twinge. It wasn't painful, but was like someone had tugged a strand of his hair. It happened again. This time, a gasp accompanied it. Going against what he was told, he peeked at Magnus, who stared at his hands. A mass of swirling darkness, consuming every bit of light hitting it, danced in the palm of Malice's hand like torch flame. As quickly as it appeared, it vanished as if it were a candle being snuffed out.

"You felt it right?" Magnus said in quiet amazement.

Unsure if he was referring to the pang or the strange feeling that flowed through his arm, Malice nodded. "The twinge?"

"Yes!" he shouted abruptly. "You did it!" Magnus grinned broadly, squishing his eyes and deepening his dimples.

Face flushing, Malice averted his gaze as butterflies returned to his chest.

Once calm, he said, "That was your core." Magnus gently poked below Malice's chest, about a hand in length above his belly button. "It's where all your magic comes from. Eventually, you'll be able to use fire, water, air, and earth as well." Adjusting his shoulders and sitting a bit straighter, Magnus spoke smugly, "Of course, so will I, since I have light magic."

"Can you teach me?" Malice asked.

"If you show me more of your magic the next time we meet, sure." Magnus, holding out his pinky, regarded Malice with a sparkle in his expecting eyes.

Malice wrapped his pinky around Magnus's, smiling. Kiran did that too every now and again. He would have to tell him about his magic and Magnus when he returned home.

"Promise me," Magnus said when he reached for his ear, plucked the earring out, and drew Malice's hand toward him, dropping it in his palm.

Malice stared at it, confused why Magnus would give him this. "I promise." He shoved the earring into his pocket. What else was he supposed to do with it?

Magnus frowned a bit. "Do you not—" he stopped himself,

looked at the floor, and quirked one end of his mouth. "Do you want to play another round?"

Is that not what I was supposed to do? Malice nodded, and Magnus went back to his side of the table to reset the board.

"Why did you give me your earring?" He didn't like Magnus's expression. It was too similar to Annabeth's false smile.

Magnus contemplated as he arranged the figures on their squares. "It's a gift," he said. "A token of our deal and friendship."

"… Thank you?" Annabeth said to use manners when he received something from another. She brought it up when he accidentally bumped into a servant in the hall, and he kept walking without apologizing. Then again, when Kiran helped read him one of his stories. She said to say thank you to show your gratitude.

"If you don't like it, you can throw it away after you leave," he said glumly, his shoulders dropping.

"But I don't want to do that." Malice took the chance to go first and moved his pawn. "If you gave it to me, I'll keep it."

His lilac eyes jerked up, brows raised briefly when his face eased. "Good."

The butterflies worsened. Shifting his posture, Malice moved another pawn, unsure how to handle the fluttering of his heart or the giddiness of his mind.

In the blink of an eye, evening had come. Felim and a dark elf named Gareth, Magnus's and Holister's right-hand man, had collected Malice and Magnus. A thick, pale scar scored the dark elf's face, from the corner of his left eye to the underside of his jaw. Felim had one too. His, however, was almost perfectly centered on his face, splitting it in two. He and Magnus had talked so much Malice's throat was sore and scratchy. The four of them headed to the ground floor and had to part ways at the arched entrance, where Holister and King Emil waited for them. Something coiled in his gut when they had to leave; Malice didn't want them to, but he watched anyway, muscles tense as he picked at his fingers.

It was neither cooler nor warmer outside than it was that morning. The trees of Dun Raik remained motionless, yet there was a quiet whistle of wind. Holister, Gareth, and Magnus headed north, while King Emil, Felim, and Malice went south. He constantly looked over his shoulder, sweat making his palms clammy. They hadn't talked about when they would see each other again. What if they never did?

Then, as if he heard Malice's thoughts, Magnus turned around. Malice's heart skipped a beat, and his mind froze. Magnus, with a slight gesture of his hand, smiled brightly. Malice couldn't help it. He grinned as he waved his hand wildly, so Magnus saw him.

Kin
IV

Twenty servants gathered and stood on either side of the path leading to the castle's front doors, five of which were holding lamps, illuminating the stone walkway. Stars glinted between passing clouds, the breeze muggy. The castle of darkness loomed over the carriage, a tree to an ant. Hastily, King Emil stepped out of the carriage and went inside. Once he helped Malice out of the cab, Felim was fast on his heel.

Annabeth rushed toward Malice. She kneeled just as quickly and embraced him, squeezing them so close he could feel her breath tickle his neck, but she made the mugginess worse, so he wiggled out of her arms. She released him and stood, offering her hand. When he shook his head, she frowned, clasped her hands in front of her, then nodded toward the big double doors carved with vines, swords, and horned skulls at every corner.

Malice, treading a little behind her, reached into his pocket, rubbing the cool gem before he held it in front of him. It was smooth like glass, the color of the night sky above. Opposite hand going to his ear, Magnus wore the twin in his lobe. Malice had seen many with jewelry dangling from their ears.

"What is that?" Annabeth asked.

Malice massaged the soft tissue between his fingers. He turned the earring over, examining the gem as closely as he could in the courtyard's dimness. It was pretty, rounded into a long teardrop shape, a thin silver stud connected to the tip by a tiny cuff. He stretched his earlobe taut, closed his eyes, and stabbed the earring through, wincing as blood streamed onto his fingers. Heat throbbed.

"Malice!" Annabeth yanked Malice's hand from his ear, tilting his head the other way. "Why would you do you this?"

Because that was what he was supposed to do. It was an earring.

She picked him up and carried him inside. His ear burned while blood raced down his neck and made him shudder as if a hair tickled him. He had made a friend, though, and Magnus gave him a gift to show it. Kiran would be excited to hear about Magnus, Malice was sure.

Annabeth's heeled shoes clacked noisily up the stairs. Malice's eyes shifted from one thing to the next. The gold railing, the grey and black marble floor polished to reflect the few light sources there were. Fur rugs blanketed the ground of the hallways leading to the eastern and western wings of the castle. They were soft, Malice knew, a pleasant sensation of his bare feet. He couldn't wait to take these boots off so he could feel the rugs again.

"Promise you'll never do something so reckless," she said on the way, reaching the third floor's platform and turning to continue the climb.

He nodded. "I promise." Something twisted his gut. He didn't like seeing Annabeth upset.

In his bedchamber, once the blood was cleaned from his neck, ear, and hair with a warm, damp cloth, Malice changed. Kiran wasn't there, although Malice expected—wanted him to be. He probably didn't know Malice was back, and that was why he hadn't come.

"Let's get you to the dining hall now," she said and gestured to the entry.

Malice followed Annabeth. "Why?" There was a chill in the dark corridor, quiet too, as if no one lived on the fourth floor. Which wasn't true. The fourth floor was the servants' living quarters.

"You'll be having dinner with your family."

Walls of desaturated red with black vines running up to the crown molding, a golden chandelier shining from the vaulted ceiling and a long table centered in the room seated the members of the Reap family. The dining hall was as gloomy as the rest of the castle. Pressure settled on Malice's shoulders as if someone were pressing down on him, the walls seemingly shrinking with every step closer to the table.

Once Annabeth seated Malice, she went to stand against the wall, her head down and her hands clasped. Malice waited for her to sit next to him, or at least stand a little closer, like she usually would. Eyebrows knitting, she shook her head, and he turned back to the table.

Queen Vendetta sat at the head. Her red hair was braided into a bun, probably so it wouldn't get in her food as she ate. Regal was the word Blodwen used one time to describe the queen. He didn't know what it meant, but it sounded right. Then his majesty, who was to her right, unmoving, his expression blank. His bleak red eyes were trained on his plate. Malice's skin crawled.

Across from King Emil was an empty chair said to have belonged to Elias, the queen's first child.

Beside the empty seat was Odovacar. Annabeth told him all the names of his siblings and what they looked like, since he had never seen any of them on the fourth floor, or anywhere else in the castle. His eyes were as black as the night sky, his skin pale like a pearl, his blood red hair mirrored Queen Vendetta's while his horns matched King Emil's.

Next to the king was Draga. Mother and daughter could be sisters, they looked so similar. In between Malice and Odovacar, was Inyene. Of everyone in the room, she resembled his majesty the most, down to her beady red eyes and dark, almost black hair.

Finally, sitting across from Malice, were Sok and Rayen, twins. They stared at Malice. Both had one crimson and one inky eye, their faces an exact copy of one another. The difference between the twins was their voice, Annabeth had said on the stairwell. Sok's was adenoidal, like his nose was constantly stuffed, while Rayen's was gravelly, as if her voice were constantly hoarse.

Malice picked at his food, his clothes uncomfortable, and his stomach queasy. He would rather go back to his room and eat with Annabeth and Kiran. Silverware clinked and scraped against the porcelain plates, wiggly snakes painted on the edges. His chest was heavy, painfully so, making it difficult to swallow the pre-cut pieces of meat and vegetables.

"Begin," her highness said, startling Malice. Eyes flitting from one family member to the next, no one else reacted. He returned to his meal.

King Emil said, the rest of his body as still as a statue, "The regions remain peaceful, prosperous. However, Queen Basia is getting restless so soon after killing her predecessor. The same can be said for Thorn." Malice didn't like his tone, uninterested, and drone. He was glad Annabeth was the one who read him bedtime stories and not his majesty. "They crave bloodshed but refuse to be the first to disrupt the peace."

"Anything we do not know?" Odovacar asked, voice much deeper and sharper, echoing off the walls.

King Emil, eyes glued on the empty chair, hands underneath the table, said, "Throughout Vinyamar, people are disappearing without a trace, few and far between as they may be."

"So insignificant yet someone felt the need to say something," Draga commented. "Who?"

"Yoon Woo Braxton."

Malice hadn't stayed long enough to hear all the ruler's names, the only one he knew being Holister.

Draga sighed, rolled her eyes, and finished the last few bites of her meal, washing it down with a draught of wine. Malice didn't have wine. Annabeth told him he wasn't old enough to drink it. Water filled his cup instead. Most of the time, it was milk or fruit juice, though.

"Is that all?" Queen Vendetta regarded the king for a moment, her eyes as dark as Dun Raik, perhaps darker.

"Yes."

"Good." She took a long, savoring sip from her goblet and licked her lips. "Eat." His majesty lifted his hands, gingerly grabbed his silverware, and began cutting the slabs of meat on his plate.

"Liar!" Sok shouted when he pointed a finger at Malice. Malice froze mid-chew like a deer caught in the middle of the woods. He swallowed. "Malice has an earring."

"Aww," Rayen joined, "did someone make a friend?"

All eyes turned to Malice like icy cold daggers sinking into his skin. He didn't dare look up, opting to watch his hands tremble in his lap.

"I thought it would be a promising idea for him to make relations with Holister Castine's son Magnus. Their relationship could come in handy one day," King Emil said, surprising everyone at the table.

The queen glanced back toward Malice, her gaze scornful. "True enough," she breathed into her cup.

"On the subject of Malice, when will his training commence?" Inyene asked, her voice dripping with amusement.

"When he finally uses magic," Queen Vendetta said.

Sok burst out laughing, dry and humorless, as Rayen blurted, "Like hell he'll ever be able to do that!"

"I bet a mouse could pull one over on you!" Sok laughed some more, combined with Rayen's as devilish smirks twisted their mouths. Malice's gut twisted once more, grinding the food he'd just eaten.

"They have a point," Odovacar glared at the twins, who instantly fell silent. "If Malice has not yet showed signs of his magical energy, he may never develop the way you want."

Intertwining her fingers, her highness rested her chin on the back of her hands, fixated on Malice. "If he proves useless, you may do whatever you please with him. I'll not have trash roaming my halls."

Heat swelled at the center of Malice's chest, spreading to his arms, making his fists ball up in his lap. But feared gripped him tighter, and forced his mouth to stay clamped, his eyes down.

"What? Does the babe have something to say?" Sok taunted.

"Well?" Rayen insisted.

"I can use… my magic," he muttered eventually, swallowing enough dread to speak, and hoped it was loud enough for everyone to hear. He didn't want to repeat himself. Better yet, he wished no one had heard him at all.

"Oh?" the twins voiced simultaneously. Malice looked up through his eyelashes, noticing the doubtful expression they shared.

With his hands on the table, Malice pushed himself up, feet coming to rest on his seat. He held out his hand, closed his eyes, and concentrated the way he had in the lounge during the summit, recalling how Magnus had breathed and the sensation that ran through his arm.

The twinge happened again. It wasn't as intense as it was a week ago, but it was there alongside the movement in his arm, as if the wind had found a way inside his body. When he opened his eyes, darkness danced in the palm of his hand like flames. It was bigger, shooting black embers into the air, devouring every bit of light. He stared at it, like everyone else in the room, awe painting their faces. Annabeth gasped behind him.

A few heartbeats went by when the darkness dissipated into nothing and Malice swayed in his chair, the room spinning as dark specks spotted his vision. Suddenly Annabeth was there, catching Malice before he fell into Inyene. The dizzy spell faded, but he had a hard time regaining his breath. Annabeth stayed, helping him back into his chair, pressing the back of her hand into his forehead to feel for a fever. Something sent her back to the wall, though she did so hesitantly, her hand lingering on his shoulder.

Sok's and Rayen's smirks had vanished, and the rest wore stupefied expressions. Malice had to stop himself from smiling and fought the urge to close his eyes. He was exhausted for some reason.

"When did you learn this?" Queen Vendetta, after a long silence, asked.

Tentatively, he answered, "At the summit."

Sok and Rayen's mouths dropped, but no words came out.

Menacing laughter crept out of the queen, sending a chill down Malice's spine. "You wanted to know about his training." She grinned. "You have your answer."

"I don't want to train," Malice blurted, and instantly shrank into his seat. Annabeth made a choked sound from the wall. Then the room was silent, frozen, picks of ice dragging across his skin. He swallowed the dryness in his mouth.

A chair scraped against the floor. Footsteps followed. They

stopped, a shadow looming over him.

"Look at me."

Malice looked up at her highness, his head tilting when she grabbed him by the neck. He squawked as his hands shot up to the queen's wrist. She lifted him from his seat. Fear raced through his veins. His heart pounded so hard it hurt. His feet dangled in the air.

"Should you disobey me, mutt," she breathed, her voice calm. Malice squirmed, but her grip tightened, forcing his breath to catch. Tears flooded and blurred his vision. He couldn't breathe anymore. "I will kill Kiran. Am I understood?"

He nodded furiously, his head on fire, the pressure threatening to pop his eyes out of his head. Flinging him, Malice crashed to the floor, a loud thud, whatever air he had knocked out of him. He retched, coughed, and spluttered, choking until he heaved and caught his breath. Body trembling, Malice didn't have the strength to run away.

"Annabeth."

"Yes!" she squealed.

"Get that mutt out of my sight," the queen said as she retook her place at the head of the table, "and get another servant to clean the mess."

"Yes, your highness."

One moment Malice was alone and the next, Annabeth was bringing him into her arms and carrying him off, the table of his family growing smaller. He sobbed, his fists bunching Annabeth's clothes. It hurt so much, throat rough like he'd swallowed a handful of pebbles, and the tears wouldn't stop.

Reaching his bedchamber, sniffling, Annabeth set Malice on his bed, got him out of his outfit and into his nightwear, then tucked him in. She turned away, and her back neared the door. Malice's heart sped.

"Wait," he said, and Annabeth stopped at the door. "Can you stay with me?"

"Of course, I will."

Annabeth had already blown out the candles, so the room was dark, light seeping from underneath the door. The sound of her taking her shoes and placing them against the wall was especially loud in the silence, her bare feet padding to the bed. She got on the mattress and shifted so she was under the covers, too. For a while, Malice listened to her breathing. When he closed his eyes, his heartbeat grew louder and matched her breaths. Her scent flowed into his nose, soap and sweet mint, which relaxed the tension throughout his body. Warmth spilled over to him, dispelling the bitter cold lingering from the queen and the dining room. Gradually, the tears slowed to a stop and Malice drifted to sleep.

Kin
"The Start"

In the southern wing of the castle, there was a room leading to the dungeons—small and closet-like, with two torches inside, next to a dark, spiraling tunnel.

Inyene glanced over her shoulder, her red beady eyes, like a rat's, glaring down at Malice before she took a torch from its holster and started down the stairwell, her footfalls quiet, while his echoed off the rocky walls. The further down they went, the cooler and smellier it became. Malice's nose crinkled as his stomach churned. He followed silently, too afraid to ask what they were doing down here. His throat was still sore from the night prior, bruises tender, and a reminder of what would happen if he voiced his thoughts.

Eventually, they reached a flat surface. Malice hurried to stay close behind Inyene, passing cell after cell. An enormous iron door blocked each chamber off, a sliding latch near the top. The torch flickered and their shadows swayed on the walls and ground and merged with the darkness behind them.

Malice almost crashed into Inyene's back when she stopped and opened a cell door with a high-pitched screech. She pointed inside with a jerk of her chin. He cautiously crossed the threshold. The walls were a mix of earth, cobblestone, and concrete, mold in the corners spreading across the ceiling, dark pools and blotches staining the floor. It stunk in here too, Malice hesitating to enter any further. His skin crawled as his mind told him to run away. How could he do that with Inyene standing there?

He turned and Inyene leaned against the door frame as she scanned Malice up and down. Her body was lean with muscle, scars tainting her knuckles. Her eyebrows were thick, her lips thin, the shape of her face as sharp as the queens, and her low cheekbones were prominent. Horns curved around her head like the king's and Odovacar's—Malice wondered if Elias had them, too.

"Show me how you conjure your magic," she said.

He didn't want to. Something told him it would cause him trouble if he did, but something even louder told him if he didn't…

Malice took several deep breaths, hand in front of him, and focused on his palm. Magnus flashed against his eyelids, his light magic a web between his fingers. Black wisps crept from Malice's hand and created a mass of darkness. Magical energy flowed through his arm like a gentle breeze racing over his skin.

"Now hold it," she ordered, a gleam of interest in her eyes. She started counting. *One, two, three…*

Annabeth taught Malice how to count to ten, taught him how to read as well, so he could keep up with Kiran's story books.

Inyene reached forty. Malice couldn't keep his magic going any longer. A pain stabbed his core, he gasped, and the darkness evaporated. Cradling his torso, a dull throb radiated through his abdomen and kept his breathing short and shallow. The pain eased soon enough, but he didn't like it, no matter how quickly it went away.

"Do it again," Inyene said.

I don't want to. Malice righted himself and concentrated again. If he didn't listen, Kiran would be in danger.

Malice's magic surged within his body, into his arm and hand, till darkness seeped out. Inyene counted to thirty this time, then thirty-five. Twenty-seven. Nineteen. Fifteen. Ten.

Little time had passed since they came down to the dungeons. Yet his core ached and burned, his limbs growing weaker and weaker. The dim room faded to black before he blinked the light back into it. Inyene doubled, blurred, tripled, and spun. His legs gave out, and he crashed to the floor, pain exploding.

*

Jolted awake, Malice's eyes darted around. It was his room. He was in bed, the blankets over his legs soft and warm. Yellow peered from under the door.

Next to him, Kiran sat up groggily, rubbing his sleepy eyes. He blinked a few times, and sprang out of bed, ran to the door, flung it open, and dashed down the hall, his feet smacking the floor the whole way. Malice shunned away from the light, confused. Soon Blodwen, Tendai, and Annabeth entered behind Kiran.

Tendai kneeled beside the bed on Malice's side, sunset-colored garments rustling, as he took Malice's wrist and pressed his fingers into the skin. He didn't look much like Kiran, his square jaw covered in a layer of dark brown stubble, coarse brows currently furrowed.

"How are you feeling?" he asked. His soft eyes were strange with horizontal pupils, eyelashes long.

Malice turned to him and opened his mouth to say he felt fine. Pain, like claws tearing at his midsection and burning the flesh, took his breath away. He doubled over onto his lap, ears ringing. Exhaustion held him tightly as he cried. It hurt.

A big hand rested on the middle of his back, and warmth soaked into his tender skin, something like a feather tickling his muscles, arms, chest, and legs. Magic, he realized. It flowed smoothly, twisting with his veins as it reached his core.

Taking shallow breaths, Malice made himself sit upright, cringing in pain as he did.

"Slowly," Tendai cautioned, his other hand supporting Malice's sternum while keeping him from moving too quickly.

One heartbeat, two, three, and the pulsing agony subsided. He finally took a full breath and flopped backward, the bed squeaking.

Kiran tore out of Blodwen's grip, fat tears rolling down his face as he rushed to the opposite side of the bed and crawled onto the mattress. He carefully sat next to Malice, eyes downcast, then grabbed Malice's hand. He was warm, which Malice liked. Without the pain, it was chillier.

"How do you feel?" Tendai repeated. "Does anything hurt?"

Malice shook his head. Blodwen and Tendai exchanged glances and looked behind them toward Annabeth, who nodded with a smile. It was small, though, the one she used when she didn't mean it. Tendai rose and ruffled Malice's hair while Blodwen gave Kiran a stern glare, both heading to the corridor. Annabeth joined them and closed the door, but not fully. Their voices filtered through the crack, quiet and incomprehensible.

Kiran yanked the blankets over their bodies and snuggled into the pillows. He was still holding Malice's hand.

"Are you sure you're okay?" Kiran whispered.

"I don't know," Malice said, his voice back to normal. He gently touched his neck, the tender bruises gone. *How did Tendai do that?* "I guess I'm okay."

Kiran lay on his side, the knubby horns on the sides of his head poking out of his curly hair. He had horizontal pupils like his parents, his face a lot rounder than theirs. In no time at all, Kiran's puffy eyes closed. For a little while longer, till he couldn't hold his eyelids up anymore, Malice stared at Kiran, glad the queen didn't do anything to him like she said she would. Why would she say something like that? He knew he shouldn't have told her no but, what had Kiran done?

Remembering last night, Malice shuddered, and his stomach twisted, the sensation of her highness's icy fingers on his neck returning.

"Malice," a voice said. It was deep and monotone, but familiar.

Malice opened his eyes, startling when he saw Odovacar looming over him. He shot out of bed to find Annabeth by the door, hands clasped to her chest, eyebrows perched with worry.

"Get up and meet me in the foyer." Odovacar turned on his heel and strode out of the room.

Annabeth walked to the closet and picked clothes out for both Malice and Kiran. Dazed, Kiran sat up too, yawning as Malice sat on the edge of the bed. He wondered when he fell asleep last night. The only thing he remembered was drawing the sheets over his head and wishing the queen's grasp would release him.

"What's going on?" Kiran yawned again.

"I have to go," Malice said, flinching at the cold floor.

"Where?"

"To the foyer."

"But why?"

Malice stood and stretched while Annabeth set the clothes on the dresser and went to the other side to get Kiran out of bed. "I don't know."

"Can I come?" he asked.

"That you can't," Annabeth answered, her voice soft. "You can stay here if you would like. Or I can take you home."

Sullenly, after a moment, Kiran said, "I'll go home."

Standing side by side, Annabeth helped them dress, brushed their hair, said, "If you're unsure of what to do next, copy someone else," and they were off. Malice would have to tell Kiran about Magnus tomorrow.

In the foyer, Odovacar waited, his posture stiff, shoulders rolled back, and his chin held high. His attention shifted when Malice approached, his dark eyes glued to him briefly. Annabeth continued to the doors with Kiran, who waved back at Malice. Shyly, Malice did the same.

"Inyene will be your teacher in the ways of magic. You started yesterday," Odovacar said as Annabeth and Kiran shrank from view. "Today, I will train you in the ways of combat." Odovacar briskly walked to the doors and through the courtyard. Malice struggled to keep up; his brother's legs were too long.

The scorching sun caused an instant discomfort as bugs screeched. Wildflowers and grass scented the air as well as a saltiness Annabeth said was from the ocean. She also said it meant it would rain soon.

Malice wondered why he had to learn about combat. He would much rather learn to read and write so he could enjoy Kiran's stories more. Maybe they could create their own fairy tale if Malice knew how to write better. His handwriting was sloppy and ugly.

"Where are we going?" Malice asked as they passed underneath an archway of the stone wall covered in vines, the castle at their backside like thousands of black spikes stabbing the heavens.

"The training grounds," Odovacar said shortly.

The training grounds were an enormous square of beaten dirt and gravel crowded with royals. They were shouting, cracks and booms echoed, fire flared further away, and a pillar of earth speared the sky. Wooden racks surrounded the yard, along with a few wooden pavilions. Odovacar explained how they stored water, food, targets, and training dummies—the racks were for weapons. Half of the royals trained in one-on-one spars, some used magic, but most were armed or fought barehanded. The other half was engaged in large group exercises, all moving in a fluid motion, mimicking the one at the head.

Malice nodded, but he didn't have the slightest clue about what Odovacar was talking about. The horrid stench, metallic and oniony, in the air, burning Malice's nostrils, didn't exactly help him focus on his brother's lessons.

"They are forming lines, attacking as a singular unit, defending flanks while remaining on offense," Odovacar said. "They are training to become a warband." Whatever a warband was.

When Odovacar and Malice approached, stepping into the field, royals acknowledged his brother with a deep bow and returned to their earlier activities. Behind him, the royals whispered amongst themselves like the servants in the castle when no one was around. One time, Annabeth had put her finger to her lips, shushing Malice, so they could listen. *"What if we're caught?"* one had said. The other responded, *"I swear, all are too busy to realize a few servants are off fu—"* Annabeth had clapped her hands over Malice's ears and yanked him away before they could finish their sentence.

In a small clearing, Odovacar turned to face Malice. His long, red shaggy hair was in a high ponytail, his clothes were plain, dirt-stained and somewhat frayed, his boots scuffed and dull. His upper body was muscular and broad, like many others wielding swords around them. A snap of his fingers summoned a royal from the crowd who handed Odovacar two wooden swords.

He threw one at Malice's feet. "Pick it up." Royals started gathering, some in shiny armor, others in leather, and a few wore clothes like Odovacar.

Malice looked down at the sword, picked it up, and held it in front of him with both hands, right above the left. *Is this right?* Peeking at Odovacar gave him no answer. He was relaxed, his body loose. A ball of nerves lodged in his throat as he watched his brother's grip tighten. Malice's did too, his knuckles whitening. He didn't think that was possible, given how pale he already was. He'd asked Annabeth why his skin and hair were as light as they were when everyone else's skin was colored and their hair dark. *You are born of snow,* she had told him. *Why don't I melt in the summer then?* Annabeth had laughed heartly at him, face red, her laugh quickly turning into a wheeze.

"You will strike me with all of your might," Odovacar said, startling Malice.

The lump in his throat went down hard. Malice ran toward his brother, hefting his sword above his head, and letting it crash into Odovacar's. Their swords clacked loudly but, with a jerk of his arm, Odovacar shoved Malice back. He fell with a yelp and dropped the wooden blade.

The gathered royals, having lost interest, returned to their own training. Malice only noticed because he knew his brother was scowling at him and he didn't want to face it.

"Get up and do it again," Odovacar barked.

Malice grabbed his sword and got to his feet, his bum sore. What was he supposed to do? Odovacar wasn't teaching him like Annabeth had. He and Kiran never did anything like this either. They preferred to forage and read and doodle. He scanned the training grounds like Annabeth told him to, then attacked, swinging his sword up diagonally instead of straight down. Odovacar parried, caught Malice's sword, twisting it to the ground, and drove the tip into the dirt.

"Again."

A few steps from the divot his sword made, Malice readied himself, a burning sensation settling in his arms. He peeked at the surrounding royals again. It was a mistake; he shouldn't have gotten distracted. Odovacar stepped forward, smacking Malice in the leg, arm, and the top of his head, all in succession of each other, causing sharp pain to burst three times. Malice winced for all of them, frowning. He didn't want to be here anymore. Odovacar wouldn't let him leave, probably. And if he ran, his brother was bigger, faster, and stronger.

Sword above his head once more, Malice charged. Odovacar barely moved his blade in front of his chest to counter. Similar to the royals across the field, Malice closed in, swung his arm in an arc, and struck Odovacar's waist, his movements sloppy. Red brows raised, Odovacar stared at the practice sword pressed against him, unmoving. Malice did as well, amazed it actually worked.

"Not bad."

Malice smiled and Odovacar pushed his sword away.

"Again."

His smile faded.

All Malice had done was strike. His arms felt like they were on fire, his skin bubbled with sweat, and the heat made it hard to catch his breath without his throat burning. Stomach rumbling, Malice wondered how much longer he had to stay here and train with Odovacar. He was hungry. But Annabeth would make him bathe before lunch, and his limbs ached from exertion.

A sharp whistle pierced the air.

Both Malice and Odovacar looked to where the sound originated. Annabeth stood in the tall grass, her hand waving wildly to catch Malice's attention. When he looked, Odovacar was already making his way deeper into the training grounds. Malice took it as permission to leave, tossed the sword on the ground, and raced toward Annabeth.

Her hand extended toward him, and he took it, arms heavy. It was good to see her again; it felt like forever since that morning.

"Is it time for lunch?" he asked. Maybe Kiran would come back or maybe Annabeth would allow him to visit Kiran's cottage and eat lunch with them. He was sure Annabeth could stay too. Blodwen and Tendai were kind.

"I'll make sure you eat as quickly as possible," she said with a slight laugh.

Beside Malice at the dining table, Annabeth cut his food into bite-sized pieces, then dug into her own plate of ham, steamed carrots, and bread smeared with garlic and butter. They never ate in the dining hall, but when Malice asked why they were here, Annabeth hadn't answered. Memories of the other night sprang to life in his head, his hunger not as strong anymore.

It didn't help that the twins sat across from him, the two inseparable. If he saw one, the other wasn't far behind. They wore the same outfit, high collared brown vests, a white blouse underneath with puffed sleeves. Sok's hair was tied into a ponytail while Rayen's came to her shoulders.

"We heard you collapsed yesterday," Sok said. He always spoke first.

"And that you were so weak today your ass made friends with the ground," Rayen teased, shoving a fork full into her mouth, both snickering to themselves.

Malice deflated a bit as he poked at his food. He and Annabeth should've left the moment they saw Sok and Rayen enter the dining hall. Why were they here in the first place? His room worked perfectly fine.

Setting his silverware down, Sok sneered, "You should really give up, don't you think? Disappear before you make a bigger fool out of yourself."

"Scum like you doesn't deserve to be heir to the throne." Rayen's jaw tensed, and she mumbled something else under her breath.

Did they not like him because of his magic or because he was their sibling? He wasn't heir to any throne either, whether they wanted to believe it or not. All they had to do was ask the queen, or anyone really, and they would say the same thing.

The twins glared at Malice as they stood, the chairs screeching against the floor, leaving their plates for the servants to clean up when they walked out of the dining hall.

Since they were gone, Malice ate, albeit sluggishly. Annabeth seethed, her grip on the knife and fork turning her knuckles white. She cursed under her breath, a sharp hiss. Not that Malice understood it. It sounded mean though, and if Annabeth didn't like them, the twins most certainly deserved it.

"I don't want to eat here anymore," he said, more to himself than to Annabeth. He would rather keep as far away from the twins as possible.

She sighed. "Then we won't."

After wiping her mouth with a napkin, she cleaned Malice's face despite how clean of an eater he was, with only a few crumbs left around his mouth or spots of grease wetting his lips. Kiran was the messy one. She got up and collected their dirty dishes, handing them off to another servant.

On the fourth floor, the servants of the castle had their own communal bathroom, a few lounges, and personal bedchambers. Malice's bedchamber was also on the fourth floor, along with a few abandoned studies used for storage. Every now and again, Annabeth, Kiran, and Malice would explore the studies. They had once found a crate of skulls Annabeth instantly covered back up.

They went to the baths where Malice washed, and Annabeth ruffled his hair dry, gave him a plain tunic to wear for bed, then guided him back to his room.

Malice gasped, his heart jumping into his throat. Kiran nearly fell out of the chair at his desk, wide-eyed, mouth open to form a high-pitched squeal. Annabeth chuckled behind Malice.

"You scared me," they said simultaneously, while the door shut and shoes clacked out of earshot.

Kiran hopped down from the chair, raced toward Malice's bed, and jumped into it, making the frame creak. He sat up and patted the sheets. Malice padded across the room, joining his friend; he didn't want to run, especially after training with Odovacar the way he had.

"Tell me about the summit," Kiran beamed. "I'm not allowed to go, so I'm curious."

Malice tilted his head. "Why can't you go?"

"I'm a commoner. It's against the rules."

"What rules?"

Kiran shrugged. "So, tell me, what was it like?" he insisted.

Malice started off by telling him about the rulers, or at least what they looked like. He only remembered Holister's name, and he hadn't stayed long enough to learn about the regions. When he brought up the barbarian with the swirl tattoos, Kiran snickered.

"You didn't know about them?"

Malice's face burned. "I haven't seen any in the castle."

Kiran giggled some more.

Changing the topic; "The castle was huge." Malice extended his arms as wide as he could. "But it was empty and half of it had collapsed." He described the amount of dust on everything and how, when he took a deep breath, he had to suppress a cough or sneeze. Not that it worked every time. Kiran listened intently, a smile on his lips and a twinkle in his eyes.

"Me and Magnus left before the summit started," he said.

"Magnus?" Kiran echoed, the wonder from his face fleeting.

Malice nodded. "Magnus is the prince of Alucard's Region. He's older than us by four or five years, I think."

"Is he your friend?" Kiran asked.

Malice, pointing to his earring, smirked. "He gave me this as a token of our friendship."

Kiran's face flashed with something, shock perhaps, when he pouted and looked away, muttering under his breath.

Malice's heart sank. "What's wrong? Was I not supposed to make a friend?" He leaned to the side and forward, trying to get a better look at Kiran's face.

"No," he grumbled. "I just wish I could've gone too."

Unsure if he should say anything at all, Malice picked at his fingernails. Magnus didn't want to make friends. His father forced him to go with Malice. It all worked out, though.

Kiran whipped back to him, startling Malice. "Well? Keep going, tell me more about Magnus." Curiosity brightened his demeanor once more.

For the first time since the summit, Malice found himself rambling about what he and Magnus discussed, about the games of chess Malice lost, which were practically all of them, and finally about their magic.

"Show me!" Kiran blurted. "Please."

Hand lifting, energy coursing through his chest into his arm and hand, darkness rose between them, jerking and flickering. He let it go until he could produce no more, the magic vanishing in a plume of shadow. A shiver raced up his spine, bumps pricking his skin. There was, however, no pain. Thankfully. Gaze sliding from the open space above their heads to the silent Kiran, Malice waited for a reaction. Heartbeats passed when a grin spread from ear to ear, creasing Kiran's eyes. Malice couldn't help but smile, too. His cheeks flushed as Kiran praised Malice's magic, but he wished Kiran could have seen Magnus's. It was better than his by a landslide. Prettier as well.

The next morning, Malice was dragged to the second floor. Malice stared at his gloomy surroundings, at the dark burgundy walls and the black floors marbled with grey clouds and white crackling lines—like a lightning storm. His eyes moved between the gold fixtures and crown molding, glancing down at the rugs of dingy teal sewn with swirls and other shapes a few shades lighter. Wax scented the air, something like lemongrass underlying it, which Malice didn't mind. They stopped halfway down the corridor and Annabeth knocked on the dark wood door.

"Enter," Draga said from within.

Stepping into the room, Annabeth presented Malice with her head bowed, one hand lifting her skirt in a curtsy. Malice copied her the best he could, but he wasn't wearing a skirt. Draga peered beyond her documents, her obsidian black eyes taking Malice in. He shivered and averted his gaze, his hands wringing themselves. She looked like her highness, a disturbing mirror raking up memories Malice would've liked to have stayed buried.

"Sit on the couch," she said dismissively, signaling for Annabeth to take her leave.

The door clicked shut and Malice sat down on the couch in front of a small table across from two armchairs. The study, with all decorations, was somehow gloomier than the rest of the castle. Skulls sat alongside jars and vials and thick-spined books amongst daggers, scrolls, and ink and feather pens.

"On the table," Draga said, upsetting the silence. Malice flinched. "There is a stack of papers. Sign your name and something you want until each sheet is full." She didn't bother looking up from her own parchment anymore, her eyes jetting across the page before she flipped to the one behind it.

The pile of blank sheets was as bulky as the books on her shelves. Malice slipped from the edge of the couch to the floor, spreading his legs underneath the table, and moved the paper closer to him. He dipped the tip of the pen, the metal body textured with whirling ridges—the one Annabeth used wasn't as fancy as Draga's— into the black liquid and wrote his name, *Malice Reap.* He paused, staring at the ink as it soaked into the paper, thinking of what he wanted. *I want to see Magnus.*

The letters were uneven, big, and small, loops too large or too narrow. Still, he continued to write because he knew he would get better like Kiran.

Halfway through the stack of parchment, Draga said, "Now switch to your left hand," her tone level as she glanced from her work.

Right hand aching and cramping, Malice was glad he could give it a much-needed break. With his left hand, he started at the top of the page. *My name is Malice Reap. I want to see Magnus.* He was much slower, and his letters were sloppier. Despite writing the same thing, the page didn't reflect it. He hoped she didn't plan to read them. She wouldn't be able to, at least not what he penned with his left hand, and he didn't want to get in trouble for it.

Annabeth began teaching him to read and write after he met Kiran. She'd used her pen and ink as an example and had him copy what she wrote using sticks of graphite which stained his fingers grey.

Then she had him follow along in the books she read aloud. One of his favorite stories was *the black throne*. It had a pleasant rhythm whenever Annabeth told it.

Again, Malice peeked at Draga scribbling across her papers, her feather pen wiggling back and forth. She dipped it in ink and resumed where she left off. She reminded Malice of Odovacar. They were both grumpy, had purplish pale skin, red hair, and black eyes. Inyene, Sok, and Rayen, on the other hand, seemed to love the sound of their own voices. Malice surely didn't. They were annoying, and Inyene was scary. Draga's attire was simple and usually one color. The only extravagant thing about her outfit was the semi-circle of gold hanging around her neck going down to her collarbone.

Still, she made Malice nervous, his hands a bit sweaty and his heart thumping in his ears.

Back to his assignment, Malice wrote despite the nag of pain in his hand and wrist and the numbness in his butt from sitting on the floor. Eventually, he finished and stood, his legs wobbly and full of pinpricks. Malice gathered the papers and hesitantly approached to place them on Draga's desk. She paid no mind to him or the work he had done.

"You are free to go," was all she said.

Relief washed over him like the warm water of a bath when he hurried out of her study.

In his bedchamber, at his desk, Malice waited for Annabeth to bring him dinner, a little disappointed he would eat alone today. *If I ask and share some of my food, maybe Annabeth will stay.*

The door opened. Malice perked his head as Kiran strode in, a silver tray of food in his hands, Annabeth right behind him. She set his tray of food on his desk once Kiran did and he went to fetch the armchair next to the closet, dragging it over. Malice smiled, sliding his chair over for Kiran. Then Kiran hopped into his seat and instantly started stuffing his gob with food. Malice questioned how Kiran stayed tidy when he ate so sloppily. Good thing he had a napkin. Though he doubted it was enough to clean Kiran's face and hands sometimes.

"You won't believe what I found today," he said in between swallows, spittle flying onto the desk.

Malice cringed a bit. "What?"

"A dragon's egg!" he declared and shoveled more food into his mouth.

"Where did you find it?" Malice, taking a bite out of his bread, asked.

Kiran hesitated and swallowed, his head swaying for a moment. "Well, maybe it's not a dragon's egg, but it's really big!" That wasn't the question, but Malice was sure he found it in the forest somewhere while exploring. His parents scolded him every time he did. They scolded Malice whenever he joined Kiran, too.

"Are you going to eat it?" Malice asked.

Kiran's head snapped toward Malice, his expression a mix of disgust and confusion. Malice snorted. "Why would I do that?"

He shrugged. "I eat eggs for breakfast all the time."

Kiran shook his head, waving his fork at Malice. "That's different. This egg will hatch into something. Mother said so."

"Are you going to keep it?" It would be neat if Kiran had a pet. They could name it together and teach it to sit and fetch things.

"No." Kiran's shoulders slouched as he nudged his food around his plate. "Mother said we should leave it in case the mother comes back. She would be furious if she found her egg missing."

Malice nodded. "Your mother's probably right."

"She's always right… Except when she's not."

Even after Annabeth came and collected their dirty dishes, Kiran blabbered about anything and everything that came to his mind. He always did. Malice liked to listen. Besides, Kiran talked enough for the both of them. Once or twice, however, he'd stopped and stared at Malice until he said something, then went on as if his mouth were a waterfall.

Little star
V

At the dining table, Magnus's mother was teaching him the chain stitch—she'd already taught him a few of the basics. Padma slept on the couch in front of the hearth, a small kindle spreading the scent of pine. Mother's cottage was small compared to his bedchamber at the castle, but Magnus preferred it this way. It was cozier. The kitchen was to their left, a counter at its center, a window above the basin for a sink. Dried herbs and flowers hung from lines of yarn on the wall.

With his own tambour frame, white cloth taut, Magnus watched as Vesh leisurely repeated the chain stitch. He'd tried a few times already, but his looked like knots while Mother's was a sage green chain off-centered on the cloth.

"Watch and listen carefully, little star." Her voice was hushed for Padma, a soothing caress to Magnus's ears.

He nodded and leaned a little closer while Vesh moved the candle toward them, shedding more light on their work.

The needle and thread followed her instructions. "Pierce the cloth downward, come back up, not through the small hole, but right next to it to grab the fabric."

She paused and shifted her eyes to watch Magnus's attempt. "So far, so good. Now wrap the thread around the needle," she said, hands delicately binding the thread. "And pull it through." Just like that, she created a loop, the first chain in the stitch.

Magnus thought he knew why his attempts were failures. He failed to hook the thread when he brought the needle back up, then he failed to be gentle, which formed a knot rather than a link. This time, he wrapped the green thread around the sharp end of the needle and softly dragged it through.

"You've got it, little star," Mother said with a smile. "Keep going and you'll have the whole chain."

Delicately, Magnus created a second loop in tandem with Vesh, whose pace was much more relaxed than it usually was. In the time it took Magnus to create a single, jagged chain stitch, his mother could have outlined the framed cloth. He was grateful for it, as he used her embroidery and handiwork as a constant reference.

"My little star," Vesh said after a time and set the wooden tambour on the table, turning slightly in her chair to face Magnus. "What happened to your earring?"

Her hand lifted to touch the blue gem dangling in his left earlobe, his right empty. They were Mother's gift for his last birthday. Suddenly, guilt sat heavy in his stomach like a rock, and he started a new line for a running stitch.

"Did you lose it?" she asked.

This was the first time he had spent more than a few hours at home with his mother and brother since before the Kings Summit. A part of Magnus was hoping she wouldn't notice the missing earring, so he wouldn't hurt her feelings. Yet, he was glad to have given it to Malice. There was something off about the white-haired boy, his name aside.

He shook his head. "I made a friend," he whispered, eyes glued to the silver needle going in and out of the ivory fabric. "Maybe."

"Did they take it?"

He shook his head again. "I gave it to him."

From his ear, Vesh's hand smoothed the back of Magnus's head as she propped her head in her palm, elbow on the table. Violet eyes stared at him. They were a much deeper and vibrant shade of purple than his were; her freckled skin was too. The biggest difference in their appearance was their hair. Magnus's was brick red while Mother's was charcoal black and coiled, currently tied up so it didn't get in her face while embroidering.

"I wanted," Magnus said, "him to feel better."

"He was upset?"

"Uncomfortable and scared. I think lonely as well." Magnus remembered his first summit only a year ago. The rulers were intimidating. They had been this year too, but not as bad only because he was prepared this time.

Lines creased the corners of his mother's mouth, finer lines at the corners of her eyes. They deepened. "What was his name?"

"Malice."

Her eyebrows twitched, but her smile remained. Father had reacted the same way. Malice, *hatred*; it was probably why none of his siblings liked him. He was made an outcast from the moment he was born.

"I can have another pair made, if you'd like."

Instantly; "No." The first set had cost months of work, if not more. With winter coming, Magnus didn't want his mother out in the cold, all because he gave her gift away. "It's still a set," he added. Separated, sure, but a set, nonetheless. It was nice to think a part of him was in another region. He would like to visit all the regions one day—in person. When he was older, he would be able to.

"All right, little star." She leaned forward to kiss his forehead, rose, and stretched her arms high.

"Momma?" Padma yawned and shuffled around the couch, rubbing his sleepy eyes with his knitted blanket of butterflies and flowers in hand. He was small, limbs chunky, cheeks round. He had Magnus's hair, red and shaggy, and bright amethyst-colored eyes, more like Mother's.

Groaning as she hefted Padma into her arms, Vesh tapped the tip of his freckled nose. "Would my little tiger like to help make dinner?"

Magnus snickered. He quite enjoyed being called little star. He assumed it was due to his magic. Unlike Padma, who was called tiger because he liked to bite and snarl whenever he threw hissy fits. "I want to help," he said as Padma bobbed his head.

Mother ruffled Magnus's hair, and started into the kitchen, Magnus dropping his thread, needle, and frame to follow. When she set Padma on the floor next to Magnus, instructions were given, supplies were found and brought out, and a meal was prepared. It would be the last one with his mother for a while. He had to return to the castle tomorrow. The thought soured his mood, so he shooed it to the back of his mind. He couldn't be sad when they had an entire night ahead of them.

But morning came too soon.

Quickly and quietly, Magnus rose, dressed, and headed for the door. He glanced over his shoulder. Padma and Mother were sound asleep in front of the hearth, embers winking within the ashes and burnt logs, both wrapped in a quilted blanket Vesh had made. Sighing,

Magnus carefully turned the knob and stepped into the crisp morning air, just as carefully latching the door.

Gold, crimson, and umber leaves littered the cobblestone streets. All the colors made autumn Magnus's favorite time of year. Although he liked the ice of winter reflecting whatever looked at it. Spring rain was refreshing and brought beautiful flowers to summer. He supposed he didn't have a favorite time of year after all.

The streets were noisy with mutters as hurried feet raced to their destinations. It was cloudy, the breeze howling, scattering the leaves on the ground. A figure to Magnus's side detached from the wall. Magnus flinched away, heart jumping into his throat, when he realized it was Gareth. He should have been used to this by now. Every time Magnus stayed the night at Mother's, Gareth was there to collect him in the morning.

Gareth smiled as he gestured to the street with a dip of his chin. "Good morning, my prince," he greeted, his voice deep and gruff.

Magnus said, "Good morning," despite its falseness. It was never a good morning when he had to leave Vesh and Padma.

In the desaturated light of early morning, Gareth's cropped hair took on more of a grey color, as did his ashen lavender skin. He wore a black padded doublet, the seams and laces royal blue, the eyelets gold, thick enough to keep the chill away. His trousers matched in color and cuffed around his boots, two swords strapped to his back via a leather harness.

From the pouch on his belt, Gareth took out a cloth, unwrapped a piece of bread, and handed it to Magnus.

"You will need it," he said. "The king expects you in the training room upon your return."

It was freshly baked, the inside slightly warm and fluffy, the golden exterior crunchy. Magnus tore chunks of the bread and popped them in his mouth. He didn't hate training, but he didn't see the point in it when Gareth or another knight would always be there to protect him. Gareth told him as much. When asked, Holister said nothing, and silence meant one of two things. *No,* or *it's none of your concern.* Good chance it meant both, depending on the topic. Solemnly, passing many citizens and patrolling royals, Magnus ate his breakfast.

The training room was a small, designated space on the first floor, eastern wing before the servants' barracks for the king. Instead of marble, the floor was wood, the walls and ceiling a plain cream.

Father was already there, waiting. With a jerk of his head, he dismissed Gareth, who promptly slid the door closed. One rack of practice swords, spears, and shields was against the leftmost wall. Holister was tan, pale compared to Magnus and his mother, and his eyes were pure white. Cinnamon hair framed his face and neck with waves and flares. Like Magnus, he wore a plain tunic with loose trousers held to his waist by a belt. Magnus had rushed to change prior to coming here.

The only way Magnus could tell his father looked him up and down was by his eyelids following the movement, almost slipping closed, then lifting. Magnus averted his gaze, one hand going to fiddle with his earring. The gem's smoothness calmed his jittering nerves some.

"Your mother," Father started, voice low and awkward, "how was—" He cut himself off and scowled at the floor. "Grab a sword," he said instead, a few moments of silence passing.

Shoes clumping across the room, Magnus asked, "Father? If someone is always there to protect me, why am I learning to fight?" Perhaps today he would finally answer the question, but he doubted it as he picked the only other practice sword and turned back to Holister.

"If you are to be king," he explained, surprising Magnus, "then you will know how to fight. If you are to know how to fight, you will learn how to kill."

Kill? Magnus halted, a wave of ice crashing into his veins. Why would he need to know how to kill? Did Father *want* him to kill?

"You are old enough to realize one day, you will have to take a life, Magnus." Holister adjusted the wooden blade in his grip, a slight twist. "Gareth can teach you to protect yourself all he wants," he said, "but what if running fails you?"

Father surged forward. Magnus reeled, his footing struggling to keep him off the floor when Holister's sword thwacked his arm. Pain bloomed and pulsed, a breath hissing through Magnus's lips.

"What if you cannot defend yourself because your enemy is too great?" Holister's tone was controlled and firm. "Because the situation demands justice over peace of mind?" Swiftly, his father slipped behind Magnus and rammed the pommel into his back, pain exploding in its wake.

Magnus stumbled forward, ground his teeth, and whipped his sword around. Father dodged it easily. Even if his slender form didn't make him agile, Magnus's attack was wild and predictable. Anyone could have evaded it.

Holister went on, only now, his expression stoney. "There will come a day you find yourself utterly alone with your back against the wall while you face the world." Shouting; "What will a measly shield do, then?"

He didn't know. To Magnus, being the king meant becoming the shield for his people. That shield would protect everyone, including Vesh and Padma. Holister was a sword, too sharp for anyone to wield and fierce, yet revered. He could never imagine being truly alone between Gareth and his mother, and Padma with his annoying little rambles, and now Malice, who he would see every year. Magnus ducked a broad swing as his father flicked his hand downward, striking Magnus's wrist. The wooden sword dropped with a clack.

"Pick it up." Glowering, Holister waited for Magnus to take up his weapon again. Once he did, their fight resumed.

Around noon, they finally stopped. Eventually, Holister's lecture had turned to silence as he focused on Magnus, and they had fallen into a rhythm. Perspiration gleamed on Holister's skin while Magnus wheezed, trying to get his breathing under control so his lungs stopped burning. Sweat steadily slipped down his nose, dripping onto the oak planks he stared at, hands on his knees. His body was on fire and his head was light, nearly spinning, and pounding if he moved too quickly.

Worn shoes stepped into view. Magnus looked up as he righted himself, Holister's hand rising to rest on his shoulder.

"Everything you're learning is only to better you," Father said. "Remember that."

Academically, no matter how boring, Magnus understood its significance. Battle wise, he didn't. Rather than voice his doubts, Magnus simply nodded. It didn't help he was in desperate need of some water. His tongue was stuck to the roof of his mouth.

Then, his father's hand glided to hold the side of Magnus's face, his touch tender and cautious, the gesture one of rarity. Eyebrows curved upward, the softness of Holister's gaze stole any thought in Magnus's head. They stared at each other for what felt like hours, and suddenly Magnus wanted to settle deep into his father's arms and talk like he could with Vesh. An urge he fought hard to keep down.

Holister breathed, "You look so much like her."

Knock, knock, knock, knock, knock. The door slid open.

"I have come to collect the prince for lunch, your majesty," Gareth said from the doorway.

For a second longer, pain morphed Holister's expression into something loving. Then it hardened, and he stepped away. "Go."

Hesitantly, Magnus met Gareth in the corridor, stupefied all the way up to his bedchamber where he bathed and clothed, during the trek down to the dining room and during the meal itself. His father was confusing if nothing else. At least he knew Vesh loved him.

Between Light and Dark
VI

The carriage rocked as Malice studied the moving terrain of Hordes Region. Flowers of pink, blue, white, and yellow pricked the grassy plains and hills. Birds occasionally zipped past his line of sight as if they were playing games of tag. Spiky trees lined the horizon, the sweet floral smell gradually transforming into mud and pine.

Felim sat next to Malice while King Emil was in front of them. The king was ghastly; the grey pits his eyes were settled in were darker than last year. Malice fiddled with his earring when he glanced at Felim. The orc's beard had grown to where it almost touched his collarbone, the scar in the middle of his face making his mustache's gap wider.

Once they reached the edge and trekked through Dun Raik, Malice's heart jittered. He could see Magnus again. Malice darted ahead of the king and his first sword, stopped, waited, feet too antsy to stay planted in the dirt. The three of them wore matching colors, black, red and gold, Malice's and his majesty's outfit identical, while Felim's was simpler and more comfortable looking. When they were close enough, Malice turned, cape whooshing, and ran onward.

Multicolored lights painted the inside of the castle and Malice's body. His and the king's shoes clacked loudly on the dull green floor.

Felim's boots were clunky. He raced up the stairs, wondering if Magnus looked different. He was probably taller now. Maybe he had more freckles.

Unlike the year prior, most every chair was occupied as King Emil, Felim, and Malice entered the great hall. Voices melded; Malice couldn't make out what anyone was saying. As his majesty took his seat, Felim gestured to the space beside him where Malice was to stand. The person next to the king had oiled jet hair, his back straight. Malice didn't recognize him, nor did he recognize the fishman to his left. His scales were the color of the sky and glistened in the sun, but green hinted under his eyes, nose, and ears. They had a kind disposition, their expressions relaxed.

It didn't take long for Malice's eyes to find Magnus on the other side of the table. With his hands at his backside, Magnus stood behind his father, Gareth on the left. He teetered in place for a moment before he noticed Malice and smiled. Malice's face warmed as he returned the gesture. Magnus had grown taller, his face not as round as it was last year. His abundance of freckles hadn't increased, but they darkened.

Eventually, the last ruler stormed into the room. She was an orc, her skin the color of moss, her tusks jutting from her lower jaw decorated with silver cuffs and rings. She threw herself into a chair by the dwarf, who shot a displeased glare in the orc's direction. Draped over her muscular body were animal hides, like some of the rugs at home.

As the elf rose at the head of the table, Magnus leaned forward and whispered into his father's ear, snatching Malice's attention. Holister frowned, shook his head, and waved Magnus back to his place. His face contorted—the same look Kiran had made when Blodwen told him he couldn't stay one night. Malice watched Magnus's fists bunch at his sides. A minute went by as the elf's voice filled the room, and Magnus sprinted to the door.

"Magnus!" Holister yelled, springing to his feet. The hall went quiet.

Malice shifted, then locked his legs in place. If he pursued Magnus, would he get in trouble? He knew the answer was yes, so he supposed the real question was what the punishment would be. And, more importantly, would the queen… would she really kill Kiran? But he wanted to follow Magnus. He'd waited a year to see him again, and he'd promised to show his magic.

He chased after Magnus. Felim's confused voice called for him. At least he wasn't angry. Yet.

The elf said, her voice light and calming, "Let the children be children. We've no need to bore them to death."

Down the stairs, heart pounding in his ears, Malice slowed and picked a direction. The rightmost wing was dark and quiet, the corridor he turned into darker still. His cautious footsteps echoed off the walls.

"Magnus?" he said to the emptiness. The further he walked, the more his skin itched. "Magnus?" he called again, louder this time, when a door at his side clicked and a hand grabbed his wrist, yanking him out of the hallway.

"Shh." Magnus put a finger to his lips once the door closed.

Malice nodded. A single candle gave the room enough light to see Magnus's grave expression. And his freckles. The corners of Malice's mouth curved a bit, chest fluttering.

In silence, they waited. No other sound came from the hallway. They let out a breath. Whatever room they were in smelled like old linen. Magnus moved to extend his legs out in front of him, pine and honey wafting toward Malice.

"Why did you follow me?" Magnus asked.

"Because I have to show you my magic," Malice said. "And we're friends."

"But you're going to get punished."

Malice averted his gaze. The floor wasn't green like it was on the first floor; it was yellow and orange like a sunset, the walls a deep red, in the dimness almost black. The queen's intense glare entered his mind, and he shuddered. He knew he would get disciplined, but maybe he could ask her to leave Kiran alone. He had never asked for anything, so she might.

"It's okay," he eventually said, eyes lifting to meet Magnus's.

It went quiet again. Magnus looked elsewhere and brought his knees to his chest. The earring dangled from his lobe, catching the candle's jittering flame. Malice unconsciously stroked his own, the gem smooth underneath his fingertips. Whenever Kiran was sad, Malice held his hand until he was ready to talk about why he was upset. Magnus probably wouldn't like that.

He tried studying the room, as if there was much to look at, but Malice's gaze continuously slipped back to Magnus. No one else had freckles like him. Not even Annabeth could compare. Malice had seen a servant with moles and beauty marks scattered across their skin. In a way, they mesmerized and fascinated Malice. In another, he was jealous. All he had was white hair. What was so special about that?

Malice counted the multitude of coffee brown specks, mouthing the numbers. He hadn't learned how to count beyond twenty yet. Kiran knew how to count to fifty! He tried anyhow, his voice growing in volume.

"What're you doing?" Magnus asked suddenly, making Malice lose his place.

"Counting your freckles." *Not that I'm good at it.*

"You can't count them," Magnus said, and he stretched his legs back out. "It's impossible."

"Why?"

"There's too many."

Malice pouted. "Can I try any—" The door burst open, light blinding the boys.

"You need to attend the summit," a deep voice rumbled. It was Gareth, Magnus's first sword—righthand man, they were called in Alucard's Region. White outlined his bulky frame, filling the doorway. "Come now, before you make things worse for yourselves."

"Please, Gareth," Magnus pleaded. "Let us stay."

Gareth's silver eyes flitted to Malice when he addressed Magnus, "How else will you learn politics?"

"Just this once?"

Malice saw the set in Gareth's jaw and knew he was about to say no—the same way Odovacar's expression became harsh whenever Malice did something he didn't approve of.

"Can't we talk awhile?" Malice asked. "Please?" He wanted the chance to tell Magnus about Kiran and Annabeth and the training. He wanted to see Magnus's magic again, and he knew, from last year, Magnus wanted to see Malice's as well.

Moments went by. Gareth ran his fingers through his midnight blue hair and groaned. "Fine. You have two hours. When I come back, I expect no complaints. Understood?"

"Yes," Malice and Magnus said.

With an easy smile, Gareth left, and the door clicked shut, his footfalls sounding down the hall. Why hadn't they heard it earlier? Was it the technique Inyene and Felim used to silence their steps? Maybe Malice would learn it one day.

Magnus got up and brushed his azure trousers off. Then he went around the small room and lit the other candles in bronze holders. Malice rose as well, excitement bubbling in his veins. He had so much he wanted to share, he could hardly hold it all in.

"He seems nice," Malice said, trying to be nice and control himself. Annabeth once said it was rude not to let the other person speak. He sat down on one of two couches centered in the room—a study from the looks of it—sneezing at the dust bursting from the cushions. Magnus nodded and took a seat across from him.

Leaning forward, Magnus's eyes sparkled. "Did you practice?" he asked eagerly.

"Yes!"

"Show me!"

To the edge of his seat, Malice held his hand out, his sleeve moving with him. Black swirls spilled from his palm into the surrounding space, Malice's brows furrowing with concentration. The darkness gathered above, abruptly moving, circling the couches, and twisting together. He jerked his wrist downward; the darkness plummeting into the table like water crashing to the ground and vanishing. Thanks to Inyene, controlling his magic was getting easier and easier.

Magnus stared at Malice, his jaw hanging loose. Winded, Malice plopped down, and the couch creaked. He still had a ways to go. Inyene explained how he had little magical energy, so it was difficult keeping his magic going for long.

"Wow," Magnus breathed. "Have you learned the four elements yet?"

That's right. Magnus mentioned the elements last year. It was another topic Inyene lectured Malice about. He shook his head. "No. I won't be able to use the main elements for years to come." He had too much to learn, Inyene had told him.

Magnus raised his eyebrow and said, "I've only learned to use fire." He flicked a finger up, a tiny flame at its tip. "I'll learn the others soon, though. I could teach you."

"Really?"

He smiled. "Do you know how to read and write?"

"Annabeth taught me," Malice answered instantly, chest fluttering, his bones growing restless.

"Good. I can tell you how through letters."

Malice's happiness dimmed. "Will… that be all right?" Would the queen allow him to write letters to Magnus? He wasn't so sure he could do that.

"Why not? My father is strict but, he can't stop what he doesn't know."

… Is that how it works? If I don't tell her highness, she can't stop me? There was still doubt in his mind, but Malice wanted to think it would be okay. "I guess."

"Promise you'll write me back." Magnus stuck out his hand, pinky extended. His lilac-colored eyes focused on Malice's.

"Promise." Malice wrapped his pinky around Magnus's.

Back and forth, Malice and Magnus talked about everything. At least, it was everything to Malice. Since his mother and younger brother lived outside of the castle, Magnus had to visit them whenever his father allowed. Padma, his brother, started using magic and had burnt a hole in his mother's curtain. He got scolded for it. When

Magnus laughed, he got scolded as well. Apparently, Magnus had done something similar by scribbling a flower onto the floor.

Kiran and Annabeth were the people Malice talked most about. He told the story of the time—times, more like—when Kiran stole his parents' books about healing and tried to explain them to Malice. He sounded ridiculous, but Malice enjoyed listening. Which only encouraged Kiran to babble even more.

Two hours passed when Gareth opened the door and momentarily interrupted their conversation about their studies, which resumed in the corridor, continued up the stairs, and ended as they walked into the great hall. Malice sullenly returned to the king and Felim while Magnus and Gareth stood behind Holister. Neither said anything to Malice. He loosely paid attention to the ruler speaking, as he was too busy thinking about what to put in his first letter to Magnus.

Between Light and Dark
"Child of Darkness"

Gripping the deep red throne adorned with spikes and skulls, the queen crushed the arm. Splinters of wood peppered the ground in a series of clacks. Malice flinched, his body trembling.

"Thinking you could treat the Kings Summit as a playground was your first mistake," she said, anger coating every word like oil on a torch. "Your second was thinking you would go unpunished."

Beside Malice were Annabeth, Felim, and King Emil, all on their hands and knees, foreheads to the ground. Malice didn't dare raise his head. It would roll if he met the queen's eyes; his gut screamed this at him and nothing else.

"Alkeim," Queen Vendetta snarled. Malice only lifted his gaze as Felim's brother stepped from the shadows behind her throne. He was big, his beard long and full, cuffs of silver and bronze interwoven throughout. Grey streaked his hair and there were creases around his mouth.

"Yes, your highness," he acknowledged the queen with a dip of his head at her side.

"Take that mongrel to the dungeons."

Malice's blood ran cold.

"No food for a week. Make sure he gets the bare minimum of water." She scowled at Malice, but he couldn't see her clearly through the tears. His chest and throat were tight, as if someone were squeezing them—as if her highness's hand were wrapped around his neck again.

"Your highness," Annabeth said. "I beg of you, have mercy. Please." She pressed her forehead further into the floor. "He is just a boy." Her voice was brittle, like how Kiran sounded right before he started crying.

Malice could do and say nothing. Fear gripped him securely, encased like a batch of cement had been poured over top of him and allowed to set… He couldn't do anything.

"You may have mercy on him now," the queen said, her tone calmer, though narrowly. "Know there will not be a next time. As you said, he is a boy, he will act out again. All children do. When he does, I will not be so kind."

Annabeth let the silence take over. Malice breathed, finding all he could do was choke, hand clinging to his shirt. *What's happening?* He didn't understand. The room got smaller, the air thicker.

"Take him, Alkeim."

No. Malice couldn't move, his legs shaking. Footsteps approached. He wanted to run, to get up and flee to the woods, hide under Kiran's bed. Alkeim stopped and lifted Malice from the ground. The orc stared at him, his deep-set eyes dark brown, warm, inviting, pitying. They walked out of the throne room, and he clutched whatever fabric his hands met. Annabeth half turned to watch while Felim and the king stayed put.

Outside of Queen Vendetta's gaze, Malice's breath finally returned in quick, shallow bursts.

"It's all right, lad," Alkeim whispered, his big hand stroking the back of Malice's head. "Breathe and cry it out."

Malice was snug against the orc, his head by Alkeim's shoulders. The scent of leather and saltiness filled his nose, tears streaming down his face. No matter how much he wanted to, Malice realized he couldn't run away.

*

The door closed behind Alkeim and Malice, and a hush suddenly overwhelmed the room. *The kid was panicking...* Felim balled his fists against the cold floor, quickly releasing them before her highness had the chance to think too much about it. Repulsion surged through his veins, for himself and for the queen, and he subdued it the best he could.

"He is getting more brazen," the queen said, startling Felim and Annabeth alike. Emil was as still as stone. "Why do you think that is?"

Felim swallowed the dryness in his mouth and throat. It did nothing but make it worse. "Magnus Castine," his voice came out unsteady, "heir to Alucard's Region, perhaps."

It could be a number of different reasons. Malice was growing bit by bit, day by day. It was nearly impossible to pinpoint the exact reason behind his development. Sneaking away from the tedious event, the Kings Summit was. Felim remembered doing much worse when he was Malice's age. Alkeim could attest to that. Would probably laugh about it too.

"Or perhaps Kiran, your highness," he said, recalling how close Malice and Kiran had gotten over the past year. It was nice to see the lads smiling, acting like kids. Once, he had heard the two of them discussing mushrooms, of all things. Kiran loved them, while Malice thought they tasted like snot. The memory almost brought a smile to his lips. Almost.

"Perhaps," her highness muttered. "No matter. That boy is still a mutt who wears a leash. You, Felim, held said leash."

Felim shivered, feeling Queen Vendetta's gaze fall upon him like a boulder.

"You allowed him leave, did you not?"

"Aye," Felim croaked, his jaw tensing as every other muscle in his being did, his body stiffer than rock, yet as fragile as glass.

"How long was he gone for, exactly?" she asked, her voice passive.

"Two hours, your highness."

"You'll receive twenty lashes. Take your shirt off and turn around."

Shaking, Felim obeyed, slid his leather vest off and undid the strings of his shirt, letting it drop in a heap at his side. Inyene stepped out of the shadows and down from the dais, grinning wickedly. *So that's why she sent Alkeim away.* The queen didn't want the big brother to see the younger getting whipped half to death, otherwise he would've stepped in. Again.

Felim turned his back to the executioner as the air chilled—her ice magic forming a whip. He folded a corner of his vest and sank his teeth into the leather. He would need it.

*

In Alkeim's arms, Malice sniffled while the odor of the dungeons engulfed him. It was dim and cold down here, despite the orc's warmth. His boots echoed off the cavernous walls. The dungeons steadily became as familiar as his bedchamber during the past year. Cobwebs collected between holsters and the wall. When it rained, water leaked, creating a rhythm of drops that distracted Malice at the worst times.

He wished it were raining, so he could hear its melody instead of Alkeim's boots and the low rambles of those left in the cells to rot.

Malice didn't think he could walk quite yet. Still, Alkeim turned into a cell and gingerly set Malice down. His legs surprisingly supported him.

After a second, the orc turned to leave, but Malice reached and caught the bottom of his shirt.

"Will Kiran be killed?" Thinking about it brought tears to his eyes again. They already burned from crying on the way to the dungeons.

Alkeim spun, shocked, and clamped his jaw, sights averted. He bent down, hand on Malice's shoulder. "No, lad, he won't."

Malice sighed, his body deflating with relief. "Good." Kiran didn't deserve to suffer because of Malice's mistakes.

With a twitch of his eyebrows, Alkeim, rising, stepped backward, closed the door, and locked it.

Already, his breathing had become excessively loud. His eyes adjusted to the darkness as he shivered. It was unusually empty—Inyene was always with him in the dungeons. He never dreamed he would miss her presence like he did. He walked to stand against the wall and plopped down. Everything was rough and icy against his back and bum, a part of him glad he got used to it in the last year. Knees to his chest, Malice inhaled deeply, mildew and iron filling his lungs, and exhaled. Exhaustion tugged his eyelids down when he pried them open. They sank once more, the week-long journey it took to get from Dun Raik to Hordes Kingdom forcing slumber on him.

Once the weariness had worn off, Malice paced alongside the walls, walking in circles—squares more like—counting how many steps it took him to reach the door again. When he had reached his starting point, he had counted to twenty three times. His feet throbbed halfway into his fourth lap, so he stopped and took his shoes off.

Malice's stomach rumbled. The last thing he ate was yesterday's dinner of roasted fish and vegetables from a tavern. Felim had eaten three whole fish and two bowls of vegetables. King Emil had less than

Malice. Thinking about food made his gut grumble and churn. He turned his attention to the door. Two holsters were on either side, where Inyene normally placed torches. He imagined the bright orange light flickering, causing shadows to waver all around while leaking the smell of burning wood and oil. It slightly warmed the cell up, too.

On the floor, legs crossed, Malice held his hand out, keeping the image of a fire in his mind. Taking measured, deep breaths, he focused on moving his magic to his hand, feeling it course through his chest, into his arm and pool in his palm, the tickle of a feather.

Nothing happened. He tried again, and again, and again, until he was out of breath, his core and arm burning. *One last time.* He had nothing else to do, anyway.

Malice remembered the fire's heat, the blue at the base fading into orange and yellow. Magical energy surged through him. The closer it got to his hand, the hotter it became. A bursting sensation spread across his palm as warmth bristled his skin. He opened his eyes. There was a small kindle, the flames calm and steady.

Excited, Malice glanced at the door, wanting to show Kiran, Annabeth, or even Inyene, but no one was there. His smile waned. Inyene had warned him about using too much of his magic, how it could kill him if he didn't know his limits. Having already experienced how painful overexerting his magic was, Malice preferred not to test his limits right now. He closed his hand around the flame, then allowed his fingers to preoccupy themselves with his shirt.

How long will it take for a week to pass? Weeks and months had always gone by fast. Malice had the feeling, however, the next seven days would be long and full to the brim with boredom.

Day Four

The silence in the cell became loud all too quickly, louder than his breathing and heartbeat at times. It kept Malice up, forbidding him to sleep for too long. All he wanted to do was sleep. The energy to walk around his cell was hard to muster now. His legs were wobbly. Every time he tried to stand, his head felt like it had spun off his neck and crashed into the wall behind him.

The queen entered his mind repeatedly. *Mutt*, she always called him. He wondered if she knew his name. She never used it. As quickly as she entered his brain, he pushed her out the best he could. Instead, he thought about Magnus or Kiran or his magic. He went as far as to sort through all the mushrooms he and Kiran found in the forest.

At least he wasn't hungry anymore. That subsided a couple of days ago, and his stomach didn't hurt either. The water Alkeim brought daily helped, he thought.

If only a little, Malice could conjure a fire a few times a day, long enough to keep the shadows in the corners of the room from creeping closer and long enough to take the chill out of his bones.

Day Six

A creak sounded before a muted thump, another screech, and then nothing. It must have been his imagination playing tricks on him, as it had been doing for a time now. Creatures stood in the corners of his cell. They were lanky things of stringy wisps, like storm clouds that had taken humanoid form. For the most part, they stayed put, observing Malice as if he were a painting on a wall. One had crept closer and closer and closer; so close Malice could smell them, feel their breath hitting him, pricking his skin with goosebumps. They smelled like rotten meat that sat in the sun too long. Blodwen had thrown out old meat from their ice chest one day. The stench was enough to make Malice and Kiran gag.

Curiosity told him to look and when he did, there was a hunk of black on the floor. Crawling toward it, he picked it up, felt it in his hands. It was spongy, the edges hard and brittle, the middle soft like fur. After a sniff, Malice realized it was moldy bread. Food.

He shoved the whole thing in his mouth, chewing and swallowing, almost coughing it up a few times until his mouth was empty. Tongue retreating to the back of his throat, he gagged but tried to keep it down. He couldn't. Bile splattered the ground. His head ached as his stomach twisted again and he heaved.

Day Seven

Eyes lazily blinking, a creature stood above Malice. He flinched and scrambled to get away, hitting the wall with a thud. The creature looked up at him, and it tilted its head as if it were confused.

"You can't stare at people like that," he told the creature. "It's rude." Annabeth had scolded him about it when an elder walked down the stairs. In his defense, he had never seen someone with so many wrinkles. Still hadn't.

Lowering its head, the creature turned, lumbered back into a corner, and merged with the shadows. Malice used the wall to help himself up. His legs were shaky, and his head pounded as his stomach lurched every which way. He took deep breaths to settle his queasiness when rattling keys came from beyond the door. It opened, light turning the cell white. As his sight gradually returned, he could make out Alkeim in the hall, but not his expression.

That didn't matter. He could finally leave. The creature of stringy wisps reappeared to wave shyly from its corner, and Malice grinned. *It's time to go,* he said to the creature. It nodded, then vanished within the wall.

Malice saw himself walk to Alkeim, down the corridor and up the stairs. He saw Kiran waiting for him on his bed when he returned to his room. Annabeth was there too, waving a letter at him. They both hugged him so tightly he couldn't breathe. Kiran put him at arms-length, his mouth moving, probably spilling a week's worth of information. *I can't hear you,* Malice said. Expression unchanging, Kiran continued, a smile on his face. Turning to Annabeth instead, Malice repeated himself. She looked at him, ruffled his hair, and left, the door swinging shut, eclipsing all the light from the hallway.

"Alkeim"

Torch in one hand, Malice unconscious in the other arm, Alkeim ran through the dungeons, up the stairs, and into the southern wing of the castle.

The prince had stood and collapsed before he managed a step. He had thinned, his cheeks and eyes sunken into grey pits, his lips cracked. His body was limp in Alkeim's arms, but he could feel the shallow movement of the lad's chest, which brought some relief.

By the time he reached the fourth floor, Alkeim was damp with sweat, panting as he headed for Malice's bedchamber. It was easier to bring him here than to the infirmary. Too many royals who would run their mouths to her highness there. Often, he had visited the servant's quarters where he'd found Annabeth lingering around Malice's door, never straying too far from it. A few times during the past week, he caught sight of a dejected boy trailing through the foyer—Kiran, the doctor's son.

Finally, the prince's room was in sight.

Annabeth was here, feather duster in hand, thank the gods. "Get Tendai!" Alkeim shouted at her. She jumped, whipping around with a scowl on her face, brown eyes alight with all the things she wanted to say. Then she realized why he shouted, and her jaw clamped. Dropping the duster, she rushed past him.

He twisted the knob and kicked the door open; it slammed against the wall. Alkeim trudged to the bed against the wall, centered in the room. Gently placing Malice down, Alkeim didn't know what else to do or if there was anything else he could do without causing more harm. He was a fighter, not a healer.

Multiple sets of hurried footsteps raced down the hall. Tendai barged in first, closely followed by Blodwen, Kiran, and Annabeth. At the entrance, however, Annabeth held Kiran back, so he didn't get in the way. He struggled in her grip, face scrunched, teeth bared, hands grasping her arms like a vise. Blodwen went to one side, Tendai the other.

"What happened?" Tendai said—panic laced his voice—while peeling off Malice's filthy clothes.

Alkeim looked away, fists clenching at his sides. "He was put in the dungeons for seven days," he said as calmly as he could. Though, to his ears, he could have sworn his voice trembled.

"What?" Blodwen stomped around the bed. "What the hell is wrong with you?" She went to grab Alkeim's collar and stopped, her jaw tensing when she took several steps back as if she remembered who she was addressing. "What could warrant that extreme of a punishment?"

"… He made a mockery of the Kings Summit." Alkeim didn't believe it, not one bit. Felim, who described the event as tedious in years past, didn't either. He glanced over at Malice, at his frail body. Not yet six years old; he was simply a child. He could imagine Malice's boredom was as intense as the others when they had attended—the queen had forced all her children to go.

Blodwen turned on her heel, cursed under her breath, and returned to the opposite side of the bed, kneeling to hold Malice's hand. Words left her lips, ramblings of a foreign tongue. Nothing Alkeim understood.

Tendai had both of his hands hovering over Malice's core, his face tight with concentration. He sighed. "Besides the obvious dehydration and malnourishment, he drained his magical energy to damn near nothing." He glared at Alkeim, his hands returned to his sides.

"I know I deserve that look," Alkeim said, "but—" He glanced over his shoulder toward the door. Just Annabeth and her worried, rigid posture, and Kiran, whose lashing anger turned to tears of frustration. He shifted back to Tendai. "I do not agree with her highness's judgement this time," he said in a low tone, almost a whisper. Queen Vendetta had eyes and ears everywhere in the castle.

Kiran finally broke free of Annabeth's grasp. She gasped, reaching for him, but he was faster. He crossed the room in a flash and joined his mother at the bedside, content now that he could see his friend up close.

"Your words are hollow," Tendai seethed as he faced Alkeim. "You have no right to feel anything but shame for what you allowed to happen."

"Aye, I can't argue when I could have suggested giving Malice a slap on the wrist." *But I am a coward.* The queen wouldn't have let Malice off easily. Perhaps she would have locked him in his bedchamber, no visitors, instead of the dungeons if he'd said something. Averting his eyes, the guilt bubbling inside was like molten iron dumped into a pail of icy water.

"Mother," Kiran said.

"So why didn't you?" Annabeth stepped further into the room, her voice brittle and distant, her hands bunched in her smock. "You're… a *father*."

Alkeim flinched. She said it as if it were an insult, a stab to his heart, as if he had not known who he was. His fists clenched.

"Mother," Kiran repeated.

"Not now," Blodwen hissed without looking at her son.

"I don't know why either," Alkeim admitted.

"Look at Malice!" Kiran shouted and finally caught everyone's attention. When all eyes settled on the bed, everyone voiced their surprise.

Alkeim stiffened, and his blood stopped.

This… this was exactly what the queen had hoped for.

Malice's skin turned to a red-grey color like mottled flesh, his nails long and black, and two knubs for horns grew from his forehead. Thin lines of blood trickled into Malice's desaturated blue hair.

The room fell silent until Tendai dropped to his knees again, a thud, and resumed feeding his magic into Malice. The clock on his desk ticked, the seconds painstakingly long. Malice's chest rose, his eyes opening for a split moment and fluttering closed. His demon features reverted to normal. Tendai got to his feet, regarding everyone in the room with a sense of shared confusion and shock.

"I've never seen a demon's true form connected to their magic," Blodwen spoke as if she wasn't sure the words coming out of her mouth were true.

Alkeim knew.

Demons, angels, and fairies were the only races able to control their appearance to some extent, mixed or otherwise. Still, they could not completely hide their true form. When Alkeim first saw Malice as a babe, he questioned whether he was a demon because of that fact, wondering if perhaps Nyx and Karlisle had adopted him, even more so after her highness said he had a small fraction of human running through his veins. He thought it was the other way around. Maybe he barely had any demon blood within his body.

His demon lineage clearly ran stronger than the fraction of human.

"Do we inform the queen?" Annabeth asked meekly.

"No," Alkeim said, startling Annabeth. "Now that his true form has manifested, it will only be a matter of time before she finds out about the lad." When he looked at Malice once more, he was reminded of his own child, his pride and joy, and shunned away, ashamed and guilt-ridden.

"But it won't be until he's stronger, older, able to handle himself a bit better."

Queen Vendetta knew this would occur, but not so soon, not while Malice was so young. If she were to find out now, her plans would only happen sooner. She would postpone them no longer. Alkeim knew how little age mattered to the queen, and it disgusted him, roaches skittering over the crevices of his brain.

"Her highness won't be too pleased if she discovers we knew and neglected to inform her." Tendai crossed his arms over his chest, shaking his head at the statement as if he could see into the future and knew the punishment they would receive.

"Aye." Recalling all the sentences he'd dealt, and all the penances he'd heard the queen give, the worst that came to mind were the few times she let Inyene do whatever she pleased. He had the displeasure of witnessing her deranged habits in the flesh. Had held it together for a while, but not long enough to escape the dungeons before his stomach emptied itself onto the floor. Alkeim shuddered at the memory.

"If she finds out now, the dungeons will become his home. Permanently." Not to mention how it would become *their* final resting place as well.

Blodwen, Tendai, and Annabeth exchanged looks. They had no clue what Alkeim was referring to. They didn't need to know the details either. They were aware of the queen's personality, her cruelty, and mulishness.

"Then we swear to keep our mouths shut for as long as possible," Annabeth said, her eyebrows deeply furrowed as her gaze fixed on Malice.

Alkeim turned, a heavy sigh escaping his lungs, "It's the best we can do," and headed to the door. If Malice were to survive beyond the age of six, something more needed to be done. Holding their tongues wouldn't be enough.

Steeling his will, Alkeim stood at the entrance to Queen Vendetta's study and knocked.

"Enter."

The dim light from a single candle dusted the surfaces nearest the desk, including her highness's sharp features, her hair the red of drying blood. He stepped in and closed the door behind him. The queen was ready for bed in her elegant, cherry blossom silk nightgown.

"So, the mutt lived?" she asked as she leaned into her chair's rest and intertwined her fingers above her stomach.

Alkeim nodded, still finding the words to say.

"Is that all? I'm sure you did not come here to brag about your heroics."

"Your highness." *Do it. Say it. Consequences be damned.* "I think you should keep Malice's age in mind when you discipline him."

"Oh?" she mused, perching an eyebrow. "If he is so weak, he ought to be left to rot." Her tone of voice did not match the words coming from her mouth. They were... cheery, almost.

He nodded as if contemplating her words and tried to keep his loathing from his tone. "As true as that may be for adults, it is not the same for children, especially those as young as he is."

She gazed at him, tilted her head ever so slightly like an owl observing a mouse running in circles.

This isn't working. "If molded and fostered properly, I think he will become exactly what you want." The tremble started in his chest and worked its way to his arms and legs. "Right now," he added, praying to any god who would listen, to let his head stay on his shoulders, "he is more likely to break."

He could hide his sweaty palms behind his back, but it did nothing to hide his quaking bones. No matter, his eyes were trained on Queen Vendetta's. *Please work.*

"I see your point, Alkeim. I do not want my toy to break before having a chance to use it. I will be sure to keep his fragility in mind henceforth," she said in the same tone as earlier; calm, elated.

It was a farce. Alkeim was sure of that, if nothing else. As sure as the sky was blue. She wanted *that* to work, meaning the chance she would heed his advice was higher than zero.

He bowed. "Thank you, your highness."

As Alkeim righted himself, all the air left his lungs, a single wheeze while they were twisted and squeezed inside his chest. The room spun, darkness creeping in from the corners of his vision. He sucked in a breath. Couldn't. Panic laced his blood like poison. Grabbing at his neck, he stumbled backward and dropped to his knees, tears stinging his eyes. Sounds of his choking packed the room, his torso constricting further, caving in on itself. A lightness made him sway. Or was the study swaying? He couldn't tell as the candlelight receded.

"Remember where you stand the next you try to offer me advice, Alkeim."

She released her first sword, all traces of formless magic vanishing within an instant. He spluttered and gasped on the floor, chest burning, ribs aching as if they were bruised. Half stumbling and half turning, he crawled to the door, weak arm reaching for the knob twisting with a click. Alkeim blinked at the corridor's orange glow. Using the frame, he got to his feet, glad the gods had listened, and his head remained on his shoulders.

Rivalry
VII

Leaves scattered the ground as Malice and Annabeth strolled to the training grounds, a coolness to the breeze. The soft grass rustled underneath and tickled Malice's bare feet.

He had grown used to the pebbles of the training grounds digging into his heels and soles. At least the sun warmed them. Royals massed the space in front of him; they were all he could see. He caught a glimpse of red hair and headed toward it. Malice took his time, toeing random stones, purposely slowing his strides. He didn't want to train today and wished he could have stayed with Kiran.

Over a month had passed since he returned from the Kings Summit, yet he still dreamed of the creatures, the shadows that came to life and haunted his nights. Malice slept with a jar of fireflies on his nightstand now—he and Kiran helped Annabeth catch them most every night. He focused on their glowing yellow bums till he drifted off to sleep.

Royals surrounded Odovacar as he spoke with a man, one Malice didn't recognize. His long hair was storm cloud grey, his skin a sickly green color, bug-like wings twitched behind him, and an extra set of hands were perched on his hips. The man's clothes were loose, his shirt seemed too big for him, and his pants were bloated, black slippers on his feet. Malice stopped in the frontmost row of royals, their conversation audible.

"It is a shame," the man said joyfully. "I would have liked to see what your kingdom had to offer."

"Mother would not allow petty squabbles," Odovacar said. "Our standing matters not."

As the man nodded thoughtfully, his eyes sliced to Malice's. He flinched and averted his gaze.

"And who is that?" the man asked.

Odovacar turned. The field remained hushed, beyond the circle surrounding Issur bubbling with energy and ever noise possible. Malice's heart thundered.

"Malice, the youngest of the Reap family."

"How old is he?"

"Five," Odovacar answered. "Six before the new year." Malice stiffened.

"Then he is the same age as my son!" the man bolstered.

Malice looked from the ground to the man, a boy now peeking from behind his legs. *This must be who Kiran was talking about.* Kiran had heard rumors—from his mother and father, he said   of a new high-ranking knight coming to Hordes Kingdom. The boy fully stepped into view. His skin was darker than Magnus's and different from the darkness of Kiran's skin. It was richer, like tree bark compared to the wet soil of the forest floor. Smoky grey hair waved and curled around his head, almost reaching his shoulders. His eyes were crimson, like blood.

"This is Zephyrus," the man said, patting his son's back. "My eldest."

Malice nodded toward Zephyrus, and he nodded back.

"So," the man said, his tone as jolly and proud as it was earlier, "does he know how to fight?"

Malice slid his foot back and gulped.

Odovacar raised an eyebrow. "A bit," he replied evenly. "Want to find out?"

"A friendly bout between comrades never hurt anyone. What do you say, son?"

Despite it being a question, it was clear neither of them had much of a choice.

"I don't mind," Zephyrus said.

I mind. The man pulled Zephyrus into his arms, turning away, and crouched down to his level. Odovacar scowled after them for a moment and, more or less, did the same, kneeling beside Malice.

"We of the Reap family cannot spar with whomever we want whenever we want. The queen must provide consent for the dispute to take place," he spoke softly. "The same goes for knights."

"Then why am I fighting?" Malice asked, matching his brother's volume.

"You are exempt because of your age, and you are not a royal." Odovacar glanced over his shoulder again, grunting. "His name is Issur Laska. I would like to spar with him myself, test his capabilities. Perhaps Mother will allow me one of these days. For now," he returned his gaze to Malice, "take this as a learning opportunity."

Odovacar stood and paced to the edge of the circle that had formed around them—which gradually shrunk as people went back to their training. Soon, Issur joined him. A quick flick of Odovacar's finger summoned a royal who provided Zephyrus and Malice with practice swords.

He didn't want to fight. Why should he? Malice's eyes darted back to Odovacar, his black orbs already fixed on Malice. He shuddered and yanked his attention back to the boy.

Zephyrus slipped into an unfamiliar stance and stared at Malice, his body parallel with the sword held near his head, his legs spread out. Malice held his wooden blade out in front of him, feet separated, shoulders hunched forward a bit, both hands on the handle, one below the guard. As Odovacar had shown him. Once. But Malice had watched other royals around the field whenever he could, and they proved to be better *teachers* than his brother.

Abruptly, Zephyrus shuffled forward and swung the sword diagonally down. Malice brought his sword up, using one arm to back it as Zephyrus' blade struck with a loud clack. It bit into his arm and left a tingling sensation behind. It wasn't as strong as Odovacar's blows, though. Malice usually avoided taking a hit directly from his brother. It was the times he couldn't, he usually ended up on his bum.

The boy moved back only to charge in again, striking from the right. Malice shifted away, dodging Zephyrus's sword. He wasn't as swift as Odovacar, either. Zephyrus lost his balance and stumbled. As quickly as he'd lost it, he regained it, frowned, and launched toward Malice.

Simple jabs, slashes and turns to gain momentum; Malice, panting, struggled to keep up. So did Zephyrus, though. His limbs began to ache and sweat trickled into his eyes, burning them. He tried to blink away the wetness. It didn't work. Releasing his sword, he used the collar of his shirt to wipe his face.

Wood drove down into Malice's shoulder. He yelped and dropped; the sword falling from his grip altogether. Tears dripped, each one hotter than the last against his overly sensitive skin. Pain pulsed from his shoulder and collarbone.

A whistle sounded, and within the minute, someone entered the circle. Malice glanced behind him. It was a healer, already stooping alongside Malice to heal him. He looked away. Zephyrus and Issur shared the same expression: slack-jawed, raised eyebrows, and parted lips. Odovacar was the only one wearing a scowl.

Malice had tried his best. He *was* trying his best.

The healer rose, bowed toward Odovacar, and scurried off while Malice got to his feet and plucked his sword from the gravel. Again, they readied themselves and attacked.

Zephyrus flung his sword left and right. Malice sidestepped the advance and scored Zephyrus across the ribs. The boy winced, biting his lips. They went on for what felt like hours. The difference was that Malice continued to get healed. Zephyrus did not.

Exhaustion didn't seem to bother Zephyrus as he hit the side of Malice's neck. His vision blackened, the ability to breathe robbed. Odovacar whistled again. Issur glared at him and opened his mouth to voice some sort of complaint. His stiff posture was strange to Malice. It reminded him of Annabeth and how she would clasp her hands whenever she was worried.

"Heal Zephyrus too," Malice said, then coughed. Panic lanced his stomach, his throat pinched like the time the queen had wrapped her hands around his neck and squeezed. He felt the damp skin of his neck just to make sure a hand *hadn't* gripped him.

The healer—a different one came every time Odovacar called— crouched between the two boys, arms extended toward them. Zephyrus's jaw dropped. The bruises blooming on his face and body, Malice was sure, faded as the pressure around Malice's throat vanished. He sighed and collapsed. A heartbeat later, the healer was gone.

The tears still flowed. He didn't want to fight anymore. He was tired of getting hit and he was tired of attacking. Pleadingly, he looked at his brother. Limbs sore, lungs strained, Malice hoped he could leave, so he could see Kiran and Annabeth.

"No more, boys." Issur's eyebrows knotted, and his arms were folded across his broad chest. "You both did good, don't you agree?" he said through clenched teeth, glaring at Odovacar.

He stayed silent, sights trained on Malice. "Yes," Odovacar eventually said. His tone was softer than Malice expected. "You did well."

Sniffling, Malice noticed Zephyrus's shakiness, the dirt on his clothes, and how low his head hung. He went to his father, bowed, and the pair walked deeper into the sea of royals. Odovacar sighed as he approached and got to one knee.

Malice reeled slightly, bracing himself for a smack that was sure to come.

It did not.

"I am sorry," was all his brother said before he rose and disappeared from Malice's sight.

Kiran wasn't there when Malice entered his bedchamber. He wanted to cry again, but he had done enough of that today and stifled the burning sensation in his eyes.

As Annabeth prepared lunch, Malice found a letter on his desk, sealed with deep blue wax in the shape of a sun. The chair screeched as he dragged it out, sat down, ripped open the side of the cream-colored envelope, and plucked out a folded piece of paper, excitement fluttering wildly in his chest.

Dear Malice, it wrote.

I hope this letter finds you well. I apologize that it's getting to you so late. When I got home, I was made to sit on a broom for so long I could barely walk for the rest of the day as punishment. I hope you did not receive one as well, but if you did, I'm sorry.

My mother and brother live in the western district of Alucard's Kingdom. I went to visit them today after what felt like forever. The three of us went for a picnic on the mainland in the meadows. This time of year is beautiful because of the changing of leaves, don't you agree? When Padma got fussy, we had to go home where Gareth was waiting to bring me back to the castle.

Studying is as boring as ever. The elder giving me lessons looks like a raisin, and they talk so fast Gareth has to explain most of everything they say. I'm sure it is as boring for you as it is for me.

As promised, everything I learned about the four elements is on the next page. I've gotten a handle on water, and I've recently started using air magic. Earth is frustrating to learn, but I'll eventually get the hang of it. If you learn earth before me, tell me, all right?

I hope to hear from you soon,

Magnus Castine.

Setting the main letter down, Malice read the instructions written in soft curves and swoops. They were the same as when Malice figured out how to use fire magic. Now he felt bad for asking Magnus to go out of his way to instruct him. On the other hand, Malice felt giddy, overjoyed Magnus didn't forget their promise.

From the drawers to his desk, Malice got out a jar of black ink, a pen, and a few sheets of paper.

Dear Magnus, he used Magnus's letter for reference, carefully penning each letter. He didn't want his first letter to be sloppy.

I'm glad you didn't forget about me and I'm sorry you had to sit on a broom. I was punished too. Also, I'm sorry for making you teach me about magic when I learned how to use fire a month ago. He spoke the words out loud as he wrote them since it was easier to sound out the tricky words.

Today I met the newest knight in Hordes Kingdom, Issur Laska. My eldest brother, Odovacar, doesn't seem to like him at all. I also met Issur's son, Zephyrus, and we fought. In Hordes Kingdom, the queen prohibits the Reap family and knights from fighting unless given permission. It was not fun.

You're right, studying is boring. Draga has me read and write at least ten pages per hand. I've gotten rather good at using my left hand because of it, though.

Kiran is always excited to hear about you. I hope one day you can meet him. I also hope your father will allow you to see your mother and brother more often. You always seem so happy whenever you talk about them.

Until the next letter,

Malice Reap.

Just as Malice set the quill near the jar of ink, the door opened, and Annabeth walked in with a tray of food.

"Dinner time," she said, smiling. Malice carefully slid his and Magnus's letters toward the wall, so Annabeth could place the tray down.

Licking his lips, his eyes darted from the roasted pig to the carrots, yams, bread, and cheese, then to the glass of juice. The smell summoned a deep growl from his stomach.

"I want to send a letter," he said as he waited for Annabeth to finish cutting his meal.

"To whom?"

Finally, she passed him the silverware, his first bite so big he almost couldn't chew properly. "My friend Magnus," Malice, swallowing a mouthful of meat, answered.

"While you're eating, would you like me to send it out?"

"No."

Silence persisted shortly. Malice picked at the purple yams until Annabeth said, "We can send it off together once you're done eating. Does that sound better?"

Nodding, Malice said, "Thank you."

A few doors before the servant's communal bathroom was a study crammed with miscellaneous things and crates. Annabeth was inside searching for an envelope, wax, a press, and a deep spoon to melt the wax in. Eventually, she found everything she was looking for and came out, walking Malice back to his bedchamber. Despite her offer to find all the supplies while Malice ate, he refused, insisting they do it together. He lit a candle—Annabeth eyed him momentarily, brows peaked. She'd never seen him use magic, he remembered. Not that what he had done was anything special—and Annabeth dropped three tiny cubes of wax into the spoon and held it over the small flame.

"You should write your friend's name on the envelope and put it inside," she said, pointing at the off-white envelope sitting on his desk.

Malice grabbed his letter, folded it as nicely as he could, and nestled it inside the envelope. When he finished carefully writing Magnus's name, the dark red wax had melted. Malice studied Annabeth closely, since he wanted to send the next letter without her help. Using her hands to flatten the flap of the envelope, Annabeth poured the wax over it in a circular motion, and let the press sink into the paper. Then they waited for it to set, peeling the press off once it had.

"Magnus *Castine*," Annabeth mumbled under her breath. "Is he from Alucard's Kingdom?"

Malice bobbed his head. "He's the prince."

"That's what I thought. I will send this on the morrow, but for now—" She looked toward Malice's closet, the clock on his desk, and back to him. "It's time to retire for the night."

Fireflies moseyed in the jar on his nightstand. Malice missed Kiran's presence. The constant warmth he provided was comforting. The moment he stopped focusing on the buzzing fireflies, all the other noises in his room grew, the darkness from the corners creeping closer. He forced his eyes closed, and let the letters consume his mind, the one he wrote and the one he'd received. One day, he would be able to see Magnus whenever he wanted, and they could talk until their voices went hoarse. One day, he would meet Vesh and Padma, and Magnus would meet Kiran.

Rivalry
"A Few Teeth Lost"

Odovacar had given the first hour of Malice's training to Zephyrus. Issur stayed close to them, observing their spars. They were even. Malice scored a few hits, then Zephyrus had.

Odovacar came back, meaning the hour was up, and told Zephyrus to go to his father. Wiping the sweat from his face, Zephyrus glanced at Malice, smiled, and left. Maybe that was his way of thanking Malice, though Malice wondered why he didn't just use words. As Zephyrus's back faded into the sea of royals, Malice shifted his attention to Odovacar, a practice sword in his hand.

He didn't like the look in his brother's eyes.

In an instant, Odovacar was in front of him, his sword bearing down on him. Malice hardly had time to defend when he brought his sword up. His blade struck, numbing and sending ripples of pinpricks through Malice's arms. Struggle caused his face to heat as he tried to hold him off. Malice's knees started quivering underneath him. Fear bubbled to the surface.

Odovacar was going to crush him.

His brother slid backward, lifting the weight off Malice, and attacked. Malice ducked and rolled, swiftly moving to Odovacar's hind side where he cut the back of Odovacar's ankles. His brother, reeling forward, swung his leg, kicking Malice square in the face, sending him flying and tumbling through the dirt.

Malice pushed himself up after a few seconds, his face

throbbing, tears in his eyes. Blood filled his mouth as his nose dripped, something hard rolling over his tongue. He spat more red and a tooth. Malice's eyes became saucers. He picked up his tooth, tonguing the hole in his gums on his upper jaw. Wincing, two more teeth fell out, and bounced once off the ground in the puddle of blood beneath him. He stared at them, lip quivering.

What had Malice done? Why was Odovacar so harsh today?

"Get up," Odovacar said as he loomed over Malice. "You lost a few teeth, not a limb."

Malice got to his feet, his nose gushing red like an angry river. He didn't bother wiping it as he picked up his sword, it suddenly feeling ten times heavier. Legs quaking, Malice attempted to hold back the water gates that were his eyes and tried to keep his grip tight around the sword. The agony of his lower face made it hard to focus, though.

Odovacar shifted, startling Malice, his wooden practice sword dropping with a clunk. Franticly, Malice gathered it again. He desperately wanted to look away, but if he did, his brother would charge. *Stay focused!* He would say.

Odovacar frowned. "Enough for today. Go," he said and spun on his heel, marching into the field.

Dumbfounded, Malice stood there, frozen, his mind blank until he returned his sword to the closest weapons rack and made his way to the castle.

*

"You don't want to fight?" Malice asked on the way to the training grounds, Kiran by his side. Occasionally, Kiran tagged along with Malice and Annabeth to the grounds so they could be together for a little longer. Annabeth hung back a few paces, her strides rustling the greenery.

"No!" Kiran said. "Mother and Father always tell me to figure my problems out with words, not blades." He huffed and looked away, his eyebrows furrowed. At his sides, his fists tensed for a heartbeat.

Head down, gaze on his dirty feet, Malice mumbled, "I'm sorry." It didn't seem like Kiran had heard him. He didn't want Kiran to be upset, so he said it again, louder, "I'm sorry."

Kiran shrugged. "I want to meet Zephyrus, that's why I'm going to the training grounds."

Malice remained silent, something bitter tugging at his chest when he tilted his head skyward. It was warm today, the sun a huge white dot in the sky, the breeze gentle. The brief time he spent outside the castle before meeting Odovacar was refreshing, one of the few times he could truly be happy and breathe.

The field was busy, like a beehive. Royals littered the grounds, healers always on standby to heal the injured, half-empty weapon racks on the outer ring of the yard. The smell of sweat and metal was strong. Malice always cringed at it.

Near the rightmost edge of the field, Malice spotted Odovacar and headed to him when he noticed Issur and Zephyrus standing with him. As they approached, Odovacar turned, his expression unchanging. Kiran averted his eyes. Malice did too, yesterday still fresh in his mind. His tongue slid across his teeth, which had grown back after a healing session. Except the canine. Annabeth said that one would grow back on its own, but he wasn't so sure if magic did nothing.

Zephyrus stared at Kiran curiously.

"This is Kiran," Malice said to Zephyrus. "He wanted to meet you."

"I'm Zephyrus Laska," Zephyrus said with an awkward smile. "Will you be staying long?"

Looking him up and down, "I'll be staying the whole time," Kiran snipped, turned, and stomped to the boundary of raised concrete, gravel, and dirt.

Issur chuckled, patted Zephyrus's shoulder, and walked away, Odovacar mirroring him.

Malice joined Kiran at the edge of the field and whispered, "Why do you want to stay?"

"I'm not sure about him," Kiran said, sights narrowed on Zephyrus's back. "Is he your friend?"

"I don't know," Malice admitted.

Moments of quiet passed when Malice returned to face Zephyrus, who handed him a practice sword. They had barely exchanged a few words. Malice sort of liked it in stark comparison to Kiran. He wouldn't use *friends* to describe what they were, but maybe they could be. He questioned, however, what Kiran saw in Zephyrus to make him so wary.

Hours went by. Malice sparred with Zephyrus, winning as much as he lost, a healer coming to remedy his injuries. And Zephyrus's. Only because he told them to, though.

Then Odovacar took over, and he was losing. He had caught glimpses of Kiran ensnared with Malice's spars, making his chest light and fluttery. Malice doubted he realized his mouth hung open near the end. Happiness to know Kiran was watching and was seemingly excited sparked Malice's heartbeat. Malice smiled and concentrated harder on his fight, tried to dodge, and land more hits on his brother. Still, training ended with Malice on his butt while Odovacar strutted away.

Kiran rushed over. "That was amazing," he said in Malice's ear as he stole the sword out of Malice's grasp and sprinted to put it on a rack—the wrong one.

Returning, he snatched Malice's hand and tugged him away from the training grounds.

When they were far enough, Kiran hastened his stride to get ahead, throwing his arms out to his sides. "Why didn't you tell me you could do that? I can't believe you were able to hold your own against Zephyrus *and* Odovacar!" he beamed.

Malice blinked at the beastman. Holding his own? He was sure his backside was caked in dirt, his limbs were sore, and he was sticky with sweat. He needed a bath. And food. Although he could let it go, considering Kiran's mood was better now. If he thought Malice was amazing, who was he to argue?

Before long, Malice's thoughts wandered back to his question and how upset Kiran became over it. "I thought you were upset?" He also recalled how Kiran had eyed Zephyrus. *Is he your friend?*

The happiness and excitement dimmed as Kiran's arms dropped. "I was…" He glanced to the left, and to the right, his hands slithering behind him. "I don't want you getting hurt. That's why I was upset." His face flushed.

Oh. Malice's face heated, and his chest tightened. He looked at the greenery. "What about Zephyrus? Why don't you like him?"

Kiran didn't answer. The boys stood amongst the long grass and wildflowers, awkwardly. Behind Malice, thumping footsteps grew louder and louder, and then they stopped, someone huffing. Malice turned to see Zephyrus hunched over, hands on his knees, while he caught his breath and stood up straight.

"Can I," he paused, his fingers twirling the bottom of his shirt, "join you for lunch?" he asked.

Malice looked over his shoulder. He didn't mind, but he wasn't sure if Kiran felt the same way. He still hadn't answered Malice's question. Maybe he didn't know either. It was Kiran, so he probably did.

"All right, but we eat in Malice's bedchamber, you know."

Malice and Zephyrus were quick to fall in pace with Kiran. "Why his bedchamber?"

"I don't like eating in the dining hall unless I have to," Malice said. He preferred eating in his room, anyway. Kiran could join him that way, and now Zephyrus could, too. Annabeth seemed more comfortable there as well. Albeit she rarely ate with Malice whether Kiran was there or not. *I already ate,* she always answered whenever he asked her to join him. "Besides, I'm usually not allowed." No thanks to the twins.

Kiran shrugged, and Zephyrus peeked at Malice.

"Her highness…" Malice muttered, "doesn't like me." None of his siblings did, for that matter.

They stopped, and Malice continued onward. Eventually, he turned. Kiran and Zephyrus stared at him, confused, perhaps; Malice didn't know the expression they were making. "If we wait any longer, Annabeth will be mad."

That put a pep in Kiran's step, who motioned for Zephyrus to follow. Together they walked to the castle, at first in silence, before Kiran blabbered about his day. Soon, Zephyrus had joined, speaking about his sister.

"She's loud," Zephyrus told them.

"Duh, she's a babe," Kiran remarked. "All babes are loud. Mother said so."

"What does she look like?" Malice had asked.

"Squishy like soft clay."

Their conversations had gone on like that long after lunch had settled in their bellies. They laughed and joked, jabbered, and laughed some more. Malice smiled so much his cheeks hurt by nightfall.

Tradition
VIII

Before autumn became winter, Sok and Rayen turned ten.

"In Hordes Region," Annabeth said as she fingered oil through Malice's hair. It smelled like mint. "When the monarch's heirs turn ten, they choose a first sword."

"Will I have to?" Malice didn't want one. He didn't think he needed one either. He guessed he was a prince because he was Queen Vendetta's child like Odovacar and Draga—royals scarcely referred to them as prince and princess. But he felt less than the servants cleaning the privies or kissing the bottom of the queen's dirt covered shoe.

"You will one day, yes." Annabeth moved back to allow Malice out of his chair. She brushed his fancy, uncomfortable clothes off and nodded her approval.

On the way to the great hall on the first floor of the castle, Annabeth rambled about how Hordes, like the other southern regions of Vinyamar, had different rankings for their military. Royals were also called something different. In Zeldine's, they were referred to as warriors instead of knights or generals. Ranks consisted of letters in the north as well as positions such as guard and knight. Meanwhile, Hordes' ranking was guard, knight, first sword, general, and commander, a commander having the highest amount of power for a combatant. When Malice furrowed his brow at the word, Annabeth said, "It means fighter." The pins, despite the lack of ranks with the titles, represented one's authority.

There were five rows of twelve royals on both sides of the rust-colored rug, each wearing the Hordes Region sigil of varying degrees—the frontmost row wore the full insignia, the profiles of three horned gold skulls with a sword down the middle. Glimmers of silver caught his eye from the center rows, the symbol that of a single sword piercing a skull. The farthest row had bronze pins, the blade removed from the skull. Four pillars of dark grey and brown granite rose to the ceiling around the base of the platform, facing the royals. The walls were dark orange like the setting sun, while the floors were the same black marble with clouds and webs of white and grey.

Annabeth guided Malice to his place next to Odovacar and his first sword. Malice had never seen the knight. He was a fairy with glinting, translucent wings and white hair. Annabeth, squeezing Malice's shoulder, walked toward the second entrance, the one they came in through, and dipped behind the corner.

Beside Odovacar was Inyene, then Draga, and finally King Emil, all accompanied by their first sword. Meaning, Felim was there too and smiled at Malice when they locked eyes.

Malice eventually looked ahead of him. He swallowed, instantly turning away. The queen, Sok, and Rayen stood on the platform while Alkeim was off to the side. He was as broad as a door. The mahogany brown leather he wore almost made him look like one, too.

Her highness watched the twins call out all the royal's names and announce their promotion. When the royals, two at a time, approached the dais and bowed, Sok and Rayen attached their new brooch to their chest, grabbing the pins from a wooden box on the pedestal separating them. Rather quickly, boredom struck like a distant bell. Adjusting his shoulders, rolling his ankles, he shifted his weight from the outside of his feet to the inside. His fingers played with the lace of his red vest; he knotted the strings just to untie them.

After a time, Queen Vendetta replaced the pedestal, her dress long and flowing, the color of a forest lit by the moon. Gold chains weaved her braided hair into a bun. All the accessories on her body—the rings, necklaces, and earrings—were sparkling gold. Sok and Rayen wore similar outfits, the color schemes switched with a few articles of clothing as if they had traded. Both wore a fitted scarlet waist coat, splitting from their shoulders was a thin fabric revealing the sleeves of their undershirt, sewn with a pale-yellow pattern. Their sepia trousers went with their newly shined shoes, and from their right shoulders flowed a fur cape pinned to their coats by a round golden brooch. Black string tied their red hair to the back of their necks.

They looked uncomfortable and silly. Malice felt bad for them, yet didn't at the same time.

Placing a hand on her children's shoulders, the queen said, voice resonating, "It is time to choose."

As loose as a brick wall, Sok and Rayen gazed over the floor of newly promoted royals. Malice was sure his breathing had started echoing, it had become so quiet.

"Xenon Lavoie, royal knight," Rayen spoke first, surprising Malice. It was always Sok who began and Rayen who finished a conversation or sentence.

Footsteps permeated the silence of the great hall as Xenon walked to the first short, wide step of the platform, sinking to one knee before Rayen with his head down. He was a fishman, his skin a cobalt blue softly glimmering in the light, four gills flared on the side of his neck every so often.

Then Sok lifted his chin. "Aglaia Kumar, royal knight," he declared.

From one of the furthest rows, a dwarf made her way to the

dais, bowing adjacent to Xenon. Her hair was dark and curly, half of it in a ponytail, her eyes deep forest green. It was a pretty color. Malice liked it better than his own, which was bright and piercing like grass in the springtime.

Simultaneously, the twins extended their hands out for Xenon and Aglaia to take, and they kissed the back of them. The knight's hands were flipped over, Sok and Rayen dragging their fingers coated in a sharp layer of ice across their palms, drawing a thin line of blood. Neither knight made any movement, no flinch or wince, their eyes steady on their palms. Maybe the ice numbed the pain. Not that Malice wanted to find out.

"Swear to become my sword, my shield, my horse," Sok said. He sounded stiff, as if reading from a script.

"Swear to serve me until one of us takes our last breath, to protect me and those I deem worthy of protection, swear to follow my orders as they are resolute," Rayen continued a tad more fluidly.

"I swear on my blood, my princess," Xenon answered. Rayen swiped her thumb across the cut on his palm, collecting his blood, and marked his forehead with two horizontal lines crossed with a third, two dots above.

"I swear on my blood, my prince," Aglaia said. Sok followed in suit, dragging his thumb across her palm and marking her forehead with the same three lines and two dots.

While the newly appointed first swords remained on their knees, her highness gingerly lifted her hands and clasped them in front of her stomach. "To all in this room," she said, her voice level as it carried. Malice involuntarily became rigid.

"Your valiant efforts have been recognized and rewarded. For that, you may take pride. Let this not create leniency, however, lest you prefer the gutters. As easily as I have given you power, I will take it away. My royals are devoted, fierce, deadly. Let that not change lest you want your head on a spike. Dismissed."

Her commands sent a wave of movement through the room, royals filing out of the great hall, quickly but orderly, boots clacking but voices nonexistent.

Malice turned to find Annabeth near the back entrance. He headed toward her as Odovacar, Inyene, Draga, and the king exited. Queen Vendetta, Sok and Rayen were the last to leave. Sok, craning forward, made a face at Malice, Rayen copying him, twisted and gloating. If not for the queen, they would have bragged about their new first swords, mocking Malice's lack thereof. Despite how he had little choice, it didn't matter to them. Shoulders deflating, he wrapped his hand around Annabeth's fingers, waiting to be escorted back to his bedchamber.

*

There were five fireflies in the jar tonight, buzzing indolently in their glass prison. Malice lay on his side, staring at the light. It wasn't so bad being in the same room as his family, like it had been after his first summit. Or like it had been in the throne room after his second. He was glad to not have stood where Sok and Rayen had, the queen's presence constantly behind them. Malice didn't think he would have been able to stand there the entire time if he had been in their shoes.

Kiran flipped to his side, making the whole bed shake. Malice turned to face him. He scowled.

"Sok and Rayen hate me," he said.

Kiran twitched and sluggishly opened his eyes. "I thought they always hated you?"

He scoffed. "They got first swords today, you know."

"I don't think that means a whole lot. Zephyrus said they're like hounds following their master."

Frown deepening, Malice realized Kiran had been spending a lot of time with Zephyrus while Malice was stuck training. Fire tickled his veins, burning the bliss of Kiran's presence. "I thought you didn't like Zephyrus," he said, tone bitter.

"I do."

Malice startled, and something wormed around in his gut. His gaze fell to the blankets. They were grey, plain, no patterns or different colors. Boring. At least they were soft and warm. "Is he your friend?"

"Yes," Kiran answered.

Malice's heart squeezed as he sat up. "Then why are you here with me?"

Kiran sat up too, his sleepiness gone. Malice wasn't weary to begin with.

"Why don't you go to Magnus?" Kiran shot back. "He's *your* friend, right?"

Malice nodded. "I can't. He lives in Alucard's Region."

"You always talk about him," Kiran said sharply. "If you can be friends with Magnus, I can be friends with Zephyrus."

"But he was my friend first."

"What about me?"

Malice turned and flinched. Tears bubbled in Kiran's eyes, his lips pressed together, and his eyebrows furrowed. His fists bunched the sheets.

"What do you mean?" Malice felt horrible now. He wanted to look away.

"We aren't friends."

Malice's blood stopped. Shifting to sit on his knees, he searched

Kiran's expression, the fireflies light not helping much. "No," he uttered. "I'm sorry. We can both be friends with Zephyrus, I promise."

Silence.

Why isn't Kiran saying anything? Did I really upset him? Malice's vision blurred. He didn't know what he wanted, but this wasn't it. He just… he just didn't want to lose Kiran. What if he did? What would he do? Panic hollowed Malice's breathing, tightened his chest, and made his head burn like all the fire in his veins surged to his brain.

"I was first," Kiran finally said.

Malice sucked in a breath, held it.

"That means we're brothers."

Suddenly stupefied, Malice didn't understand. They weren't brothers. Not only did they look nothing alike, but they also had different parents. "We can't be brothers," he croaked, trying to ignore how nice it sounded. Kiran would be a much better brother than Sok or Odovacar. Then Kiran could go to the summits with Malice and meet Magnus. He would be able to join his training sessions with his siblings as well.

Kiran pouted. "Why?"

"Because we don't share the same blood."

"If blood didn't matter, would we be brothers?"

"Of course."

"Mother said," Kiran reached and grabbed Malice's hand, "that blood doesn't matter. It's what the heart wants that does."

Hearts have thoughts?

"Do you want to be my brother?" Kiran asked, his eyes now on Malice's, expectantly.

"Yes, very much so." He did, he really did. Maybe if they were brothers, her highness couldn't hurt him, no matter what Malice did or said.

"Me too. Which means we're brothers. Got it?"

"You and me?"

Kiran nodded. "You and me."

Kiran and Malice laid back down, pulling the sheets to their necks as Kiran nestled into the pillow. His eyelids slipped close, his hand still holding Malice's. Malice didn't want to let it go yet, either. *We are brothers*. He smiled. The terrible feeling that had wormed in his stomach earlier was gone, replaced by a lightness. The same sensation he got when he was here with Kiran and Zephyrus, talking the afternoon away. Abruptly, he was tired, and the word eluded him.

Healing a Mockingbird
IX

Spring was muggy and hot. Kiran's daishiki stuck to his skin as if covered in sap. The fabric was a thin cotton, and colorful shapes patterned it. At least the trees provided some shade, not that it was much cooler than when he stood in the sun. It was why winter was so nice. The day was tolerable, pleasant, while the night was chilly.

Malice sat beside him on the forest floor, sweat making his pale skin shimmer. He wore an oversized tunic, something Kiran saw him wear less often since he started training with his brother and sisters. He wasn't jealous of Malice one bit when it came to his studies, despite Kiran's disappointment about not spending as much time with him because of it. Instead, he was spending more time with Zephyrus, who was fun, especially when Kiran could visit his home in the kingdom, but he wasn't Malice.

A full basket of herbs and fungus rested on Kiran's lap. Mother had sent them out after lunch.

Rising with the basket, Kiran said, "We should go home." Malice had to return soon to study with Draga, anyway.

Malice nodded and got to his feet when a loud squawk stopped them both. They looked at each other and another screech echoed through the forest. Together, they followed the sound, eventually finding a bird on the ground. It flapped and jerked, one of its wings angled strangely.

"Should we leave it?" Malice asked, as he bent down to inspect it.

Blodwen had said to leave a bird if it fell from a tree because the mother was the one who pushed it. But it was hurt. "No, let's take it to Mother and Father. They can heal it."

Carefully, Malice gathered the bird into his hands and brought it to his chest. It must really be in pain to not struggle at all. Kiran and Malice hurried through the oak trees and burst into the cottage. Freshly baked bread hit Kiran, instantly making his mouth water. He unfortunately had to ignore it for now. The windows provided the perfect amount of light, touching everything in the living space with soft clarity, shadows elusive.

"Mother," he said and closed the door. He would get yelled at if he left it open again.

She peeked around the kitchen counter, slicing the bread into thick slabs. "Quite the harvest," she said with an impressed grin.

On his tiptoes, Kiran set and slid the basket onto the counter. "We found a bird."

"It hurt its wing." Malice opened his cupped hands, moving them away from his chest to reveal the small creature.

"That's no good," Father's voice came from the hallway as he walked into the living space and crouched to inspect the bird.

"What do we do?" Kiran didn't like that it was in pain. The bird's feathers of greyish blue were ruffled, and its eyes were half open. It had a slender body, a small head, and a long, thin beak.

"You can heal it," Blodwen suggested, put the knife down, and joined them by the entrance.

Malice extended his hands toward Tendai.

"Why don't you try to heal it, Kiran?" Father asked, the corners of his mouth curved.

"But I don't know how," Kiran mumbled. And he didn't want to hurt it any further.

"I'll teach you."

His father moved closer to Malice, shifting him so his body was facing the living room, then gestured for Kiran to come closer. He did, the tips of their bare and dirty toes nearly touching.

"Place your hands over Malice's," he said.

Hesitantly, Kiran listened.

"From here," Tendai poked Kiran's stomach, and he giggled, "all the way to here," his finger traced up to his shoulder, down his arm, to the back of his hand, "feel your magic flow within your body."

Kiran breathed in through the nose and out through the mouth, like Blodwen had taught him. The first time he used magic, it was like a tug in his sternum, Malice had explained. A few months ago, Kiran had experienced the same sensation, as if someone had snagged a strand of his hair.

Magic ran through his torso, arm, and hand, the energy tickling yet gently tugging at his muscles and veins.

"Now release it into the mockingbird," Mother said from behind Malice.

Maybe because he was nervous, when his magic reached his fingertips, it died. Kiran started anew, eyebrows furrowed in concentration. Again, magic sparked and flowed, but this time, he let it go into the little creature. The mockingbird twitched, startling Kiran and Malice.

"It's all right," Tendai whispered. "Keep going."

Magic soaked into the bird. Moments went by. Kiran held his breath, his eyes trained on the bird resting in Malice's pale hand. Its wing flexed, jerked, and righted itself. Kiran wanted to look away, but didn't. Then, with a few tweets, the bird perked up, head moving all around, blinking. It shook, hopped in Malice's palm, and flapped its wings as if to test them.

Tendai caught it, stood, and hurried outside, Kiran and Malice on his heels. Father released the mockingbird, and it soared toward the trees, singing.

Kiran grinned as his heart danced. He turned to Malice, whose face was light with surprise.

"You saved it!" Malice exclaimed.

"Great job, son," Father said, the door clicking shut. He smiled down at Kiran.

As she nodded toward the kitchen, Blodwen asked, "How about a treat to celebrate?"

I saved it! "You should learn too, Malice!"

The three of them joined Blodwen in the kitchen, Kiran and Malice climbing into the stools on the other side of the oak counter.

Malice shrugged, gaze on the wood. "Maybe."

Maybe wasn't no, so it was good enough for now.

Mother slathered the bread with honey and berries, then sprinkled it with cinnamon, put the slabs on plates and handed them out. Kiran gobbled it up, juice and honey running down his chin. Malice was a slow eater, and his face was always clean. Kiran, adjusting his posture, wiped his mouth, and matched Malice's pace as he sank his teeth into the rest of his dessert. He was older than him, yet ate like a toddler.

"That was very impressive," Father said, ruffling Kiran's hair. "Would you like to learn more about healing and medicine?"

"Yes!" Kiran said with a full mouth.

"What about you, Malice?"

Malice did nothing for a second, aside from staring absently at his treat. In his stillness, Kiran observed him, confused why he didn't say yes. His white hair loosely coiled to his shoulders, random clusters extra fuzzy from their time outside, and his lips were pouted. He had long eyelashes, Kiran noticed, like daisy petals above grass.

Eventually, Malice nodded.

"We can start tomorrow."

Excitement bubbled in Kiran's stomach. If he could save a bird, surely he could save a cat, a flower, maybe a bug, though he wasn't sure why a bug would need to be saved. One day, he might heal Malice and Zephyrus during their spars. They would become a team, Malice and Zephyrus fighting and Kiran making sure they were okay afterward. That sounded good to him. Zephyrus would agree, he was positive. He just needed to convince Malice his caution was unwarranted.

Hidden Past
X

"There was a surge of fish this year," the barbarian with tattoos said. "As much as we thank the seas, we aren't eating 'em fast enough and they're stinking our docks."

A child stood at Anselm's backside, one big pale blotch on his face, almost like Kiran's, except the boys—Leontios, Malice believed his name was—was shaped like a skull. Malice guessed he couldn't have been much older than him, a year or two, yet not as old as Magnus.

The dark elf, who always sat by Caroline, the elf at the head of the table, said, "We shall send more convoys throughout the year. Help rid you of some of the surplus." His voice was like gravel underneath Malice's boot.

Draga had tasked him to learn all the ruler's names this year. *You will recite them upon your return,* she had warned. Listening to solely avoid punishment, standing beside Felim, Malice patiently waited for each ruler's name to be said as they droned on about trade, coin, and other boring matters. All of which flew over Malice's head. The only reprieve, snatching his attention like a fish on a hook, was Magnus across the table, the blue gem sparkling in his ear, the same as Malice's.

"… raise the taxes," the giant said—Malice didn't catch the first half—his grey hair in a knot on top of his head, shielded by a transparent black hat.

"Have I not raised them enough?" Surin the fishman, King of Raelle's Region, shot back, delicate brows of coral orange furrowed, scales shimmering, gills flaring steadily. "I'll find another way to compensate for the loss of our harvest. The urchins were like roaches. We'll be better prepared for them next year."

Eventually, Malice caught every name and title. It had only taken till high noon to do so.

He sullenly ventured down to the first floor. Magnus, confirming with a small shake of his head, couldn't join Malice like he had previously. Still, delight fluttered in his chest, filling his veins as he swung around the railing, made his way to the twin slabs of wood beyond the stairs, and opened it to the library. A musty smell hit him instantaneously. His nostrils flared, and he sneezed.

Rows of empty cases and coves obscured the floor of emerald, black, and gold solid and dotted lines, which created a map. Not that Malice knew what the map was of. His eyes drew skyward, his jaw nearly dropping to the ground for a moment. There was a mural of a battle between all twelve species and many others he didn't recognize. It was dingy, old, cracks spreading through it like a spider web. Lamps, candelabrums, fixtures on the tables in the center of the library matched the old softness of every other gold thing in the castle.

Malice walked between the cases, running his finger on the shelf, his skin now dirty with dust. Wiping it on his pants left grey scuff marks. Annabeth wouldn't be happy about that. The walls were sage green, vines of white crawling to the crown molding. He went deeper into the library, going up and down the book aisles until he reached the back wall.

Three stone statues stood. One was like the sculpture in the foyer, the second too small to be any of the races Malice knew, yet its wings resembled a fairy's, and the third was too monstrous to be a demon. Their muscles, skin folds, wrinkles, and curves made it seem as if they were about to take a breath and stretch their stiff limbs.

Moseying around the angel-like one on the right, Malice's foot hit something, almost tripping him if he hadn't caught himself. A metal latch stuck out from a wooden square door painted to blend in with the floor at first glance. He bent down and opened it with a grunt. It was a pitch-dark tunnel, the first few stairs of earth illuminated by the library's light. For a while, Malice stared into the tunnel, his heart whispering in his ear to go down there, his mind telling him to close it and return to the summit. He had stayed with the king and Felim for a while. That should have been good enough for Draga, right?

Turning to peek around the statue, no one had followed him. Malice, swallowing his nerves, held his hand out. Fire burst in his palm, and he started down the stairs.

The dark passageway swallowed up all the light, only exposing a meter or so in front of and behind Malice. His footsteps were dull, unlike the dungeons, making the beat of his heart distracting. It smelled of dirt, rich and minerally. The stairwell was straight, going ever further underneath the castle, steadily dropping in temperature—he shivered. Soon, he saw an end, and the firelight bled into open space, outlining the frame of a smoothly carved archway.

The sound his shoe made when it hit the floor changed, a high-pitched clack, similar to the sound of marble. Holding the flames to the side while his other hand stayed against the wall, Malice cautiously walked along the edge of the room. Which was different as well. It was perfectly flat, whereas in the stairwell, the walls were rough.

The contour of a table caught Malice's eye. On it were two candles he lit, taking one to the others. Each table was full of things: scrolls, wax, ink and pens, books, parchment, clocks, and ball-like maps. There were trinkets galore like a small handheld watch that sprung open when Malice pressed the button on top. The minute-hand and hour-hand no longer ticked.

The walls were slabs of cool grey stone; the floor of jade ribboned with white like soap foaming in the bath. Spaced at even intervals across the room were five jade pillars, the bases carved with birds, wider than any tree trunk he had ever seen. Twenty bookcases sat beyond the pillars. The cases must have been taller than the first floor of the castle, yet the tops of them were nowhere near touching the ceiling of this hidden archive. Taking a lamp, Malice explored the closest aisle.

Books crammed the shelves, some threatening to fall out at the slightest disturbance. Malice stopped a ways down and grabbed one as carefully as he would write a letter to Magnus. The cover was black leather imprinted with symbols that looked more like Kiran's scribbles than words. He opened it, eyes gliding up and down. Understanding nothing, he put it back and continued.

On the opposite side of the library, Malice found a section of books, mixed with scrolls and loose papers, he could read. At random, he picked five books, stacked them in his arms, and rushed to a table, slamming them down. He startled; the reverberating thud was much louder than he thought it would be. Malice sat down and slipped the top book in front of him as his feet swung back and forth.

Land of Deserts: The Continent of Strvey. The cover read above the name *Eskender Torok.* He flipped to the first page. *Journal Entry I.* Skipping through the pages, Malice stopped and read periodically. He set the book opposite the stack, slid the second down, and opened it. There were pictures of creatures inside. At the top of a page, below *Goliath,* was a rough drawing of the creature. It was huge, the size of an oak tree, its limbs long and profuse with muscle, its facial features sharply pronounced, eyes sunken into dark pits, its physique like a door, broad and bulky. Malice didn't like it—it made his skin prickle— so he slammed the book shut and got the third one.

Sheets had been torn out of it, ripped, or dyed with ink, concealing the words underneath a veil of black. He closed the leather-bound book, disappointed he wasn't able to read, and put it on the growing stack as he grabbed the fourth from his right. It was the same; the inside torn and stained, the sentence structure strange like the books Annabeth said were too difficult for Malice to read quite yet. The fifth was no different.

Books three through five were shoved to the center of the table, keeping the first two to his left. Malice pushed his chair out, hopped down, and went to find more books. The more stories he found, the more he could share with Zephyrus and Kiran when he returned and could write about in his next letter to Magnus. He was sure Annabeth would be interested in what he'd learned as well; she always liked to listen.

Out of all the books he grabbed, one held his attention the most, refusing to let it go. It was the biggest, the spine as big as his palm. The leather of the cover was old, worn, damaged at the edges, and scratched. Maybe a cat got ahold of it at some point. The first five pages were blank before he reached the start. Turning sheet after sheet, illustrations of wings, eyes, then hands, and other symbols, reminding Malice of the different region's insignias disassembled, filled the spaces between paragraphs. Near the middle, across two pages, was a drawing of an angel-like creature, beautifully horrifying, a mirror of the statues in the foyer and the library above.

Abruptly, it all shifted. Everything flipped upside down, the text reading from right to left instead of left to right. Malice spun it around. The page layout, however, was almost exactly the same, the difference being the creatures shown on this side of the book. Their eyes, hands, wings, and horns all emulated that of a demon's, yet was somehow more grotesque. Again, spanning two pages close to the center, the creature illustrated twinned the figure in the library. On a single page, dead center of the book, was the simple title, *Archangels and Devils*.

Malice stared at the book's cover for a time, feeling drawn to it, like a string was wrapped around his brain, and the book was drawing it in. The illustrations inside flashing inside his head were strange. Alluring. Scary. Curious. Annoyance ebbed his dazed state. He couldn't read much of its content, the words holding little if any meaning. Frowning at the aged leather, no doubt older than him, his expression eased, and he sighed. Huge as it was, he might be able to stow it home so he could read it when he was ready.

That was theft. Not only would Annabeth be upset with him, the queen would have his bum on a silver platter. Not such a pleasant thought.

Letting the idea fester, Malice stood, yanked the book to the edge of the table, and pressed it tightly against his torso. His shoes smacked the jade floors as he hurried to put out all the candles, then came to the archway and looked over his shoulder. Bitterness coated his tongue, sadness squeezing his heart. He forced his legs up the stairs. *I'll come back next year.*

*

Servants waited and greeted their king, his first sword, and Malice. King Emil and Felim strode inside, leaving Malice to his jumbled thoughts and anxieties, and Annabeth. She asked what the book was in his arms.

"It's a book I found," he mumbled. Despite how true it was, the way his heart skipped a beat when she asked proved differently.

Her kind brown eyes lingered curiously on him, but she dropped the matter and rushed him inside to the fourth floor for a bath.

Once Malice changed into a soft linen shirt and loose trousers held to his waist by a belt, a knock came to his bedchamber door. Annabeth opened it, the door screeching as she did, uncovering the bulk of Alkeim.

Alkeim solemnly nodded toward the hallway. "Come on lad, it's time for dinner."

Malice stole a glance at the book on his desk, then at Annabeth, her complexion suddenly pale. Why had Alkeim come to collect him? *Her highness knows*, Malice realized, his blood as cold as stone in the winter. His feet carried him to the door nevertheless, oblivious to the churning dread in his stomach, and followed Alkeim through the corridor, Annabeth trailing. His heart, at the rate it was going, would pound its way out of his chest before he reached the dining room. Maybe that wasn't such a bad thing. The thought of dinner knotted his intestines, but he knew he wouldn't be eating tonight, bringing a sense of relief that vanished as quickly as it appeared.

Annabeth stood against the wall of the dining hall, her head down and her hands in front of her, clasped tightly, knuckles white. Alkeim brought Malice to the head of the table beside the queen, taking his place behind her seat. She cut her steak, the meat pink and overflowing with juices, the top peppered with herbs. Her gaze sliced to Malice. He shuddered as his legs gave and he instantly dropped to his hands and knees, breath shallow. Queen Vendetta continued slicing. She stabbed the bite-sized chunks of beef and ate while the rest of the table remained silent.

When her plate was half empty, she moved on to her side dishes. "You thought it wise to disregard the summit? Again?" she said without looking at Malice.

He couldn't speak and wouldn't even if he thought it wise.

"I was told you went as far as to steal a book from the castle… Inyene."

Inyene perked up. "Yes?"

"How is the mutts' regeneration?"

Her daughter shrugged, tone passive and unimpressed. "So so. Better than the twins, I'll admit."

"Annabeth." The queen snapped her finger. Annabeth flinched. "Go fetch Tendai. He ought to still be in the infirmary."

Annabeth didn't ask why or refuse. She practically sprinted out of the dining room and rather swiftly returned with Tendai. As Annabeth went back to her place, Tendai crossed the room, stopping on the opposite side of Malice, and bowed.

"You called for me?" he asked politely.

"Stand there for now." Sticking a cube of pumpkin with her fork, she addressed Malice, "Do you know how we punish thieves?"

"… No," Malice uttered, his entire body trembling. He didn't want to find out.

Inyene chugged her goblet of ale, slammed it on the table, and stood, almost knocking her chair back. She walked over briskly. When she hoisted Malice to his feet, she shoved him face first onto the table, her hand encasing his forearms. Shackles of ice glued him to the table. He struggled and yanked his arms, but the ice burned, ripping the skin underneath. Grimly, pain searing his wrists, Malice turned his head toward his sister, a grin so twisted on her face it made him want to retch.

Despite his blurred vision, Malice looked toward Alkeim, his head averted, and his expression screwed. He glanced at Tendai, whose head was low, and his eyes were elsewhere.

"Must we do this at the table?" Draga intervened as she wiped the corners of her mouth with a napkin. She glared at Malice. "It will create a mess… and a headache."

Inyene raised her arm. A cleaver of ice manifested. "Of course, we do."

It whistled as she brought it down. With a *thunk,* it bit the table. He screamed. His hand jumped forward, blood spraying the contents spread on the table in front of him. His periphery went fuzzy as Draga and the king swayed. She hefted the cleaver once more, severing Malice's left hand from his forearm. He let a gut-curdling shriek, his ears reverberating the noise, rattling his chest, quaking his bones. Pain throbbed; blood pulsed in rhythm with his speeding heartbeat. He was short of breath. Tears, more like droplets of fire, rolled down his cheeks.

Smiling deliriously, Inyene returned to her seat, probably glad she'd finished eating since crimson splattered her empty plate. The strength in his legs fleeted, and Malice slumped over the side of the table. A voice, somewhat deep and concerned, spoke, then another, higher pitched, carped at the first. Forcing his heavy head toward the voices, it was Tendai and her highness. He suddenly felt silly, thinking they could have been someone else. Over his shoulder, Annabeth sobbed into her hands as quietly as she could, but she couldn't hide the heaving of her diaphragm or the violent shaking of her extremities.

After what seemed like hours, Tendai finally received permission to reattach Malice's hands and heal him. The pain lessened but did not fully disappear when the doctor finished.

"Now leave. Let us enjoy the rest of our meal in peace," the queen said.

Inyene released the ice around Malice's forearms, it melting into puddles. He slipped to the floor as Annabeth rushed to his aid, lifting him into her arms, and left with Tendai. Malice watched the table of his kin shrink, the door closing on them. As if lead weighed them down, Malice couldn't keep his eyelids open any longer, and the corridor faded to nothing.

Groggily, he sat up, the fireflies in the jar dim on his nightstand and hardly flapping about. His room was empty, warm, yet cold at the same time. He threw his blankets off and swung his legs over the edge of the bed, his feet not able to touch the ground. Kiran couldn't either, though.

Reaching to scratch an itch on his head, he paused. Malice gasped and grabbed his forearm, eyes like the full moon. His hand was gone. Severed at the wrist. Blood flowed down his arm onto the bed and floor like a river of red. He screwed his eyes shut, hoping it was his imagination. But he opened them, and his other hand was gone too. The room spun.

He bolted out of bed, slipped on the blood, fell, and biffed his chin on the floor. Pain spiked through his tongue and a metallic taste coated his mouth as tears rushed to his eyes. Malice struggled to stand upright. His bedchamber swayed like tall grass. Agony pulsed beyond his arms into his chest and head, the door so close and so far. It was shut. He couldn't turn the doorknob. He couldn't breathe. His knees were trembling.

Malice banged on the door. *Open the door! Someone! Annabeth! Kiran! Please help me!* Opening his mouth to scream only produced a strangled groan of noise.

Footsteps sounded outside.

"Malice?" Annabeth.

As he stepped away, Annabeth opened the door, dropping to her knees in an instant, her face twisted with concern.

"What's wrong?" she asked frantically, grabbing Malice's face to steady it, and brushed his hair aside. "Breathe, you're safe."

Malice gripped her shoulders tightly, making her wince. He wanted to yell at her, tell her to look at his—his hands? They were gone? Spun around, he searched for the pool of blood he had slipped in seconds ago to find nothing.

"My hands," he croaked, the lump in his throat a jagged rock.

Annabeth flinched, her mouth ajar for a split second before she drew Malice into her warm embrace, kissing the side of his head as she whispered, "It's all right now. You're okay."

Over and over, she recited words of comfort until Malice sank into her arms, exhausted, all the strength in his body slithering away. Finally, he took a full breath, taking in Annabeth's smell of honey and mint. Still, his body trembled. His hands… they *were* gone. He'd seen the blood on the floor, felt the warmth spill down his arms. He'd slipped in it.

Peeking at his desk, the large spined book stared back at him, the old leather dully gleaming. His mind went blank, his body cold, chest constricting. He turned and stuffed his face in the crook of Annabeth's neck where it met the shoulder. She was warm. Very warm.

"Can you eat?" she asked in a brittle voice.

Malice didn't want to eat, but the tension in his stomach told him he should. He nodded. Annabeth, her hand stroking his hair, kissed his forehead, the warmth of her lips lingering when she pulled away. She helped him to his feet, caressed his cheek with her thumb, and left.

Annabeth soon returned with a tray of fruits and two bowls of hot oats. And Kiran. He sat at the desk while Annabeth placed the tray of food down and stood by the door afterward. He was glad she didn't leave. Unhurriedly plucking blueberries, blackberries, orange and banana slices from the big wooden bowl, Malice regarded Kiran. He was quiet, reserved, almost seemed nervous, like he was walking on eggshells. Malice didn't know whether he appreciated the silence or if he preferred Kiran's rambling.

Kiran had followed Malice everywhere he went. Today he studied with Draga. Kiran sat next to him the whole time, peeking at his papers and books without saying a word. Draga didn't protest to Kiran's presence either, she simply gave Malice his first instruction.

When evening rolled around, Kiran ate dinner with Malice in

his bedchamber. Then they bathed, all of it a silent blur of activity.

They crawled into the bed that was too big for Malice, Malice lying on his back while Kiran lay on his side. Kiran searched for Malice's hand, gripped it underneath the blankets, and drifted to sleep as quickly as he always did.

Malice had stuffed the book inside his closet, hidden underneath his clothes. He didn't want to look at it ever again. *I should've left it.*

Commands of the Eldest
XI

Malice stumbled to close the closet door leading to the dungeons, his mind fuzzy, his core aching. Inyene had let him go early. He didn't question it. Why would he?

He took a breath and leaned against the wall of the entrance. Forcing him to go to his limits when Inyene was the one who'd warned about the consequences of doing so made little sense. In spite of his muddled mind, he was sure there were other ways he could improve his magic. Malice remembered there was a letter waiting in his room from Magnus and kicked off the wall.

As familiar as these halls were, there was always a sense of foreboding, a cold eeriness, whispers telling him to run grating his eardrums. It was dark in the southern wing of the castle, only two torches lighting the hall, one on each side. He passed very few doors, since the rooms on the first floor were huge, unlike the many studies, storerooms, and bedchambers of the upper floors.

Servants went about their evening rituals, Malice sticking close to the wall so he didn't get in the way or get bumped into. His legs were weak, and the trek up the stairs made his muscles numb. If someone knocked him down, he probably wouldn't get back up for a while.

Light flooded from his bedchamber's cracked doorway. Hand on the knob, Malice froze, one foot in his room. Books were thrown all over the place, clothes scattered across the floor, his mattress hanging off the bedframe, the armchairs tipped over. The armoire fell with a boom. Malice jumped. Sok and Rayen turned to him, grins on their faces, their first swords standing idly against the furthest wall.

His mouth hung ajar, wide-eyed, head fuddled.

"Oops," Sok said with a shrug.

"Guess we're caught," Rayen added slyly.

"Why?" Malice breathed.

"Why?" Sok echoed and tilted his head, an eyebrow cocked.

Rayen grunted a laugh. "Why not?"

"But if you want the real reason, we can tell you," Sok went on. "For a price."

Malice slid his foot backward, his thoughts coming back to him. "What do you want?" He didn't care what their reasoning was, he wanted them gone so he could clean up this mess and find Magnus's letter.

The twins looked at one another, exchanging devious smiles, and turned back to Malice. His blood ran cold. They both moved forward, inching closer to Malice.

"Don't you get it by now?" Sok asked.

"You," Rayen joined, "deserve a punishment for keeping secrets from Mother."

"What secrets?" He tensed.

"Your letters," Sok said as he yanked an envelope out of his warm grey coat, wagging it in the air. Malice's name stained the back of it, and when he turned it over, Alucard's Regions sigil sealed it.

Malice lurched forward. "Give it back," he snarled, reaching for the letter. His fingertips grazed it as something hit him, hard, and he sprawled to the floor.

His cheek throbbed, blood filling his mouth. The twins stood over him. Rayen's fist was bunched at her side, her knuckles a few shades darker than her sickly blue skin tone.

"We'll give it back," said Sok, that smile having never left his mouth. "After we've dealt a proper punishment for your foolhardiness."

At the same time, Sok and Rayen kicked Malice, slamming their heeled shoes into his ribs, chest—everywhere. He braced himself, curling into a ball, hands over his head, each hit rattling his body. The thought of fighting back briefly crossed his mind, but what could he do if Aglaia and Xenon stepped in, upheld their oath, and protected the twins?

Rayen took Malice by the back of his shirt's collar, hoisting him off the ground, and choked him. Malice huffed and thrashed, pain stabbing all over his body. She only tightened her grip. Darkness danced across his vision. A white rectangle stayed in Sok's grip as he drew his opposite fist back. Malice needed to get the letter back. He needed to read what Magnus wrote. When Sok's fist flew, Malice reached for the envelope.

Then a voice gasped at the door, and footsteps pounded nearer. Kiran tackled Sok to the ground, both grunting. Rayen's vise-like hold lightened a smidge.

"How dare you!" Sok bellowed as he grabbed fistfuls of Kiran's hair and hit him over and over again.

Kiran, eyes screwed shut, jaw clenched, tried to keep Sok pinned to the ground. Winces and hisses of pain slipped from his sealed lips.

"Let go!" Malice said and wrenched himself free of Rayen's

grip.

He dropped and sprang forward, scooping the letter that had fallen from Sok's hand. Rayen snarled behind him. She stomped, her hand landing on Malice's shoulder, before she whipped him around and punched Malice. His nose crunched, tears sprang to his eyes instantly, and blood poured down his face. She punched again. This time, her fist hit Malice's hands. His palms stung.

"Can you not handle a calf by yourself?" Rayen asked gruffly, her chest heaving. "Seriously, Sok, do I have to come to your rescue? Again?"

"NO!" Sok shouted and bit Kiran, who yelped. Shoving him off, he straddled the beastman and wailed on him. Left and right, his fists becoming bloodier and bloodier.

Despite the agony coursing through every inch of his body, Malice's heart tightened at the sight of Kiran's swelling face as tears ran to the floor. His veins burned, his lungs taking in fire instead of air. Teeth gritting, Malice returned Rayen's punch, which made her stumble backwards, stunned. Sok was next as Malice kicked him off Kiran and hauled him away, the action too rough as they teetered and fell. *Wait.* Something was off. *The letter!* It wasn't in his hand.

"Looking for something?" Rayen sneered, her teeth stained red, as she got her bearings, holding the slightly crumpled envelope up for Malice to see.

He glanced down at Kiran, his bloodied face already bruised. Malice held him upright for a moment and let go. Kiran stayed put, wheezing as crimson dripped from various cuts on his face. He looked worse than a good number of the royals Malice had seen at the training grounds. With a deep breath, Malice got to his feet. Sok rose as well. Eyes darting between the two of them, Malice lunged at Sok, raking his nails over his face. Sok shrieked and reeled, eyes screwed shut. Rayen grunted as she closed in. Thin marks on Sok's face beaded with tiny dots of blood.

Malice twisted just in time, reaching for her shoulder, when Rayen drove her fist into Malice's gut. He doubled over, suddenly winded, and crashed, pain shooting into thighs and calves. He swallowed repeatedly to keep the fluid in his stomach while wetness blurred the floor. Rayen looked over Sok's injuries.

"You're fine," she told him.

Folded over on himself, shuddering, Malice smiled through the tears. He pressed the envelope into his chest. As breath came to him in shallow gasps, Malice crawled to Kiran and blocked him from the twins. He was in better shape than Kiran, anyway. Thanks to his training with Odovacar, he could take a few more hits. Probably.

Their faces flushed with anger, reflections of each other. Yet, the longer he stared, Malice could see a bit more harshness in Rayen's snarl, a darkness in her gaze Sok didn't have. Xenon and Aglaia still stood motionless against the wall. But then they stiffened, their relaxed posture going rigidly straight, complexions paling.

"Enough," a deep voice commanded.

The twins froze.

"How much longer will you let your immaturity win?" It was Odovacar. But why?

Malice glanced at the door. Odovacar leaned against the frame, arms crossed, feet bare, wearing loose linen meant for bed. If he was ready to retire, Malice wondered what he was doing in the servant's quarters. His siblings didn't sleep here. Annabeth said they were on the third floor.

Rayen snipped, "What's it to you, brother?"

"Why not let us be for once?" Sok asked, his tone sharp and irritated.

"Do you think mother will tolerate this childishness for long?" Odovacar asked. "I am giving you a chance to leave. Right your mistake before you can no longer take it back."

"You have no right to tell us what to do!" Sok barked, his bloodied fists trembling at his sides.

"As your elder brother, I do. As a general, I do. As Prince, I do. Heed my advice and leave lest you want this to reach Mother." His eyes scanned the room, passing over the first swords, the wreckage, and falling to Malice and Kiran. "Do not make me do more than this."

Sok's jaw strained. Rayen huffed. Both stormed out of the room, slinking around Odovacar, soon followed by Xenon and Aglaia. They kept their heads down, shoulders slumped, unlike the twins. The general stayed a moment longer, observing the bedchamber and everything in it.

Malice didn't know what to do. Pain pulsed throughout his body, making it hard to see, let alone piece together his thoughts. Kiran sat in front of him, his breathing haggard. Malice grimaced.

"Thank y—"

"Do not thank me," Odovacar interrupted. "I did not do this to help you. I did it to keep those two redeemable and so you could come to me in your best condition tomorrow."

Malice hoped it was out of kindness, even if it was a fraction of his reason. He was wrong and bitterness coated the inside of his mouth. Or perhaps it was the blood.

"Why did you not fight back?" Odovacar asked, catching Malice by surprise. "You know how to, and you would have been able to fend off the twins."

"It was four against one," Malice answered, unsure, brain pinching. "Then it was two against four." Besides, he fought back. He slugged Rayen a good one and kicked Sok hard enough to put him on his bum.

Odovacar's black eyes twitched. "What makes you think they would have joined Sok and Rayen?"

"They swore to protect them, not me." The knights hadn't helped… Maybe they were ordered not to, but how was Malice supposed to know?

Odovacar grunted, turned, and vanished into the hall.

As Malice helped Kiran to his feet, they cringed and groaned through the pain. Unsteady, Malice observed his bedchamber, tears ready to fall at any moment.

Everything hurt. Crimson stained his clothes, skin, and the floor. His right eye was swollen shut, his face throbbed, his chest burned, sending a shock of pain every time he breathed wrong. Malice knew Kiran was in a lot of pain as well, yelping as often as he was. Still, they cleaned his room, righted the chairs, struggled, but eventually got the armoire up, collected papers and clothes, putting them in their respective places. They heaved and shoved the mattress back onto the frame and made the bed. In a pile outside the door against the wall, they threw what couldn't be spared and what was dirty out.

When all was said and done, Malice was exhausted. Kiran was too, his eyes half closed, both of them breathless. He stumbled, then crashed onto the bed. Malice joined him. As sleep began to take him, someone entered the room. They approached, so he reluctantly sat up. Tendai looked between Kiran and Malice, surprised. Sadness took over; squished his eyebrows and softened his gaze.

He kneeled in front of Malice, healed him, and stood to heal Kiran. Silently, which was curious. Malice expected questions, but got none. Tendai left soon after. He didn't say goodnight. Annabeth hadn't come either.

Flipping onto his side, Malice studied Kiran—the bruises were gone but blood remained, dried and cracked. Why did he come to his rescue? He hated violence, yet didn't hesitate to help Malice. Was it because they were brothers? Was that what brothers did for one another? Malice would do it. He would help Kiran. It didn't matter if he would get in trouble. Malice would come to Kiran's rescue, no matter what.

"Odovacar"

The Twins tormented Malice simply because he existed. Malice was younger than them by five years. Albeit negative, he got more attention from the queen as well. Odovacar did not doubt Sok and Rayen subjected Malice to their menace for that reason. He could not know for sure, however, and did not want to find whether his theory was true or false.

Luckily, on the way down to the third floor, there was a servant. *Fetch Dr. Tendai and send him to Malice's room,* he told them. They obeyed, spinning to trudge back down the stairs.

Odovacar veered to the western wing, to his bedchamber. Draga's was on this floor as well, as were Inyene's, Alkeim's and Felim's. And the undisturbed solace of Elias's room. He passed his late brother's door, his reputation now on Odovacar's shoulders and his legacy left for him to fulfill. They were proving difficult to live up to.

His door was beyond Elias's, and it opened to a bleak room, dark and mostly empty aside from the essentials. A bed, closet, table, armoire, chest, and a bookcase. He wondered if the twins would tell Mother of what he did. If so, what would the queen do to him? If Sok and Rayen were to snitch, they would rat themselves out as well, so it was unlikely they would say anything. The same could not be said for Xenon or Aglaia. Loyalty, depending on how much they had toward the twins, would be the only thing preventing them from telling her highness.

Sighing, Odovacar sat on the chest at the foot of his bed. It was packed with extra covers and sheets, thin and thick for the changing seasons.

All of Queen Vendetta's children had been through what Malice was going through in her attempt to make a more powerful version of Elias. Draga and Inyene, being the eldest, had suffered at the hands of Father, while Odovacar, Sok and Rayen had suffered via Inyene's crueler methods. Mother had always told Odovacar every way he lacked when compared to his deceased brother. Every way he had become a disappointment.

He felt the only reason the twins listened to him was out of some shred of gratitude, small as it may be. He did for them what he was doing for Malice. But how much longer could he protect Malice, go easy on him before the queen would not tolerate it anymore? There was only so much he could do, only so much he could withstand.

Odovacar stood and stripped, catching sight of himself in the mirror across the room. The scars on his back itched. They had not healed properly and tugged with most of his movements. The discomfort was something he had learned to live with. They were nasty looking, dark, puffy slashes going from side to side, marking his youth's discipline, reminding him of it always.

He tore his eyes away and crawled into bed, covering his legs with the top blanket. Once he was comfortable, the lashings he received as an adolescent entered his mind, the itch refusing to leave, worsening. He was flogged, then kept on the wooden post for days without food or water. The reason ludicrous. Odovacar had not run his blade through an opponent who did not deserve death simply because he thought himself better than his actual skill set. Defeat and a verbal slating would have been punishment enough for such arrogance, but her highness could not have disagreed more. Voicing his opposition earned him a session with the whip and had taught him a valuable lesson.

Never speak against your mother.

Breaking the Soul
XII

Part I

It was cold and stormy outside; the winds beating against the castle, howling as if mourning a lost lover. The mass of ominous, swirling clouds turned evening to night, flashing white, deep rumbles quaking the earth.

Vendetta closed the curtains to one of the few unbarred windows in the castle, looking out to the northern grounds, the greenery vibrant and lush, and sat at her desk.

A few candles flickered inside her study, elongating the swaying shadows across the burgundy walls. The room matched the interior of the rest of the castle; the floor mirroring the angry clouds outside, the furniture's wood stained rich brown. Darkness was comforting, an embrace of the familiar.

On cushions of red in front of Vendetta's desk sat Draga, lips to a pipe, releasing a long breath of smoke, the smell of mugwort earthy and herbal. Alongside her was Odovacar, his posture rigid as it always was. In the armchair opposite the couch, Inyene had her feet on the table, a goblet of ale in hand. Languid, confident, arrogant; Inyene was never one to show her vulnerability, a quality Vendetta was glad she inherited.

"How goes the twins' training?" Vendetta asked as she reclined into her chair, her eyes moving from one of her children to the next.

"Disappointing," Draga said, taking another drag off her pipe, exhaling the grey cloud as she spoke. "Neither has the wits to outsmart a rat."

Inyene smirked and eyed her drink as it tempted the confines of her cup. "Rayen's temperamental, easy to rile." She shrugged. "Can't say much else."

"Sok is no different," Odovacar said monotonously. "The control he has over his magic can best a handful of green royals. His talent stops there."

Sighing, Vendetta massaged the bridge of her nose. "Will they become a hindrance, or can they yet prove themselves useful?" *The rotten apples must be removed from the crop.* As she had said about the mutt; she would not have trash walking her halls.

"As of now, they are as useful as they are useless." Draga tapped the step of her pipe with her finger, emptying the chamber. "It can go either way."

The twins were once promising. An ounce of praise inflated their egos. If she had not pushed them out herself, Vendetta would have sworn they were children of nobles with their pompous conceit over a touch of leniency. Gave an inch and they took a mile. They would much rather spend their time tormenting the mutt than sharpening their skills. Recently turned twelve, Sok and Rayen had the chance to be salvaged, to be useful in some way.

Each of her children was a fraction of a whole. None were well rounded, versatile, or adaptable as they ought to be, as Vendetta wanted them to be. Her late son Elias, on the other hand, had been. He had the mind of a scholar, the brawns of a commander, and the stony heart of an executioner. All he lacked was power and said deficiency killed him whilst on a campaign a little over forty years ago.

"What of the mutt?" There was still hope in giving one of her children everything: power, intelligence, strength, a killer's touch. Hope she could mold something to her standards.

"Everything I have given to him, he has done without complaint and has needed little help." A smile teased the corners of Draga's mouth. "For such a young child, he is quite the problem solver."

Odovacar carried on. "His development has far exceeded my expectations." He looked down at his calloused hands, little white scars painting his flesh as if someone dragged a fine tipped brush across them. Vendetta remembered most of the orders given to create those scars.

"He is evenly matched with Issur's son," he added.

"His magic?" Vendetta said.

After a draught of her ale, Inyene sat forward and replenished her goblet from the pitcher on the table. "He excels," she crooned.

"How?"

Inyene sat back, crossing her legs as her heel slammed into the table again. "The control he has over his magic is impressive, more so than what I can say for the twins. However," she switched the position of her feet around, "the way he has improved over the past three years is… strange to me. It seems he wants to put on a show."

"Sounds as if Malice found someone to impress," Draga said and glanced from her sister to Vendetta. "My guess would be Kiran or Magnus, perhaps Zephyrus."

Vendetta grunted, nails drumming the arm of her seat. Kiran was Blodwen's child, a smart little beast, but weak and sensitive. Allowing Kiran to befriend the mutt added another pawn she could later manipulate him with. She had done it once, threatening Kiran. She would do it again should the need arise. Same went for Zephyrus. He, conversely, would be much easier to control, as he wanted to follow in his father's footsteps. The brat would have no choice but to obey her orders as a royal of Hordes Region. Albeit Magnus, Holister's spawn, was out of the question. She could not reach him if she wanted to.

"He can also use fire, earth, and water magic," Inyene sang.

"What?" Odovacar reeled, his arched brows poised. "He was not supposed to learn the elements until he was ten."

Inyene nodded, a flicker in her amused expression Vendetta could not quite pin meaning to. "I'm aware, which is why I said what I said. He wants to show off, not to fight."

"I assumed it was a one-sided puppy love." Leaning forward, Vendetta placed her elbows on the surface of her desk, fingers entwining under her chin. The heat of the candle flame licked her skin.

Magnus took a liking to his new pet, a bit surprising, but not something Vendetta could not deal with. "What do you think of their letters?"

"I don't think it is anything of concern," Draga said. "They exchange mundane routines, happenings, and not much else."

Vendetta quirked an eyebrow. "You intercepted one?"

She nodded.

"We will leave them then," she decided.

Vendetta scowled at her desk. Alucard's military was large, better known for its Units and their versatility. The prior monarch, Holister's father, King Jaci Castine, made it so. Disease took him some years ago, a short time before Magnus's birth, if she remembered correctly. As unfortunate as it was that she had never had the opportunity to meet him; good riddance. His death had weakened Holister, making his region gradually deteriorate alongside him. With their connection, it would be little trouble to convince Magnus through Malice to form an alliance. A true alliance. Perhaps she ought to marry

Rayen off to Magnus, have her produce an heir or two, solidifying the Reap's claim to Alucard's Region. Which, in turn, would make sinking her claws into the land of angels that much simpler. By then, should Magnus and Holister refuse, her gathered forces ought to be more than enough to overthrow the abated throne.

"What do you think about Malice's true form, Mother?" Inyene asked, breaking Vendetta away from her thoughts. "Do you think he has one?"

She sighed. The mutt had the three great bloodlines running through him. "It will manifest." *But one day isn't fast enough.* "He needs something to get him there. He has been too safe thus far."

It was her fault. She had allowed her children to train a mutt with gentle hands and a slack leash. He needed fear.

"Leave, all of you." Pointedly at Odovacar, as he rose, she said, "Send for Annabeth. I have a task for her."

A Tale of Origins

"Alkeim"

Alkeim enjoyed the crisp chill of winter nights in Hordes Region, giving him a reprieve from the heat bearing down on him during the day. The grass underneath his feet was frost bitten, crunching with every step. A full moon painted the world a dull blue, and stars glittered in the north. It was beautiful, serene.

The enormous stone castle had windows, like gleaming eyes, but they were only for show. Inside, all were barred and covered with dense black curtains, keeping the light of day from entering. Depressing and oppressive.

Alkeim walked into the front courtyard, following the granite path, climbing the shallow, wide steps, and entering the castle. Through the dimly lit foyer, he made his way to the second floor, assuming the queen was about to leave or had already left her study to retire for the night. His own bedchamber was on the third floor, along with Felim and the queen's children. First swords had the option of living in the castle if they desired. Alkeim had come to regret that decision.

Once he reached the top of the staircase, there was a certain drag in his limbs, a weight he could usually ignore, yet tonight, an ache accompanied the pressure, crawling up his torso, nestling inside the cavity of his chest. He glanced toward her highness's study. Padded footsteps sounded from his right. He whipped his head around, his heart skipping a beat. The queen's silhouette strutted down the corridor, nearing her bedchamber.

"Your highness," he called out as he approached.

She turned. There was no change in her neutral expression upon seeing him. What else had he expected? The queen still wore a dress with a diamond opening on her bust, the shoulders puffed, while the sleeves flared around both sets of forearms. The rest was form fitting, flowing onto the ground, veiling her shoes. There were probably little openings in the back, pulled tight with laces, for her plum-colored bat-like wings. They flapped once as they stretched out to her sides, then retracted as if his gaze triggered their movement.

Alkeim bowed at the waist. "Turning in for the night?"

"Indeed," she said. "But I'm glad you are here."

"What is it, your highness?" he tried to keep the nerves from his voice. The way she smiled made his palms damp with sweat and the hairs on his arms stand on edge, every muscle tensing.

"Throw the mutt into Mutuwa tonight."

As if punched, Alkeim recoiled, shook his head, and stared blankly at the queen. She was not jesting.

"But your highness," he protested, despite knowing if he went on, he would most likely receive a lashing of some sort on the morrow. "He's *seven*." Mutuwa was a death sentence for anyone, no less a child.

She scowled, her lip flaring. "Have I not let you off easy?"

Alkeim blinked.

"After you brought him from the dungeons, his true form had manifested."

His knees almost gave out, and he teetered. *How did she find out? Who told her?*

"What he needs is not time, it is danger." Queen Vendetta stepped closer, Alkeim flinching back, as her hand shot up, and suddenly, Alkeim was utterly stuck, frozen, his muscles stone. All he could move were his eyes—he could hardly breathe.

"I've made all the necessary preparations," she said, fingers curling in on themselves. Alkeim's stomach twisted, agony blooming so horrendously, his scream manifested as a prolonged groan through his clamped jaw. "Unless you want Blodwen, Tendai, and everyone else who was in that room and neglected to tell me flogged alongside you, follow your orders."

Queen Vendetta marched to her bedchamber, releasing Alkeim of her vile blood magic. He staggered and clutched his gut. At her door, the queen halted and turned.

"I've grown fond of you, Alkeim," she said, her voice cold. "So, believe me when I tell you; this is the last time I will show you kindness. Disobey, speak out, or abandon your tasks again, you will wake to your wife's and daughter's heads on your chest."

She slammed her bedroom door, the bang echoing.

Icy sweat beaded on his forehead and back, slipping down his skin. It took a time, but eventually the pain eased enough so he could at least stand properly and narrowly collect himself. Alkeim rushed the way he came and hiked up the stairs. Images of his wife and child flashed in his mind's eye, distant clouds warning him of a brewing storm. As well as Malice.

Which poison to take? Kill Malice or kill his family?

He gathered two royals lingering in the halls and paused at the top of the fourth floor's platform, eyes glued to his brown leather boots. How could he do that to a child? How could her highness do that to her *own* child? Guilt, hesitance, and shame were one and the same as they swirled viciously inside Alkeim like the storm he'd ignored and was now a typhoon of misery.

He sighed, attempting to master the trembling of his hands, and walked toward Malice's door, the royals behind him.

"Get him," Alkeim ordered one of the two guards, not caring who went in and grabbed the prince. He… couldn't be the one to do it. Not again.

Both looked at one another, sharing quick, confused glances. The bigger of the two opened the prince's door, stalked in, hoisted Malice into his arms, and returned to the corridor.

Alkeim whispered, "I'm sorry lad," while caressing the boy's hair. It was soft, tightly curled, as pure as fresh snow. But something… was wrong. He should have twitched or stirred from Alkeim's touch. Alkeim gently shook the lad's shoulders, to no response.

"He's drugged," a feminine voice said, startling the royals and Alkeim.

He swiveled. Annabeth stood there, where she came from, Alkeim didn't know. Her hands were clasped in front of her, her shoulders bunched, making her look small and defeated. There was a hollowness to her features he could almost feel resonating within his own.

"I'm not sure what the queen had me give him, but he won't wake anytime soon," Annabeth said.

Alkeim stared at the servant, the one who had raised Malice since he and his brother brought him here. The sight of her disgusted him.

But how could he say anything?

He took in a shuddering breath and said, "On the queen's orders, take him to Mutuwa." Alkeim fought the urge to snatch Malice back and hide him somewhere, anywhere. He would have done it for his daughter Shohre in a heartbeat, even faster if he could.

With a dip of their heads, the two guards were off, disappearing beyond the wall. All Alkeim could do was watch, heart wringing itself as if the queen had a hold of him again. When he glanced over his shoulder, Annabeth had vanished. One mention of Queen Vendetta was enough to scatter an entire warband or put them into action. Fear drove them.

Those royals were no different. Neither was Annabeth.

Alkeim was no different.

"Malice"

The bed was cold, damp, and bumpy. Malice wriggled in place but didn't want to open his eyes yet. His body was heavy, his limbs refusing to move. It smelled of earth and moss, which he found sort of comforting, like spending time with Kiran in his forest. Eventually, he blinked. It was bright. Too bright.

A pain stabbed his leg. Malice, wincing, watched a centipede, at least a meter, its segmented leather black body twitching as its yellowish cream legs jerked one by one, gnawed on his leg. The orange antennae squirmed over Malice's thigh, a rope dragging across his skin. Its mandible sunk deeper into Malice's calf. He yelped and kicked the thing, the centipede screeching and skittering into the forest.

Forest?

There were trees above him, light breaking through the foliage. They were different though, bigger, moss and vines hanging off branches, and the flowers weren't the same. He wasn't in Kiran's forest.

Sharp pain cut his thoughts off. Malice glanced at the two punctures in his leg, the redness around them forming a V-shape. The pain radiated into the rest of his leg, his body tensing with every wave. Malice focused his magical energy on his calf to close the wounds, blood steadily oozing out of them. Recently, Inyene had started teaching Malice regeneration, although he knew the concept from Kiran. After a while, the bleeding stopped, yet did nothing for the pain.

Snap. Malice's head jolted, eyes narrowing on a tree. He couldn't see anything through the shadows of the woods. When he stood, he looked around again, then made his way into the forest. He didn't know where he was or what direction he needed to go in.

Why am I here? Fear coiled in his gut and his legs—pain aside—were weak. Malice had done nothing. He had been listening and following his siblings' lessons. He had won three times in a row against Zephyrus during their last spar. And he could almost count to one hundred now. He didn't need to read out loud as often. Draga had introduced math equations, and Malice wasn't half bad at them. He had to use his fingers to count sometimes; Draga hadn't seemed to mind.

Did someone take me? But who? Malice couldn't think of anything or anyone. Right now, he needed to walk, just walk until he found something. The foliage changed, most everything around him became big and leafy, vivid, lush green and dripping with wetness.

Clutching his shirt, bare feet moving faster, he didn't recognize anything. He was hoping it was a part of Kiran's forest they hadn't ventured into. It may not have been big, but Blodwen didn't like it when they explored too far southward. So they never did. He couldn't tell which way he was going, the impenetrable canopy of green keeping the sun's position hidden from him.

Malice's head spun abruptly, forcing him to stop. Every sound penetrated his ears, as if knives were stabbing right into his brain. It was warm, the air a sopping, musty, hot cloth clinging to him. His leg distracted him further, the throbbing pain like waves of red-hot needles surging through his limb.

If you ever get lost, stay put and wait. Someone will find you. Tendai's tender voice cut through the fog of his mind. Blinking away the tears Malice didn't realize had started falling, he tried to collect himself. He remembered getting lost in the woods and sitting at the base of a tree until Blodwen found him.

Find a hiding place, he told himself. There were too many chitters and rattles, despite the bird song and whizzing bugs, for Malice to feel safe out in the open.

Mouth dry, his stomach rumbled. When he found a sapling, he

placed his hand on its thin trunk. Magic flowed through his arm into the tree before he guided out a small undulating orb of water, slurping it from the air. It was warm and tacky, like the juice from a red apple.

He stayed there a moment longer, shaking off as much fear as he could. Onward, limping, Malice watched his feet, since he would prefer not to step on a centipede and suffer another bite. It didn't take long to find a cluster of small mushrooms. Kiran loved them and had shown Malice a hundred times which ones he could and couldn't eat. Malice didn't like them. They were slimy or spongy and tasted like moldy dirt. He bent down, ripped the cluster from the earth and sniffed, his nose crinkling as he retreated. They were rich and slightly pungent, meaning they were old. The ones that smelled like fish, Kiran had said, were poisonous. Even if they weren't, they would probably taste bad.

Reluctantly, Malice ate the mushrooms, the nasty things crumbling inside his mouth. Once he finished—and took another draught of water to get the taste out of his mouth—he trudged through the woods, stepping over roots and plants.

Surely, someone would come for him if he found a spot and stayed put.

Life Goes on
XIII

Malice was dead, of that Alkeim was certain. Experienced woodsmen, hunters, veteran royals, and mercenaries had gone into Mutuwa and had never come out. The few who had hadn't been breathing or whole. Onyimyths, the greatest ambush predators on Vinyamar, were to blame. He wouldn't be surprised if the queen had forgotten about sending her own child to his death a week ago.

Alkeim couldn't stand being in the same room as her highness, almost as much as he couldn't stand looking at himself in the mirror. He stood behind her as she worked at her desk, a constant switch between writing and reading, his mind deluded with guilt and shame.

Unlike Dun Raik, where the trees were so tightly wound horses couldn't get through, Mutuwa was perfect. It never got cold enough for animals to migrate. During winter, everything from the north flocked to it. The rift splitting Mutuwa in two allowed for centipedes, dragons, bears, panthers, and whatever else liked the cold and damp to make homes within the caves of the cliffs. Howlers, known to thrive in the north, made burrows within the forest for the plentiful prey. Besides animals, Mutuwa had the highest concentration of poisonous plants.

There was no safety.

Alkeim suddenly felt sick to his stomach, nausea taking hold of him.

He peeked at the content of her highness's documents to take his mind off Malice. A trade in about two weeks for newly developed elixirs in exchange for wealth. The merchant purchasing the poison belonged to Cain's Region in the northwest, and they would travel by boat—faster and easier to escape curious eyes, he knew.

The letter was signed in heavy-handed loops at the bottom of the page, *Wallace*. He scowled at the name. A nobleman, no question, cluelessly serving a monster.

"Is there a problem, Alkeim?" the queen asked, breaking the quiet and startling her first sword.

"No, your highness," he answered instantly, jerking his sights to the shelves built into the walls.

"Good. You will have no issue checking in on Blodwen and her progress, then." She tapped the paper. "I need to know when the new batch will be finished."

"Of course not."

Blodwen was a witch doctor, using medicinal herbs and recites to heal. Her kin specialized in poisons and had been working closely with the Reap family for generations, receiving something close to nobility without the title in return. When he married Blodwen, Tendai started working within the castle, treating the wounded royals that trickled in.

Walking through the field of wildflowers and grass outside the castle's grounds, Alkeim found himself staring westward. At Mutuwa, a dark smudge on the horizon. He frowned and continued into the woods.

The cottage had not changed save for a bit more moss growing on the outside of the rounded stout house and the roof. He went up to the door, keeping his feet on the stone path, and knocked. It squeaked open moments later. Kiran stared up at Alkeim, his big brown eyes curious.

"Where's Malice?" he asked.

A lump caught in Alkeim's throat.

"Can I see him?" Kiran hadn't given Alkeim a chance to answer. Then again, he couldn't speak as Tendai appeared behind the lad, scowling.

"What brings you here?" Tendai said as he guided Kiran back inside, leaned against the door frame, and crossed his arms.

"I've come for a status report on her highness's order." Alkeim didn't want to be here anymore than they did. After what Annabeth said the night Malice was taken, he could only assume Blodwen supplied the drug he'd been given. No one had kept their promise to the young prince. There was a bitterness in Alkeim's chest that rolled onto his tongue, forcing him to suppress the cringe coming with it.

Tendai's eyes flickered, his brows furrowed. He nodded inside, stepping away from the door. "Come in and see for yourself."

Alkeim looked around the warm, inviting home teeming with books, papers, and plants, the smell of various herbs heavy in the atmosphere. Candles throughout the living space washed everything in warmth, but made the shadows hard and ominous.

Blodwen poked out of the hallway in front of him, her expression serious. She turned as quickly as she emerged, disappearing into the room. He glanced at Tendai, and he tilted his head in her direction, giving him permission. Alkeim headed toward Blodwen. The floor creaked under his weight.

A table spanned the walls of the room, a window in the back, the desks cluttered. There were four crates covered with white linen in the furthest corner from the door.

Blodwen gestured to the crates. "I'll need another week to finish the last of it. You can collect it then." She was reaching her middle years. Signs of it, however, were few and far between.

Shelves on walls held vials, bottles, various sized mortars and pestles, and labeled clay jars. On the table to his right were old, worn books, probably ones that had been passed down through the generations. Pens filled a wooden cup, feathered and otherwise, while jars of ink were spread about it. To his left, papers scattered the surface of another table. Most were written on and most looked to be the recipes for her tonics.

Alkeim squeezed his eyes shut, then peeled them open, fixing on Blodwen's gaze. "Was it your drug Malice was given?"

Blodwen flinched, her proud shoulders bunching defensively.

"What does that mean?" Kiran said from the doorway.

Alkeim spun around. He didn't know the lad was there. Kids and their sneaky little feet! He looked back at Blodwen, who had gone stiff, a muscle rippling in her jaw, and her face was grim.

"Malice couldn't sleep," Tendai said as he scooped Kiran into his arms with a grunt. "So, your mother gave him a spoonful of syrup."

"Can I have some?"

"You wouldn't like it. It's sour."

Kiran grunted, puckered, and shook his head. "I don't like sour things," he said.

"I know." Tendai's eyes flicked from Alkeim to Blodwen, landing back on Alkeim with a sternness he didn't present to his wife—Alkeim couldn't blame him, he would never look at his own wife the way Tendai glared at him—before he went back to the living room.

Their voices danced through the house, Kiran's much louder and eager, followed by the clunks of pots or skillets. Alkeim swallowed, the tension in his shoulders easing for a second.

He shifted to face Blodwen again. "Did you tell the queen about Malice's true form?" He kept his volume low.

Blodwen grimaced. "What choice did I have?"

Alkeim's teeth ground, jaw sliding, when his wife's voice entered his head and told him to stop. "You could have stayed silent."

"And risk her killing *my* son?" she hissed back. "Do not put the blame solely on me. You're the one who collected him. You didn't bother talking the queen down, did you?"

"I'm trying to protect my family."

"So am I!" Blodwen shouted. The cottage fell silent. Heartbeats passed, every thump stronger and louder than the previous. Movement from the kitchen resumed, a knife clacking against wood, voices talking back and forth.

"If that's all, leave," Blodwen said sharply.

Alkeim turned on his heel and stomped toward the exit. Kiran was helping Tendai in the kitchen, probably standing on a stool so he could reach the countertop. Tendai didn't acknowledge Alkeim on the way out. An air of controlled rage shrouded the beastman. One his son couldn't sense as Kiran waved his small hand goodbye. Alkeim shunned away, his chest heavy, an ache building and clawing its way up his throat.

"Odovacar"

Dodging the broad swing of a spear, Odovacar rushed in, striking the right side of the royal's ribs, then twice more on the left. He slunk around their body and put the edge of his blade to their throat.

The spar concluded, his opponent admitting defeat and walking in the opposite direction with their head down as Odovacar wiped his face with his shirt. His eyes swept the field until he spotted Issur. His long grey hair was tied back, posture easy, expression even more so. Zephyrus attacked with a wooden practice sword. The two traded blows. Eventually, Issur whacked Zephyrus's wrist just right, sending the wooden sword flying out of his grip. The half-breed laughed, his smile bearing all his pointed teeth. Zephyrus, on the other hand, was not so amused, but plucked his sword from the dirt, likely asking for a rematch.

He looked elsewhere before they resumed their sparring session. Something about the field felt emptier than usual. It was an emptiness he would have to grow accustomed to as well.

Odovacar swung his sword, changing his grip so the blade was behind him, pommel forward, and swung it back. He had always liked the weight of a sword—of steel—in his hands. The burn it caused his arms the more he wielded it; the precision and power he gave it. Unlike Inyene, Odovacar had never been one for magic. It was tiring in a way fighting was not. Neither was it so easily recovered. He was efficient in using his ice, but only when he had to.

Mother had been kind enough to inform her children about Malice a few days after the fact. Almost a month had passed since. Odovacar did not care enough to be worried now, but when he was told, he had been sick to his stomach. It was brief, however, a wave of nausea crashing into him as the ocean would the shore. He understood and pitied Malice—pity for the mess he was dragged into and pity for his future as the queen's toy.

Yet, Odovacar was glad the role would not be his to play.

If he wanted to survive, he had learned long ago he needed to appease his mother without going out of his way to be outstanding. Had he practiced magic, he knew he would have been better than Inyene. Had he studied, he would have been at Draga's level of book intelligence. Odovacar would have had and would have been everything his mother wanted had he been blind to her hunger.

A royal approached him, a smug look on her face as she readied herself. Odovacar mindlessly countered her attacks, blocked them, and drove her off, switching between offense and defense, and finally delivering a fatal blow. If the swords were steel and if Odovacar had not halted prior to contact, that was.

The defeated royal cursed as she walked away, which was common enough he could easily tune them out.

Odovacar recalled a lesson he learned as a boy from a knight, the same knight following orders from Queen Vendetta like a broken, loyal hound. *Sparring is a chance to learn, experiment; failing is simply another lesson. A fight is meant to hand out death like candy; it's kill or be killed lad. Never forget that.*

His mother had told him three years ago, *aim to kill him,* when Malice's training began. It contradicted the very essence of what he had been taught, but Odovacar did not argue. He did not follow those instructions wholeheartedly, either. The queen was less than pleased to hear Odovacar had used wooden practice swords instead of real ones and allowed Malice to strike as he wanted, without striking back until the end. It had been one of the few mercies Odovacar could give, with little consequence. Short-lived as it was.

There was no longer any mercy to give when the receiving was dead.

Odovacar walked to the weapons rack, leaned his sword into place, and made his way to the castle. He was tired, not physically, but tired, nonetheless.

"Kiran"

The new year had come and gone, but people still celebrated throughout the kingdom, taverns busy all day into the night before curfew. Venders and merchants crammed the streets, making it difficult not to bump into people, selling candies and freshly baked goods, jewelry, and beadwork.

The excitement of the new year seemed to reach everyone but Kiran.

He looked at the dazzling colors, the miniature flags flapping in the wind, the banners going from lamp to lamp, in all shades of the rainbow. People chatted and laughed all around him. Other children ran through the streets. But amid it all, something was missing. *Someone* was missing.

Kiran gripped his father's hand tighter as they walked in the middle of the bustling road, a cloak wrapped around his shoulders. It had been a little over a month since Malice disappeared. No one knew where Malice went off to, or how much longer he would be gone for. Not even his parents knew. Kiran visited Malice's room often—a few letters stacked on his desk—so he could be there in case Malice burst through the doors. Every time he didn't, Kiran's entire body shrunk with disappointment.

The sadness dissipated with hope at first, but now it was as heavy as a boulder and impossible to overlook.

Zephyrus was in the same boat the last Kiran saw him looking for Malice at the training grounds. One day he saw the future royal searching around—Kiran was there with his parents helping restock the pavilions medical supplies—going up to the others and asking about Malice until he reached Odovacar. Odovacar scowled, mouthed something Kiran couldn't make out, then sent Zephyrus to his father, a devastated look on his face as he trudged away.

"Do you think he's all right?" Kiran asked while looking at the vender ahead of them, carving little wooden figures of animals. The one they were working on was a cat. They were all cats, he realized as he squinted at them.

Father glanced down at him, eyebrows twitching, hand squeezing Kiran's. "We can hope," he said sullenly.

Kiran's eyes moved to the granite street, tears blurring his vision, a tightness in his chest. *What if Malice never comes back?* Kiran shoved the thought out of his brain. Of course, Malice would come back. He had to. They had so many things to do yet. Blodwen promised to teach them how to swim, and Malice wanted to learn about the herbs she used to heal people. Kiran had to convince Malice to learn how to heal too, but he was so stubborn, saying he wasn't allowed. *Ask!* Kiran had told him. Malice shook his head, though.

That wasn't all of it either, so Malice had to come back. Kiran needed him to come home.

Breaking the Soul
XIV

Part II

No one's coming for me.

Malice had never been more sure of anything, as sure as the fog blanketing the forest floor. He also guessed he was in Mutuwa, the only other forest he'd ever heard about—save for Dun Raik, but he knew the path he walked every year with the king and Felim rather well.

The milky white haze hovered around his knees. Gaze shifting, he breathed deeply, salt entering his lungs. He tugged his tattered and stained shirt away from his chest, the air sticky. Kiran had shown Malice illustrations of the south. Stony faced cliffs kept Hordes Region above the ocean, but only in the south, the land descending the closer you got to Dun Raik, as if the continent was a massive bowl. Blodwen had always told them not to head south, so he spun the opposite way.

Eventually, earth and flowers were all he could smell, his clothes no longer glued to his skin. All good signs, considering it was hard to get a grasp of the location in this stinking forest! Or maybe he wasn't very good with his directions. Dung wafted and attacked his nose. As his nostrils flared, he searched, found, and avoided the pile. Some gigantic beast that would happily eat Malice probably left it.

Malice abandoned his original hiding spot, a burrow, when he decided to try to find his way home. His heart seemed to shrink that day, keeping him short of breath, making sure pain radiated in tandem with his pulse.

He stopped near a tree, its trunk wider than his arm span, its roots creating an arch for an entrance to a hole. He prodded the inside with a stick to make sure nothing lived there, then crawled into the cavity. Straw, dead grass, and tiny twigs littered the spongy ground, smelling of wood and dirt. Whatever had lived here, Malice hoped it wouldn't come back.

He popped his head outside as a droplet hit his nose.

Soon, a heavy downpour started, lightning flashed, followed by a crack, a boom, and a rumble. He didn't mind the rain; the scent was soothing, and it cooled the heat, sending a shiver through his body. The sound of pitter-pattering raindrops put him at ease. At least it had.

The storm lulled all other sounds, so if something were to come, Malice wouldn't hear it.

Malice gathered the debris into a pile before him and lit it on fire. Smoke pulled away from him as if the rain lured it outside.

He brought his knees to his chest and stared at his calf. The puncture wounds from the centipede were gone thanks to his regeneration. The pain too. They were minor injuries anyway, like all the cuts and bruises from shrubs and branches, and from him tripping. He didn't know where some of them came from. They had appeared and vanished within a day.

Head on his knees, Malice wanted to sleep but was too scared. He wanted to cry but didn't have the strength to muster the tears; he wanted to scream but knew it was best not to.

It was morning, songbirds chirping outside the split tree, dew dripping off leaves, while the sun warmed the air. Malice blinked a few times, his neck and back sore from sleeping upright and his butt numb. He stretched his limbs. Leaves and grass rustled beyond the trunk's arch, Malice freezing. A rabbit, its coat brown, grey and tan, hopped in front of him. Nose twitching, the rabbit's ear turned before its head. Their gazes locked. Malice held his breath, remaining as still as the tree he sat in.

He swallowed the hunger tearing its way through his intestines. All he had been eating were mushrooms because he didn't know what else was edible. Moving his hand further, ever so slightly, from his body, Malice extended all of his fingers, one by one, and clamped his fist shut. Nothing happened. Not so much as a tickle in his core. He frowned.

He tried again, and this time the rabbit struggled, squealing. It kicked and flailed, but Malice's air magic wrapped around it, pinning it to the ground. Air was tricky to control and use. His face scrunched in concentration, his entire body tense.

If he were to kill it, he would finally have some decent food!

Fixated on the rabbit's eyes, he willed his hand to close, but the fear within the sea of brown… were the same shade as Kiran's; rich and laced with a tan that turned to gold in the sunlight. Malice couldn't do it and the rabbit darted off.

Over the cliff side, the water sparkled as fish swam near the surface, making it ripple. Malice sat on the edge, watching the orange, brown, yellow, and multicolored fish, big and small, chase one another in games of tag. He could have fish if only he could reach the water. And if the water was shallow. He didn't know how to swim.

Along the valley's steep walls, ledges had nests, caves were black pits, and further to the south were one or two pockets of water as if someone had carved bathtubs on the side of the cliffs. Malice wouldn't mind a bath. He stunk and his skin wasn't pale anymore, it was so caked in filth.

After a time, Malice rose and walked along the cliff's edge. If he kept walking, he'd probably run into someone or some sort of town. At least he hoped he would. The longer he spent trudging through Mutuwa, the less he was confident he would make it out.

Malice stopped dead in his tracks, his blood running cold, icicles stabbing his insides. Coiled between a ring of trees was a giant lizard. He made to step backward, but paused when he recognized it from one of Kiran's books—it was a wyvern. Clawed wings wrapped around its enormous body, acting like a blanket. Its wedge-shaped head faced Malice. Sharp scales protruded around its mandible, going to its neck and smoothing out along the rest of its dried rose-colored body.

Malice, hands trembling, continued forward and lowered himself to the ground, his eyes constantly shifting from the beast behind him to what was in front of him. He didn't want to make any unnecessary sound. He also wanted to make sure he caught the slightest hint of movement so he could run before it noticed him. Maybe then he would actually have the chance to escape.

However, once he had gotten a certain distance away, he turned around. Why would a wyvern sleep in the middle of the day? Malice certainly didn't want to, no matter the time of day, not with the monsters running around. His mind and body betrayed him often, however, and demanded sleep. He surveyed the area again. Nothing was in sight, but trees and plants Malice didn't know the name of. Kiran probably wouldn't either.

Malice, searching, picked up a rock the size of his palm. He may not hit the wyvern, but he should get the rock close enough to make it startle. He threw it with all his might. The rock bounced off a tree, tumbled down a huge leafy shrub, and thudded to the ground. It didn't move. It was completely still.

Is... it dead?

Closer to the wyvern, crows cawed above the canopy, their inky bodies zipping behind leaves. Heart pounding, Malice drew nearer and stopped about five trees away, peeking around the trunk of another. He waited a time, holding his breath in case the beast could hear it. The wyvern still didn't move. It was dead. This close, Malice should have been able to see the rise and fall of the beast's back as it breathed.

Depending on how dead it was, maybe he could eat it. The thought made his mouth water, and he licked his dry lips. He was tired of mushrooms. Mostly, he missed the meals Annabeth brought him, and he missed eating with Kiran, sometimes Zephyrus.

It wouldn't hurt to check.

Malice approached the beast, sniffed the air, and stepped closer still. It didn't stink like rotten meat, which was good. It didn't smell good either, an irony fog surrounding it. When he poked it, it had a hint of warmth left. At least it was fresh. He stalked around the dead wyvern, trying to see where it got hurt. Maybe it died of old age. Then he saw it. Its underside was red with blood. The ground was tacky with it, too. Malice swallowed the nausea, the stench of blood, like rancid fruit, striking him.

Shuffling backward, he tripped and slammed into the ground with a wet thump. Crimson soaked his already nasty clothes. He shot to his feet and tried wiping his face off, but his hands were bloody as well, his shirt and trousers clinging to his skin. The sensation was vile, Malice's stomach twisting so viciously, he was sure it had knotted itself.

Something gleamed out of the corner of his eye, prompting a slight turn of Malice's head. Underneath the wyvern, bumpy pink things, like thick rope, spilled from its insides, blue veins crept along the fleshy cords.

Malice's gut untied itself to empty onto the earth, tears stinging his eyes, the bile burning every inch of his throat and nose. This wasn't such a good idea. He had to be like Kiran, curiously reckless and optimistic.

Malice stood. A sound halted him. Twigs broke. More cracked. Low growls and snarls reached his ears, each a jagged melody of rocks grinding together. Slowly, he glanced at the trees. There was nothing. If he couldn't see them, maybe they couldn't see him.

Malice, avoiding the wyvern's corpse, ran through Mutuwa. He didn't care about food or where he was going, he only knew he needed to run. He stumbled over a root, caught himself, and pressed on, sticks and pebbles jabbing at the soles of his feet. The heat burned his lungs, every deepening breath like inhaling fire, sweat beading on his skin and streaking the blood, the smell of rusted metal reignited. Fear pulsed through his veins, making his feet pound the ground faster and harder. Leaves smacked his face. Bugs pelted his body. Still, he kept running. And running. And running.

It was well past dusk, the moon high in the sky, when Malice stopped running. He was out of breath, damp with sweat and blood, which had crusted his hair to his forehead, his garments just as stiff. Using his earth magic, Malice stomped and forced his hands apart, creating a little burrow. One hand holding out a fire, he crawled in. It was cool down here, relieving the overwhelming warmth of Malice's body. Once he situated himself in the tight space, he closed the forest floor above his head, leaving a sliver to see out of.

Heaving yet, Malice jerked his hand across the ground to give himself more room. The earth grumbled in response, reminding him of his bedframe groaning with most every movement.

All he smelled was blood when he desperately wanted his nostrils to be saturated with earth's aroma. He *tasted* it. He regretted not getting water from a nearby tree, his mouth too dry to swallow properly. It was too late now; he was settled, the ground sheltering him, and his limbs screamed for rest. Exhaustion held Malice down and coerced him to sleep.

Crunch.

Malice startled awake, hitting his head on the ground above, an instant spike of pain making him yelp. White light came through the opening he had left last night. Shifting so his legs were underneath him, he peeked outside. Leaves, grass, flowers, trees, and bushes. Then paws walked across his view. He lurched backward, slapping his hands over his mouth. They were huge, probably bigger than his head.

More came. Seven creatures in total stalked around him. Bears. Body trembling, he guessed these were the beasts he'd heard yesterday, maybe the ones that tore into the wyvern. And if they could kill a wyvern, they could do worse to Malice. He had to run or go deeper, and running wasn't an option with those monsters outside. Perhaps he could dig far enough to emerge a good mile away from these beasts.

Light erupted from multiple places before he had the chance to turn, dirt burying him, huffs and snarls surrounding Malice.

Malice frantically wiggled and fought out of the dirt so he could breathe. As he hacked up debris, his fingers tore at the fresh air, giving his legs the strength they needed to breakout out of his own grave.

They weren't bears. Their backs were hunched as if overly stuffed with cotton, their tawny fur like bristles. Their heads were too narrow and too long to be like the drawings of bears in Kiran's books. Saliva dangled in clumps, viscous strings dripping from their too large fangs, their eyes a milky white. Gore painted their muzzles.

Run, a voice said. How? Seven huge beasts walled him in, an impenetrable shield of tans, creams, and greys. He was dead. They would tear him apart and devour him.

One from the right howled a high-pitched screech. Malice winced away, his ears ringing. It pounced, jaw snapping, spittle flying. Malice swung his arm and fire shot out in an arc. The beast snipped and retreated, whining as it pawed at the smoking bits of fur on its face. Without thinking too much, Malice extended both his hands and released his magic. Fire spread around him and consumed the top layer of the forest floor. It blazed strong, despite how his magic had ceased, smoke rising. The beasts stayed back and snarled at the fire. Eventually, the wolf-bears withdrew into the trees, sinking into the shadows deepened by the flames.

Malice stood, wobbled, and fell back to his bum. His legs were numb, yet ached from running the day prior. But he had to run. Now, before the fire died out and the beasts returned. Punching his thighs, Malice ground his teeth. *Get up!* He pushed himself to his feet and stepped toward the blazing ring. The heat burned what little wetness was in his mouth, pricking his skin. Maybe it was the anxiety hatching within the fibers of his being like spider eggs, or maybe it was fire keeping him short of breath, his head light and fuzzy. No matter, Malice checked to make sure they were really gone.

Please move, Malice pleaded with his legs. *Just run.* The flames would hurt, but what choice did he have?

Eyes screwed shut, Malice sprinted through the fire. The blaze scorched his clothes and hair some. No time to worry if any embers caught to his person. He dashed around trees. Avoided roots and plants. Weaved through the trunks so he might lose the wolf-bears. Air came to Malice's burning lungs in strained gasps, his body screaming in too many places for him to know what hurt more. He wasn't fast enough, not with how fatigued he was.

Heavy bounds grew closer and closer, breaking anything they trampled on.

Suddenly, his knee buckled, and he crashed to the forest floor, grimacing, tumbled until he hit a tree, and pain exploded throughout his back. Malice rested against the trunk. The bark dug into his back, moss wafted toward him, the potent odor of smoke smothering him. Howls echoed and birds fled from the treetops. How far were they? Facing the direction he ran in, there was little to see. The breeze didn't rustle the foliage, either. Had he imagined how close they were? Did it matter? There was nowhere else for him to run. His arms no longer had the strength to tremble, let alone his legs.

Why didn't someone save me? Tears blurred his vision. Almost every night, he had wished someone would find him and bring him home. He would happily deal with the training, and Sok and Rayen's torment if he meant he could have escaped Mutuwa. *What did I do?* Malice asked himself time and time again. No answer came to him, so why was he here?

Wails, shrill, bone chilling screeches, rang, reaching Malice's ears like daggers. The distance he put between them was waning.

Malice stared blankly at the environment, tears no longer falling. The bright green grass and the mushrooms scattered about, dried and dead leaves littering the ground, the flowers of mauve, scarlet, and vibrant blue. The bugs stayed to provide a constant buzz. No other creature was brazen or stupid enough to linger.

They came back. Not every night, but most of them. The creatures of darkness he saw in the dungeon three years ago, after his first summit. They kept him company when he couldn't sleep. Instead of speaking, they tilted their heads in response or gestured loosely with their lanky, three-fingered hands. He probably would have seen them last night had he not fallen asleep so quickly. They were smart for leaving him be right now.

The undergrowth, in all directions, shook and splintered.

Malice wouldn't live much longer. He closed his eyes, taking in the smell of wet earth, salty mist, and sweet flowers. And blood, the heavy, foul stench of blood.

Don't you want to live? the same voice that told him to run said. It was familiar and, simultaneously, unknown.

Not having enough energy to move his head anymore, he let his eyes wander.

If you've done nothing to deserve this, why should you perish? The voice resonated in Malice's ears.

"I want to live," Malice said, voice hardly a crackly whisper. He wanted to see Kiran and learn how to swim. He wanted to spar with Zephyrus at the training grounds and listen to Annabeth's stories. He wanted to learn about the plants Blodwen used to heal people, and he wanted to read Magnus's letters.

What was the point of it now? Malice's limbs refused to listen, and he struggled to keep his eyes focused on the forest in front of him. The wolf-bears were nearing. Prowling out of the forest, muzzle dripping red, one faced Malice hungrily. Its jaw jittered, teeth clacking, rolling laughter sputtering out of its throat as if too excited to control itself.

Tell me what you want, and I'll make it happen. I'll save you, Malice.

"Save me, please!" Malice sobbed. He wanted nothing more than to leave, to curl up in a ball on his bed and weep beside Kiran.

Crack!

Breath hitched at the back of Malice's throat as he lowered his head. His leg twisted unnaturally, his toes curling inward, his foot itself condensing, morphing into a hoof, the noise reminiscent of when he ground his teeth too hard. Agony didn't just blossom, it crashed into his body like a boulder plummeting down a mountain. He screamed, the world going black for a second. Bones started breaking, grinding, cracking. Blood dripped into his eyes from his forehead. Something split through his back, shoving him forward onto the ground, teeth ripping meat from bone. The pain was overwhelming. All thoughts evaporated. Even his heartbeat seemed to cower in the face of his blood thrumming in his ears. Then the forest vanished.

Silas Johnson

"Vendetta"

A deep, sudden chill had penetrated Vendetta's bones that morning, daggers piercing further into her soul.

On horseback, Vendetta rode toward Mutuwa, the plains of Hordes Region undulating beyond her sights, the green vivid, flowers pricking the land. The breeze was gentle and cool, a crystalline sky housing the blinding sun. Her children and their first swords cantered behind her, alongside Emil, and brothers Felim and Alkeim. Birds sang in the distance until a flock screeched out of the forest, a cluster of dark dots racing northeast.

About a hundred meters from the edge of Mutuwa, Vendetta stopped, a shiver raking her body, the daggers growing barbs to truly embed themselves. A subtle scream, perhaps a roar, broke the quiet, alerting those at her backside. The horses stamped as whinnies drifted to her ears. Restlessness. All fell silent when the breeze died off completely, the calm before the storm. Vendetta's lips curved into a thin smile.

Something burst through the trees, flew past, and, flying upwards, descending in an arc, disappeared once more. Vendetta looked over her shoulder. Sok's and Rayen's heads slipped from their shoulders, the movement sluggish as if their bodies hadn't realized the lack of thought. At this distance, the sound their heads made as they hit the ground were muted, quiet thumps. Their bodies tilted forward, Rayen's slipping off the side and getting stuck in the stirrup, hanging limply. Sok's simply slumped forward. The horse stayed put since the action was so composed, it probably seemed like an act of affection. Ichor seeped from their necks, Sok's spilling onto his horse, creeping down its brown and white coat into the grass, tainting the vibrancy with death.

First swords Aglaia and Xenon made for their master's, but Vendetta waved them off. They halted. Obedient enough to not let their inner emotions shine and outweigh her commands. Odovacar stiffened, his horse nickering and shifting impatiently. Draga looked elsewhere to keep her expression unreadable, yet her horse was as anxious as Odovacar's. Meanwhile, a grin split Inyene's lips. She was amused, happy Vendetta would say. Both Alkeim and Felim, however, wore disturbed faces, their features taut and ghastly, as if neither had seen a headless body.

Dismounting, Vendetta left her horse. Alkeim rushed forward to grab a hold of the stallion's reins as she walked toward Mutuwa.

"Your highness," Alkeim said.

"Lest you be next," she said, "stay put."

With plenty of distance between her and her party, Vendetta stood amongst the tall grass and wildflowers, waiting for the mutt to unveil himself, to stop using the trees of Mutuwa as a curtain to hide behind. Had she not gotten the gut-wrenching feeling, she would have presumed him dead the moment he'd awoken in the depths of that hell. She would have accepted his death and moved on, starting anew to get what she wanted was little trouble. Nyx was alive, after all.

The mutt appeared in a dark blur of motion, as if her thoughts summoned him. She lifted her hand, palm facing him. He stopped tens of meters away, halted in midair, like he had hit a wall. Vendetta's magic was one of a kind, something she'd spent decades refining, replacing the water magic she once had.

Vendetta's theory was proven correct. He needed genuine danger. Three years ago, the mutt knew his time in the dungeons would end; all he had to do was survive hunger and boredom. Despite the pain, she was sure he had an inkling his hands would be reattached, miraculously, when Inyene severed them. A savior in every instance that ought to have brought about a significant change. Mutuwa was oh so different. There was no escape. No rescue. No end.

However, he was nothing like Blodwen had described.

Vendetta lowered her arm, the mutt following as she brought him closer, her hand nearing her chest. She grinned as he snarled, all four of his arms reaching and clawing for her. The boy had become a hideous little thing. She swallowed the sensation of maggots crawling up her throat. A tail, resembling a lizard's, whipped behind him as his wings strained at his sides. His skin was the red of deluded blood, his hair a similar shade of midnight blue, slightly curved horns grew from his forehead, streaking his face with crimson. His legs were that of a goat's, his feet now hooves.

Truly an ugly creature.

It was what Vendetta had hoped for.

She twisted her hand. Malice's body contorted. His screams resounded as his bones shattered like pottery. She released him then, his body dropping lifelessly. Not dead, but close enough.

Vendetta waited a good while for the mutt to move, to go berserk. Considering his lineage, since his true form had manifested, there was no telling where his limits lied. It was far from a stretch to believe he could regenerate every bit of damage she caused in the matter of a second, should his power be as lethally potent as she thought. When he didn't, she turned, grabbed her horse from Alkeim and said, "Retrieve him."

Alkeim was in shock. His deep brown eyes were doubled, his mouth gaping open, tusks on full display, shoulders slumped.

"He needs to be contained," she added, voice sharp. "Else he wakes in another fit of rage."

Her tone having broken his daze, the orc ushered his horse to the mutt, hopped down, and picked him up, remounting his steed crudely. Anyone and everyone were threats. Till his senses graced him once more, he needed a place free of outside contact.

Vendetta passed the corpses of Sok and Rayen, their horses grazing. It would be a shame to lose them.

"Xenon, Aglaia." The two first swords swung their attention toward her, expressions terrified, posture as stiff as a board. Briefly, she wondered where their composure wandered off to. "Collect the horses."

Xenon gazed at the twins' bodies. "What about their…" he trailed.

"Leave them," Vendetta said. "What good will cadavers do me?"

Vendetta spurred her horse on, the wind beating her face and stirring her hair, her movement in sync with the horse beneath her. Sok and Rayen were failures of which her court had no room.

She looked over her shoulder at Alkeim and the creature sitting in front of him in the saddle. Blodwen and Annabeth had described his skin tone, hair, and horns, but nothing else. Vendetta doubted they withheld information, meaning it was a fraction of his true form. It was likely this, too, was only a fraction of the whole.

Valor, Reap, and Apostolov; the concentration of the three great bloodlines made him something entirely different. The manifestation of his *demon* form piqued Vendetta's interest. Demons could not change their appearance, aspects of it perhaps—Vendetta cared not about concealing her attributes whatsoever, though few shared her ideology—but not everything.

Hooves thundered behind her, everyone in her company silent. The distant sound of squawking gulls and waves crashing onto the shore imbued the emptiness with a lullaby. *It was a good day.*

Slaves to Power
XV

The Reap line, the most prominent demon line in Vinyamar, was known for its dark magic. So far, any with Reap blood had inherited dark magic. The element was arguably the most powerful magic known to man. Apostolov's could regenerate and heal, their core capable of handling both when, for all else, it was one or the other. Finally, Valor, for their unique ability to house four elements in their core. The most a core could handle was two, the trait giving one the title of wielder. Still, one element was always superior. Rumor once said, the Valors could control the four main elements equally.

The greatest traits seemed to have been passed down to the mutt.

Close to Vendetta was Alkeim, the bulky orc staring solemnly through the slot of the metal door. The mutt was inside, slamming himself against the walls and door, releasing absurd amounts of magic that had nowhere to escape. He moved aside for Vendetta to peek into the cell. As insane as he was the day prior, he would eventually tire.

Metal slit scraping shut, Vendetta turned down the corridor, and followed it up to the stairwell, Alkeim on her heels.

Two more seats were permanently empty next to Draga at the dining table. Vendetta wondered who would be the next to perish and join Elias in the grave.

"Since Malice can regenerate," Inyene said, "I want to experiment. I've had a few ideas circling my head."

"Keep him alive," Vendetta said warningly, though, truth be told, his limits invoked her inquisitiveness as well. "Otherwise, do what you want."

Always the eccentric one. Inyene's passion exceeded anyone else's, making her second to none in her field of expertise. Vendetta found her commitment to torture without killing impressive and repulsive—so long as she coaxed the needed information, there was little reason to care about the method. Years of studying the anatomy of all twelve species did her good. Perhaps having the mutt learn the same would be equally beneficial.

"What of his academics?"

"I've not much else to teach." Draga sipped her wine. Outwardly, she was as stoic as a portrait, forever frozen in time.

"He is not taking your lessons to become a scholar," Vendetta reminded. Malice needed to know more than books. He needed to know how to talk to compel someone, to turn their words against them, to instill fear or courage. He needed to learn to use his voice as a weapon, be it dagger or poison.

Draga inclined her head. "I'll alter my plans."

"Same goes for you, Odovacar." Vendetta moved her attention to her son. He stopped cutting and looked at her through his eyelashes. "He is not learning the sword to become a royal."

"Yes, Mother," he said simply.

Vendetta lingered on her son and could not believe how much

Odovacar resembled Elias, save for his personality. Odovacar was stiff, his emotions controlled, a stickler for the rules. Elias was hot-headed, governed by his heart, which made him more likeable to most, more approachable. If it meant saving a few more lives, Elias had been more than happy to break the laws or disobey his mother. It left a bitter taste on her tongue.

She had warned Elias he was not powerful enough to stand against an army thrice the size of his own. He had thought otherwise and paid the price with his life, of course.

At her husband—sitting to her right—a once muscular man was now reduced to skin and bone. Vendetta pitied him.

"A new shipment of slaves is to come from Wolfgang's Region in a week's time, sooner if the seas are good," Draga said and put her napkin adjacent to her chalice.

"What was his name again… Roach?"

"Roch," Draga corrected.

"Yes, Roch," she echoed, disgust thick in her voice, cringing at the thought of the tradesmen. "What does he want this time?"

"Coin, jewels, gold."

"How many are in the shipment?"

"Seventy-two."

"Two chests of coin ought to suffice," she said dismissively.

The coin she received from Wallace in exchange for crates of poison two weeks ago would be handed off. Wallace, a nobleman from Cain's Region, in stark comparison to Roch, was a man Vendetta would not mind having a cup of tea with from time to time. Albeit, Roch's work ethic was not something she could entirely criticize. Whatever needed to be done, he did it. Complained to high heaven while doing so, but, nevertheless, the job was never left unfinished, and she was never left without slaves.

"I think we should call in Tendai." Odovacar abruptly changed the topic. "You do not want Malice to drop dead the moment he returns to normal, do you?"

Vendetta sighed. "Call him in tomorrow and tell him to keep a close eye on the mutt."

"Understood." Odovacar nodded and stood to leave.

So much like Elias… Vendetta watched her son cross the room and disappear beyond the closing doors. If there was anything he refused to do, it was get his hands dirty with slaves. Some were products of lost battles over holds, loss of wealth, unpaid debts, some were born into it. While some lost everything and had no other choice if they wanted to live.

*

The ever-moving water glittered white from the sun, mist spraying as waves smothered the beach. Clouds moseyed in the azure sky above, the call of gulls surrounding Vendetta and her party. Four docks at equal distances spread across the beach into the water, barnacles, and algae masking the posts.

The smell of salt and rancid seaweed was none too pleasant, yet so different she dared to call it refreshing.

On the grass bank before the sand was Draga, and her first sword, a dark elf in chain-mail. Nearby, Alkeim was in his usual grey tunic, trousers, and worn leather boots, adorned with a belt, old gauntlets, and a holster for his sword. Four wagons waited on the bank behind them, one with the chests of coin, the others empty. A few royals stood beside them.

From the northeast, black dots appeared on the horizon, two deep bellied transporters, a single mast at its center. The closer they got, the more visible the sail became. A wolf's head twice speared waved in the breeze, the symbol of Roch and his crew. A blatant display of impertinence for their homeland's monarch. Vendetta would happily hang each and every one of Roch's crew with their own sail if he ever grew the balls to do such a thing.

Swerving into the bay, men climbed over and into smaller row boats, lugging heavy ropes with them. They reached the docks. One jumped off and quickly tied the bowline to the dock cleat, while the second secured the spring line to a cleat closest to the stern. Crewmen from the second transporter mirrored the first with practiced ease and rhythm. Soon, from the hullo of the ship, gangplanks hit the docks noisily.

Roch spilled into Vendetta's view. She almost gagged at the sight of the fat tradesmen. He stalked across the pier, his grungy rat-like features becoming all too clear. He hawked and spat a greyish green gunk as he lumbered toward Vendetta, then bowed halfheartedly, and smiled, most of his teeth missing.

"Nice to see you again, milady," he said with a lisp.

Up close, he was more disgusting, his shirt threadbare, stained with sweat and grease. His pants barely stayed on his ass with a belt on the first loop, certainly not enough to keep the bottom of his stomach from bulging out. His wiry mustache and beard, rings tangled within, were full of crumbs. The little hair he had on his head was oiled back.

Vendetta said nothing and glanced at the ships swaying with the tide, gulls circling the masts and perching on the yards.

"Don't you worry 'bout a thing," he said. "Seventy-two slaves ripe for the taking."

Vendetta turned. She would rather speak to a rock fully expecting an intelligent conversation than to exchange a few words with the tradesmen. She waved to the four royals by the wagons, all stepping into motion at her command. Pairs of two hauled the chests to the beach, placing them in front of the docks for Roch's crew to collect.

Roch shouted orders. His men scattering, most disappeared below deck, and returned to the surface, followed by rows of people chained together. His band of goons guided the slaves onto the sand where Vendetta's royals took over their handling, bringing them to the bank and loading them onto the wagons.

Women, men, children, and elderly of all races passed Vendetta. Those who had been purchased were clean, wearing gold chains around their necks instead of iron around their wrists. Dirt and grime caked a good handful of slave's skin, smelling of the sea, feces, and urine. Feet dragging, there was no more pride left in their posture. They were fear stricken as their hands trembled and their knees quaked, a ghostly look on their faces, chains clinking.

The trade had concluded faster than Vendetta anticipated. Two bobbing ships rowed out of the bay. The sails unfurled to catch the winds, and float somewhere she could no longer perceive them. With the help of Alkeim, Vendetta climbed onto the bench of the creaky wagon, and the orc hopped on. Reins cracking, the wagons rocked into motion as the wheels struck every stone and divot.

The sun blazed. Sweat beaded on her forehead, her skin aflame. She gazed over her shoulder at the slaves for a moment, each face a mirror of the one at its side, lacking details, save for their horror brimmed eyes. The unclaimed would be auctioned off. If they were lucky, a few avaricious nobles might buy them in addition to their previously bought merchandise. Pity, the need or want for an extra set of hands, unspoken potential; reasons aside, Vendetta expected the unclaimed bunch to be cut in half before the auction in four days.

A horde of servants gathered in front of the castle, mingling with one another like ants in the nest when Vendetta arrived. Slaves were lined in front of the dark-faced castle like wares displayed on a table at a market. Nobles, woodsmen, mercenaries—anyone with the coin to buy—could grab their goods whilst inspecting the unclaimed. None had the nerve to stand toe to toe with Vendetta, to thank her for her deeds, not in the flesh. She would receive plenty of thanks via scribbles on paper in a few days' time. Like rats, customers retrieved their slaves, snatching them, bringing them to their carriages, carts, or horses and fleeing. Few lingered, eyeing the unclaimed hungrily, greedily.

By evening, all seventy-two slaves had been purchased, leaving Vendetta auction free for a while. If not for the profit, she would have ceased the trading of slaves some time ago, the swine who bought summoning disgust from the depths of her being. She sighed on her way toward the entrance, ready to soak in a warm bath as she sipped on honey mead. The doors opened, a servant standing in the foyer, panting as if she had run down the four flights of stairs.

In an instant, the servant dropped to her knees. "Your highness," she squealed. "Malice has regained his human form and has been moved to his bedchamber. Dr. Tendai says he needs rest for at least two days."

Vendetta dismissed the servant. "So be it."

She rose and rushed off. Vendetta continued through the castle, half expecting such news, but impatience was a difficult thing to ward. *What do a few more days hurt? Let the mutt rest for another week, he'll need it.*

Vendetta sank into the standing tub, candles dim throughout the bathroom, the milky water warm and soothing. The tiled floor of gold was almost bronze in this light, gleaming with the flicker of flames. Incense filled the room, a mix of lavender and citrus, the white smoke swirling toward the coffered ceiling. Her left was open to the bedchamber, a folding partition depicting a snake coiling around a tiger acting as a wall.

Emil sat on the edge of her round bed. Still in his day attire, he wore an over shirt of burgundy that laced up his arms, front and back, making it tedious to put on and take off. His trousers were of the same color, and stiff, accentuating his lanky limbs. At times, she could not tell if he was breathing due to how still and quiet he was.

"Get dressed and speak freely," Vendetta said.

He rose, stalked to the closet on the opposite side of the room, and stripped with practiced ease. Servants were no longer allowed in her bedchamber past nine. She hardly tolerated their lowly hands on her whilst they attended her in the mornings. She refused to have them in the evenings as well. Emil's skin was a sickly blue color, his hair cobalt, and his eyes as red as a rat's, most similar to Inyene except for the musculature. Once he had been bulky from decades as a woodsman. It was her fault, forcing him to stay in this room, only permitting him to leave for meals and the summit.

The rulers knew of her, the home-bound wife, yet she refused to attend the Kings Summit. Not for her less than desirable personality— though truly, she could only feign so much in the face of gathered idiocy—but for her reputation. She needed to be known as the wife, a powerless queen to an ill-disposed king. Should a coincidence occur, should the rulers use their combined ounce of intelligence and deem Hordes Region a threat, blame would lie on Emil's shoulders and punishment would befall him. Her plans, however, would then be awry and require hastening. He was, for all intents and purposes, her greatest scapegoat.

Besides that, Alucard's yet remained her biggest enemy. The first and last time she had attended the summit, she was just shy of twenty. There, she had seen Jaci Castine, grandson of Alucard, a veritable force of nature whom Thorn admired likely more than his own father. Holister had Jaci's harrowing touch and a charm Jaci never bothered with. While Holister could sweet talk his way out of damn near every situation thinkable, Jaci needed only to scoff and heads bowed his pardon. Vendetta could promise Basia and Thorn violence and earn their allegiance, neutralizing their threat. The Castine's were not so easily bought. It was oh so easy to gain their animosity, of which Vendetta had no room.

"How are the children?" Emil asked.

Vendetta glanced from the hazy water to the partition, slight regret forming. She ought to have stifled his speech till she finished soaking. "Sok and Rayen are dead," she answered. Rarely, he took his freedom of speech and utilized it. He was silent, answering with a movement of his head or when he was spoken to.

Back turned, Vendetta did not see her husband's expression, but she noticed the way his body reacted. The quake of his shoulders, the bunching of what little muscle he had, the expansion of his diaphragm, and the release.

"Do not feel sorrow for them. They were weak, their potential withered, never having the chance to bloom."

Emil said nothing as he pulled his arms through the sleeves of his nightwear, the silk holding a soft glint.

Vendetta was rather pleased the mutt had killed them. Two issues scratched off her list. She had given up on the idea of reforming those two. There was no point in wasting her energy when they would have only become disappointments like the rest of her children.

"Who killed them?" Emil finally asked and started toward his bedroll near the couches on the left side of the bedchamber.

"The mutt."

"He will not stop there," Emil said and stopped, turning to face Vendetta. "Malice will kill all of us."

"You put too much faith in him," Vendetta countered, a blade suddenly pressed against her spine.

"I believe he will discover what makes you tick, Vendetta."

Her blood sped. "Enough."

"He will find your weakness and use it against you."

"I said enough." Vendetta shot up, the water sloshing and splashing to the floor, her fists clenched at her sides.

"And I hope he does."

"You will not be exempt!"

Emil regarded her with those blood-shot eyes of his, hollow and bleak, then laid down and drew the covers over his body. "I know."

Out of the tub, Vendetta yanked the towel from its stand near a small table of soaps and cloths and dried herself. Her teeth ground. Blood magic controlled Emil, his actions, but not his eyes or his mind. She marched to the wall where hooks held robes, choosing a soft, fur lined one to put on and secure to her waist.

Vendetta glowered at the man on the floor as she crawled into bed, rage boiling her stomach acid. Emil knew nothing of what he spoke of. He hadn't a clue how hard she had worked; how much she had done to ensure success. The mutts magic would be hers. Formidable as blood magic was, as powerful as she had made it, it could not compete with darkness. Subsequently, the mutt would become a puppet, sent off to only the gods know where to do her bidding as she saw fit. With dark magic backing the Reap name as it once had, the Castine line would learn what it was to fear, and the continent could finally come under one rule. Under her. A single monarch was what Vinyamar needed, not this ludicrous excuse the twelve regions called peace.

Emil didn't know how much Vendetta would sacrifice to get what she wanted, how much she already had to get to this point.

Malice could never kill her, could never destroy what she had built, or take that for which she had killed.

Breaking the Soul
XVI

Part III

When Mutuwa blackened, Malice's pain had disappeared too. He was just floating somewhere for a while, warm as if being embraced, and calm, his head as clear as the sky in the middle of summer. It was nice, so much so he didn't want it to end.

Then he saw Sok and Rayen's heads slip from their necks and fall to the ground.

Malice's eyes fluttered open. There was softness underneath and around him. His bedchamber glowed a delicate orange like it always did, the closet door open to display all his and Kiran's clothes, his desk neatly arranged, a short stack of letters on it now. Malice took his time sitting up, adjusting to the familiarity of his room that didn't feel so familiar anymore.

He blinked the grogginess away, noticing a figure at his side, and flinched. The queen was there poised on his desk chair, staring at him, her black eyes bleak in the dim room. He swallowed hard and his hands trembled instantly despite him telling them not to.

"The mutt wakes," she said, her voice chilling and distant. "I was curious to see how human you still looked."

She reached for him. Malice jerked away, but her highness caught his chin with the other hand and steadied his head. "Your eyes have changed." Then an arm from her second set grabbed one of his hands, holding it up for Malice to see. "So have your nails." She released him completely.

Awkwardly, he sat there, back hunched, while he fiddled with the blankets. He couldn't and didn't want to meet her eyes. His fingers stopped working the blanket's fabric. His nails had changed. They were black as night, long, and pointed.

Silence continued as Malice's skin prickled under the queen's heavy gaze. Not in the least bit curious, he wanted her to leave and for Kiran to replace her presence in his room. He had letters to read, and his stomach was tensing from hunger.

"I ordered you sent to Mutuwa."

Malice shifted away from Queen Vendetta, mouth dry, the tension of hunger transforming into daggers slicing his throat.

"I had a theory about you," she explained, her tone hinting at a smile. Malice refused to look at her because of it. Instead, the source of pain distracting, he dug his nail into his palm. "Putting you in danger would prove it false or correct. Your survival was pure luck, but I commend you for it all the same."

Gathering his courage, Malice asked, "Were you going to save me?" He glanced at her highness. The hunger plummeted to the deepest crevices of his intestines, smacking him with a wave of nausea. Her lip flared, eyebrows scrunched, head slightly reeled; a look of utter and pure disgust.

"No." She rose. "Why would I save something as pathetic and loathsome as you?" She left, shoes clacking, and the door slammed shut behind her.

I tried, or *I wanted to*, was what Malice had hoped she would say. She was his mother, wasn't she? A throb in his chest made it difficult to take a deep breath. His blood boiled fiercely, like he stood too close to a torch. Yet, Malice felt like crying.

Soon, or maybe after a while, three people entered his bedchamber while one stayed by the door. It took a moment to register it was Annabeth who had not come in and Kiran, Blodwen, and Tendai were the ones surrounding him, talking, asking questions. Their voices were lost to him, muffled gibberish. Briefly, a hand touched his shoulder, he thought, and hesitated to release him, but did.

What have I done? Again, and again, and again, he asked himself. If he was so loathsome and pathetic, why hadn't the queen killed him already? Or let him die? Why had Sok and Rayen been able to run around and torment everyone in the castle, but Malice wasn't allowed to sneak out of the summit without punishment? Why couldn't he go into the kingdom? Kiran's cottage was the farthest beyond the castle grounds he was allowed to go.

After however much time had passed—he never noticed Kiran and his parents had left—Malice laid back to stare at his ceiling.

Your eyes have changed and so have your nails.

He got out of bed, padded to his desk where the mirror was perched against the wall, and looked at himself. His skin wasn't so pale anymore, nor was he covered in dirt and blood. His white hair was still curly but longer, dipping below his shoulders. There was a hollowness to his face that reminded him of Emil. Then his eyes, the green more vibrant and his pupil a slit like a cat's.

Malice deflated. There was no resemblance to Queen Vendetta. Sighing, he turned, dragged the chair back to the desk, and sat down. What could he do now? If he didn't listen, Kiran, and likely Zephyrus, would be in danger. But if he wasn't meeting the queen's expectations anyway, why did it matter what he did? He should've asked her while she was here, since he doubted he would see her anytime soon. He *hoped* he wouldn't have to see her anytime soon.

Eventually, freeing himself of his mind, Malice spread the letters from Magnus out on his desk. At the corner of each letter was a tick. Annabeth was probably to thank for that. Tearing the envelope with a single mark, Malice spent his night reading. It was better than doing nothing. Or sleeping. Or crying.

"Magnus"

One month earlier

Snow covered the ground in a generous layer of white, like a fur rug on the floor. The sun was warm against Magnus's rosy cheeks but not warm enough to melt the fountain's frozen water in the castle's garden. Sitting on the fountain's ledge, the ice reflected Magnus's purple eyes and abundant freckles. The statue at its center was beautiful, her figure curvy and full, her curly hair flowing past her shoulder blades while covering her breasts. Most of the plants were dead, their brown skeletons peeking through the snow except for an assortment of pansies and white snowdrops.

Gareth, swathed in fur, came into the garden before noon. He looked at Magnus, then nodded toward the stone path he had come from. Magnus rose as he rubbed his numb hands together from spending all morning outside.

Tables of knights, enjoying alcohol and food that warmed their guts all the same, surrounded Magnus and Gareth as they ate their meal in the dining hall. Afterward, stomach full, Magnus headed to the second floor's library, Gareth behind him.

The library was grand; the wood carved with grapevines, the back wall nothing but windows overlooking the castle's garden. On either side of the center, occupied with desks, were neatly packed bookcases. A balcony rimmed the library walls, coves of books filling the shorter space between the terrace and ceiling. Like many other rooms in the castle, the floor illustrated a map of the region in solid and dotted gold lines against blue marble. The walls were pastel sage green, a refreshing lightness.

Paper, writing utensils, and books waited for Magnus at one of the desks, but his usual teacher was nowhere to be seen. They were a few hundred years old, their skin like leather branded with the black swirls most adult barbarians had. Half fairy, their small wings mirrored a honey bee's. To this day, the elder had yet to tell Magnus their name. He doubted Gareth knew it, either.

There was a note on top of the books, he noticed as he took his seat, telling him he was on his own today. The elders didn't care much for Magnus, almost as much as he didn't care for them. Gareth sat next to him and sighed as he situated himself. It was quiet, his breath and the movement of materials echoing in his skull.

Math equations turned to writing formal mock correspondences. Father insisted on the importance of tone while speaking with the rulers as he shared his intentions and concerns. *Never let them show they get to you,* he said. *It's a sign of weakness, one they will exploit.* Magnus slid page after page toward Gareth, who checked them over, creating two piles in front of him. One was quite a bit thinner than the other, which was a good sign.

Unbidden, his mind wandered to the letter he sent a week ago. Malice should have received and responded by now. He tried to imagine if anything he said would have upset Malice, but he wasn't the type to leave Magnus high and dry if he was upset. Leaned back into his chair, eyes scanning his finished document, he concluded Malice must be busy. He was a prince.

Hands free of graphite, his handkerchief now grey, Magnus glanced at the three books and grabbed the first. *The History of Cytor* read the title, a fishing kingdom to the northeast on the mainland. Another thing his father told him was if he were to become king, he needed to know the histories of all his kingdoms. Magnus couldn't argue with that, but it didn't make it any less boring.

Outside, the desaturated world of winter gradually became bright with gold as the sun began to set. The ticking clock on the table was a constant reminder of what today was.

Gareth placed two papers beside Magnus's book, a few equations marked incorrectly. While Gareth explained why they were wrong and how to fix them, Magnus's leg bounced violently under the table, his heel tapping the floor. The second Gareth's mouth closed, Magnus quickly corrected all he'd pointed out, his stick of graphite wagging.

Finally, Magnus shoved the parchment back toward Gareth, his bones ready to jump out of his skin, he was so restless.

With a smirk, Gareth looked them over. "You are free to go," he said.

Magnus jumped out of his seat, knocking his chair back, and ran to the doors. In the hallway already, he raced to the stairs and almost tripped down them. Narrowly steering clear of servants, Magnus sprinted out of the castle and into the cold of winter, a burst of icy wind hitting his face with pin pricks. He was quickly out of the castle grounds and on the streets of Alucard's Kingdom, his breath fogging. Snow packed the cobblestone streets, crunching under his feet.

People smiled at Magnus as he passed. Some waved, and a few tried to talk, but Magnus didn't have time to stop and chat today. It had been months since he had seen Vesh and Padma. He was nearing the western district. The houses and cottages were smaller than anywhere else in the kingdom, the streets a smidge dirtier, and the people a tad grungier in appearance. Magnus swore a long time ago to make the western district a nicer place for his mother and brother to live, no matter if they were to come live in the castle when he became king.

Soon enough, his mother's small cottage was in sight, smoke billowing from the chimney, ginger illuminating the square windows. Her home was the same as the rest: roof of thatch, tan concrete walls, wooden beams, molding, and doors.

The icy air stung Magnus's lungs, eyes, and cheeks, but he

didn't care. He slowed a few houses down, heaving. He would probably sweat if it weren't so cold. Although, now that he wasn't moving so much, he shivered, the winter chill suddenly freezing. He went to pull his cloak tighter around himself, only there wasn't anything to pull. In his haste, he'd forgotten his cloak and sighed. Good thing Holister wasn't around to see it. The cloak was embroidered with the insignia of Alucard's Kingdom, a triple winged sun with an eye in the middle. Hopefully, his mother had a spare he could borrow, or, better yet, he could stay the night, and Gareth would bring the cloak tomorrow morning. He smiled at the idea.

At the entry, thuds sounded alongside incoherent ranting. Magnus opened the door with a drawn-out creak. Knees buckling, he barcly caught himself on the doorframe as his chest and stomach knotted together.

Holister stood over Vesh, kicking her head into the floor like she was a kindle needing to be stomped out. Blood splattered the ground. Her body was limp, jerking every time his father kicked. The wet cracking noise changed to mush as if he stepped in mud. There was a bottle in Holister's hand, empty, cork on the floor, his face red and delirious from alcohol.

A gust of icicles rushed into the house. Father stopped and lazily turned his head toward the door.

"What'cha standing there for?" he said, his words a long slur. "Get inside before you freeze us out!"

Magnus stepped in, wobbly, his legs numb, and the knob clicked into place. His feet inched closer, the smell of blood and urine making him cringe.

"Stop," he heard himself say, or maybe he thought it because his father showed no reaction.

Holister sneered when he looked at Vesh, flared his lip, hawked, and spat at her. "You stupid bitch!" He lifted his boot.

"Stop!" Magnus shouted, startling Holister into snapping toward him. Magnus flinched, his feet firmly in place.

"Stop?" Holister echoed. "Why should I? This filthy wretch talked back to me. *Me? The king?*" With all his might, he brought his foot down. Blood and gore spurted out from under Mother's head. Magnus's stomach lurched at the muted, wet thump. He twisted away and vomited, the pressure bringing tears to his eyes.

Father kicked her again. Vesh slumped to the side, revealing a smaller body. Padma. Magnus teetered as all the air left his lungs as if someone punched him in the diaphragm, pain blooming. Bruises of black and blue colored the small amount of visible skin. He was… Padma was just a boy. He was six. And Mother—

Sucking in a breath, Magnus forced himself toward his father and yanked his arm. "Enough!" His voice trembled. "They're dead. You killed them. Isn't that enough?"

Holister swung his free arm around, smacking Magnus to the hardwood floor. "Bastard!" he hissed.

Metal coated his mouth. Magnus must've bitten the inside of his cheek as he spat and stood, blood dribbling from his nose. Without thinking, Magnus lunged, slammed into his father, and wrapped his arms around the drunkard's torso, tearing him away from Mother. They both fell, Holister grunting as they hit the ground. He struggled free of Magnus's grip, flipped, and climbed on top of him. He wrenched his fist back, Magnus's arms flying to protect his face. Fear coated his thoughts, flayed his rationality till it was gone. Father paused. But only for a moment before he let loose a flurry of punches. Each hit felt like it was breaking bone, his tense muscles distributing the impact into his arms and shoulders.

"You despicable child!" Holister bellowed, spittle spraying. "I gave you everything! Took you in! Raised you like a prince!" He kept punching, right and left, Magnus's arms ready to give any second. "I'm the one who gave you a better chance at life, yet you cling to your whore mother?"

Grinding back shrieks of pain, Magnus caught one of Holister's fists, wrenched it to the side, and hauled himself out from under his father, getting to his feet as quickly as he could. His arms throbbed, pulsed with burning agony. He tried to wiggle his fingers and couldn't, instead pain shot up his arms, white sparking his vision.

Father stood unsteadily. Magnus crept backward until he was on the other side of the counter in the middle of the kitchen. He knew Holister had a temper, most everyone did, especially when he drank. Never had Magnus ever seen him, his own father, become so violent. His heart wanted to know what caused it. Why had his father lost control? Fury engulfed his mind in a red-hot rush, a blaze licking his insides.

Holister pushed his brown hair, soaked with sweat, back, chest heaving. His eyes emanated such animosity Magnus could have sworn he was looking at the most heinous criminal there ever was.

"You ruined us," he said, stepping closer, voice smoother and crueler than earlier. "Killed my father. Destroyed my legacy." Holister halted and swayed, glowering at Magnus. "I should have let you rot in the gutters with your damned mother and brother."

His words hurt like a knife, leisurely penetrating Magnus's heart, briefly fueling the flames of anger. Confusion struck him second like a pickaxe of ice smashing his skull.

"You, Magnus."

Magnus remained still because his legs were stuck, set in concrete, body like a statue, forever cursed to stay unchanged. Father closed the distance between them.

"Are my greatest mistake."

Magnus noticed the glint of metal on the counter. He reached for the cutting board with partially chopped carrots on its surface while Holister rammed his fist into Magnus's gut, Magnus doubling over. His heart pounded violently. Dragging himself, Magnus tried to flee when Holister kicked his back, sending him sprawling to the floor, chin bucking the wood.

"You can't blame me," Father said as he loomed over him. "Your cunt of a mother should've miscarried you and kept her mouth shut."

Magnus wanted to yell, scream at his father, but he couldn't muster his voice. Holister kneeled and snatched Magnus's neck, fingers wrapping around him. He squeezed. Magnus wrenched backward, so he was on his back and Holister was on top of him. His vision clouded, his ears rang as he scratched Holister's arm, the warmth of blood welling under his fingernails, legs flailing in hopes of kicking his groin. He did. Holister yelped, his grip gone in an instant. Magnus scrambled away, back slamming against the cupboards, choking on his breaths like a fish on land.

The throbbing of his head made his eyes feel as though they were bulging, ready to pop out of his skull as the room spun. Magnus glanced at his arms, surprised he could use them. He wasn't as bad at regeneration as he thought.

Holister got to his feet, stumbled, then used the counter as a brace, his expression pure rage. Magnus searched and grabbed a knife from the sink. It was dirty, dried juice and blood from butchered meat on the sharp edge. Holister screamed, his mouth wide enough to see the back of his throat, veins bulging on his forehead and neck.

Father rushed toward Magnus. He startled into the counter and cabinets, the edge stabbing his lower back, as his father cocked his fist. Panic gripped him tighter than his father's hand around his neck had, his blood halting. Magnus lunged anyway, got low, and to the side, and buried the knife deep into Holister's stomach.

Holister staggered backward, surprised. His hand dropped to the hole in his gut, which came back bloody.

I... stabbed him.

Drawing his hand back with a snarl, light emanated from his palm. Before it could fully manifest, Magnus tackled him to the floor, knife plunging deep into Holister's core. He swiftly sat up, lifting the blade over his head and sinking it into Father's chest again and again and again. Each time met the resistance of bone.

"YOU KILLED MY MOTHER!" Magnus screamed over his father's volatile shrieks of pain and horror. His fingers gouged the flesh from Magnus's face and neck to stop him as his legs thrashed and thudded against the floor. Squeals turned to gargles. His legs had eventually gone limp, and his arms fell to his sides. Ichor spilled from the corners of his mouth.

Still, Magnus stabbed. And he kept stabbing as every bit of anger evaporated like clouds in the dead of summer.

Panting, Magnus stared down at his father, his eyes dim, glazed over. Blood pooled beneath him, soaking through Magnus's pants. He was exhausted. Every place Holister struck was a searing throb or ache, wrecking his mind whenever the pain spiked. Magnus stood and noticed the red splattering his clothes, his hands, felt the wetness on his face, and clumping his hair. There were too many holes in his father's chest to count.

Abruptly, Magnus whipped around and vomited into the sink, everything he didn't throw up earlier coming up now. Tears stung his eyes, and bile burned his already sore throat. When he stopped, he lurched upright, tripped over his father, slipping on the blood, and stood at the edge of the counter, the house completely still. Quiet. Chilled.

Vesh and Padma were greying, their bodies probably void of warmth. He wanted to sink down next to them, hold his mother and younger brother in his arms one last time. What right did he have? If what his father said was true, Magnus was nothing but a burden, a misery to them both.

Knock, knock, knock, knock, knock. The door squeaked open, a gust of ice-cold wind following, and a gasp. Something dropped, like a blanket crumbling to the floor. After the door closed, footsteps hurried inside, paused, and changed direction. Boots entered Magnus's view of the crimson-stained wooden planks. A big, warm hand rested on Magnus's shoulders, the other hand gently taking the knife from his grip. They tugged Magnus into their embrace, his head pressing against their abdomen. For an instant, the scent of pine and leather overwhelmed the smell of blood. Gareth.

They stood there for a while, Magnus gradually coming to his senses as he focused on the sound of Gareth's steady breathing. Gareth stepped away and picked up what he had dropped, then slung it over Magnus's shoulders, fitting the hood over his head. The cloak he'd left behind.

Gareth tried to guide Magnus to the door, but once again, his legs were stuck, frozen in a bath of ice. Bending down, Gareth lifted Magnus into his arms like he was a toddler who weighed nothing.

They walked toward the sound of howling wind and the indistinct murmurs of people lingering in the streets. Magnus watched Vesh's and Padma's bodies disappear beyond the closing door.

A Tale of Origins

"Gareth"

Up the stairs to the second floor, the tips of Gareth's pointed ears and nose were still numb. Once Magnus was settled in his room, Gareth gathered a few royals, one of which was a healer and another was his subordinate, Ahenobarbus Narine, a lush of an angel. Barbus helped transport the bodies of Padma, Vesh, and Holister to the morgue, east of the castle. If they had not been dead by the time they had returned to Vesh's home, they would not have lasted long. All their injuries were too extensive to heal, considering how much time had passed.

Gareth felt the Castine's death like a sack of bricks had fallen on his shoulders as a dagger churned his gut. He had watched his majesty Holister grow from a babe, stood by his side as his right-hand man for over twenty years.

When King Jaci died of disease, King Holister, prince at the time, fell into a never-ending cycle of self-loathing, regret, and sorrow, alcohol becoming his escape from the cruel reality. Prior to his father's passing, his majesty had sworn off alcohol when he had hit an innocent servant whilst drunk. Alcohol had always made his majesty violent. It was why he kept to himself, locked in his bedchamber or study, far from anyone he could lash out at. He wished he knew why King Holister went to Vesh's after all this time.

Down the hall of the second floor, a maid, a tray of food in her hands, paced in front of Magnus's bedchamber. Gareth started toward her.

The maid turned, jolted, then bowed upon seeing Gareth. "Sir Gareth," she squawked. "The prince refuses to eat. He's never done this. I'm concerned—"

"Please try not to worry," Gareth interrupted as he looked at the

227

door, grapevines carved into the wood. "He will most likely not have an appetite for a while."

"Why is that?" She peered at Gareth, her eyes big and curious.

The truth will eventually come out. Might as well be the one to say it. "King Holi—"

The door swung open, startling the maid. Magnus stood in the entry, calm, composed, his expression neutral. Gareth knew better as he stared into the prince's dead eyes. Without a word, Magnus snatched the tray of food from the servant's hands and slammed the door on them.

"We must have been talking too loud," Gareth said, and patted the servant's shoulder. "I will announce something soon, but for now, let it be. All right?"

Confused, the maid nodded, curtsied, and walked around Gareth. With an inhale and exhale, he gathered himself and entered the prince's bedchamber.

The room was big, not as big as the kings but certainly bigger than his own on the floor above. A fur rug covered most of the ground. To his right was a bed too big for a child, nightstands on either side, both of which had unlit lamps. A long dresser sat against the wall, a mirror hanging above it, while a few small jewelry boxes were on the dresser's surface. There were spools of thread, needles, and a tambour on the furthest edge. A sewing station of sorts. To his left was an armoire, a bulky piece of furniture, a couch with dark blue cushions, a bookshelf for the random things Magnus had collected and games. The set of chess pieces his mother gave him years ago was displayed on the fourth shelf from the top. They were made of marble, each one hand carved. Vesh had saved a year or two worth of coin for the set and Magnus was ecstatic when he returned, showing it off to everyone he passed before arranging them on his shelf.

Across the bedchamber, Magnus sat at a round table with three chairs encompassing it, lit candles at the center, casting dark shadows around the space. Gareth dragged a chair out from the table, scraping the legs on the marble floor, and sat down. Magnus had not touched his food, simply stared at it, disgusted.

"When will the funeral be held?" Magnus asked, breaking the silence and surprising Gareth. "Which of the elders will step in as regent until I'm old enough?" His head moved toward Gareth. His eyes had trailed behind, all the life drained from his features.

Gareth found himself struggling to formulate an answer. "Whenever you are ready," he intoned.

"In three days." Magnus looked away, as if searching for something. "I want them buried separately. My father will be put to rest in the ruler's mausoleum along with his crown, but I want my mother and brother buried elsewhere."

"Where?"

Magnus took a moment to think. "There's a place on the mainland she used to love. I'll have to find it tomorrow and mark the spot."

"You do not want them buried in the churchyard?" He doubted Vesh and Padma would have been buried with Holister, since he never declared them as his wife and son or opposing desire—he was king, his reason for having peasants buried with him did not need to be shared. They were not the queen and youngest prince. They were peasants. Holister cared more about how his reputation would suffer marriage to a former prostitute and peasant, how it would dampen his authority, than the well-being of his sons and wife.

"No," he said bluntly.

Gareth nodded, not knowing what else to do. "As for your other question; the decision is yours as well."

"Yeong-Suk Dahl," Magnus answered rather fast. "She's been

watching the rulers since she was my age, starting with my grandfather. At the very least, she won't do any harm."

True enough. Yeong-Suk was about twenty-five years older than Gareth, close to her hundreds by now, but she was still the youngest elder in Alucard's Kingdom. She was not so stuck in her ways. However, she was timid like a mouse, just as quiet too. Her lack of confidence could prove to be an issue in the future with resolving conflicts or controlling the royals. It would be difficult to tell if she were in the room, if not for her size. Being a full-blooded giant, Yeong-Suk stood taller than Gareth by at least half a meter.

"It will probably be for the best," Gareth said eventually. "I cannot imagine any other old piece of leather being able to handle the throne." He had hoped to see Magnus crack a smile for his jab at the elders. He did not and continued to stare at the wall, absent-mindedly.

"What will you say about Father's death?" Magnus asked, his voice quiet.

"I… can take the blame," Gareth said. "I would have to retire, run, or sit in prison until pardoned." That was the nice way of putting things. Treason for killing the king, a ruler, would put him to death. No trial, no sitting and waiting in a cell, no chance to run. He would receive a painful execution where the core would be wounded beyond repair. One he would gladly accept, for Magnus's sake.

Magnus frowned. "No." He paused as if to ponder his next choice of words. "The people should know what type of man Holister was, what type of king he was. I don't care if you fabricate his death— accident, suicide, an assassination—but don't cover up what he did to my mother or Padma." Anger scrunched the prince's face, bunched his fists on the table before he let his breath go and slumped in his chair.

Gareth considered Magnus for a time. Confusion was not the right word for what he was feeling, nor was shock. It felt unreal to be having this conversation with Magnus, with the prince, a child.

"All right," was all he managed to say.

"Magnus"

When the light from the hallway reduced to nothing, Magnus picked up his tray, stood, and dumped the food into the empty hearth. He threw a ball of fire inside. It hungrily consumed his meal and the wood, spitting and sizzling, as Magnus set the tray on the table and crossed the room to his desk.

Once he gathered his supplies, the pungent smell of ink assaulting his nose, he put pen tip to paper. It all happened so fast it was laborious in his memories. Minutes swelled into hours. The stench of death was suffocating, gut-wrenching. His lungs seized for a moment as he thought back on it.

Vesh's lifeless body over the top of his brother's corpse, an image seared into his mind, one he doubted he could ever forget. The warmth of blood when it splattered his face and washed over his hands—he had scrubbed his hands for what felt like hours, yet the sensation was vividly there.

Holister deserved his death. Deserved to meet a painful end. Magnus thought it a shame his father wasn't able to experience the same agony he inflicted on Vesh and Padma. Scowling at the words on the page, Magnus didn't want to think like that. Holister was his father, his blood. Father had his good moments, the times he cared enough to ask about Vesh or Padma, explain his reasoning, or soften his tone. He had wanted Holister to be proud of him, and proud to make Magnus his heir. How could he have been so wrong?

Magnus finished his letter to Malice, corking the jar of ink and fishing out an envelope from the second drawer, along with some wax. Eyes fixed on the parchment, body weary, mind even more so, Magnus figured he could seal it tomorrow.

Magnus rose from the chair and put out the fire with a wave of his hand. He flopped backward onto his bed. He ran his hands up and down his forearms, touched his fingers to his cheek, and to his neck. Nothing remained. Between regeneration and the healer Gareth called in, all his injuries were gone.

The bed was cold, sending a shiver up Magnus's spine when he turned to his side. The sound of his mother's skull being smashed in corrupted his ears as if his pillow had captured the moment and was reminding Magnus. He clenched his jaw, screwing his eyes shut, and anger gathered like hundreds of jittering ants cramped in their nest.

He jolted upright, grabbed one of the many pillows at the head of his bed, and chucked it across the room. Then another. Every pillow thrown was another insult his father spat, like he, his mother, and Padma were less than the dirt he walked on. He ran out of pillows far too quickly. Magnus's body felt feverish, boiling with rage. Holister had slaughtered them! It was his fault! He chose to raise Magnus when Magnus would've been happier if he had left him with Vesh. This wouldn't have happened if Magnus wasn't the prince. If Magnus hadn't been born, all would be fine.

Bottom lip trembling, Magnus found it hard to breathe all of a sudden, his chest caving in from guilt. Pain pulsed into the rest of his body, a giant wave of grief spreading to the tips of his fingers and toes. He choked out a sob, gripping the sheets at his sides and bunching them to his face, where he wept. His body convulsed and shuddered with every cry. He wished his mother were here to hug him and that Gareth hadn't left so he could be angry and sad with someone. If only Malice were here, he wouldn't be alone.

Blade
XVII

Malice crumbled the letters between his hands.

Blinking, he frantically tried to smooth the wrinkles back out, pressing the paper on the edge of the desk as he moved it back and forth. He glared at them for what seemed like hours, the clock on the edge of the desk ticking the silence away. After a few deep breaths, Malice focused on the positive. Yeong-Suk Dahl accepted her role as regent, stepping in for Magnus until he could take the throne in four years. The funerals went well, at least. Most of all, Magnus was alive.

He grabbed out all the materials he needed—Annabeth had made sure there was a wealthy supply of wax, paper, ink, and envelopes in Malice's desk drawers—and spilled his guts, too. Memories dredged from the shallow graves he buried them in. How the light dappled the forest floor, bugs constantly screeched, the foliage always rustled, how the twigs stabbed his feet tickled his senses once more, the scent of wet soil and moss entering his nose. Then blood. Horrid, vile, ichor.

Gore dripping down their elongated teeth, the wolf-bears struck his mind. Malice flinched as his stomach twisted, his throat tightening.

He went on, reliving every moment like a night terror. Before long, there was nothing left to write. Parchment sealed and signed, he slid it forward and brought his opposite hand to thumb the tiny divot in his earlobe.

In the last drawer, Malice found the blue teardrop earring Magnus gave him. He only wore it when he went to the Kings Summit because that was the only place he knew it would be safe. He guided the earring through his lobe, squeezed the backing into place, and enjoyed feeling its presence in his ear.

Malice stood to go to bed, fingers rubbing the smooth gem, and crawled under the covers. The mattress was uncomfortable, as if he were sinking into the stuffing, as if he were going to drown in it. Sitting up, he closed his fingers, and the tiny flame on the candle's wick vanished, leaving a trail of white smoke spiraling toward the ceiling. It was pitch dark and silent.

Beyond the cage of his ribs, his heart pounded loudly, the darkness enveloping him. He pulled his legs to his chest, ear resting on his knee, and wished he could see the stars or moon. They were always bright enough on the nights it didn't rain, and the breeze was strong enough to move the treetops. Thinking back, a part of him wished he would have been able to stay in that glade for a night. The sky would have been breathtaking, he was sure. Although, it was probably better he didn't, wolf-bears aside. He would miss it too much if he had.

*

The morning air bit Malice's skin on the way to the dovecotes. A false dawn painted the sky and clouds, the dark blue fading to a pale yellow. The birds sang, and the breeze blew Malice's hair all around.

He couldn't sleep any longer. The same nightmare made him toss and turn—Queen Vendetta commanding a pack of wolf-bears after him every time he closed his eyes as she laughed hysterically—and wake to overheated, sweat-dampened skin. Sleep was near impossible to hold on to.

Located in the southeastern courtyard, three big, rounded stone buildings housed all the messenger birds. Annabeth had shown Malice a few times. From watching her, he knew how to call for the ravens instead of the falcons or doves—falcons delivered letters to other realms while the doves were used within the region. Ravens were for the Reap family exclusively, Annabeth had explained.

Four short whistles, tweets really, with a five second rest before he did it again to call a raven from the third dovecote. He grabbed the letter out of his cloak and held his opposite arm out for the bird to perch. A blur of black burst out of the rounded building, circled, and dove, landing, its talons kissing his forearm. It tilted its head. He stared at the raven's glittering inky eyes, admiring its midnight feathers. When he held the letter for the bird to take, it jerked its head and examined the envelope, then snatched it.

"To Alucard's Kingdom," Malice said as he moved his arm upward, prompting the raven to take off with a squawk.

How the bird understood those commands, Malice didn't know, but his letters always found their way to Magnus, so he guessed it didn't matter whether he understood or not.

The wind blew Malice's cloak away from his body. He inhaled deeply, expecting the air to be refreshing. It wasn't. Everything was too familiar, too much to be reminded of the people who hated him, and of the pain those people caused. Glancing back toward the castle of many peaks and ridges where all the windows were blacked out, and the stone was darkening with time, he didn't want to go back.

This early in the morning, the field of beaten dirt and gravel was empty of royals. Quiet and motionless. Malice wasn't sure how to feel about it. He'd gotten used to the never-still forest. If not the forest, when he hid, his heart had raced, and his body had trembled, so he was never able to stop moving, either.

Racks upon racks lined the edges of the training grounds. Targets and dummies, untouched from the day prior, were spaced evenly on the north side. Healers would wait in the two pavilions on the west and east sides of the grounds, running out to heal whoever needed it. One day, he was sure Kiran would be there too, answering as many calls as he could.

Malice walked across the field to the rack of swords, gazing at the blades. They were well taken care of, the edge sharp and smooth. The guard, however, was rough from years of use. A few were longer than his body. Fewer yet had bronze blades curved to create an incomplete circle, and there were some about the size of his forearms. Dual swords connected by chains, long and thin-bladed swords with daintier handles; there were so many his eyes jetted back and forth. At least once he had seen a royal use every single one.

Do not pick up a blade if you do not intend to kill. The same goes for any weapon. Odovacar's voice echoed in his ears. The weapons displayed throughout the training grounds were nothing more than decorations for Malice. Yet, he couldn't resist running his finger down the cool steel of a common sword, wondering how heavy it was compared to a wooden one. Hand gliding past the guard to the handle, Malice wrapped his fingers around the worn leather.

He whipped toward the practice swords, grabbed one, and walked across the field to the padded dummies, steps crunching. He didn't want and wouldn't be a murderer. Standing in front of it, Malice studied the dummy, the wooden grip a familiar sensation against his palms. It was almost soothing.

Useless, the queen hissed. Malice flinched backward. Queen Vendetta glared down at him. Her cold eyes bore holes in his face, forcing him to look at the ground. *Pathetic*, she said. Heat swelled in Malice's chest and hands, boiling up his arms and into his throat. Her lower set of hands reached for him, for his neck, but he retreated and swung his sword. If Odovacar were here, he would have scolded

Malice for what he did—the attack was too loose, broad, and held little power. She swatted the wooden stick as if it were an annoying pest. *Mutt!* she growled.

Breath hitching, Malice stepped forward and jabbed her highness in the stomach. She grimaced, her claws swiping. He dodged, rolled on his heels, and snapped the blade, striking her ribs.

This will not go unpunished!

Why should he care? Malice attacked in every way he knew, the queen wincing, blood oozing from the wounds he left. He'd done everything right and still, he was punished. To Queen Vendetta, he was exactly as she called him, a mutt in need of training. But for what and why would Malice care if everything he did was wrong anyhow?

The first voices sounded behind Malice, blabbering royals idly making their way to whatever stations there were on the training grounds. Malice halted; the dummy returned to its normal state. No wounds or blood, just a lifeless doll, and let his arm drop as Kiran entered his mind. *I will kill Kiran.* Malice had no reason to doubt her anymore, never had one to begin with besides stupid, blind hope her highness actually loved for him.

The sun was above the horizon, warmth clinging from the little exercise he did. He glanced around. Since no one paid him any attention, he slinked to the outskirts of the field and waited for Odovacar. It was probably too late to head back to his bedchamber, not that he was going to sleep.

Eyes roaming the grounds, he landed on the dummy that turned into the queen. How many times over had he killed her? Why had he kept going?

Why did it feel so good?

A flash of red caught Malice's attention. He shifted as Odovacar marched toward him, his face scrunched. Malice watched until their eyes met, and his brother's severe expression lessened. Relief? Malice averted his gaze, gut wringing itself.

When Odovacar approached, wearing loose, simple black garments and scuffed boots, he examined Malice, lingered on the practice sword for a moment, then drew his own from the scabbard on his hip. The sound rang in Malice's ears. The pommel was a skull with horns and fangs, coiling snakes made the guard, and thick, mahogany leather bound the grip, while the steel itself glinted. Lifting the sword so the tip leveled beneath Malice's chin, Odovacar discarded any softness Malice thought he saw. This was what he was used to.

"Attack," he demanded.

His gut curdled at his brother's command, a sudden urge to say no rushing to his tongue. He knew better than to say anything. Malice's heart thumped before he took a step back and brought his wooden blade up, making sure his hold was tight.

Malice attacked, driving his sword into Odovacar's gut, but he had turned his body to evade the strike. In a swift movement, Odovacar chopped the wooden practice sword, over half of it falling to the dirt. Malice stumbled to a stop, inches from his brother's blade.

Then Odovacar stalked to the racks, grabbed a sword, and shoved it in Malice's face.

"I don't—"

"A few nicks will do you no harm," he interrupted. "Grab it and attack me."

Reluctantly, Malice discarded what was left of his practice sword and took up the common blade. It hit the ground. He struggled to heft it up and hold it steady; the end kept quivering. Odovacar slammed his sword down, knocking Malice's from his grip, the steel clanging as it hit gravel.

"Pick. It. Up."

He did and turned to Odovacar, who rammed the pommel into his forehead. Malice staggered, the sword dropping, and his head throbbed, eyes watery and blurry now.

"Surviving gave you stones, Malice," Odovacar said, "but you need to be reminded of your place."

Again, and again, and again, Malice's sword left his hands, and a fresh cut or bruise brought more pain. Odovacar hesitated at each sniffle Malice couldn't contain, jaw sliding tersely. By the time it was noon, he couldn't walk or lift his arms, tears streamed down his face, and blood stained his clothes. Odovacar grimaced as he stomped the opposite way and called a healer. It was as if it pained him to see Malice in the sorry state he was in. Which made little sense. It was Odovacar's fault to begin with.

The healer rushed to Malice's side, dropped, and healed him. Magic surged through his body, easing his aching muscles on the way.

Reminded of your place. What was Malice's place? He wasn't treated like a prince, so that couldn't be it. If he were training to be a royal like Zephyrus, he would spend more time with them. He didn't know what he was supposed to do, or who he was supposed to be. Outside of nothing, since that was how he was treated most of the time.

To his feet, Malice dusted his soiled clothes off the best he could and started his trek to the castle. Alone. He scanned the grass and flowers. There were no signs of Annabeth despite how she would usually come to collect him around this time. Tightness began in his chest and further slumped his shoulders.

Footsteps bounded closer, the foliage rustling, when Malice spun. Zephyrus barreled toward him, threw his arms out, and hugged Malice, squeezing him tightly. He wheezed and embraced Zephyrus. He smelled like metal and grass, not usually pleasant, but Malice liked it. Then he shoved Malice away, eyes narrowed as he looked him up and down, hands on his shoulders.

"What happened to you?" he asked in a breathy way, his chest rising and falling rapidly. "Are you all right?"

Malice averted his gaze. He didn't want to revisit the memory again. He also didn't want to lie… "The queen sent me away to train."

"… If you say so," Zephyrus said, holding Malice for a moment longer and releasing him. "You didn't answer my other question, though."

"I'm fine," he lied. "What have you've been up to?"

Zephyrus shrugged as they walked through the open plain between the castle and the training grounds. "Training with Father, so nothing new. Kiran started teaching me about medicine."

"Will you learn to heal, too?" Kiran had asked Malice repeatedly to learn how to heal with him, but Malice kept refusing. He knew—at least his gut told him—the queen wouldn't want him to be a healer.

"Nah." Zephyrus shook his head. "As a royal, I need to focus on myself."

"You're not a royal yet," Malice reminded.

"Yet."

They went back and forth for a while, Kiran joining when they reached Malice's bedchamber for lunch. Malice didn't realize how much he had longed for this. How much he missed Kiran and Zephyrus jabbering on about their days while he listened because nothing new ever happened to Malice.

Annabeth, as quick as a hare, delivered their plates of food and left, saying nothing with her head bowed. She looked in pain, like all her muscles ached. Then his attention fell to his plate and his stomach twisted. Mushrooms sat overtop a slab of beef. Suddenly lightheaded, his tongue retreated to the back of his throat. He stood and rushed to the side of his desk where a small trash bin was. He vomited, heaved, coughed, and vomited some more.

He wanted to forget, thought he would be able to for a second as the hours slipped by. Every day for almost two months, he had run and hid in any crevice he could find. He had eaten only what he knew, which was everything Kiran had shown him. And when he finally escaped, there wasn't any evidence. All his wounds were gone, healed or regenerated. It was like he had never been trapped in Mutuwa. Like it was some horrible dream.

Kiran and Zephyrus were silent at his desk, the silverware no longer scraping against the porcelain plates.

"Malice?" Kiran said, and the chair screeched as he pushed it out, followed by Zephyrus.

Queasy, Malice sat back on his heels as Zephyrus got to the floor in front of him, Kiran at his side. He spilled as much as he could tolerate, leaving out that it was her highness who had sent him to Mutuwa. It would be better if they thought he was kidnapped or one of the royals went rogue. He didn't think he could handle them knowing the truth. *He* could hardly handle the truth. The hope someone would save him may have died eventually, but another part of him had believed someone *wanted* to find him. To learn even that wasn't true hurt worse than a hit to the diaphragm.

Explaining his time in Mutuwa, Malice trembled, knees to his chest, eyes on his feet. His toenails were black too, slightly pointed. Kiran and Zephyrus wore white socks, their shoes nestled by his closet door. Their feet were slightly bigger than his, as were their persons, despite how they were practically the same age. Once his mouth closed, Malice sucked in and released a long, haggard breath. His bedchamber was quiet for too long.

Kiran cried at Malice's side, his face scrunched as if he were trying to hold in the tears, so he sat there sniveling instead. Zephyrus extended a hand and placed it on Malice's, his red eyes on the desk.

It felt good to say it all out loud, he supposed. It would feel better if his chest didn't burn, and his heart didn't beat brutally against his ribs, trying to flee. He *was* angry and scared and hurt. With little he could do, Malice locked those feelings away.

Lie and Strategize
XVIII

Annabeth had ushered Kiran and Zephyrus out after lunch, telling Malice Draga had summoned him. Confused, he followed her to the second floor, and she continued to the first, leaving Malice alone.

Annabeth had become distant since he returned from Mutuwa. Every time he tried to talk to her, she ignored him. She no longer helped pick out his clothes or do his hair. Someone else took over. A demon servant in their twenties with emerald skin and jagged horns resembling gems. They were nice, Malice guessed, but they weren't Annabeth.

In the western wing, he knocked on the study's door and waited till he heard her voice.

Draga's blood red hair was in a bun, strands falling from the front to frame her face. She was always reading something when he arrived. Today was no different, as a few documents were in her hands, her eyes racing across the page. Malice closed the door and sat on the couch when she finally looked up from her papers, set them aside, and perched her elbows on the desk, delicate fingers interlocking.

That was new. She'd rarely paid Malice much attention, save for giving him assignments. He didn't like it.

"Lie to me," she said, her expression completely serious.

Malice blinked, pondered, then glanced at the table. "Odovacar is the weakest royal." It probably wasn't true, but Malice hadn't seen him spar with anyone else, so it might have been.

"You looked elsewhere before you spoke. Keep eye contact and try again." Her posture was refined yet relaxed, her chin tilted ever so slightly.

"… The sky is red." Keeping eye contact with Draga's obsidian orbs knotted Malice's gut. He averted his gaze, sights falling on the stormy marble floor.

"You hesitated." She gestured the walls. "These white walls get dirty far too quickly." As if her hand compelled him, Malice peeked at the dark burgundy walls. "I should have painted them black, so the dust would not be so obvious."

Draga retracted her hand, and once again laced it with the other. "Lying is simple and easy, as is making it believable."

Malice frowned at his lap, his cheeks burning. Clear as it was, he felt the need to check.

"You could not tell I was lying, correct?"

Malice nodded.

"I know my habits whilst lying and can control them. On the outside." She tapped her chest. "Inside or out, there will always be an indication of deception."

"Why do I have to lie?" Maybe to make someone feel better, but that was the only reason Malice could think of.

"There will come a time when a situation calls for it," Draga said as she reclined, moving her seat back and crossing her legs. "You should know how to convince whoever you need, and you should know when someone else is dishonest."

"Isn't the truth better?" Annabeth had said lying was bad and the truth should always come first. Malice knew he wasn't doing a very good job, though, with how many lies he had told Kiran and Zephyrus. He didn't inherently mean to, but the truth was painful. Sometimes too painful.

Draga dipped her head. "It can be, but it can also be harmful. It is up to your discretion when and where you think a lie is necessary."

I'm... getting a choice? Something about it sat wrong with him, like worms squirming underneath the skin. He'd never gotten a choice, at least not much of one. Why was he getting one now?

The next morning, the demon servant, Shevanti was her name, instructed Malice to go straight to Draga's study after breakfast.

Four lamps sat on the corners of the coffee table in the middle of the room, holding the edges of a map down. Draga loomed over it, tucking her hair behind her ear when she straightened herself. Her dress of plum purple rustled as it moved with her, skirting the ground, sleeves like mini tunnels around her arms. Malice came in and closed the door. Now sitting on the armchair's rest, Draga gestured to the couch across from her, and Malice took his seat.

"These are the kingdoms of Hordes Region," Draga said, pointing to four miniature castles on the map. "Name them."

"Bextierther." Malice placed his finger on the cold marble castle near Dun Raik in the north. Amongst the books Draga had Malice reading, a few were about the kingdoms and their locations. Despite there being no illustrations, the books detailed their surroundings. Bextierther was the furthest north, and it was also the only kingdom to experience snow in winter.

"Estera." He touched the figure east of Mutuwa on the Nameless Lake's northern edge. The body of water wasn't named because no one thought it was of importance or had anything valuable. "Mondlesgrave." The only kingdom on an island to the east. "And Ryzion." Directly south of Hordes Kingdom and the oldest of the cities, as the book described.

"These four kingdoms are at war. What would you do?" Her arms folded over her chest as she gazed at Malice.

"Tell them to stop?"

"If that did not work?"

"… Try to fix the issue for them," Malice guessed.

"How?" she pressed.

Malice looked between the white marble castles, veins of smoky grey like webs on their surfaces. "I would… try to figure out why they started fighting in the first place."

Draga remained silent, waiting for Malice to continue.

"Once I know the reason, I would find a solution or compromise, so everyone's happy." A peaceful ending where no one got hurt. Malice thought it was correct and smart, but the unimpressed look on Draga's face had him questioning his answer.

"What if there could be no compromise? No resolution to reach? Whose side would you pick?"

Malice's eyebrows twitched. No matter who he stood behind, someone would be angry or disappointed. It was a tricky question, like asking him if he would choose between Zephyrus or Kiran. Kiran was his brother, while Zephyrus was his only friend in Hordes.

"Whichever kingdom has shown the most support or Ryzion since it's the oldest." There was no good solution. Sullenly, Malice glanced at Draga for her response.

"Suitable answers," she praised dryly.

Different scenarios involving the kingdoms occupied the rest of the afternoon. A few involved the other regions as well. She didn't like his answer when they got to Alucard's Region and Malice said he'd support Magnus no matter what.

Talking back and forth with Draga felt strange. He couldn't recall ever hearing Draga's voice as much as he had between today and yesterday. Her tone wasn't much different, but there was a subtle softness in the way she talked that a sharpness replaced in front of the queen. He wondered if she knew of the habit. She probably did. Draga was as controlled and level-headed as a perfectly weighed scale.

To his feet, stretching, Malice looked at the clock on the many shelves against the wall, abundant with knick-knacks and parchment. It was mid evening. Dinner. A perfectly timed grumble from his stomach confirmed it. Before he reached the door, he paused and turned back to Draga.

"Am I coming back tomorrow?" he asked.

"No," she replied instantly. "Inyene will be returning later tonight. You will spend your time with her when she calls for you."

Shuddering, mouth dry, chest tightening, Malice tried his best to swallow the sudden tidal wave of fear consuming him. "All right."

The hallways were quiet and mostly empty. The eastern wing of the second floor was a mystery to Malice. He assumed it was where his siblings slept, or perhaps Felim and Alkeim. Now that he was thinking about it, he believed they were on the third floor. *Why am I on the fourth when everyone else is on the third?*

He didn't care about the stairs. Annabeth, on the other hand, must've been tired from carrying him when he was younger. It was nice not being close to his siblings, so he didn't mind. Although, without Sok and Rayen, it wouldn't have been terrible if he had to. Inyene, Odovacar, and Draga probably had better things to do than spend their time pestering Malice more than they had to. Still, it was a shame he couldn't live with Kiran.

*

As Malice put his shoes underneath his hanging clothes, they thumped against something. He moved them a smidge and tried again, but they wouldn't budge. Putting his shoes aside, he felt then slid out what his shoes were catching on. It was the book he'd stolen from the Barren Circle. He had forgotten about it.

Book in hand, Malice rose, trudged to his desk and plopped in the chair, moving the candle closer. Apprehension stopped him from opening the book while his fingers glided over the leather cover. His hands had been chopped off for this book. The sensation rushed back to his wrists, the searing pain of a blade slicing skin. Muscles stiffening, he rubbed his wrists to rid the chilliness from his bones.

A few deep breaths allowed Malice to gather himself. It'd been over a year since he had stolen the book, yet he hadn't opened it once. All that trouble to not look inside? Kiran would surely be disappointed in him for not peeking. If it hadn't been hidden all this time, Kiran would have already whisked it away, read it, and driveled about the contents.

He opened to the middle of the book, where it wrote *Archangels and Devils*. Deciding to start with the archangel portion, Malice read out loud. It was easier to pronounce words he didn't know, and no one was in his bedchamber, anyway.

"Archangels are an immortal species," he read, "and are an epicene race." Malice could pronounce *epicene*—probably incorrectly—but he had no clue what it meant.

He got through about ten pages when his eyelids, vision fogging, started to slide and fling back open, his head bobbing. The jumbled words made it impossible to comprehend what the book actually said. Malice grabbed an envelope from the drawer and placed it in the spine's nook, closing the book with a heavy thud. He had a long way to go.

Yawning, Malice crawled into bed, still in his day attire, as he wondered when the archangels went extinct. Were the drawings in the book accurate or had the archangels looked completely different? Had they lived in Vinyamar, or elsewhere? Were any alive?

Daughter of Insanity
XIX

Malice hoped he wouldn't have to see the dungeons any more after Mutuwa. He was wrong.

The clacks of his shoes echoed louder than his thundering heart. It was cool and foul smelling down here, his skin crawling, intestines knotting like string. Malice faced the corridor. At the opposite end, Inyene watched, her beady red eyes seemingly glowing in the dim torchlight. Trembling as he walked toward her, he knew if he ran, she would catch him.

She smiled at him, her hand gesturing to the open cell and the chair within. Blood stained the floor, blotched the walls, and splattered the ceiling. A single flame flickered beside the heavy metal door, warming the space only in color.

Malice willingly sat down as Inyene closed the door behind her, her footsteps silent when she approached and crouched in front of his feet. She placed her hands on his ankles, sweeping her thumbs across. Ice burned his skin, him grimacing, and cuffed him to the chair. She did the same to his wrists. He tensed again. If he moved too much, his skin would peel as if he were a shedding lizard.

"There's no point in trying to break free." She said, "You'll hurt yourself," and grinned.

Despite having done nothing, Malice was short of breath. Fear broiled in the pits of his stomach.

Inyene stared up at him, her gaze unnervingly delighted. He looked away, goosebumps racing over his arms. The tightness in his chest returned, squeezing his heart and lungs like a vise. Gently, Inyene caressed Malice's hand, and her rough fingers glided over his till she grabbed his index finger. She broke it like a twig. A single snap. Malice screamed as a scorching pain vibrated through his hand into his arm. She moved on to the next one, then the next and the next, circling back to his thumb.

All of Malice's fingers were twisted and bent backwards, tears streaking his cheeks. He had bitten his lip so hard, a metallic taste coated his mouth. His head throbbed and the pulsating room spun. Tremors raked his body. He should have run away… but… what would have been the point? He would have had to return at some point, meaning he still would have ended up in this chair. Prolonged the inevitable was all he would have done.

"You," Malice shuddered a breath, "insane bitch." His mind was fuzzy, thoughts a chaotic mess inside his skull.

Inyene simply cackled in response. He observed the floor because it was better than looking at his sister and tried to stop the flow of tears. He was tired of crying.

"Don't be so foolish, Malice," she said. "The only one who refuses to see reality is you. Define insanity, if not that."

"What reality?"

"No one in this castle cares for you, and no one will rescue you."

She was right. In the castle, no one cared for Malice. But that was in the castle.

Inyene broke every finger on Malice's right hand. One by one, five consecutive cracks, five consecutive bursts of agony. When she was done, she departed without so much as a glance over her shoulder.

A part of Malice was relieved. The pain made it difficult, though. His breathing was sharp and raspy, his vision of the stone floor hazy and unsteady. The ice around his wrists and ankles melted, creating puddles below him. At least he wouldn't be stuck here.

Directing magic to his hands, each finger broke into place. He gasped and bit the pain back the best he could, sweat dripping from his nose onto his lap. Healing was different, gentler than regeneration, for some reason.

Although he could barely move his hands, they were restored. Wobbly, Malice stood and staggered to the door, leaned against the frame for a moment, and continued down the corridor, the smell of sweat, dirt, and mold making him cringe. The climb to the fourth floor winded him, and his legs burned. Malice's hands struggled to open his bedroom door.

It was quiet, cold, and dark. Kiran wasn't here tonight. So badly had Malice wanted to see him. His knees almost buckled from disappointment, but he forced himself to take a step and close the door.

Glancing toward his desk to see if Magnus had replied yet, he crashed onto his bed like a sack of potatoes. His clothes rubbed against his skin, the sensation of sludge and gravel, but he didn't have the energy to change. As he turned onto his back, he wished there were a window or mural on the ceiling or wall, something more interesting to look at. He didn't know, however, what he would want. Perhaps he would let Kiran pick. They could both enjoy the sleepless nights then.

The subtle roar of the waves crashing against rocks while bugs hummed, and the leaves rustled, returned to Malice's senses, soothing him some. He had grown used to the star-dusted sky and the bright moon washing everything in light blue. Grown used to the muggy heat, not that he liked it, and the multitude of smells he couldn't quite place.

One day, this castle would have hundreds of windows, so he could stare at the evening sky, count the stars, or guess the shapes of clouds as they drifted by.

Recorded Truth
XX

In Holister's place sat an old woman, taller than those who sat beside her, her legs unable to fit under the table like Yoon Woo's. Her name was Yeong-Suk Dahl, Magnus's regent for the time being. He talked very little of her in his letters. Her hair was silver, wiry, going past her broad shoulders. Her skin was tan and leathery, her jawline sagging. Yeong-Suk's attire was simple, two layers of clothes—the bottom a dark sapphire blue and the top robe folded across her chest was the color of snow edged with gold.

Gareth stood on her left, his midnight sky hair oiled back, his expression stern. Magnus was to her right, his face thinner, and there was a darkness to his features. Malice's heart ached for him, yet danced at the sight of him. He must be exhausted. Worse, Malice could do nothing for him like he could with Kiran or Zephyrus. He knew how to make them feel better, but not Magnus.

Not long after the rulers began talking, Malice bolted. The library underneath the Barren Circle had to have more books, like the one about archangels and devils. With how huge it was, how couldn't it? Recently, he got to the devil's portion of the book and his curiosity was piqued. What else could he learn from the archive?

Candles lit the enormous library, which was as he left it from the year prior. The candlesticks were halfway melted in their candelabras, pillars of wax touching the surface they sat on. The books he stacked were still on the table to the right of the archway. Running his fingers over the cover of a book, it was dusty. If anyone had been down here in the past year, all they did was look around.

Malice went off to the section of books he could read, plucking three down from the over-packed shelves carefully, so nothing toppled over. He flipped through them, looking for damaged pages. Luckily, none did.

At the same table, chair loosely pushed in, Malice froze as a set of cautious feet came down the stairwell. The silence amplified the thumping of his heart. Maybe it was Felim. Maybe he'd grown tired of Malice's antics. None of the rulers seemed to mind Malice's absence. He assumed most actually preferred it that way since he was a child. The footsteps stopped at the archway. Malice's gaze jerked to the book in front of him and he opened it, the smell of old paper wafting. He couldn't help himself, though, and peeped at the stairwell.

Sparkly eyes wide, mouth open, Magnus took in the massive cavern of the library. Malice blinked. Of all people, he didn't think Magnus would've followed him. Without his father, Malice realized, he wouldn't get in trouble.

Magnus's attire was blue like the ocean, gold stars and crescent moons scattered on the surface, gold lining the collar and cuffs. He silently made his way over, still gawking at the shelves, coves of books and scrolls, and the trinkets masking the multitude of tables. He pulled out the chair across from Malice, gingerly sat down, looked at the stack of books, and slid the top one in front of him.

For a moment, Malice considered asking why he was here. Did he want to talk? If he did, Malice would shove the books aside to listen. Would he tell anyone about the library? Malice shook off his doubt. This was Magnus he was thinking about. He wouldn't rat Malice out, just like he wouldn't rat Magnus out. They were friends. Malice didn't say anything, and instead smiled, reading his own book. It was nice to be in Magnus's presence again.

Compared to most of the books he'd seen, this one seemed relatively new. Only had a handful of scuffs and scratches on the leather, the pages untainted by grubby hands. Past the beginning of blank pages, he recognized the name of the first title. *Florence Ezhil*, the founding ruler of Florence's Region. Draga switched between games of strategy and lessons about history during his studies, tossing in a few lies to throw him off. It was frustrating.

He skimmed over about twenty pages until he reached the next chapter, titled *Jared Boon*. Another twenty pages, *Dieu Maziar, Alucard Castine*. He stopped. *Hordes Reap*. The man who ended the war of species six hundred years ago and died a century afterward alongside the other founding rulers.

Hordes Reap had no heirs, meaning his throne went to the next of kin, his cousins, Vendetta's great grandparents. Draga said that made Hordes Malice's great-great-great uncle. That was what all the history books Draga had given to him said, and it was in the books Kiran had as well.

Yet, that wasn't what was written.

Hordes Reap produced an heir with the Lady of Ryzion, Hyacinthia Valor. They had a daughter, Nyx Reap. Early in adulthood, Nyx left her life as a princess behind and that was where the information about the throne's heirs stopped. The next paragraph spoke of Hordes' last century as King of Hordes Region before moving onto *Hyeon Braxton*.

Malice wondered if the queen knew about Nyx. He also questioned how true the book was. All he'd ever read and known said it was false, yet something told him it was true. A strange feeling in the back of his mind and in the pits of his stomach. It'd probably been sitting down here for decades based on the layers of dust so thick a broom couldn't clean them, which was sort of gross. Queen Vendetta knew everything, making it unlikely she didn't know about Nyx.

Nothing about what he read made sense. The only way to prove them pretend or otherwise was by asking her highness. He doubted it would end well if he did, considering all the punishments he had and would receive for skipping the summit.

Slouching in his chair, Malice sighed, closed the book, and opened the second one. Inside his home, he had no one to go to with these questions. Not even Annabeth. Not anymore, anyway—tears stung his eyes for a second when he blinked them away. Outside, on the other hand, maybe Blodwen or Tendai knew something, maybe Issur, Zephyrus's father. The question there was, would they tell the queen? It all pointed back to Queen Vendetta.

Anger swelled in Malice's chest, bringing with it a heat that rivaled a Hordes Region summer.

Then Magnus looked up from his book and smiled warmly, every bit of anger melting. They stared at each other, Magnus's eyes a soft lilac purple. Malice's pulse slowed and the chill of the archive caressed his skin, mind clearing. He smiled back, chest brimmed with the flutters of butterflies. They continued reading in quiet, the flames flickering, the silence peaceful.

*

Why wasn't I punished?

Malice lay in bed, Kiran snoring at his side. He hadn't attended the summit. The queen should have demanded discipline. She hadn't called him to the dining hall. If not tonight, when would it come? He wouldn't get away with treating the Kings Summit like a joke. The past proved it. So, why?

He turned to his side and chewed his black nails. Kiran mentioned something about a true form before Malice was sent to

Mutuwa. He didn't believe him. Demons didn't have true forms. Inyene taught him as much. Was that another lie Malice had been fed or was Kiran right? Perhaps that was why Draga was teaching him how to lie, so he could recognize all the ones he had already been told.

It hurt a bit, like someone digging their finger into his flesh, to know his family hadn't been truthful. His annoyance was stronger. He couldn't see the point in anything the queen or his siblings were doing to him. If Malice was so useless, why keep training him? If he was so pathetic, why continue sending him to the summit? If he was so much of a burden, they'd had plenty of opportunities to let him die.

The more he thought about it, the more his throat closed, suffocating him, chest caving.

The answers were somewhere. Malice simply had to look… had to be *willing* to look. He wasn't too sure if he was ready to confront whatever he might find, like how he wasn't ready to sleep without fireflies.

Gaining an Equal
XXI

From head to toe, Malice wore stiff, uncomfortable clothes, raven black accenting wine red in multiple stuffy layers. His outfit reminded him of Sok's and Rayen's when it was time for them to choose their first swords.

The mirror reflected a prince, a ridiculous prince. Annabeth stood behind him, using a comb to lather oil in Malice's hair, slicking it back. Her dull orange and silver hair was braided into a bun. It had been quite some time since he last saw her. There were bags under her eyes, and a hollowness to her cheeks. Even the freckles dusting her cheeks and nose seemed to have faded.

He averted his eyes.

Hair done, Annabeth stepped backward as Malice rose. The layers of clothing were already too warm for his liking. The first comprised his undergarments and a strange fitted shirt stopping below his chin, trousers, and a ruffled shirt. Then a two-piece corset beneath a cape flaring past his knees cuffed to his shoulders, each patterned with silver swords, roses, and swirls of vines.

It took an hour to get dressed. Malice was glad he did *not* have to dress up often.

Each step in the corridor was an annoying sharp click thanks to his heeled shoes. Annabeth led the way, trekking down four flights of stairs. Sighing, Malice's eyes wandered to the lofty ceilings, beams of black creating an ornate design that made him dizzy if he stared too long.

Shevanti explained what he should do and the process of the Royal's Ceremony. She also gave him a list of names and titles he needed to memorize a few days ago. What he didn't understand was why he couldn't hold up the list and read from it. The entire ordeal would be easier if that were the case. He memorized it, nevertheless. Probably.

The great hall had fewer royals than it did five years ago—less than seventy. Behind him stood King Emil and Felim, then Draga, Inyene, Odovacar, and their first swords. If they were still alive, Sok and Rayen would have stood next to Odovacar. Alkeim was close, near the edge of the platform between him and his siblings, his outfit not quite matching his bulky frame.

Nothing had changed.

His eyes swept over the royals. Malice had called each of their names, surprised he had recited them all. Of course, with the ceremony over, if someone were to ask him to repeat five of them, he wouldn't be able to. Most had simply gained a new pin; a handful had become knights. Fewer looked older than Draga, but none were as young as Magnus, who was fifteen.

"Choose," the queen, standing behind Malice, said, her bitter voice echoing into the great hall.

A shiver raced through his body. Focusing on the royals made him forget she was there, but now he was all too aware of her. She never had punished him after the Kings Summit. The thought weighed heavily on his mind. *When will it come? How? Why has she waited so long?* Malice didn't dare ask anyone because a part of him was rather happy her highness had let it go.

Malice gazed at the royals once more. Names—as he predicted—eluded him like he hadn't spent the last few days reading and rereading them, committing them to memory. Perhaps he could say he didn't want one. That posed two problems. The queen's anger and Malice would pass up the opportunity to get help. He needed someone on his side who had the capability of walking freely around the castle and kingdom. No responsibilities. Both were a privilege he hadn't received and likely wouldn't. Someone who didn't need to report every little thing to the queen, if anything at all. There were too many mysteries, too many questions to answer. He needed eyes and ears of his own.

"Eunice Baklav," he said the moment it entered his mind.

From the middle row on the right side, a short beastman made her way down the aisle, which split the room. Malice instantly recognized her. She was one of the few who became a knight, a shiny gold brooch on her chest. Eunice's features were rounded, pudgy, her skin a rich brown like black tea, her hair like an inky cloud. Reaching the first step of the platform, Eunice bowed, lowering herself to one knee, her head dipped.

Malice glanced over his shoulder. Queen Vendetta's expression was cynical. He assumed she had not wanted him to have a first sword, but didn't want to diverge from tradition. Or maybe she truly didn't like Eunice. Either way, satisfaction rooted in Malice's stomach, blooming into his chest.

Jaw clenching, her highness turned. "Dismissed."

A wave of whispers flooded the room, royals confused but unwilling to disobey as they started filing out of the great hall. The most confused out of everyone was Eunice, her head moving between Malice and the queen at the other entrance, the end trail of her dress kissing the floor.

Eunice remained still, so Malice took the chance to study her. She was muscular but not bulky like Basia, the Queen of Zeldine's Region. With no weapon on her person, she probably fought with magic or her fists. More likely, she left her weapon behind for the ceremony. A glint of silver caught his eye, leading to her left hand where a band shimmered on her ring finger. Alkeim had a ring like that, too.

The room emptied in a matter of minutes. Malice let his shoulders drop.

"You can stand now," he told Eunice, and, still in a daze, she rose. "We'll talk in my room."

She nodded questioningly. Malice strutted toward the exit, footsteps following him. Knowing it was Eunice behind him didn't stop the anxiety wriggling through his veins. With a breath, he peeked at her, and, to his relief, Eunice's attention was elsewhere. He slowed to walk beside her, hands tensing and stretching at his sides, bones and muscles rolling beneath the surface.

Eunice entered his bedchamber while Malice lit the candles scattered about the room and closed the door. She looked around, her posture stiff. Malice strode past and dragged the chair from his desk closer to his bedside. Frame squeaking as he sat, he gestured to her seat. "Sit and speak quietly."

Hesitantly, she crossed the room, settling into the chair as if it were going to bite her. It wasn't. He sat in it enough times to know for certain. So had Kiran and Zephyrus. Neither of them were ever bitten.

"What did you call me here for, my prince?" Eunice asked after a moment of contemplation.

He said, "We need to swear an oath to one another, don't we?"

Narrowing her dark eyes, Eunice inclined her head.

"You'll be my bodyguard for a while."

"And that would be my honor," she replied.

"Sure," he said dismissively. He didn't believe it based on the lack of change in her demeanor. That was something else Draga had taught him. "I need ears, eyes, and an extra set of hands."

"Gathering information," Eunice said, "is a part of the job description, my prince."

"You won't question me?" He raised an eyebrow.

"Why should I? I was chosen for the honor of becoming your first sword. Whatever you need of me, I will do to the best of my abilities."

Malice looked her up and down. "Even if it meant angering the queen?"

Eunice didn't answer right away, though her body went rigid, a ripple of terror before she reined it in. Everyone reacted like that when her highness was mentioned, including Malice. Especially him. Admittedly, it wasn't so bad now. Fear was there, clawing at his insides like those wolf-bears in Mutuwa, but calmer and half of the time swapped with an immense, nearly unbearable rage.

"What information do you want to find?" she asked.

"Things don't align," he said vaguely. "I'm not comfortable telling you anything yet." Not that he had learned much.

"But you plan to tell me?"

"Yes. Keeping you in the dark would be pointless when I need your eyes most of all." Eventually, Malice would tell her, hopefully soon. Trust, however, came first. He needed to know she was on his side.

Deep in thought, Eunice sat there, unmoving for a time, silence heavy between them. Then she straightened her back, sat forward in the chair, and stated, "I swear to become your first sword."

Extending his hand, Malice motioned for Eunice to give him hers, and she did. He slid his nail across her palm; her eyebrows twitched. He cut his as well, blood welling from both. First, taking his blood and smearing it in hers, Malice marked her forehead. A simple line at the center of her forehead going to the bridge of her nose. It wasn't proper, but it would work for them.

"Do the same to me," he said.

Frantically, jaw dropping, she shook her head. "I can't."

He paused, peeked at their hands, and looked at Eunice's dumbfounded expression. "Right now, we are equals."

As if to say something else, her lips parted but sealed again in an instant, sights darting to her right. "Why?" she asked instead.

Because, if I'm not considered a prince by the queen, how can I be anyone else's? "Because I have little power and influence. I'm a child. I can't give you anything in return besides my oath to be on your side if you'll be on mine."

He thought of Alkeim and Felim, of Aglaia and Xenon. Their free will had been taken from them. Familiar with the reflection in the mirror, Malice knew they were following orders because they were scared. Above all else, he refused to become like her highness. He wouldn't have his first sword obey his commands because she feared him. He wanted her to trust him and believe in him.

After several quiet moments, the candles casting a steady, undisturbed light, Eunice shifted. She dragged her thumb over Malice's palm and marked his forehead. A single line just like hers.

"One day," Eunice said, her voice soft, "I hope to be someone you can rely on."

Uncomfortable in his own skin, Malice swallowed, needing to look away, but didn't break their eye contact. "I hope to become a worthy prince."

Malice wasn't used to the awkward silence of strangers; he was used to the unnerving solace of Draga's study or his bedchamber when Kiran wasn't there.

"For now," Malice said, "you're dismissed."

She rose, bowed, and stepped away from the chair, heading for the door. The cut on Malice's hand regenerated as Eunice stepped into the hallway and the blood on his forehead was crusting.

The First of Many
XXII

"A group of bandits is running amuck in the northeast, near the border. You seven will resolve the issue." On top of her throne of black crystals, Queen Vendetta glared down at the six royals kneeling before her and Malice. Alkeim stood by the throne, hands behind his back. If his face couldn't gain anymore worry-induced wrinkles, Malice's skin couldn't get any paler.

"With all due respect, your highness," Toussaint said, an angel with black wings and scars wherever skin peeked through clothes. "How are we supposed to bring a child with us?" Toussaint glanced at Malice, his eyes narrowing for a split second. He snapped his head away.

If it made the angel feel better, Malice didn't want to go, either.

"You leave in three days." Tone and expression contemptuous, her posture was poised, an imposing statue of grace and cruelty.

"Yes, your highness." Toussaint, alongside his Squad of five royals, rose, conveyed their respects to the queen, and left.

"This is an opportunity to prove useful, mutt," she said, her voice cold and harsh. "Do not waste it."

"Yes, your highness." Once he got to his feet, Malice bowed at the waist, copying Toussaint, and promptly took his leave—the sooner he got out of that suffocating room, the better.

His hands shook at his sides, his heart hammering. He would get to see more of the region outside the path he always traveled to reach Dun Raik. Flutters tickled his chest at the thought. They might explore the kingdom a bit! Based, however, on the glare Toussaint shot him, he doubted it. Excitement cooling, he wondered how long the mission would last. How dangerous would it be? Would he make it back or was the queen intending for his death, like she had with Mutuwa?

If it were the latter, Malice wanted to return so he could rub it in her face afterward. Not that he would say anything, of course. He could hardly hold eye contact, let alone speak freely to her. Still, his mere existence might annoy her a little if this was meant to kill him and didn't.

It had been two months since Eunice became Malice's first sword. During the day, she roamed about the castle, helping the servants with random tasks or at the training grounds. Malice had asked her to do it, asked her to goad any information on the queen she could. So far, whatever the servants spoke of, which was usually very little, was common knowledge. Useless. Malice had Eunice make nice with the servants all the same. One was bound to know something, and one was bound to spill if there was someone trustworthy to spill the information to. That someone would be Eunice.

Malice hoped it would eventually be him, but he didn't have the time, not when he was busy with Draga, Odovacar, Inyene, and now the mission. He had very little time to spend with Kiran and Zephyrus.

Through the castle's archway, Malice made his way to the stone wall, the grass damp and the violets and daisies budding. Fast moving dark clouds rumbled overhead, the salty smelling wind whistling in Malice's ear. He passed the spot where he and Kiran had met, the memory hazy.

Then Malice was on the rolling plains, saturated with blooming flowers and untamed grass. Mutuwa was a dark stain on the land, a wall of danger on the horizon. Yet, there was some beauty, like the clearing he'd found near the cliff-side. It would be the only thing he would return to should he ever go back.

Into the forest, he trekked to the Pretorius cottage. The outside was the same as it was six years ago when he first saw it. Moss covered the foundation and roof, rounded windows made the house look like a cross-eyed toad. Further into the woods, four raised garden beds provided fruit, vegetables, and herbs all year round. Malice had struggled to pull a carrot the size of his forearm out of the dirt, landing on his butt once he did. Kiran had laughed so hard he sent himself into a hacking fit and hadn't stopped for a while.

Malice knocked. Soon enough, footsteps sounded, unhurried and soft, probably Blodwen's. Kiran stomped wherever he went. He learned it from Tendai, who was also heavy-footed.

The door creaked open. "Malice." Blodwen smiled. "Come on in, sweetheart. I made some fresh tea and sweetmeats."

"Is Kiran here?" Malice asked hastily.

"No, but you can still enjoy a cup of—"

"That's all right," Malice interrupted, his gaze fixed on the floorboards and Blodwen's toes sparkling with bronze rings. "I only came to tell him something."

"I can relay the message for you. What is it?"

He stood there like a statue while thunder boomed and lightning cracked across the sky. *This is an opportunity to prove useful, mutt. Do not waste it.*

He was going to die.

The cottage and Blodwen swayed. Malice's mouth went bone

dry, his blood stopping, a chill goose-bumping his skin.

"Malice?"

The queen really *did* want to kill him. Truly, once and for all. He couldn't think straight. The only thing he knew was he didn't want to go on that mission. At least he could still see Kiran and Zephyrus if he were locked up in the castle.

Malice turned and ran the way he came, his feet drumming on the forest floor as Blodwen called after him. Raindrops started to fall, hitting Malice's face as it gradually came down heavier. Twigs and rocks jabbed the bottom of his feet, but he didn't care. His chest was heavy and his guts twisted, making him nauseous and lightheaded.

Out of breath, feet aching, lungs burning, Malice flung his bedroom door open and slammed it shut. He pressed his back against the cold wood, sliding down to the floor, sopping wet.

"Malice?" a quiet, panicky voice said.

To his feet, Malice shoved his hand out in front of him as a ball of fire erupted in his palm. Kiran stood defensively next to Malice's bed. His big brown eyes were searching, and his posture was slumped. Malice immediately eased and planted his bum on the marble floor again.

"I'm sorry." Kiran took a step forward. "I didn't mean to startle you."

Flicking the fire in his hand to the candles around the room, Malice sighed, shadows dancing beyond his bed and in the closet. He forced his eyes to his legs, fearful if he stared too long, the shadows would come to life. Kiran crossed the room and bent down in front of Malice, sitting, so their feet and legs touched.

"What's wrong? You look pale." He tilted his head. "And you're soaked."

Malice ground his teeth as he studied the square patterns on Kiran's shirt for a moment and breathed in the smell of herbs, which distracted him some. "I'm going on a mission in three days."

Kiran gasped, then grabbed Malice's shoulders, fingers tight around his flesh. "But why?"

Head, heart, core; always remember those three points. Abruptly, Inyene loomed over Kiran, smirking, arms crossed. *If, for whatever reason, those places aren't so accessible.* She crouched and rested a hand on Kiran's shoulder, Malice shuddering as if the touch transmitted to him. *Tire them out, drain them of blood and magic, make it painful, Malice.*

"… To kill…" Malice realized, the words churning his stomach. "I don't know if I will survive." He wasn't a murderer like Inyene. He didn't enjoy seeing others in pain, watching the agony contort their faces so badly they become unrecognizable. Hesitation, as Odovacar liked to remind him, would get him killed in actual combat and that probably meant he wasn't a good fighter, either.

"No! You will survive and you'll—"

"If I don't survive," Malice said in a louder but shaky voice, "then everything I have is yours."

"It won't be," he protested. "I don't want anything of yours because you *will* come back, and you *will* be fine."

"Please." Malice looked at Kiran. "Everything that is mine will be yours, so please just take it." There was no choice in this. He had to go, no matter how much he wished he could hide somewhere and pretend her highness truly cared for him. It might ultimately be better to pretend he had a different *mother* altogether. One who didn't require him to choose between ending his own life or someone else's.

He couldn't think of any other reason the queen would send him on a mission outside the kingdom. Perhaps it was to learn to work with a Squad, fight alongside others, or how to apply theory to practice, but he could do all of those things while patrolling the streets of Hordes Kingdom. Draga said he would start there once he was old enough. She had promised him. Said it was possible he would be stationed with Zephyrus.

Liars! Every one of them! Malice didn't understand. Lying felt horrible. He hated it. Why would they keep doing it to him? Was it so hard to speak the truth?

"I refuse." Kiran scooted closer and moved their legs side-by-side. "I don't want you to die." He wrapped his arms around Malice and squeezed.

Malice squirmed, trying to shove Kiran away. It felt like an insult to be pitied. An even bigger insult to reject the damn offer outright when they were brothers. But Kiran's grip didn't lessen.

"Let go of me," he said through clenched teeth, his words a tremble. If he wouldn't accept what Malice was giving him, why should he accept his hug?

"No," Kiran said.

With a huff, Malice gave up. The run from Kiran's cottage to his bedchamber tired him out. There was no more strength in his limbs or his mind. Besides, he didn't want to hurt Kiran accidentally with his thrashing.

Tears welled and overflowed. "I don't want to die." Malice gripped the back of Kiran's shirt and Kiran's hold tightened. "I don't want to die." *I don't want to kill.*

It was all that filled his head.

I don't want to die. I don't want to kill.

Every shuddering breath hurt. Malice couldn't explain the type of pain it was. Kiran sobbed into Malice's shoulder, his tears and snot further soaking his shirt, but Malice did the same to Kiran's.

I don't want to become like Mother.

*

"My mission is in two days," Malice told Eunice, who stood at the doorframe. The idea still felt like swallowing a handful of nails. Bawling in Kiran's arms last night allowed him to gather whatever will and composure he had. Which wasn't much, if he were being honest.

Her jaw went slack, her eyes searching Malice's. He looked away, a tightness in his chest burning his throat.

"You won't be coming. I'll be traveling with Toussaint and his Squad to the northeast. Apparently, bandits have been causing trouble."

At a loss for words, Eunice stared at Malice. "What do you want me to do here?"

He was glad she didn't protest like Kiran had. He hardly had enough courage to tell her as it was.

"Nothing really." Malice glanced over his shoulder at his desk, at the open letter from Magnus he had yet to reply to. "If I don't return, I want you to become Kiran's first sword, or at least something like his protector."

"Who?"

"The beastman that's always around. Blodwen and Tendai's son, Kiran Pretorius."

Her eyebrows jumped, like she finally understood who Malice was talking about. "Is he important?"

"He is my brother," he said defensively.

"… Is that all?"

"Yes."

Eunice dipped her head. "Then I wish you the best of luck, Prince Malice."

Malice smiled weakly as Eunice turned around and left.

The First of Many
"Taste of Freedom"

The air was muggy, like hot breath sticking to the back of Malice's neck. Morning songbirds sang all around the paddocks in the west, the dovecotes greyish mounds against the exterior of the castle, the training grounds in the distance to the north.

Malice watched Toussaint and his royals saddle their horses, two of which would tow a wagon of supplies—tents, food, ale, and fur bedrolls from what he could see so far.

The horses were big, muscular, their manes and tails cut short or braided. They didn't look to have been bred for speed, but for transporting goods over long distances. Albeit, Malice knew little about horses. He had never ridden one either.

"Who am I riding with?" Malice asked when he walked over and admired the mount's shiny, dark brown coat, while Toussaint threw a rug over the horse's back, then a saddle.

Eyebrow perched, Toussaint glanced down at him. "You'll be walking, so try to keep up," he said with a laugh. "We won't stop or slow down for you."

As Toussaint fastened some straps across the animal's underside, Malice stormed off. Not that he went too far.

If he could control it, he would bring his wings out and fly above them. There were some aspects of his true form he could control, his nails being one of them and his horns, neither serving any real purpose. His tail had come out randomly during his spars with

Odovacar, as if it had a mind of its own.

Soon enough, mounted and ready with two horses hooked up to the wagon, Toussaint was at the front, his royals were on either side of the cart, and one was in the rearguard.

The Squad trotted through the courtyard into the kingdom streets, Malice trailing behind them. The roads were granite, dull and roughly textured underneath his shoes. People moved out of the way, most smiling, waving, and sending well wishes to the knights as they passed. Houses and shops were built of clay, red or sand white, dark timber framing them. Every dozen paces or so was a metal lamppost, a lantern with a candle inside. He never grew tired of seeing Hordes Kingdom from the carriage but, to witness the people and buildings, the smells and noises outside four walls were enough to make Malice's chest flutter.

It was huge, roads stretching beyond his view. Pointed roofs that twinned the castle's sharp, melancholy architecture jutted above the houses and establishments. Malice spotted a few people who frowned, mumbled, or cursed something under their breath before turning away or glowering at the head of the group. He shared their sentiments. Toussaint was a jerk. At the same time, without him, Malice wouldn't have been able to see his own kingdom.

When they reached the open plains and meadows of long grass and wildflowers, Toussaint broke for the northeast toward rolling hills and the Nameless Lake. Malice, dumbfounded for a brief second, ran. The sun's intensity differed from what it was at the training grounds or in Hordes Kingdom's streets, instantly burning his throat and lungs, forcing him to squint to keep an eye on the Squad as they sped off. They inched further and further out of sight. Malice struggled through the reeds that smacked him relentlessly. He knew they would be gone in no time and hoped he could follow their trail of disturbed grass.

*

The moon was high in the star-dusted sky by the time Malice caught a glimmer of orange light.

Toussaint's makeshift camp looked like heaven. Smelled like it too.

Malice wobbled toward it, his legs both numb and on fire. His breathing was haggard and shallow, wheezy, as if he'd caught the fever. Collapsing near the crackling blaze, Malice was too tired to make a face at the snorting royals around him. Then his stomach roared, which caused the royals to laugh harder and his face to flush. No matter, it felt good to let his muscles utterly give out and completely relax in the soft greenery of the land.

Malice could have fallen asleep right there if someone hadn't tossed a waterskin in front of him. Licking his chapped lips, he snatched it, unscrewed the top, and guzzled until he swallowed wrong and started hacking. The royal to his left chuckled some more, whacking Malice on the back, Malice spluttering. His back stung now. The same person handed him a steaming roasted pig leg.

Malice's mouth watered, his stomach leaping for joy. He hadn't eaten since that morning. But he hesitated and peeked at Toussaint.

"Your reward." The angel grinned from across the fire. "For keeping up with us. Or at least finding us at the end of the day." Laughter rose within the small group once more.

Scowling, Malice sank his teeth into the pig's leg. Juices exploded over his tongue, the tender flesh tearing easily. Each bite was quicker than the last, wetness streaming down his chin. The last time he ate this ravenously was after Mutuwa. He probably looked like Kiran right now.

The pain of hunger subsided some. Thankfully. Malice looked up at the group and threw the bone into the fire, embers shooting into the air. They passed along another skin, each taking a long savoring draught.

"Here kid." The one who passed him the pig's leg offered the skin to Malice—Buhle was his name.

He was a fairy, his translucent wings shimmering in the firelight, his hair a fair pink. His skin was just as pale but spotted with dark tan patches. Frame large and muscular, he reminded Malice of Alkeim.

He took the skin, sniffed the spout, sipped, and spat it out. It was disgusting. He thrust the drink to the next person, aggressively wiping his mouth to rid his lips of the taste. The ale was strong, yeasty like dough with a tang he didn't care for—too much like the moldy bread he ate in the dungeons.

To his right sat Iqaluk, who gave the skin to Duncan. Iqaluk was a barbarian fishman hybrid, tattoos covering his entire face. His ears were webbed with spines poking out like fins, his fingers were as well. Through his sheer shirt, it looked like someone had carved the flesh out of his ribs to create gills. Iqaluk was thinner, his muscles wiry and woven underneath his scaly skin.

Duncan leaned back into his arms, his legs stretched out before him. He was half beastman, half orc, his body fuzzy with an abundance of dark curly hair. Top and bottom canines protruded from his mouth at all times, the bottom more like tusks, while the top resembled a howler's—the wolf-bears Malice had seen in Mutuwa, Kiran had shown him. Duncan's grey-blue eyes bulged when the ale was returned to him, and he gulped down the remainder.

Next to Toussaint, Malice observed the other demon in the group, her skin green like the grasshoppers he and Kiran found in the forest. Her jet-black hair was wavy, two sets of horns sprouting from the sides of her head. The front most set went to the back of her head and the bottom curled around her ears. Tumelo. She was pretty, Malice guessed, her features softer than Draga's or the queen's, her eyes the same dark red as the castle's walls.

But she wasn't as pretty as Magnus.

Finally, between Tumelo and Buhle, there was the dwarf, Sonam. They were shorter than Malice—and he hadn't hit a growth spurt yet, as Kiran liked to remind him. Their expression was a permanent scowl, whether they smiled or not. With their legs crossed, one hand on their knee, the other gesturing wildly in the air, they told a tale of the beasts they had slain. Their hair was braided in three sections to their nape, gold ornaments dangling around their face, and gold jewelry around their neck, wrists, and ankles. Seemed too flashy for a mission, but what did Malice know?

"Let's get some shuteye," Toussaint said, tearing Malice from Sonam. "We've a long day ahead of us."

Knee as his aid, Toussaint rose, stretched his arms and wings as far as they could, his inky wings eventually flapping closed. He turned on his heel and headed for the biggest tent, everyone else, Tumelo putting the fire out, quick to follow.

Malice fell back, the cold earth comforting. He tried connecting the dots of white in the sky and create figures, so he could show them to Kiran and Zephyrus, maybe Magnus too. One was a five-petaled flower. Kiran would like that one. He found a sword next, then a book—or a rectangle, but Malice liked to think of it as a book. On and on he went until sleep finally took him.

Fog encased the ground, making everything damp, including Malice. He was the first to rise, the sky still dark and the camp quiet. The horses were standing a little ways from the tents, motionless. Was that how they slept?

After a time, Malice got to his feet and fell right back down, his legs turned into a puddle. Despite his lack of surprise, he frowned. Eyes darting from one pitched canvas to the next, he landed on the mostly empty wagon.

The Squad wasn't awake.

He crawled toward the cart. The grass stains would be a pain to get out later. He would have to apologize to Shevanti and Annabeth.

When he reached the wagon, Malice pulled himself up and used the bed as a brace. At the corner there was a folded cowhide to cover the supplies during rainstorms. As he climbed onto the bed, the wagon creaked. He froze, whipping around. No movement. Up the rest of the way, Malice chose his spot in the corner and sat on top of the cowhide.

He would absolutely not be running again today. Even if he wanted to, he doubted his legs would allow him. Besides, he was small, so he wouldn't add much more weight for the horses to haul. No matter what way Malice thought about it, he would be the one most inconvenienced. The tents would squash him when they were packed. Toussaint would likely get a laugh out of that, and so would the others.

Birds and insects were as noisy as ever come morning when the dew lay thick on the grass from the fog. Everyone woke around the same time, coming out of their tents, quickly relieving themselves, and getting to work.

Buhle cooked, reigniting last night's charred logs with a skillet sitting on the flames. Sonam helped Toussaint take down the tents and fold them up, while Duncan did the task on his own. Iqaluk and Tumelo got the horses ready beyond the camp, rounded them up, gave them water, and brought them to the wagon. Before loading everything onto the cart, the Squad sat down to eat what looked like oats, bread, and cheese.

The smell wafted every so often toward Malice, his stomach growling. He willed it to be silent. Not that it ever listened.

When they finished, the dirty skillet was tucked behind a crate of perfectly smooth rectangular rocks. Buhle winked at Malice as he walked to his horse. Malice hunkered down, brows furrowing. If someone were going to move him, he wouldn't go without a fight. The rest started piling up their supplies on the wagon's bed, which forced Malice to bring his legs up to his chest.

Toussaint strode past and dropped a hunk of bread in Malice's lap, a smirk on his face. Malice glared at him but said nothing and ate his food. It was better than being thrown off. Or given nothing to eat.

The wagon rocked into motion. Malice clutched the side of it, his knuckles turning white, so he wouldn't fall off. Duncan rode alongside him, his horse keeping with the cart, Sunam on the opposite side, Buhle, and Tumelo at the head, and Iqaluk in the rear. Same formation they left in.

Clouds gathered in the east, the easy breeze carrying a salty mist. Their pace was as measured as the Squads. Malice relaxed some and no longer held the wagon's side like a vise. Excitement gradually returning, he felt comfortable enough to turn in place and gaze at the land. Draga once said there weren't many farms because of the type of soil in Hordes, so flowers of all colors pricked the hills, grass undulating like long hair on a windy day. Out here, the air was fresh. The sun, blinding and harsh as it was yesterday, wasn't so bad, either.

Malice settled his chin on his forearm resting on the wagon's edge and glanced behind them. The castle speared the sky, black daggers reducing to needles the further they got. In front of them, however, the Nameless Lake was a broadening line of slate blue, towering beyond it was the city of Estera. Malice ignored his left. He knew what lay in the west.

Humming reached his ears over the rhythm of hooves and the creaking of the cart. He peeked over his shoulder as Sonam bobbed their head and rocked back and forth with their melody.

"Lest you grow such mighty horns," they sang, voice hearty and rough, "I'll not fear your bullheadedness! Till you grow your promised fangs and claws, I'll not give you your reprieve!" They continued their little jig, and Malice went back to the open grasslands.

"For I've seen your kind all too often," Buhle joined and was much more pleasant to listen to.

Then Tumelo added her voice, a high melody complimenting the others. "So take your strength, your grit, your pride and throw it to the howling winds."

Let the earth swallow you whole and spit you out,

For I am your end and salvation,

Lest you grow your wings and take to the heavens,

Oh, mighty beast, shall you be cast down,

So I might begin the chase once more.

From there, the song's lyrics repeated, the entire Squad singing along with Sonam. Malice didn't not like it, but he found it strange, nothing like the lullabies or stories Annabeth had told him. His favorite was *the black throne*, only realizing it was his favorite because of Annabeth when Shevanti tried telling the tale and Malice didn't enjoy it the same.

Bloated, dark clouds turned day into night. The wind growing stronger and chillier, a low whine turning to a sharp whistle. The landscape hadn't changed much: rolling meadows, scattered trees, a pond, a river to trot beside for a short while. Hordes Region was a relatively flat realm, no mountains, only hills.

In the distance, there was a silhouette against the horizon of a tower, and a shorter building surrounding it, another one off to the right. Toussaint called a halt when it was spotted, and everyone dismounted to break camp. Malice did too, since his legs finally decided to work.

"We'll plan to ambush them tomorrow night," Toussaint said as he pet the bridge of his horse's nose.

Tents were laid flat against the ground instead of pitched, while, once they were stripped of their saddles, the horses were let loose to graze. Malice assumed it was to make them appear wild instead of tamed. They started a small fire, enough to provide some light, maybe cook a fish or two, but no bigger. The tall grass and hills would help protect them from being seen, but it was no wall.

The Squad sat on a canvas with cards in their hands, bowls of food between them, a waterskin regularly moving around. Malice was also given a bowl of food earlier; he'd gobbled it up in minutes.

Lifting his head when a gust swept through, the scent of rain was heavy. He quite liked the smell. Although, it would make things difficult come tomorrow.

Malice looked back toward the camp, gaze falling on Toussaint. His eyes were a sea of white and nothing else, as all full-blooded angels were. Unlike most angels, however, his wings were burnt black—it was rare for an angel to have dark wings, let alone black ones—big, easily twice his height, feathery, and sprawled out behind him as if he were shielding his Squad. His build resembled Odovacar's, lean, muscular, but Toussaint was taller, his legs longer than his torso.

The Squad was friendly like Malice, Zephyrus and Kiran were. Malice's heart suddenly ached. He flopped backward and sighed, wishing he could've brought Zephyrus for some company. He didn't think Kiran would have been so eager to join because of the purpose of their travels.

Kiran and Malice had fallen asleep on the floor the night he told Kiran about the mission. His eyes were swollen the next morning, they had stung too. Then Kiran left to go home. Later, at the training grounds, Malice told Zephyrus. His reaction was so different, it shocked Malice. Zephyrus was excited for him, jealous even. Which made sense now that he was thinking about it. Zephyrus wanted to become a royal, go on missions, protect the kingdom, and all that. Malice hadn't, yet here he was while Zephyrus was stuck in Hordes

Kingdom.

The next day, there was nothing to do but wait. At first, Malice was restless. He usually sparred with Odovacar, studied Draga's lessons, and received whatever beating Inyene had in mind.

He didn't have to do any of it.

The restlessness quickly became excitement. He was outside. No one was watching him, insulting him, or had expectations for him. The grass whipped with the breeze, bugs hopping from one green blade to the next. Flowers were abundant. He could only name a few thanks to Kiran—heather, coneflowers, daisies, lilacs, too. Beneath his bare feet, the earth was pleasantly warm, in some spots cool.

Mostly, Malice ignored Toussaint and his royals, and they ignored him. He ventured around the bowl-like landscape they were camped in because he could. It was a shame his friends weren't here to experience it with him. He would make sure they could one day.

Even without them, he felt lighter, no longer fatigued from the days of riding in the cramped wagon or running.

Malice felt good in a way he never had.

He wondered what it was called, the fluttering and dancing in his stomach and bones, not just in his chest. As he lay on his back, the sun baking his skin, the air caressing his body, he didn't think it really mattered.

Kill or be Killed
XXIII

Rectangular windows glowed yellow from the first and second floors of a barracks close to the northeastern border.

Duncan flared his cloak backward as he crouched behind Toussaint, dark fabric blanketing the ground. "The watchtower and stables are empty, save for some horses," he reported quietly.

Toussaint nodded, rose from his belly, and waded through the grass, everyone following, the foliage rustling. Clouds hid the moon, which made it extremely dark, but Malice could see well enough. After Mutuwa, his sight improved some. Probably due to his *true form,* which refused to manifest outside of inconvenient times.

The plan was simple: locate the bandits, wait a few hours for their guards to go down, then bombard them with attacks. Go wild without a care in the world or any real strategy, Malice surmised. If he were in charge, the plan would be different, efficient. Divide and conquer, a strategy Draga had taught him. He would split the seven of them up, two going into the plains and causing a racket, drawing a few of the bandits out of the hold. Two would be stationed further from the barracks for stragglers, while the last three dealt with the bandits inside.

Simple and effective. A sure way to ensure victory when outnumbered, as Draga had explained it. Malice tried to say something, too, but no one listened. Why listen to a *child*?

Drawing near, the smell of urine overpowered the saltiness in the air. Malice's nostrils flared. His heart pounded as fast as his feet moved to keep up with the Squad. How had his elation morphed into dread so quickly? *Prove yourself useful, mutt.* He hadn't done much of anything. Although, he wasn't in the way either. Maybe that was what Queen Vendetta meant, to not be a hinderance, doubtful as the idea was.

Now pressed against the side of the barracks, the rough texture of the bricks caught Malice's clothes. Toussaint gave the signal to start the assault, a double jerk of his hand toward the door. Buhle, the biggest in the Squad, rose from his crouched position, lumbered to the door, and broke it down with a grunt.

Malice flinched.

Chaos erupted inside when Buhle shouted, guttural and feral, and charged. Bangs and crashes rattling the walls eclipsed commands. Malice stayed underneath the windowsill, his breaths harder to catch.

The earth rumbled when glass shattered above him. He covered his head, shards hitting and bouncing off his arms before he darted up the hill. His feet slipped a few times underneath him and he crashed to his knees, mud stuffing his nose and mouth. He pushed himself up, spitting and blowing the dirt out, and turned.

A huge spike of wood projected from the holds roof, a body dangling off the tip like a banner, falling silently. Malice's stomach lurched into his throat. Another person crashed through the wall, skidded across the earth when they rolled to their feet and flung their hands backward, pillars of fire surging out of their palms, propelling toward the barracks.

Mind blank, Malice watched as tremors raked his body. It was loud, the screams and booms echoing. Fire spread. The barracks and tower crumbled like the stick castles he and Kiran had built in the forest. Horses dashed up the hills, their wails more horrific than a howler's, curls of smoke glowing red on their backs.

The rain was abrupt and heavy, thunder booming, and instantly soaked Malice's clothes. He wanted to run—he *should* run while the Squad was busy. By the time they realized he was gone, it would be too late—but he couldn't peel his eyes off the destruction of the barracks. Amazed at how a building of stone, mortar, and timber could be so easily wrecked, Malice was hardly aware of the gradual hush descending upon the hills.

Six people strutting out of the decrepitude building broke him out of his stupor like a smack to the back of the head.

"It's time to do you part, runt," Toussaint barked as he led his royals closer and closer toward Malice, firelight licking their backsides, darkening the shadows on their faces.

Breath hitching, Malice scrambled backward. The job was done. They hadn't needed him. He didn't want to go down there. "I don't want to."

For a moment, when he stopped in front of Malice, Toussaint seemed to wrestle with that. His jaw clenched repeatedly, expression twitching from one emotion to the next until he landed on something cold and resolute.

"I will not risk the lives of my royals for you," he said, hand reaching for Malice's collar. "You should know by now; her highness keeps her promises."

Toussaint yanked Malice off the hill as he struggled, kicking and punching the knight, swearing the curses he'd heard others use. He *did* know that, and he knew it well. He'd lost his hands, starved in a dungeon, was thrown in Mutuwa. This was her punishment for the last summit. It had to be, and it was all the more reason he regretted not running when he had the chance.

They swiftly reached the hold being swallowed by hungry

flames and Toussaint, huffing, tossed Malice inside like a sack of potatoes. Hitting the ground took his breath and doubled the wood planked floor. Then he stood, eyes flicking to the leftovers surrounding him. Seven of them.

He couldn't look back to check if Toussaint and the Squad were still there or had escaped. It went against everything Odovacar taught him. With a swallow of nerves, Malice needed to assess the situation the best he could, ignoring the growing talons of fear sinking into his spine. He was weaponless, outnumbered, and had zero experience. He'd never fought outside of a spar. As still as his body would allow, which was the equivalent of a leaf in a storm, Malice waited for someone to move, so he could dart through the opening and flee. What else could he do? He couldn't fight them.

He couldn't fight them *and* win.

"It's a child," one said.

"So?" another scoffed.

"Clearly, the royal bastards didn't like the child too much if they threw her into the lion's den," someone else cackled.

"Who sent you, girly?" The leader, most likely, stepped forth, eyeing Malice as she closed the distance between them in a single stride. "Which kingdom?" Her voice was husky. Age and sun left her skin leathery, tanned, and freckled. Her pulled back hair was more grey than it was brown, and her eyes were an icy blue.

"Hordes Kingdom," Malice said meekly.

"So, the queen caught wind of us, did she." The leader, grunting, swiveled. "Kill the girl. You two with me," she ordered.

Take me with you, rushed to the tip of his tongue, yet his mouth remained clamped. Anywhere was better than in Queen Vendetta's impossibly strong grasp. Legs trembling, Malice stared at her withdrawing back, unsure of what he could possibly do when horror dug into his vertebrae, paralyzing him.

Two left the circle surrounding Malice and joined their leader, leaving four to take care of him. One bandit relaxed, shoulders drooping as a smile spread across his thin lips, and walked toward Malice. The bandit's pungent odor hit him, burning his nostrils, clearing some of the disarray of his mind. There were stains all over his shirt and pants, his gut hanging out of the bottom of his shirt, rings along his fingers and pointed ears.

He swallowed, conscious of each breath he was taking.

Kill them, a voice said, rousing a memory. *Remember how good it felt?* the voice asked. Malice remembered how he pretended a training dummy was his mother, how he had killed her time and time again. Goose bumps crawled over his skin as he recalled the satisfaction it brought him.

Kill them.

Malice stepped forward. As if drunk, the man reeled in surprise. A sword of darkness materialized in his hands, magic prickling his veins, and he thrust the blade up into the bandit's head. The tip of his sword met the resistance of bone and cartilage and punctured the skull. When he yanked it free, crimson followed the blade's trail. Blood gushed from the bottom of the man's head, a river of ichor splashing onto the ground and staining his shoes. He dropped weightlessly and slumped to the pool of blood like a rag doll.

The room spun. The metallic tang of blood overwhelmed Malice. His stomach wrung itself.

Booming thunder and the rhythmic patter of rain as lightning branched across the sky permeated the silence.

He knew leaving wasn't an option yet and there wasn't much time to think. Three bandits still contained him, three more were close by. Shuffling his feet, Malice slashed the neck of the fishman to his right. They dropped to their knees, hands trying to contain the blood streaming from their throat. Malice plunged his blade into the bandit's sternum. The bandit twitched, spasmed, then collapsed, red spilling ceaselessly.

Head, heart, core, Inyene had said. *Tire them out, drain them of blood and magic, make it painful, Malice.*

The orc broke from the circle, punching the air, water following like arrows. Malice ducked, flung himself across the floor and swept his legs, knocking the bandit off his feet. Hand raised, a sword of darkness appeared above the bandit. Malice flung his arm down. The sword speared the bandit's core. As the orc spluttered and tore at his sternum, Malice got to his feet, curling his fingers. The darkness responded. It wiggled. Jerking his finger downward, it shrank as if the orc's chest absorbed his magic. With a snap of his fingers, the man's chest inflated, a soft thump, and caved.

Inyene hadn't shown or explained this… How much could he do with his magic?

The last three charged Malice. One had an axe, another, a pig beastman, summoned chunks of earth to their side, while the third drew twin swords, the latter two having detached themselves from the leader.

Axe swinging, Malice ducked, and the steel edge embedded itself into the beastman, rocks dropping with loud bangs, bone crunching. Blood sprayed. Warmth painted Malice from head to toe as the bandit howled over the other.

Despite the waves of nausea coursing through him and the violent shaking of his extremities, Malice reminded himself, *don't think about it. Kill them. Prove yourself. Live.*

Malice, teeth gritting, lunged and chopped the axe man's ankle, severing a foot. He dropped heavily, a hiss of pain escaping him. Before the man could turn, Malice stabbed the middle of his back and wrenched the blade of darkness down, cutting through organs, muscle, and bone.

Overheated and sweaty, Malice's clothes stuck to him like sap. His stomach curdled every time he glimpsed the bodies littering the floor. *Don't look. Don't look. Don't look.*

He sucked in a breath through his mouth so he didn't have to smell the blood. A shiver raked his spine. Malice spun on his heels and dodged simultaneously. A blade whistled past him, but the other slashed his chest. Pain seared and bloomed, wetness dripping along his torso. It was shallow, though, meaning it would regenerate fast. Odovacar had given worse, as had Inyene.

The giant cursed and drew back one of her blades as if connected to a string. The handle met her palm so perfectly, Malice stared in awe for a moment. As she stepped forward and swung, Malice stowed his astonishment and attacked. Their swords connected and were oddly silent. She was strong regardless of what her frail appearance let on.

No, she wasn't, Malice realized. She was using air magic to reinforce her blows, making up for her lack of strength. Each hit brought a small gust, like someone had blown on his face.

Malice charged. Startled, she staggered, quickly regained her footing, and struck once more. She may not have been as strong as Odovacar, but she was faster, and her blade work was strange, hard to follow. Her sequence of blows cut Malice's arms and abdomen as if he were a piece of meat needing the fat trimmed off.

He had calmed down a smidge, the knot of his stomach no longer unbearably tight. It helped he wasn't dealing with multiple people anymore. Their shock had benefited him, that much he knew. Had they been able to regain composure any faster, he would have been dead.

Malice saw the leader in the corner of his eye, who had done nothing so far. Which made little sense. How many times could she have taken Malice's head or gone after Toussaint? Or both? Too many to count.

The giant shouted, snatching Malice's attention, and sprinted for him. Her patience was lost. Zephyrus, more often than not, had also lost his temper during a spar. Despite pointing it out many times, Zephyrus hadn't seen it.

She thrust and whipped her swords left and right, all the while cursing at Malice. When she lifted both of her hands above her head, Malice darted, driving his black sword into the bandit's gut. She gasped. He ripped it free. Organs spilled out as she bellowed.

Malice stepped away, watching the bandit writhe on the ground, a scarlet pool expanding at an alarming rate. He didn't know blood could flow so quickly.

Slowly, turning toward the leader, she glowered fiercely back at Malice. He recognized something more in her gaze. Caution… *Is she scared of me?* Malice shivered at the thought. Ears ringing, heart thundering, the smell of ichor so was profound he gagged on it.

The leader threw her hands backward, then forward, a wall of smoke brewing like foamy waves and crashing into Malice. He collided with what was left of the wall. All the air in his lungs evaporated, and he dropped to the floor, heaving, his vision dark and hazy.

Footsteps clunked closer. She grabbed a fistful of hair, lifted Malice, and banged his head against the wall. Plaster crumbled. She doubled and tripled as his head throbbed against the cage of his skull.

Malice slammed his palms against her ears. She winced, released Malice, and staggered, fingers to the sides of her head. The leader moved them away, and they were red. With a snarl, she lashed a rope of smoke at Malice, slicing his cheek. Blood trickled down his face. Ignoring it, he hit the floor in one heaving blow, magic blasting into the earth. The ground trembled. The leader went still. A diversion.

Malice rushed her, but he wasn't fast enough. She recovered swiftly. *Damnit!* She punched the air, fists of smoke hurtling toward Malice. He leaped, tumbling, and kicked her knees with such force they gave instantly, and she fell to the floor with a hard thud.

Half-ass getting to his feet, Malice grabbed her face, his hand too small to encase more than her mouth. She gripped his forearm, nails digging in. It hurt, but at least she couldn't break his arm.

The fear he had seen earlier was entirely alone, completely overtaking everything about her expression. A fluttering sensation burst inside his chest, his head floating. He locked the feeling deep within him; he had to.

Head, heart, core.

Fire engulfed the leader's head, her screams muffled by Malice's hand as her nails created long gashes in his arm. He grimaced and resisted the urge to jerk away. Then her screams went silent, her arms falling limp to her sides. He let go. Her face was nothing but a lump of charred skin and bone. Burnt flesh, hair, and more ichor than Malice had ever wanted to see overwhelmed him, consumed him, stripped him of whatever mask he had managed to put on as he fought.

Malice stumbled backward and collapsed to his knees. Everything he had been holding down rushed to his mouth, burning his throat. He coughed and gagged. He couldn't tell where his vomit began, and the blood ended. At the stench, his stomach turned inside out again. The world flashed white as thunder boomed, shaking the barracks. The blaze had mostly been extinguished. Smoldering timber and embers dancing around raindrops stung his eyes.

I killed them. All of them. Seven people and I killed them.

He retched again.

What would Kiran say? Or Zephyrus? They would despise him! Only Magnus would understand, right? He'd had no choice when he killed his father. And Malice had had no choice tonight. He would have died if he hadn't killed them. There was no other way, right?

No one's voice comforted Malice in his mind. Who would? Especially after what he had done.

Deliberate, loud claps lanced the air. Malice startled, his eyes and head darting around the destroyed living space of the barracks. There was nothing other than the corpses and no one living outside of Malice.

"Children of darkness never cease to impress me," a voice said. It was silvery, almost sarcastic, and shrill.

Malice stared in the direction it came from, sights narrowing till the shadow grew outward. He scrambled to get away, slipping in blood. Lanky fingered hands formed, stretched, and grabbed the plaster walls. Then a foot emerged and the other, the entirety of the shadow removing itself from the corner.

"It seems you've been left all alone, child," it leered, lumbering toward Malice. "I can get you out of here, back to Hordes Kingdom long before the others."

Malice hit the wall.

Crouching, knees nearly passing its shoulders, the creature tilted its head, a face shrouded in darkness exposing itself, the features unsettlingly vague. The shadowy creatures that visited him in the dungeons and Mutuwa had long, as if weighted, simple faces with orbs of ink for eyes.

"Who are you?" Malice said through the lump in his throat. Body shivering as it was, one would think he was in the brutal cold of the north. That would be better, actually, than where he was right now.

"Who I am is of little relevance."

This isn't the queen, he told himself. "Are you my enemy?"

Despite the elusiveness of the creature's face, Malice clearly saw a grin expand as it chuckled. "For now, I would consider myself an ally."

"I want out of here then," Malice said abruptly.

He couldn't stand being surrounded by corpses anymore. People he had killed. The blood beneath him, veiling the floor, was already cool, his clothes and skin tacky with it. Iron coated the inside of his mouth. It was all he could smell, all he could see and taste and hear, as if the bandit's blood still thrummed through their veins.

"You do not wish to know why?" it questioned.

"I don't care!" Malice barked. "I just want to leave!"

A hand clamped around his wrist. Malice jumped and yanked it free. He spotted who had grabbed it. The bandit's leader, her burnt head cocked toward him.

"I'll do anything you want. Let me leave. Please!" he said and crawled toward the creature, tears threatening to fall.

The creature righted its posture and was taller than any giant or beast Malice had seen. Good thing there wasn't a roof on the barracks, not much of one anyway. Black embers shot off its body like Malice's dark magic.

The creature extended its hand. "To your feet, child."

Exhaustion was heavy in his limbs, and his head was fuzzy. "Take me outside the castle. There's a small forest to the southwest of it. Take me there instead," he pleaded.

Malice took its hand, and it hoisted him up. The creature stalked to the corner it came from, its grip firm on Malice's hand, though he didn't fight it. Until its foot disappeared into the shadow.

Digging his heels into the floor, tension rippled across his upper back and warped his stomach. The creature didn't seem to notice

Malice's piddly attempt to stop. Along with the creature's, darkness absorbed Malice's hand. He struggled to get out of its grip as shadows consumed the rest of his body. He felt nothing, smelled nothing, heard nothing, almost as if suspended in water at the same temperature as the surrounding air.

Against his wishes, his body relaxed, his muscles easing. The few seconds it took to reach the forest were blissful in a way. Then his feet slipped on the wet grass. Luckily, the creature was still holding his hand and kept Malice upright.

The fresh, earthy, floral scent of the woods and plains flooded Malice's nose. The cool breeze caressed his skin, clouds gathering in the north. He looked around; the wall surrounding the castle's courtyard tens of meters away, the castle itself imminent. The forest was there when Malice turned, a dark mass of trees broken by soft beams of light. Someplace he was familiar with.

Relief rushed through his veins.

"How did you do that?" Malice heard himself ask once the creature finally let go of his hand.

"You must let the darkness become one with you," it said, "and it will let you use it."

As if that made sense, Malice nodded.

"Your name, child?"

"I am of little relevance."

A low grumble of a laugh leaked out of the creature, chilling Malice's bones. "I am called Lazarus, a voident."

"I'm Malice Reap."

"Malice," Lazarus drawled.

His fear returned as quickly as it fled, daggers of anxiety

twisting his barely calmed mind.

"Of course, you are a *Reap*," Lazarus said. "Remember our little deal, child."

Deal? You do not wish to know why? His ears reminded him. "What do I have to do?"

"Kill."

Putting his trembling hands behind his back, Malice averted his gaze. "What if I forget?"

"*You* will die."

After a moment, Malice mustered the courage to look at the voident, but he was already gone. Deal or not, if this was how he needed to prove himself useful, the queen wouldn't allow for anything different.

Momentary Solace
XXIV

Malice made his way to Kiran's cottage. Toussaint and his Squad wouldn't return for days, which meant it was probably for the best to stay out of sight until then. Even if it wasn't for the best, it didn't feel right to return. More like he didn't want to go back and face her highness.

It was late, well into the early hours of the morning, but he knocked anyway, hoping someone would come to the door. His wet clothes made it difficult to control the random shivers. He stunk of smoke, blood and bile, a wicked combination.

Floorboards creaked from within. They were wary steps. As Malice slid backward, the door flung open, Tendai standing with a kitchen knife in his hand. He looked wildly into the forest before his eyes fell on Malice. The knife clattered to the ground.

Tendai grabbed Malice by the shoulders and yanked him inside, wrapping his long arms around him. He was warm, smelled of oak and herbs. Silently, Tendai started stroking the back of Malice's head, and he sank deeper into Tendai's embrace.

He had never hugged Malice, and it made him wonder if Kiran told his parents about the mission. Of course he would. There was no reason not to, and Kiran was a rambler.

"Tendai?" Blodwen called from the back of the house, her footsteps approaching. "Are you all right? I heard a thud—" She gasped.

Racing to her husband, she dropped beside him while Malice sluggishly moved his head away from Tendai's chest. Her eyes considered Malice for a time when her expression contorted with pity and concern. A look he had seen far too often from those who actually looked at him.

But Malice was tired, and he didn't have the energy to cry or to be angry. Kiran had the crying part covered, though. He rushed in after hearing a commotion and upon seeing Malice the waterworks began. Throwing himself in between Blodwen and Tendai, Kiran sobbed, still shoving his father to get to Malice.

It was nice. Malice couldn't stop his aching muscles from relaxing, nor could he stop the tears from blurring his vision. When Tendai shifted, Malice clutched the soft material of his shirt. He wasn't ready to let go yet.

He didn't know if he would be able to, either. Head so full, yet so blank, Malice was a mess. There was a tearing sensation in his chest, the pain radiating to his intestines. A multitude of spots all over his body hadn't fully regenerated and hurt in some way or another.

Kiran eventually moved away. Malice reached for him before he could stop it. But, noticing the flare of Kiran's nostrils and the crease of his brow, Malice retracted his hand. His stench was hard to ignore. So Malice let go of Tendai and pushed himself to his feet.

"We'll give you a good scrubbing tomorrow, but for now, rest." Tendai stood and helped Blodwen up as well. "And get into a clean set of clothes," he added with a smirk.

Kiran took that as a sign to drag Malice to his room and close the door. Crossing the floor to his dresser, he dug out a fresh set of garments for Malice. This wasn't the first time Malice had been in

Kiran's room, but it was the first time he would spend the night.

In the kitchen, Blodwen's and Tendai's voices were an exchange of murmurs.

Lines pointing to notes on the drawings of animals and plants hung all around the room. His bed was in the corner, a nightstand at the head, giving the middle of the room more space. The dresser was opposite of the door and to the left was a desk bombarded with books, writing utensils, and random things like rocks, dried plants, feathers, and whatever else Kiran liked to collect.

Once he handed Malice a balled-up pile of clothes, Kiran plodded to the bed, crawled close to the wall, threw the sheets back, and laid down. With his growing horns, Malice didn't understand why Kiran refused to lie on his back. It would probably be more comfortable.

Malice quickly changed, peeling the bloody, dirt stained, ripped clothes off his body and kicked his shoes off. The fur rug felt strange between his toes. He couldn't describe the difference to those in the castle, but he sort of liked it.

Malice settled next to Kiran, who was having a tough time keeping his eyes open. He yanked the blankets up, covering both him and Malice, then stuffed his arm under his head. Always so quick to fall asleep; Malice was jealous.

Slumber wouldn't come. Instead, he studied Kiran or the drawings he could make out or the wood beams of the ceiling.

Kiran snored while noises started coming from the kitchen. Warm light streamed through the window above the dresser. A savory smell, like meat searing in a skillet, soon invaded Kiran's room.

Carefully getting out of bed, Malice winced at the tens of random pains and aches throughout his body from the night prior. As he stood, the floor creaked and Kiran stirred, stopping Malice in his tracks. He glanced over his shoulder. Kiran was still asleep.

Malice gradually released the knob when the door closed, so it didn't make too much sound, and padded into the kitchen off the hallway.

Blodwen leaned over the counter, her elbows resting on the oak surface, a cup of something steaming in her hands, a silk robe tight to her waist. Kiran, Malice thought, looked most like her, with their shared paleness clouding their skin. Tendai stood in front of the wood stove, a fire blazing within as a skillet sizzled on top. That was where the smell came from. Pork.

Malice's stomach grumbled.

He pulled out the stool by Blodwen and climbed into it, his mouth watering.

"Good morning," Blodwen said, smiling, as she ruffled Malice's hair. Or tried, but his hair was a rat's nest, clumped and matted with dirt and blood.

"Good morning."

Skillet removed from the stove, Tendai placed it on top of a crocheted mitt on the counter and took four plates from the cupboard. He slid a piece of ham, a portion of eggs, toast, and griddlecakes onto each. The beastman was thin but had wide shoulders, wisps of hair on his jaw, cheeks, and upper lip. Blodwen shifted away from the counter to stretch her arms above her head, grunting. She shuffled toward Kiran's room. Meanwhile, Tendai poured two cups of orange juice, one for Malice and one for Kiran.

Groggily, Kiran walked into the kitchen, Blodwen behind him, hands on his shoulders. He was half asleep, his eyes lazy and puffy, a streak of wetness trailing from the corner of his mouth down his chin. His arms swayed loosely at his sides, too. After Blodwen slid a stool out for Kiran, she took her seat.

Kiran yawned as he clambered into the chair. He blinked a few times, then lit up. Without a word, he started devouring his food as if he had never eaten.

"Kiran," Blodwen said. "Manners."

He paused, gulped, and glanced at his father. "Thank you." He grinned.

Chuckling, Tendai shook his head and gestured to Kiran's plate. "Eat up."

Kiran didn't need to be told twice.

Malice looked down at his own plate and cut into the ham. Most of the surface was perfectly golden brown and crispy, the inside pink like flesh.

He spun his plate and ate the griddlecakes, but they stuck to every corner of his mouth. He took a sip of juice, which, gratefully, was very refreshing. Strawberry chunks riddled the jam on top of his toast. He sank his teeth down. It crunched, and he chewed.

Sweet…

It was metallic.

As he drew the toast from his mouth, dark red liquid ran off the sides and spilled onto his plate. Malice dropped it in his eggs, cracking the yolks open. Warm, thick blood stained his hands. He swallowed hard; the toast going down roughly, grating the back of his throat. He tried to wipe his hands off on his borrowed shirt, but he only stained it.

"Sorry," he mumbled, glancing around the counter for a napkin or towel to clean his hands. Panic settled underneath his skin like howlers getting ready to pounce. His eyes eventually landed on his plate again, and he pushed it forward. "I need a towel."

"Malice."

He looked up. Tendai stared at him, those horizontal pupils fixed on Malice.

"Are you all right?" he asked.

When he glanced down at his hands again, the blood had vanished. Blodwen and Kiran stopped eating as well, expressions glum. Malice had no intention of making them worry. He felt disgusted, the hunger absent now, replaced with a churning. The dirt and blood, dried and cracked on his skin, felt like maggots wiggling over his bones. Malice recalled every gruesome way he killed those bandits last night. The smell of iron, burnt wood, and rain suddenly flooded his nose. He tensed.

"Malice?" Kiran questioned.

"I'm fine," Malice said, the corners of his mouth lifted into a small, false smile. He relaxed his shoulders too, slouching similarly to Kiran. Draga had taught him how to feign certain emotions.

Blodwen stroked the back of Malice's hair as she said, "If something is wrong, you can tell us."

"I know." Malice picked up his piece of toast and ate it, fighting the urge to vomit.

Kiran lingered for a moment, shrugged, and went back to his meal. Malice focused on keeping his food down. *Toast done, now the eggs.* Seasoned with salt and pepper, they weren't as bad. Lastly, the ham. He stuffed it all in his mouth and chewed as fast as he could.

Belly full, plate cleared, Malice slipped from the stool. "I should return to the castle."

"Are you sure you don't want to bathe first?" Blodwen asked, while carrying dishes to the sink.

Malice shook his head. "I don't want to get in trouble for

arriving without the Squad." He would probably get in trouble whether he was with them or not. "Besides, Kiran's clothes are too big on me."

Looking at himself, then at Malice, Kiran pouted. He was taller and chubbier than Malice. Blodwen snickered as she handed a stack of plates to Tendai at the sink. Malice hesitated. What if he stayed here forever? Blodwen and Tendai seemed to like him enough, and he and Kiran were brothers.

Queen Vendetta knew where they lived, making the entire notion nothing but a silly dream. She kept her promises.

Malice went to open the door, but Kiran stopped him. "What about your shoes?" His eyes darted to the floor.

"Toss them." Malice had another pair, he thought. But if he didn't, he enjoyed being barefoot anyway.

Kiran fiddled with the bottom of his shirt. He took a deep breath and marched toward Malice, throwing his arms around him, squeezing with all his might. Malice wheezed. Kiran's breath hit Malice's shoulders as his chin moved.

"What did you say?"

"Nothing," Kiran said. "You should get going, so you don't get in trouble."

Malice, not having the courage to smile anymore, waved goodbye to Blodwen and Tendai in the kitchen. He considered Kiran one last time and left.

No one batted an eye when Malice trudged through the castle. He was thankful his soreness from the morning had dissipated, considering he had to hike up four flights of stairs.

Malice's bedchamber was untouched since the moment he left over a week ago. He was thoroughly disappointed to see there wasn't an envelope on his desk. He had hoped Magnus's letter would cheer him up.

With his night attire in hand, it was time to bathe. If there was one thing he needed, it was that.

Roses and peppermint perfumed the pools. It was empty, not a soul in sight. On damp tiles, Malice's dirty feet left footprints. Inside the stalled showers was a bucket of soap with a sponge and a washrag. He stripped off Kiran's clothes, deciding to throw them out since they were exposed to so much blood and grime. He turned the faucet on, perfectly warm water pouring from the rounded shower head.

Under the stream, Malice ran his fingers through his hair, catching snarls he eventually untangled after a few tugs. With how gross he was, he poured a wealthy amount of soap onto the rag and scrubbed and scrubbed and scrubbed.

The bandit's faces flashed before him, their lifeless eyes gawking at Malice, their blood becoming a slippery mess on the tiled floor. Ichor overpowered the scent of wet earth and smoke clinging to his skin.

You could have run, the axe man said. *Instead, I killed my friend because of you.*

You watched, the giant with dual swords hissed, *as I writhed in pain. Giving me such an agonizing death, your sister taught you well.*

The leader chimed in, her voice clawing at Malice's eardrums, *What you should have done was let us kill you, little brat! We're all dead because of you... You're just like your mother.*

Malice flinched. His arm was red, beads of blood popping where he scrubbed. In a heartbeat, the redness faded, and the blood washed away.

Malice flopped onto his bed the moment he returned to his room and rolled onto his back. He wept into Kiran's arms. He was so concerned about his own death, it seemed like he had a tantrum in hindsight. Inyene had warned him multiple times that one day it would be his life or someone else's. He should've believed her.

At the back of his mind, the bandit's voices screamed, *Murderer!*

He tossed to his side, forcing his eyes shut and waited to be found, to be brought in front of the queen for his punishment.

Kill or be Killed
"Judgement"

He had watched every member of Toussaint's Squad walk through the large doors of the throne room, ornately carved with the region's sigil and serpents. No one lifted their gaze until they were below the queens on their hands and knees.

There was a chill in the air, or perhaps it was just Odovacar. Inyene and Draga stood to his right, Alkeim at Mother's side. If they were alive, Sok and Rayen would be on his left. They stood behind the throne of black crystals at the shadow's edge. This vantage point allowed him to see every tremble, scowl, or lip curl one might have. Seldom had someone relinquished control over their extremities in front of her highness.

Malice and his first sword, Eunice, were the last to arrive. The boy looked tired, haggard. Odovacar remembered the first time he had taken a life, remembered how much of a toll it took on him. He felt bad for Malice in a way he never had. The young prince had been sent on that mission to see if he could and would kill someone. It was his purpose. He excelled.

"You disappoint me, Toussaint," Mother said, her voice daggers of ice. "I did not tell you to burn a mile of land in pursuit of the bandit's death."

"I apologize," Toussaint said feebly.

Toussaint was not fit to lead; Odovacar, alongside a majority of the generals, had shared his opinion on the matter. Whether his royals cared for him was of little importance when his top priority was fun over efficiency. The most useful place for someone like him would be in an attack force or warband, a sheep, not the shepherd. Coordinated missions were out of his realm of capabilities.

Queen Vendetta wanted yet another plaything, making his opinion as significant as the water current to a bird.

"You understand your mistake?" she said.

"I do, your highness."

"But you will not learn from it."

Silence.

"If you were to learn from the mistakes you keep making—of which there are plenty—my land would not be blackened."

One thing Odovacar liked about where he stood was he could not see the queen's expression. He could only imagine the look of death on her face, and thankfully, he had a poor imagination.

"What would you have me do?" Toussaint asked, his head still low.

"You?" Mother mused. "Are your royals unable to take accountability for their own actions?"

"They," Toussaint swallowed, "were following my orders, your highness. I should be the one to take responsibility."

"How commendable," she said sarcastically. "As their leader, are you prepared to take all of your royals' penances? Whatever they might be?"

For a time, Toussaint said nothing. Tension riddled his back, muscles knotted beneath his tunic. "Yes."

Every member reacted as if dealt a blow so painful they could not help themselves, yet none were willing to speak against the queen's verdict.

"You burned my lands," the queen said with light amusement. "So, you, too, shall burn. Experience it yourself. Maybe then you will think twice about setting my land aflame."

"Thank you, your highness." Toussaint pressed his head to the floor and kept it there. Smart.

"Now." Queen Vendetta's head shifted slightly. "Mutt."

Malice baulked.

"I hear you killed seven bandits."

Hesitantly, Malice brought his eyes up, meeting the queens. Odovacar perched an eyebrow, impressed he could meet his mother's unyielding and vicious gaze. "Yes," he said. "I did."

This time, it was Eunice who startled.

"Let me ask you this; what are you?" There was an edge to her voice, one Odovacar heard in his nightmares, scars suddenly itching on his back. "Prince is far too kind. You are not yet a royal, so what gave you any right to kill?"

"What?" Malice went still, very still like the calm of leaves without a breeze. "You said… you wanted me to prove myself."

"Yes?" A level of mirth entered her tone, a velvety sheen coating her acidic words. "Could you not do that by aiding in hunting? Cleaning? Breaking camp? Had you not any ideas to keep them from burning my fields?"

Terror wholly took over Malice's expression, stealing what little control he had.

"Inyene." She emerged from the shadows. "The mutt disregards life so easily. You ought to give him a taste of death for everyone he took."

"No," Malice breathed. "But, but—I—I would have died!"

"Then you should have accepted your fate," Mother said.

"Why should I have to die?" he shouted, tears glistening and breaking from the pools in his eyes.

"Why should you live?" the queen countered.

Malice scrambled backward as Inyene stalked closer and closer. "I did what you asked!"

Odovacar closed his eyes and turned his head away, his scars throbbing as if they had their own heartbeat, clashing with the frenzied state of the one inside his chest.

"Look," Draga hissed at his side. "You cannot close your eyes to everything."

Clenching his jaw, Odovacar forced himself to look at Malice. She was right. He needed to *see* what he had helped create, face the consequences of his inaction.

"I proved myself!"

Inyene drew nearer still, her footfalls silent, a technique every royal knew as it was standard practice. Finally, she reached Malice, walked past him, and grabbed the back of his collar, dragging him to the door.

"Please!" He kicked and thrashed. "I won't do it again! I'll listen! I promise!" The desperation in his voice stung like a poison-laced blade, sinking as deep as it could into his gut. "Please, forgive me! I didn't want to die!"

He continued after the doors closed, his voice loud, fearful, but losing determination because he knew he would not get away. No one had been able to. Odovacar's breath hitched, his knees close to buckling under his weight as the throbbing of his back radiated to the rest of his body, centipedes gnawing at his mind. He felt sick to his stomach. The amount of agony and horror on Malice's face—in his body—was visceral to Odovacar as if transmitted directly to his bones.

"Eunice!" the queen carped. Odovacar flinched.

Deliberately, like it took a tremendous amount of effort, Malice's first sword pried her head from the door, her eyes wild, her jaw slack.

"Just this once, you may talk freely, without consequence."

"You vile wretch!" Eunice seethed much to Odovacar's surprise. His mother liked to offer the opportunity to speak one's mind to watch them struggle with the concept.

"To your son, your blood, your CHILD! How could you ever treat him as if he were nothing but a tool?" She rose at a steady pace, her chest heaving.

Odovacar may not have been able to see his mother's face, but he knew she was smiling, a thin, sinister grin. Rarely had one disregarded their fear in such a way. Odovacar had only seen it once, and there had been nothing left to bury once Inyene had finished with them.

"When a dog yips; there are means to yet break it."

Now, the beastman was standing upright, fists balled at her sides, eyes so full of rage he could feel their intensity cross the distance between them and stir the dread deeply nestled inside his veins. Savagery enveloped her, reminding him of a cornered animal in the woods, desperate to survive; desperate for the kill.

"I do not serve you," Eunice spat.

The room changed. Odovacar's blood ran cold.

"I will never take another word from you. It is him I serve, and it is him I will follow. No matter where it leads me."

"Your time," Queen Vendetta said, her smile surely wiped from her lips, her voice barely containing her smoldering rage, "is up, beasty. Leave my sight."

Seconds, which felt like minutes, went by. Eunice and the queen glared at one another. The conflict in the atmosphere was denser than the earth. She turned and stalked out of the throne room, her boots a loud clunk on the marble.

"The same goes for your lot. Get out."

Toussaint and his Squad left promptly, the doors hardly closing all the way before they were flung back open. The dreadful silence returned momentarily, but Mother stood and then she was gone as well.

Suddenly, the strength vanished from Odovacar's legs. He swayed and stumbled when a hand clamped around his arm, righting him.

"Do not falter," Draga told him, her voice distant.

Sucking in a strained breath, Odovacar gathered himself. Whatever was left of him, anyhow. His hands quaked as every fiber of body screamed to run like the child he was in his mother's presence.

"He will become nothing," he uttered into the still space of the throne room.

"He won't," Draga said.

"What makes you say that?" Had she not seen the same thing Odovacar had? Not witnessed the same absolute terror in Malice as he had?

"He struggled," she said plainly. "He has never *struggled* while receiving his punishment."

The ache of his back eased; the chittering of centipedes calmed.

"Malice got a taste of freedom, Odovacar." She turned to him. "He got a taste of what life could be without the queen. This will not break him. It will be another hammer strike that forges the sword.”

The sweetness of the world outside this castle… was one Odovacar took every chance to indulge in. Malice had seen the kingdom, the people, the flowers, and plains. Had seen how big the sky was when the castle did not loom over him.

“He will kill us,” Odovacar whispered. Never had he heard such tenderness in his own voice.

Draga stepped down from the dais, her dress sweeping the floor. “I will not fight it if he does.” The door closed behind her.

Nor would he.

Odovacar lingered for a while, dreaming of when that day would come, ignoring the pain of which would surely accompany him and looking forward to the bliss afterward. When his heart finally stopped, and he took his last breath.

*

Without consequence. Eunice repeated the phrase over and over and over again. A chant. A melody continuing to feed her rage. Her feet carried her to the southern wing of the castle, down the stone stairwell, into the catacombs of prisoners. She wasn't angry. Anger did not cover what she felt. It was too soft of a word, too gentle. *Without consequence*, her highness had said. She was right. Eunice would not face the consequences. Vendetta would.

Muffled screams twisted Eunice's gut, the stench of death heavy. Then, as if her emotions were felt through the compact walls of stone and earth, Inyene emerged from a cell. Sweat glistened on the executioner's icy blue skin, her red eyes bright. She smiled at Eunice.

“Let him go!” Eunice demanded. She stopped short, making sure there was plenty of space between her and the monster in front of her.

"Why?" Inyene cocked her head, and the smile vanished. Her expression hardened. Eunice shivered. "You think Malice is so special, don't you?"

"That doesn't matter, he is—"

"He is going through what we all went through," Inyene snarled. "The only difference is Malice has me where I had my father."

Eunice reeled.

"I took over so Father could save a shred of himself. Not that it mattered in the long run. He's practically dead by now." Inyene stepped forth. "Malice will continue to endure whatever the hell I decide to put him through. I—" Inyene's shoes tapped the tips of Eunice's—"will break Malice until there is nothing left to break." Her voice was low, gravelly yet sweet, as if she were talking to a lover, as if the words leaving her mouth were flowers instead of venom.

"I won't let you," Eunice matched her tone, eyes fixing on the beady red of Inyene's.

"Fine," Inyene said. "We can trade."

"What do you want?" Eunice had only met Malice a handful of months ago, but he was a child. Innocent. Undeserving of the hell his own kin were putting him through. And for what?

"Cut your hand off and we'll call it a deal."

Mind blank, her ears rang for a split second. Her hand? Eunice extended it, fingers twitching. Inyene placed a knife of ice in her palm. She gripped it, the bitter cold biting her skin. As she lifted her opposite arm, Eunice held the knife to her wrist, the blade kissing the flesh. It was a hand. She could have it reattached, but would Inyene allow it? Even so, a hand for a life wasn't terrible. She could use magic to replace the appendage. Edge sinking a hair further, Eunice stared at the thin line of red starting. *Malice doesn't deserve this.* She ground her teeth, sights glued to her hand, breathing deeply.

What would her wife say? What would Helle do?

Averting her eyes, Eunice dropped the knife, which shattered upon hitting the stony ground.

"Better luck next time, beasty."

The cell door closed. Her superficial cut regenerated.

Screams began.

Besting the Arrogant
XXV

Zephyrus groaned and dramatically collapsed onto his back, letting his arms flare out to either side of him. Chuckling under his breath, Malice joined him on the cool ground, which instantly sent a shiver down his spine.

They were both sweaty as their chests heaved from sparring all morning. The trees in the glade provided some shade, but it was the beginning of summer, the air still muggy from spring and overwhelming. They sat near the edge of the cliff overlooking the clear water at the bottom of the dell, the smell of wet earth strong.

The first time he and Zephyrus ventured into Mutuwa, they had stayed in the glade for half an hour, maybe less, but no more. The second time they had spent an hour here, then two and three. Despite inviting Kiran every time, he always declined. They had been coming more often, too. It was hard to believe the forest's reputation was entirely accurate or deserved. However, a bit older and not so fearful, Malice understood how Mutuwa had once terrified him. The circumstances in which he came to know it hadn't helped. At least in the glade, there was serenity and beauty undermining Mutuwa's fearsome repute.

Odovacar, surprisingly, allowed Malice to go a few days out of the month, so long as he and Zephyrus were training. And they did… most of the time.

It was like a reward for completing his first mission a year ago.

Salty winds whistling, clouds growing abundant, Malice guessed it would rain here soon.

"What do you want to do?" Zephyrus interrupted the quiet, his voice still shaky from catching his breath, startling Malice. "When you become king," he clarified.

"I don't want to become *king*," he said. "I know that much."

"Why not?"

Malice was silent for a moment. If it meant becoming anything like Emil, a ghost, or Vendetta, a monster, he refused. He would destroy the throne and crown to spite them if he had to. Running away was an option, too. He would have to convince Kiran and Zephyrus to join him. That in of itself posed issues.

"If I were king," Zephyrus lurched upright, "I would change this region for the better."

"Why?" Besides replacing the queen, Malice could not imagine a way for the region to improve. Not that he knew what needed to be improved to begin with.

"My father says there are… dealings underground poisoning the land."

Malice raised an eyebrow.

He shrugged. "Mother said something about slaves. From overrun villages, strongholds, other kingdoms, and regions, but I don't know how true it is."

Slaves? "Do you want to become a ruler?" Malice asked as he wiggled his fingers. Every so often, they felt numb.

Zephyrus snickered at the question and looked at Malice, a gleam in his crimson eyes. "If I say yes, will you give me the throne?"

As obvious as his sarcasm was, "I would," Malice said and sat up alongside his friend.

Zephyrus whipped toward Malice so fast Malice thought his head would fly off his neck.

"As long as you prove yourself. I can't give the crown to any dimwit I come across." He grinned.

His bewildered stare shifted to a smirk. "Of course not. Father says if I want something, I must earn it."

"How would you do it?"

"I would teach those pesky nobles a lesson." He glared at the sky, his tone aggressive and disgusted. "They prance around all day, acting as if their power exceeds their castle. They portray themselves as high and mighty when they don't have any ground to stand on."

Zephyrus spat and paused, sighed, then went on, "Most don't let their power go to their heads, but a lot do, and they're the ones who need a good smack to the head… two for good measure."

"You hate nobles that much?" Malice couldn't say a whole lot on the subject. He had never met a noble. Didn't exactly want to either. He had met the rulers, though, and doubted there was much difference between them.

"Yes. I do!" Zephyrus snapped, his brows furrowed as his lip flared. "The noble of Mondlesgrave banished us because she no longer liked my father or my mother. And do you know what she said?" He turned to Malice. "She called my parent's bastards, liars, and honorless wenches," he said, as if the words were poison. To him, they probably were.

"We were happy on the island, not too far from the kingdom,

about a day's ride on horseback. Father was a guard while Mother was a fisherwoman." His sullen tone hardened again. "The Lady burned our house, stables, and docks, slaughtered our livestock, then sent us off to the mainland. She put a bounty on my parent's heads, saying if they were ever spotted in Mondlesgrave again—" Zephyrus stopped himself, anger brewing like a storm throughout his tensed body.

He deliberately breathed out, drawing out his release of breath, eyes closing. "Since coming here, our lives have improved some. Father is a knight. Mother is a shipwright now. My sister will go to school in the next few years, and I'll become a royal soon."

Turning, Zephyrus smiled at Malice. A hint of sadness dimmed the sharp red of his irises. He must have loved Mondlesgrave, a chunk of land between Hordes region and Zeldine's in the east. The Apostolov bloodline governed the city, making Mondlesgrave the second eldest kingdom behind Ryzion.

"If I become king," Malice said absently, "I'll pardon you and your family so you can return to Mondlesgrave if you want."

Whether he did or not, he would find some way to pardon Zephyrus. It wasn't fair. The noble was wrong, and the queen was wrong for letting her banish Zephyrus's family. The how part could come later when Malice had the ability to do more than walk freely around the castle grounds. He'd recently gained the privilege of entering the kingdom to meet his assigned Squad for missions and nothing more.

Zephyrus's eyes flickered with excitement. "I'll hold you to it."

*

With the constant threat of rain, it was either cool or sticky. No in between. Bugs were also constant, buzzing around Malice as they bit and bounced off him. Comfortable had become a foreign word the moment Malice stepped out of the castle. It didn't help the training grounds were always full, royals drenched in sweat, himself included.

Zephyrus was across the field, sparring with his father, his smoky grey hair pulled tight to his scalp. Eunice was close by, wearing a sleeveless tunic, and a pair of trousers coming to her knees, slippers on her feet. She had cut her hair a while ago in preparation for the heat to come. Malice saw the sweat glimmering on her dark skin as she practiced defensive maneuvers.

In front of Malice, Odovacar stood shirtless, as many others did. His body was chiseled, scars latticed his torso but were more so concentrated on his back. Malice wondered how many of those were results of the queen's punishments or from his missions. Odovacar's long red hair was also up in a bun to keep it from touching his nape.

With a nod, Odovacar sank into his position, the grip on his sword tightening, his eyes focusing like a predator readying itself to attack its prey. Malice did the same, everything around them fading to oblivion—that was the part Malice enjoyed the most. He could forget for a little while.

"Why not switch it up?" Inyene's voice broke Malice's concentration instantly, his body going rigid.

He turned with a scowl. Her presence was a thorn in every inch of his skin. Inyene's weight shifted to one side, arms folded across her chest, and a smirk curved her vile lips.

"Switch what up?" Odovacar asked shortly.

Inyene gestured at Malice and Odovacar as a whole. "Switch who he spars with."

"You want to have a go at him?"

As if she didn't do that enough.

"No," she half chuckled. "I'm sure, however, a few others would love to. So, why not give him a taste of defeat, hmm?"

Malice, for one, thought he knew defeat rather well. He would go as far as to say they were close friends with how often Odovacar easily bested him. Inyene's gaze sliced toward the field, landing on someone who she flagged down. A royal rushed up to Inyene a minute later, bowing. When he turned, Malice recognized him. Rayen's former first sword. His heart skipped a beat.

"Let Xenon take your place, little brother." She narrowed her eyes, her tone changing into a command rather than a suggestion.

Odovacar's jaw slid, a vein spasming in his neck. He approached Inyene, whispered in her ear, and stomped not too far off.

Xenon was lean, his figure smaller, his muscles stringy underneath cobalt blue scales—unlike Odovacar or Eunice, who were bulkier. The gills on the sides of his neck flared every few seconds. His face was narrow, his hooked nose long, and his dark eyes down-turned.

The fishman's brow furrowed and his lip flared into a slight snarl. "I'll gladly fight him," he said.

Malice returned the glower. "You actually cared for Rayen?" he asked, though his tone came out more venomous than he intended. A lot more. Shoulder's slumping, he held eye contact with Xenon, despite how he wanted to slink away.

"She was a child!"

Malice reeled. Was he not also a child? Had Xenon completely forgotten about what Sok and Rayen did to him over a *letter*? What they did to Kiran when he only wanted to protect Malice? *No one in this castle cares for you*, Inyene once said.

Malice crouched and held his sword up. There was no point delaying any further. If he wasn't a child in his eyes, he might as well act like it. The sooner he could end this, the better.

Erecting a sword of yellow lightning from his palm, static encased the blade and Xenon's hand like pulsing waves of light. The air vibrated between them, *zips* and *zaps* sounding.

Malice righted his posture and walked to the edge of the ring—one always formed whenever he and Odovacar sparred—and stabbed his sword into the ground. A stomp of his foot conjured a blade of earth that jumped into his hand, forming to his grip perfectly. Inyene eyed him. Malice fought the urge to make a face at her. There was something about the way she stood, watching Malice as if she were taunting him.

Anger flared in the pit of his stomach, flickering to his chest. Teeth clenched, Malice waited for Xenon to attack first.

After what seemed like an eternity, the fishman finally moved, lunging toward Malice like a spear hurtling toward a target. He thrust his sword in a series of jabs, none of which hit Malice as he retreated. Using the generous space left by the curious royals was something Malice learned to take advantage of a while ago. It was really the only way he could avoid Odovacar on a bad day. On a good one, Malice had no chance.

Xenon swiveled, swinging his sword up diagonally, narrowly missing Malice's neck. Just as quickly, it came back around, hitting Malice's sword of earth against his chest. It lacked the power Odovacar's blows had, which made sense. Xenon was scrawny.

Xenon's scaled face flashed with irritation when he backed off, adjusting his shoulders. He stalked around Malice like a wolf. Their swords of magic cancelled each other. Xenon wasn't stupid enough not to realize that and probably thought to change tactics. Xenon was faster than Malice, much faster. He could overwhelm Malice easily if he wanted too but Malice would recover quickly. Everyone he sparred against was better than him at something. Experience, speed, strength, agility, magic.

That didn't mean, Odovacar aside, Malice lost very often anymore.

Malice got behind the fishman, aiming to attack his kidneys, but Xenon glided around Malice. His sword arced over his head and came down onto Malice's collarbone. Malice moved his shoulder away, switched his sword between his hands, and caught Xenon's blade. Pain exploded as blood ran down his arm, dripping onto the gravel. He yanked Xenon forward and kicked his ribs, Xenon skidding across the dirt. The fishman rolled to his feet, dirt streaked his torso, arms, and pants.

Malice's right hand tingled and twitched, red fleshy bubbles on his palm, each brought a pulsing, searing pain. Luckily, the blisters were gone in a few heartbeats, but the jerking persisted. He scoffed. The power he had with two hands was gone. A stupid move on his part, Malice admitted.

He needed to truly *study* the way Xenon moved, his agility and speed, his flexibility during an attack. If Xenon were only slightly better in one or two aspects than Odovacar, he wouldn't win. Malice refused to let him win. Refused to give Inyene that satisfaction, either.

Take it slow, watch, learn, break him down.

"Eunice"

Eunice moved to the edge of the field when she saw Odovacar replaced by a royal. Xenon Lavoie, the former first sword of the late Princess Rayen.

He was fast, able to maneuver around Malice easily. A part of Eunice believed it was because of Malice's size. Despite his age, he had grown little during the past year and a half, unlike Kiran and Zephyrus. Nevertheless, his spars were always an interesting spectacle. Someone so young, so gifted.

"Interesting lad, isn't he?" a gruff voice said behind Eunice. She jumped out of her skin and spun, almost clocking Sir Alkeim in the face with her fist. He glanced at her knuckles, hardly an inch from his cheek, and gave a squeamish smile.

Eunice, sighing, turned back to her previous spot. "That he is, but what brings you here, Sir Alkeim?"

"Out for some fresh air, I suppose." He shrugged his broad shoulders and watched Malice like a hawk.

Sir Alkeim was the queen's first sword, a gentle giant, as most of the servants liked to call him. Eunice was inclined to agree. Royals, especially knights, had this air of ferocity about them. If you so much as looked at them wrong, they would break you like a twig, but Sir Alkeim was different, with an ever-constant aura of kindness about him. Perhaps that came with fatherhood.

Her attention returned to Malice, who was calm, his eyes fixated on Xenon's movements as if he were studying him. He *was* studying Xenon.

"What do you make of how Malice spars?" Alkeim asked.

"I don't think I can place my finger on a particular technique he uses," she said. "He's like a sponge, soaking up everything he sees and using it." Often, she'd caught his eyes darting around the field before he'd attacked, looking for inspiration.

Alkeim chuckled, a tender rumble. "Aye."

Malice ducked an overhead swing, crouched, sidestepped, and kicked Xenon's legs out from under him. His opponent on the ground, Malice threw his arm in the air and stabbed his sword of earth into the dirt, Xenon rolling away in the nick of time as the blade would've impaled his forehead.

Creating an earth sword to combat Xenon's lightning was sensible. Most, if not all, of the advantage Xenon had magic wise disappeared.

Alkeim said, his voice quiet as if from another room, Eunice enthralled by the spar, "Malice is like a spider waiting at the top of his web in the shadows."

Malice dodged a series of blows, Xenon losing his temper as each of his swings missed. His gills flared to uncover the red, sinewy flesh of his neck, brows scrunched so deeply they were nearly in his mouth.

"He waits patiently, as long as it takes, for his prey, the moth, to get tangled in his web."

Xenon cursed, spittle sprayed, veins pulsed on his arms, dare Eunice say even his scales were flushed. He sliced at Malice's side, lightning flying off his blade like stray hairs in the wind.

"The moth beats its wing fiercely, trying to break free while Malice watches."

Left and right, Xenon's movements became erratic, uncoordinated, his chest heaving from loss of breath, his body covered in dirt and scrapes. Panic underlined his features, like an external force had yanked them taut, adding darkness to the crevices of his face. Eunice shifted and rolled her shoulders, eyes fleeting to the most probable reason. Inyene stood patiently alongside her brother. Eunice was glad she couldn't see the executioner's wretched expression, because if she could see Inyene, Inyene could see her, and she would rather not get on the Reap's bad side any more than she already had.

Two heads of grey snagged her eyes for a moment. Zephyrus and Issur, deep in the sea of royals. Issur was gesturing, Zephyrus nodding, as he explained something. Then another boy in all white was there and held his hands out for them to take. They did. A heartbeat later, the boy released them, lingered a moment longer, and turned around. It was Kiran. His pale face marking was as recognizable as a mountain on the horizon. Eunice watched until he vanished into one of four wooden pavilions edging the grounds.

Alkeim said, "Malice waits for the moth to lose its strength and will to fight, and that is when he delivers the final fatal blow, savoring his victory."

Weaving between the flurry of slashes, Malice found an opening, rushed forward, and rammed his shoulder into Xenon's sternum. Xenon recoiled, the blow to his diaphragm taking his breath away, as it would for many. Malice shifted around the fishman, holding his sword horizontal to his body, so the blade rested between two of Xenon's gills.

Moments passed when Malice relented and let his sword droop. He whirled toward Inyene, wearing a triumphant smirk.

"With what you saw, would you say Malice has any weakness?" Alkeim peeled his eyes from Malice and looked down at Eunice, curiosity painting his olive-green face.

He did, more than Eunice cared to count, but… "He adapts better than anyone I've seen."

"He does," Alkeim said bluntly, a sudden seriousness to his tone hardening his gaze and mouth. "Her highness knows of them. She knows them well."

Eunice frowned. *What is that supposed to mean?*

"One day, sooner rather than later, she will use them against the lad." He dipped his head and turned, striding through the swaying tall grass and wildflowers back to the castle, his figure gradually receding.

*

It was early evening when Eunice headed to Malice's bedchamber. He returned soon after his spar with Xenon. Eunice had tried to follow, but Malice told her to go cool off or go home for the day, one of the two.

She did neither.

Eunice stayed at the grounds and continued to spar, asking her opponents questions about Queen Vendetta while they were distracted. She knew the technique worked since her wife used it with Eunice on the occasions she didn't feel like talking, usually because of a rough day. Helle always knew to put her to work though, let her get invested in the task, then lay the questions out in the open and Eunice, despite herself, spewed answers like a waterspout. It worked with the royals as well, but they spoke of information she already knew. A waste of time, for the most part. Meanwhile, Alkeim's words hung over her head all day like a fog.

Down the hall, his door was wide open. Sounds of distress and laughter echoed into the hallway, which was followed by a thud. She rushed to the door. With his arms encasing Zephyrus's head, legs wrapped around his torso, Malice had Zephyrus in a tight hold, restricting his movements. Kiran sat on the edge of the bed, snickering.

"Come on, say it," Malice taunted. "Say you surrender."

It always amazed Eunice how much energy children had.

"Never!" Zephyrus grunted as he started pushing himself up

from the floor, rising further to his feet, Malice's eyebrows jumping

Malice tightened his arms around Zephyrus's head, jerked his body in such a way it brought the both of them crashing to the floor again, Malice on his back. Eyes bulging, choking, Zephyrus frantically tapped Malice's arms.

"I yield," he croaked, and Malice released him.

Scrambling away, Zephyrus caught his breath while Malice, smug as all get out, sat up and crossed his legs, leaning back into his arms.

"You caught me by surprise. It wasn't a fair fight. If it was—"

"I still would've won," Malice interrupted, grinning.

"Is that your way of telling me you want to go another round?" Zephyrus sneered.

"Sure. I know how much you like getting your ass handed to you."

Kiran broke out into laughter, falling back onto the bed, his hands on his jiggling gut. Zephyrus pouted. Malice was giggling too—a sight seldom glimpsed, making Eunice forget why she was here. He was someone else completely with these two, a child.

Footsteps hurried down the hallway. "Boys!" a servant yelled, stopping at Eunice's side in the doorframe, hands on her hips. "How many times have I told you to stop wrestling in the castle?"

Kiran shot up, wiping the tears from his eyes. Zephyrus went rigid, and Malice got to his feet. "We're sorry," the three boys said in unison.

Eyes moving from child to child, Shevanti sighed and shook her head. "Come now, it's time for dinner. I'll be back in a moment with your food. Get yourselves ready." On the way out, the emerald demon curtseyed toward Eunice.

Eunice thought Annabeth was Malice's caretaker, but it seemed she had been relieved of the duty. Mostly. She'd caught the servant loitering about the fourth floor's eastern wing a handful of times, attending tasks someone else had previously completed. Eunice had once seen her staring at Malice's door, her expression haunted.

"Wait." Kiran stopped Malice and Zephyrus on their way to the desk. "Let me heal you."

"You healed us at the training grounds," Zephyrus commented.

Frowning, Kiran said, "It's for practice."

Hands enclosing the boys' biceps, Kiran closed his eyes, breathed deeply, and let his magic flow into them—Eunice knew the procedure, but felt nothing that indicated Kiran did anything. It had only taken a second before Kiran let go and shooed them to their prior objectives. Zephyrus gathered two chairs near the closet and set them next to the desk while Malice decluttered the surface for them to eat. Finally, when Kiran and Zephyrus were seated, Malice noticed Eunice's presence. She bowed her head instantly, dipping out of the doorframe as he made his way to the corridor.

"I thought I told you to go home today?" he questioned quietly.

"I decided to stay and help around the training grounds. Was that a problem?"

"No." He peeked toward the stairwell, clacks resonating and growing in volume. "Make it quick," he demanded.

"I came here to tell you not to let your guard down."

Malice blinked at her.

Eunice recalled her conversation with Alkeim, shoulders rolling gingerly. "Her highness—" She swallowed the rising fire from the depths of her stomach at the thought of the queen—"I think she's planning something, my prince."

"That so."

Either he believed her and didn't care or didn't believe her and still didn't care.

"Stay outside until we're done," Malice said. His gaze shifted from Eunice to Shevanti, who came down the hall with a tray of food in her hands, concentration thick on her face. "I have questions for you."

Absently, she nodded, stepped aside for the servant, then stood against the wall on the opposite side between two doors. Soon after Malice went in, Shevanti left, greeting Eunice all the same.

She sighed.

To her surprise, when the boys finished eating, Kiran and Zephyrus were sullenly sent on their way. Malice motioned for Eunice as if she were the next in line for an audience. She supposed she was.

Two chairs now sat in front of the desk, the other returned to its original place by the closet. Malice sat first while Eunice took in the room. Malice was rather cleanly for a child and a boy. Books, few in quantity, were neatly placed on the bookshelf. His bed was made, pillows organized from biggest to smallest against the headboard. Shoes rested below his array of mostly black garments. Papers were on the left side of his desk, but far from the edge. The corked jar of ink was beside a cup of writing utensils, and the ticking dust-free clock. Closest to her was a bulky-spined book aligned with the corners.

Eunice took her seat, the cushion firm underneath her.

"Since you're my first sword," Malice said, "your loyalty lies solely with me."

Eunice made a face at him.

"Meaning, you will not take orders from the queen, you will not report to her, you will barely interact with her unless necessary. The queen is an obsolete figure to you."

She moved back. What she needed wasn't clarity, it was context. Why state the obvious? He didn't know what she had proclaimed to the Reap family after Inyene dragged him away. And how could he? Should she mention it? *I will never take another word from you. It is him I serve, and it is him I will follow. No matter where it leads me.* As stunned as she was by her own audacity in hindsight, she meant every word.

"And?"

"Everything discussed in this room tonight stays between us."

"It will." That was a given.

"How is Vendetta involved with slaves and what does it have to do with underground dealings?" he asked. Everything about him turned to stone, resolute and still, those bright green eyes piercing.

Muscles stiffening, a shiver raced up her body. *How does he know about that?* Queen Vendetta would happily cut a royal's tongue out before she would ever allow them to utter a word about her commerce. Whoever talked better hope her highness never caught wind. Eunice's gut, considering who the information reached, told her a tongue wouldn't be sufficient.

Rolling her shoulders, she shifted once more and suppressed the tide-like disgust rising into her throat. "I had helped transport slaves from the docks to the kingdom three, four years ago," she said and looked at the gloomy marble floor. "Slave trade is only a part of what she does. It's her biggest export."

Malice set his back against the chair. "Do... the people know?" he asked, awe-stricken. Then Malice answered himself, "No, they can't know. Why would they sit and watch it happen if they knew?"

In all honesty, she wasn't aware of how much the kingdom was involved. She doubted everyone, but suspected a good number of people stood behind the queen. If not for the coin, for the satisfaction it brought their corrupt ways. They lived lavishly because of it, too. Liking to think otherwise didn't change how Eunice wasn't much different.

"What else do you know about her highness? About her trades?"

"Not as much as you're hoping for," Eunice exhaled, the tension in her shoulders worsening where not even rolling them lessened the discomfort. "I know what she gains from the slaves. Coin, jewels, devotion, poison, weapons."

"Devotion from who?"

"From whoever buys the slaves and swears to keep their lips sealed," she said. Slave trade was made illegal over five hundred years ago thanks to the founding ruler, Hyeon Braxton. Few clans, giant, dwarf, and dark elf being the primary sources, during the war of species depended on their slave-culture, but it was enough of an issue to outlaw.

"Do you know where she's getting the poison and weapons from?" Malice asked, his posture changed as he leaned to his side, hand supporting his chin, elbow on the armrest.

Eunice shook her head. "Weapons; my guess would be everywhere. Vendetta has ties in most every region. Poison, on the other hand, is… local."

"Most? What regions has she left alone?"

"Alucard's, Zeldine's, and Maziar's Regions. Probably." They were powerhouses Vendetta couldn't handle without the support of another region. Support she didn't have as far as Eunice was aware.

For a reason Eunice didn't know, Malice visibly relaxed when she mentioned Alucard's Region.

"What do you mean by local for the poisons?" he asked. "You know who her supplier is?"

Eunice did. And so did he. She stared at Malice, observed the soft, boyishness of his features, how the candle made his white hair bright like flames. To the fairness of his pale eyebrows, almost nonexistent against his pearl white skin. Her stomach dropped. "It's Blodwen Pretorius."

Malice froze. "You're sure?"

She nodded. "I am."

Head moving without his eyes, Malice let the room grow silent as his posture slumped. It must have felt horrible, a dagger to the heart. He was close to the Pretorius's. Hell, he'd asked her to protect Kiran if he hadn't returned from his first mission. She could only imagine the betrayal he must have felt, the confusion.

"Well," he said after a time, voice unnervingly steady yet monotonous, "go on. What else do you know?"

It wasn't much, Malice soon learned, but it was enough to give him a head start, she was sure. They had talked for hours. She could feel it in the rigidity of her muscles. A tiredness settled into her bones as well. She fought it the best she could.

Malice appeared lost in thought, the room quiet again, so Eunice closed her eyes. Just for a moment. She couldn't tell whether it felt good to get everything off her chest or if it would all come back to bite her in the ass later. Still, her mind was a little clearer now, her shoulders not so tense.

"I want," Malice said, startling Eunice, her eyes flinging open, "to go around the kingdom. Helping where I can, gaining the people's trust, respect, admiration, anything that draws them to my side."

Eunice looked curiously at Malice. "It almost sounds as if… you plan to go against her highness."

"What did Alkeim warn you about during training?" he asked, changing the subject.

She frowned. "He warned me about your weaknesses, how the queen knows them, and how she plans to use them against you." There was no point in keeping this from him when she basically spilled her guts moments earlier.

"Then I do plan to go against her," he said simply, nothing about his tone or demeanor changing.

"What?"

"With everything you told me—which is likely only a fraction of her deeds—I have every right to." He sat up straighter and came to the edge of his seat. "If I'm going to have any real chance at dethroning her, I need the people on my side. A kingdom is nothing without its people and neither is a ruler."

"Wanting to revolt the queen is easier said than done."

"I'm aware."

Reclining, Eunice couldn't argue with his reasoning. The illogical side of her agreed. The support of those who would be most affected by a change in rule, at least, if not the entire region, would be imperative. He was aiming small right now, but he would quickly need to gain favor with the other kingdoms. Sooner rather than later.

The logical side of her wondered; "Is the throne worth it?" If there was anything Malice truly needed to consider, sit on, let roll around his skull, it was this. Eunice was in the same boat: was following Malice, if he decided to go against the queen, worth putting her wife in danger?

"It has nothing to do with the throne," he snipped. "I don't want it. I plan to hand it off as soon as I can, but I won't give it to some pompous monkey who thinks the world revolves around them."

Eunice, a little taken aback, said carefully, "You want to find someone worthy of the crown?"

"Yes." Malice stood, stepped away from the chair, and paced. "Why would I go through all the trouble of saving the region from the queen to pass it on some halfwit with their foot up their ass?" His gaze sliced to Eunice, anger warming the coldness of his serpent green eyes.

She smiled slightly. "As your first sword, I'll help in any way I can," she said.

"I need more information."

"I can only dig into the servants so much before they get suspicious." There were a few she was lucky didn't tell her highness about Eunice pestering them. Nothing had happened to her wife, and it was how she knew they hadn't.

Malice waved his hand toward her, a flippant gesture. "I know," he said, then halted. "I want you to search Queen Vendetta's study."

Eunice's jaw dropped as words refused to enter her mind, let alone leave her mouth.

"Draga has accounts for everything, from her diet to what she taught me. Draga not giving the queen any information? No records of their trades and deals or a list of partners, established and potential? Who their enemies might be?" He raised an eyebrow. "I'm not asking you to ransack her study, nor am I asking you to look through her stuff." He continued to pace. "Look at what's on the desk and on the shelves. In and out."

"That's it?" It sounded too simple for what he wanted to do.

Malice nodded. "That's it. Once you're out of there, you need to tell me the general contents of what you found. Big or small, doesn't matter."

"And what will you do?"

"When I know there are records in her study, I'll find a time to get in there and trace the parchment."

Eunice shot out of her chair. "That is about the stupidest thing I've heard. Are you looking to get yourself killed before you have the chance to knock her down?"

If someone caught him, if the queen suspected anything and had him tailed, she would have enough of an excuse to dampen the good reputation he planned to build. *If* she chose to be merciful. A liar, a deceiver, a traitor; the people wouldn't know who to trust but they would know Malice wouldn't be it. Eunice could take the fall. Both she and Malice could say she disobeyed Malice's orders and went rogue. Malice would dismiss Eunice as his first sword, solidifying the accusation. She and Helle would flee, get as far away from the queen as possible.

"I know what you're thinking," Malice said.

"Do you?"

He shrugged. "Maybe. But I'm saying this not because I don't think I'll get caught."

Perhaps they were on the same page, albeit reading different paragraphs.

"I have a way in and out. No one will see me leave, no one will see me enter. I go in, get the information, and leave. Simple."

"… And this way in is what, exactly? A miracle?"

Malice walked to the furthest end of the room, beyond the bed. He stood there for a moment. Was his plan to stick to the shadows? If that was the case, he was in for a rude awakening. That white hair of his would give him away, no matter how silent he was.

Suddenly, he sank lower and lower, until he disappeared. Eunice blinked at the empty corner when a hand grabbed her ankle. She shrieked, jumping, and made to stomp on the hand as Malice climbed out from under the desk, stopping her foot midair. Eunice, frozen, watched the prince crawl on the floor, stand, and present himself to her as if to say, *see?*

"What was that?" she breathed and lowered her foot, unsure whether she needed to be amused, scared, or utterly confused. Frankly, she was all three.

"Dark magic," he said and leaned against the desk. "It's how I'll get in and out without being seen."

She didn't want to question things further, not with his magic. She had the feeling it would give her a headache. "Why do you need me?" Using darkness to travel seemed to be a pretty sure way to keep himself out of harm's way. Eunice no longer fit into his plans.

"I don't have the time to look around." He sounded exasperated, as if Eunice should have known. She pulled a face at him, to which he pulled one on her. "Inyene, Odovacar, and Draga kept me busy enough. And now I'm sent on missions at random."

He would need a damn good excuse to ditch his siblings' lessons. If one existed. "Fine," she sighed. "When?"

"Soon. Whenever you feel you can get in there, do it. Don't waste an opportunity because you think there might be a better one. Chances are, there won't be."

"Find you afterward?"

He nodded.

They had discussed so much, and every topic swirled in her head, her brain throbbing. "Is that all?" she asked.

"For now, it is."

"I'll take my leave."

She passed the prince and headed to the door, closing it behind her as she stepped to the side and slid down the wall. Head in her hands, she took a few deep breaths, the reality of what she was going to do hitting her like a war hammer. She was going to sneak into Queen Vendetta's study, snoop around, then walk out unscathed with her head still on her shoulders. And she had agreed to it.

What would Helle think? Eunice had to warn her wife, tell her what might happen, and tell her what she should do if something happened to Eunice. Something most certainly would happen to her. It was a question of what.

Fatigued and frustrated, rolling her shoulders, Eunice pushed herself off the wall. It was late and there was much left to do.

Saved by Luck or Fate
XXVI

The time to act came sooner than Eunice expected, sooner than she had wanted it to come. The queen alongside Draga, Inyene, and Alkeim were scheduled to leave the kingdom in the morning, Eunice guessed, to retrieve a shipment of slaves. That left the queen's study vacant for the morning and afternoon.

The issue, of which she could think of several, was getting past servants in such a way it wouldn't make Eunice suspect. Royals, gratefully, wouldn't be a problem. They would think Malice had sent his first sword on a fool's errand. He more or less did, making Eunice the biggest fool for accepting. The mornings were too busy, servants crawling around the castle like ants hurrying from one chore to the next. Noon would be the best time.

And Eunice was right.

Up the stairwell from the first floor, she passed one servant with a pail of water, a towel, and soap in hand. The servant smiled at Eunice, and she smiled back, reaching the platform and turning toward the eastern wing. She stopped, looked at either end of the corridor, and went left, magic coating the bottom of her feet to keep her steps silent.

The dark stained door carved with thorns and swords opened silently to a gloomy study of reds and blacks. Wax, jasmine and something foul, like blood, were thick in the air.

Once inside, Eunice waited for her sight to adjust, then crossed the floor, eyes meticulously picking apart the contents lying on the desk, ignoring the tension riddling her body. Like Malice, the queen was well organized. Papers both blank and scribbled upon sat on the right side of the desk. Pens, feathered, black, gold, bronze, and silver, rested in the clay cup shaped to resemble a crow, wings pressed to the sides, the beak its handle. Shadowy ink sat next to it. New candles had been placed in the rusty gold colored candelabra, the white wax and wicks untainted by flame. A few books or journals occupied the left side, untitled, as well as a collection of scrolls held together by coarse string.

There was a wrongness in everything her sights landed on, the queen's very essence embedded within the objects of her study. The essence of her highness, however, was much more palatable than seeing her in the flesh. Eunice locked the unease creeping underneath her skin, inside her bones.

Shelves built into the walls held decorations, trinkets, more books, and scrolls. Most of the back wall was open, the bottom having a shelf crammed and stacked high with parchment, old and new, loose-leaf and bonded, a curtained window above. Row after row, shelf after shelf, Eunice found nothing exposed, which wasn't surprising. Only a fool would keep their secrets on display.

If she could shift through the study, take everything from her highness's desk and shelves to examine them, she could find something proving Queen Vendetta's transgressions. As was, Eunice wouldn't find a damn thing, and this would have been a waste of time.

With a sigh, knelt in front of the bench on the back wall, Eunice conducted her final search, eyes jerking from one document to the next. She paused, reached for a discolored set of papers bound with red string, and stopped herself.

Could she leave the first thing to warrant suspicion alone?

No, she couldn't. Not if she wanted to make this endeavor worth it. One thing out of place could be blamed on a servant using too much force while dusting. Provided Queen Vendetta permitted servants to enter her study.

Carefully, Eunice tugged the makeshift journal out of its confinement. She held it for a moment, feeling the weight of it in her hands, knowing if she opened and read the material or shoved it back into place, there was no going back. She'd disobeyed Malice's orders by touching the queen's possessions. Worse, she *had* touched the queen's possessions. Rolling her shoulders, she flipped the leather cover. They were letters. Every other one was addressed to Vendetta, the handwriting small and sharp, others unknown. As she skimmed over the contents, a name appeared on the second to last page in the third paragraph.

To break your word means to break the cradle of security I offer. I thought wiser of you, Hyacinthia, considering your prior title of noble and as a Valor.

Eunice went to the next letter.

You left wisdom to the wind the moment you stole my grandson. I kept the peace for sake of Nyx and only her. Think not that I would hesitate to drag you down to the depths of hell should your thinly veiled threats occur, and your even thinner swathe of protection be ripped from them. If violence is what you desire, shall I invoke history, send upon you the might of Alucard's? As this was your final warning, let this be mine; leave Malice and Nyx alone, else death befalls you and your kin.

Hyacinthia Valor, the former Noble of Ryzion, was said to have relinquished her nobility to live her elder years in peace. That, however, didn't seem to be the case. It probably never was. More importantly, Malice was mentioned. He was her grandson, Nyx his mother—Eunice presumed Queen Vendetta had not birthed Malice or had an affair since

Malice's appearance was so different, but to think Malice was grandson to Hordes Reap, father of Nyx, founding ruler of Hordes Region and the biggest reason the war of species was ended.

Not only did this make Malice a genuine contender for the throne, it made him the *only* true heir.

So many questions berated her head. How had Vendetta's predecessors come to rule if the Reap line hadn't died with Hordes? Where was Nyx? Where was Hyacinthia, who traded her nobility to keep her daughter and Malice safe? Not that it worked. Malice was as safe as a sheep in a dragon's den. This may not have been what Malice was looking for to incriminate her highness, but it would work better to gain favor with the people and nobles.

Shoving the letters back into place, Eunice hurried to the door, almost ramming her hip into the corner of the desk.

Voices carried, nearing the door from the hallway. Eunice stopped dead in her tracks. They were familiar. Draga. Inyene. Queen Vendetta. *Fuck.* Eunice sucked in a breath, held it, her body tight with dread and fear, the muscles of her shoulders bunching so tightly they were close to cramping. She probably reeked of terror. Swiftly, she pressed herself flat against the wall beside the entry. *I'm fucked. I should've left half an hour ago. A quick look. That was all I was supposed to do. This is it; this is where I die. Damnit, damnit, damnit!*

Draga sounded similar to the queen but was higher pitched, while Inyene's tone was harsh.

"Blodwen is a smart girl," the queen said. It was the first thing Eunice could fully make out, which meant they were closer still.

Right outside the door, their voices were clear, as if they were speaking face-to-face. *I'm sorry, Helle.* Eunice screwed her eyes shut, preparing for her highness to walk in, notice Eunice, and take her head from her shoulders without asking, wanting an explanation, or a second thought. A servant would then be called to take her body away, another to clean her blood off the marble floor.

"Your highness," a panicked voice said, a man, perhaps. "His majesty has the fever. We have been trying, but it has yet to lessen."

Heart pounding, breath lodged in her throat, Eunice waited on pin pricks for what was to come.

The queen sighed. "Fine, take me to him. The two of you leave, rest, I care not what you do." Footsteps carried away from the study.

"Don't have to tell me twice," Inyene said with a grunt and, presumably, left. Another set followed in suit.

Minutes went by, yet Eunice remained stiff as a blade. Afraid her sigh of relief would be too loud, Eunice held her breath as she stepped off the wall, turned the knob, and opened the door.

Draga stared down at her, eyes as black as a cloudy night. Eunice gasped, her entire body rigid with the realization death loomed over her. The princess looked regal, her velvet dress of lilac purple embroidered with green flowers trailing up the skirt and sleeves, straight red hair falling around her shoulders. Their gazes met. Eunice didn't know what face she was making, but gods did she hope it was pitiful. Just then might Draga let her go. Or make her death painless.

Eventually, Draga smirked. "Here I expected to see Malice," she said and stalked off toward her own study a few doors down.

Not willing to waste another second, Eunice ran, her mind racing faster than her feet carried her. It was mid-afternoon. Where would Malice be? Avoiding servants on the way to the fourth floor, Eunice, as thankful as she was, couldn't help but question Draga's motives. Why would she let her go? Why did she expect to see Malice? Was she on Malice's side, or did she want to be the one to dish out his punishment? Did she know about his parentage?

Thank gods. Eunice, panting, stopped at Malice's doorway. Three boys sat at the desk, chatting, laughing, eating. She waited a moment to catch her breath and collect herself.

"But why?" Zephyrus questioned as he sank his teeth into a chunk of beef. Clearly, she had come in the middle of a conversation.

Kiran shrugged. "Not sure. At least, not entirely. Mother wants me to focus on herbal medicine."

"Well," Malice chimed in, wiping his mouth with a napkin, "you aren't training to become a field medic, are you?"

"No," the beastmen admitted. "But it would still be nice to learn in case extra hands are ever needed."

Finally, breathing settled, Eunice stepped into the room, catching the boy's attention and silencing them.

"Lady Eunice?" Kiran asked sweetly, eyes big and brown, nose somewhat flat, face rounded. He was only a year older than Malice at thirteen. Unlike Malice, however, he had entered adulthood, though barely. She could hear it whenever he spoke for a prolonged time, his voice cracking often.

Zephyrus sat by Kiran, the same age as Malice, his voice a bit deeper, a few red blotches on his face, wisps of facial hair starting on his upper lip. He resembled his father to his crimson eyes and smoke-grey hair to their face shape—squared. Issur's had a sharpness Zephyrus didn't yet, youth keeping his features pudgy.

"Is something wrong?" Malice was the one to ask this time, his tone nothing like Kiran's; plain.

"Yes," she said. "I apologize for interrupting your lunch, but I found something you should hear, my prince."

He raised a white eyebrow. "Can it wait till we've fin—"

"It cannot." She did not get caught to wait for them to eat their mostly full dishes. "I don't have a problem with sharing in front of your friends if you want to continue stuffing your face." Mentally, she scolded herself. Her manner was far too snippy for whom she was talking. Still, her patience was waning, and he *needed* to know what she found. Now, rather than later.

Despite Kiran and Zephyrus exchanging glances with one another and looking between Malice and Eunice, the prince's eyes held Eunice's.

"You guys should leave," he said finally to his friends, both of which nodded, stood with their trays of food, and departed. Kiran lingered at the door as if to ask, *are you sure,* until Malice smiled at him.

Eunice closed the door while Malice cut the lamb chop on his plate into small chunks. The smell of seared meat, herbs and spices, and vegetables reminded her of how she had only eaten an apple at home that morning. Of course, Helle lectured her about it, but Eunice had promised she would eat at the castle. She hadn't, but she would.

Malice gestured to the chair at his side, biting a fork full of meat.

Eunice shook her head. "I'll stand."

He said after he swallowed, "I assume you got into her highness's study?"

For now, she thought it best to keep Draga catching her to herself. "Malice."

Malice flinched at his name and set his utensils down, pushing his plate away. Apparently, her tone was hard to ignore. She couldn't hear it herself. Or perhaps it was the sound of his name coming from someone other than his friends.

"There was nothing out in the open," she reported. "But I found a collection of letters on the bench behind her desk."

"Go on."

"When I grabbed them out—" Malice frowned. He didn't want her to touch anything almost as much as she didn't want to. At the moment and in hindsight, she had little choice—"Vendetta was speaking with the prior noble of Ryzion, Hyacinthia." The shock having had time to wear off, her mind could process how fucked the situation truly was. Queen Vendetta abducted Malice, and, based on the letters, proceeded to threaten Nyx's life and break her agreement with Hyacinthia.

Eunice had always believed Vendetta simply wanted power; she had it. How did Malice, a child who would have likely never come within an inch of the crown if not for her, play into that? She compromised her precious throne all by herself when she decided abducting Malice was a necessity.

"Eunice?" Malice said.

"Hyacinthia Valor is your grandmother," she blurted. "Your grandfather is Hordes Reap."

Malice's eyes widened to a saucer.

"She gave up her nobility to protect you and your mother—your birth mother. Vendetta hasn't been holding up her end of the deal."

"You… read of the letters?" he asked slowly, carefully, as if the words would bite him if he spoke too quickly.

"No, only a few. It was the last thing I found. I ran out of time."

"Do you know where the queen is?"

"In her bedchamber. King Emil caught the fever," she said.

"Tonight," he said, his disbelief coming under control, "I'll get those letters."

Between Brothers
XXVII

Part I

Malice couldn't look at those letters anymore.

It was morning already. He had read them over and over and over, trying to make sense of them. Now his head throbbed violently. He couldn't see straight, like the world was pulsating.

A knock came to the door. Jolting, he flipped and thrust the letters across his desk when it opened. He expected to see Eunice, but she waited for permission to enter. Zephyrus never came on his own, and Kiran usually barged right in.

Odovacar, wearing his riding gear of dark brown leather, stood in the hallway's light, red hair in a ponytail. Malice winced away from the brightness, head aching.

"What do you want?" Malice asked, blinking his brother—not brother now, he supposed—into focus. The last time Odovacar visited his chambers like this was when the twins were alive, beating him and Kiran. The memory ignited a brief kindle inside his veins, but he had been the one who killed them. His anger was no longer warranted, he supposed.

"You and I are to go on a mission," he said simply. "We leave in an hour.”

“When did you receive the order and why wasn’t I told?”

“I was given the mission four days ago,” he said, adding, “and I *am* telling you.”

Malice shot his glare at the floor. “Do I have a choice?”

“No.”

Of course not. “I’ll be down in ten minutes.”

“Your horse will be packed by then.”

“How kind. I’m actually getting a horse this time.”

Queen Vendetta had been sending Malice on missions since he was ten, but never had he been given a horse of his own. He was stuck in a wagon, behind some oaf, or was made to walk. He had brought his wings out and flew above his Squad twice in the last two years. Knowing the sensation didn’t mean he knew how to bring any aspect of his true form out on command. He didn’t know where to start or who to ask, either.

“I still need to change,” Malice told his brother, since he wore a long shirt that passed for a dress. “Will you tell me anything about the mission?”

“Eventually.” With that, Odovacar took his leave, his boots plodding down the hall in deliberate strides.

Malice had searched the stables near the dovecotes, Odovacar nowhere in sight. Venturing to the eastern, more southeastern, side of the castle revealed a second paddock and stable. Malice didn’t know there was another. It was smaller, the wood darker, and carved with serpents and daggers. The rafters were also more intricate, the beams resembling the ceiling in the foyer.

Odovacar's horse was saddled and ready to be mounted. There was a second horse out of its stall, also saddled, a step stool beside its belly, which Malice assumed would be his. Both had two pouches on their sides, bedrolls behind the saddle, and a few other things strapped to the horses. A servant quietly waited near Odovacar, head down, something in their hands. Leather, perhaps; it was sepia colored.

Hay and dung mingled with the salty breeze for an unpleasant stench. The difference, however, from what he usually smelled in the castle, was refreshing, so he didn't mind. Six horses whinnied in their stalls. Birds sat in the rafters, despite the little space, nests of dead grass and twigs peeking from the top. Malice's shoes crunched and rustled straw, the boots uncomfortable thanks to his clawed feet.

The servant noticed Malice before Odovacar had. Or he simply didn't bother acknowledging Malice's approach. The second option seemed more plausible.

Bowing, the servant said, "Young prince, I am here to dress you in your riding gear."

Malice halted and blinked. "Really?"

"We do not have all day," Odovacar said, his voice on the gruff side when it wasn't talking over royals.

Malice lifted his arms for the servant to guide a leather jacket over his head, and fastened the laces on top of his shoulders, underneath his arms, down the sides, and in the front. Breeches with open pant legs were put on next, the servant seamlessly weaving the laces through the eyelets then tying it at his hips. Lastly, the servant had Malice lean forward and balance on one foot while his hands held onto their shoulders so they could take off his current boots. Apparently, they weren't good enough. Boots going to his knees—with even more straps and laces—were slid over his feet and secured. When the servant finally rose, they handed Malice a pair of gloves, to which he declined. Gloves and shoes were one and the same because of his long nails. He tried to keep them trimmed, but they grew back within the hour.

The servant left soon after, bowing and hurrying toward the castle.

"Saddle up," Odovacar said as he hopped, one foot in the stirrup, into his saddle, reins in hands.

Malice stepped onto the stool, grabbed the saddle's horn, shoved his foot into the stirrup and mounted the mare, settling himself as he grabbed the straps. The seat was much harder than he thought it would be.

"Her name is Snow," Odovacar mentioned as he ushered his horse forward, passing Malice. The sunlight engulfed him outside the stable.

Fitting, he thought and tugged the reins in Odovacar's direction.

Uncomfortable and hot, Malice and Odovacar made their way through the castle grounds to the kingdom. People greeted them with smiles and waving hands. By them, it was mostly Malice. Quite a few came up to his horse and shot the breeze—them talking, Malice listening—or thanked him for one thing or another as he flashed a smile. Odovacar did no such thing, ignoring those around him, back straight, head forward until they were amidst the grass and flowers.

Malice trotted up alongside him, his horse veering a little when he drew her back. He was lucky Snow was trained because he certainly wasn't.

At Odovacar's side, Malice saw the relaxed nature of his expression, the hardness in his features melting like ice in the heat, his shoulders slumping. Odovacar closed his eyes and inhaled, grip loose on the reins. He looked young. Malice had never thought he looked older till now. The darkness and solemnity he came to associate with Odovacar aged him well beyond his years when he was only twenty-six. Memories dredging, Malice remembered this version of his brother from the first time he'd gone to the dining hall at four. Youthful, not yet so defeated.

"It is nice to escape the kingdom every now and again," Odovacar said, voice gentle.

Malice, returning his attention to what lay in front of him, agreed to an extent. The true escape came when he could go to the Kings Summit and see Magnus. He wasn't about to say that out loud, though. "Sure," he said instead.

Their travels were spent in silence. Across the undulating plains of Hordes Region, butterflies flapped around heather, jasmine, ginger lilies, and others while bees lazily buzzed close by. Birds flew overhead, one, a couple, a flock. It was paradise outside of hell.

Evening painted the sky scarlet, pink, and lavender, the clouds pastel orange and yellow, a subtle breeze swaying the grass. Odovacar altered his direction closer to the Nameless Lake almost at the center of the region. It was huge, the calm water reflecting the sky above.

"We will make camp here," he said and dismounted.

Malice wasn't aware they could make camp. It didn't seem like their horses were packed with enough supplies for them to stop anytime soon. He thought they would get said supplies from Estera, the outline of the city beyond the northern end of the lake.

As Malice jumped down, swinging his leg over and taking his foot from the stirrup, he asked, "Are we sleeping outside of tents?" With a stomp of his foot, he created a stump of earth he stepped on to reach the sacks and bedroll on Snow's hindquarters.

"Do you not like sleeping under the stars?" Odovacar had done the same, though faster, all his supplies already off the horse and spread out on the grass. He started unbuckling the straps to the saddle and bridle.

"You're letting them loose?" Malice stamped the stub back into the ground, bedroll in his arms, and turned to set it by the rest of their belongings.

"They are trained to stay close to their riders and come when called," Odovacar said. That explained why Toussaint had been so comfortable doing the same.

Once Odovacar had finished his task, he came over to Snow and showed Malice how to undo the straps, take off the saddle and bridle, then how to take off his riding gear. While Odovacar headed to the lake, pant legs rolled up to his knees, to hunt for fish, Malice was tasked with starting a fire.

The sky darkened as flames crackled in a shallow pit and their horses roamed and grazed, tails flicking. Odovacar returned with five fish on a spear of ice, stabbed them again with a stick, and shoved those into the dirt to roast the fish. He turned toward his things, grabbed his sword and a leather satchel. Pulling a whetstone out of the bag and the blade from its scabbard, he poured some water from his skin over the stone. In long, diagonal movements, blade slightly tilted, it made a rather satisfying scraping sound as he began the sharpening process.

Malice observed the purposeful movement. The re-wetting of the stone before he switched, and went the opposite way to hone the other side. Everything Odovacar had done so far was with practiced ease and speed, as if this were routine for him. Based on how he relaxed immediately after leaving the kingdom, perhaps it was routine. And more of an escape than Malice gave it credit for.

The fish sizzled and popped over the fire. It was pungent, but not horrible. Crickets chirped, while an owl or some other bird hooted in the distance.

"Why am I here?" he asked, breaking the solace between them.

Without looking up from his broadsword, Odovacar said, "To complete a mission." The warmth of the fire made his ashen skin tone fleshy in color. If not for his ridged horns, Odovacar could have been mistaken for a human.

"Answer the question seriously."

"We are to deal with a potential threat to the queen covertly," he finally explained.

Malice leaned back, using his hands to support himself. "How is *she* in danger?"

"Danger and threat are two different things." Obsidian eyes sliced from his blade to the campfire when Odovacar, a smirk on his face, placed his sword down and removed the fish from the fire, staking them in the earth to his right, somewhat closer to Malice. "We believe a group of royals from one of the kingdoms has gone rogue. They have sent letters stating their desire to attack Hordes Kingdom."

"What do they want?" From the sounds of it, they wanted to negotiate, money perhaps, or escort to a different region. *You leave us alone, we'll leave you alone* premise. Didn't seem like there was much to bargain with though.

"Escort to Cain's Region and a pardon."

"On what ground do they have to ask for that?" Malice questioned, somewhat surprised he was correct.

"None," Odovacar said as he plucked a stick from the dirt and felt the fish to see how hot it was. "But who is to say they will not act whether her highness agrees to their demands or not."

"What's our destination?"

"Directly east of Estera. There is a patch of woodland where the rogues are hiding." He sank his teeth into the soft meat of the fish, steam pouring out as he tore his mouth from the body.

Scooting closer so he could reach them, Malice also took a stick. He let his cool down a bit more. "Where do I fit in?" The mission was simple, a one-man job, perfect for Odovacar to handle on his own.

"Is it hard to believe Mother would send us on a mission together?" Odovacar asked, his tone almost amused.

"It is."

"You are right," he admitted as he wiped juice from his lip. "She did, however, say I could bring along anyone I wanted."

"Again, why me?"

"You are skilled, Malice." It was strange to hear his name from the voices of his kin—or not kin. Every time he did, it sent shivers down his spine. "I have heard reports of your competence during missions. Think of this as an evaluation. Should you do well, you will go on missions alone."

Malice's eyebrows shot up. "You don't think I'd use the opportunity to be a thorn in the queen's side?"

"Would you?"

He looked away. He valued his life enough to not let it end by her highness's hands if he could help it. It was a glorious idea, nonetheless. He could imagine the pissed off look she would have if he were to derail a mission so bad it couldn't be repaired, and her reputation would take one hell of a hit. One day, he would do something of that caliber. It wouldn't be in the near future. He needed more time, more power and influence, more people on his side. The longer he waited, the more she corrupted the land. Exhaling, Malice gobbled up his fish, avoiding the bones the best he could. A few still stabbed his gums.

"You hate her that much?" Odovacar asked, throwing the stick and fish skeleton into the fire. A cloud of embers exploded.

"As much as she hates me."

"She does not hate you," he said.

Malice grunted a laugh. His name was evidence enough of how she felt toward him—no wonder Holister reacted the way he did all those years ago. "There's no point in sugarcoating the truth." The sudden urge to ask Odovacar if he knew about his origins was hard to choke down. The reality of who he came from was a tricky thing to grasp, difficult to process. Malice *was* the grandson of Hordes Reap, he *was* heir to the throne, and—as the letters stated—Queen Vendetta had no right to rule over the region. The whole story of how the queen's line came to power was patchy and incomplete. Just another thing on Malice's to-do list.

Odovacar averted his gaze momentarily and took another fish. "She raised you—"

"She didn't raise me! Annabeth did. Blodwen and Tendai did. You and Draga raised me more the Queen Vendetta. No." *All she did was use me to release her frustrations. A tool is what she made me.* Malice clenched his jaw, glaring at the swaying orange flames tipped with red.

When he eventually peeked at his brother, Odovacar blinked at him, the light glimmering in his eyes as if they were glass. They stared at one another, silent, Odovacar probably searching for something within Malice that wasn't there.

"We should rest. We have a long day ahead of us," he said after a while.

Between Brothers
XXVIII

Part II

It was a laborious five-day ride to the east of Estera, the youngest kingdom in Hordes Region, the city of magic. Unlike most kingdoms throughout Vinyamar, magic reigned supreme in Estera, governed social class, lit the streetlamps, built the roads and houses, determined the weight of one's pocket.

Odovacar and Malice rode through it, their destination beyond its outskirts. The streets were massive slabs of rock. The lamps of metal, shaped into a bird cage with a sparrow on the outside, contorted over the streets like upside down hooks, fire dancing inside. Houses and stores, even the castle, were solid buildings erected from the earth or smoothed stone as if someone swept away the impurities.

As they trotted by, people used magic for basic tasks: drying laundry, washing dishes, blowing debris from their shop's entrance, watering their plants, roasting meat. At first, Malice seemed curious. If Odovacar did not know any better, he would have said Malice was excited, and perhaps he was. However, the further they traveled, the more his infatuation turned to annoyance. Odovacar shared the sentiment.

The use of magic within Estera, as incredible as it was, was reckless. If Estera were to come under attack, the people would be too tired from overexerting their magic to defend themselves. The entire city would cease to function and fall.

Outside the kingdom, the sun bleeding into night, Odovacar and Malice spotted the small forest, a cluster of black plum and Marula trees. They stopped, dismounted, and continued approaching the forest on foot. It was warm, warmer still with leather on. They were closer to the sea now, the air briny.

Despite choosing Malice over his own first sword, who was rather distraught about it, Odovacar had his reservations about using him on the mission. He was proficient, yes, but a child. As they weaved around trees, Odovacar glanced at Malice. His white hair was whipped back from days on the saddle, his skin a bit red. If he asked, he doubted Malice would sit idly outside while Odovacar handled the rogues inside. He sighed, motioning for Malice to take cover behind a tree trunk.

The boy nodded and pressed his back into the nearest Marula tree. Odovacar joined him and stared at Malice as he considered asking him to stay put.

Instead, he whispered, "We are here to kill them and get out. Understood?"

"Is… that the entire plan?" he asked, green eyes narrowing.

"No." He was not Toussaint.

It was simple. Odovacar was bait. He would go in through the front door, cause a commotion and kill as many as he could while Malice snuck in some other way. The most he knew about the location was it was a two-story outpost. With his dark magic, Malice should have little trouble getting in. Malice agreed.

Again, they shifted through the trees, both applying the silent walk technique Inyene had taught them. Unlike Inyene, silent walking never became an unconscious habit. Odovacar had to concentrate on the thin layer of magic coating the bottom of his feet. He knew Malice had to do the same, as he was relatively new to the skill.

Soon enough, they spotted a wooden house with two windows, light emanating from within, and a thatch roof. The outpost. There was no door on the side facing them. A shadow passed over one window, however. About thirty meters out, Odovacar now saw how old the outpost was, moss growing on the shabby, faded wood, thinned patches of thatch making the roof jagged like a poorly paved road.

Hairs on the back of Odovacar's neck stood, the scars on his back aching when he dragged a blade of ice from the scabbard on his hip. Malice's head flicked to him. Odovacar nodded, and he was off. Odovacar, once Malice was out of sight, stayed low as he crept around the house, finding the front door. Chatter and rolling dice sounded inside before the familiar clunk of a goblet slamming on a table.

Straightening his hunched posture, facing the door as if he were about to knock, Odovacar kicked it. The hinges rattled. All went silent. He kicked again; the wood cracked. Kicked a third time when, finally, the door flew, skidding across the foyer's floor and crashing into the wall joint connected to a staircase. Warmth rushed out in a wave as the smell of alcohol, pungent body odor, and mugwort overwhelmed him. Odovacar almost turned away.

He entered the room as if it were his and surveyed the space. The ceiling was lower than the standard four meters, so giants could walk freely without concern of hitting their head. To his right was a table, half of the rogues standing, the other half sitting, all in casual garments. Though, Odovacar's riding leather was not so different.

Still in shock, it took a moment for any of them to realize Odovacar had a weapon, even longer to realize the weapon had left his hand, impaling a dark elf's forehead, and then a few more seconds to recognize who he was and what the queen had decided. The dark elf thudded to the floorboards. All turned to chaos.

One shrieked the horror of their comrade's death, while a group of them shouted and cursed Odovacar. The other three ducked behind the back wall, leaving nine to face him. Four hung back as five charged, Odovacar rushing them as well. The closest went down easily, a fluid slice across the jugular, crimson flowing at an impossible rate. The next parried Odovacar's strike while the third, a fishman, got behind him.

Odovacar shifted as the rogue in front of him slipped on the growing pool of blood and crashed into the one after his backside. He stabbed the fairy who slipped, the blade of ice meeting resistance, then freedom and resistance again as it penetrated the fishman. Her brows knotted, dead weight forcing her to the ground.

Thuds and booms rattled the ceiling. Sounded as if Malice was busy as well. When Odovacar wrenched his blade free and turned, an arrow of wood whistled past him, *thunked* into the wall. It was close and well timed.

Footsteps thundered down the stairs. Glancing, Odovacar reeled as water surged from the stairwell, Malice at the front of the wave, getting consumed. The rogues near the back raced toward him simultaneously.

Ice encased Odovacar's feet in a heartbeat, and the water slammed into him like a wall. Pain burst throughout his body, taking his breath away. He immediately clamped his jaw. He glimpsed Malice. Odovacar stretched his arm and hoped Malice would see before it was too late. He did. Malice grabbed Odovacar's hand, Odovacar grasping him like a vise.

Turning away from Odovacar, Malice held his free arm out, fingers extended. Seconds passed as a tightness grew in Odovacar's chest, the need to breathe becoming increasingly more difficult to suppress. The ice on his feet needed to go, and the door needed to be open, so they could… escape? He peeked over his shoulder. The door was indeed open, but the water was not flowing out. *Damnit.* Someone still controlled it. Freezing the water would not solve the situation, it would only make it worse. He was useless.

Red strands flowed around Odovacar's head, startling him, but it was only his hair. The water moved the way it originated. Then, as if ripped from the first floor, the water shot out of the door and windows, random planks of wood missing from the walls and floor.

Malice fell to the ground and Odovacar's knees buckled when he caught himself, both spluttering for air. The pain persisted, the burning in his lungs not so intense, yet the aching of his back worsened enough to keep him short of breath.

Wobbly, Malice rose, stumbled, and faced the stairs, a sword of darkness manifesting his hands. Voices and feet clamored to the stairwell. As he went to step forward, Malice collapsed, gasping. The sword dissipated. He used too much magic reversing the wave. Taking control of someone else's magic while it was in its elemental form required twice the energy, and was almost as hard as controlling the four types of formless magic. Malice had exceeded his limits.

Odovacar pulled one arm back while lifting the other, an arrow of ice fashioning between the bow and string. The first rogue appeared, fell with an arrow jutting from their core. The next with an ice pick through an eye. They all rushed down the stairs and they all fell, one by one, the moment Odovacar's eyes landed on them. Now lay a pile of bleeding corpses at the bottom of the stairs.

"There were," Malice said abruptly, forcing Odovacar's attention from the accumulated bodies, "a total of fifty upstairs hiding in the bedrooms." He faced Odovacar, clothes and hair dripping, a single shiver raking his body. "They were expecting us."

His eyebrow quirked. "That so?"

Malice shrugged. "They would've been fools if they hadn't, considering they threatened the queen."

"Bastards," a haggard voice said.

Malice and Odovacar spun to meet the one who spoke. They tried to push themselves off the soggy floorboards, arms trembling, eyes glowing with defiance.

"You'll follow the devil, so long as she keeps your pockets full of coin!" they snarled.

If only it were that simple. Moving to finish the rest of the rogues, something whirled past Odovacar, hitting flesh with a smack, and a thud from the rogue hitting the ground. They fell face first, ramming the blade further into their skull, red oozing to the wooden planks. Malice sauntered toward them, yanked his knife out, and slid it back into the holster on his belt.

"We should set the outpost ablaze, save us some work," Malice suggested and walked outside, his riding gear squeaking.

Odovacar, taking in the state of the house, turned and followed, his own garments stiff and heavy.

"Do you have enough magic to do so?" The structure was soaked. It would take a time or a lot of power to get it burning.

Wordlessly, Malice pressed his palm into the outpost. Sparks painted his hand yellow and orange. Fire burst, spread and engulfed the wooden building, those inside oblivious, but not for long. They backed themselves to the edge of the glade, settling beside a tree trunk. The fire was warm and had, surprisingly, no issue with staying ignited. The blaze turned night to day, everything in the immediate vicinity tawny. Those inside had begun to scream.

The reality of what had just happened sunk in, liquid steel simmering as it cooled. There were fifty upstairs, fourteen down. Three vanished. Odovacar had killed five, then the seven from the second floor. Malice, on the other hand, killed thirty-four rogues.

Odovacar was outclassed tonight.

Leaning into the rough bark of the tree, Odovacar chuckled under his breath and gazed at the stars beyond the growing cloud of smoke. At least, he could not say it was the messiest mission he had ever been on. That title belonged to his first over ten years ago.

Next to him, Malice lifted and closed his fist, wincing as the fire dwindled to embers and smoking debris. Odovacar did not realize the rogues had stopped crying out, snips and crackles echoing, feeding the sounds of nature.

"We should find a place to make camp," Malice said and stood with a groan.

Odovacar mirrored his younger brother, both treading into the forest.

Finding an inn with two rooms available and warm baths once they reached Estera again was easy enough. There were stables for the horses as well. Using his title as prince helped, Odovacar had to admit, it also made the stay cheaper.

In the common area, they ate a meal of smoked venison, flaky bread, and fruits, then bathed, and slept. At dawn, they rode out and followed the eastern coast. Malice may have been all over Hordes Region due to his missions, but Odovacar doubted he had ever gotten the opportunity to see his land in a relaxed manner.

It seemed Odovacar was right.

Three days into their travels home, they trotted a mile from the coastline, the ocean a shimmering slate-blue horizon, a salty breeze peppering their faces. Odovacar soaked it all in, knowing it would be awhile before he could do so again. The ocean always calmed him like a lullaby to a babe, settled the worry and dread that never ceased to nestle itself within the tunnels of his veins. It also eased the tugging ache of his back.

Glancing at his side, Malice gazed at the sea. The look was of admiration rather than awe or curiosity. Odovacar could not help the smirk curving his lips as he looked ahead of them.

Near high noon, they crossed the river feeding into the Nameless Lake; Hordes Kingdom was three days away at the pace they were going, a day and a half if they overexerted their horses. Although, if he truly wanted, Odovacar could easily make three days into four. And he might.

*

As Odovacar and Malice cantered into the kingdom, their horse's hooves clacking on the granite, the streets were, as usual, packed. Clay and freshly baked goods scented the air, a floral fragrance overwhelming them as the wind picked up and died. Civilians took notice of their princes and gathered around them, slowing them further. Noise overwhelmed his ears and gradually dulled the sound of hoofbeats.

Odovacar was there, his hair fire red in the sunlight, his leathers embroidered with Hordes Kingdom's sigil, his skin a pale lavender, all indicators of his lineage and status. Yet none of the focus was on him. He was simply there, a presence blocking the right side of the road from viewing the one they truly wished to see. On a horse of white, in leathers un-adorned with insignias or patterns, his features so different from what they were used to, Malice likely glowed in the eyes of the people. His snowy hair was windblown, his skin rosy from weeks in the sun, those green eyes bright as they scanned the crowd. Malice had been making an effort to get the kingdom on his side, to help wherever he could, and paint himself in a better light. And so far, he had succeeded.

Odovacar let it continue. The people and Malice deserved a bit of a reprieve from the normal fear and oppression given to them by Mother. Malice especially.

Summer would be upon them soon, as would the Kings Summit. Malice was to attend. Odovacar suddenly felt more exhausted at the thought of the tediousness of the event. Malice found enjoyment in it where Odovacar had never. He was rather glad when Sok and Rayen took his place. They were five at the time, he was fourteen, only a couple of years older than Malice was now. Thinking back, however, reminded him of how he had admired Thusitha Cain, the prior ruler of Cain's Region and Decimus Cain's father. He had a great mind for strategy, like his son, and was someone who had valued other's opinions no matter their rank. He'd often asked the first swords, right-hand men, and children about their views.

Odovacar's gut curdled, his back suddenly searing as if daggers raked the length of him. If only he had had a parent like that, how different would his life be?

The Time to Rise
XXIX

Magnus knew who stared back at him in the mirror, his eyes a perfect blend of Holister's ghastly white and Vesh's deep violet. But the one he saw was a stranger, his red hair longer and unkempt, his multitude of freckles darker than the year prior, his broadening shoulders slumped. He was sixteen now. Too old to be a child and too young to be an adult, yet able to sit on the throne and rule over an entire realm. Taking a deep breath, Magnus knew this day would come eventually. It was what his father had been preparing him for. In the four years since his family's death, he'd taken to shadowing Yeong-Suk during her regency, and dove into the memoirs and journals of his predecessors to learn how to handle certain situations should they arise.

To say he was excited to be crowned at last wasn't exactly right. Happiness was a part of what he felt, he thought, but there was a bitterness inside his chest and a tightness in his throat.

What if I'm no better than my father?

Five knocks came to the door, tearing Magnus from his mind, and he turned in his seat. It opened as Gareth stepped in. From head to toe, he was dressed in his finest garments, which looked strange on someone so rugged. They were a mix of modern and traditional. Underneath he wore a fine blouse with ballooned sleeves in the same shade of blue as the castle floors, laces tying the front of it closed, and gold embroidered stars and moons from the collar down to the hem. His trousers were white, his knee-high boots black. On top of it all was a thick robe stopping at the knees, went over his left shoulder, and was held to his waist by a wrap. Geometric shapes masked the fabric in an array of colors and stitched beads ran along the edges. The last thing was his golden three-winged, one-eyed sun brooch pinned to the folds of the robe.

His boots clicked as he crossed the room and stood beside Magnus. When he smiled down at Magnus, the scar across his face moved as well.

"Are you ready?" Gareth asked, his voice soft.

Swallowing, Magnus rose, only wearing a white tunic and pants, both oversized, his feet bare. He wore nothing else, not even the earring from his mother. Instead, the glue gem sat on the surface of his vanity, sparkling in the light. Tradition demanded no embellishments. Magnus would abide, but gods, he wished today, of all days, he could wear that earring. To feel a hint of Vesh's presence would remedy the acid burning in his throat.

"Yes," he said, despite how far from the truth it was.

Every knight with the rank of S, the elders, and the prior ruler—or regent—were to follow Magnus while he strode through Alucard's Kingdom to the mainland. There in the open field beyond the strait, the nobles of the region would join their soon-to-be king for the coronation. It was a sign of respect and trust for both the prince and the nobles to meet outside their kingdoms.

Citizens gathered behind Magnus's party, the cobblestone streets warmed by the sun and the breeze almost non-existent. Voices quickly became loud as footsteps thundered. Salt and leather permeated the ground, a smell forever baked in the stone. Magnus had hoped when this day came, Vesh would walk alongside him, Padma next to Gareth and Father on his left. No one walked at his sides. Becoming a ruler wasn't meant to be a solitary ordeal. At least that was what he had read in his grandfather's and great grandfather's journals. Both their parents had stood with them—none of Magnus's predecessors had siblings. If they had, they would walk behind them as next in line. Padma would have been the first to take up the position. Magnus's entire body tensed, a pain pulsing through his chest. Desperately, he wanted them both to be here, almost a need like his knees would lock if they didn't show, as if he were a toddler throwing a tantrum. Was it so bad that he didn't want to be alone?

Salty mist hit Magnus's face as he crossed the white stone bridge, hundreds of people trailing to the mainland. The water below shimmered, fish swimming all around. In the distance, figures grew from the north, northeast, south, and southwest. Six kingdoms had come to give their blessings and pledge themselves to Magnus.

The sun was high when the nobles met him in long grass and daisies. Clouds passed overhead, creating a wall of shadow. Stragglers and guards filtered in from behind the carriages.

Cytor was the eldest city outside of Alucard's and from the carriage of daffodil yellow emerged Lord Gazika and Lady Zoja, both decorated in their kingdom's colors, periwinkle blue and gold, the most similar to Alucard's. Then Lord Abel of Ntesal, wearing an assortment of browns and tans to match his hair and skin. Lady Iset from Anddulia was the eldest of the nobles, a mix of angel and dwarf. Liotkin's nobles, the house of Bosch, brought their entire family. The cleanliness of their clothes was a stark difference to their location nestled at the base of the mountains. Chestimir was the Lord of Ivory's Kingdom and the only human amongst the nobles. Finally, hailing from the youngest kingdom, came Lady Thais, dressed in the blazing colors of a fire. She couldn't have been more than five years older than Magnus, yet she looked fierce and above all the others.

Magnus walked into the opening left by the nobles, followed by Yeong-Suk, who had carried a bowl of charcoal paint. The giant's feet were also bare, their dirtiness matching Magnus's. She towered over Magnus, though, her shadow twice as long as his.

"We've gathered to witness the birth of a new king," she said, her voice resonating, silencing whatever talk there may have been. Regency gave her some much-needed confidence. "Step forth nobles of the region and give your blessings and loyalty or state your disaccord."

While the head of each kingdom drew nearer, Magnus stripped his tunic, let it drop, and got down to his knees, hands on his thighs. Nobles, as much as anyone else, had the right to voice their thoughts about their new monarch. They were encouraged to do so. Positive or otherwise. Magnus had done little for his people since his father's passing. He didn't make a mockery of himself either. Their thoughts would likely be few and neutral. That was what he was hoping for, anyhow.

Lord Gazika, as the head of his house, was the one to give his blessing and was first to dip his hand in the charcoal. "Young prince," he said, his voice weathered but orotund. "I believe you will make a fine ruler." Lord Gazika bent down and placed a wrinkly hand over Magnus's heart, the cool paint making him shiver, sending goosebumps all over his body. He stayed there for a moment. "Despite your relation, you gave your father justice and your mother peace."

Magnus's jaw clenched.

"You will lead with a strong heart," Lord Gazika said, then stood and returned to his place, a black handprint on Magnus's pectoral.

Lady Thais came forth, dipping her fingers in the paint. "I trust in your head; let your mind guide your hand, young prince, not your heart," she said with a smirk and dragged her fingers down Magnus's face, his eyes closing.

May strength give you many victories, Lord Chestimir had said. *Learn well from the past,* Lady Iset told Magnus as she dipped both hands in the charcoal and placed them around his neck. Lord Joan Bosch had marked Magnus's stomach and said, *I pray you will be blessed with fertility and prosperity.* Finally, Lord Abel gave fidelity. *For your future, may your shoulders remain proud and your head high.*

Briefly, Magnus stayed on his knees, allowing the paint to dry and become tight on his skin. The silence left by the nobles—his nobles, he supposed—tickled his ears as nature took over. Birds tweeted in the distance, a howl echoing, and water constantly undulated, a melody which brought hot tears to his eyes and was hard to choke down. As much as he loved these meadows and fields, he hated them for reminding him of his mother at a time like this. He had to ignore Vesh's soothing lullaby the moment the breeze picked up and infected his mind with her voice.

Magnus got to his feet, his shoulders back, his chin tilted, bare torso covered in inky marks. There was a lingering sting behind his eyelids. Yeong-Suk moved to his front, her gentle face aged with creases and spots. She smiled at him and submerged her thumb into the charcoal, drawing a symbol on his forehead which stood for the people. A solemn vow to have their best interest at the foremost of his mind and heart, no matter which he led with. To protect them as they would protect him. To treat their trust and loyalty as though it was sacred because it could be easily lost and hard to regain.

Once the bowl was handed off to Gareth, Yeong-Suk kneeled. Magnus gently took the crown from her head, felt the weight of the gold feathers in his hands, and placed it on his own—a duty normally performed by the prior ruler or one's parent.

Standing alone, Magnus had become the king of Alucard's Region.

The field erupted in cheers and shouts. Nobles, commoners, and royals became one and the same as they mingled and rejoiced before the crowd swept Magnus back into the streets of his city. After a coronation, the region would feast and party for days until the newly appointed monarch called its end—it was tradition. One started not by Alucard himself but by another ruler, Hordes. In his journals, Alucard wrote how much of a nuisance it was, yet he let Hordes do whatever he pleased.

Only the best wines, ales and meads were brought and shared, or so their bringers proclaimed. Alcohol flowed like a fountain; Magnus wasn't entirely sure the fountain in the garden *hadn't* flowed red from all the spilled wine. The castle was full to bursting at the seams. The royals' and servants' barracks never stilled, the foyer, dining hall, ballroom, nearly every room bustling with bodies and laughter, food and drink, music and dance. Surprisingly, Gareth managed to stay next to Magnus no matter where he went or how rowdy the crowd was.

Households and nobles introduced their children to Magnus, prospects for marriage. It made his heart pound wildly. That might have been all the wine he drank tonight, though. Gareth, a little smile on his face, stood behind him, a hand on Magnus's shoulder to keep him steady. They were in the foyer, right off the stairwell. Some wealthy merchant was talking, but his words were a slurry, jumbled mess in Magnus's ears. He was drunk to high heavens. Not his fault, though. How could he refuse every goblet someone shoved in his hands? Those he didn't drink, Gareth or some other royal did. He wondered how many got drunk that way and why Gareth wasn't. Unless he was also passing the drinks along so he could stay sober.

"You need not marry her, your majesty," the merchant said with a wide grin creasing his eyes into crescent shapes. What was his name… Stewart? Magnus couldn't remember but, did it matter? "I wish to offer her to you for the night to do whatever you please." He leaned closer, his breath foul and pungently fishy. Magnus resisted the very immediate urge to vomit. "She's been well trained in bed, your majesty," he whispered, winking as he slinked away.

Magnus swallowed, his face hot as he looked away. "You… want me to copulate with your daughter?" he asked.

Gareth's grip tightened slightly, but he said nothing. Magnus was not so naïve as to not know how many people around his age were bedding someone new each night. No longer a child but not quite an adult; what a strange age sixteen was.

"If it is what you desire, of course!" Stewart laughed and wrapped his arm around his daughter's shoulders.

Magnus finally looked at her, too. She was shorter than him, her frame reminding him of the statue in the garden's fountain. Her breasts were plump beneath the material of her chiton and her hips were wide. Long, wavy hair, half braided into a bun, spilled over her shoulders. Bright jewels in her ears, around her neck and wrists, caught the warm candlelight. She was pretty, Magnus had to admit, but he was inexperienced.

"But—"

"I'll make it worth your while, your majesty," the girl said, stepping close enough for her breasts to press against Magnus's chest. "Everything you want, I can do. And if you don't know, I'll teach you."

Magnus couldn't speak as he stared down into her green orbs. Behind him, Gareth had let go of Magnus's shoulder and his presence left his backside.

"His bedchamber is on the third floor. A servant will guide you from there," Gareth said, and dipped to speak directly into Magnus's ear. "I can also send her away, if you want."

After a quick look, Magnus shook his head and ignored his apprehension. This was bound to happen eventually, right? He might as well get it over with.

Gareth addressed the girl; "His majesty has had quite a bit to drink. Will you be able to handle him?"

The girl smirked, her hand clasping his. "I will," she said.

A servant guided the girl and Magnus up the flights of stairs and pointed to a door on the left. Magnus's chamber was on the second floor. The room they gestured to belonged to Magnus's father and grandfather, probably his great grandfather too. It wasn't his yet. Despite that, when the girl opened the door, all of his belongings were there, replacing whatever might have been Holister's. The girl gasped as she marveled at the bedchamber, which was the size of a cottage. Magnus mirrored her astonishment. Though, her awe didn't last long before the door clicked shut and she tugged Magnus to the enormous bed centered on the right wall.

"My name is Lilith," she said, guiding Magnus backward onto the mattress. "You are very handsome."

"Am I?" His voice cracked a bit when she began undoing the buttons of his shirt. She grunted softly, her eyes raking Magnus's torso.

He hadn't forgone his training, so he was muscular in a soft sort of way. Unlike Gareth, whose build was forged from decades of diligence and experience. Dragging him back from his thoughts, Lilith's hands, soft and warm, explored his stomach and chest, feeling the grooves of his muscles. She straddled his lap and kissed him. Lips against his, her breath tickled his face, mint washing over him. When she drew backward, she opened her eyes and Magnus froze.

"Wai—"

She kissed him again, this time slipping her tongue inside his mouth. Those eyes were a vibrant green like grass in the spring. Too similar to Malice's.

It *felt* like he was kissing Malice.

Magnus, as gently as he could, tried to push Lilith away. "Please," he breathed in between kisses. He didn't want this. To be reminded of Malice, twisted his stomach with both disgust and shame.

"Stop, Lilith."

She didn't listen and started to grind against him, small gasps and moans escaping from the back of her throat. Her voice was pitched, her breasts squishing against Magnus, her warmth fueling his alcohol induced temperature. Momentarily, he stopped fighting, allowed the sensations to flow over him. It was pleasant, subtle tingles washing over him, spiking as Lilith teased him. Until Vesh rushed from the deepest corners of his brain. Her bashed in head splattered the floorboards because of him. Because she had a child. If they continued, if they had sex, would Lilith become another Vesh? Would Magnus end up just like his father?

"Stop!" Magnus shoved Lilith off his lap, chest heaving, bile threatening to jump into his throat from the abrupt wave of queasiness crashing into him like a boulder

As she hit the floor, she yelped. Magnus frantically got to the ground. "I'm sorry," he said, his voice weak and breathy. "I just—I can't—I've no experience and I—" What could he say to make this better? "I—"

"It's… all right," she said.

"Are you hurt?" Finally, something other than nonsense left his mouth.

Lilith shook her head. He helped her to her feet, but she moved away from him, eyes on the floor, and wrapped her arms around herself. She turned and ran, her bare feet smacking the floor.

Falling onto the edge of the bed, Magnus buried his head in his hands. He didn't want to hurt her, but he couldn't keep going. She bore little resemblance to Malice, yet it was enough to make everything feel so wrong and dirty and then… Magnus couldn't live with himself if he had forced a child onto Lilith. He didn't want that child to destroy Lilith's life like he had destroyed his mothers.

A time had passed when footsteps approached his bedchamber. Magnus looked up from his hands, his eyes stung from crying. Though, his whole body ached and was uncomfortably warm. Gareth stood in the doorway. He startled and rushed to Magnus's side, dropping to his knees.

"What is wrong?" Gareth asked, his hands coming to rest on Magnus's shoulders. "Are you all right? Did she hurt you? Force you to do something? Tell me what happened so I can fix it."

"No," Magnus sighed, "she didn't hurt me." It was the opposite, actually.

"What is wrong?" he pressed, his tone as tender as it was this morning.

Magnus met Gareth's unwavering gaze, his silver eyes like the moon on a clear night. "I… couldn't do it," he said, the words uncomfortable to get out.

"Could not… bed her?" Gareth questioned cautiously.

Magnus nodded. "I'm too drunk. What—what if—I couldn't live—another Mother—" His throat tightened, his chest caved as if a dragon had sat on it. Tears blurred and dripped from his eyes again like molten lava, burning his skin every inch they slid.

"Magnus," Gareth said as he guided Magnus into his arms. "You are not your father. Alcohol does not blind you the way it did Holister, nor do you surrender to it." He moved to cup Magnus's face, the rough skin of his thumbs wiping the tears away. "Your father did not goad Vesh into motherhood, either. She wanted you."

A few sniffles later, Magnus took in a deep breath and let it go. He knew Father hadn't forced Mother to lie with him, but he hadn't made her life any easier because Magnus was growing inside of her.

How had she not resented Magnus when he caused her pain and suffering? And how could he do that to another?

"How do you know?" Magnus asked meekly.

"Because she told me," he said. "Your father had asked me to watch over Vesh whenever I could the moment he found out. She talked, I listened. They both talked, and I listened."

Magnus wished he could believe Gareth—his heart wanted to—but his gut couldn't. He grabbed and pulled Gareth's hands from his face, too tired to fix his posture. He smiled, but the movement felt far too stiff, as if his face turned to stone, and he knew Gareth could see how fake it was. "I think I'd like to rest."

Gareth returned the smile, nodded, and rose. "I will collect you in the morning," he said and left, closing the door shut as Magnus crawled to his pillows.

Alone
XXX

Since his mission with Odovacar, Malice had been sent out on two more by himself. Every time, his heart and mind waged war inside him. His mind hated it. Not only was he doing exactly what Queen Vendetta wanted, he had to leave Kiran, Zephyrus, everyone to the queen's devices. While he was in the castle, he could protect them. She seemed content with tacking on their punishments to his own, and he was glad to take them.

The moment he stepped foot outside the castle, that protection vanished like a candle flame in the wind. He hated it.

His heart, conversely, sang with the breeze. He could escape, feel the sun warm his cold skin, allow the fresh air to fully inflate his lungs. He was free from her highness. The cost of freedom was still leaving his brother, his best friend, and first sword behind. No amount of bliss changed that. Now was no different.

Only, he wouldn't be truly alone this time around. The queen had sent Toussaint to escort her new contract to Mondlesgrave and gather information on him. Sarkis Evers, Head of House Evers in Raelle's Region, gave five ships to the queen's naval fleet for land and wealth, which also added seven hundred men to her army. In celebration of a deal well made, Sarkis was said to be in Mondlesgrave, taking full advantage of the island's nightlife. Toussaint was to confirm this, track his movements, and tell Malice at the rendezvous point, the southern docks.

At the edge of the strait, not far off from the opening channel, Malice glimpsed pale orange and blue lights undulating beneath the water's surface. Mondlesgrave had the highest population of fishmen and was the only kingdom in Hordes extending into the sea. He looked toward the five walkways spanning the gap between the island and the mainland, each probably erected from the ocean floor. Bridges would've been better. At certain times of day, the tide would submerge and disable these paths. On either side of him, the moonlight sparked the water like white fire. Salt overwhelmed his nose, the misting from the waves cool on his face. Beyond the strait, Mondlesgrave shone, muffled sounds reaching him all the way out here. Nothing like Hordes Kingdom, which was dead at this time of night.

He peeked southward. Toussaint should be there by now, meaning Malice should meet with his contact, get the information he needed, and carry on with the mission. Should. He had nothing, per se, against Toussaint. But Malice had ears of his own sent out at the same time Toussaint had departed and she returned two nights before Malice left. Eunice told him everything he needed to know without deceit. Who knew what lies Queen Vendetta might have fed Toussaint so Malice would purposely fail the mission, giving her a reason to do whatever her heart felt like. She had done it on his first mission. She would do it again. It would have been a well thought out trap had Malice not learned from his mistakes.

Across the earth bridges and through the grass humming with insects, fireflies pricking the landscape with dots of yellow, Malice's boots clumped onto wooden planks. Bronze bowls of fire on posts lined the streets. Performers dressed in brightly colored, flowing dresses, skirts, and robes danced in the middle of the road as musicians pounded drums and blew on flutes. Silver twinkled in their ears, on their wrists and necks, everywhere. Pressing deeper, Malice dodged the twirl of a baton as the warmth tickled his skin, the ends flaming green, the heavy, smoky scent of oil briefly filling his nose. Huddled in groups, closer to the red clay buildings, people gambled with cards and dice, exchanging coin, weapons, and jewels. Malice watched a man offer a young woman, wearing nothing but a silk wrap, who then slunk her way into a deer beastman's lap.

Despite the chaos and the ringing of his ears, there was laughter too, and smiles so wide they bore all the teeth one could have. He paused, absorbing what his own kingdom could be, but wasn't because of her highness. He, too, could laugh with his friends, yet he had to protect them instead. Bitterness clawed at his throat, and he compelled himself forward. He had a mission to complete.

Not much further were the taverns. Patrons packed the tables out front, their doors and windows open, the smell of savory gravy, seared meat, and mead overriding the scent of brine. Vines cascaded from and coiled around trellises over the patrons, bronze lanterns hanging above them.

Eunice had said Sarkis frequented the brothels in the southern district after he drowned himself in alcohol during the evening hours. So that was where Malice was headed.

The quality of light changed, the blaring pastel yellow turned to a mellow intimate vermillion, the noise reduced to whispers, groans, and the soft melody of a lyre. The air shifted to jasmine and oysters, a sweet fishy aroma. Malice's face may not be well known, but his appearance and name were spreading faster the more he helped those in Hordes. He thought the cloak concealing him would be too conspicuous. In this part of town, however, he blended in well. There were too many high-profile people who didn't want to be recognized.

The planks of wood gave his step a certain quality of clacks, low and dull yet loud. Which wasn't a problem, but it would be soon enough. Buildings were made of clay with dome roofs, eaves like rolling hills, rounded walls, and stained-glass windows. Instead of blazes that could rival campfires, kindles equivalent to hearth fires bathed the surrounding streets in orange. The people were less crowded in the southern district; he didn't have to worm or shove his way through.

Den of Furs read a hanging sign over the door to the brothel Sarkis was supposedly at. It was a two-story maroon building with curtained windows on its face and sides. Rather boring, but he assumed the decor inside would be anything but. He dipped into an alley two establishments before the brothel and sank into the shadows, darkness racing to consume every inch of his person. Emerging, he found himself in a broom closet—literally. There were eight brooms leaning against the wall in front of him. Light bled through the frame's gaps, the sound penetrating the door as clear as day. He must be near the entrance. A cordial voice spoke to a deeper, slurred one, and sent them to the second floor, room twenty-three. Eunice hadn't learned which room Sarkis was in.

One eye closed, hand pressed to the wall, the other to the door, Malice peeked into the lobby. A back obstructed his view, so he waited till it moved. When it did, though only slightly, he got a better view of the dim space swathed in sheen curtains, pearls and gold, candles melting on whatever surface they could. The ambiance was soft and breathy, as if the musician and their instrument were whispering to each other. Perfect, he guessed, for the environment he was in.

Eventually, when the person stepped away, Malice opened the door a crack, then a bit more, craning his neck to see the open book on the desk's surface. A quick scan of the page, a third of the way filled, revealed nothing. He glanced at his surroundings, twitched his finger, and turned the page. Sarkis had been in Mondlesgrave for seven days. Tomorrow was supposed to be his last. He found the name eight pages back. Written across from it was room eleven on the first floor.

Malice closed the broom closet's door, sighed, and stepped toward the center of the box-like space. If the common areas were in the front, the rooms were upstairs and toward the back of the brothel. Not that he knew any better where Sarkis's room was. He would have to take a shot in the dark and hope for the best. Malice was too young to walk around freely. He would be thrown out in an instant. Doubtless, he would pass as the servant who beat dirty linen. If only his appearance suggested he was in his twenties, lying through his teeth would be easy, getting in even easier.

Once again, he sank, rising in the corner of a pitch-black room. Against the wall, Malice felt his way around, magic coating the soles of his feet, silencing his footfalls. Although whoever was sleeping snored loud enough, Malice's steps probably wouldn't be heard. His hand brushed and followed the curve of a cold knob, the smallest amount of light glowing underneath the door. Swiftly, holding his breath, he opened, stepped into the corridor, and closed the door. With his back pressed against the cool wood, he paused, waiting to hear if there was any movement in the hall or in the room he came out of.

Nothing. Good.

Malice's head swiveled from the left to the right. Room eleven was four doors down on the opposite side. Allowing his sights to narrow on the mahogany door with bronze numbering and a worn handle, he inhaled slowly, exhaled just as slowly. He returned to the sleeping guests' room, only to be swallowed by the darkness.

Sarkis Evers, head of his house, was a sell-sword whose lips were a little too loose for the queen's liking. Eunice confirmed as much from her recon. Queen Vendetta had gotten her soldiers and boats. Sarkis was an extra, unnecessary expense.

Inside, Malice found himself huddled in the corner next to a giant brick hearth. Logs crackled within, pine and roses scenting the room. Two voices murmured into the quiet. One giggled while the other whispered. Carefully, he looked beyond the corner. A fishman and a giant lay in bed, neither clothed, the blankets crumpled on the floor beside the frame. It was bigger than Malice had ever seen. The same curtains which draped the frame covered the windows and adorned the walls. Twin couches were angled toward each other in front of the hearth, a fur rug beneath it.

The fishman was Sarkis. The giant, however, was unknown. After one more glance at the cozy couple, Malice noticed the bed wasn't against the wall. He guessed there to be at most a meter of space between them. Good way to keep the frame from knocking against the wall.

As he stepped backward, the floor disappeared, and black dragged him down. Then Malice hauled himself up from the shadow behind the headboard.

"What will you do now?" the giant questioned, her voice velvety.

"With the queen's money," Sarkis replied, his tone matching hers, "we can go anywhere. Do anything. Be anything. What do you say?" he asked. "Want to be anything with me?"

Malice hesitated when the giant's face glowed and the sheer joy in her eyes darkened some part of Malice's heart. They sat up at the same time to embrace one another, chuckling as the giant breathed a litany of yeses, smiles on their lips. Malice's chest constricted.

They chose the wrong queen.

Wall at his backside, Malice used a burst of air to kick the bed forward, the legs screeching. Sarkis and the giant gasped as their heads whipped toward him. He was already jumping over the headboard, a blade of darkness manifesting in his hands. In a single fluid motion, he cut their heads off. Warm blood sprayed and their bodies fell limp onto the mattress while their heads thumped to the floor. Quick. Quiet. Efficient. Inyene and her highness would be so proud.

Malice stared at the ichor seeping into the bedsheets, and with it, their happiness, a metallic scent mixing with the pine and roses.

They would be cold before anyone found them, and Malice would be gone, likely in his bedchamber. Once he climbed off the bed, he slipped into the shadows and stepped into the alley. The first few times he'd shadow traveled, he had hesitated, fought the darkness ensnaring him in its embrace. He got used to the sensation faster than he would have thought possible, so now, it was as effortless as taking Sarkis' head from his shoulders.

The air was fresh compared to the brothel, damp and chilled, fishy yet sweet from the mead and perfume. Malice started toward the streets when a pain lanced his core. His breath evaporated in his lungs. He wobbled and propped himself against the wall. Black coated his nails, creeping up his fingers like a droplet of ink in water. The further it climbed, the more intense the pain in his core became. Every muscle tightened, threatening to shred themselves if they didn't relax.

What was happening? His magic had never done this. Had he used too much of it? He'd done that many times, but the darkness never consumed him for it.

Suddenly, when it reached his wrist, the black leaped to the crook of his arm, the speed at which it was devouring him unsullied now. Talons raked his arms. Glowing hot knives twisted his flesh. Centipedes crawled, gnawed and injected their poison into him. He screamed, vision swaying, and dropped to the ground. The darkness viciously tore at his shoulders, collarbone, neck, then chest and stomach. All the while, the misery in his core worsened as if Inyene peeled his skin layer by layer and poured boiling oil over him. That would be better than this. Anything would be better than this.

He wanted it to end. Why wouldn't it? *Please... make it stop.*

Jolting upright, sunlight blinded Malice. He shunned away, eyes screwed shut, a dull ache radiating from his head down to the rest of his body.

"Are you all right, young man?" a brittle voice asked.

Rapidly blinking, Malice looked at the old lady staring down at him, the sky bright blue behind her wrinkled face. When did he pass out last night? He turned his hands over, flexed his fingers. The black had returned to his long, claw-like nails. With a sigh, he ran a hand over his face, which was sticky with sweat. After a time and a slight movement from the elderly lady, Malice nodded.

"I'm all right."

"Good," she said, righting herself. "Now get. I got a business to run, and I can't have mongrels sleeping outside my store." She hobbled toward the road with a huff and turned the corner.

There was a limit to magic, as it was not infinite nor kind. Malice had just learned the limit, and he would be damned if he ever crossed that line again. He would rather suffer at Inyene's hand a thousand times over than experience the hell he'd gone through last night. Gathering his bearings, Malice stood, his body trembling like a leaf, and made his way into the busy streets. Good thing he mirrored the drunkards who stumbled their way home or to their businesses.

He wondered if Magnus knew about this, since their magic was similar. He needed to know. Malice didn't wish that sort of pain on anyone, the queen included. His core throbbed as he walked through the morning chaos of Mondlesgrave. By the time he reached the river, he would be fine. Until then, he needed some food and something to drink. It was a long way home.

Eye to Eye
XXXI

When the afternoon shifted to evening, Malice and Eunice were called to the throne room.

Dread and anxiety sank to the pits of Malice's stomach, chest tight. Had they been caught? Did the queen figure out they had been in her study? Many questions overwhelmed his senses, his ability to think straight nonexistent on the way to the first floor.

Eunice strode beside him, rolling her shoulders constantly as if there was a knot she couldn't get rid of. Based on the sweat trickling down her forehead, she was probably in the same state he was.

Malice's and Eunice's boots resonated off the stairwell into the foyer. Since it was always so dark within the castle, it was jarring whenever he stepped outside, the bright sun striking. The walls of burgundy never ceased to remind Malice of drying blood, a bitter taste coating his tongue in an instant. Above hung a silver chandelier, providing a surprising amount of light. Yet, Malice was sure the torches, candles and lamps scattered about were the main reason he could see a meter in front of him.

Into the eastern wing, side by side, Malice and Eunice entered the throne room. Malice stopped dead in his tracks.

They weren't the only ones who had been summoned.

The Pretorius and Laska families knelt before the dais the queen's black throne sat on. Toussaint was there too, his person sticking out like a sore thumb. Eunice halted as well, her focus on a woman. Her wife, he could only assume.

Why are they here? He didn't understand. If Queen Vendetta knew about their trespassing, why involve innocent people? Malice was the sole person to blame. Every fiber of his being shook. Violently. He was drowning in the emotions, the strongest of them dragging him deeper.

Alkeim stood to the throne's right while his majesty and Felim were to its left—King Emil was almost as surprising to see as everyone else. Draga, Odovacar, and Inyene were also out of the shadows. He was used to the dire or impassive expressions Draga and Odovacar wore. The seriousness of Inyene's features, however, which were normally alight with glee, stuffed his stomach with rocks.

The only set of eyes moving were the queens, and they were nothing short of ice. She smiled, her lips thin, her eyes creasing.

Malice's pulsed quickened.

Together, he and Eunice joined the line of people on the floor, Eunice bowing adjacent to her wife. There was one spot left. Malice kneeled in the center of the room, the cold marble sending a shiver through his body.

"So, the mutt finally graces us with his presence," the queen said. "How benevolent of you."

He was even more confused.

"I have heard things, mutt."

Jaw tensed, he hoped it was not what he was thinking.

"You think it wise to utterly abandon the procedure of your missions?"

Relief washed over Malice, the rigidity in his limbs melting. "No," he said far too quickly.

"Oh?" she mused. "Then what of your beasty pestering my servants?"

The relief vanished. Malice needed to be careful, to choose his next words as if his life depended on it. Frankly, it did. "I… wanted to know more about your duties, your highness." He lifted his head enough to meet the queen's gaze. "If I am to rule one day, I thought I should learn all I could."

One arched brow jumped. "Rule one day," she echoed. "You? A useless mutt thinks he can take my place?"

Despite the powerful urge to look away, Malice forced his eyes to stay on hers—they were blacker than the night. "I don't."

Her highness stirred, crossing her legs to reveal a crimson heeled shoe which matched her dress. "Ah, I know. You must think yourself untouchable simply because of how much I've allowed you to get away with."

Malice's heart sank with the sudden realization Queen Vendetta knew everything. How often he left the castle, how many meals he ate, or how many baths he took. How many falcons he'd sent to Alucard's Region.

He no longer fought the need to look away, his view now the grey, white, and black of the floor.

"Have I not been lenient with you, mutt?"

She had been.

"Have I not kept you fed, bathed, clothed?"

She had done that too.

"Yet deception is how I am repaid." She grunted a laugh. "You ought to be thankful I've allowed you to send your precious letters."

Something settled upon him, forcing him ever so slightly closer to the ground.

"That I've allowed you to wander about the castle, and recently the kingdom, with absolute freedom. What of the privilege of having a first sword, hmm? You've used the poor beasty, convinced her you are the best master to serve."

Malice didn't need, or want, to lift his sights to confirm the smile on her highness's face. He could hear it, a soft, satisfied hum to her words. More like the careful work of needles driving into his ears, further into his nerves, wrenching his ribcage closer to restrain his breathing.

"Now look at where she has landed," the queen went on. "Truly, you ought to apologize for forcing my hand—I've had to bring her wife to show exactly where she stands in this court."

He didn't want to be right about that woman being Eunice's wife.

The needles increased and yanked his muscles tight.

"Shall I mention how I've allowed you the concession of friends?" Her bottom right hand gestured loosely to Malice's left. "Sparring with the son of one of my knights. Visiting the son of my personal doctors, are these not things you ought to be grateful for?"

Malice's head seized, a corrosive pain spreading through his chest.

"Mutt."

"I should be," he croaked. "I… I'm sorry."

"I'm glad we see eye to eye," she said. "You will cease all activity outside this castle. You will no longer engage with Zephyrus or Kiran. Your first sword will step down. You will burn every letter you have received and will receive. No longer are you to write Magnus. No longer are you permitted to go on missions."

A small gasp reached Malice's ears. He assumed it was Kiran. Or perhaps it was his own.

"For encouraging such behavior, everyone gathered afore me will receive twenty lashings."

Silence. It rang. It lasted. The final stitches cut off Malice's blood flow, muscles wound together, chest like a vise. When he sucked in a breath, a scorching heat replaced the weight bearing down on him and burned the threads of his crippling defeat.

"They will not," he heard himself say.

"What?" the queen's voice bounced off the empty walls.

"They," Malice got to his feet, gradually, almost losing his balance on the way, "will not."

Vendetta stood as well, brows furrowed. Behind her, shock pulled expressions taut and stiffened postures.

"They did nothing," Malice said.

"They," her highness snarled, "are the cause."

Malice should have stopped the words tumbling from his lips, but he didn't want to. "Everything I've done has been to spite you."

Queen Vendetta stepped down as Malice stepped forward.

"Eunice doesn't want to serve you. You never deserved her service."

Another step.

"You brought her wife here to scare them but all you've done is prove how easy it is to hate you. What privilege is there in being locked in this castle? This cage?" His voice grew in volume and confidence, fueled by a rage he had never felt. It was as if he was about to be consumed by it, the heat scorching his insides.

Her highness strode closer. Anger twisted her expression the same as it twisted Malice's.

"I made friends despite my *privileges*," he continued. "And I would rather rot in the dungeons than let you touch so much as a hair on their heads."

Now, in the extensive space between those who groveled and the throne of crystal skulls, Malice stood toe-to-toe with his so-called mother. Unafraid. Wrathful.

"Or what?" she growled, her hands twitching at her sides.

"I'll earn my sessions with Inyene. Earn those twenty lashings." Malice certainly had enough pent-up fury to make it so. He would relish every moment, no matter the reprimands. He would laugh in her face as he destroyed everything he possibly could.

The tension was concentrated, palpable. Yet Malice felt nothing but ire. She had sentenced his loved ones, few as they may be, to something they had nothing to do with and expected him to let it happen.

"Are you threatening me?" she asked in a low tone. A slight flare of her lip uncovered her sharp canine.

"Promising."

As Kiran taught him, blood didn't matter. Malice was Queen Vendetta's son, and he could be as horrific as she was. He could be so much worse. He *wanted* to be so much worse just to watch her writhe.

For a long while, Malice stared up into the queen's obsidian eyes. Rage creased her brow, darkened the shadows of her sharp cheekbones and straight nose. Despite her unwavering gaze, it felt like she was contemplating him and what to do next. Malice didn't know what his next move was, either. Head a bit clearer, he was more concerned about leaving the throne room alive. Everything he had said and done could be considered treason. There was the perfect executioner standing next to the throne as well, probably beside herself with joy, expecting full well to torture Malice to death as soon as the queen gave the word.

Her highness's hand shot up, hooking Malice's bottom jaw by piercing the underside of his chin into his mouth. He yelped as she lifted him off the ground. His feet flailed. Blood flooded his mouth and throat, and pain exploded.

"I hope the audacity you've gained," she said, "will be worth it."

Wide-eyed, Malice gripped the queen's wrist, and she hissed. Blood welled where his nails bit into her flesh. For a split second, his mind hollowed. She could bleed? He didn't know why it came as a surprise, but it did. She *could* bleed.

Queen Vendetta threw him, his shoulder and head smacking the ground, the room flashing white as his brain throbbed against his skull. The room doubled and spun, including the queen, who headed back to the throne. As she took her seat, Malice pushed himself up, stood unsteadily, and stumbled on his weak legs.

"Are we done here, *Mother*?" he asked cynically. The queen, nor anyone else on the dais, was clear, each one shrouded in a haze.

"Leave my sight. Else I lose what little patience and mercy I have left," she said, venom lacing her voice.

No one needed to be told twice. Gasps and huffs sounded before the scampering of feet.

Malice was the last to leave, glaring at the queen, hoping she read the wrath in his eyes. The underside of his chin was already healed, and he hoped she saw that too. Above all else, Malice hoped she had figured out he was no longer afraid of her.

"Zephyrus"

Fool! How could Malice do that? Talk back to the queen, his *mother*, like that? He must have been out of his mind. What else could explain his actions? And what was that pressure in the atmosphere? As if the air itself became sludge, suffocating him, squeezing his lungs.

Everyone was gathered in the foyer, reeling from what was witnessed. Zephyrus stopped pacing. He had never seen Malice look so… defeated, then so angry. They were both a new side of Malice Zephyrus didn't know existed. As much as he understood the frustration of the situation, a bigger part of him knew how insane Malice's outburst was. He was lucky to be alive.

Footsteps grew closer.

Zephyrus whipped around as Malice walked into the foyer. He darted toward Malice, who looked at Zephyrus with a growing smile when Zephyrus punched his shoulder, hard, which actually hurt his hand. Pain pinched Malice's face.

"What were you thinking?" Zephyrus barely kept his voice from a shout. "Do you not have any intelligence left in that head of yours?"

Over his much deserved ridicule, Zephyrus had not heard the clacks behind him until someone punched him, too, and he stumbled forward. He spun to meet Kiran's furrowed brow.

"Don't hit him when he's injured!" Kiran snapped.

"He deserves it!" Zephyrus countered.

"I'm fine," Malice cut in. "See?"

Malice tilted his head and gestured to the bottom of his jaw, where two holes should have been.

Kiran punched the same shoulder Zephyrus had. "You're out of your mind!"

After a glance behind him, Malice asked, "Can you lecture me upstairs?"

Zephyrus nodded. It would be terrible to run into the queen and her children when they exited the throne room. Malice saved them from a lashing once. Zephyrus doubted he could do it again.

Upstairs in Malice's bedchamber, his family, Kiran's, and Eunice and her wife crowded the space. No one was comfortable, and it felt awkward to berate Malice with the mountain of insults forming in his head. For some of those insults, his parents would surely make him eat soap when they got home.

Eunice sighed heavily and leaned against the wall, arms crossed. Her wife was at her side, caressing the beastman's shoulder. "What now?" She broke the silence.

"We have to move quicker," Malice said, walking the little space there was at the center of the room. He rubbed his hands together, none too gently either, fingers cracking, twisting, and squishing around one another. "I doubt the queen will let this be… there has to be more."

"More what?" Mother asked. Fausta stood next to the bed, her chestnut hair braided in rows along her scalp, tied in the back with a string, his little sister Ester behind her legs. Mother always wore straps around her waist to hoist up her skirts, which were down at the moment.

"More of a punishment," Malice said.

"She planned to give us all twenty lashings," Tendai said. "Is that not enough?"

"Not for you, for me," he replied, tone distant, as if lost in his thoughts. "That was a slap on the wrist compared to what she normally does."

Recoiling, Zephyrus looked at Eunice, whose expression darkened as she turned her head shamefully. So, it was true. Zephyrus knew her highness's discipline toward Malice was harsh, but he never thought it was plain torture and yet, that was what it sounded like Malice was implying.

"Does she," he spoke softly, making Malice stop in his tracks and face Zephyrus. "Does—you know—does she… torture you?" The words sat rancidly on his tongue.

Malice stared for a moment. The room was quiet, lethally so, yet extremely loud. His eyes fell to the floor. "Is it important right now?"

"She does." Zephyrus stepped closer.

"It's not important."

"Then what is important?" Zephyrus said. "You won't tell us anything. Why do you have to hurry? What are your plans? And why can't you tell us? Aren't we friends?"

Hurt scrunched Malice's face, fists clenching at his sides. "I can't tell you because I don't want you to get hurt."

"But we're—"

"That doesn't matter!" he barked. "Did you not hear what she said? None of you have done anything, yet the queen was more than happy to flog you for simply being in my presence. I'm trying to protect you."

"We don't want your protection," Kiran joined Zephyrus.

"You need it." Malice glanced around the room, his chest rising and falling rapidly. "You don't understand. My mother—not my mother—" He groaned, head shaking as if it would help the jumbling of his thoughts settle.

What was that supposed to mean? Not his mother? "Is the queen not—"

Malice, slightly panicked, cut him off, "She will not allow a swift or kind death. Inyene will make sure you feel every ounce of agony your body can tolerate. Even then, she'll push you to your limits. You would be lucky if she stopped at physical pain."

"Slow down," Fausta said, hand motioning to emphasize the phrase. "You said, 'not my mother.' Care to explain?"

Eyes dropping, flinging back to Fausta, Malice wiggled his fingers at his sides. "She's not," he hesitated. "She's not my blood mother."

No one made to move or speak for a while. The air was uncomfortable, thick with unease, fear, disgust, confusion. Malice had no intention of telling anyone—outside of Eunice, who already knew—what his plans were or what he'd found out about the queen, and it wounded Zephyrus. A stab to the chest. Zephyrus thought they were closer than that. He thought it didn't matter what happened because they would stick together. He swallowed the lump in his throat and struggled to keep the welling tears at bay.

"The queen," Malice said, reverting the topic, "will do something else. Sooner rather than later… I don't know if it will be me or if she'll involve all of you as well."

"We can cross that bridge when we get there," Issur said.

Malice grunted a humorless laugh. "You don't have a bridge to cross."

We'll fight rushed to his lips but, Zephyrus knew better. They couldn't win against Queen Vendetta. It would be a death sentence.

"I don't think she'll come for us," Blodwen said. "When she

delivers her judgments, she likes to watch the recipient's reaction."

"And?" Malice questioned.

"Her eyes were on you, Malice, and you alone."

Realization lit his face. "You think it was a scare tactic?"

She nodded, and something seemed to lift from Malice's shoulder. He swayed a bit, but regained composure in an instant. Zephyrus's heart ached.

"Still," he added, "I won't risk your safety by telling you my plans."

Eunice's wife said quietly, "That might be for the best, young prince."

"I think it is time to retire for the night," Tendai said.

"I want to stay," Zephyrus said.

Kiran didn't move either, his eyes having been glued to Malice the entire time.

When Malice didn't refuse, the adults and Zephyrus's little sister left, filing out of the bedchamber. He felt he could breathe again. Although, sadness remained a heavy weight on his chest.

To the closet, Malice gathered three sets of night clothes. Both Kiran and Zephyrus had their section in Malice's closet. After handing them out, Malice turned his back to them and changed. Zephyrus did the same, Kiran too. It was silent. When they crawled into the huge bed that comfortably fit the three of them, it was still quiet. Zephyrus couldn't tell if Malice simply didn't want to talk—his stubbornness and all—or if he had too much going on in his head to speak.

Zephyrus guessed none of them would fall asleep for a while. He knew Kiran wasn't. He always snored, and Malice jolted awake at random, usually taking him a moment to fall back asleep. Though

Zephyrus supposed he knew why now. He simply thought Malice was prone to night terrors. Zephyrus had gotten them a few times, but not every night like Malice.

"Does it hurt?" Kiran whispered.

Probably, Zephyrus thought. It was the type of question which had an obvious answer, yet one couldn't help but ask it. Malice didn't answer.

How often? He wanted to ask. *Do you resent us for not realizing?* The ache returned, making Zephyrus grimace. If only he had known, he would have been there to help ease Malice's pain however he could. Be the ear he might've needed, so he could rant or cry or be silent like he was doing now. Just anything.

"Yes," Malice eventually said.

"I'm sorry," Kiran sniffled.

Zephyrus's lip quivered. He wanted to say it too, opened his mouth, but nothing came out, which made him feel one hundred times worse. Instead, since his limbs listened to him, he reached for and found Malice's hand underneath the blankets. He flipped it over and wrote, *I'm sorry* on his palm with his finger. Malice caught and squeezed Zephyrus' hand in response, a slight hitch leaving his throat like he was choking back tears.

The next thing he knew, the three of them were crying because they were scared. They were anxious and angry and sad and weak because they were children. Zephyrus hated how he could do nothing to help. He could only watch as Malice fought alone, hoping one day he might become someone worthy of the throne, so Malice didn't have to fight anymore.

Zephyrus, however, wasn't special. Trying his damnedest during training was getting him nowhere. His father wouldn't help because Zephyrus had to earn his place amongst the royals. He wasn't old enough to go on missions either. He'd be lucky if he could join a Squad at thirteen. Next year. Could Malice hold out that long? He was tough, probably the toughest person—aside from Mother and Father—Zephyrus knew.

Time was working against everyone, in that it wasn't moving fast enough.

Death of a Boy
XXXII

Part I

Three knocks rapped on Malice's door.

"Enter," he said, expecting to see Eunice.

It squeaked and revealed the bulk of Alkeim instead.

Setting the quill down on the surface of his desk, Malice turned slightly in his chair to give the orc his full attention.

"The queen demands your audience," Alkeim said, his voice gruff, his line of sight aimed for something beyond Malice. For quite some time, Malice noticed the queen's first sword had had trouble looking at Malice. Was his guilt getting too tough to swallow? Perhaps he should choke on it then.

Malice, forcing those thoughts away, nodded and rose when Eunice peeked her head around the door frame and disappeared again.

The dreadful halls never changed. Candles and lamps were the only source of light shining off the polished floors where dark rugs didn't hide them. His frequent missions, prior to when the queen had revoked his privileges weeks ago, made it increasingly difficult to feel refreshed in the castle. As if the walls constantly threatened to cave in, limiting his air flow.

Alkeim led the way to the second floor as Malice glided his hand over the icy gold railing, the rough texture running across his fingers and palm. The staircase bled into the lower floors, a rounded turn at each platform.

When they reached her highness's study, Eunice sucked in a breath behind Malice. He felt the need to do the same, but couldn't.

A heartbeat passed as his eyes adjusted to the dimness of the study. Queen Vendetta sat at her desk, her thin, sharp features highlighted by the single candle to her left. She was as pristine as a painting. Her dark eyes followed Malice as he walked toward her. Eunice stayed by the door beside Alkeim. Malice bowed.

"You have a week to gather a warband before I send you north," her highness cut to the chase. Extending an arm, she tapped a few papers with a pointed nail.

Malice slid them forward and flipped through the pages.

"Reports say there are mercenaries terrorizing the region and our neighboring realms. Years of bouncing between Hordes, Zeldine's, Florence's, and Braxton's Regions, yet it is only now they have become brazen."

Murder, illegal trade, rape, thievery, and arson, common bandits from what the reports stated. He glanced at her highness and her calm, borderline disinterested conduct. They were small fish in the ocean. Why send an entire warband to take care of them? Why send Malice, someone who had no experience with leadership, someone, to her standards, was untrustworthy if it was of that much concern? Why send the very person she'd told was no longer permitted to go on missions?

The queen said, "I want you to find them, flush them out, kill every last one of them. They've used what little freedom I've given them and thrown it to the wind."

Malice frowned. "Is that all?"

"This is your last chance, mutt, lest you want to test the limits of my generosity. Do not waste it. Now leave."

Since one bow was plenty, Malice turned on his heel and left, Eunice trailing behind him. He heard the door shut as he treaded to the stairs and back to his bedchamber.

The bed was made, the floors clean, his clothes neatly placed inside his closet, the letter he was writing to Magnus on his desk, all of it unbothered. No one went through his belongings.

"The reports say those mercenaries are nothing more than herded bandits," Malice said while Eunice took her place next to his desk. She refused to stand or sit anywhere else most of the time.

"A warband seems excessive," she said, folding her arms across her leather cuirass, her black eyes narrowed. "Sending someone with little experience—"

"No experience."

"No experience," she corrected, "is reckless for everyone involved. Sir Ushas' Squad would be better suited for numbers."

Malice nodded and sat on the edge of his bed, the frame making sounds of protest. "It's been nearly a month since I threatened her. This is her punishment. She needed to wait for the right time."

"Now it is."

"The queen doesn't want us to succeed come next week," Malice said, leg bouncing. "She wants to humiliate me, if not completely defeat me." *She wants me dead,* Malice thought of saying, but he guessed Eunice already knew. It wasn't exactly a secret anymore.

"Using your incompetence won't bode well when she informs the kingdoms."

Malice's brows jumped. "*Incompetence?*"

Eunice chuckled underneath her breath, shaking her head. "I believe she'll try to brand you a liar and a traitor after hearing the rumors spreading through the region."

Kin slayer, monster: she stole the crown from the young prince. Rumors were like rats. Once they multiplied, it was hard to get them back under control. Malice had said nothing. He didn't need to. Between Kiran, Zephyrus, and their families, and Eunice working with Malice around the kingdom, a few mentions of Malice's true heritage had a handful of people believing he was the rightful heir. Then a dozen, two dozen, fifty, hundreds. Never once had anyone slandered her highness's name. Her reputation did that all on its own.

"What do we do?" Eunice asked.

"We prepare as if we know nothing. Gather as many royals as you can in the next week." They would need quantity and quality.

Malice stopped shaking his leg, straightened his back, and stared at his desk. He'd been to the north many times. Not once had there been remnants of a large warband camping or traveling.

Her highness wanting his death was becoming more and more likely. And the cards were stacked against him. He had no royals of his own, aside from Eunice. He hadn't been playing nicely during training, either. How many would actually rally to his cause? How many would go on a campaign that was almost certainly a deathtrap? Eunice was good, but not good enough to gather a sizable warband who would side against their queen in a week.

"You should tell your wife you might not make it home," Malice muttered into the silence, gaze sliding to Eunice.

Expression blank, the beastman said nothing for a time. The room went still and uncomfortably quiet. It was a terrible thing to say, he knew, but he wasn't wrong. She knew the risks of what was to come, meaning she probably knew it was also for the best to prepare for the worst. Or step down as Malice's first sword. Either way worked.

Then she stood to leave, "You're right," and hurried out of the bedchamber.

*

In the stables, he watched the stable master Gwen clean, trim, file, and shoe his horse, Snow. She was bathed and brushed, her mane and tail braided like a fishnet. Odovacar gave Malice the morning to get ready. Between Shevanti having the oils for his hair splayed across his desk, riding leathers out and ready, and Eunice preparing the warband she'd scrounged up, he didn't need to do much. Finally, the mare was bridled, strapped, and saddled before he mounted his steed of winter.

Malice veered around the castle into the courtyard where eighty-four royals gathered, Eunice at the front, facing them. Two wagons waited on the opposite side, the coachmen chatting. Eunice's midnight armor, simple in design and appearance, glinted in the early morning sun—black armor was Hordes Region's standard with a red sigil on the breastplate. The white and grey speckled horse underneath Eunice was slender, her frame smaller, her muscles rippling with every impatient stomp. She was busy convincing royals to join his warband until last night. There was no time to practice drills, to become a team, a proper Squad. Malice didn't recognize the faces assembled in the courtyard. They all, however, knew his.

Near Eunice was one of the queen's generals, a friend of Alkeim's, Charikleia Tor, an older woman, lines creasing her face, her dark brown hair streaked with white. For a mortal, she was on the wrong side of forty. A big stocky horse neighed and shook his head, his coat auburn brown, his tail and mane cropped. Charikleia glared at Malice, her mouth drawn in a hard line. At the very least, she could hide her less than happy attitude about joining the campaign, per Alkeim's request. She could have said no. Malice would have preferred it that way.

He cantered next to Eunice, nodded to her, and turned toward his warband. If it could be called that. When he spoke, he was surprised to hear his voice could be so loud outside his screams of pain. "Royals." The bustling courtyard fell silent, and all heads swiveled toward him. "I am Malice Reap. While on this campaign, I am no longer your prince. I am your commander. I expect to be treated as such." Charikleia huffed her disapproval.

Snow stamped underneath Malice as if to emphasize his point. "Our ride north will take four weeks. Mercenaries are not only threatening us, they're threatening our neighbors. We are to hunt them down and eradicate them." He peeked at his first sword. "Lady Eunice's words are as absolute as mine. Command falls to her in my absence."

Briefly, Malice let his gaze sweep over the gathered royals. It wouldn't take a month to reach the northern border if they traveled at a decent pace, but he needed time to train these royals on the drills he'd read from a handful of books over this past week. Most of the royals knew a select amount of formations and lines—not the ones he had in his head or the ones he had read about, albeit—Malice was the one who didn't. He hadn't gotten that far with Odovacar yet, and he needed to learn *with* his warband.

He glanced at the castle's doors. His family was nowhere in sight. He would get no goodbyes or sendoffs, no speech or word of advice.

Turning his mare toward the gate, he said, "Move out."

Rolling hills and meadows surrounded them, wildflowers in constant bloom spreading their sweet scent, bugs humming. The gentle breeze would have been nice if it didn't feel like hot breath washing over Malice. In this heat, it might take a month to reach the north after all.

The northern border was a vague juxtaposition though, a twenty-mile stretch of woods between Hordes and Zeldine's Regions, kissing the backside of Bextierther. Having studied maps religiously with Draga before he had started going on missions, Malice knew Hordes Region like the back of his hand. Estera was the only kingdom ahead of the warband, and it was where they would stop tonight. Could they make it under these conditions? There were hours till high noon, yet Snow's coat was damp with sweat.

A quick look over his shoulder summoned Eunice to his side.

"We won't be able to travel during the height of the day," he said. The royals were also of concern. Most wore armor the same as Eunice, while everyone else wore leather like Malice. Both were great insulators, trapping heat like ovens.

She nodded as she observed the warband and the terrain. "You want to find a campsite?"

"We can travel during the evening, night, and morning. The afternoon will only lead to exhaustion. Remember why we're here." They can't afford to be exhausted.

"Oh, I remember perfectly," she said, and rolled her shoulders.

"What's the holdup?" Charikleia rode up on Malice's left, scowling as if Malice had insulted her entire bloodline.

"We'll be stopping to make camp soon," Malice answered.

"Why?" she snipped. "We're fine as is. Can't you handle a bit of heat?"

Anger licked at his ribcage, and he gripped the reins that much harder. "I'm worried about the horses."

"Then we stop more frequently."

The three of them had come to a halt, forcing the rest of the warband to stop as well, a litany of hooves pounding the earth. Charikleia's inky armor was ornate compared to Eunice's, snakes winding down the breastplate from the gorget, continuing onto the pauldrons, daggers and thorny vines entwining them. It was as if the queen personally carved the details, marking the general as her own.

Eunice shifted, her horse moving to stand between Malice and Charikleia. "If we travel at night, we'll avoid the heat. Everyone, including the horses, will stay in good health," she said flatly.

"We need to continue traveling during the day," Charikleia pressed, her tone harsh and judgmental. "It's better to have broad daylight guiding us than torches." She glowered at Malice. "These royals need to thicken their skin and apparently, so do you."

"Why are you arguing so passionately? Traveling at night is the best solution," Eunice said.

The general studied them both for a moment, scoffed, and reeled back to the head of her column. *Not even noon, and she's giving me strife.* He and Eunice exchanged glances and gave the order. The warband quickly broke formation and started pitching tents, creating a shelter for the horses, gathering water and wood. Within the hour, camp was made, and most everyone disappeared inside their tents to escape the sun.

The only reprieve the south of Vinyamar got from the scorching temperatures was during winter, when the nights were cool enough to leave frost. In the north, close to Dun Raik, it would snow lightly. Yeager's Region, however, was a desert, the weather so hot it could melt skin off the bone, or so Malice had heard from many drunken royals wandering the castle and training grounds.

Malice and Eunice shared a tent, despite how Malice insisted she had her own quarters. Her argument was someone might try to kill him at his most vulnerable.

She'd stripped her armor off, let her chain-mail fall to a heap on the ground, and took a seat at the table close to the tent's pole. There wasn't much to look at. He had a low bed covered in furs to the left of the entrance, Eunice's on the right, their belongings at the foot of their beds in trunks. Malice had unlaced the top layer of his riding gear and plopped onto his bed, which was surprisingly more comfortable than his mattress at the castle.

"Something's wrong," Eunice said after a while.

"I doubt Charikleia would act this way if Alkeim was the one who asked her to join the campaign," Malice said as he toed his boots off, assuming that was what she was talking about. "She's a veteran. I have a hard time believing my being in charge would get under her skin this much."

Eunice teetered on her chair, her body stiff and her face drawn tight with concentration as her eyes remained on the table. "Should we kill her?"

It was worth considering. Charikleia might be the signal the mercenaries need to attack. She might have a rendezvous with a contact, spilling his strategies, making it easier to take down his warband. She might be the one meant to kill Malice. There were many possibilities, yet nothing was concrete, and it was pissing him off.

"No," he said at last. "Don't get me wrong, I want to. It'd be easier in the long run."

"In more ways than one," Eunice commented.

"Nothing is certain." He scowled at the grass beneath his feet, the softness of it the only thing soothing him at the moment. "If she values Alkeim's friendship, perhaps we can convince her to our side. Or get more information.”

“You truly think the queen told her anything?” It was a sarcastic and rhetorical statement, and Malice knew the answer was no.

“We can’t kill everyone who’s annoying, and that’s exactly what it would look like to the royals.” They knew little about the relationship between Vendetta and her children, other than it was shit. To them, it would seem like Malice killed Charikleia because she voiced her concerns, and he didn’t agree with them, making Malice no better than Queen Vendetta. “Leave her be for now.”

“If you say so.” Eunice stood and lay down on her cot, her back facing Malice.

Charikleia’s attitude was sour from the moment she had approached Malice the night before they set off. He had come from the dungeons when she stopped him on the first floor and told him about Alkeim. She was fidgety, her eyes never locking onto Malice’s for more than two or three heartbeats, sweat beading on her forehead as if she had finished at the training grounds. As suspicious as he was, Malice was tired, his bones screaming at him, his head throbbing. His *organs* had ached. He’d had no energy to question her. He should have, anyway.

In the early evening, Malice rounded up his warband, explained the drills, and led them. The first of which were lines. They needed to hold them, move with them, attack and defend with them. This was the easiest part, the fundamentals already applied to their daily training. It was when he instructed an unfamiliar maneuver that difficulty arose. Lines broke. They were sluggish and uncoordinated. Royals got hurt as a result, but Malice had expected it.

The techniques he implemented were meant to handle a force thrice the size of what he had, at least fend them off for a while. Shields formed the outermost circle, every other royal holding their shield over their head rather than in front of them. Swords were positioned right behind them, protected by the shields as they stabbed through the gaps. At the center there were archers to rain arrows upon the enemy, healers racing in between the rings to heal whoever needed it. Finally, there were four royals—the most proficient and talented with magic—within the circle meant to create large-scale attacks or add another shield overtop the entire warband.

It was one of the few maneuvers Malice had found. The warband would learn all of them before they reached the north, and hopefully, one kept them alive.

*

Metal clashed, magic flowed freely, and fists battered their opponent. Malice observed his royals, watching them spar one on one for now. Once food filled bellies, it would be time for drills and lines.

Charikleia stood on the other side of the training area, arms crossed, watching Malice like a hawk would a rabbit. Eunice was with the royals, currently handing one their ass on a silver platter. The desire to join them was strong. After riding for two weeks, training eased his stiff muscles and helped return the feeling to his numb ass. He would join them later.

The general eventually made her way toward Malice. Eunice broke away from her sparring partner, sweaty and panting, her sights fixed on Charikleia.

"You are tiring out your royals," she said as she stomped closer to Malice. "What would you do if someone attacked you? Right here and now? You would be a sitting duck."

Eunice inserted herself between them, stinking of metal and body odor.

"We cannot sit idly for twelve hours," Malice said. "It's better to keep our muscles awake than to let ourselves become indolent. *That* would make us sitting ducks." They went from training every day to riding, making camp, and sleeping. To keep a blade sharp and in good condition, one must sharpen and use it; these royals would rust and dull if they were to do nothing.

She frowned. "You will be the death of your warband."

"I think that role belongs to you," he said. Charikleia flinched, wild-eyed for a split second, then stormed to her tent.

"She has taken orders from the queen," Eunice said, and kept scowling at Charikleia after she vanished beyond a row of pitched canvas.

"Doesn't really matter. We need to carry out the campaign."

Eunice shifted, her eyes falling to Malice. "We leave now, the queen will have our heads. We don't, we walk right into a trap. We're dead either way."

"Seems like it." Malice gazed at his royals, who were trained to kill and trained to keep fighting no matter what happened to them. "At least we won't die alone."

Eunice smirked.

*

Three weeks had passed since leaving Hordes Kingdom. Hills and plains surrounded the encampment, Estera a week behind them. From the north, a breeze came, spreading the scent of flowers, sun baked clothes, and leather, salt wafting every so often. Malice took it in, a deep inhale followed by an exhale. He blinked sweat from his eyes and wiped his face with his sleeve.

In the saddle of four hills, he watched a royal throw a beastman twice their size over their shoulder as if it was nothing, then laugh. The beastman snarled his defeat but accepted the hand the smaller royal offered him. Once they were on their feet, they began sparring again.

Eunice chuckled to Malice's side. Maybe she'd enjoyed the same spar as he did. As it turned out, she was a joy to converse with and easy to get along. In the castle, they hardly had the time to talk beyond planning how to stay alive as they snuck behind Queen Vendetta's back. While with the warband slept and patrolled, after they finished discussing tactics and the behavior of the royals, Eunice spoke fondly of her wife. Malice didn't entirely think she realized she did it. And Malice shared his ideas for the future, not his, per se, but Zephyrus's and Kiran's.

Charikleia was nowhere to be seen. It seemed she left once they settled here for camp. Anticipation made his nerves sing, his foot tapping the earth, head constantly moving to survey the land. It was also why he had kept Eunice from sparring. Her keen senses would help spot any irregularities.

Should he stop the training and prepare for battle? What if the queen's forces never came and Malice was paranoid for no reason? Charikleia could have lost heart and ran ahead of schedule. If they were going to be attacked, he wished the enemy would hurry and get it over with. A swift, meaningless death. Queen Vendetta probably wanted that, provided she had truly prepared an army to take on Malice's pitiful warband.

High noon brought the harshest of heat, the sun unsullied by clouds. Even birds refused to fly right now. Bugs, on the other hand, screeched to no end. Malice wiped more sweat from his face and neck, used the dampness to plaster his hair back.

"My Prince," Eunice said, placing a hand on Malice's shoulder.

He peeked at her dark eyes, sparked with amber in the sun, and followed her line of sight to the horizon. There was nothing when he squinted.

A single white dot appeared and another. Within a few moments, the horizon was a white shimmering line. Malice's heart dropped into his stomach, chest fluttering.

"Call a halt and prepare for battle," he said smoothly, which surprised him a bit. He expected his voice to crack.

Eunice's commands carried, forcing all royals to stop and race up the hill, shooting past Eunice and Malice. Weapons clanged while armor clunked, and boots pounded the soil.

He stared, awestruck, at the skyline. More kept coming, hundreds, perhaps thousands, a sea of glinting metal. A hick caught in the back of Malice's throat. He had *less* than one hundred men. Queen Vendetta didn't mean to defeat or simply kill him; she wanted him slaughtered.

"You too," he said to Eunice. "Go get your armor on." She needed to fight. Her strength was not something this warband could go without, not with so few.

"What about you?"

"What about me?" Glancing at Eunice, Malice knew what she meant, but there wasn't time to search for bits and pieces of leather and metal to fit Malice with a full suit of protection. He never had armor, the queen never allowed it. "There isn't time," he said, matching Eunice's glare.

Her frown deepened. "I will get you a shield. It's better than nothing."

Malice waved at her. After a final look, brimmed with reluctance, she turned and hurried to their tent. The enemy was still filling the horizon, the first lines clearer. All were on horseback, no banners or emblems flapping in the wind, armor a common silver. As if that would fool him. Her highness had rounded up those men. There were probably a good number of Hordes Kingdom royals thrown in the mix as well. Pitting his own people against him. Malice couldn't blame her, as he had done the same. An eye for an eye, he supposed. More like a life for a life.

Quite the fuss just to kill—Malice let his gaze drop slightly. Rock overflowed from the cavity of his chest, his ears ringing, the world dimming. He toppled forward; the stake driving deeper through his body, blood gurgling as it painted the grass. There was so much pain he couldn't feel it anymore. Maybe they should have run when they had the chance. The queen had let them go… they could have… escaped…

Death of a Boy
"Embracing one's true self"

Malice's head jerked forward as if he were nodding off. He was on his feet, clothes and chest intact. All around the world had turned white, an unsettling, untainted white. Lifting his hand, Malice was the only source of impure color, his skin ivory underneath black leather. The warmth gradually grew colder, like evening fading to night. There was no scent either, no sound besides the pumping of his blood through his veins.

Time to choose.

Flesh prickling, Malice whipped around, eyes darting to find anything within the sea of white.

The voice came again; *There is always more than one side. Whose will you choose?*

"Sides?" Malice turned back to his original position, an unnatural calmness settling on his shoulders.

Us or them, the voice echoed, bouncing off nonexistent walls.

As if that cleared any of his confusion. Maybe it did. He had this vague understanding of what the voice referred to, almost like he knew he would have to decide sooner or later and had been putting it off.

"Who is them?"

You and I. Suddenly, the voice was near. *Or them.*

A foggy apparition materialized in front of Malice, then a

second and third. Haze clearing, Malice put faces to the images. Queen Vendetta was first with her unmistakable long, blood red hair, obsidian eyes, sickly pale skin, her posture of elegance and arrogance, her pallid expression.

The subtle chill turned bitter.

Inyene and Draga, Odovacar, King Emil, Felim, Alkeim, Annabeth. Kiran and Zephyrus manifested as well. Magnus was last.

An icy hand crept up Malice's shoulder. He yanked it away and spun. The voice belonged to a child, the same height, age, and build as Malice. His hair was murky, like the sea during a storm, his skin tone a dull, muted reddish color. His sclerae were orange, but the irises were the same vibrant shade of green as Malice's.

It's me, he realized.

Go on, Malice's mirrored self tilted his head. *Choose.*

Looking beyond himself, Malice asked, "… Why should I?"

Must I explain everything to you? He stalked around Malice, his strides deliberate and long, a grin twisting his lips.

"Yes." Malice was dying, if not dead already. Why else was he here? And for what other reason, at the peak of heat, would Malice feel as though he were soaking in a basin of ice? Random bursts of shivers made his entire body convulse.

What have they done to you except cause you pain? Why let them live?

"I won't kill them."

The copy groaned. *Think about yourself for once. What do you want? What do we want, hmm? We know to live and breathe the same as they do should not incur such wrath, yet here we are. On the brink of death.*

Malice laughed humorlessly. All he had ever done was think of himself. Zephyrus, Kiran, Eunice, everyone had almost suffered the consequences for it. This campaign was retribution. Malice's twin slipped from his side. They were face to face, but Malice felt nothing from him, no warmth or puff of breath. There were two moles underneath his copies' right eye. Did Malice have those as well? He never paid much attention to his features.

Come now, he drawled, the smile gone. *Don't be so naïve, Malice. You know they won't stop until you're mindless like poor Emil or you're dead. Why put up with it? Why deny what you truly want?*

"I want something?" He did, he realized. Malice wanted to keep those he cared for out of harm's way. "The best way to do that is for me to…"

Shaking his head, Malice's mirror stepped backward and put his hands behind his back. *There's more to it. Say it, Malice. Stop* denying *what we want.*

What would saying it out loud do? Make him feel better? He was dead and no one would bat an eye. Although, that might be why he should say it. No one would hear him. There was no one to tell him he was nothing but a mutt who hardly deserved the dirt he walked on.

Malice breathed as if there wasn't a hole in his chest outside of whatever realm he was in. "Fear." The twisted smile returned to his twin's face, turning his eyes into crescents. "The power to best them—to be worse than them."

I'll give it to you, the copy said instantly and calmly, a fact. *Everything is what you'll have.*

"But?"

What are we?

Malice quirked an eyebrow, the question not quite making sense. He was a child, a demon, a wannabe prince, and a dead boy.

You are *a child, a wannabe prince, and a dead boy,* he said. *Yet, we're more than that.*

A monster.

Not quite. I think you know what you are, but you keep refusing it. You keep rejecting me. And I can't save you this time unless you accept me.

This time, Malice thought.

All the books he had read over the years flashed in his mind, the ones in different languages, with torn pages, and the ones he only understood once he got a little older. The book, tome more like, of archangels and devils joined by two others on the bookshelf in his bedchamber. The thick spine had steadily gained more creases.

Despite how little it made sense, Malice knew what his mirrored self was talking about. Knew everything, as he knew the cold spreading from his chest into his neck and legs. His time was running out.

The figures behind his copy were fading, a numbness encasing Malice's body, the white world dimming.

Malice held his hand out for his twin to clasp it. Darkness consumed his other self, smokey tendrils climbing dingy red skin until it was all black. Like water soaking into dry dirt that finally gave in and accepted hydration, Malice took in what he had done, weathered it, and closed his eyes.

Victory Through Mistakes
XXXIII

Water struck Eunice's ribs, broke them, and sent her tumbling across dirt and grass. Biting back the pain, she steadied herself then propelled forward, using a burst of smoke from her heels. A bannerless royal shot another spear of water. Eunice dodged as an axe of grey solidified in her grasp. Hefting the weapon above her head, she cleaved the traitorous bastard in two, blood sprayed, bones crunched, and guts spilled onto the earth before two halves of a body fell in opposite directions.

With every strained breath, Eunice's diaphragm burst with pain. One or two ribs probably stabbed her lungs as well. Her body apparently felt the need to prove her hypothesis when she coughed up blood, iron coating the inside of her mouth.

It hadn't been long since Malice's death and the first wave of enemies hit. The bodies littering the ground suggested otherwise. Around her, battle waged on, the warband holding their own thanks to Malice's drills. It wouldn't last much longer. His drills were meant to handle an army of no more than three hundred. Thousands of men ran the green meadows silver. On the hilltop overlooking the saddle, Eunice stayed close to protect Malice's corpse. She scowled over her shoulder at his small, unmoving body. *I should've dragged him with me.* Teeth grinding, Eunice forced her eyes to what was in front of her. Slain enemies who signed their life to the wrong Reap.

Ribs mostly regenerated, Eunice tightened her grip on the axe of smoke while a group of ten mercenaries broke from the queen's army, heading straight for Eunice. She spat the excess blood in her mouth, sucked in a deep breath, held it, and hurled the axe. It whistled through the air and sank into the chest of the first mercenary. He fell, making two behind him trip over his carcass. Seven more continued on their path. Until she snapped her fingers, and the axe exploded, launching them all in multiple directions, each one bouncing off the ground like pebbles.

Exhaustion and adrenaline coexisted. She had the energy to keep fighting for hours to come, despite how quickly her limbs were becoming lead. Those who had tried to single her out were strewn about the surrounding area. One would think Queen Vendetta's men would get the idea. Yet they kept coming. An annoyingly smart decision on their part, considering their numbers exceeded her own one hundred times over and then some.

Magic depleted, a new batch of enemies approaching, an army of thousands swarming the plains of Hordes Region, Eunice pulled the sword from the scabbard on her hip.

The smell of death was rancid, a heavy fog that, if she thought about for too long, made her gag. Her ears rang with the clamor of battle. Screams were cut short. Metal clanged and sparked. Magic rumbled the earth, thinned and dried the air, shot waves of heats like that from a forge. Footsteps thundered and her own ichor thrummed in her veins. Eunice had always dreamed of being triumphant in battle and returning home with the honor one only heard about in legend.

Victory may not come today, but Eunice and her men wouldn't go down without a fight.

Ignoring the sharp pain of her ribs as she inhaled, Eunice screamed till her lungs were void of air. The queen's men closing in stopped in their tracks, their faces suddenly gone pale. One dropped their weapon, another stumbled backward and hit the grass, the rest turned and ran. For such a small beastman, she must be more terrifying in her half-deranged state than she gave herself credit for. Helle would surely laugh if she'd heard Eunice say that aloud.

A shiver crawled up her spine, a centipede scaling her back, tension stiffening her shoulders. Instinct told her to look down. Her shadow had grown three times larger as wings spread out to either side of her and a set of limbs below the top cracked its wrists in circular motions. Pops sounded behind her.

Eunice, against her better judgment, turned around, her head tilting back to see the creature in full. One of four hands reached for his chest, fingers gliding over thin muscle as if to make sure everything was there. Four eyes peered down at Eunice, each one green like sprouting grass, the sclerae orange. His skin was muddy red, his hair a desaturated blue. A long, bulky tail, barbed at the tip, lazily swung back and forth behind him, his legs that of a goat's.

She returned to those eyes, noticing two small dots underneath his right eye. "Malice?" she croaked.

Just then a mouth split the skin of his torso, razor-like teeth piercing flesh and wriggling as they fit themselves into place, blood trickling. She gagged.

Knees buckling, Eunice hardly caught herself when Malice surveyed the land, lingering on the battlefield. She was… was too stunned to think behind the question of how? Why? Her reeling mind couldn't make sense of what she was seeing. Her injured body didn't help clear the confusion. Either she was dead or hallucinating. Could she be both?

"Call the warband to you," he said. Eunice flinched.

All she could do was nod as she stared blankly at the teeth, consuming what had once been Malice's mouth. Taking several steps back, Malice crouched and leapt into the air, his wings flapping, launching him over the hills in a heartbeat. His tail, horns, and wings were the only aspects of his true form she had seen, most of which were uncontrolled appearances from what Malice had told her.

Shaking her alarm off as much as possible, Eunice shouted, "To me!" hoping one person heard. During training, it was rare for more than a few royals to catch a command. Those around who gave the order might hear and pass the message along. If not, royals simply followed the leader and the herd. And that was in a controlled environment. Her words had to travel over the chaos of an army overwhelming a warband twenty times its size.

BOOM!

Activity ceased. The hills went silent. A horn blasted from the north.

"TO ME!" Eunice repeated, her voice carrying this time.

Heads swiveled toward her and toward the north, enemy and ally alike. Moments of uncertainty passed. The mass around the warband broke apart and, as a single entity, Malice's royals cut their way through the southern wall of Queen Vendetta's men. More and more of the enemy split off when another boom rumbled the ground beneath Eunice's feet. A pillar of earth impaled the heavens. Red glowed in the northwest, smoke billowing upward. It didn't take long for the screams to reach her. But she had other matters to attend. Her royals finally broke through the army's barricade.

Eventually, the warband approached Eunice, who had had enough time to regain her composure. She took up a shield, sending the royal to the second ring of swords.

"Formation defense," she called, the shields moving to flank her while the swords and archers remained at her backside.

Those at her sides were heaving, glistening with sweat and blood, yet they stood, and they stood proudly at that.

"What's going on, Lady Eunice?" the one to her left, Jayesh, asked.

"Malice…" she hesitated. "Malice took the fight to their head."

Jayesh's head whipped toward her as a small yip leaked out of him. "He's alive?"

She swallowed, "Apparently," and returned her attention to the fleeting army. "For now, we need to focus on staying out of our graves."

"Yes, ma'am."

The mass of enemies moved slowly. It was one of the problems with large groups, too many feet stuck together to move as efficiently as they should, especially without proper training. While Malice was at the head of the army, they needed to attack the rear. The opening was ripe for the taking and, despite the barrage, they hadn't fought long enough to truly become tired and require rest. She could feel it. Rage and adrenaline vibrated the air.

"Forward march," she commanded and rolled her shoulders.

Boots stepped forward as one, a single beat turning into the melody of a drum, signaling impending doom. Heart speeding, Eunice clutched the leather strap of her wooden shield, shaped like a sharp, elongated oval, metal edges, the field of it plain. It was dense, making it heavy, which was a good thing, despite how her arms would soon disagree with her.

Upon reaching the last lines of her highness's army, the royals at her sides huffing, she braced herself. "Advance."

Enemies turned too late as Eunice and the line of shields slammed into them, swords jutting between the spaces. Cries rang, faces reduced to surprise and pain. At the height the swords were stabbing, their cores were penetrated, making for swift, albeit painful, deaths. If the sword didn't work, the ever-moving sabatons stomped out what little life remained. Arrows rained down further ahead, dividing the queen's army. Chaos was no more. Not for her band, anyhow. The upper hand was nowhere near theirs, but they had gathered their wits, regrouped, and struck first, this time around.

Horns blasted once more, different ones from the earlier call for retreat. "Halt," Eunice said, the warband rippling to a stop as well. "Raise shields."

As she shifted to follow her own demands, she slunk behind the second row of royals, allowing them to replace the front lines. Pain pulsed throughout her whole body like waves crashing onto the shore. She wasn't all that experienced in combat. The missions she'd went on prior to becoming a knight were simple, rounding up mercenaries who crossed the queen, capturing thieves and the like, patrolling the kingdom. Her stamina was waning, her magic faster still.

Eunice rolled her shoulders and peeked around the front row of bodies, then through the cracks of the shield roof. The horns sounded for an aerial assault. Fleshy and feathered wings zipped back and forth. *Shit*.

Queen Vendetta's army dwindled, mostly thanks to Malice at the head, massacring everyone he could. Eunice, however, liked to think she and the warband made a good enough dent in her forces. After the queen's army sent winged royals to the sky's, their speed was reduced considerably, and they were attacked from every angle. Which was a little too much like the initial barrage, but Malice *was* the difference. His resurrection caused panic, his death-dealing planting seeds of fear. Both grew and spread like a plague. Slaying her highness's army was easier said than done, yet easier than Eunice imagined it could ever be.

Cries gradually died as the earth calmed, and the columns of smoke blew away. It reeked of iron, defecation, burnt flesh, and mud. Red painted the green of the grassy plains. Crows circled overhead, vultures above them. If they stayed long enough, howlers would stalk out of their faraway dens to partake in such an easy meal. Good chance an onyimyth or two would as well with this much to feast on.

Motionless, weapons and guards up, they waited while all sounds ceased. Even the wind was absent. Eunice caught a trace of scarlet in the distance, squinting as it gained shape. Breaking from the warband, she stepped over a body lying face down, another headless, the ground squishing and squelching.

It was Malice staggering over the hills, covered in blood, hair too weighed down to so much as twitch with the gust of howling wind. When they were within a few tens of meters of one another, she realized he was naked and averted her eyes.

"You should stay behind me until you can get something to cover yourself," she said, to which Malice simply laughed an exhausted sound.

He didn't refute, though, and stayed in her shadow. "Fetch some clothes for the prince!" A royal peeled away and rushed to what remained of the camp.

Thankfully, it didn't take long like she'd expected considering the camp was in ruins, half of it smoldering, the other half trampled, the horses gone. In his human form again, Malice picked chunks of organs and flesh off his body, his bottom half wrapped in a torn and blackened canvas. She supposed it was better than nothing.

"Are you hurt?" was the first thing she asked. He shook his head, so she said, "Are you without a brain?"

Malice blinked at her.

"Not only did you refuse armor, but you attacked the head of an army. Alone." She was grateful to be alive, but he *had* died. His body had grown cold, his heart no more, every ounce of his blood soaking into the dirt. Perhaps accepting armor would have saved him, since it would have required him to follow Eunice to their tent. Then, of course, he thought the smartest thing to do was challenge an army by himself.

"You're alive," he said, his voice deeper than it was this morning. "They're alive." He gestured to the disbanding royals. "I'm alive."

"You died," she reminded with a flare of her lip and a roll of her shoulders.

He gave Eunice a measuring look, one hand reaching to feel the center of his chest. "Almost."

Evening passed in the blink of an eye, and night had descended. Amidst the remnants of camp, a fire pit blazed, painting the warband orange and bathing them in the warmth the battle likely drained from them as it had Eunice once cleanup began. It crackled and snapped as crickets chirped. Occasionally, Eunice heard the unmistakable sounds of teeth sinking into and tearing meat from the northern hilltops, smelled the fresh waves of blood ride the breeze.

Malice sat next to her on a rock bench erected from the ground. He was clean enough for now. At least his skin was pale again and his hair white. The stench of death lingered yet. He was one of the first to bathe in a pond made by a royal at Eunice's request. The patch of greenery the royal took the water from was now brown and dry. It was easier to use and manipulate what already existed than to create an element from nothing. It was why she wished she had earth or air magic. Both were so easily accessible and not so taxing on one's magical energy.

Unfortunately, it was late, no wooded areas for some distance, meaning no food. Water had replenished skins and had been passed around, treated as if it were the finest alcohol. After the day they had, it might as well have been. Still, water could only quench hunger for so long. Eunice figured she would take about ten royals with her at dawn to hunt down some food. She was too tired to do anymore tonight and so was everyone else.

Ahem.

Eunice turned her head. A royal stood at the edge of the bench, slouching.

"My prince, my lady," they said.

"How many remain?" Malice asked.

The royal's eyes darted to him and fell to the ground. "We've… gained sixteen more, my prince."

When? she almost blurted. The answer was obvious. She had been so focused on protecting Malice's body she hardly paid attention to the warband after the first set of commands were given. Deserters could have joined their company at any point.

Teeth grinding, she glared into the blaze.

"Bring them to the fire." Malice sat straighter. Not only had Malice's voice dropped, he was also taller by a good inch or two.

Eventually, sixteen royals lined themselves in front of the bonfire, two rows of eight, one stepping nearer. Eunice jumped to her feet, metal scraping as she ripped her sword from its scabbard, stopping the fairy in his tracks. Malice died once today, she would be damned if she let it happen again.

Malice took in the newest royals before he spoke loud enough for all to hear. "You swore fidelity to my mother. What makes you think you're welcomed here?"

The front most royal, oddly familiar now that she saw him up close, dropped to a knee, head bowed. The rest followed, a series of clunks as armor hit the earth. "We are not a part of the queen's service. You," he looked up at Malice through fallen locks of white hair, "don't recognize me?"

Nikanor? Eunice vaguely remembered him now.

"Odovacar's first sword," Malice muttered. Louder; "Why would he have you join Queen Vendetta's army?"

The knight got to his feet, his Squad, too. "Sir Odovacar wanted us to save as many as we could when we arrived on the battlefield. Sneak you and your royals away from the hills." He paused and glanced around the blaze at the many faces staring back at him. "We were with the second wave of attacks. We cut our way to you, joined your band, and fought alongside you the best we could." Nikanor gave a rueful smile and added, "Your advances were… a bit tricky to execute."

"Where were you in all of this?" Malice asked, green eyes on her.

Instinctively, she wanted to defend herself as a white-hot anger curled her fingers into her palms and coiled the muscles in her back. As quickly as it ignited, it quelled because Eunice was meant to lead when Malice could not. Ashamed, plopping beside him, her sights dropped to Malice's bare feet, scuffed and streaked with dirt and grass.

"I," she found it difficult to spit out the truth, "thought you were dead, my prince. I wanted to protect your body, so if I survived, I could give you a proper burial." Her own reason made it seem like she wanted nothing to do with the fight.

For a long time, Malice simply observed Eunice. She could feel the sting of his eyes on her, as if he couldn't understand her motive. Perhaps he didn't.

"You swore your oaths to my brother, not me," Malice said at last, voice bitter.

Right in time, Eunice lifted her gaze to see Odovacar's first sword reel slightly and his expression sour.

Nikanor said, "You would be surprised, perhaps well-pleased, to know there are many more than what Lady Eunice gathered who wish to be free of the queen's cruelty."

Wishing to be free was a hell of a lot different from actively trying to get said freedom. They could wish all they wanted. Unless they stepped up and acted upon those wishes, they would never achieve them. Aside from having a week on top of her regular duties, Eunice had trouble convincing those she had to fight after having their courage and pride ripped from them time and time again.

"Thank you," Malice said. Nikanor deserved thanks, Eunice guessed, but she was glad she wasn't the one who had to give it. "Without your aid, eighty-four royals would likely be dead."

Face lightening, the knight smiled tenderly and inclined his head.

"If you see my brother before I do," Malice mused as he relaxed back into his propped arms, "tell him to keep his nose out of my business."

Nikanor perched a white eyebrow.

"We go on one mission together and he thinks we're buddies now."

Snickers sounded all around them. The knight couldn't help but chuckle, too. They were all lacking the necessary sanity to realize laughter wasn't the most appropriate at the moment. The one lacking it most being Malice. They had almost met a horrible demise, while Malice *had* met a horrible demise. Maybe that explained his strange jesting mood. Their survival was funny, Eunice had to admit. Miraculous and utterly due to luck.

Malice went on, "I would offer food, but as you can see, we've just run out." More laughter, Eunice included, which eased the tension in the company.

"Not to worry," Nikanor said. "We brought along a few wagons of supplies, figuring you would need it."

"How did you keep it safe?" Eunice asked as the stiffness in her back faded.

"Sixteen royals disappearing for a time among ten thousand usually go unnoticed." He winked.

"Take as many as you need to get the wagons here. I'm starving."

The fairy nodded, gathered up an additional five royals, and headed north.

Stomachs full, the fire perfectly warm, the stars twinkling, chatter packed the night as jugs of ale were passed from person to person. Looking at the joyous expressions surrounding her, feeling the elation in the atmosphere made it difficult to believe they had escaped death that afternoon.

The royals didn't know who attacked them today. And she had nearly forgotten. The addition of sixteen royals could have been an over-bearing brother caring for his younger brother, trying to support his first campaign.

She glanced at Malice, who was in conversation with Nikanor. He was a fairy born in Florence's Region, which explained the accent he had. His voice was very melodic, his pronunciation of *s*'s and *j*'s odd for Hordes. Florence's was Hordes western neighbor, home of wine, olives, and marble temples where fairies and other folk born of the land walked around naked because clothes were like shackles. Nikanor's hair was the same white as Malice's. His skin, however, was tanned, his eyes black orbs. Unlike most fairies, he was rather masculine—fae were androgenous in every aspect—square jaw, sharp cheekbones, full lips and shoulder length curly hair. Muscular too. Nikanor *was* a part of Odovacar's service. The general was anything but lenient when it came to training.

Finally, Nikanor got up and joined his fifteen royals at the other end of the camp—it only took him what felt like hours. The supplies from the wagons he brought rejuvenated what had been lost, so most everyone had a tent, while very few had to share.

"Odovacar has good taste in royals," Malice commented.

"What was that?" Eunice asked, unable to hold the question back any longer. The mouth splitting Malice's torso in half was seared into her brain, the grotesque teeth squirming as blood dribbled down his flesh. The way his jaw had reformed itself, unhinging like a snake's, growing sharp, canine-like teeth. A part of her was amazed at how well her brain accepted what happened until the high of survival vanished and food gave her some energy to think properly.

"A conversation?" Malice answered half-assed mockingly, paused when Eunice scowled, then sighed. "I died."

"I'm aware."

"You mean my true form?"

"What are you?"

"… Not a demon," he said shortly.

His tone suggested the end of the conversation, but all it did was introduce more questions. If not a demon, what else could he be? A hybrid of some sort? Hybrid or not, what species on Vinyamar looked like that—could create someone who looked like that? Eunice was better off not knowing.

"You're… still you… right?"

Malice met her gaze. "Worried I'll become like Mother?"

"Yes." She would not give her life to serve another monarch like Vendetta. She would run if she had to. Take her wife and become a fugitive. At worst, she would kill herself and unchain Helle completely from Eunice.

His expression darkened. "I won't. That I assure you."

You've already changed. For better or for worse, Malice wouldn't be the same when they returned to the kingdom. They regarded one another for a while, thoughts swirling in Eunice's head like a typhoon. Malice would let her walk away right this minute if she said she wanted to. Somewhere deep within the cavity of her chest, a little tug, she did. Stronger and louder was the desire to continue as Malice's first sword. He came back from death and the first thing he did was make sure his warband got to safety. If anything was in order, it was her gratitude and respect. Had it not been for Malice, they would all be in some scavengers' gut by now.

Swiftly, Eunice slipped from the bench onto her knees in front of Malice. "Thank you, my liege."

Blaze sputtering, timber scenting the air, the camp briefly fell silent when a wave of rustling grass and thuds resounded behind her. For the queen, bending the knee was always a symbol of submission, surrender, and fear. It was one of the few ways to stay alive. Eunice felt strongly in that no one here, kneeling in front of the rightful heir, was doing so out of dread or compliance. Appreciation and reverence brought knees to the ground.

Malice stood, clawed feet shifting. "It is I who owes you gratitude. You listened to Lady Eunice, blindly followed us to a deathtrap, and fought in my name," he said, voice carrying. "I have no way of showing my gratefulness right now, but know upon our return, you will be rewarded."

Let that reward be our heads remaining intact when we face the queen.

*

Eunice sat up and rubbed the sleep from her eyes. A thousand different places ached or throbbed, despite the healers running well into the night to tend to everyone. With so few, they had to heal the most severe, leaving minor injuries to regeneration. Most of her pain, thankfully, was from sleeping on the ground without so much as a blanket. She didn't remember falling asleep.

Once she got to her feet, yawned, and stretched, she made her way to the pond and knelt at the edge. She paused, remembering the entire warband bathed in the pool yesterday.

"Don't worry. The water has been changed," a royal said as they came up alongside her, crouched, and cupped water to splash their face.

A moment of skepticism later, Eunice did the same. The water was refreshing, goosebumps racing down her arms.

Eunice returned to the firepit, the inside black with burnt logs, and spotted Malice, his white head easy to spot at the other end of camp. He was giving an order to a royal mounted on a saddleless horse. *Found a horse that didn't scamper too far. If there's one, there might be more.* The royal nodded to whatever he said, spun her horse around, and galloped south.

"Where did you send her?" Eunice asked as she joined Malice.

"To Hordes Kingdom," he replied. "I want to know what her highness thinks of our death."

Eyebrow flared, she eyed Malice. It didn't look like he had slept. His clothes were as wrinkled as they were last night and his eyes had dark circles under them, slightly aging his youthful face.

"When I flew to the enemy's head, I found their leader. I kept him alive for the sole purpose of feeding Queen Vendetta false information."

"You think he'll do it?" It was quite the assumption and quite the leap of faith if you asked Eunice.

"Of course not," Malice grunted with a smirk. "He'll die in five days when I crush his heart."

Eunice opened her mouth to question him, but thought better of it. He had transformed into a monster the day prior after his chest was obliterated. He could do anything he wanted.

*

The moon was high, matching the intensity of the dancing flames' light, the breeze salty, hinting a storm was coming. The rider Malice sent to Hordes Kingdom came back a week later.

"The queen thinks us dead, young prince," the royal said frantically, her face dripping with perspiration and taut with worry. The horse was breathing heavily as well, nostrils flaring, coat slick from sweat.

Malice, petting the horse's neck, laughed heartily, which startled Eunice and the royal. "We will ride out tomorrow," he said.

When the warband gathered, Malice explained his suspicions prior to the campaign, Charikleia's role and why she had joined their company, then what the queen had announced to the kingdom, further solidifying his assumptions.

"You're telling us," Nikanor stepped closer to the bench Malice and Eunice were seated on, his brows furrowed, "her highness—she wanted you dead?"

If Eunice hadn't been Malice's first sword for three years, she would have had the same reaction. A mother pinning an army against her son, whose voice had barely started to deepen, was unthinkable, disgusting to anyone with a heart, and, for those with half a brain, she was not worth following.

Silence sat heavily on the warband, an impenetrable fog snuffing the life out of the royals. It didn't help Malice had the look of death on his face as he stared into the fire. Such pure hatred and anger could kill in an instant if anyone were to look Malice in the eyes.

She leaned close to him and whispered, "My liege."

Malice glowered for a moment longer, took a deep breath as he closed his eyes. He opened them, the tension lifting. *Was that… intimidation?* Eunice had never felt the effects of formless magic. Beyond a wide-scale attack, formless magic wasn't used. Too dangerous and unpredictable. If she *had* ever felt magical energy, it wasn't potent enough to warrant concern. Malice's was something else entirely. Eunice swallowed the unsettling lump that had formed in her throat and rolled the discomfort out of her shoulders.

"Me or Vendetta," Malice said, scanning the clustered royals, his green irises specked with copper. "Before we ride out tomorrow, I expect an answer. Whose side will you choose? Mine or the queens?"

A few gasps made their way to Eunice.

"I won't blame you if you want to run, as it's also an option, nor do I blame you for wanting to stay with the queen. I won't make you an oath breaker if you don't want to become one."

In this situation, Eunice wouldn't have given these royals an alternative; follow her or die. There was far too much Malice had shared to make letting them walk safe. Thinking about it like that, however, she understood why Malice gave them the right.

The queen didn't give choices.

"I've told you all I know, but I'm sure some of you have experienced her highness's commerce for yourself." Grim faces nodded, while most remained statuesque.

"What if," a voice called from beyond the front rows of people, "we tell the queen what you plan to do?"

"I won't stop you."

Are you trying to dig your grave? Eunice's head jerked toward the foolish prince. If he were sleep-deprived, this ordeal should wait till the morning so he could think straight. Clearly, he was not doing so right now. Eyes boring holes into the side of his skull, she cleared her throat.

"Allow me to tell you one last thing," Malice said as he peeked at her. Then he righted his posture, his head just above Eunice's, completely ignoring her. "There is a *possibility* if you join me, you will die by Queen Vendetta's hand." His gaze turned to stone, petrifying those who stood directly in front of him. Nikanor slid a sabaton backward.

"If you stay with Queen Vendetta, you *will* die by my hand."

The corners of Eunice's mouth curved into a smirk. *A threat promising temporary safety. He's good with his words, I'll give him that. Still out of his mind, though.*

The hundred royals surrounding them had witnessed the massacre Malice inflicted on the queen's army. Heard the screams. Tasted the death, it stunk so terribly. Saw the result of Malice picking chunks of flesh off his body like one would pick dirt from their clothes. Listened to scavengers' feast over the meal.

Malice's statement wasn't merely a threat, it was a guarantee. And a damn good one.

Pride swelled in her gut. Comparing the boy she had met three years ago to the boy she knew now was like comparing a cat to a panther. He was coming into his own, fangs and claws and all.

"Which poison to drink," someone said. "*That* is what you're telling us to choose between."

"I've drunk mine. It's time you drank yours."

As the crickets filled the void left by the warband, Eunice studied the doubtful expressions highlighted by the fire, unsurprised by their hesitation. Malice, despite all he had done last week, was a child. If she let herself forget, she could believe Malice was a rebellious son trying to prove something to his strict mother. If Eunice could do that after seeing all she had, she could only imagine what these royals were thinking. It was hard to view him as a hazard, a true competitor in Queen Vendetta's game.

Nikanor approached, fixed his sights on Malice, and dropped to his knees at the prince's feet, the fire making his white hair glow orange. "To give my service to the true heir of Hordes Region would be my honor," Odovacar's first sword proclaimed. "I swear fidelity to Malice Reap, future king of Hordes Region."

Malice's expression went blank. Eunice guessed Malice hadn't expected another man's royal, no less first sword, to give themselves to him. Neither had Eunice. Odovacar was a respectable general, better than her highness or any of his other siblings. Yet today he lost his entire Squad. The fifteen in Nikanor's party followed their leader, each bowing and reciting Nikanor's little speech.

Then, in a cacophony of voices, eighty-four royals swore themselves to Malice over their queen. Chose the possibility of freedom over absolute oppression. Whether the risks were worth it, they wouldn't know till Malice took the throne, but Eunice had the gut-wrenching feeling it wouldn't take long if the queen had anything to do with it.

As if unsure, Malice steadily rose, and seemingly absorbed the new oaths sworn tonight, the moon as their witness, and accepted he was already king to the warband he trained, protected, and fought for.

"If we win," he said, his chest inflating, "you will reap the benefits. If we die, know I was the first and know I left a wound

Vendetta will never get rid of."

"To the king!"

Cheers echoed into the night, waking the dead, no doubt. Faces were bright, tones were cheerful while the ale was poured from barrels and handed out like candy at a festival. Royals came up to and complimented or congratulated Malice, many slapping his shoulder or back in good sportsmanship. The mood was so ecstatic it was hard not to get swept up in it all and enjoy their last night of relaxation.

Eventually, Nikanor gave Malice a skin of ale. Eunice went to take it from him when Malice chugged the entire thing, liquid spilling from the corners of his mouth. Nikanor, snowy brows nearly in his hairline, was slack-jawed, and so was Eunice. Subsequently, no one else offered Malice a drink.

Wiping his mouth, Malice passed the empty skin back to a chuckling Nikanor, who inserted himself into a conversation a few meters away. Still staring, Malice had either drunk before or he was feigning sobriety. Both were impressive for his age. Then he spun, teetered, and almost fell backwards. Luckily, Eunice caught and righted him.

"You're drunk," she said, getting a better look at his half-closed eyelids and flushed complexion.

"Yes," he said. "I downed a whole skin of ale… I've never had alcohol."

Containing her laughter, "I can see that," Eunice, hands on Malice's shoulders, guided him from the campfire. He willingly let her walk to their tent, get him out of his oversized tunic, and put him to bed.

The alcohol was probably hitting him harder and faster due to his lack of sleep over the past week. Night terrors kept him from getting more than an hour or two. He had jolted upright, stiff as a board until he had lied back down or stayed awake.

After drawing the fur blanket up to his waist, Eunice turned, but Malice caught her wrist. "Stay," he said.

I'll be right outside, she almost said, since it was the original plan in case any of the royals needed her. She nodded instead, "all right," and sat on the cool ground, her back against her cot on the other side of the tent, legs sprawled out in front of her.

Their belongings were destroyed during the battle, so nothing in their tent was theirs. The trunks at the foot of their beds had clothes that didn't fit either of them very well. Centered in the space was a table, four chairs on each side. Linseed oil lamps kept the map on its surface flat, as well as a jar of ink and a dagger. Otherwise, their canvas home was bare.

The royal's liveliness continued, Eunice assumed, till dawn. None were happy when morning brought hangovers, vomiting, and hunger.

Duties were, nonetheless, performed without complaint. Rounding any remaining horses was one of those duties, ending with a total of thirty-two. Royals who were still injured got the horses, along with Malice, Eunice, Jayesh, and Nikanor. They set a relaxed pace since most of the warband was on foot. Heat was as much of a concern as it was weeks ago. Malice made it clear they would travel for long as possible this time around. There was no reason to delay their return.

Those salty gusts Eunice had smelled brought a few days of constant storms. The rain was heavy, wind whipping in all directions, lightning cracking in blinding flashes, thunder booming, and rattling the ground like an earthquake. The warband pressed onwards.

Supplies were restocked in Estera and horses were bought— more like loaned. Malice had charmed his way into the biggest inn he could find capable of housing one hundred royals. Then charmed five local farmers and stables into selling him all their horses, so each royal had a mount. It was probably the first and last time Eunice would ever see him swindle someone like a merchant trying to get a customer to buy a chipped sword—he had promised ten sacks of coin these poor people probably wouldn't see for years to come. Good thing the warband only stayed for a night and left at dawn the next morning.

Although, the inn keeper especially loved the sound of another *Prince* having stayed at her inn.

A rock settled in the pit of Eunice's stomach when Hordes Kingdom loomed over the horizon like a dark ominous wall, tension bunching her back and shoulders. Not only were Malice and his warband alive and well, thousands of the queen's gathered forces had been desecrated.

Malice rode proudly next to Eunice, his expression aloof, but she saw the trembling of his hands more than once, her own hands matching. Whether it was fear or anger, Eunice didn't know, and she didn't ask. It didn't matter. He would be a fool not to know the hell he would walk into by the end of the day.

Malice was a target Vendetta had been getting her subjects to shoot at. He had given more than a justified reason for her highness to take aim herself, and Eunice doubted Vendetta would miss.

Victory Through Mistakes
"Claiming what is mine"

Malice had practically been shitting bricks since he and the warband left the streets of Estera. The nerves jumbling his thoughts were as strong as the rage curdling in the pits of his stomach. At least he wasn't alone.

Almost every time he glanced at Eunice, her hands trembled, her body rigid with anxiety, a muscle in her jaw twitching often. Nikanor's expression was distant, as if he were contemplating his life and what he needed to do before death caught up to him.

People flocked to the warband within five minutes of hooves clattering the granite streets, cheering, smiling, welcoming them home, overrunning the road. Their upbeat attitude infected the royals as they waved back, laughed, spoke to the people as if they were old friends. Any feelings of negativity blew away in the breeze. Malice let it infect him, too. It was nice to be wanted by his people.

Deeper into the kingdom, the castle was an ominous dark structure of ornately carved stone and towers piercing the sky like spearheads. Malice couldn't count the number of patterns, ridges, spirals and arches, even if he tried. Beautifully intimidating.

The further they went, the thinner the warband's entourage became, though it never truly disappeared. A few stragglers remained.

Malice spoke quietly, almost a whisper, knowing Eunice would hear, "Stay with the royals in the courtyard."

Eunice peeked his way, an eyebrow lifted.

"Then take them to the taverns, relax, unwind, have some drinks—good drinks—and food. Keep away from the castle for a while."

Malice didn't look at her directly when she nodded. He was unsettlingly calm. The elated crowd must have stolen his nervousness and anger. Wondering why would lead to overthinking and would allow those feelings back tenfold, so Malice focused on what was in front of him. The streets, being high noon, would empty soon to avoid the heat of the day. Each establishment was different. Some were built of stone and wood like architecture in the north, some of plaster like houses in the southwest. Very few were made entirely of wood, like those in the east, while red clay was most abundant. Windows weren't so common depending on the structure and if they were, they were small and rounded. He looked at the few people going about their business. A woman, perhaps a human, swept off the walkway in front of her shop. A fishman watered their plants and headed for shade when they finished. Soil and wood wafted, hoofbeats drowning most other noises. Sweat beaded on Malice's skin, trickled down his face, tasted salty on his lips.

The courtyard was peaceful and vivid compared to the gothic design of the castle, flowers in bloom, the bushes, trees, and shrubs trimmed and rounded. Snow's hooves clumped on the stone path leading toward the front doors.

They opened.

Vendetta stood in the foyer's shadow, her long crimson hair braided and resting against the black of her dress. Draga was on her right, almost an exact mirror of her mother, her attire a softer red. Then Odovacar, and Inyene to Vendetta's left, both wearing loose, simple garments. Odovacar was in dusty violet whereas Inyene's clothes matched the vibrancy of her beady eyes.

Malice had convinced himself he was calm as he stopped halfway to the wide, shallow stairs.

But he made the mistake of averting his sights from the queen and his siblings to find a lone boy standing in the eastern courtyard. The boy dropped his basket of plants. It was Kiran, his skin a rich umber in the sunlight, a slight twinkle from his curving horns. Malice flung his eyes back to the castle's entrance, his heart pounding like a war drum. His blood stopped and his lungs squeezed. Breath caught in the back of his throat.

Why was he here? Of all places, of all times, why now?

"So, the mutt lives," her highness called, voice harsh.

"The campaign was successful," Malice said, struggling to collect himself, his mare shuffling underneath him. "The mercenaries are no more."

Queen Vendetta's eye twitched and a prolonged silence settled, as if she were expecting Malice to say something else. He glimpsed a movement from Odovacar, his skin ashen. Those inky eyes were on Nikanor beside Eunice at the gate. Odovacar's prior first sword had thrown any sigil or emblem into the fire the night he pledged himself to Malice.

"Does that matter when you've killed your own royals?" Her second set of long-fingered hands extended to her sides, gesturing to what lay around her. "This was but a test for you, Malice. Yet you took it upon yourself to kill thousands of royals. Your title as prince will save you the judgement of treason, but it will not save you entirely." She smiled, a thin, horrendous thing. "Inyene."

Malice reflected her grin. "Those royals were traitors, attacking their own prince and royals. It was self-defense. You've no right to punish me," he countered and Inyene stopped dead in her tracks, shock pulling her features long.

"I told you to rid the region of the mercenaries, not six thousand of your own men. Of my men," Vendetta said slowly, carefully, a single spasm raking her body.

"They were sent on your orders, weren't they?" he asked, confidence building in his chest like fluttering butterfly wings. "If they went off on their own accord, they had become rogues you would've wanted me to kill, anyway."

"I gave you the chance to excel, to show brilliance, to earn your place in my court." She took a single step into the light, the gold jewels hanging around her dainty wrists and neck gleaming. "You've squandered it."

"Why do I need to earn my place when it's my birthright?" Nothing could have prepared Malice for the reaction his kin gave. Outrage, understanding, devastation. Malice jolted upright in his saddle, fighting the urge to smile like a madman. His muscles stiffened in that split second, the fluttering exploding, reaching every corner of his being. He had gotten past her highness's defenses, had sparked a nerve, destroyed her image of him.

And he loved it.

Malice dismounted, letting go of Snow's reins when a whistle tweeted behind him and she stalked toward Eunice. "I saved my warband from annihilation. I killed those threatening the precious power you think is yours. I passed your test and led my royals to victory. *Your* men met their makers because you underestimated me."

"Enough… *child*," the queen ground out. "Accept your mistakes gracefully." Her face was of barely controlled wrath, a fire in her black eyes blazing stronger than Malice had ever seen. Vendetta, mighty Queen of Hordes Region, was rattled by her own mutt.

"The court you say I need to earn my place in is mine," he went on. "The throne, the crown, the kingdom and region, they are all mine."

"Of course they are yours," Vendetta huffed, stepping down to the first stair. "You are my *son*, and that is the only reason your head has remained on your shoulders."

"I am no son of yours, Vendetta Claymore. I am the grandson of Hordes Reap, true heir of Hordes Region. My birthright is the very air you breathe, the dirt you walk on, the food and drink you fill your stomach with."

The atmosphere was dense, hefty on Malice's shoulders, but he didn't mind. It was the weight of victory, small as it was. He continued toward the stone steps, climbed them, his boots clacking. "I have taken every single one of your challenges head on," he said as he passed

Through the space between Draga and her siblings, Malice marched into the foyer and headed for the dungeons. He knew what was to come and would rather not struggle against Inyene. He had nowhere else to go either, at least no place the queen wouldn't know to look and hurt those harboring him.

He met the darkness of the tunnel leading to his prison with his chin high and his shoulders proud, breathing in the stench of mold and death.

The stragglers would spread his declaration, and so would his warband. Whether anything detrimental happened because of it didn't matter, that wasn't Malice's intention. He wanted Queen Vendetta to know what he had done and what he planned to do. Malice *needed* her to know he had taken up a bow, had nocked an arrow to the string, and was aiming at her. The difference between them? Malice wouldn't miss.

Death of a Boy
XXXIV

Part II

Two weeks before Malice's campaign

"Finally became a royal, huh?" Malice mused, his voice breathy and fast. Sweat trickled down his pale skin. He was smiling, his green eyes steady on Zephyrus as the dagger of darkness in his hand shot embers of black.

"Don't worry, I'll be able to help your sorry ass out on missions soon enough," Zephyrus retorted.

Malice laughed mockingly, his shoulders shaking. "You say that as if you can beat me in a spar." He cracked his neck, two loud pops. "Beat me here and I might let you join me on a mission or two."

Zephyrus squeezed the grip of his sword, glided his other hand past the guard as if he were feeling the smooth edge of a sword. Lava slithered and bubbled, following Zephyrus's hand as it formed a blade. Lava wasn't the easiest element to control, and it was about as rare as smoke magic, Malice's first sword Eunice being the only one he knew to have it. The blade of lava let off a steady amount of steam, heat smothering him worse than Mutuwa's muggy air.

A second dagger manifested in Malice's off-hand. He propped his arms in front of his chest and face as if they were about to spar barehanded. Training with Malice was interesting, yet annoying. He never stuck to one technique, so Zephyrus never learned his habits.

Malice was fast when he swooped in low and swung at Zephyrus's ribs. He reeled, the dagger grazing his shirt. Zephyrus hefted his sword over his head and brought it down. Malice caught it with both daggers. Left, then right, in a series of four, five, six blows, Zephyrus hacked, but Malice parried each strike.

He thought to create a pit of lava behind Malice. It would be enough for a distraction, but it was a fleeting thought. The scale of the attack would drain too much of his energy and take too much of his focus off Malice. *Magic isn't a save-all.*

Behind him, Malice's back crashed into Zephyrus. The butt of Malice's dagger jammed into his kidney, pain bursting and robbing him of breath. He jerked and swung his sword wide, too wide. Malice got in Zephyrus's guard, rushed forward to throw Zephyrus off balance, then, a black dagger vanishing, Malice gripped the collar of Zephyrus's sweat-soaked tunic, the other hand pressing a blade to his throat. Malice smirked.

"Guess you're stuck with a Squad for now," the cheeky brat said as he steadied Zephyrus.

"Yeah, yeah," Zephyrus huffed.

Lava solidified, Zephyrus stabbed his sword into the ground and surveyed the oasis, taking in moss, salt water, the sweetness of wildflowers, and sap.

Within Mutuwa, it was surprisingly quiet. As they caught their breath, he admired the lethal tranquility of the forest. Bright green leaves, big and small, created a meter tall canopy above the ground for the critters and bugs, beams of light penetrating the true canopy well beyond the height Zephyrus was willing to climb. Despite his warranted hesitation, he enjoyed being here and spending time with Malice outside the castle, away from the queen.

Stretching his arms high, Zephyrus got a sudden whiff of his stench and recoiled, arms dropping back down. He was, without a doubt, bathing when he returned home. He peeked at Malice to see if he saw what had happened. Thankfully, it didn't seem he did. The demon fixated on the underbrush, his expression serious, which allowed Zephyrus to stare a bit longer. He frowned.

They were the same age, yet Zephyrus was the one who stunk, whose clothes fit awkwardly and whose skin was riddled with bumps. His voice cracked at the worst times, yet Malice hadn't changed much, his voice high, his skin pristine, his attire perfectly fitted to his small body. Kiran was in the same boat as Zephyrus, so he guessed Malice was the odd one out.

"Up for another round?" he asked, snatching Malice's attention.

"Hand to hand?" Malice quirked an eyebrow.

"Afraid I might actually beat you?"

"Not a chance." Malice put a bit of space between them, a grin on his smug face.

Zephyrus returned the sneer. "We'll see."

Zephyrus, with a sore ass, walked through the grass and wildflowers outside Mutuwa, heading back to the castle, Malice at his side. He had *not* won. He truly thought he had a chance! Especially when Zephyrus landed a solid punch on Malice's face. Malice just had to return the blow and now blood stained their shirts. Still, it was fun.

"Did I," Malice said into their shared silence, "do something to Kiran?"

Initially, Zephyrus didn't understand. They were two peas in a pod. Zephyrus would have guessed they were brothers because of it if he didn't know better. Then it dawned on him, and he sighed.

"Not directly," he said. "He…" How could he phrase the truth without hurting Malice's feelings? "Doesn't like what the queen has you doing." That sounded all right.

"He's scared."

Zephyrus didn't respond.

Malice had killed on his first mission three years ago. Not having a choice in the matter didn't change the fact of. He knew how to kill, knew where to aim to end someone's life. Zephyrus saw it sometimes; how Malice changed the angle of his weapon during a spar to keep it from being deadly or stopping short of delivering a fatal blow. It scared him too if he were being honest, like a howler's screech in the night, a bone-chilling sensation freezing his blood. Zephyrus knew how to live with it, he was surrounded by royals most of the time. Kiran didn't.

The long grass was damp, the ground somewhat spongy with weeds. The breeze was stronger out of the forest, saltier too, and rustled the greenery, clouds passing overhead and blocking the sun. Hordes Kingdom was a half a mile or so in front of them when Malice stopped, Zephyrus as well. They looked at one another, the intensity of Malice's green eyes stronger than the plants they stood in.

"You really want to become king?" he asked out of nowhere.

"Yes." There was zero hesitation. Zephyrus saw the problems all around him, but he was forced to live with or ignore them. Royals were too vicious when they should be the protectors of the people. The nobles were arrogant. Mother and Father struggled to pay taxes. The people were scared to mention the lack of imported goods to keep their businesses afloat. Zephyrus would change it all if he had the chance.

"I'll make you king." Malice brought his fist up, letting it thump against Zephyrus's heart, keeping it there as he said, "Give me three years and the throne will be yours."

One needed to be sixteen to ascend the throne. They were too young to claim it now. Butterflies in his stomach, Zephyrus held back his smile to match the sincerity of Malice's demeanor.

Placing his fist on Malice's heart, he said, "Give me three years to become worthy of that throne."

While the birds pervaded the quiet, Zephyrus clasped Malice's hand. They smiled, lingered in the field between the kingdom and Mutuwa, then continued on their way, a comfortable silence persisting.

At the castle gates, Zephyrus watched Malice enter his gloomy home before he started toward the north, where the dining hall was. Evening was fast approaching, and after training with Malice all morning, he was starved.

Zephyrus hadn't gotten far when a hand clamped down on his shoulder. Heart leaping into his throat, he whipped around and slapped the hand away, letting his own hover over the sword hilt in his belt. The person stepped back, hands up, eyebrows almost in their hairline.

"Good response, kid," they snickered.

"Who're you?" Zephyrus snipped.

"Name's Nor Leroux." Giddily, they tapped the brooch pinned to their leather jerkin over their left breast. The gold was shiny, a single-horned skull with a sword through it, a partial Hordes Region sigil. "I'm a newly promoted knight myself."

He eyed them suspiciously, letting his hand relax to his side. *Newly* promoted? Since the youngest of the Reap family had already reached the age of ten, the ranking ceremony was held a little after the new year. It was spring. "What do you want with me?"

"Wary of strangers, not a bad thing there, kid." With a quick clearing of their throat, they said, "Sir Ushas is waiting for us at the dining hall. Better not keep him waiting either, kid."

The crowded dining hall was deafening with chatter and laughter, the smell of food and alcohol hardly covering the musk of sweat. Weaving through the crowd, Nor and Zephyrus grabbed a plate from the back wall where a table always had a spread of food. Meat, fruits, vegetables, cheese, bread, along with jugs of water, wine, ale, mead, fruit juice of some sort, and goat or cow milk. They both stuffed their plates. Nor's was so full, their food threatened to fall to the floor more than once.

Nor brought Zephyrus to a table on the far side of the dining hall. The table was quieter than the rest, reserved. Nor leaned over and whispered something into the ear of a big fishman. They turned, winked at Zephyrus, and made their way to an empty spot on the other side. The fishman inclined his head and the royal to his right slid over to make room for Zephyrus. Hesitantly, he sat next to the big fishman, trying not to touch either person at his side.

"Little sprout," the fishman said, his voice a deep grumble, "welcome to the Squad!" From ear to ear, a grin showed shark-like teeth as Sir Ushas slapped Zephyrus's back with a webbed hand.

He winced, a stinging pain blooming between his shoulder blades. The rest of the table shouted a welcome, thrust their goblets into the air, their drinks splashing out, and threw them back, gulping every drop until their cups were empty. Three different pitchers were passed around the table to refill goblets.

Sir Ushas leaned down to murmur, "From here on, we're not *just* a team, we are *family*. We fight together, help one another, cover what someone else lacks. This Squad looks out for one another. Got it, little sprout?"

"Got it, sir." Zephyrus nodded and Sir Ushas went back to gobbling his food and drink, chatting with his royals.

In Hordes Region, Squads were composed of knights and guards, typically led by a knight, rarely by a general—they led armies and special attack forces. It allowed royals to gain experience while surrounded by those who were stronger, battle-hardened, and able to pull the rookie from danger if need be. It also allowed royals to become competitive, shoot for greater feats or succumb to their limitations and leave. This system weeded out the weak and cultivated the strong, Nor had explained on the way to the dining hall.

Sir Ushas was one of the highest-ranking knights in the region, a man Zephyrus's father had a lot of respect for. And probably one of the best knights to take tutelage from. Father said he'd declined the offer to become a general, so he could continue training young royals. He had four red gills on the side of his neck, his skin a slate grey color, his eyes almost completely black. The big man was bald, had holes where his ears should be, and scars running long ways across his face, chest, and neck, each one pasty and protruding as if they didn't heal right. Ushas was bulky and tall, a mix of fat and muscle making him as large as a tree trunk.

As he ate, Zephyrus got a kick out of watching his new comrades match the energy of the other tables, sometimes besting their loudness. He laughed with them, enjoyed the stories they told oh so proudly, whether they were true or not. Quite a few seemed rather far-fetched. He wished Malice and Kiran were here to experience it with him.

Once bellies were stuffed and all that was left were mostly drunk goblets, Sir Ushas went over the details of their mission. They departed in two weeks.

*

A few miles south from the coast, Zephyrus and his new Squad captured eight traders, three of which had put up a struggle and were bound hand and foot to the wagons.

It was dark, as Sir Ushas wanted the element of surprise and with as big of a company as they had, night was the best time for an ambush. Nor and a few others kept a flame in their palms, lighting the traders and their luggage. The air was salty; it coated the inside of his mouth and dried his tongue out.

Zephyrus, unlike the others who were older and more experienced, was one of five scouts. Two watched over the captured traders on the ground. Each had their hands secured—except those three tied to the wagons, who were *extra* secure. Everyone else in Sir Ushas's Squad, a total of nineteen, searched and placed all the wares from two carts on the grass. The lot was divided between weapons, minerals, and jewels Nor said were from northern Vinyamar. Specifically, Wolfgang's and Jared's Regions. A bunch of rocks was what Zephyrus saw. The weapons would be useful since they looked to be in good condition. And there were tiny sacks, every other one clinking as it was transported.

Zephyrus shuffled a little closer to see what was inside the pouches. Corked vials, powder, dried leaves and flowers. Stuff to make tea or herbal medicines. One he recognized thanks to Kiran and his parents, burdock, good for fever and pain. Wait—he inched closer, squinting. It was belladonna nightshade, a highly poisonous plant that was difficult to harvest with bare hands, since the toxins could seep through skin. Understanding flashed across Sir Ushas's and a few other's faces. Anger darkened them.

"Poison," a royal confirmed.

Zephyrus jerked his head forward. The coast met the horizon, a harsh line against the shimmering ocean. *Why would they have so much?* Sir Ushas had the same question, but he actually asked it, and when he didn't get answers… he became persuasive. Turned out, a few good blows to the head could produce some answers.

No one liked them, though.

"They're to be delivered to Yvonne Apostolov," one trader, a human, blurted, her voice shaky.

Rage sparked and raced through Zephyrus's veins. He knew that name very well. The Apostolov's were the nobles of Mondlesgrave. Anything said afterward, Zephyrus didn't catch over the drumming of his heartbeat.

Nor was the one who broke him out of his dazed state; it was time to break camp. They would stay there tonight and head out at dawn.

This was why he wanted to become king. He wanted to root out nobles like Yvonne, who had no business commissioning poison. Clients weren't required to share the reason for their order, or so the one giant amongst the traders explained to the royals during further questioning. Zephyrus hadn't believed it. Neither had Sir Ushas based on how scrunched his face was.

The traders continued spilling all they knew throughout the night for food, water, and blankets. The poisons had been collected all over Vinyamar. Many mercenaries, nobles, and ordinary civilians with a grudge would pay and had paid good money to kill whoever they wanted without getting their hands dirty and without getting caught. The weapons, minerals, and jewels were for show, had to seem like a normal trader's setup, making it easier to travel through kingdoms and not rouse suspicion.

"Who ordered you?" Sir Ushas asked again, only this time, his tone was harsh and guttural, a growl from a wolf.

"We already told you," the trader Borch said, an elf with a missing ear. "Lady Yvonne commissioned the poisons."

"Who." Sir Ushas extended his webbed hand, grabbing Borch's collar and lifting the trader off the ground as he stood. "Ordered. You?"

A single shudder ran through Borch's body, his complexion gone stark white. He gulped. "I—don't make—can't say or—why would you stop us—we're all—all… we're all," he spiraled, words growing quieter and slower. Moments passed, tension heavy in the air, the fire the Squad sat around crackling, crickets chirping.

"She'll kill us all if I say!" Borch shouted, writhing in Sir Ushas's grip. He flung the trader to the ground and stomped toward his tent, yanking the flap open, the canvas falling behind him.

She *sounds an awful lot like Yvonne, but would Sir Ushas react like that if it were?*

Malice's words trickled into his ears. *I can't tell you because I don't want you guys to get hurt.* Zephyrus swallowed. Malice and he had left on their missions around the same time, Malice leaving a few days earlier. He recalled their last conversation.

"If I don't make it back, there's another way you can become king, but you're not going to like it," Malice had said lightly.

"You'll make it back," Zephyrus had chuckled. *"You're too stubborn not to."*

Malice hadn't laughed. *"Kill the queen."* Malice's gaze met Zephyrus's confused stare. *"If you kill her, you can claim her throne like they do in Zeldine's Region."*

Zephyrus hadn't taken it seriously then, but maybe he should have. Maybe he should've paid more attention to what Malice was doing and saying. Read a bit deeper. Was it too late to start?

*

Trotting through the granite paved streets, people greeted Sir Ushas's Squad on the way to the castle. Zephyrus's lips spread into a grin as he waved, eyes darting from person to person. He hoped to see his kin. Carefully, he scanned the crowded streets, looking for the head of smoky grey belonging to his father or his mother's brown hair or his sister's toothy grin. He didn't see them.

It had been a little over two months since he left on the mission. He'd never been away from home for so long, a few nights at most. His heart sank the closer the Squad got to the castle positioned in the kingdom's south. It had also been two months since he last saw Malice and Kiran and he missed them too, missed their banter and shared meals.

Sir Ushas was the only one to enter the courtyard and deliver the traders to a group of royals near the entrance, each branded with Hordes Kingdom sigil on their breastplates. Next, they were off to the royals' paddock—Malice said there were two, the second being for the Reap family exclusively—and then to the dining hall.

The dining hall was a long, wide building of timber, inside and out. There were four stained glass windows on its face, but that was it color wise. Tables, chairs, beams, plates, cups—everything was wood. At midday, most royals were out training, on a mission, or patrolling the kingdom, so the noise was bearable.

Roasted and baked food overwhelmed Zephyrus's senses, causing a rumble in his stomach. Like the others, he hurried to the back counter, made sure his plate overflowed with food, and joined his Squad at a table to scarf down his meal. Not that he was entirely thrilled about sitting again. His ass was sore enough from the ride back to Hordes Kingdom.

Hunger subsiding, meaning he no longer ate like a hog, Zephyrus let the chatter of the hall fill his ears, sipping from his goblet of water. *These youths aren't what they used to be*, a haggard voice proclaimed. Another voice was just a voice, their words too slurred together to make out what was being said. Zephyrus set his cup down and focused on the whispers of the table next to theirs.

"I still can't believe it," a demon said.

The one across from him shook her head. "What I can't believe is how the queen sent him on another mission a day or two ago."

"Didn't he murder an army?" the demon shot back and huffed. "How much slack will the queen allow her mutt to have?"

"Enough to allow nonsense to be spewed!" She slammed her fist onto the table, the dining hall falling silent for a moment. Quieter, leaning across the table, she said, "He went as far as to proclaim himself heir! That runt doesn't deserve the title of prince if he's going to act like this."

"Agreed."

Runt. Mutt. Prince. Malice. They were talking about Malice. He returned? When? Before that, he—he killed an entire army? Well, how big was an army to those two? Zephyrus knew about Malice's campaign, but was that why he had warned him about the possibility of not returning? Because he knew he was going to face an army once he left the kingdom?

Why had he proclaimed himself as the heir? Zephyrus understood he had only recently become a royal, but he thought Malice meant what he promised.

Teeth grinding, the urge to stomp back to the castle, storm to the fourth floor, and demand answers from Malice took a minute to push down. If he had returned, Zephyrus could do that tomorrow. Today, he wanted to see his family.

Truth Obscured by Death
XXXV

One month before Zephyrus's return, the night of Malice's declaration

The cold and damp familiarity of the dungeons underneath the castle eased Malice strangely enough. What eased him more was the fact that he'd gained an edge against Vendetta. Whether he died in this cell or not, he'd done what he had promised his royals. *If we die, know I was the first and know I left a wound Vendetta will never get rid of.* The truth was out there. Her false claim of the Reap name was on the wind, Eunice and his royals would spread it further yet. That was the wound he inflicted. Although, he liked being a thorn in her side better, brief as the moment may have been.

With his arms and legs cuffed to a heavy oak chair, Malice couldn't move. He *could* break free if he wanted to. Being down here, waiting for Inyene, however, gave him time to think. Malice didn't escape because he knew the consequences would fall onto those closest to him. He didn't fight back simply because he knew death was a heartbeat away.

The thing was, he had died already.

Dread and fear once consumed him, drove him at times. What

about now? Anger? Sure, to an extent. There was something else, a need for something, and it was powerful. Tearing up his throat, fogging his mind like a morning haze over the land, an itch in his veins he couldn't scratch, a constant skittering resonating through his skull.

The metal door opened, a high-pitched squeal like a pig making Malice's ears ring as light flooded the cell. Inyene placed the torch in the holster adjacent to the doorframe, her red eyes gleaming with excitement. When the door closed, Inyene exchanged no pleasantries. It seemed she had been looking forward to Malice's homecoming more than anyone else and dove into her routine.

Knuckle by knuckle, joint by joint, his appendages fell to the floor, each time a wet thump, the enclosed space making the smell of blood as strong as it was on those hills. It was only his blood this time, whereas it had been thousands upon thousands of bodies Malice had slaughtered on the hills north of Estera. Faces he didn't recognize, all blurs in his memory. Yet he remembered his actions so pristinely. *He* was the one in control that time; *he* had killed the queen's army; *he* had worn a smile as he ripped organs from torsos and cut heads from shoulders.

Malice broke from his thoughts when the sounds of flesh hitting stone stopped. Confused, he blinked up at Inyene, expecting more because it always progressed; beatings, burning, icing, drowning, crushing his bones with a wooden hammer with however many strikes it took, seeing how much flesh she could peel off in a single sheet, and then how far she could skin him before he passed out.

Instead, his elder sister stood there, the dingy blue of her skin warmed by torchlight, her eyes searching. Stepping forward, Inyene pressed a knife to Malice's wrist. He jerked, the cuff restricting him as metal kissed the paleness of his skin.

"Don't look away," Inyene hissed and put her weight into cutting his hand off, the knife sinking deeper until it hit the arm of the chair and Malice's hand slipped to the floor. Sometimes blood sprayed, sometimes it didn't. Like paint flowing over a canvas, crimson poured onto the ground.

He swallowed hard, heart hammering inside his chest, breathing unevenly. Bone sprouted anew, tendons, veins, muscle, and skin following, fibrous tissue weaving and stitching itself together to regenerate what had not disappeared but laid on the stone next to his foot. Malice stared at his hands, the new and old.

Inyene stumbled backward a bit, dazed. "You can't feel pain?"

He couldn't?

"What the hell happened?"

"I… died," he breathed, wiggling his fingers, closing and opening his fist, cracking his knuckles. He had done the motion so many times to make sure his hand was still there, and every time it was.

"Died," Inyene echoed.

"My heart was obliterated." Malice had had to tear the sharpened pillar of earth from his chest when he got to his feet. From its size, it wouldn't have been a stretch to believe his heart and lungs, even his stomach, had been destroyed.

Inyene took another step back, an involuntary action, like prey backing away from the starving predator. "The queen was right about you," she eventually said. "You have become the truest definition of immortality."

What? His thoughts and muscles seized.

As she spun and strode to the door, she added, "If not through pain, I will find another way to break you." The door slammed shut, deafening Malice for a split second.

He didn't know how much time had passed, but he stared at the slab of dark metal, unmoving and absentminded, as if Inyene stole it on her way out.

Eyes gradually falling to his left hand, Malice pulled against the shackles. And pulled. Bones popped; resistance momentarily lapsed. His skin bunched against the chipped and scratched cuff. Flesh ripped like paper torn in two, blood welled. Upper lip flaring, Malice gave it a final yank, and his hand jumped from the armrest. It hit the floor, ichor spraying the ground and wall. Again, he watched his hand regenerate.

No pain. None.

The tug, the sensation of his skin and muscles tearing and his bones dislodging were there, yet there was no pain. The lack thereof was disorienting, his head swimming, heartbeat rapid. He knew what it was supposed to feel like. He expected it, wanted it. The agony. The gut curdling, blood stopping, vision blackening pain Inyene rained down on him every single day he was in this cell.

What happened to it? Why did it leave Malice?

Was this what Malice had been denying for so long? Refusing to accept what was? He knew he had changed after he died. His true form was different. His human form was different. Like clothes he suddenly grew out of, he could feel the difference in how he walked, sat, ate, slept, spoke. His own skin felt strange to be in, as if he had to learn how to do all basic functions again. Did he have to learn how to feel pain again?

Tilting his head back, Malice forced his thoughts elsewhere.

On the night of Zephyrus's birthday, Zephyrus, Kiran, and Malice visited the Nameless Lake, north of Hordes Kingdom. The body of water was huge, spanning further than Malice could see and grazing the city of Estera, a black smudge against a canvas of dark green.

Eunice had tagged along to keep an eye on the boys and keep their parents' minds at ease.

The clear water reflected the moon and stars like a mirror, rippling when a bug skidded across, or a fish skirted the surface. Iris's, forget-me-nots, and spider lilies surrounded the outer bank of the lake while lotus flowers floated in the water.

The smell of sulfur and flowers came back to Malice intensely.

They had stayed out all night, lying in the grass, star gazing, chasing one another around, swimming in the water day had warmed. Before the sun rose, Eunice brought them back to the castle, Kiran and Zephyrus passing out as soon as their heads hit the pillow. Malice hadn't slept that night. In the morning, he had read a letter from Magnus and wrote back to him.

Magnus was well, his crown uncomfortable on his brow, but he was getting used to it. The Games of Retribution were doing better than Magnus hoped and had become quite a spectacle for the people, and for those outside of Alucard's Region as well. Basia, Queen of Zeldine's Region, asked to witness the Games firsthand. Magnus refused. If Thorn, King of Maziar's Region, had asked too, he would have told the dark elf no, all the same. Malice thought it was a good idea to keep the Games localized to Alucard's Region. Introducing two of the most bloodthirsty rulers to the Games would likely end in disaster.

Malice kept his thoughts busy, bouncing between every person he knew until his mind became numb.

"Zephyrus"

Day of Zephyrus's return

Zephyrus remembered the timber and rock of his old home and how cocoons scattered the walls during the spring and summer months. His mother had tried her best to keep the caterpillars off her plants and, out of annoyance, flicked a good number of cocoons off the walls, grumbling under her breath as she did.

Compared to the hold Issur and Fausta had built, their current house was small and insignificant. But it was better than a tent big enough for one barely fitting a family of four.

During the sleeping hours, his home had gone up in flames, the blaze hungrily engulfing everything there was. The house, the barn, and stables, the well and barges near the coastal for tarring and repairing boats. Not even the holds skeleton remained, the fields of lush green, black and barren.

Zephyrus trudged through the granite streets, scowling.

He was getting closer to home; he could not only feel it but smell the familiar scent of freshly baked pastries and bread, and the flowers from nearby shops. A wave of excitement put a pep in his step. Children ran up and down the road, avoiding the wagons and carriages trotting in the middle, the coachmen cursing at them. The kingdom always brimmed with life while the sun was up, but when night came, the threat of the curfew killed off almost all activity. It was another thing he would change when, or if, he became king.

Down the way, he saw the concrete walls, and terracotta roof of his home, windows trimmed with dark stained wood, two flower beds on either side of the front door, and a flagstone pathway leading to the entrance. Lights painted the curtains yellow. Issur and Fausta were probably cooking while Ester played with her wooden blocks, creating towers and castles of her own.

Almost tripping when he picked up his pace, Zephyrus hurried, his shoes clapping against the pathway, his hand on the slightly warmed knob. The door opened. He reeled, a horrid stench punching him in the face. He dropped to his knees, and his stomach emptied onto the flagstone.

Panic slithered across his body like a snake as he caught his breath, and tears burned his eyes. Zephyrus crawled into his home, the odor worsening. He gagged but pressed forward. There was a candle almost completely melted in its pricket, flickering on the counter. Then a pair of bare feet entered his vision, the dark skin mottled.

Issur lay dead. His blistering body was sprawled, dried blood pooled around him. Zephyrus cautiously made his way over, his heart the only sound. He placed his hands on his father's face, felt the chill penetrate his palm, wiped the cracked blood from the corner of his father's mouth. Zephyrus put his ear to Issur's chest. Still. Silent.

He rose steadily, turned, and walked to the dining room, where a second corpse lay face down on the round table. Plans for a ship design were crumpled and black underneath Fausta's head. A tower of wooden blocks were knocked over beside his sister's swelled body in the living room. Eyes sweeping the entirety of the home, nothing else was out of place, nothing stolen from Zephyrus's memory. They hadn't been robbed.

They'd been dead for a while, Zephyrus concluded. The hole in Fausta's head festered with maggots. The slit running from ear to ear across Ester's neck also squirmed with bugs. His family's flesh was rotting, their bodies unnaturally shaped as decomposition settled in. Ichor no longer ran through them. Their hearts would never beat again. Their lungs would never take in air.

Breath forcibly left Zephyrus, leaving him wheezing and

swaying. His ribcage constricted and the thundering of his heart shook his entire body.

Quietly, sluggishly, Zephyrus went to the back of the house, collected blankets, and covered his father, mother, and sister as if he were tucking them in for bed. He could pretend he was. After a long day of training, he came home to find his family had fallen asleep waiting for him; that was what he told himself as he stood in the entrance, observing the cleanliness and undisturbed solace of his house.

Whoever killed them had been invited in. Had been welcomed. Issur would have fought otherwise, while Fausta took Ester and ran. Whoever killed them did so with deadly precision and speed.

Time passed. Zephyrus found himself entranced by the single candle left, the flame the only source of light. It jerked, then calmed, as if returning his gaze, whispering in his ear.

People darted past him, shouting. His shadow danced in front of him. The house he came to like was a blaze steadily consuming his neighbors' homes as well. Royals ran to the fire, giving commands while Zephyrus walked on.

He felt hollow and lost. He stopped amidst the chaos and looked skyward, grey pillars forming new clouds. Suddenly, his view blurred, wetness trickled down his cheeks, his jaw and neck.

Whoever had killed his kin had been invited into his home. Had been shown Fausta's work and Ester's toys. Had been allowed inside the kitchen as Issur cooked. Had eaten with them, had laughed, only to slaughter them like animals.

Whoever had killed them had been considered a brother.

Birth of a King
XXXVI

Zephyrus stepped beyond the southern gate to the castle's courtyard, the forest Kiran lived in skirting the grounds. He came for someone, and he didn't have to look hard.

Malice stood in the middle of the courtyard, head of loose, white curls tilted up, eyes closed. His ruffled white shirt was tucked into black trousers, his bare feet and hands tainted with black scuffs, his pale skin glowing in the sunlight. His friend. His brother.

Bitterness twisted Zephyrus's gut as anger burned a hole in his chest, his mind clearer than it had ever been.

As if he sensed Zephyrus's presence, Malice turned, lit up, and started toward him. Fists bunched, Zephyrus's heart thumped wildly as his eyes burned. He met the prince halfway, stopping six paces from him. *He's happy... My family is dead, and he's happy.*

Grass swayed gently with the breeze, caressing Zephyrus's shins. The sweet scent of lavender, hibiscus, and jasmine were sickening.

"Why?" he asked before Malice got a word out.

Malice's face screwed with concern. "What happened, you look—"

"Why did you kill them?" Zephyrs shouted, the tears he desperately tried to keep at bay rushing back to his eyes.

The distant sound of elevated voices grew when the wind died, the birds still tweeting obliviously.

"Kill who," Malice said at last, a hardness to him that wasn't there moments earlier.

"Don't," Zephyrus said through clenched teeth, "lie to me. Don't play coy either." Malice simply blinked. "What did they do to you or the queen? Did they threaten you? Did I? Was the idea I could become a greater king than you so terrible?" He stopped to catch his breath, the horrified look on Malice's face wrenching his heart out of place, a dagger scoring his flesh.

"You returned weeks ago. Was it solely to kill my family? Or did you want to relax first? Perhaps you expected me there too and your *mother* forget to tell you I hadn't come back yet."

Zephyrus caved in on himself, the dagger sinking into his sternum. *Don't look at me like that. You killed them, so you have no right to be surprised... You... you killed them...*

There was a slip in Malice's expression, and a seething hatred distorted his features. Zephyrus shuddered, an earthquake.

"What do you want?" Malice asked, pain lacing his voice, his body as riddled with tension as Zephyrus's. *Tell me you want your family avenged. Tell me you want to find them and banish them, kill them. Anything and I'll make it happen.*

Another silence descended. Every muscle, every bone, and fiber of Zephyrus ached. He wanted the truth, but when he opened his mouth; "I want a duel."

A duel in Hordes Region was an honorable way for royals to claim revenge. He'd watched a mother covered in blood challenge a fellow royal and kill him for raping her daughter who died giving birth.

When death came, so had the truth. The royal told every gruesome detail of what he did to the woman's daughter.

That was at the end of winter, hardly six months ago.

Truth would come, Zephyrus would have it now or when Malice drew his final breath.

Eyes bloodshot, Malice regarded Zephyrus as if silently pleading with him. *Please don't make me do this. Rescind your request and I'll let it go. Don't make me fight you. Please, Zephyrus.*

"Here and now, I claim my right to avenge my kin," Zephyrus said and grabbed the hilt from the sheath on his belt. "Malice reap, Prince of Hordes Region, I challenge you to a duel." Chin up, Zephyrus waited for Malice's refusal, waited for him to turn and walk away, waited for the truth. For something. *Come on, Malice, say it. Prove me wrong. Tell me it was the queen. Tell me anything and I'll believe it!* A part of him wanted to hear nothing. Yet he wanted to hear everything. He was more torn than Mutuwa, the rift growing between them wider than Zephyrus could ever have imagined.

Despite holding his head high, Zephyrus's lips quivered, his brows furrowed. Pain like a vise encased him, making him short of breath. *Please.*

Malice closed his eyes, his head drooping to the side a bit, his chest deflating in a trembling exhale. *You want a scapegoat? You want someone to hate, to blame for your family's death? So be it.* Malice chuckled, head shaking. *Ignorance is bliss.*

Malice's face turned stony when he looked at Zephyrus, his eyes detached, body easing into the more arrogant stance Zephyrus always saw during their spars. "You want it your way, fine. Let's have it your way, Zephyrus."

White-hot anger exploding, he snarled, "You won't deny your crimes?"

"Prepare yourself," Malice said flatly, "or die."

Lifting his left hand, Malice flicked his wrist to the sky, clamping his fist in a fluid motion. At first, nothing happened. Agonizing pain surged up Zephyrus's arm into his chest, red-hot swords fresh from the furnace carving his arm. He screamed, his head snapping toward it. Darkness raced up his forearm as his hand disintegrated in its wake.

In the blink of an eye, Malice was there. "Let me help," he said, one hand gripped Zephyrus's good arm, and held him in place. Malice dug his claws into Zephyrus's bicep, his fingers forcing themselves deeper. He ripped the decaying arm off.

Zephyrus screeched. Pain flashed the world white. Pressure crunched his chest, cracks echoed to his ears as Malice broke his sternum, knocking him back a few tens of meters. Crashing to the ground, rolling to his back, Zephyrus gasped while pain stabbed his chest and arm like thousands of knives. Air refused to enter his lungs for a moment.

"Did you think I would go easy on you if you challenged me?" Malice seethed, his approach measured. "Did you think I wouldn't give you someone to hate if you wanted it so badly?" He loomed over Zephyrus. "I am a *Reap*. I have a reputation to uphold."

He allowed Zephyrus to get to his feet, blood gushing, and he swayed, body trembling like a leaf. Zephyrus stepped forward, swung his right arm, and felt his fist bump into Malice.

"You son of a bitch," Zephyrs croaked, trying to keep his vision steady on Malice, who slapped Zephyrus as if he were swatting a fly. Everything to his left vanished.

He staggered backward, brought his right hand up to his face. A huge gash went from his chin up into his hairline and flowed with warm, viscous ichor. Right then and there, Zephyrus realized, with sickening defeat, Malice had always let Zephyrus win. He never had a chance.

"Zephyrus Laska—" Never had Zephyrus thought such coldness could be in Malice's voice, but it was—"I hereby strip you of your royal title and exile you from Hordes Kingdom." In the same tone as if their past never existed; "Should I ever see you in my kingdom again, I will not be as kind as I was today, nor will I show hesitation."

Malice turned on his heel and walked off, his back grown doubled and hazy.

Zephyrus turned only to fall, head throbbing, and hit the ground with a thud. The archway was still in view. Legs driving as his right hand helped drag his body, Zephyrus had nowhere to go, had nothing left, not even his honor, since Malice didn't uphold the traditions of a duel, not his home or family.

The pain gradually melted away, or Zephyrus had become numb by the time he got into the forest and leaned his back against the first tree he could. Light broke through the foliage, scattering white beams. The summer air was smoldering but, in the shade, it was warm. Perhaps it wasn't so hot because Zephyrus was losing that much blood, cooling his body bit by bit.

World silencing, Zephyrus closed his eyes for a moment, taking a deep breath—which wasn't deep at all—the smell of moss masking the metal scent of his blood briefly.

"You poor thing," someone leered. They were close, as their softened tone could be heard perfectly. "Do you want to live?"

Live? What do I have to live for now? His mouth fell ajar, and the person laughed.

"Can't make a sound? Malice sure did a number on you, didn't he, Zephyrus?"

How do they know Malice? Or my name, for that matter? Forcing his eyes open, Zephyrus looked at the person, unable to tell if what he saw was reality or if his dying brain was jesting. What crouched before him was a wall of darkness, a large creature, horns twisting around its head, the face vague, almost featureless. *Who are you?*

"I can save you, give you power, give you a chance to kill Malice." It paused and considered Zephyrus. "Is that not what you wanted? Revenge? I can give it to you. All you need to do is grab my hand." The creature waited, its clawed hand extended.

Didn't I tell you already? I have nothing left to live for anymore. You should leave me here so I can die in peace. His body betrayed his thoughts, and he reached for the expecting long-fingered hand. The creature caught and squeezed Zephyrus's hand, its expression changing. His eyelids were heavy, too heavy for him to hold open anymore.

Between Brothers
XXXVII

Part III

Alkeim knew. He knew who Malice was, who he came from. It was a shock to hear him declare his right to the throne not only in front of the queen, but out in the open where anyone could hear. Where everyone had heard. He stood right outside of view, beyond the front doors against the wall, Felim beside him.

They had argued that night, he and his little brother, about whose side to take. *He is the rightful heir,* Alkeim had said. *The queen will kill us all.* Felim had been and was still swayed by fear. *I do not want to lose you, brother,* he had told Alkeim and left.

They'd accidentally heard Malice's and Zephyrus's duel from the shadows, the declaration, the silence, the cries of pain. It was quick, lasting no more than five minutes. Alkeim peeked around the corner to see Zephyrus alive and crawling toward the gate, leaving a trail of red behind him. Alkeim wouldn't have let the lad be as Malice had. He would've sent him to the afterlife with his pride and honor whole. Now Zephyrus had to live with the loss of his dignity and his kin, the truth forever unknown, no matter how short his time was.

Malice didn't kill the lad's kin, though. How could he when he was in the dungeons till this morning?

The one who had killed the Laska's was the very man Alkeim turned toward.

"You did it on the queen's order?" Alkeim asked. He wanted to hear his brother admit it.

"Aye." Felim nodded, his warriors' braids shifting with the movement. The same ones Alkeim had in his hair. Felim had fewer simply because Alkeim had been a royal longer.

"We could run."

"I'll not be breaking my oath."

Alkeim scowled. "Then you'd rather stay with Vendetta? You, who felt her actions against Malice, were unjust. You, who are as terrified as me. You would rather forsake your own blood than join Malice's cause?"

"Look at who raised him! You think he'll show mercy when he finds out we're the reason he's here? I think not, brother," Felim said, his brow deep in furrow. "You put too much faith in the lad. He's a wain, a boy not yet affected by adulthood, and you would follow him to the grave for what? Pride? A conscience?" He scoffed and turned simultaneously, wiping his face down with his hand. He sighed.

"Yes, I do this out of guilt," Alkeim said. "But I do this because I think it's right. Do you? Do you think following Vendetta is the right thing to do?"

"'Course not!" Felim whipped and spat.

"Then join me!"

"No!"

Brothers stared at each other, unspoken words of a time long ago lingering in the air between them. Alkeim knew his brother felt inferior to him, felt jealous he became a knight so young. That he became Vendetta's first sword while he became the first sword to a puppet. Felim was envious Alkeim had started a family while he could not. Alkeim tried his best to never outdo his brother, tried his best to keep by his side. He tried to have him be a part of his family so he could watch his niece grow. Felim's stubbornness was like a shell of diamond, near impossible to break.

"Don't stand in my way any longer, brother," Felim eventually said. "I'm going to stop Malice before he can think of going near the queen."

Alkeim watched his brother's feet move, a war inside him. Let his brother go or protect Malice to let him do what needed to be done. Break his oath to Vendetta, break his oath to his mother and father, or make a new one with Malice. Kill his brother or kill his wife and child.

Grinding his teeth, Alkeim drew his sword from the scabbard on his hip, letting the blade create an arc to his side, blocking Felim's path. "Things need changin'." He fixed his gaze on his brother's dark eyes, mirroring their mothers. "Malice is going to be the one to bring about that change."

Felim reeled, forehead wrinkled, and his mouth ajar. Alkeim never faced his brother with a real sword, nor had he ever pointed it at him as he was doing now. The tip of the blade hovered at Felim's collarbone.

"Are you challenging me?" Felim almost choked from the sound of it, as if he had to force the question from his lips.

Alkeim's heart ached. "Yes."

The last his father told, his dying breath, in Zeldine's Region was, *Keep your brother safe. Protect him. He's all you have and you're all he has.* They'd fled after that. Alkeim had sworn on his parents' graves. But now Felim stared down his brother's sword. And Alkeim stared at a man he no longer recognized.

Felim stepped further back, drawing his own blade, holding it two handed as Alkeim did. Their father taught them to use the bow and arrow, the spear, and a fishing rod. It was their mother who taught them to throw a punch, taught them how to use knives and swords, how to parry and attack.

"I won't hold back," he said.

"I wouldn't expect you to," Alkeim returned.

The breeze picked up and died, the air salty and floral at the same time, the sky bright and calm. Yet nothing brought comfort to the war tearing his insides to shreds.

Felim started the onslaught. He launched forward, his sword above his head, and came down fast. Alkeim countered, their swords struck, metal grating metal, sparks flew. They stepped away, briefly, when Alkeim attacked left and right, Felim dodging or deflecting. They danced around the southern courtyard and, despite the coolness of the shadow, sweat accumulated on his skin, dripping into his eyes that he had to blink away.

After a time, they both paused, nicks and cuts all over their bodies, beading red, staining their clothes, their breathing heavier.

"Enough pussyfooting around," Felim barked, his lips drawn back in a snarl. "If you don't finish this, I will and you will die by my blade, brother!"

He sprinted, attacked from the right, feigned, then caught Alkeim's ribs when he attempted to defend himself. They cracked and pain burst, whiteness taking his vision for a split second. Warmth ran down his side.

Felim continued, but not without the slightest hint of hesitation. Alkeim ducked a horizontal swing, shuffled into his defense and head-butted Felim's chin. He staggered back, spat blood, and glowered at Alkeim. He, too, faltered. Alkeim couldn't drive his sword through his little brother's core.

Felim could. Except he missed the core and impaled Alkeim's stomach. He gripped Felim's shoulder with one hand, hissing back the pain, and thrust his sword through his brother's sternum, watched his eyes grow wide.

Unaware of how long, they stood there, staring into each other's eyes, swords embedded in one another's bodies as blood seemed to flow endlessly from the wounds. Alkeim's stomach was already regenerating, magic pulsing through him as sinew stitched together. Felim did not. Instead, sweat rolled down his paling olive-green skin. His sharp eyes darkened into pits.

Alkeim's chin quivered. Tears stung his eyes and slipped down his cold cheeks.

Felim's eyebrows shot up, a smile creeping onto his face. "I didn't know… you knew how to cry, big brother."

Felim's legs gave out underneath him, his arms gone limp, hands releasing the sword in Alkeim's gut. He caught and helped Felim to the ground as he held his brother as close as possible with a sword protruding from his torso. He simply held him. Brushed his hair out of his face. Squeezed the hand now lying on his chest. In silence, in the lull of late morning, Alkeim felt the weight of death take Felim, gloss his eyes over, and steal the warmth of his body.

Birth of a King
XXXVIII

Part II

Malice paced down the hall to Draga's study and opened the door, surprising Draga as her head jerked up from her papers.

Despite appearing like sisters, Draga had softer features, her skin smooth where Vendetta had faint lines in between her brows from scowling, her skin not as vibrant as it likely was.

"What gives you the right to barge in here like this?" she asked, frowning, her tone sharp.

"The death of the Laska family." Malice crossed the room in a few strides. "Why?"

Her eyebrow twitched, and she leaned back into her chair. "What makes you think I would tell you?"

"The magic in your body." Malice tensed his fingers at his side. Draga jumped as her hand snapped to her core, her inky orbs rounding. "Is not entirely yours." He twisted his wrist as if he were opening a jar.

She gasped, pain striking her face in a pale rush.

He wasn't in his right mind. That familiar out-of-body sensation had started pricking his spine during his duel with Zephyrus.

"I could kill you slowly. Painfully," Malice said with a level of calmness Draga apparently found appalling as her body stiffened. "Or I could kill you quickly and painlessly. The choice is yours."

Inyene taught him well, but his experience taught him better. He had plenty of time in those dungeons where rats and prisoners had no escape, and Malice did. Learning to condense his magic, Malice injected formless energy into living things. If he let it fester, it acted like poison, eventually killing the rat. If he controlled it, he could attack the core directly. An instant but still very painful death—the prisoners' screams couldn't be heard outside the dungeons. With no outward injuries, Inyene was none the wiser.

For a time, Draga studied Malice, her raven black eyes flickering with indecision, doubt, fear.

"Felim was sent two days ago," Draga said, her entire body settling into a practiced, calm position; weight shifted to one side, her arms on the rests of her chair. "The purpose was rather simple, though I advised Mother against it; we wanted to rid you of any reason to rebel."

"You killed them and turned Zephyrus against me." Malice tilted his head. "What a mistake to make." He had figured he caused their death. Zephyrus had been right to blame Malice.

"Mother thought if you were to lose a close friend you would fall into despair, become easier to control in your grief," Draga added and sighed. "If you are going to kill me, get it over with."

"Why not fight back?" Inyene had.

"Why would I fight for my death to be an agonized one?" She regarded Malice solemnly, the most emotion he had ever seen from her in one day. "We have all been watching you. Mother thought you could still be tamed, the rest of us knew otherwise and expected one day you would come for our heads."

Us? Malice had nothing more to say or ask. The anger in his chest went out, a candle flame deprived of oxygen. He extended all his fingers and closed his hand into a fist, crushing Draga's core. Pain lit her face and vanished as she slumped, her head lolling forward.

Malice's eyes lingered on the motionless body of his eldest sister. He killed another of his kin. Inyene was first—it was the only way he could escape her torture. He had not been as kind to her as he had been to Draga. His nostrils were still tainted by smoke and burnt flesh. Malice turned, walked to the other side of the couch, stepped into the shadow, and sank down.

He wondered, briefly, how close his sanity was to breaking. Had it already shattered, and he hadn't realized? Maybe that was why he felt so at peace, the undisturbed solace of an oasis, his head as clear as the sky at high noon during summer.

He rose behind Vendetta's desk. Her study was darker than even the dungeons. Six elders spoke to one another, each looking like sacks of sun damaged leather, each keeping their volume controlled in the presence of their queen. Smart. It was strange no one knew of the fire he started in the dungeons. Enough time had passed for it to have spread by now.

One spotted him. They jerked, opening their mouths to announce his arrival, when Malice flung his arms out and up, brought them closer, and thrust them downward. Darkness, like a tidal wave, shot out from under the couch and armchairs and soundlessly crashed into them. Letting the darkness settle into the cushions and seams of the furniture, the elders were gone. Silence charged the study, thorns scratching his eardrums, while Vendetta sat unmoving and calm.

Once again, he sank down and climbed out into the hallway a few rooms from Vendetta's.

"I know it is you, mutt," Vendetta said from within her study as his footfalls neared, her tone playful.

Malice, walking through the threshold, faced his mother. In the dim light, her expression soft, Vendetta took on a youthful quality. Not that it affected her heavy presence.

She gestured loosely to her missing audience. "You killed them. I wonder why."

"Tit for tat," Malice replied with a shrug. "You killed the Laska's."

"Indeed…" She let the quiet become unsettling, the atmosphere sharp, acutely dangerous. "Have you come to kill me?"

Malice didn't answer as he tried to keep most emotion—keep the anger and disgust—from his features.

"Do tell."

"Do I need a reason?"

Vendetta chuckled as she looked elsewhere momentarily, then regarded Malice with an amused grin. "You and I may need no reason to kill one another, but the region does."

"I have plenty of reasons to give the people. You don't need to worry about that."

"Oh, really?" she mused. "Enlighten me, mutt."

"Ha." Malice shifted. "You think you deserve anything other than a painful death?"

"How defiant you've become." Her midnight eyes narrowed.

"You enjoy having a disobedient son. It keeps you entertained, doesn't it," Malice said like poison had coated his tongue, "*Mother*?"

Vendetta's wall of composure cracked; anger washed over her. A surge of joy raced through Malice, making the hairs on his arms and nape stand on edge. As quickly as it came, her anger was veiled with placidity. Malice couldn't help nor stop the hammering of his heart or the adrenaline coursing through him, excitement fluttering his chest like it caged furious moths trying to escape.

"I cannot say you are wrong," Vendetta said.

"What did you want from me?"

"Your magic," she answered. "If you were to become like Emil, the perfect puppet, I would have had you feed your magic into my core, replacing it with darkness."

Malice startled. Memories of the one time he'd lost control of his magic flooded his mind. It was painful, like his own magic was thousands of centipedes eating his flesh before the darkness finally came back under his control. His body was made to handle darkness. He could only imagine what it would be like for someone else.

"It is truly unfortunate you did not work." Vendetta rose from her chair, a vicious grin on her face. "I have other options to exercise."

Bringing her hand up and twisting, Malice's head lurched skyward, all the air suddenly fleeing his lungs. With her second hand, she lifted Malice off the ground, gradually bringing her lower set of arms together. His shoulders crunched together, his back twisted and cracked as his legs broke. It was as if she was dismantling his body to shove him inside a tiny box.

He gasped, blood flowing up his throat, choking him. The stomach lurching sound of his bones breaking and his flesh tearing filled the room. Wax and rosemary scented the study, iron joining the smell as more ichor escaped his body.

All he needed was to move his hand, a single jerk.

One of Vendetta's fingers twitched, and Malice's right arm turned into a wrung-out towel, crimson spraying in all directions, splattering the walls. He noticed her expression of disbelief. Ah. Inyene hadn't told Mother of her theory about Malice's inability to feel pain. Vendetta had wished to observe the agony contort his expression, to ruin him. Now that it hadn't, she looked as shocked as Inyene had when he locked her inside the cell she always kept him in. And torched her.

Finally, using Vendetta's pause, Malice's hand jolted. Vendetta recoiled like an arrow had shot her. Malice dropped to the floor with a wet thud, his body swiftly regenerating. The vile noise of bones fracturing and muscles squelching was loud in Malice's ears. He had grown used to the sound of regenerating, his tendons and skin mending, the cracks and crunches of his bones, the pressure and release. It was nauseating at first in the dungeons when Inyene was finished with him, watching as his body grew from nothing. The pain had almost been as bad as the injury itself, yet bearable.

"What did you do?" The little color in her skin drained as she grasped at her chest, face warped with madness. Her breathing was strained and raspy. She swayed on her feet, catching herself.

He stood and cracked his newly regenerated fingers, joints popping.

"Answer me, damn it!" Vendetta snarled and collapsed to the ground; her legs must've given out.

"What I did to Draga." Malice put the back of his hands together. Leisurely, he pried them apart, his fingers curving.

Vendetta screamed, a horrific screech comparable to a howler's.

"Could you ever imagine a pain such as this?" Malice asked normally, his voice unable to break through Mother's cries. Her body convulsed on the floor, sweat beading and dripping.

"The core is the most sensitive part of the body. Any damage, permanent or temporary, causes so much agony people beg for their death." Malice had begged the only time Inyene had targeted his core. Boiling in oil was a kinder experience, one he would gladly go through again if it meant he could avoid his core being tampered with.

He crouched in front of Vendetta, her eyelids flickering to stay conscious, various muscles spasming. She was tough. Anger and hatred flashed across her expression when the pain wasn't overwhelming her completely.

Placing a hand on her sweat slicked head, Malice gently caressed her smooth, crimson hair as he had seen Kiran's and Zephyrus's parents do, as Annabeth had to him. "If you wanted to control me, you should have confined me, broken my mind before my body. Your mistake," he said softly, like Annabeth had the one time he broke a vase. *It's all right. It was an accident,* she had said, then checked Malice over for cuts from the porcelain shards.

"My mind grew as you thought you were breaking my body," he went on in the same tone. "You let me feel, gave me a first sword, an ally, allowed me to communicate with another region's prince. You allowed me friends. All the while, you kept telling yourself later, didn't you? I'll break him later, I'll take everything from him later, I'll make him miserable later. Later, later, later. Another mistake."

"My submission was for survival, but you thought otherwise. Mistake. My obedience was to make you believe your leash on me had not frayed. Not your last mistake, but close to it."

He looked down at his mother as she peered up at him. He was surprised she had the strength to do so. For a time, she twitched and eventually Vendetta was motionless, her eyes glazed over.

Rising, Malice thought to make sure she was dead, something Vendetta apparently never had the patience to do with him. He supposed he was never meant to die in the first place, just meant to break. He lifted his leg and slammed his foot into her skull, brains splaying to either side of her caved-in head. He brought his foot down again and again, each time her brains and skull getting mushier and mushier. Each wet thud was more gratifying than the last.

When a chunk hit his face, he stopped. Mother's head was nothing but a pulpy mess, her hair matted with pink, veiny globs. An eye rolled away, which left a trail of fluid. With his sleeve, he wiped his cheek. His white shirt was very red. It wouldn't be surprising if his hair were redder than a strawberry as well.

He spun around and walked into the hallway, where Eunice stood at the corner leading to the stairwell, torchlight warming her already rich skin tone. Her determined expression faltered at the sight of Malice.

"My liege," she said as she approached. "Are you all—"

"I need you to do something for me," he cut her off. There was this… serenity upon him right now, a weightlessness to his limbs he didn't want to disturb.

Eunice, though suspiciously, nodded.

"I want you to find Odovacar and bring him to Vendetta's study in twenty minutes."

Without question, Eunice left and walked down the corridor to the stairs.

Malice went on his way, too. He hated these walls. The darkness constantly wrapping around him, smothering him, draining his energy with every step. His footfalls echoed to the high ceiling until he stopped in front of the door he believed was Vendetta's bedchamber.

The room quietly opened to reveal a candlelit chamber thrice the size of his own. At the center was a round bed, sheer curtains draped around it, a bench at the foot of it, while a nightstand of metal framework and marble stood on either side. There was a fireplace on the back wall, logs stacked neatly within but never burned. Multiple sets of chairs, vanities, couches, and armoires occupied the space, a giant fur rug, tan, white, and brown, spanning the length of the room, going underneath the bed and out the other side.

On the couch beside a small table, a tray of sweets and a jug of water displayed on it, was Emil. His expression was vacant, yet something about his blank stare was off, as if he were finally alert to his surroundings.

In time, Emil brought his gaze up to meet Malice's, still disoriented, his eyes unfocused.

"Is," Emil said, his voice a tremble, "is she dead?"

Malice nodded, and something drained from Emil as he reclined on the couch. He looked… free. Life returned to the king, his eyes sparkling, tears streaking his hollowed cheeks.

The eldest servant in the castle, a fairy half-blood over two hundred years old, one Malice had become acquainted with not too long ago, was a chatty old woman. She blabbered on about the king and queens 'love' story so often he might be able to recite her story word for word if someone asked him to. Emil was a common woodsman in the northeast, crossing into Zeldine's region for the abundance of trees along the border. He was a romantic at heart, and Vendetta, once he fell head over heels in love with her, played him like a lyre. He had quickly become the figurehead of Hordes Region, so Vendetta could stay in the shadows playing puppet master.

"What of my children?" Emil asked. "Have you killed them too?"

"Draga and Inyene are dead," Malice answered.

A shudder raked Emil's thin body before he sucked in measured, steadying breaths. "Kill me. I know well enough you will spare no one under the queen."

Malice tilted his head.

Emil smiled meekly. "I do not have the strength to go on living. Not after knowing everything I've done and everything I haven't."

"You couldn't have done anything if you wanted," Malice countered.

What made Vendetta formidable, forced the eldest of royals to bow their heads and tremble in fear at her feet, was her power. Blood magic. Magical energy was not concrete. New elements could be derived from old at any given moment. Blood was a sub element of water, as lightning was of fire. Still, there were limits. It was one or the other. If one learned the sub element, they couldn't wield the main. It was a trade, not an addition. This, of course, excluded those with light and dark magic who had use of the four main elements. He and Magnus couldn't trade whatsoever. Malice would have been jealous too, but Vendetta had the right idea. Dark magic was powerful, inherently so. It was capable of things he doubted the other elements could do, and the only limit he knew of was his own creativity. Save for light magic. Light could always conquer the darkness.

"I did. Desperately, I wanted to do something. It does not change the fact that I watched. All these years I've done nothing but watch. I could have fought back, could have worked around her to repair the damage she inflicted, but I did not because I was a coward. Because I feared she would use my children against me as she used Elias. I let her manipulate me because I could not *hurt* my own children any longer. Because I had hoped, one day, she would come back to her senses, go back to being the woman I fell in love with. I was wrong." Wincing, he closed his eyes, memories stirring deep within him, causing physical pain; Malice could see it with every flinch.

The woman Emil dreamed of never existed. Of that, Malice was sure.

"I hold as much fault as Vendetta, Odovacar, Draga, and Inyene. Sok and Rayen would have led the same path of misery had you not—" he paused.

Malice stared for a bit, studying the shortness of Emil's raggedy, dark blue hair, the dimness in those scarlet eyes, and how his clothes barely fit the slenderness of his body. Defeated by everything he held dear; Emil was a shell of the man he once was.

"Any last requests?"

"Make it painless. I think I have had enough pain to last me centuries in the afterlife." He locked eyes with Malice. "Please."

Rising, Emil was exhausted, truly a husk. Malice brought his hand up, but Emil caught it and gently pushed it away.

"Wait," he mumbled. "I know this will mean nothing to you, but I am *truly* sorry, Berhane."

He was right. His apology meant as much as throwing a pebble against a mountain, expecting it to tremble.

Berhane?

Silence stretched between them as Malice searched for meaning behind the name. It was not his, not the one Vendetta had given him anyhow. Yet, Emil said it with such certainty Malice assumed *Berhane* was his name at some point. About to ask, he stopped himself, the longing in the king's eyes forcing his mouth shut. The longing for death.

Darkness grew from Malice's hand, turning into a blade. Painless was what Emil wanted, so it was what he was going to get. Gliding back, Malice altered his weight and swung his arm, slicing Emil's head from his shoulders. It slipped, bloody, and splattered on the ground, rolled to a stop at Malice's clawed feet. He bent down to pick it up. It was heavier than he thought it would be. He searched for a clock and found one on the mantle across the room.

Fifteen minutes left.

"Eunice"

Odovacar hadn't struggled when Eunice collected him from the training grounds. The mention of Malice's name both enticed and ebbed his curiosity.

They climbed the stairs, Odovacar trailing behind her, their echoing shoes the only sound, as her mind wandered to Malice repeatedly. He was covered head to toe in blood. She smelled the vile metallic odor from the foyer. As she had been doing for the past week to see if he had been released from the dungeons, she was on her way to his bedchamber when she had coincidentally seen Malice out of the corner of her eye.

So many things had swirled in her head upon seeing him. *Why are you covered in blood? Whose blood is it? Great news! Most, if not all, of Hordes Kingdom is on your side, wanting the rightful heir to take his place after nearly six hundred years. The plan worked flawlessly.* She was sent away before she could spit any of it out.

Ichor wafted down the western corridor again as she and Odovacar reached the studies and Vendetta's chambers. It was thick, oppressive, a trail of red leading from the south end of the hallway to Vendetta's study.

Eunice apprehensively opened the door, her stomach instantly lurching to her throat, the pungent smell practically choking her. Iron, rotten sweetness, and burnt flesh and hair. The world swayed for a moment. Eunice wrestled out of her dismay. At least tried to. Odovacar gagged behind her but did not step back. Forcing herself to stay and look at was in front of her took a tremendous effort.

The study was fully lit, with multiple candles burning, which was something Eunice had never seen.

Bodies sat on the couches, four of them, two on each side. To the left, the bodies were headless, one bashed in, fragments of bone and flesh making for an unrecognizable blob. It was the dress Eunice recognized as Vendetta's—the material was a lavish red velvet with puffed sleeves and a deep *V* neckline, black patterns embellished the sides of the dress. The other had his head in his lap, eyes still open and soulless. Emil. On the right sat Draga, her body slouched, her pale skin greying, her lips tinting blue. Finally, a burnt lump of flesh was next to Draga, blackened. Skin and muscle curled and red hair was burnt to the slightly charred, pinkish grey skull. Even the tongue from inside the gaping toothy mouth was a hunk of discolored, shriveled meat.

It took everything Eunice had not to retch. She stepped inside, Odovacar's arm in hand, dragging him with her. The door remained open.

"You may leave if you want, Eunice," Malice said, breaking the disturbing silence.

As disgusted as she was, she felt she needed to be here, witness what was about to happen. She shook her head, and Malice shrugged.

"You killed them," Odovacar muttered, more to himself than to Malice, it seemed.

"If you expected anything else, Draga's a liar."

The general's eyes twitched. "She told you."

"That you anticipated my coming to hunt you down? Yes, she did. If only Inyene and Vendetta were smart enough to let it happen." Malice passed a look over the burnt corpse of Inyene and the nearly headless body of Vendetta. "Instead, they fought."

"What do you want from me?" Odovacar asked. He wasn't trying to hide the trembling of his body or the brittleness of his voice. He was genuinely terrified right now. Eunice was too. Her shaking hands were simply behind her back and her jaw was fastened.

"I want you to serve me as you served your mother," Malice said, surprising Eunice. She wasn't the only one.

Odovacar went incredibly still, black eyes like a saucer. "Why keep me alive? I resolved myself long ago, accepted I would die by yours or my mother's hand."

"You want death?"

"I have never wanted anything more." It was the first time Eunice had heard such raw, heartfelt emotion in his voice and seen it on his face, as if his words were being ripped from the deepest crevices of his soul. "I had lost the will to live long ago, but never had the courage to end it myself."

"You truly are a pathetic lot."

Odovacar averted his gaze.

"Emil wanted the same, you know," Malice said. "Unlike you, he had little choice, so I fulfilled his request. Quick and painless." He gestured toward Emil.

More than what he had done, Eunice was appalled by how Malice was speaking. The lethal calmness of his voice as if he couldn't care less, as if these people, volatile as they were, didn't raise him. There was an underlying spark in his green eyes, too, one of pure delight. At that moment, Eunice wished she had run when Malice told her to collect Odovacar.

"You want death," Malice repeated. "You should have had the courage to do so before today." He rose.

Eunice and Odovacar flinched, her heart threatening to break her ribcage, it beat so hard, as Malice crossed the room and stood toe-to-toe with his brother.

"Kill yourself, Odovacar." Malice took the general's hand. He jerked, but Malice's grip was tight. The moment it manifested, he placed a dagger of darkness in Odovacar's palm. "If you truly don't want the chance to start over, to serve under me, then kill yourself. Prove how *mighty* a general of Hordes Region is."

Gradually, Odovacar's breathing became heavy and rough. Sweat pricked his pale lavender skin. The muscles in his jaw spasmed time and time again. Malice guided the knife in Odovacar's grip to his neck and pressed. A single droplet of blood ran down his throat, his tunic soaking it up.

"What's wrong? Why hesitate?" Malice added a touch more strength, the blade biting deeper, a new pulse of red further staining Odovacar's collar. "Isn't this what you wanted? Exactly like your father. Aren't I showing mercy by giving you what you want?"

Eunice wanted to tell Malice that was enough. He had proved his point, whatever it might be. He had Odovacar. It was right at the tip of her tongue; her grinding teeth was the only thing keeping it in.

"Come on, Odovacar," Malice insisted. "Kill yourself."

Truth be told, fear held her tighter than Malice's grip on the general. The room felt like it was closing in on her, and those corpses—if she looked away for too long, they turned to scorn her. It was as if she was trying to swim to a surface that didn't exist.

"I can't," Odovacar finally sobbed, knees buckling as the knife in Malice's hand vanished and he crumbled to the ground. "I can't." Tears flowed down his cheeks, body shivering and caving in on itself.

Malice had just broken a man. Broke a general who had survived the brutality of Vendetta for twenty-seven years in less than five minutes.

"What will you do?" Malice sat on the coffee table between the couches. "I'm giving you a choice because you treated me like a person." Malice sounded humane again, as if the bodies he brutally murdered weren't sitting at his sides, as if he weren't covered in their blood, as if he didn't tell his own brother to kill himself.

"I," Odovacar breathed, "will serve you, my liege."

Seconds ticked by. Malice's eyes were glued on Odovacar's still shaking and slumped over position, the silence ringing in Eunice's ears.

"Leave," he said at last. "Take him with you. I want this castle empty by the end of the day."

Eunice hauled Odovacar out of the room, not bothering to get him on his feet as she raced into the hall, down the stairs, and into the foyer, where she dropped him and dropped to the floor herself.

They both heaved, albeit for different reasons.

That was Malice, Eunice reminded herself. That was the prince and soon to be king of Hordes Region. In the three years Eunice had been Malice's first sword, she had never felt fear like this. Never had she felt this terror for anything or anyone else. Not even Vendetta all those years ago. Whoever led the warband a month ago and spent the nights talking with her was not the person she saw today. That person, *that boy,* was dead.

Why me?
XXXIX

Madness seeped from Malice, like dirt releasing from skin in a warm bath, as he waited in Vendetta's empty study. He'd let his magic consume the Claymore line. The servants didn't deserve to clean that up, and they didn't *truly* deserve a proper burial, now did they?

He stalked up the stairs, stagnant lead in every inch of his body, forcing him to drag his feet through the vacant castle. Gloom surrounded him. Silence grated at his ears. The clear-headedness he thought he had was nothing short of a delusion. Now, however, his head *was* clear. It was terrible. He wished the insanity would come back to him.

Odovacar was alive against Malice's worst judgment, which was to cut his head off and put it alongside his mothers. Rationality won out. Thankfully. Odovacar held a plethora of information about Vendetta and what she had been doing during her reign. Malice needed said information. Besides, he couldn't kill Odovacar without possibly losing too many of the royals. Odovacar was a pillar, a leader. He was respectable and capable. To tear him from what he had helped create would turn too many against Malice.

Eunice wouldn't be one of them. She might retire, anyhow. The reason being Malice. And he couldn't blame her one bit. Couldn't blame anyone for wanting to break their oaths to him. He would be alone, a cold crown on his head, a mountain of corpses beneath him, and he would have no one else to blame than himself.

Bedroom door slamming, Malice's heart pounded violently as he slumped to the floor. He couldn't calm down. It had worsened during his trek up here. Thoughts raced through his head like a rabbit running from a fox. There was much to be done. He needed to appear before the kingdoms, tell them of Vendetta's crimes, tell them of her false lineage and of the Claymore's deaths—the rulers needed to be informed too. He needed to gather the nobles of the region. Would he keep the throne empty or put a regent in his place until he was old enough, like Magnus? Could he do that? Would anyone be competent enough and allow him to ascend when the time came without struggle? What of those who were still sworn to Vendetta, would he kill them, let them walk free, recruit them?

Malice crawled to his desk, where a letter lay on its surface. The cream white envelope, his name penned on one side, sealed with dark royal blue wax in the shape of a sun, was all so intensely familiar. Relief gave him the strength to stand and open it.

Dear Malice, the single, creased piece of paper read.

I hope this letter finds you well and I hope your campaign was a success.

Since the last Kings Summit, I've come to a decision: I'll no longer be writing you. I know of the feelings you have and they're wrong. On both ends. Our short time together will be something I cherish.

From the bottom of my heart, I thank you for all you have done for me.

Silas Johnson

Goodbye Malice,

Magnus Castine

What feelings? As though he had been struck, Malice staggered backward, his world turning upside down for the third time that day. *What did I do?* Was it punishment for killing Vendetta? Or Emil and his sisters? Was it because he *hadn't* killed Zephyrus during their duel? Why?

Malice's heart wrenched and tore at his ribcage. He crashed to his knees with a heavy thud, clutching at the strange pain in his chest. Pain? He could feel it? Why now, when all he wanted was to feel nothing? He would give anything to get rid of the agony coursing through his body. He tried to control his wheezy breaths. Couldn't. Instead, his vision of the marble floor and wood desk blurred.

He had gained everything! The crown, the throne, the kingdom and region, he had gained all Vendetta had to offer! Only to lose Zephyrus? Lose Magnus? In what world was *fucking power* worth having when he'd lost Zephyrus and Magnus and Annabeth, his childhood, his sanity?

Malice attempted to reach for the drawer containing his writing utensils; his arm refused to listen. He didn't understand. What was so wrong about wanting friends? About wanting to exist without so much misery?

Choking on the air his lungs needed, Malice doubled over, forehead pressed against the cold floor. Tears spilled, plopping as they hit the ground. They were red from the blood caking his skin. It was Inyene's blood. Zephyrus's. Vendetta's, Draga's, Emil's, Sok's and Rayen's, it was those seven bandits he'd killed three years ago. It was the blood of the couple he slaughtered in their bed. It was the blood of six thousand royals from Vendetta's army she had sent to kill him.

It was *his* blood.

Message
XL

"The Laska's are dead," Malice said.

Kiran sat on the edge of his bed, Malice standing in front of him, expression dazed. "I… don't understand."

Neither did Malice, not really, anyhow. Recalling what had happened in the last three months, the campaign, the month in solitude, his duel with Zephyrus, killing his family, it all had felt as though he'd watched a play. Witnessed the demented tales of someone else's mind instead of experiencing his own cruel reality. He hadn't told Kiran much of anything outside of that he murdered Vendetta, Draga, Emil, and Inyene, yet kept Odovacar alive. He didn't have the strength to delve into any more detail.

Doubt crept in at the idea of sharing what had truly conspired last week. What if Kiran hated him for accepting Zephyrus's duel? Malice fought and left Zephyrus for dead, disregarding the traditions of a duel and depriving him of any shred of honor he had. Blood trailed into the forest, stopping at the base of a tree outside the castle grounds, his body gone. Howlers likely got to him and Malice only hoped when they did, he had already perished. What if Kiran abandoned him, too? Malice had lost too much, everything, besides Kiran. To lose him would make all of his actions up to this point meaningless. What purpose would he have to continue breathing then?

"Become my advisor," Malice said abruptly, eyes on his one *true* brother's hands trembling in his lap.

Kiran's head snapped up to him, eyes wide, mouth gaping, tears glistening. "Did you kill them?" he asked in hushed disbelief.

Malice's entire body constricted. "No," he answered. It was a half-truth because Kiran didn't ask right and Malice wouldn't elaborate, refused to. "And I don't know who did either." He dropped to his knees and, placing his hands on Kiran's, gripped his pant legs. "But please, Kiran. Stay by my side. Become my advisor." He was close to breaking again. Even after a week, he was fragile. He was weak and helpless and utterly alone without Kiran.

"I'm not—"

"It doesn't matter," Malice cut him off, head jerking upwards. Their gazes met. "I couldn't protect Zephyrus." Kiran's expression morphed, scrunched with misery. "I can—*I need* to protect you, and this is the best way possible. You'll learn as you go, like me. Your parents can live in the castle too. Just," Malice choked, *"don't leave me."*

*

In his study on the fourth floor, one he had cleaned and claimed as his own, Malice sat at his desk, tapping his finger impatiently, waiting for his ragtag council to arrive. Priscilla Wheelock, as the eldest servant of the castle, became the sole elder of Hordes Kingdom. Kiran accepted the title of Malice's advisor and regent should he need one. Alkeim remained a knight, training the royals alongside Odovacar.

Before the new year, Malice would be crowned king.

The servants and royals flooded the castle upon returning, getting back to their usual duties when Malice sent the word. Most everyone returned. Only a few had the gull to run away. The western wing of the second floor was avoided like the plague. He was fine with that, despite not requesting it.

Reclined into his chair, pinching the bridge of his nose, Malice found it difficult to stop thinking about Zephyrus and Magnus, causing a headache to form. Inyene had jumped the wagon in her diagnosis of Malice's inability to feel pain, and he had jumped with her.

A knock came to the door, quick and loud, and it swung open. Eunice dipped her head and stepped aside. Priscilla hobbled in, hands behind her back, dressed in green velvet robes which swept the floor. She smiled, exposing her toothy grin, and sat with a groan. She was old, nearing two hundred-fifty, wrinkled skin sagged wherever it could, and her wiry hair was a yellowish silver color.

Alkeim entered next, bowing his respects, a haunted demeanor weighing his proud shoulders down. He sat beside the elder as Kiran strutted in, his face bright as he smiled at Malice and chose his spot behind the couch. Kiran was different, like he had matured overnight since taking on the role of Malice's advisor. His cassock robe, the color of pale-yellow daisies, had been steamed smooth and his hair was as neat as he could get it—a few stubborn curls stuck out at random.

Odovacar was the last to enter, black eyes downcast, his face hollowed some. He sat gingerly in one of two armchairs, as if he were afraid of making too much noise.

Malice almost felt he should be.

Then, closing the door, Eunice took her seat in the armchair closest to his desk. Malice looked at each one of them, contemplating where to start. He had many questions, most of which were answered thanks to Draga's habit of writing everything down—she had a journal dedicated to how often she trimmed her nails.

"Alkeim," Malice eventually said. "I have a personal question. One to appease my curiosity."

"I shall answer whatever it may be, my liege," he dipped his head, his tone strained. He was nervous, scared even.

"Why did Emil call me Berhane?" Malice wasn't so daft as to not gather Berhane was the name Nyx and whoever his father was had given him. He supposed it was why he was asking, to learn who else handed him over to Vendetta for a better life.

All the color drained from Alkeim's olive-green skin. He swallowed, unable to meet Malice's gaze. "It was your first name," he said in a meek tone, like a mouse. "My brother and I…" His hesitation began to wear at Malice's nerves. "Took you from your blood parents when you were a babe, two months old. The queen had found out about your existence and could not let you go to waste."

"Get to the point," Malice said. Vendetta had been kind enough to tell him that herself.

Alkeim finally looked at Malice. "Your blood parents are Nyx Reap and Karlisle Apostolov."

The Apostolov bloodline were the nobles ruling Mondlesgrave in the east, the ones who burned the Laska's land and exiled them to the mainland. His blood spiked at the thought. The Apostolov's were known for their regenerative abilities. They could be a healer and still regenerate moderate injuries, not severe, but it was better than what most healers could do. If his father really were Karlisle Apostolov, it would explain Malice's own regeneration. He rubbed his wrists and open and closed his fist, his skin cooler than the room's atmosphere.

"Thank you," he said plainly. Alkeim nodded. "Who hasn't Vendetta sunk her daggers into?" *She had a good century to spread her roots beyond Hordes Region. She would have been a fool not to take advantage of that time.*

Eunice assumed, when Malice first brought the notion to her attention, Vendetta hadn't touched Alucard's, Maziar's and Zeldine's. He needed confirmation, details, and an explanation. More so with Zeldine's and Maziar's. Their rulers loved violence based on Draga's journals and rumors. Vendetta might have been able to convince them to her side, promised they could have as many battles as they could tolerate. Unless… she feared them. Was that why she wanted his magic?

"I think there is all but one or two she didn't dare touch." Priscilla brought her hand to her chin, maneuvering her drooping skin in all directions. "One of them was Alucard's Region. Holister and his father Jaci were powers to be reckoned with. Shame they're dead."

"Silence," Malice spat and scowled at Priscilla. She didn't know a thing and had no right to talk about Holister as if she did. "You will not speak unless spoken to."

Startled, Priscilla nodded and let her head droop as she picked at her cuticles.

"Odovacar."

"Vendetta had not dared to mess with Alucard's, Zeldine's or Maziar's Regions due to who ruled them," Odovacar confirmed. "They have the biggest military influence on the continent, standing toe to toe with us. Vendetta could not afford a war when no one would side with her."

Malice was right. Vendetta was cautious of her ill nature. Emil was under her strict control and couldn't foster friendlier relationships with any of the rulers because of it. A hindrance in the long run, all because Vendetta refused to ease her hold on her husband. He was an empty figurehead. Basia and Thorn were stubborn and extremely dominant. He doubted they would have allowed two words from Emil's mouth before they refused his proposal. Vendetta was as well. If she couldn't manipulate with fear, death was the only alternative. Neither would have worked on Basia or Thorn.

Malice glimpsed Kiran, who seemed to be deep in thought. It was one of the few times his face ever pinched, as if frustrated. "What are you thinking about, Kiran?"

Kiran jolted out of his thoughts, glanced about the room, and shook his head. "Nothing."

He lingered on the beastman for a moment longer. They hadn't talked in days, not since Malice told him about the Claymores, Zephyrus, and he accepted his position as advisor. "What of Vendetta's trades?" And they couldn't talk right now; it brought a dull ache to his chest.

Alkeim and Odovacar glanced at one another, then to Malice.

Alkeim explained the multitude of crimes Vendetta had endorsed and partaken in over the decades, her reach branching out, her poison soaking into the soil. Odovacar added what he knew but admitted he hadn't contributed, so his knowledge about the topic was limited.

"I told you about when I helped retrieve a shipment of slaves, yes?" Eunice asked after Alkeim and Odovacar had finished speaking. Malice nodded. "I didn't tell you about the time I was sent underground."

Malice raised an eyebrow.

"Underneath Hordes Kingdom is a city built for criminals, slaves, whores, exiled nobles, and so on," she said, shifting. "It thrives off the money brought in from the illegal trades, nobles who paid for the queen's silence or protection, criminals who signed their life away so they didn't have to rot in a cell. Fighting pits bring in just as much profit. Elderly, retired royals, mercenaries, prisoners, slaves, women, children; doesn't matter who, so long as they can make some coin. They're thrown into a pit and made to fight to the death."

"You know how to get there?" Malice asked.

Eunice hesitated, her eyes falling to the ground for a split second, shoulders adjusting. "The entrance is the last cell in the dungeons."

He had spent at least a year in accumulated time in that cell. It was where buckets of his blood had been spilled. It was where he learned to control his magic. With his focus always elsewhere, he believed it was probably an easy detail to miss. Still, there were enough times where he couldn't do anything but study the four walls around him, yet he never noticed this supposed entrance to the underground city?

"We can't attack it yet," Kiran blurted, catching Malice's attention. "This underground city is like the base of a tree. If the roots survive, so could the base."

... *Let it go.* Malice breathed deeply. "I need to rid the other regions of Vendetta's poison first."

"You need to inform the rulers of your intentions and get their permission," Odovacar said.

"I suggest starting with Ruler Valentine," Eunice said. "They'll be the easiest to deal with."

"Valentine will be first. Yoon Woo next."

"What?" Eunice looked at him, brows furrowed with disbelief.

"Neighbors first. It'll be easier, allows me to travel back to Hordes in a timely manner. When I go for the northern, eastern, and western regions, I might as well get it done all at once." He would get their permission, act as swiftly as possible, and leave. Convincing the rulers would be as difficult as finding Vendetta's rat dens. They were well hidden if the others hadn't found traces of Vendetta's activity in their regions, which didn't bode well for Malice. But he wouldn't know until he spoke with them.

"You'll be gone for months," Kiran mumbled.

"I have no choice."

"You should start local," Alkeim said, his nerves settled now.

"Start drawing out Vendetta's connections before you go anywhere else."

Malice asked, "Who is one of her most trusted or used partner?"

"Roch Van Rossem," Odovacar answered.

"We'll deal with him first, acting as the bait," Eunice said, crossing her legs with her arms on the rests of the chair.

"He'll be the one who sends a message to them all," Malice confirmed. "When is the next shipment from Roch?"

Alkeim pondered for a moment. "Two weeks, perhaps a few days sooner, if the waters are calm."

"He comes by boat?"

"Aye." Alkeim nodded. "He is based in Wolfgang's Region. It's too easy to get caught on land, so he goes by sea."

"The southeastern docks were constructed for him," Malice muttered under his breath. He'd seen them in the distance, but never visited them in person. On all the maps of the region Draga had ever shown him, the southeastern docks were always marked below Mondlesgrave. Ryzion governed the biggest port of Hordes, which was also marked on every map he'd studied, importing and distributing wares to and from other regions. When Draga had explained how Ryzion's port was Hordes' only one, Malice should have realized the significance of those docks and felt incredibly stupid for not doing so till now.

*

It was high noon when Malice and his company reached the southeastern beach where the docks came onto shore. Four wagons stayed on the grass bank for the shipment of slaves, two of which had empty crates in the bed covered with sheets. Four royals sat coach, Nikanor being one of them, taking the opportunity to laze.

White shimmered on the blue water, the call of gulls surrounded the beach, the smell of salty water and seaweed heavy in the air while the sun blazed. Sweat trickled down his back, a disgusting sensation Malice had to ignore.

Eunice stared out to sea at his side, growing anxious, constantly shifting her weight from one leg to the other as she rolled her shoulders as if her jerkin were uncomfortable. Malice assumed it was, considering she wore a long-sleeved blouse underneath. Further up on the bank were Kiran, Alkeim, and Odovacar. Alkeim wore a tunic, a simple pair of tan trousers, and a sword on his hip. He was ready for this heat, whereas Kiran underestimated it. Wearing long robes of red wine and a cowl, he tugged his clothes away from his body. Odovacar seemed unbothered by the heat, in spite of his black riding leather.

Off the horizon, a fleet of ships were a dark smudge on the water, four brigs coming from the north. Soon, the boats docked, men running all over the decks, securing one thing and another.

After a time, Roch Van Rossem finally marched from his boat onto the dock and toward Malice. The fat man looked as clean as the sewer, his clothes stained, torn, and frayed at the edges, his shirt too small, allowing his gut to hang out. His wiry beard was streaked with grey and incrusted with morsels.

Roch smiled at Alkeim, showing what remained of his yellow, brown, and almost black teeth. He spied Kiran next to the bulky orc, but paid no mind to him. Settled on Odovacar as if he saw the similarity to Vendetta—probably did. Mother and son shared many features—then his eyes moved to Eunice, licking his lips as he eyed her like a perfectly seared piece of meat. Malice felt her reaction, an impulse of disgust and the will to suppress it. Malice shared the sentiment when Roch finally landed on him and sized him up all the same.

"Where's her highness? I was hoping to get my fix today." He snorted to himself.

"I was sent in her stead," Malice said as he bowed his head.

"And the little princess is?"

"Prince and heir of Hordes Region, Sir Roch. My mother thought it best if I were to come, start learning her way of ruling and politicking." It *was* why he had been sent to the Kings Summit.

"Prince?" Roch's eyebrows shot up as his head tilted, hand rising to catch and stroke his beard. "You sure about that?" he asked, though he wasn't looking at Malice. Eunice's expression hardened.

"I don't think I follow," Malice played innocent, nudging Eunice with the tip of his shoe.

Sweeping close, Roch's breath hit Malice like a wall of pungent garlic and fish. "I'm asking if your stones have dropped. I'd be more than happy to check."

"Do you have our salves?" Malice gritted out.

He contemplated while Malice ignored the burning of his nostrils, resisting the desire to rip Roch's esophagus from his neck.

"You got our goods then, yeah?" Roch said, righting himself with a tug of his beard.

"Of course." Malice nodded toward the bank. "It wouldn't be much of a trade without it."

Sights narrowed on Malice, Roch chuckled and gently caressed Malice's shoulder. "I like you, princess." He promptly turned and shouted at his crew.

Malice was thankful he hadn't eaten, otherwise, he would've thrown it all up.

Everyone from the first two ships burst into movement, following their captain's orders to retrieve the slaves. Roch stayed put, hands on the rolls one would call a waist, spilling over his pants. Rather swiftly, crew members started to haul lines of slaves onto the beach, chains clinking.

"Here's the deal, princess." Roch whipped around to face Malice. "A few of the slaves caught the fever and died on the way over, but you still have about forty here."

"Forty? Out of the biggest shipment you've delivered. Fifty out of ninety slaves perished?" Malice said, flabbergasted. Eunice gasped as well.

Roch shook his head and hands, appearing animated. "Listen, I'm as upset as you are. You know how much extra work it was to take care of those damn slaves only for them to die on me?"

"They died on your watch."

"I can't do anything about the fever, princess. It's just how it is."

"You don't expect me to give you full payment, do you?" Malice gestured to the ships. "Over half of our goods are fish food because of your misinformation."

When he grabbed the waistband of his pants, Roch wiggled them up into place. "Of course, I do. My men and I should be compensated for the journey and for the loss of supplies."

Malice sighed and massaged the bridge of his nose. Glancing toward Eunice, their eyes met briefly. Nothing needed to be said. She rolled her shoulders and jerked them downward, popping.

"Too bad." Malice shrugged. "Alkeim. Odovacar."

The two trudged down the bank, coming to stand next to Eunice.

"Burn their ships and kill the crew, leave no survivors. Odovacar, take the slaves up to the wagons." The three of them went off in different directions. Kiran also made his way to the beach to help

Odovacar gather the slaves.

"What do you think you're doing, princess?" Roch snarled and clamped his hand around Malice's shoulder. "I made a deal with the queen!"

"You did, but she's dead." In one swift movement, Malice took Roch's hand, twisted it, yanked it down as he brought his knee up, snapping his elbow. "This *princess* is now your king, and you didn't make a deal with him."

Roch bellowed and dropped to the sand, cradling his broken arm. "How dare you betray us!" he shouted, spittle flying, eyes bulging. If they bulged any more, the tendrils keeping them in his skull would give.

"Nothing personal, Roch." Malice placed his foot against Roch's chest. "I need to send a message, and you happen to be the perfect messenger."

Leg cocked like an arrow to a bow, Malice kicked Roch halfway to the water. The fat man propped himself on his forearms, hacking up sand, and he got to his feet. His regeneration was impressive if his arm was up to par already. Roch flung his hands backward with a roar, his legs spread, then thrust them toward Malice. Water surged onto the shore, avoiding an archway around Roch. Malice threw his hands up and the water came to a halt an arm-length's out, Roch gasped, his face quickly flushing red and scrunching. He shouted some more, calling more crew to his aid, but no one answered. Alkeim and Eunice were quick. Any who dared set foot on the beach met their blades and lay on the shore as nothing but a corpse.

Salt and metal mingled. It wasn't so different from the smell of blood spilled on grass and earth or stone. Sometimes, alone in his bedchamber, the scent returned to Malice. He had gotten used to it, the smell a part of him as much as his limbs were.

Gaze slicing to his side, horror struck Roch's features like a slap to the face at Eunice's and Alkeim's carnage. When Eunice looked at the tradesmen, he flinched, head jerking to the ground to avoid eye contact. Malice grinned.

Breathing heavily, eyes wild, Roch darted to the last ship free of fire. Malice stared, rather dumbfounded by his cowardice. Moving his arm in a semi-circle one way, then turning it the other direction, Malice whipped his arm, a rope of water wrapping around Roch and yanking him back. He tumbled to Malice's feet, groaning as Alkeim set fire to the last ship and Eunice ran a crewman clean through with her sword. All slaves were on the bank where Odovacar and Kiran watched.

"Like I said, Roch." Malice looked down on the man. "It's nothing personal."

In a last-ditch effort, Roch leapt and reached for Malice's throat, yelling like it was the only thing he knew how to do. Before his sausage fingers enclosed around his neck, Malice caught him by the face. Magic tickled his veins, coursing from his core, down his arm, and into his—He froze.

Roch Van Rossum. One of the queen's most *trusted*, or at least used, partners…

"Change of plans," Malice said over the crackling and crashing of the burning ships. Eunice turned toward him. No one else heard. "We're taking Roch prisoner." *He has information and his confinement sends the same message.*

Eunice blinked at him for a short time. She dipped her head and kicked a crewman to the bloodied, foaming waters.

Malice released Roch, the sand dampening the fall. Desperately trying to flee, Roch headed into the ocean. As Malice stepped forward, Roch slung fistfuls of sand, all of which hit a shield of air.

When seawater crashed against his back, submerging his lower half, Roch stopped moving. There was nowhere for him to go. Malice walked into the warm, pinkish water, it instantly filling his shoes, his breeches clinging to his legs. Malice slipped his hand underneath Roch's beard, fingers brushing past greasy, stiff strands of hair. Roch was as unmoving as a mountain, allowing Malice's hand to wrap around his neck and push him below the water's surface. The sequence was so tediously slow, their eyes locked, waves rocking against his legs.

Roch struggled, his legs kicking fruitlessly, hands clawing at Malice's arms. Gouges formed, welled with blood, and regenerated painlessly. It took most of Malice's strength to hold the fat man down, his face a blur as air bubbled to the surface like boiling water.

Heartbeats passed when Roch went limp and Malice pulled him out, hauling him up onto the beach by his beard. He was heavier now that he was unconscious and wet.

Bodies littered the ground, the shore absorbing every bit of ichor, leaking red into the sea. Alkeim heaved as he wiped sweat and blood from his face. Eunice stood straight-backed, chin held high, her breathing as rapid as Alkeim's. Their job was completed.

The slaves on the bank settled into the wagons, their chains having been cut from their limbs and discarded. Malice returned to solid ground while Eunice and Alkeim worked to move bodies into the ocean. The fish would be well fed today. Ships blazed over his shoulder, each like a miniature sun providing ample warmth and light, burning wood and tar overpowering every other scent.

Kiran was busy treating any injuries the slaves might have had while Odovacar was making conversation with a few others, his expression somber. Around the group huddled close to the wagons, Malice dropped Roch and hopped onto the bench, startling the royal already there.

"When we return to Hordes Kingdom," he said loud and clear, making all heads turn toward him as a hush fell upon the bank, gulls unaware as they circled the crackling ships. "You are free. You can leave, you can stay, you can live or die. No matter what you choose to do, for the time being, all will be given sanctuary, food, clothes, and money."

Compared to what these people had been through, it was the least Malice could do. "If you wish to return home, I will have you safely escorted to your region."

Gasps rippled among the crowd, shock, anger, and grief painting expressions. Then relief took over. Although, in most eyes, there was caution, the hesitance of a scared animal. Rightfully so.

"I know your doubt, and I cannot blame you for it." His gaze swept the gathered bodies. "The queen is dead; her reign is over. Believe me or don't, but know I will not go back on my word. I promised you sanctuary and I plan to bring you there."

Malice turned and sat. "Tie him to the wagon," he ordered the royal at his side, who was still a bit groggy. They obeyed, clambered down, found a rope from another wagon, and tied Roch to the one Malice was in. A few cuts and scrapes would hardly do anything to someone as thick-skinned as Roch.

Eventually Eunice, Alkeim, Odovacar and Kiran took their seats next to the coachmen, and the wagons rocked into motion.

*

"Are you sure about this?" Eunice asked on the way down to the dungeons.

"Yes," Malice answered for the fourth time in the last five minutes. "Roch has worked with the queen for many years. He's bound to know something."

Eunice went silent. He couldn't see her expression—she was behind him, after all—but he assumed she was frowning.

Mildew and feces were stenches Malice was familiar with; the burnt flesh, on the other hand, was new. These stone walls, some charred black, had changed very little since he was a boy. Iron doors were still dark, a slot at the top Malice still couldn't reach unless he had a stool to step on or strained on his tiptoes. No wonder Roch thought he was a girl.

They stopped at the seventh cell from the dungeon's entrance. It creaked open, Roch inside. Malice handed the keys off to Eunice. He'd gone two days without food or water and looked miserable because of it. A wretched odor hit Malice, forcing him to turn away. Urine and excrement.

Roch sat on a wooden chair in the middle of the cell, shackled, chains connecting to the loops in the wall behind him. Like the ones Malice had struggled against so many times. In the back of his mind, Malice hoped this cell would look different from the one he'd spent his childhood in. Maybe that would make it special. It didn't.

The tradesman was asleep when Malice crossed the threshold of the chamber. Eunice stayed at the door. He slapped Roch, the smack echoing into the halls. He startled and spluttered awake, eyes frantic. Once he understood where he was and who was with him, Roch settled into a feigned relaxed posture, his legs spread, his back hunched. Malice knew better. He noticed the lines of tension creasing his face and kept his fingers tightly wrapped around the arms of the chair.

"Traitor," he said and spat at Malice, a white glob on his black shirt. "I won't say shit!"

"I haven't asked anything yet," Malice said calmly.

"Doesn't matter. Unless you guarantee my freedom and riches, I ain't telling you anything." Roch leaned forward, straining his bonds. "Princess," he sneered.

"You'll be getting neither. What I can give is imprisonment or a painful death."

Roch cackled a dry noise. "You couldn't kill me at the beach. Why should I believe you can kill me now?"

"I won't kill you now." Malice crouched, placing his hand on Roch's knee. "I would keep you alive for weeks, make death a release you came to yearn for."

There was a point two fingers in width down from the kneecap toward the inside of the knee; Malice dug his thumb into it. Roch jerked and winced. Inyene liked to see how far she could dig her finger in, as if trying to worm her fingernail beneath his kneecap, and how often Malice would react to the pain of it. The only time he didn't was when he was unconscious.

"I know." Malice rose and found a similar trigger point on Roch's arm, behind the crook near the elbow. "Most every spot." He jabbed his finger into the softness between two bones. Again, Roch grimaced, flinching backward. "To inflict the most pain without drawing blood, without you passing out, without killing you." It was Inyene's expertise.

He walked to Roch's backside, ducking under a chain. He could see Eunice now and her expression was firm, fists clenched at her sides.

"Where is the fun in that?" Malice stabbed his long nail into Roch's neck, missing the jugular. Eunice's gaze remained on his, unyielding, fierce. Her jaw tightened.

He ripped his nail free, blood trickling down the tradesmen's neck in a steady stream, dripping to the floor.

"You should leave," he suggested. "It won't take me long."

There was a moment's hesitation, a look of concern and disgust, then she was gone. The door closed. Darkness enveloped the cell.

To be honest, Malice was enjoying himself. It was a sick and twisted satisfaction to be the one finally inflicting pain after so many years of receiving it. He knew how deranged he must seem, must look, but didn't care. Why should he? No one else had cared as Inyene put him through hell. As Vendetta tried to rip everything from him. As Odovacar stretched him beyond his limits.

"Will you talk?" Malice asked, tossing a flame to the corner of the room, orange dousing the four walls.

"No," Roch said.

"Good." Underneath Malice's hand, Roch twitched. "Have you ever had your fingers and toes cut off? Knuckle by knuckle?"

Roch was trembling now, tensing in his cuffs, the chains clinking ever so slightly. Malice shuddered. He had reacted similarly whenever Inyene spoke of what she would do in that elusively tempting tone of hers, a controlled excitement as if she were explaining what she planned for an afternoon picnic. He emulated it.

"Have you ever been burned?"

Silence.

"I asked a question."

"No," Roch whispered, a shudder raking his body.

"The heat of flame would make your skin blister and sizzle. It would smell horrid at first, then it would remind you of pork over an open fire." Malice still had a hard time looking at a boar—alive or skinned and ready to be cooked—let alone eat one. "Ice would send you nerves screaming. It would hurt worse than the fire." It always had, hence why it came second.

"B-bl-bluffs!" Roch shouted. "All of it, lies!"

Malice shifted to Roch's front and looked into his ugly, shit brown eyes brimming with fear. Malice smiled. Roch's expression went stark, eyes doubled in size, mouth falling open. His shoulders slumped.

Tilting Roch's head back, Malice held it in place. "Are they?"

Stiffening his first two fingers and thumb, Malice's nails sunk into the socket and ripped his right eye out. Roch screamed, his body lurching all around. The white ball was wet and quickly drying, veins and nerves dangling from the back.

Malice's own green eyes, handed to him by Inyene, entered his mind. How many had she yanked from his head? How many times had he reacted exactly like Roch, only to realize it did him no good?

"What do you know of Vendetta's other *partners*?" Malice asked, rolling Roch's eye between his fingers, the surface tacky.

"Nothing!" he blubbered. "I swear it!"

Malice shoved the eye down Roch's throat, and forced his jaw shut, one hand underneath the chin, the other over the mouth. Gagging and weeping, Roch choked, but his jaw closed once, twice. His eyeball popped. He heaved again, swallowing multiple times to keep it down. When Malice moved away, Roch couldn't hold it in and vomited.

Fortunately, Inyene had never thought of feeding Malice his own eyes or any other part of himself.

"She has fourteen scattered throughout regions," Roch spluttered, his breathing haggard, his face blotched with red and pricked with sweat. Bile stained his shirt and pants, broken chunks of white in his lap.

He gave up rather quickly. Malice was disappointed. "How many in Hordes?"

"Five," he rasped.

One in every region save for Alucard's, Zeldine's, and Maziar's. "What else?" Malice doubted they worked alone, so he wanted to know about groups, warbands, strongholds. Vendetta had to have had followers, those who worked alone, or those who refused to be anything less than her equal.

Roch spilled all he knew. Malice didn't have to torture the tradesman further, so by the end of the hour, he killed him. Took his head from his shoulders and let his dark magic consume the body. The servants didn't deserve to clean up that mess.

*

"Did you have to kill them?" Kiran asked, back against the wall as Malice changed for the night. His short white hair dripped from his bath yet, mint scenting the air.

He was disgusted by what he saw at the beach, horrified to learn *more* people like Vendetta existed, but did that warrant death? Torture?

"Do you think talking will resolve every mess? Especially the ones Vendetta left behind?" Malice snipped. Kiran stiffened. Regret immediately washed over Malice's face, body caving as he looked to the floor. "I may be able to persuade a good number of people to my side, or convince them to turn themselves in, make it easier for everyone. But what of the rest? What of the ones who refuse to back down so easily?" Malice glanced at Kiran then, pleadingly, as if begging him to understand where he was coming from.

And Kiran did, to an extent. His jaw clenched as he wrapped his arms around himself. It was hard to argue when Malice looked at him like that; broken. Vendetta collected followers who were only slightly less stubborn than her, making negotiating nearly impossible. He understood that words only fixed so much, but it was the effort Kiran sought because he didn't understand the need to jump to violence first. He didn't want death, pain, and destruction to be Malice's solution to his problems like it had been for Vendetta.

"Did you kill Roch too?"

"Look at the people we saved and tell me Roch was worthy of mercy."

They all doubted the fifty people who caught the fever *actually* caught the fever and died. Odovacar and Eunice had their theories; perhaps the slaves got too rowdy, and Rock sent them overboard. Eunice believed Rock had simply been bored and killed them for entertainment. Some darkening part of Kiran thought it was both.

For a long while, Kiran stayed silent. Misery twisted his guts. "I can't."

"… I know."

Land of Marble and Fae
XLI

Unless Malice wanted to carry Eunice over Mutuwa to reach Florence's Region, they would have to travel around the forest by carriage or boat. Malice opted for the boat.

Ryzion, the eldest kingdom in Hordes Region, owned and operated the only port on the southern coast. Malice had requested a boat and a captain the week of the summit. In nine years, it was the first time Malice wouldn't attend the summit. He couldn't face Magnus. His last letter was still a raw, throbbing wound, refusing to heal. Despite proclaiming himself otherwise in front of Roch, Malice wasn't king yet. He would be facing the rulers in a place meant for rulers as a princeling.

Greeted and chaperoned by the noble of Ryzion himself, Malice had spent hours with Sophronius. He was younger than Malice had expected, long, blonde hair framing his thin face, body scrawny as if he had never touched a plate of meat in his life. He was kind, soft-spoken, and apparently new to the life of nobility, as Malice was new to the life of a monarch. The noble was easy to get along with, which was pleasant, and a sharp contrast to what Zephyrus had warned him about.

Sophronius waved Malice and Eunice off at the port as salt water sprayed their faces. The trip wasn't so bad, the waters calm.

Eunice wouldn't have said the same, as her first day was spent spewing off the side of the ship. Two days later, they docked in the bay between two islands and the mainland of Florence's Region—had they chosen to go by land, two days would've been closer to three weeks, if not longer.

Having sent word when he requested the boat from Ryzion, a carriage waited for Malice and Eunice the moment they stepped from the gangplank. It was pastel green encased with metal veins, flowers blooming all over the body. The coachmen, a weasel beastman with buck teeth, a high pointed nose, and a long, bushy tail, opened the carriage doors for them and, once inside, they were off to the main kingdom.

The carriage nearly lurched to a stop, throwing Malice and Eunice forward, then continued at a snail-like pace. Malice jerked the curtain back, the evening sun almost blinding. They trotted down a street of beaten dirt. Homes were built of white stone with terracotta roofs, laundry flowing in the breeze from second-story balconies, one or two thin rectangular windows on the front. Buildings—which were closer to temples—were also stone, but much larger. Pillars of white held the ceiling while wares crowded the inside. Mixed in were mounds of earth with doors and windows, brick towers overlooking the streets, and oak framed concrete inns.

Most people, fairy or not, were naked right down to their earth-stained feet. Some wore jewelry of gold and silver, chains spilling over their curves or cuffs around their limbs. If clothes were worn, they were white chitons held to waists by a band of some sort; the skirts sweeping the ground or stopping at the knees, shoulders and collarbones exposed.

Malice would've been more surprised had Nikanor not explained the customs of his homeland before Malice left. He read about them in books, but reading and seeing were two different things.

Finally, they reached an enormous, hollowed hill. The

coachmen stopped near the expansive, tall archway where statues valiantly kept the entrance from collapsing. He and Eunice stepped out of the carriage to be hit by the smell of rich soil and sweet perfume. Vines, flowers, and vibrant grass coated the hill—palace, Malice assumed.

A servant hurried toward and bowed to them. "Prince Malice, Lady Eunice, I'll be escorting to you to their majesty," she said quickly, voice pitched.

Outside in no way did the inside justice. It was magnificent. Malice took a deep breath, enjoying the overwhelming scent of flowers and mint. Fountains on either side of the foyer—it might have been too incredible to be called that—had sculptures, copies of one another, holding a basket with which water poured from, fish swimming in the pool and hiding underneath lily pads. Benches were everywhere, inciting visitors to sit. Many of the same flowers Malice saw in Hordes Region bloomed and flourished all around him.

Jealousy flickered in his veins. He could *breathe* here. The walls weren't closing in on him and the colors weren't draining his life away. He could… exist.

They walked up a set of stairs built from the walls, most likely erected by earth magic, moss in the corners, lightened prints showing the path of feet. Suddenly, their guide turned into another open space. People chatted and drank, nearly every table in the room occupied. Pillows scattered the floor, naked bodies sprawled upon them, goblets of wine in hands, while hammocks swung from the ceiling, limbs dangling outside the fabric confinements.

Malice, Eunice, and their guide continued their march upward. He glanced down at his garments—black, ornate, and sharp—and knew how out-of-place he looked. He *felt* out-of-place like a weed.

Eventually, passing bustling room after bustling room, one of which had at least ten individuals indulging in one another's bodies, they reached their destination.

The guide had informed Malice and Eunice they were on the topmost floor of the palace when they entered a high-ceilinged room, fireflies buzzing about, candles and lanterns lit for ample light. Soft moss carpeted the ground, silencing their steps. On the farthest side of the wooden doors, there was a wall of succulents, green and vibrant, spiny, leafy, or with strange foliage. At the center of the room, facing the wall of windows to Malice's left, was a huge round bed sitting low to the floor. Pillows galore covered the bed's surface, fur blankets peeking out from underneath and spilling to the moss at the sides. Within it all was a head of long, daisy blonde waves.

"Prince Malice and Lady Eunice of Hordes Region, your majesty," the guide declared and took her leave. The doors closed to complete a depiction of the region's sigil, the tree of life. At this size, it was more detailed as the mural had buds at the ends of branches, flowers scattered amongst the leaves, forest animals grazing or frolicking at the tree's base.

The head of yellow turned, a smile on Ruler Valentine's soft face. "Welcome, please come and join me."

Malice and Eunice did, crossing the room to stand next to the luxurious bed.

"How was your trip?" they asked, gesturing for them to sit. Malice took up the offer and sank into the mattress, the supple material instantly relaxing Malice, coaxing him to recline further until his head rested on one of many pillows. Eunice remained standing.

"They were fine," Malice said and made himself sit up. "Thanks to your guides."

"I am glad their use extended to you as well. Would either of you like refreshments? Food perhaps, after your travels?" they offered, completely relaxed, legs off to the side to hide their genitals, arms draped over pillows, their small breasts the only thing exposed.

"Later, preferably," he said.

"Of course." They smiled sweetly. Unlike Vendetta, their majesty's appearance showed nothing of their age as an immortal. Vendetta's habit of constantly scowling didn't help. Malice believed they were in their three or four hundreds, yet seemed no older than twenty. "You are here to talk, yes?"

Not wasting a second more, Malice spoke about why he requested to meet Ruler Valentine. Granted, he didn't go too far into the details. They, as well as the other rulers, didn't need to know the full scope of what he or Vendetta had done these past few years. A part of him didn't want to deal with their potential scorn and disgust. Or sympathy. He didn't need the monarch's trust, per se, just their permission. Once he had finished, their majesty frowned, their delicate brows furrowed.

They stood, revealing the fullness of their nudity. Malice averted his gaze. He had forgotten how fairies were intersex. Valentine's *friend* was on as full of a display as their breasts were. When he looked back at Eunice, she had turned around, hands behind her back.

Ruler Valentine, butterfly-like wings flapping, glided to the edge of the bed and landed gently on the floor. Fairy wings were never big enough or strong enough to do more than hover. Half of the winged population for angels and demons were the same, like Vendetta, whose wings had been far too small to make her float.

"That is concerning," they said as they walked toward a table near the wall of succulents. "And you are sure of this?"

Malice rose to follow. "Yes."

"You are the true heir." They swiveled to face Malice. He nodded. They said, "I give you permission to rid my region of your mother's influence." Rosy pink eyes darting to the floor, their majesty sighed and met Malice's gaze once more. "Know you will not have help from my hoplites."

"I didn't expect it," Malice returned. "This is my mess to clean." In all reality, it wasn't. He could easily leave the other rulers to fend for themselves, but Malice would never truly be free of his mother if he did. As the future king of Hordes and as the one who killed Vendetta, he had to be the one to take responsibility.

They closed the distance between, smelling of pomegranates and rosemary. Ruler Valentine, placing a tender hand on his shoulder, asked, "Do the others know?"

"You are the first."

"If you'd like, I can be the one to inform them."

"No. They need to be told in person."

With a nod, "All right. I wish you the best of luck, young king," they brought their hand up and caressed Malice's cheek with their thumb, the gesture reminding him of Annabeth.

He leaned into the warmth of their palm as his eyes slid shut. Malice couldn't remember the last time he had had a positive physical interaction with another. For a while, it had all been pain and death. It felt good. Surprisingly, their majesty let him. More jarring than surprising, it made him feel small and helpless. Malice shifted backward as his chest fluttered with a churning anxiety, but they pulled him into their embrace. His eyes flung open, the sensation of a hug so alien yet so familiar. Kiran and Annabeth flooded his mind, the churning morphing into a whirlpool of emotions.

"You poor child," he heard them mutter as they rubbed his back.

Heat surged and disrupted the current of emotion behind his ribcage. *Poor child.* Malice stepped out of their arms, bowed, "Thank you," and made a hasty retreat.

*

Ruler Valentine had provided Eunice and Malice with separate rooms, both elegantly simple and huge, vines adorned the walls, marble encased the low, round bed, and all furniture was cherry oak, the cushions emerald green. If it weren't for the fireflies, Malice wouldn't have been able to sleep the four nights they stayed in the palace. He didn't know why he had bothered bringing the bottle of lavender and chamomile tonic. It helped at first, putting and keeping him asleep. Until it hadn't and the nightmares violently ripped him from slumber most every night. The more he drank, the more it helped, though only for a short time. He thought if he were out of that castle, the sleep tonic would work again. It had the first night, the second brought little sleep, and by the third, it hadn't.

Instead, he gazed out of the balcony opposite the entry, looking out over the undulating land clustered with trees, rivers, a shimmering lake, and the smallest mountain range in Vinyamar. He could have stared out of the balcony windows for hours. A part of him wanted to as he waited for his royals to arrive, who were also traveling by boat. Going around Mutuwa with a hundred men would have taken an additional two months.

Specifically, Malice wanted Nikanor here, since he was born in Florence's Region, meaning he knew the land well. Eunice had agreed.

Nikanor, alongside Malice's warband, brought a fleet of horses. Memory served him well in guiding the company to his home village northwest of Florence's Kingdom.

It was quaint, the houses of plaster and thatch two stories, clothes swaying on lines, the smell of straw and dung strong. Nikanor did most of the talking—asking—while the warband lingered on the village's outskirts. The streets were too small to fit a warband, anyway. Despite, technically, how small the band was.

On the way out, Nikanor said, "Florence's Region has impeccable defenses, my liege."

The warm air chilled the moment a cloud moseyed in front of the sun. Malice welcomed it. "Should be easier to find Vendetta's rats' nest then."

Nikanor nodded, black eyes wandering his homeland.

"Why did you come to Hordes Region?" Malice asked.

The fairy flinched, remained silent, sighed, and looked down at his horse, a rueful smile on his face. "I… I was the bastard son. Unwanted and about as useful as dung stuck to your shoe."

"You wanted something better?"

"I wanted to be needed. For my worth to be acknowledged." His shoulders adjusted. "Odovacar had seen my skills and chose me as his first sword."

And I took you from him. Malice didn't say that and let the silence stretch, horse hooves clapping the beaten path, the warband growing as they got closer. Guilt wasn't quite what he felt, and if it was, it was very minute. He didn't force Nikanor to relinquish his title as first sword; he did it of his own volition. Malice had asked for loyalty. Could someone not be loyal to more than one person?

With the warband, Nikanor went over the information he gathered from the villagers. There was a stronghold erected within the last twenty years, a peculiarity in both appearance and location. It was made of stone rather than marble or clay, the usual construction materials. The few times it had been searched, it had been empty long enough for dust and cobwebs to collect.

"That's where we go," Malice said. "Unlike the hoplites, they won't know who we are even if they know we're coming."

"Where is it?" Eunice asked, looking at Nikanor.

"Base of the mountain range, right outside of Mutuwa," he answered and tapped a map of the region their majesty had provided prior to setting out. It differed from what he was used to seeing in Hordes. The paper itself was so rich it was nearly orange, mountains, forests, bodies of water and more silhouetted, outlining the details, the edges elaborately patterned.

They were hunched over a table in a tent surrounded by tents, in the middle of a field of daisies outside Nikanor's home village. The sun was quickly setting, so a lit candle was placed on the edge of the map. Sounds of an active camp filtered through the canvas, royals checking equipment, preparing food, and scouting.

Malice grunted. "Closer to Hordes than I thought."

Nikanor dragged a chair to his backside with his foot and plopped heavily into it. "What's the plan, my liege?"

"I want them detained and questioned," he said flatly. "The stronghold is to be destroyed. Any who still swear themselves to Vendetta are to be killed."

"Those who cooperate?" Eunice questioned.

"They can live out their days in a cell." It was mercy, in a way. Many would choose prison over death, and just as many would choose the latter.

"The plan of attack," Nikanor clarified, pitching Malice a raised eyebrow.

"Encompass the stronghold," Malice said, raising his eyebrow in return. "Call for a surrender. If they don't concede, we invade and apprehend everyone inside. Simple."

Nikanor's hands shot up, a smile on his lips, head shaking. "You're good."

"This is nothing."

"You're too modest."

"What's modesty?"

Eunice and Nikanor chuckled as Malice turned to leave. "We leave at dawn." The tent flaps closed behind him.

*

Sleep must've damned Malice. Not that it was anything new. He had hoped he would've been able to get some shuteye since he was outside, amidst the constant ambiance of nature, and had downed one of the five sleep tonics he'd brought. Two remained. There was also a candle at his bedside. Nothing changed how alone he was, though.

Groaning, Malice shot up, rubbed his face down, and threw his legs over the edge of his cot. Twenty royals patrolled and scouted the campsite, their torches illuminated his tent every hour. He watched one pass, swift footsteps rustling the grass. The orange light glinted off something behind them. Wings? Malice guessed it was Nikanor patrolling. But why was he in a rush? Just then, a second set of feet hurried to catch up with Nikanor, wings sparkling on the canvas. There were a total of five fairies in his warband, and only one had wings at all, no less like that of a dragonfly.

Carefully, Malice rose and shuffled to the tent's flaps, peeking his head out. Eyes darting the way they came, he glanced toward Nikanor's fleeting back, sparkling wings twitching as if irritated. Behind him, a daintier figure made itself clear, Malice's vision having become accustomed to the dark. He yanked himself inward and held the flaps closed. It was Ruler Valentine. Malice could recognize their hair and gait anywhere, as he had yet to meet another who had the easy grace their majesty had.

As he stepped backward, Malice stopped, torn by indecision. He was curious. How couldn't he be? A ruler visited a lowly knight from another region. At the same time, how was Nikanor's business any of Malice's?

He *was* Malice's lowly knight, that was how.

After a quick survey of the tents in front of his—the camp was laid out with him and Eunice at the head, everyone else's in five rows of twenty beyond theirs, an aisle of sorts splitting them to act as a commune area—Malice slunk around the entrance, sticking to the shadows. It wasn't easy with no other structures to provide said shadow. Eunice's tent lay to the left of Malice's. Nikanor and Valentine headed to the right. So long as he didn't overdo it, his dark magic would keep him concealed.

Closer he crept, their voices growing the further from camp they got. Both of their tones were very pleasant to listen to, melodic and comforting, like a lullaby. Eventually, with the base of the mountains peaking in the distance, Mutuwa a harsh black wall to the east, Nikanor whipped around to face Valentine. Malice halted and, stupidly, looked for a spot to hide. There was nothing out here besides the ever-moving grass and flowers tickling his legs.

"Enough," Nikanor snipped. "Can't you see? I've made a life for myself in spite of you and father. Must you impose on me now, of all times?"

"I," Ruler Valentine hesitated. "I only wish to explain myself."

Nikanor scoffed and shifted to rest a hand on his hip as the other covered his face. "You've had plenty of chances."

"How so, when Pontos never told me of your birth? He vanished one day. What else was I supposed to believe other than he wanted nothing more to do with me?" their majesty said pleadingly, their voice nearly trembling.

Malice wanted to get closer to see their expressions, but thought better of it and sank into the earth, their voices silencing. Hand reaching upward, he grabbed his cot and heaved himself out from underneath it. The moment was a bit too personal for him to eavesdrop. He *had* a sense of decency, no matter how trivial it was. He had learned all he needed to know and plopped onto his bed, a bit awe-stricken if he were being honest. Malice never would've thought Nikanor's resemblance to Ruler Valentine—which he only connected in that instance—wasn't coincidence. What a secret to have.

*

The plan was executed without a hitch. Thirty-seven followers were found in a vine-riddled stone stronghold. All came out willingly, weaponless, and immediately dropped to their knees. From the youngest to the eldest, they had answered Malice's questions. No hesitation or resistance, no beating around the bush. When they were bound by rope and put in the back of wagons, they did so without protest. Their compliance was more suspicious than if they had fought. Malice knew better than to trust their obedience blindly.

Malice hopped onto one of the five wagons with Vendetta's followers, three more beyond them, stuffed with the warband's supplies. The followers hadn't reacted to Malice joining or when he sat by the eldest of them, a hunchbacked giant with hooded eyelids and blotchy skin.

He looked at Malice, dim eyes leisurely scanning him up and down.

"Why are you cooperating?" Malice asked, his sights on everyone else. Some flinched, others remained statuesque.

"Why'd you pick me?" the old giant returned, his voice as battered as his wrinkled face looked.

"Elderly are opinionated."

He grunted.

"And have little left to lose."

The giant didn't respond. Moments passed, tense moments where those his gaze touched started fidgeting, sweating, licking their lips. They didn't like his presence so much anymore.

"We believe the new ruler will take over where the queen left off," the old giant finally said.

"And who is this new ruler?" Malice hadn't announced himself yet. He hadn't made a name for himself outside his region either. All Vendetta's followers knew was she was dead. Which, in turn, meant someone new would promptly take over.

"One of her children." The old giant shifted and groaned, face twisting as if a pain stabbed his back. "My hope is Draga or Odovacar. Inyene's too twisted and Sok and Rayen are too immature."

Malice compelled his body to be still, and said, "You believe one of them will set you free?"

Face reddening, the giant said through gritted teeth, "We've been devoted to her cause for decades! Our freedom is the least we deserve. Waiting won't kill us none."

You'll be waiting in vain. Standing, Malice didn't have to avoid feet as he walked and jumped from the wagon bed—the followers had pulled their knees to their chests to clear his path.

The warband's journey would circumvent the limestone mountain range where the stronghold stood, steering clear of Mutuwa to enter Hordes Region through the northwestern border close to Bextierther and Dun Raik. And during the two and a half months it took to return, Vendetta's followers were questioned thoroughly. Locations were revealed and marked on maps. Names and numbers were given. Permission from the rulers became a formality rather than a necessity; Malice knew where to strike. With or without consent, Vendetta's followers would soon be eradicated.

City's Heart
XLII

Part I

It was a string of commands, chaos, debris, and blood. The prisoners from Florence's Region were sent to the dungeons. For the first time in months, the castle had barred its doors, also on Malice's word. Malice stayed and fought alongside his royals. They swiftly performed the drills he had taught, Malice leading, Eunice and Nikanor at his sides. Arrows loosed from the second story, muted thuds sounding as each victim was struck, various elements and wooden rods protruding from sternums. When Malice peeked at the dark-faced castle, Odovacar drew another arrow of ice, released, and shot down a fox beastman.

The battle was over quickly. A little over a hundred dead bodies strewn about the courtyard like patches of decay gradually corrupting the surrounding life, the lush grass crimson. As he took in the wreckage, the doors opened, and Odovacar ran toward Malice. Eunice stepped between them, blocked Odovacar's path, and flung her hand out. Odovacar suddenly met a wall of smoke, stopping dead, and grimaced.

"You let them come!" she roared, eyebrows furrowed, body heaving from exertion and covered in blood.

"Where's Kiran?" Malice asked, stepping out from behind Eunice.

Before he could answer or defend himself, Nikanor, as grimy as Eunice, put himself in the middle. He gently pushed Odovacar back as he guided his arm around his neck, his broad frame supporting Odovacar.

"No one… saw them," Odovacar wheezed as he clutched his chest and Nikanor's shoulder. "They just… appeared." He looked at Malice, gaze firm. "Kiran and his parents are safe."

The relief surging through Malice's veins was strong. He released a breath.

"They couldn't have appeared out of thin air! They were here!"

Perhaps they could have. It was hardly past dawn, and Odovacar was still in his sleeping garments: silk trousers, black slippers, and a bare torso, exposing his multitude of angry looking scars. His well-kept hair was snarled and wild from sleep, too.

"Eunice," Malice said, "drop it for now. The courtyard needs to be cleaned up."

"But—"

Malice dropped his tone. "I will speak to him. Alone."

Eyes searching, Eunice nodded stiffly after a moment, rolled her shoulders, and turned. The order for clean-up bounced off the castle, echoing beyond the courtyard.

Malice passed Odovacar.

"They came from underground," Odovacar said.

Malice's study had been kept clean while he was in Florence's Region. Candle wax scented the air. Since the windows were no longer blocked, however, the sun illuminated the room. He sat on the edge of his desk while Odovacar occupied the couch. His elbows rested on his knees and his head hung low, fingers interlocked. Swooping and flaring red hair veiled his face.

"Slowly crawling out of the dungeons," Malice carried on Odovacar's assumption, crossing his arms. "With that many, it probably only took a night. An hour to hide themselves in the courtyard. It was smart."

Malice turned and glanced outside, watching his royal's pile the bodies. They dug ditches—more like graves given their shape and depth—along the gardens and under shrubs to conceal themselves, easily ambushing a travel-exhausted warband. A single royal broke from the mass, armor glinting, strutted toward the trenches, swept their foot across the ground, and sealed the dugouts.

"It's likely to happen again," Malice voiced his thoughts. "Considering we've done nothing with the underground city." Despite the recent attack, he couldn't do anything until he cut off the roots, like Kiran had advised. It was the best course of action and the gentlest.

Unless he didn't need to be so gentle.

The underground city wasn't the base, it was the heart. Crush the heart to stop the flow of blood, kill off the tendrils. Limbs could regenerate, stitched back to the main body, or replaced with magic. Head, heart and core. An agonizing death, if not an instant one. Kiran's way was harder, would take too much time and threaten the safety of the castle's residents. Sooner rather than later, it would affect the kingdom as well. Somewhere in the back of his head, a voice urged him to stick to Kiran's plan. It wasn't wrong to avoid bloodshed and violence. *Kiran wasn't wrong.* But it was more complicated than that. Vendetta had made sure it was more complicated than that.

"Why didn't they attack the servants?" Malice mumbled.

"Perhaps they were waiting for you," Odovacar said.

"Again, why?"

"Did you recognize any of them?"

Malice briefly closed his eyes, the faces he had slain all but flashes in his mind. "No."

"Many were from Roch's crew."

He frowned. "We killed them on the beach."

Odovacar leaned back against the couch, his intertwined fingers in his lap. "He never brought his full crew to a trade-off. Repulsive as he was, he was not stupid."

"Someone survived that day," Malice said. "Had to of to make it back to Wolfgang's and inform the others."

"Or," Odovacar looked away, "traitors are amongst your men, relaying information to the regions."

Malice sat with the idea for a moment, let it sink in, let it roll around in his skull, and agreed. Which also meant there was a secondary entrance to the underground city. Roch's men wouldn't have been able to slip through the castle to get to the dungeons otherwise. It was rather redundant to sneak through the castle so they could sneak back to the courtyard.

"Any prospects?"

"How could you be sure it is not me?"

Malice paused and observed his brother. Odovacar was looking at him already, black eyes resolute. His expression was the firmest Malice had seen from him in a while. Unconsciously, he'd grown used to the timidness Odovacar adopted since his kin's death, making it strange to see a smidge of his former confidence straighten his shoulders. It suited him as a general. Yet, he twitched as if suppressing a shudder when Malice gave him his full attention.

"Deep down, you know what I'm doing is right," Malice said. "You hated what your mother was doing more than I did—more than I do. Why impede my work if our interests align?" He regarded Odovacar with a coolness Draga had often presented to everything.

Tension overwhelmed the space dividing them, adding a chill to the air, the study void of sound.

"There have been a handful of royals, five or six, who have avoided the training grounds since Mother's death," Odovacar said after a while.

Malice nodded. "Gather and question them."

He hesitated. "That is all you want done?"

"Until we get back from the underground city, yes."

"We?"

"*We* should see what *our* mother created."

"Kiran"

This was where Malice was kept… and tortured. A dim, damp, stone cell where black, flaking marks painted the walls, floor, and ceiling. Kiran gulped, trying to keep himself from breathing too deeply because of the stench. Right now, he hated his heightened sense of smell—he could *taste* the air heavy with excrement, mold, and blood.

Malice was the first to step inside the cell. That had been a few minutes ago, however. He just stood there, unmoving, shoulders stiff. To blend in, their company wore their worst garments—Malice was in an old, oversized tunic and patched trousers. It brought back memories, as he was sure this cell was doing for Malice.

Kiran stepped forward, shoes clacking, stopped at Malice's side, and gave his hand a gentle squeeze. Those green eyes flitted to Kiran, the hallway light not reaching them, so they were dark and stormy, like a forest caught in the rain. He offered a weak smile, but knew it would do little to comfort Malice. Or maybe it did more than he thought. Malice sucked in a breath, righted his posture, and moved to the wall.

His pale hand brushed over the surface and paused near the left side. With a jerk to the right, the wall rumbled open, unearthing a wide, shadowy, spiraling tunnel. Kiran gulped down the lump in his throat, which crashed into his stomach as a boulder. He had wanted to believe Eunice was mistaken about what she saw years ago. Now that it glowered at him, how could he?

"You're sure you want to do this?" Eunice's voice echoed slightly, expressing the question that had formed in Kiran's head and likely everyone else's.

"It needs to be done." Fire bursting in his palm, Malice entered the tunnel, his head of white quickly disappearing beyond the curve of the stairwell.

Kiran followed, not wanting to lose the light source Malice had. Malice was correct, too. Kiran was the fool who'd suggested going about this in such a tedious manner. No matter the path they chose, lives would be lost. Whose lives were the question: Kiran, those he loved, and the innocents of Hordes. Or strangers who had sworn themselves to Vendetta, had fed her the support she needed to expand and sink her fangs into the realms. The answer was obvious.

Footsteps clambered loudly, every noise amplified by the cramped space. The further down they went, the cooler it became, and the more the smell of wet soil entered Kiran's nose. Eunice's presence was at his backside, a comforting fact. She was nice, capable, and strong. Odovacar, Nikanor, and a few others had joined them. Their mission, per se, was to get a general idea of what was down there, get an estimate of the population, and find the secondary entrance.

When nerves made his hands tremble, Kiran forced his mind to Malice. He hadn't grown much, was a hair taller than Eunice, and she was short. Granted, she wasn't as short as a dwarf. Besides, Kiran liked being multiple inches taller than Malice. It made resting his arm on his shoulder easier. It was about the only superiority Kiran had. His smile diminished some and his thoughts wandered to places he wished it wouldn't.

Once, they'd spoken about Zephyrus, and it was when Malice said he'd died. Kiran's chest suddenly felt hollow. He missed Zephyrus. Missed the days they'd spent wandering the kingdom while Malice was away or confined to the castle. Zephyrus and Malice had also been the reason Kiran had fought to train alongside the healers at the training grounds, but now that Malice didn't need healing and Zephyrus was dead, he had no cause to return.

Malice's wavering flame made their shadows on the wall squirm as warmth steadily crept back into the air. They were getting closer. Soon, Kiran caught a foul stench like rotten mushrooms. His nose crinkled. The company had walked in silence and continued doing so even when the platform was in sight. An eerie, dim blue glow instead of warm orange firelight greeted them.

Malice extinguished his fire as he set foot on the flat surface, then stepped aside so everyone could file out of the stairwell. It didn't take as long as Kiran had thought to reach the city. Immediately, something wormed inside of his gut. About five meters in front of him, the ground vanished, an icy blue cloud forming a rug. Shuffling forward, Kiran peeked over the edge, leaning as far as his balance allowed, so he didn't have to get too close. They were on a ledge, while the city must have been several miles below them yet.

Wind sweeping his hair out of his face, Kiran sniffed. Clusters of mushrooms provided the blue light—gleaming spots scattered over the cavernous walls and ridges. Kiran recognized it as the glow mushroom which was known to only grow in Dun Raik at the center of the continent. Either the fact had become false, or they were brought to Hordes Region and cultivated. The mushrooms explained the rotting smell, though.

Kiran slid backward and ran into someone, his heart leaping out of his chest as he whipped around. Malice raised an eyebrow, eyes big, his slit pupils enlarged.

"There are ledges all around," Nikanor said as he approached. "A few with stronger lights, most empty." With his chin, the fairy pointed to one across the haze, higher up, the ridge looking like a crumpled wad of paper jutting from the cliff's surface. They all thought the underground city was more like a rat's nest, but it seemed to be an ant hive instead.

"We get to the city first," Malice said. "Then we check the ledges."

"You think there might be more entrances?" Eunice asked, head swiveling to survey the massive cave.

Before Malice could say anything, orange light flickered and spilled from the ridge Nikanor had pointed out. Everyone went as still as a statue, sights on the ledge. Kiran held his breath, his blood thrumming through his veins. Voices echoed, cheery ones, when a head peered at the city's entrance and disappeared again. Seconds went by. Then two people jumped. Kiran's hands shot up to his mouth to keep his gasp from escaping. Wings spread behind both of them, the whooshes resounding as they flew higher, circled back, and launched themselves downward. They were flashes of darkness, encompassed by the blue fog.

He supposed that answered their suspicions about other entrances.

Stomach dancing with his heartbeat, Kiran's hands fell to his sides as his feet carried him back to the fringe. He wondered how it felt to fly. How exhilarating would it be?

"Kiran," Malice said.

Kiran's state of awe broke like shards of ice. Malice gestured toward the path leading to the city, a flat, declining shelf following the curve of the cave. The other ledges had them as well.

Kiran walked alongside Odovacar, Nikanor in front of them, four royals behind, Malice and Eunice leading. Their footfalls rebounded worse here than it had in the stairwell. He looked beyond the bulk of Nikanor as Malice glanced over the edge. For a moment, his gaze lingered, as if he wanted nothing more than to jump like those people had. He had wings, so he certainly could. The only other person in the company who had wings was Nikanor. Fairy anatomy didn't allow for their wings to grow big or strong enough to support them in flight—Nikanor's wings were no more than decoration.

"You should do it," Kiran said, everyone's attention snapping to him as the group came to a halt.

Malice turned, but not all the way. "I won't leave you behind," he said.

"You don't have to," Kiran countered. "Fly down, fly back up and rejoin us."

Malice's eyes jerked to the blanketed hole, then to Kiran. Kiran nodded. After everything Malice had been through, perhaps a brief flight would do him some good. Admittedly, a cave wasn't the most ideal place. Nor were the circumstances. But there had been a rigidness in Malice since… since *it* happened, a growing, ever-consuming tension. Curiosity was a part of it as well; Kiran had never seen Malice's wings. Demons normally didn't have feathery wings. Maybe Malice was the exception. Were they the pallor of his skin or as dark as his nails?

More than curiosity, Kiran was concerned that if Malice didn't have an outlet… he would—"We'll be fine," Kiran cut off his train of thought. Malice would never hurt him. They were brothers.

Out of the corner of Kiran's eye, Odovacar folded his arms over his chest. Odovacar and Sok were Malice's brothers. Zephyrus was like Malice's brother, too. Kiran gulped and shifted his sight, so he wasn't staring into Malice's eyes anymore. *He was different.*

"Don't think we can handle ourselves?" Eunice said playfully.

Malice stared a moment longer, then walked through his company the way they had come. They hadn't gotten far from the platform, anyhow. By the time Kiran turned around, Malice had discarded his shirt and handed it to the last royal. Reaching the ledge, bulges moved and expanded from under Malice's shoulder blades until wings sprouted. Kiran cringed. Had half the mind to look away and gag when the sounds of bone grinding together reached his ears, blood wafting. Maybe not having wings wasn't such a bad thing.

At this angle, Kiran couldn't gauge the mass of Malice's wings. With a flap, he was in the air and his wings were thrice the size of his body. Mouth gaping, Kiran watched the gentle sweeping motion of Malice's dragon-like wings, blue shimmering off the midnight scales. One more flap brought him high enough for Kiran to have to tilt his head back—everyone's head was tilted matter of fact. In the air, Malice embodied an ethereal beauty, his skin taking on the azure hue of the glow mushrooms. If he didn't know better, Kiran could imagine Malice was a deity of myth.

Kiran glimpsed a smile on Malice's face when he relaxed his wings and plummeted toward the unseen bottom, the cloud swallowing him whole. The company waited a short time and resumed their descent.

"I'm jealous," he muttered under his breath, a wry smile on his lips, his eyes on the haze of blue above the city.

Nikanor said, his head in the same direction as Kiran's, "I think it's better to not have wings, so flying wasn't a possibility, than to have wings that are useless." Defeated bitterness coated the fairy's words and Kiran's heart ached for him.

Soundlessly, in the blink of an eye, Nikanor was off the ground and gone. His screams resonated off the walls, then ceased as if he were—were… killed. Everyone froze. Eunice signaled for the company to press themselves against the wall as her opposite hand guided her sword out of the scabbard on her hip, the metal ringing, the noise scraping Kiran's eardrums.

The rock was rough against Kiran's back, a chill seeping through his clothes. Eunice's head jerked to one side. Kiran couldn't hear anything. His heart was thundering too loud. Cautiously, Malice's first sword returned her weapon to its sheath. The moment the hilt clicked, she vanished, like Nikanor had.

Odovacar put his hand out in front of Kiran, ice forming a sword in the hardened grip of the other. In the matter of a minute, the person soared well above the path and lowered themselves for all the company to see.

Malice extended his hand toward his royals, waiting till one took it, a smirk on his face. After yanking them to his person, they were off, falling to the depths once more.

Head blank, Kiran sank to the ground, releasing a tremble of a breath. Zephyrus was right, Malice was out of his mind.

One by one, Malice took his royals down to the city. The knight prior to Odovacar hooted and hollered on the way. When it was Odovacar's turn, he was hesitant. *At least he wasn't stolen like poor Nikanor was.* Somehow, Eunice knew who it was and let him take her. Kiran guessed her sense of smell was to blame. Bears had extremely sensitive noses, and she *was* a bear beastman.

Eventually, Kiran's time arrived. Malice's wings beat steadily behind him, making him bob slightly in the air as if he were in water trying to stay afloat. Kiran got to his feet and stepped toward Malice.

"Ready?" he asked.

"You didn't ask the others if they were?" Kiran squeezed Malice's outstretched hand as tightly as he could.

Malice shrugged and pulled Kiran from the ledge, his other hand quickly holding Kiran's body up. Kiran's arms wrapped around Malice's shoulders as his fingers instantly curled against Malice's warm back. The whooshing of his wings was quite a bit louder now that Kiran was close enough to feel every breath Malice took.

"Fast or slow?" Malice's voice vibrated in his chest.

"Both."

Chin lifting, hold strengthening, Malice floated close to the ceiling. Kiran felt and saw the exact moment Malice's back muscles and wings relaxed, allowing them to freefall. The wind howled, the ceiling shrinking. Blue fog encased them, a damp cold making Kiran shiver as every fiber of his being screamed. Fear or excitement, he couldn't tell which was rowdier. The indigo cloud turned into a secondary ceiling and the wind lessened.

"Look," Malice said.

So Kiran did, releasing Malice a hair to look over his shoulder. It truly was a city. Blue and orange mingled like meandering fireflies. Chatter rose and fell over the deafening sound of Malice's wings. Buildings were tiny squares or mounds on the ground, in the walls of the chasm, at the peaks of stone pillars and stalactites. Kiran thought the hole above them was massive, and it was, but this… this was something else entirely. Easily, the underground exceeded the size of Hordes Kingdom.

His breath caught at its sheer magnificence. Surface drawing near, Kiran saw the people and their simple garments, their friendly smiles, and their linked arms or clasped hands. They were happy, as if Vendetta hadn't put them down here. His next thought was like a knife to his brain: how long had it been since the underground city was constructed? How many generations had lived and died here?

Nikanor, behind a line of tiny homes, waved them down. His white hair matched Malice's, making him easy to spot nearly anywhere. Malice set Kiran down first. His legs almost gave out, and he faltered. Luckily, Odovacar was there to catch him.

"They did the same thing," Nikanor snickered and gestured to the royals with his thumb.

"Says the one who was wiping bile off his lips when I got down here," Eunice said off-handedly, and looked toward Malice as he landed a few meters away, dust billowing.

Nikanor scoffed. Odovacar smiled at him.

They had landed behind a series of clay houses, simple and small, each a little different in design. It seemed more on accident than on purpose, though, as if most of them were built by inexperienced hands and minds. The limestone beneath his feet was smoothed, yet the walls remained jagged. The air was pleasantly warm, not obscenely hot like what it was on the surface. Various things scented the draft; bread, burning timber, stagnant water, dung. Immediately, Kiran missed the sweetness always in the air from the flowers in constant bloom.

"Eunice," Malice said, while throwing on his oversized tunic. "You've been here. You'll lead the way."

City's Heart
XLIII

Part II

Reckless. Idiotic. Insane.

Needless to say, Eunice didn't like Malice's plan.

Factions divided the underground city. The deeper one went, the more horrid the faction became. The first few were fine, peaceful, the equivalent of life on the surface. Faction eight, second to last, held the fighting pits. Finally, the gallows where all the waste and bodies were dumped. Eunice smelled it as soon as Malice had set her down in faction one.

People trickled into the underground city and never left, meaning, especially in latter factions, faces were known. Eunice was known. Odovacar wasn't. Unfortunately, he bared quite the resemblance to his mother. The citizens would figure out his identity in the blink of an eye. Kiran thought it would be a hindrance. Eunice had concurred. Malice said they could use it to their advantage.

Bound with rope by wrist and ankle, Malice and Kiran walked between Eunice and Odovacar, the rest of the company following. Kiran slouched, fingers woven in front of him, trembling. He certainly looked the part, though he didn't need to act—Kiran was genuinely terrified. If there was one person who might have been able to disagree and persuade Malice toward another course of action, it would have been Kiran. Still, everyone had reluctantly agreed.

In faction seven, the people were filthy, smelled even worse, and wore torn bits of fabric she supposed passed for clothes if they wore anything at all. Glares burned her skin. Snarls and insults drifted to her ears. Nothing intelligent or eloquent. Homes and trades were smaller, shabbier, sheets for doors, crooked windows half falling out of the clay walls, the ground no longer smooth. Most of the light was residual from the lesser factions behind them. So far, they had gone past two buildings with a lantern illuminating the entrance. Of course, one was a brothel.

Eunice had lost count of the number of times she'd heard the mumbling of disapproval from a royal at her backside. Hell, she'd heard one of them gag when a one-winged angel shoved a greyish-brown goop-like substance into their mouth. They had proceeded to defensively huddle closer to the wall to protect their meal. She was disgusted sure, but she mostly felt guilt and pity. Eunice had put people in a place like this to secure her and her wife's life. If push came to shove, she would do it a hundred times over for Helle.

Peeking at Malice, he was calm, eyes sweeping the last stretch of faction seven. It had taken an hour of walking to get to this point. After another half an hour, through crowds of people avoiding the company like they were a disease, the pits were in sight. Metal latticed domes covered five holes, about ten meters deep, three meters wide. Eunice's stomach twisted, the discomfort scrambling into the rest of her body like disgruntled rats. She remembered what it was like all those years ago. Each face seared into her brain, each scream so different from the last.

"Calm down." Malice's voice broke her out of her thoughts.

Taking a deep breath, she realized how flush her knuckles had become and loosened her grip on the rope around Malice's hands and feet. So close to the gallows, her nostrils flared at the odor and hoped no one in the company spewed their breakfasts.

Clay braziers surrounded the pits, shedding more light than Eunice had seen since they first arrived in the city. It took a moment for her eyes to adjust. A quick glance to the side; Malice was scowling, his green eyes bright with anger. Kiran, on the other hand, was pale and sweaty. Odovacar didn't seem much better. Precipitation stuck his long hair to his neck and forehead in clumps. Odovacar must've buried his anxiety and revulsion as he set his shoulders and stared ahead of him, expressionless. Eunice checked on the others over her shoulder, all of which steeled themselves as well. Time to put Malice's plan into action and pray it worked.

The pits were empty. Thank the gods. A guard, quickly approaching, spied them from across the vastness of faction eight at the same time Eunice spotted her. The guard's style of armor didn't belong to Hordes Region. Bronze scales reinforced the leather tunic. Thick linseed strips covered her waist and stopped above the knees. There was a short spear in her off-hand while the burgundy wrap kept a sickle pressed to her hip. She hailed from Yeager's Region, the land of deserts and dwarves.

"What's the queen's dogs doing here?" the guard asked, brows furrowed, lip curled.

"To deliver these criminals," Eunice answered, gesturing to the boys with a point of her chin.

"I ain't talking to the beast." Her sights jerked to Odovacar. "I'm talking to the queen's spawn. The son of cowardice."

Odovacar's jaw clenched. "I thought it time I step into my role as prince."

Eyes raking Odovacar, the guard spat at his shoes and transferred her attention to Kiran and Malice. Kiran flinched under her gaze, shrinking into himself.

"What'd 'a couple of kids do, eh?'"

"We're not at liberty to discuss," Eunice said. "Not with someone as low on the food chain as you."

The guard lunged, almost taking Eunice by the neck with the short spear, had she not backed up in time.

"Wretched bitch," she fumed and swung.

Eunice caught the wooden shaft, released the rope, and punched the guard, wrenching the spear from her grasp. Eunice broke the guard's weapon in two, tossing it aside, and retook the rope. Blood gushed from the guard's nose and split lip. Glaring, the guard reached for her sickle, an incomplete circle of bronze with a leather-bound handle.

"Try it," Eunice said as smoke formed a sword at her fingertips. She caught it, spun an arc, and abruptly altered the sword's path. The blade whistled through the air, stopping to kiss the guard's neck. Odovacar's broadsword joined Eunice's. The ice caused goosebumps to appear on the guard's tanned skin.

None of the royals in Malice's company had brought a weapon to keep themselves as inconspicuous as they could while exploring the factions. At least, that *was* the original plan. Conflict was severe and oppressive between them, the pressure of water when light couldn't reach the bottom. If more guards were to come, they would be outnumbered and fucked.

"Enough, Heba. Release our guests," a feminine voice called out.

Eunice shuddered. *Freya.* Beyond Heba, who put her hands out and backed away, Eunice made out the silhouette of the underground city's leader. Odovacar's ice retracted into the palm of his hand, and Eunice's smoke dispersed. Freya drew near. Fur hides adorned her shoulders, and her velvet green dress had a sheen to it, following the curves of her body. Her skin was the color of a red grape, her hair the fair shade of periwinkle. And those eyes were as inky as Odovacar's and Vendetta's; deep, intense, brooding. Silver sparkled in her low-pointed ears.

"Ah." Freya smiled, revealing two gold upper canines. "If it isn't Eunice. And at last, Prince Odovacar has graced the underworld with his presence," she drawled.

Stopping in front of them, her eyes quickly fell on Kiran and Malice. "What fine specimen you've brought me." Delicate fingers raised Kiran's chin, his eyes firmly screwed shut, mouth a hard line. Freya chuckled and moved onto Malice, grabbing his jaw between her thumb and index finger, tilting his head one way and the other. Malice's expression, unlike Kiran's, was unreadable. Any shred of anger he felt earlier, he bottled.

"So, tell me, Eunice," she said, "what did these two sweethearts do?"

Eunice opened her mouth, but Malice spoke first, voice like the cold simplicity of steel. "Killed the queen."

Freya blinked at Malice, then burst into laughter, taking a few steps backward. He glanced at Eunice and nodded. With a tug in the right place, his bindings came undone and slipped to the limestone. Odovacar did the same for Kiran and ushered the young beastman behind him. Nikanor and another royal acted as his protectors while Malice stayed put, stretching his arms high, his back and shoulders popping. Despite his youth, Eunice was surprised by how often and loudly he cracked his joints, like an eighty-something-year-old mortal.

Freya stopped laughing, the ease of her facial expression morphing into understanding, and lastly defiance. This time, Heba yanked her sickle out, stance defensive at Freya's side.

"The rumors were true," Freya muttered. The alluring nature of her tone vanished, replaced by an odd firmness.

Malice said, "Depends on what they say and what you've heard." There was nothing Eunice hated about Malice except for that tone, vindictive, cold, because it was so precisely Vendetta's yet so perfectly did it fit Malice.

Freya was affected, too, her body remembering what the queen was like, her poised demeanor becoming as rigid as the walls surrounding them. "You killed the Reap line," she said. "And were coming for our heads next."

"Vendetta was no Reap, neither were her children." He shrugged. "Your information was false."

"Perhaps we can strike a deal? I keep my life in exchange for whatever you wish." She plastered on a fake smile if Eunice had ever seen one, displaying her gold teeth and pale pink gums.

"And what do you have that is of value to me?"

Gesturing, she said stiffly, "The pits."

Malice's head lazily followed the direction Freya's hand was pointing, gaze locking on the metal cages, which kept spectators at bay and combatants from escaping. "Right… the pits."

Eunice's blood churned, her back muscles constricting. Memories of his bloodstained body sitting on the coffee table with his dead kin perched on the furniture beside him slammed against her skull. Her stomach jumped into her throat and her legs spasmed as she suppressed the urge to run away.

He returned his attention to Freya. "Which brings you more coin, slaves or the pits?" he asked.

Hesitantly, she answered, "They are equal."

"You'll have neither."

Freya's fists clenched and her brows knotted. Something like relief but not quite eased Eunice's tense muscles. Malice was Malice, not the reflection of a boy void of sanity.

"I'll give you two options. Die alongside your subordinates. Or adhere to my terms and live," he said. "Your choice."

"What are your," she gritted out, "*terms*?"

"That's not how this works."

"You want me to choose blindly?"

"Life or death. What's there to think about?"

What terms are you speaking of? Malice had said nothing about negotiating with these people when they had reached the city, nor had he said anything before they left. What could the underground city provide if he wanted to rid Hordes Region of Vendetta? Her hands built it, her mind cultivated the factions, and her actions lured the residents into their barely habitable shelters. Eunice would happily raze everything in sight as her own way to spiting Vendetta in the afterlife. Behind her eyelids, however, Helle glared at her, her mouth wiggling the way it did before she lectured Eunice. Children ran around the first few factions. She thought about their smiles and the established livelihoods of thousands. Even if his goal was to save their home, four factions were inhabitable for non-savages.

"Life," Freya gave in, head dipping, eyes on the ground as if she were also swearing fidelity to Malice. Yet, her stance was not completely below his line of sight and her knee had not sunk to the ground.

"Every non-criminal will be released and put in a home," Malice said as he stepped away from the company and headed toward the pits, everyone moving with him. "I want details on all the crimes that sentenced these people down here. My advisor and I will decide if their punishment is ethical."

Glancing over her shoulder, at being called his advisor, there was a shy smile on Kiran's face.

"What of those whose reprimands were just, your majesty?" Freya's tune changed awfully quick.

The group stopped at the first pit. Inside, blood splattered the cream walls, the floor no longer tan. Two metal gates were on either side, a weapons rack against the wall facing the company. There was a shield, a spear, a sword, a dagger, and a sickle, a war hammer, an axe, and a club which looked to be carved out of bone.

"Keep them here. Continue your fighting pits."

Kiran gasped. When heads swiveled toward him, he turned away, hands gripping his tunic.

Flabbergasted, Freya said, "I don't understand."

"Another ruler has something similar, something on a much grander, public scale than this and it has worked flawlessly," Malice said. "The amount of criminals in their prison steadily decreased. Overall, crime is lower."

Magnus was the only ruler Eunice knew Malice was in constant contact with. She'd never heard of this *grand* event and supposed that was the intent.

"We'll do the same, but won't make it public," he went on, slipping from the pit to the next one, shoes echoing. "I want factions three through seven cleaned, repaired, and livable."

"You... want to establish the underworld as a kingdom?" Freya said deliberately, seemingly trying to make sense of the prospect.

"Do you have an objection?" Spinning on his heel, Malice stopped Freya dead in her tracks, his posture proud. Like a king.

Unable, for some reason, to hold his gaze, Freya's eyes fell to the limestone. "Of course not."

"Great," he said and strode past her. "I also want a map of the city and its entrances."

With a snap of her fingers, Freya said, "You'll have it." Heba hurried toward the mound in the distance, vanished, and raced back within a few minutes. She put a scroll in Freya's outstretched hand, who then offered it to Malice. "This map is the most relevant, as we've established four new routes within the last four months."

Malice handed the map off to Eunice. Out of curiosity, she unfurled it a bit, revealed the latter few factions of the city, and rolled it up again.

"Prove your worth, Freya Venczel."

The dark elf flinched. Eunice looked between the two of them, fists bunching at her sides. He knew. This was his plan the entire time.

Malice said, "Should your loyalty still lie with my mother, you'll receive the same fate I gave her."

Taking the hint, Freya and Heba dropped to one knee, heads lowered. "I swear my service to you, your majesty."

Eunice stared at the pair. They bent the knee without a second thought. Yes, Malice had given them a choice, whereas Vendetta likely hadn't, but Eunice's suspicion was roused. *Service* Freya had said.

Without a word, Malice turned his back to her and walked the way Eunice and Odovacar brought them, the company trailing behind him. She lingered a second longer, whipped around, and stomped toward Malice. Eunice was more enraged than she was curious about Freya's motives. Beyond that. How could he not inform his own first sword of his intentions? His advisor? Anyone? No one would have refuted the idea because of how beneficial it would be. They could have been better prepared, mentally. Perhaps they could have brought a troop of royals to help with construction and clean-up, gather the criminals from wherever they were being held.

When Freya and Heba were out of sight, Eunice grabbed Malice by the arm, dragged him to a house and threw him against the wall, keeping her hands on his shoulders to keep him pinned. He scowled at her in return.

"Why didn't you tell us anything?" she hissed. Voices murmured around the corners, gradually increasing in volume.

"Eunice." Odovacar. "Now is not the time for this."

She ignored him. "*When* were you planning on telling us? Had you ever planned to tell us?"

"I found out this morning," he said and jerked his shoulder, but Eunice was stronger. His scowl worsened. "I thought you already knew about Freya, so I didn't think to tell you."

"I'm not talking about her." She slammed him again, a hollow thud from his back hitting the mud packed wall.

"Eunice," came Kiran's cautioning voice.

"The fighting pits? It was a spur-of-the-moment decision."

"Bullshit."

"If I had known before we left, I would have gathered the warband," Malice snipped. "Came down with the intention of taking the city by force if necessary. I would've had the criminals found and escorted to the surface for a retrial. All of us would have been prepared, suited and equipped for conquering an entire city not dressed in rags and weaponless."

The green glaring back at her burned with wrath. Eunice's anger fueled the pounding of her heart, bunched every muscle in her back, the tension threatening to snap them like string. She released him and stepped away. Chest rising with measured inhales, Eunice studied Malice and knew he was right. He had done so for the campaign, prepared himself and his warband for the possibility of an ambush and for the possibility of being outnumbered ten to one. He knew how to plan ahead and did it well. Which made it equally hard to believe his plan was impulsive or deliberately withheld it.

When did reason ever quell the blaze of fury, though?

The tedious trek through the city and up the cavern walls was silent. Eunice was in no mood to find a middle ground with Malice. Apparently, neither was he. Disgust broiled in her guts; Malice had *slaughtered* his family yet hesitated when it came to Freya? A woman who earned a vicious death because her actions were as heinous as Vendetta's? Fear crashed and wrestled with her repulsion and wrath. Malice had nearly lost control. Eunice felt it in every fiber of her being, her instinct shouting so profusely it lost its voice. If he had, who would he have gone after? She tried to rationalize his actions and did. Tried to defend him and, once again, did that too. Vendetta could not be spared, used, or changed. She would have only caused more pain if she had been kept alive. Freya was different in that she could change, she could right her wrongs, and commit herself to the region Malice wanted to build.

Upon reaching the surface, Malice dispersed everyone while Eunice had come to a decision. Whereas Vendetta's cruelty had no limits and seemingly no purpose, so as long as Eunice could see Malice's objective, she could live with and stand by his cruelty.

Den of Wolves
XLIV

Seventy 'criminals' were released from the underground prison. Malice and Kiran deemed their crimes too light to fight in the pits. Odovacar agreed after reading a few mishaps they had committed. Theft of bread, a necklace, or a wooden practice sword. Talking out of turn in front of the queen. Abandoning a mission that was almost certain death. The list went on. Over two hundred criminals remained, however, meant to be executed in a hole by fellow lowlifes.

Odovacar helped with cleanup and construction for the underground city as often as he could. Houses were rebuilt, streets smoothed, lamps placed, waste turned into compost, and wells were dug. There was much to be done. The underground city was the size of Hordes Kingdom, Ryzion, and Bextierther combined, quite possibly making it the largest in Vinyamar. It would not be an operable city for another six months to a year.

Malice certainly knew how to keep his people busy. Odovacar was hardly complaining as it kept his mind preoccupied and his body sound. He liked physical labor, liked how he was truly helping after so many years of destroying or doing nothing. He could escape the castle of nightmares and forget the memories haunting his every waking moment.

Until it was time to meet the northern rulers. Malice wanted Odovacar to accompany him instead of Eunice. When asked why, Malice had not given a reason, and Odovacar had not pressed for one.

Three regions lie between Hordes and Wolfgang's. Dun Raik, with the proximity of trees, forbade travel, thus forcing all who were not on foot to go around the massive forest at the continent's heart. Going through Dun Raik would have shaved two or three weeks off their seven-week timeline. Flying was not an option, considering how long they planned to be in the north. Malice could not carry Odovacar and their supplies over the regions.

The carriage stuck to Dun Raik's fringe, so they avoided Zeldine's Kingdom and the regions swamps, the coves of Raelle's Region, and the twin mountain ranges of Wolfgang's and Jared's, divided by a valley, similar to Mutuwa with its cavern of brackish water.

Malice had his nose in Draga's journals and books, religiously studying her notes. It was a habit the queen also tried to instill in Odovacar—out of some shred of defiance—Inyene, and the twins to no avail. Meanwhile, Odovacar was content sitting in silence, watching the world outside the window, glad he could venture outside his motherland. He half expected Malice to look outside with as much wonder as him, seeing as how he had never been to the north. Odovacar should have figured it out by now; Malice was unpredictable.

A storm in Raelle's Region halted their voyage and drove them to settle in a rundown inn amidst an equally rundown village. The folk were old, weathered, but kind and cheap.

There were five rooms available. The coachman, who had been caught in the storm trying to get them to shelter and had been dripping wet, got a room of their own. They deserved it, no matter how much they argued otherwise. Malice requested another with two beds rather than separate sleeping quarters. The innkeeper obliged, and Odovacar did not argue.

It was a decent room, the beds big enough so a giant's feet would not dangle off the end. Quilted blankets were neatly folded at the foot of each mattress. A vanity sat against the wall, a window in between the beds, while two oversized trunks rested on the opposite side. The fur rug on the floor was soft, and the space smelled of wax from the candles on the vanity, a hint of saltiness from the storm.

Malice set his belongings on a chest, slid out of his shoes, and claimed the rightmost bed. They were alone, it was quiet, and the inn was asleep. If Odovacar had questions, now was the time to ask them.

Following suit, Odovacar put his sack on the second trunk—they had grabbed a night's worth of supplies and left the rest in the chests on the carriage—and stripped, changing into a pair of linen trousers. He blew out the candles, then made his way to the surprisingly quiet bed. It was warm enough, so he left the blanket where it was.

"Why are we sharing a room?" he asked first and foremost.

Malice shifted, the sheets rustling.

"Afraid?"

"…"

Odovacar shot up, head whipping toward Malice. He *was* scared but of what? With a sigh, he pushed himself against the wall and crossed his legs. Pin pricks raced through the scars on his back from the coldness of the wall. Jaw tightening, he stayed until the sensation passed.

"Why bring me instead of Eunice?" Odovacar let the other matter go, returning to a subject Malice refused to answer before they had left. Perhaps one day, Malice would share his fears.

Again, Odovacar met a barrier of silence. He was not asleep. Odovacar saw the rigidity of Malice's body and the quickness of his breath. They had fought, per se, in the underground city, and it was the only explanation he could think of for Malice not bringing his first sword.

"Helle caught the fever," Malice said at last. "Eunice wanted to stay by her side."

Head against the wall, Odovacar understood. The fever was deadly. If he had a lover and if they caught the fever, he would do the same. Still; "There are others." Malice had taken a fancy to Nikanor, Nikanor to Malice.

Odovacar would be lying if he said Nikanor's defection did not sting. No. The pain was worse, like Nikanor had ripped something from Odovacar's body and had yet to return it. Pristinely, Odovacar remembered the day he chose Nikanor as his first sword. The one he'd selected on his tenth birthday lasted four years. Then Queen Vendetta took her head from her shoulders—the knight had glowered at the queen during a time she did not have the patience for it. Nikanor had just become a royal. Odovacar witnessed his sparring match against Alkeim days prior to when he would have been placed in a Squad, and knew he would have no one else by his side.

"None like you," Malice said flatly.

Odovacar held back an exasperated sigh at Malice's false adulation. "How do you see me, Malice?"

"Do you resent me?" he shot back.

The storm outside howled and thundered, rain pelting the inn, lightning flashing the room white. Neither had answered each other's questions for a while. Odovacar thought he would resent Malice, would hate him in some way or another. Malice had killed his kin. Slaughtered them in the worst ways possible. He told him to kill himself and meant it. Malice was everything Odovacar had never been in his mother's eyes.

Yet, he did not. Could not.

Odovacar watched the hands that had molded him, sculpted him, only to destroy and build him again in the never-ending cycle of his childhood. His own hands helped create who Malice was. A part of Odovacar could not help but view Malice as a reflection of someone who had experienced everything he had and of someone he could never be.

Odovacar said, the words slipping off his lips like raindrops on the windows; easily, "I do not resent you."

Quietly, the storm dampening most sounds, Malice said, "You are my brother."

Odovacar's heart squeezed, robbing him of breath, scars pinching. "You should not see me like that."

"And you should resent me, but here we are."

What a strange pair of brothers they were. Joined by false lineage with a sense of shared misery. Odovacar laughed because it was ludicrous. Because they were both idiots. Because they did not know any better, and it was evident. Soon enough, Malice laughed too, probably realizing the same thing.

"Did she ever love me?"

Odovacar continued laughing like a madman. The answer was simple yet so complicated and applied to all of Vendetta's children. "She loved your potential, Malice. Loved you like one would their favorite trinket. When the trinket breaks, there is sadness for a brief time. Then one moves on to get another." It was the debilitating truth.

He did not realize they had both stopped laughing until the room was uncomfortably silent. The raging winds and berating rain seemed affected as well, suddenly calm.

"You knew that," Odovacar guessed.

"Yes."

"Does it hurt?"

"No," Malice said. "I wanted to humanize Vendetta, I suppose."

So had Odovacar when he was younger. He had wanted to believe deep down his own mother loved him, the punishments were truly deserved, and she was preparing him for the difficulties of kingship. When Sok and Rayen came of age, he gave the notion up. Once more, had he let go of the idea when Malice was of age. Each time was like another piece of his soul shattering as reality settled in the gaps and cracks. Odovacar had never looked at his mother the same. That, too, was painful.

Odovacar laid on his side and spread the blanket over his legs, a chill having goose-bumped his skin.

"I'm afraid of the dark," was the last thing Malice said.

Me too.

*

Holds of stone and brick dotted the snowy landscape of Wolfgang's Region. The kingdoms were clusters of homes low to the ground, cylindrical, and made of rock and wood to keep the warmth in and the cold out during the winter months. Others, which Odovacar assumed were shops, were slightly taller and rectangular.

He shivered constantly; hands numb despite the several layers of heavy clothing he wore. He hated the cold, was not made for it. Malice, on the other hand, was unbothered. His pale skin was rosy, the wool and fur covering his body making him look like a small child.

It was always frigid in the northern regions, always snowing. Odovacar had not believed it, as he had not believed how hot it was in Yeager's Region. Until he experienced the extremes on opposite ends of Vinyamar and understood how the rumors were hardly exaggerated.

The main kingdom was a fortress of dark stone and timber like the rest, simply grander in scale. The coachman stopped at the courtyard where servants and guards bustled, the cobbled ground resonating their busy feet. The fortress was a good five meters off the ground and encased the courtyard, curtained windows facing them. Rocky beams held the structure up, the space underneath completely open and full of warriors going about their duties. Everyone Odovacar's eyes landed on wore heavy breeches, padded doublets, or cloaks. Further ahead, a group huddled around something. A furnace to an outdoor forge, he assumed, based on the grindstone and the hanging weapons surrounding the group.

Through the courtyard to the entrance, welded metal depicted two wolves battling on the wooden double doors. They opened at Odovacar's and Malice's approach, a servant dipping into a curtsy.

"This way," she said and turned on her heel.

While Malice followed the guide, Odovacar delayed at the chestnut doors. Foreboding settled in the furthest reaches of his mind, his instinct whispering cautions like sweet nothings.

The fortress was not as lavish as Odovacar thought it would be. He was used to the extravagant taste of Hordes Region. A single embroidered rug of reds, oranges, and greens in alternating geometric patterns covered the floor. From the ceiling hung a chandelier of antlers. To the left of the foyer was a hearth with furniture around it, same to the right. Doors encompassed the back walls and greeting them was a wide staircase leading to the second floor.

They reached a counsel room. Plainly brown with a long table at the center, candles spread on its surface, and cushioned chairs seated at the edges. The servant departed swiftly.

Clawed hands behind his back, ears flicking backward as the doors clicked shut, the king stood in front of the window. Ko's head turned, lip instantly curling at the sight of Malice. It was as if he had not seen Odovacar and he was grateful for it.

"What displeasure brings you to my home?" he asked, his voice deep and scratchy.

Odovacar frowned. The king's tone was displeasing and, as far as he knew, unwarranted.

"Vendetta," Malice said as Odovacar took in the strange array of colors Ko wore.

His attire consisted of four layers—first a high-collared white shirt, and a robe patterned with ferns. The third was a deep maroon with yellow overlapping triangles and finally a midnight blue coat, white deer jumping along the bottom helm. Ko was massive for a beastman, broad-shouldered and looming, brindled fur of greys and tans adding to his girth. His height neared King Yoon Woo's, who was a giant well over two meters tall.

"What of her?" he grumbled.

"She's dead."

Ko's bright yellow eyes expanded to show the whites. He looked away. "I am sorry to hear that."

"Don't be," Malice said. "I killed her."

Odovacar blinked at Malice, shocked by his candor, worried about Ko's reaction as his hand tensed over his sword.

"What?" the beastman replied.

"I'm here for other reasons."

Ko, wearing a deep scowl, studied Malice, then Odovacar. He

stood slightly behind Malice as a guard might because today, he was one. Odovacar's title as prince meant nothing; he was never a true prince, anyhow. His title of general, however, might have some effect on Ko. Through the Kings Summit, Odovacar had learned of Ko's respect and admiration for royals in the early days of his kingship. It was, from his understanding, one of, if not the biggest reason Ko and Yoon Woo got along as well as they did.

"Speak your motives," Ko said as he sat at the head of the table. "Quickly."

Odovacar and Malice remained standing. "Vendetta was in control of the exportation of slaves. Her biggest shipments came from your region." Malice glanced out of the window at the wintery landscape. "Slaves were only one of things she dealt with. Money, weapons, poisons, and more have been traded under your nose."

Malice could try a gentler approach. He had, Eunice said, with southern monarchs.

The beastman looked ready to shout his contempt, barely containing his temper, making him snarl and expose his jutting canines.

"I'm here to right her mistakes. I'd like your permission to search for her remaining devotees and bring them to justice."

In silence, Ko intertwined his fingers, placed his furry chin on the back of them, eyebrows furrowed. Odovacar could not think of a reason for refusal. Accepting would do no harm. If Ko were suspicious, it would be little trouble to send his own royals to accompany Odovacar and Malice.

"Your request is denied," Ko eventually said.

Odovacar fought and swallowed his initial alarm, his expression deadpan and his body still. He actually declined…

"I don't think you understand the gravity of her grievances, Ko—"

"Here, you will address me as king," he growled. "I will not tolerate you, a child, probing about my region. How can I trust you at your word? You've admitted to killing your own mother, then spewed lies about slaves, which, might I remind you, was a practice outlawed centuries ago."

"I did what had to be done," Malice said calmly, eyes steady, shoulders relaxed. "And if laws prohibited every crime from being carried out, what need would we have for royals?"

Intending to insult Malice was not a bright idea, nor was insulting Odovacar. They had survived a childhood of degradation from Queen Vendetta. It would take creativity to truly hurt either of them, Odovacar thought.

Malice added, "I will address you however I please. You and I are equals."

"Are we?" Ko stood, shoving his chair back, and strode toward Malice. Odovacar stepped closer. The king stopped.

"You have no crown on your head. You sit not on a throne. You are a prince, at best, a boy-king." He paused and looked down at Malice—down *on* Malice—yellow orbs gleaming. "Tell me, boy-king, how are we equals?"

To Odovacar, as a child, Ko was intimidating. The wolf's sharp eyes had never ceased to pierce Odovacar's flesh, and his canines peeked from his lips whenever he spoke. The growl at the back of his throat and his sheer size reminded Odovacar of what he was. A beast. Now, as an adult, the fear was gone. Slight annoyance replaced it. Ko was reaching his middle years and with it came arrogance. Not the best of combinations.

"There are many ways to ascend the throne," Malice said. "I followed the law. I killed the prior ruler. With or without a coronation, I am king." Malice met Ko's disdainful gaze. "That is how you and I are equals."

For a time, Ko regarded Malice as one would regard an immoveable object. He stepped backward and said, "What of your *guard*? Has your title of prince fallen to the gutters as well?"

Odovacar startled slightly. This entire time he had been ignored, to be addressed so abruptly, temporarily voided his mind of intelligence. Clearing his throat, he answered, "I was never a prince, your majesty. I am and shall remain a general of Hordes Region." Odovacar topped it off with a gentle bow, his arm pressed against his torso as his head lowered.

Ko grunted. "Your opinion on the matter, Odovacar, speak it plainly."

He dipped his head again. "I support my liege's will. I believe we must eradicate Vendetta's presence from the continent for it to prosper as it once did." Amongst these two, Odovacar was no one. His opinion was only wanted because he was an adult and a voice to oppose Malice. Yet, he felt like himself, a general, a brother, a man. Not an object before his mother that could be shattered if she looked at him right.

"My answer is still no. Leave my region. You are no longer welcome, kin-slayer."

Malice, Odovacar on his heel, departed. Either Ko's region would fall, or Malice had a secondary plan. No matter which it was, Odovacar would not mind. Ko had earned either result, and his juvenile behavior was to blame.

*

Predictably, Malice was not without a substitute plan.

Faces unknown, it was easy to walk around in broad daylight, traveling from one locale to the next, all of which Roch had told Malice of months ago and all of which were accurate. Roch's crew was double the size Odovacar had previously believed, but he was not the only band of miscreants who had sworn themselves to Vendetta. Wolfgang's Region was infested, meaning Odovacar and Malice had to stay in the brutal cold for an additional two weeks. Ko was an ignorant ruler, painfully unaware of how effortlessly Vendetta could have invaded, taken over, and claimed Wolfgang's Region for her own.

If Wolfgang's was in such a state, dread nestled deep inside his bones at the thought of what the other regions were like. They had been outnumbered a thousand to one. Yet, it meant nothing when the quality of Roch's men was abysmal. And the same could be said about the other regions, which brought a strange respite, as if his dread had shrunk only to fit something he could not place his finger on. Odovacar preferred it that way, however, as it made his and Malice's work of Vendetta's servants easier and quicker.

Odovacar rested his head against the carriage's window. He watched the snowy world of the north melt, transform into hills, slump into swamps and eventually level into the flatlands of Hordes Region. Bextierther was on the horizon, a stone fort meant to keep the citizens in and everyone else out. The nobleman, Balios, was a paranoid human, always fretting over when and how Mother would rip the peace from his desperate grasp.

Malice sat quietly across from him, the leather of the seats contrasting with his pale skin. His hair was long, white waves reaching past his shoulders. Hair was once sacred amongst demons. He'd read how each clan was different. Those of Reap blood kept their hair long to show they were leaders, chieftains, and generals. To cut one's hair meant dishonor. To shave one's head meant exile. How true that was, Odovacar did not know and there was no one left alive to tell him otherwise, save for Hyacinthia. Wherever she was.

Lazily, Malice's head shifted toward Odovacar, green eyes passing over him, before he returned his gaze to the outside, as if he thought better of speaking. Odovacar was not sure why, but the silence between them was comfortable.

Onyimyth
XLV

The cold of winter followed Malice from Wolfgang's Region. With the new year a little less than a month away, and Malice's birthday less than two weeks, the time for his coronation had come.

Malice dreaded the thought of the crown being laid atop his brow. Worse, Vendetta had worn it. The people wouldn't see it as a symbol of peace and prosperity, of safety and a new beginning. They would see it as a constant reminder of what Vendetta had enforced. The pain and fear she instilled in the very land of Hordes Region. It would be a constant reminder to Malice as well, a nightmare he would never get rid of. What could he do? It had been passed down through generations of rulers.

Setting his back against the wood of the chair, Malice sighed and looked at the ticking clock hands on his desk. Physically, he was drained from spending months traversing northern Vinyamar. Mentally, even more so.

Thankfully, a weight off his shoulders, the underground city—named Khuomouth—was nearing completion. Freya seemed content to become the unofficial 'noble' of Khuomouth. When all was said and done, construction complete, and Malice on the throne, her title wouldn't be so empty.

Knocks sounded. Eunice's voice followed with, "You have a visitor, my liege."

Malice sighed, "Come in."

The door opened, Eunice stepping aside to allow the visitor in. A woman of average height and build, her skin a few shades darker than Malice's but ashen, as if she bathed in grey watercolor. As Eunice closed the door behind the woman, Malice stood and tucked his hand underneath the desk, fingers tense.

"You are?"

Four maroon eyes scanned Malice. The second set's placement was just above the point of her cheekbones, like Malice's in his true form.

"Hyacinthia Valor," she said.

Malice slid backward, and his hand relaxed, heartbeat a sickening thud in his chest. For a while, they stared at one another. Malice knew her, and she knew him. Hyacinthia Valor, former noble of Ryzion, mother of Nyx Reap, and the woman who struggled to keep Malice and Nyx safe from Vendetta's torment. He never thought he would meet his blood kin. Nor did he really want to. He was content with what he had, happy with those he called family.

"Why are you here?" he asked.

"I've heard of your wishes to be crowned by the new year." Hyacinthia made to step forward, but a quick motion of his hand stopped her dead. "I've come to request something of you."

"What right do you have?" Malice hissed. Her good intentions did nothing to save him from a childhood of pain. Words and threats would have never been enough to hold Vendetta to her vows. Anyone who had the displeasure of interacting with her would have known that.

Expression twisting, her gaze fell to the floor. "May I sit?" Malice nodded, so she did, gingerly taking up a cushion on the couch. The skirt of her long dashiki inflated slightly, and she smoothed it out. "Perhaps my being your grandmother would be a sufficient price for your ears, but I realize it is not. So I ask you instead to consider my request in the name of your grandfather."

Cautiously, Malice retook his seat, his clothes rubbing against his skin like thorns.

"The Claymore's ripped tradition from this land," Hyacinthia said with a furrow of her brow. "To become a leader, it was more than putting a crown on one's head and drinking till the fountains ran red with wine. Before Hordes was put on the throne, he competed in a hunt. He painted the bodies of his chieftains and in turn they painted him in front of a spitfire, cooking the beast he had hunted." She spoke proudly, shoulders back, chin held high. "To show his faith and fortitude, he cut his hair in front of his people and let it burn."

Each major clan treated their hair differently. The Valor's braided theirs, each braid signifying an accomplishment. Hyacinthia's silver hair was a collection of thick plaits running down to her lower back, smaller braids woven throughout. Malice had read a few books about it. One stated each plait meant a victory in battle; another said it was for every decade one lived. If one's head was adorned with ornaments, it represented their social status, of which Hyacinthia wore none.

"I want you to bring them back," she said, eyes steady on Malice, hands laid on top of one another in her lap. "To honor Hordes and to restore what has long since been buried."

Malice asked, "If I say no?"

"You are no better than Vendetta."

Malice laughed dryly. "I never claimed to be better than her." Matter of fact, he had claimed the opposite. He wanted to become something worse and was almost certain he had done just that.

But that was when she was alive, and he was full of indescribable rage. Now, he didn't know what he wanted. Everything was working itself out, the continent continued on. Life refused to stop and let Malice catch his breath.

"Describe the ceremonies," Malice said, apparently much to her surprise.

Despite the brief stint of wariness, Hyacinthia seemed relieved to share her memories of Hordes. Malice was happy to listen. Hordes was a man who had earned his throne, had proved himself worthy of the people's respect and admiration. Jealousy stirred. Malice had done none of those things. He wasn't a man who deserved the loyalty his royals gave and the smiles his people wore.

He was a boy with blood-stained hands and luck.

"In return," Hyacinthia went on, shifting to fetch something from her dress pocket. "I'll give you this." Standing, she handed a rolled piece of parchment to Malice. "It is the draft for the kingdom Hordes initially wanted built. He never..." she trailed. "I thought you might want it."

Once the string was untied, he unrolled the parchment, which was the length of his arm. The high points of twelve towers, the courtyard at the castle's heart, the materials listed on the right-hand side, the library—in the castle and underground—all touched a part of Malice's memory. The kingdom Hordes wanted was based on the Barren Circle's castle, right down to the stained-glass murals and jade floors. Mouth ajar, he studied the paper, each line and note jotted down in soft, elegant handwriting, each detail welding the species' cultures together. Hordes wanted a kingdom to be home for everyone. *This* was his grandfather.

"I do," he muttered. "I'll reintroduce the coronation ceremony." Malice rolled the parchment up, tied it with the string, and set it on his desk. "If you attend as well."

"I'll not become a noble again," she said shortly.

"I'm not asking that of you."

She blinked.

Malice shrugged. "I thought you would want to see the past brought to life."

Sighing a chuckle, the wrinkles on Hyacinthia's face deepened as she smiled wryly. "Very much so."

*

Kiran and Alkeim were against the hunt specifically. Being so close to Malice's coronation, neither wanted anything to happen to him or those with which he would hunt. Eunice and Odovacar believed it was a good chance for Malice to bond with his people, maybe make a few friends closer to his age outside of Kiran. The deciding factor had been Priscilla.

"I'm old," she had said. "I doubt I'll be able to see a hunt such as this again before I kick the bucket."

Now, a week later—the day he was supposed to be crowned— Malice stood alongside thirteen participants for the hunt outside Mutuwa. Ten meters behind them were the spectators, all standing or on horseback, which included citizens, royals, and nobles. The voices were indistinguishable and loud, almost deafening. Within the first row of the crowd, Malice spotted Eunice and Helle, who had recovered fine from the fever. Unlike Helle's flowing dress, Eunice wore her usual doublet with her sword on her hip. Odovacar and Nikanor were side by side, the fairy's wings sparkling in the sun while Odovacar's bright hair was up.

Priscilla and Alkeim were in the front row, as were Kiran, Blodwen, Tendai, and Hyacinthia. So many familiar faces mingled with the unknown; the ones he was competing against were strangers.

Malice was the youngest by at least two years and the smallest by at least fifteen centimeters.

Sun still rising, the sky clear and blinding, the breeze salty, a rider cantered from the north, a horn in one hand. Their horse stamped and went into a light trot but never stopped moving, the proximity to Mutuwa getting to the animal.

"Hunters," the royal shouted. "You have till high noon to capture and kill a beast within Mutuwa. It is not a hunt of speed but of quality. The hunter who returns with the biggest and mightiest beast will be thrown a feast and rewarded with coin." Steed prancing back and forth, the royal brought the horn to their lips, waited, and blew.

They were off. Weaponless, armor-less, and mount-less, the hunters would plunge into Mutuwa with nothing but the clothes on their back and the shoes on their feet. Save for Malice, he left his shoes behind. At the forest's edge, everyone split, heads vanishing beyond a tree trunk or a massive leaf.

He slowed and took in the location. He'd never entered Mutuwa from this point, directly across from the meadow outside of Hordes Kingdom. Not much was different. Light dappled through the canopy, birds tweeted, moss, leaves, and flowers veiled the ground while bugs smacked into Malice. It was muggier in the forest, the air like mucus on his skin.

With a thin layer of magic underneath his feet, at least his steps were silent. There were so many beasts in this forest it was hard to choose which one to hunt. A bear would suffice, he was sure. Howlers had probably found their dens and retired already. Wyverns were an option as well, but Malice didn't know where to look since he'd only ever seen a dead one. An onyimyth was out of the question. As he moved a branch out of his path, he figured whichever one he found first would work.

The sight of mushrooms clustered in the disjointed bark of a tree churned Malice's stomach. He fought the urge to look away and quicken his pace. This was a forest and mushrooms were everywhere.

Time passed almost laboriously, Malice's thoughts spiraling. Every tedious moment since Vendetta's death resulted from Malice's lack of planning. He never thought he would be the one to become a monarch. Zephyrus, the moment he said he wanted it, was clearly the best candidate. In more ways than Malice cared to count, Zephyrus would have made a superior king.

High noon rapidly approached, yet he had found nothing. Not even a squirrel. When he stopped and truly focused on the environment, all the hairs on his body raised, the sensation of worms wriggling up his spine. It was silent aside from the breeze rustling the leaves above. Birds no longer sang. Little crunches and snaps from the foliage disappeared.

Allowing his mind to wander was a mistake. And he knew better. Instinct told him to turn and run, the hunt be damned. Facing an army who were easily swayed by the fear of death was one thing. Facing a beast whose only goal was to find its next meal and wouldn't stop till it got said meal was something entirely different.

Heart beating unnervingly quick, Malice shifted his foot to turn the way he came. He froze. Clicks echoed. He whipped around, eyes raking the trees, ground, and plants. It came again, closer this time, the sound a series of low ticks. To the south; nothing but a motionless abundance of green with splashes of red and purple.

Malice's breathing was deep rather than shallow, so he could be as quiet as possible. He swallowed and slightly lowered himself, hands perched at his sides, as he scanned Mutuwa. Sound reverberated incredibly well in forests, making it hard to guess how close the creature was. Perhaps there was a way to know for sure, but he wasn't aware of it.

When the next set of clicks sounded, breath came with it, a wall of foul-smelling warmth hitting Malice's backside. Ice replaced the blood flowing through his veins. Why hadn't he heard its approach? Based on the amount of breath that had struck him, it was safe to say this creature was by no means small.

Known for their stealth and unique way of communication, onyimyths are Vinyamar's most deadly monster, Kiran read from his plethora of books. Their nights together were spent sleeping or Kiran teaching Malice about whatever his heart desired.

Despite what one would think, an onyimyth's size didn't hinder its ability to traverse the most labyrinthian of landscapes. That wasn't what had Malice's knees locked in place. *If you can hear an onyimyth's click, it's too late. It saw you before you could see it, and once the dragon finds its prey, it gets it.*

This monster gave Mutuwa its reputation, Malice realized. Not the howlers, centipedes, or wyrms. The onyimyth.

Another breath. Malice screwed his eyes shut, every muscle bunching. He exhaled. Unhurried as a snail, Malice turned. The onyimyth's jaw clattered, its overgrown yellowish razors for teeth like rocks grating together. Plated scales of a dull, muted green covered its head, steadily shifting to murky umber. Webbed spines followed its vertebrae to its whip-like tail, lazily waving behind it. Four legs bent, belly almost to the ground, the onyimyth's head was angled downward, fire orange eyes observing Malice.

Low clicks emanated from the onyimyth's throat as it crept backward, Mutuwa's undergrowth engulfing it.

Malice spun and darted into the forest, heels striking the earth, lungs straining from the foggy heat. The greens and yellows and blues were blurred as branches and fronds beat him. A thorn bit into his flesh, fluid dripped down his arm, and the cut regenerated. The onyimyth relinquished its stealth. Its weight forced saplings to bend and break, trunks the height of a house to crack in two and topple. Snaps and chatter reached Malice's ears over his labored breathing and thundering heart. Claws racked trees, the sound almost like a crunch.

Up ahead, a patch of forest brightened. A clearing. Malice pushed himself to go faster, jump over a fallen log, avoid a low-hanging limb. Without the slightest clue as to what he was doing, Malice dug his heels into the grass of the glade, swiveling, and thrust his hands forward. The onyimyth burst through the trees as spears of earth shot up, one of them catching the dragon's shoulder. The disjointed shriek it made rained a thousand icicles onto Malice as birds scattered.

Jaws nipping at the pillar, the onyimyth writhed and jerked violently, one claw scoring the pillar, gashes carving deeper and deeper. Malice slid his foot across the ground and punched the air, another spear stabbing the onyimyth. He did it again, the fourth bigger, taking up most of its chest. The dragon still fought, body twitching, blood oozing and pooling so quickly the dirt couldn't absorb it yet.

Eventually, the onyimyth's head and limbs drooped, random muscles jerking.

Malice wheezed. The chase suddenly caught him like a fishnet trap. His chest constricted, a weight not allowing him to take a full breath. How many times would luck get him out of a near-death situation? He hadn't the slightest clue what he was doing out here. He'd never hunted. When he was trapped in this hell for weeks, he was too weak to kill an animal, a rabbit, of all things.

A horn blared, and birds squawked in response, as if annoyed by the disruption of their peace. It was high noon. Malice ground his teeth and glared at the onyimyth's corpse. What was done was done. He killed a mighty beast, he supposed.

Wings sprouting from his back, Malice stretched his scaly appendages out. Assuming his true form during the campaign gave him some control over his appearance. Learning to control all of it, however, was a process he didn't have the time for. He crouched and leapt, hands down and rising to his midsection. Hefty as it was, Malice lugged the dragon's body through the trees and above Mutuwa, his air magic carrying it. As quickly as sweat beaded, it blew away.

Hordes Kingdom lay in front of him, dark and menacing. Closer was the gathered mass of the region. He was rather glad he hadn't covered too much distance. The onyimyth was heavy despite it being an adolescent, which was half the size of an adult.

Malice's arms trembled. His wings faltered, and he lost some height, branches snagging the beast. Forcing himself higher, Malice would have to land at Mutuwa's fringe. His nails dug into his palms as the tension in his shoulders, arms, and wings grew stronger. Just a little further. The crowd was increasing in size. Still, he was too far to hear its roar.

Once he reached the precipice, Malice released his magic, and the dragon plummeted, landing in the meadow with a boom, petals and dirt clouding it. Malice's wasn't far behind, since he couldn't feel his wings anymore. Keeping them spread allowed his descent to be gradual and calm. Yet he landed terribly, tripping and tumbling across the grass as if his legs were new.

Screams and cheers of the spectators penetrated Malice's eardrums while flowers flooded his nostrils, figuratively and literally. At least he wouldn't reek of sweat. He would smell floral and grassy. He would also be coughing up bouquets for the next week. Steadily, Malice got to his feet, trying to brush off as much green as he could when feet bounded closer.

Malice looked from his soiled clothes to the crowd. Kiran ran toward him, face alight. He caught Malice in his embrace, bodies colliding, squeezed, spun, then put him down again. Kiran was smiling and laughing, hand in Malice's, trying to drag him toward the onyimyth. *I haven't seen him smile like that since… Zephyrus was alive.* Whatever was to come, Malice wanted Kiran to keep smiling so brightly, so genuinely. He didn't know how to make it happen, but he would try. Kiran's joy was always infectious. Malice felt his frustration fading, a smile slipping onto his face, his body lightening with every step.

Hair and Paint
XLVI

The fire jumped and flared, grease spitting from the onyimyth's roasting legs. Two more blazes created a triangle, the second and third having the dragon's hind and head—the beast was too big to roast over a single fire. Young oak logs scented the air of the meadow outside the castle's grounds, Mutuwa at the feast's backside.

Wine derived from sugar cane filled cups. Malice refrained from drinking the sweet liquid. He preferred to be sober when the time came to be crowned. Drums, fiddles, and lyres played melodies people, shoeless, some clothes-less, and carefree, frolicked to. Above the celebration, stars twinkled, hazes of plum and azure dusting the night sky. Crickets chirped, owls hooted, howlers laughed.

Malice turned as ginger steps approached. Hyacinthia smiled at him, hands tucked behind her back. The fire made her maroon eyes orange, her skin and hair vibrant with life as it probably had been centuries ago.

The thought appeared like a lightning bolt inside his head, sudden and intense, disrupting the calm he clung to. *Does Nyx look like her or Hordes?*

"I've something to give you," she said, her dress brushing against his leg. From her backside, she presented Malice with a tooth longer than her hand, almost as wide too. "It is tradition."

Malice took it, surprised by the weight, and turned it over in his grip. "From the onyimyth?"

She nodded. "Hordes had killed one as well. Hunters are encouraged to keep a relic from their hunt. After having it dyed red, Hordes wore the onyimyth's teeth in his ears."

The look he gave made her chuckle.

"I do not expect you to do the same," she said. "I wanted you to have it."

Malice said as he slipped the tooth inside of his pocket, "There was more to this hunt, wasn't there?"

This entire affair would have been a hunt for the glory of the act more than the result, like the ones in Cain's Region. Instead, it was a game where all the participants were on the precipice of adulthood, hunting beasts in the most dangerous forest on the continent. Alkeim and Eunice were right in that it was too dangerous for the future king, but Hyacinthia didn't tell him everything when she requested the ceremonies return.

Eyes flitting to the side, she said, "It is a rite of passage into adulthood."

"You could have said so."

"I… did not know how you would react—did not know you."

Malice regarded her with a blank expression, then looked to the blaze shooting embers into the sky, each becoming a star for a heartbeat, and subsequently dying out. "Do you know me now?"

"Not in the least."

Neither did he.

Later, nobles were brought to the fires while Malice was stripped of clothing per Hyacinthia's instructions. The feast fell silent as a path toward the flames opened.

Breathing in the smell of cooking meat, adjusting his shoulders, Malice strode through the crowded people of his region. Eyes followed curiously as grass cushioned his steps and the heat intensified, prickling his skin. Naked for all to see, he came to a halt in front of the first blaze. He found the same faces in the mass of bodies as he had for the hunt. It was a good thing he was this close to the fire; the warmth gave an excuse to the flush of his skin.

Before his embarrassment truly settled in and made Malice's straight-backed posture falter, a noble walked around the licking flames, a bowl of paint in hand. The first to mark Malice was the youngest of the nobles and the only one he'd ever met in person prior to today. Sophronius's blonde hair was like wisps of gold, framing his thin face. He wore plain trousers and a white dashiki which sagged below his clavicle, acting like a low-collared dress.

They came toe to toe, Sophronius a head taller, a hue of red tinting his pale cheeks. Malice couldn't tell if it was because he was naked or because of the fire. Both, probably. Sophronius avoided looking too far down as he dipped his fingers into the black fluid and painted Malice's chest. The paint was cold, Malice shivering.

Eyebrows upturned, Sophronius shifted backward with a meek smile. "I'm no artist," he whispered shyly, which was almost too quiet to hear over the steady beat of the drums and inclined his head.

Malice submerged all five fingers, lifted, and dragged them down Sophronius's face, long black streaks tainting his pure skin. Hyacinthia had told him to paint the nobles' shirts. The nobles could paint his flesh, yet he couldn't do the same? Was he not swearing himself to his nobles as much as they were to him? If Sophronius was shirtless, Malice would have drawn a sword on his chest, a partial Hordes Region sigil, just as the noble had painted Ryzion's insignia on him. Because Malice wasn't suited for defense. The role of a shield sat on Eunice's and Odovacar's shoulders. Nor was he the gentle touch one needed while healing like Kiran was. He was the bloodied blade keeping enemies wary, the refined edge to never dull, the weapon which never failed to kill.

Paint met and chilled his body once more as the second noble continued to decorate his chest. It was awkward to stare at them, so he gazed at the stars. Embers made it difficult to find any constellations, though. Focusing on the sky lessened the embarrassment of his bare ass on display, he guessed. Not that it soothed the subtle ache in his chest as Magnus came to mind, the stars resembling his abundance of freckles Malice tried to count.

He couldn't help but want a letter to appear on his desk one day, Alucard's emblem pressed into the wax seal. He knew it would never come, yet hope refused to die, no matter how much Malice wished it would. Whatever wrong he had done was unforgiveable, and their friendship was over.

A part of Malice was surprised to see how many supported him taking the throne. Look at all he had done to get here. Drove his two closest friends away, killed his own kin, murdered some more. The nobles were, nevertheless, pledging themselves to him, marking the pallor of his body with their own sigils. The people smiled at him, praised and thanked him. How much of it did he truly deserve?

Eventually, the last noble lifted their fingers from Malice's back and shifted to stand in front of him. As he had done for the others, he swept his charcoal-soaked fingers down their face, and they joined the others at the edge of the crowd.

Bextierther's symbol was a sword crossing a shield branded with the stone fortress. Estera had a left facing profile of a horned skull, tulips sprouting behind it. Mirroring Estera, Mondlesgrave's insignia was the right facing horned skull with a cichlid, a species of fish only found in the eastern waters of Hordes Region, swimming around it. Finally, Ryzion had a full portrait of a horned skull in the jaws of an onyimyth. Sloppy renditions of each sigil were drying across his torso, one on his back, tightening his skin.

At last, Hyacinthia detached from the rows of people, a blade in her hands. Usually, the parent would do what she was about to. Nyx nor Karlisle were present—his blood parents—and neither were Vendetta and Emil, so his grandmother sufficed. When she placed herself behind him, she undid the string tying Malice's hair up, but didn't let it fall completely undone. Knife pressing against his hair, the sound was like thousands of threads snapping in rapid succession. Hair tickled his shoulders, and it quickly became an itch. Lock after lock fell to the ground, his head growing lighter and lighter. Now that he was thinking about it, he'd never cut his hair. It had only remained shorter thanks to Inyene's torture.

Willfully allowing his hair to be cut felt different, like throwing out old torn and stained garments instead of his favorite tunic being ripped from his hands. Malice understood, if only a fraction, why demons once cherished their hair as they had.

Then it was done and Hyacinthia backed away as Malice's hand went up to feel the transition from nape to the back of his fuzzy head to the top, where his hair was an inch or so long. The draft against his usually blanketed skin gave him goosebumps.

Tonight, however, was far from over. In front of his entire region, next to the onyimyth he killed, adorned with the oaths of fidelity from his nobles, a crown still had to put on his head, and he had one more vow to make.

Down to one knee, Elder Priscilla fixed a thin, obsidian crown on his brow. Veins of violet snaked throughout the branches, forming an incomplete circle, black cherry blossoms at the ends. Rising to face the masses, Malice's voice carried, telling of how he would change the region for the better, clean what his predecessors had left behind, and to rule beside them—he took inspiration from Zephyrus's speech when they were eleven. He meant those promises. Except, deep inside, it felt like he was lying to himself. Even when smiles brightened the faces around him and the celebration was revitalized, Malice felt dirty and wrong. He may be the region's sword, but he was corrupted beyond saving, as if his words were poison seeping down his throat, the paint of his chest and back like acid gradually stripping flesh from muscle, then muscle from bone.

He shouldn't have been the one crowned tonight.

Fabric suddenly wrapped around his shoulders, sweeping past his knees. It was soft and warm, the wool heavy. Kiran tugged it over his chest, tied the string going across it, properly covering his body. His brown eyes gleamed, the ridges of his horns on the sides of his head catching the light. At fifteen, Kiran had begun the trials and tribulations of becoming a witch doctor, earning his first piercing, which was a small bronze hook in his nostril. He smiled.

"I have a gift for you," Kiran said. From an inside pocket of his ornately designed robe, he pulled out a little jewelry box and offered it to Malice. "They'll match your crown."

Small hoop earrings of obsidian. The difference was the earrings were pure black like the sky on a moonless night, orange from the fire adding precise highlighted lines.

Hands behind his back, Kiran said, "I didn't think you'd be one for big. I thought earrings would be simple and wouldn't get in the way."

"Thank you." The box closed with a clack, and he slipped it into his cloak's pocket. He would put them in tomorrow.

"You like it?"

Malice nodded.

"Really?"

"Yes." He tilted his head.

For a moment, it seemed like Kiran wanted to say more, eyes moving back and forth, smile fading, but he didn't. There were a few unspoken topics hanging in the air, and neither of them was quite ready to address those topics. It created friction between them, the desire to speak or walk away an unsettling sensation in his gut. It was probably the same for Kiran as well. One day, they *would* talk about Zephyrus and his family. Discuss what Malice had done during the week he had the castle emptied. Explain what had happened on the campaign and what had happened with Magnus. Just not right now, not while the wounds were still fresh.

Malice was the first to look away. "Go have fun," he said to the ground.

Wordlessly, Kiran left to join the celebration. He was tired in every way imaginable, every muscle screaming at him to rest, his mind leaking from his ears. If he had to guess, it was hardly past midnight, and this party would last till dawn. He couldn't ditch his own celebration.

Running From Pain
XLVII

The marble floor had warmed, but what else did Malice expect when he and Kiran had been lying there since half past ten? With Kiran beside him, Malice breathed in the scent of honey and herbs, mint to be exact. It changed constantly as Kiran worked with different combinations every day. Candle flame provided a soft light from the desk. Unlike most in the castle, the ceiling in his bedchamber was plain and flat.

Hands resting on his stomach, Malice lifted one to gesture about the blankness above them. "What if you painted flowers?" he suggested.

Light no longer kept the nightmares away. They haunted him, never let him get more than a couple of hours of sleep before he woke to a sweat-dampened pillow. Herbal tonics did nothing, either. He'd tried stronger concoctions, but Blodwen had started asking questions, pity so thick in her tone and gaze he had practically choked on it. He'd thought, fleetingly, about asking Kiran. To admit his nightmares had gotten to that point wasn't something Malice was ready to do. Instead, he resorted to medicinal books from the kingdom's shops and the short stints he would spend alone. Malice mentioned wanting to stare at something during the nights he had nothing better to do and sleep told him to fuck off, no matter what mixture he chugged. Eunice had found a local artist who was decently priced, and that was when Kiran interjected.

"What kind?" Kiran asked, his voice gentle.

"Lilacs," Malice answered instantly. Because they would remind him of Magnus. "Butterfly weed." For Annabeth's orange hair. "Amaryllis." They were Kiran's favorite as they came from Fae folklore. Where the nymph queen's blood fell, flowers had bloomed, so went the short version.

"Sunflowers?"

Malice turned his head toward Kiran. "What do they look like?" He'd heard of them but had never seen one. The climate of Hordes Region didn't allow for the plant to flourish like it did in the north.

"It's big," he said, extending his hands to approximate the size. "Tens of yellow petals surround the seeds at the center. You can eat the seeds."

"Really?"

"They're sort of nutty."

He looked back toward the ceiling. "A few."

"Anything else?" Kiran stuffed his arms underneath his head. Using his horns to support his head couldn't be comfortable, certainly didn't seem like it was.

"I want the sky to go from evening to night," Malice said, arm sweeping left to right.

"Because of the stars?"

Malice nodded. "Add whatever constellation you want, but don't tell me. I want to find it on my own."

Imagining what the ceiling would become, they slipped into a comfortable silence. It had been a while since they'd done nothing together and enjoyed each other's company like they had as children. Malice supposed they still were, to some extent. More him than Kiran. Adulthood deepened Kiran's voice, so he sounded more and more like his father every day. Malice could tell whenever Kiran was overwhelmed since he wouldn't have the time to shave the slight stubble on his chin. Shifting to lie on his side, Malice remembered the softness of Kiran's features, the roundness of his cheeks and gut, how big and bright his eyes were. He was steadily losing them. A pale birthmark painted a stripe of his chestnut brown hair cream, the mark forming a bumpy *v* shape down his face, stopping at his lip. The edges of his eyebrows, too, were whitened. The kindness of his dark eyes was the same.

Kiran turned, somewhat startling Malice. They stared at each other, Kiran's folded arm supporting his head and keeping his horn from the ground. Malice wondered what he looked like to Kiran. Had he changed any? Were his boyish features fading too? How much did he remind Kiran of his mother? Would he ever forget the fear Malice had inadvertently planted in his mind?

"Coin for your thoughts?" Kiran whispered, his breath caressing Malice's face.

Kiran spent too much time with the royals if he spoke like that. Malice smiled, then frowned. "You should stay here tomorrow. All of you should."

"You want to go to the Kings Summit alone?" Kiran spoke quickly, brows knitting.

"Yes." Malice tried to hold Kiran's concerned gaze. Ultimately, his sights dropped to the cloudy floor.

His mouth opened, snapped shut, and he flipped to his back, releasing a drawn-out sigh. Kiran wanted to argue. *You need protection,* would probably be his first point, but did Malice really need it? *You're king now. It's proper to have your first sword with you,* he would say second, and Malice would say neither Queen Basia nor King Thorn brought their first swords. *But you're too young to go without*, would be Kiran's final case, but Malice's age meant nothing, and they both knew it.

Malice turned to his back as well. The thought of returning to the Kings Summit was not a happy one. He dreaded it. News of how he had earned his crown spread, which meant it reached Basia's and Thorn's ears. What if they wanted to *test* just how mighty Malice was if he supposedly killed the entire *Reap* line? There were many things Malice was confident in, winning against either of them was not one. Then there was Ko, who hated Malice as much as Malice hated him. What of Valentine? Malice had leaned into their touch like some needy child desperate for the smallest amount of attention from a parent. A year later and embarrassment still colored his cheeks. Caroline was worse in her pity and that… His stomach had burned through the lining that day, raced through his veins, and almost left his tongue in the form of insults.

When Malice closed his eyes, the words of Magnus's last letter painted his eyelids. *I'm sorry*, Malice had eventually responded with. He couldn't say anything more. The pain of no longer having Magnus's friendship was like a stab wound, refusing to heal. Despite how much time had passed, Malice didn't think he could face Magnus tomorrow. Didn't think he could tolerate being in the same room as him, but what choice did he have? He was king now. It was his duty to attend.

"If," Kiran said, "you change your mind, you'll let me know, right?"

"I will."

He hadn't changed his mind. Solemnly and silently, Kiran had watched Shevanti pick out Malice's attire, dress him, and style his hair, which was more or less brushing out a few snarls since it wasn't long enough to do much of anything else. He'd followed Malice down to the foyer, where Eunice sent him off.

A carriage of black and red waited outside on the stone path. Malice waved the coachmen off. There was a reason he'd asked for an open-backed shirt and waited till the *day of* to leave, crown strapped to his belt. While hooves clattered and stomped beyond the castle, wings broke through skin, whooshing as they stretched at Malice's sides. They were dark, but in the sun, the thin, scaly flesh took on a blush red color. It felt good to fully extend them, like the first stretch after you wake in the morning. Muscles released their tension between his shoulder blades and lower back. The breeze caressed him, billowing his wings and rustling his clothes, making the grass and bushes of the courtyard sway.

Knowing who would send him off, Malice didn't bother looking behind him and took off. Within a few heartbeats, he was above the kingdom, all sounds consumed by the beating of his wings. Higher, the air was fresh, like he was breathing in the north's atmosphere without its bitter cold biting his skin. Although he liked the cold.

Soon, the cities of his region became dots of warm grey on rolling green hills. The Lake of Zephyrus was the greenish blue of algae, shimmering with white. A flock of birds drifted over the enormity of Mutuwa toward Florence's Region. In the north was the Barren Circle, the ruined castle, and the mountain range of Wolfgang's and Jared's Regions peaking amongst the clouds. Slightly east, Malice connected the tiny islands making up Oakens Region at the edge of Raelle's. West was the more desolate lands of Vinyamar where the climates were their harshest between the scorching heat of Yeager's and the tundra of Maziar's.

If only he could stay up here, make his home in the clouds, and ride them anywhere.

Malice descended, avoiding Dun Raik and landing on the gravel in the circle. His boots crunched as plumes of dust surrounded him and dissipated. Hopefully, his attire wasn't too soiled.

The castle was the same as it had been two years ago. The white stone of the towers and parapets hardly yielded to time, the foundation likely as solid as it was centuries ago. Gold emphasized the cloisters at ground level, the corbels above those, and the machicolations below the towers, windows scattered everywhere.

Nothing was ever out of place. A profuse layer of dust still coated the empty shelves and crevasses of the doors, dulling the floors and gold accents around the foyer. He was sure the library would be the same. Despite the never-changing state of the castle, admiration flourished in his chest, butterflies dancing against his ribs. Except now, anxiety accompanied it. The clacking of his shoes on the jade floors didn't help, as it was one step closer to the great hall. One step closer to the rulers.

At the top of the third staircase, Malice sucked in a breath, let his shoulders drop for a relaxed disposition, and unclipped the obsidian crown from his belt, placing it on his head. He was sure he looked as stupid as he felt.

Exhaling, flexing his fingers and wrists, Malice strode into the Kings Summit.

All heads turned when he stopped halfway to the table. Shivers raked Malice's body like talons. He ignored the sensation and, instead, looked over the rulers. If not big, eyes were expectant, mouths gaped, a few heads were cocked, while Ko wore a scowl. Malice couldn't blame him. Their last encounter was rather sour. There was an empty seat between Valentine and Surin Raelle, probably for him.

Then he saw Magnus, and his heart spasmed. He was beautiful. From his rich brown, freckled skin to his lilac eyes to his pristine royal blue attire, Magnus was like dusk, where gold bathed the world. For a moment, Malice could forget everything. Could fool himself into believing he *was* here to attend as King of Hordes Region and truly take part in the summit, that everything over these past two years was a nightmare. Then Magnus looked away, misery darkening his gaze and shrinking his posture.

Malice's chest caved, but he tried to keep it from showing as he ignored the will of his limbs. He wouldn't run.

"How fares Hordes Region?" Caroline asked, breaking Malice away from Magnus. Her elegant attire fit her kind appearance; flowers embroidered her flowing dress of pastel green, gold decorated her long neck and high pointed ears, more flowers secured a section of pale blonde hair to the side of her head. There were slight lines at the corners of her soft eyes and around her mouth.

"Fine," Malice choked out, hoping his tone was normal. "Everything is nearing its completion."

"That is good to hear." She smiled and gestured to the empty seat. "Please, join us, Malice."

"I think not," Ko snipped. "At least Magnus waited till he came of age. But you wish to have a child sit amongst us? To act as our equal?" Drawn into a snarl, Ko bared his teeth, eyes gleaming, fists bunched on the table.

"Why not?" Basia, Queen of Zeldine's Region, shrugged, her arms crossed. "He's earned it." Her grin revealed the lowest parts of her tusks adorned with rings of silver and gold.

"I didn't come to sit and chat," Malice said before anyone else threw their opinion out in the open. "My region is not as stable as I'd like it."

"You're admitting to your ineptitude," Ko grumbled.

Temper spiking, Malice wanted to rub how close that wolf was to losing his throne and life to Vendetta in his face. He swallowed it. "I have spent the last two years cleaning my mother's mess. It's not something one can recover from easily. While my people and I are recuperating, I want independence from you." Malice's thoughts were suddenly swimming, his heart hammering in his ears.

"What?" someone said.

He went on, "I don't need obligations to you whilst worrying about whether my region will crumble."

He recognized the next ruler to speak. "You realize this opens you up for attack, don't you, lad?" Basia, her voice devoid of concern. "You're vulnerable."

"I killed the Claymore line," Malice nearly shouted, face flushed with heat that rolled into the rest of his body. "If you think I will not do the same to you, feel free to test your theory, but know I am not my mother." Through the fog and mayhem of his mind, Malice gathered enough wits to meet Basia's gaze and hold it. "I do not fear my neighbors. If it's a fight you want, it'll be a fight you get."

Intense brown eyes stared back at Malice. Basia's green skin contrasted with the dark fur hides dressing her muscular body. They were similar, as they both killed the prior ruler to get the throne. In Zeldine's Region, however, it was tradition and celebrated. Perhaps Malice could have commemorated the death of his mother. The people would have supported it. The thing was, no matter how good it felt to kill her, he'd lost too much to consider Vendetta's demise anything worth honoring.

Moments went by as silence lapsed. She laughed. Malice startled. It was a deep, hearty laugh, echoing off the walls of the great hall.

His head wasn't getting any clearer. Every time he looked in Magnus's direction, his chest constricted as if in a vise, and the room spun. He turned on his heel.

Voices called after him, but to stand there any longer meant he would break. He would break in front of the rulers. Right now, more than ever, he couldn't break. He'd spent so long filling in the fractures and still hadn't repaired them all. It hurt to see Magnus follow through with what he'd written in his letter. It hurt to realize Magnus would never come to know Kiran and Zephyrus and Annabeth and Eunice, as Malice had dreamed about for years. He was infuriated by how little his traveling to each region, slaughtering the last of Vendetta's followers, did. And the worry in some ruler's eyes was sickening. Anger he could withstand, sympathy, not so much.

The second his boot touched dry soil, Malice took to the sky where his responsibilities disappeared, and his mind dispelled the unease.

Tears ripped from his eyes as he flew over the lands. Forgetting wasn't an option, and neither was running away. He couldn't face it, so Malice decided as Hordes Region drew closer to let it seep into his marrow. At least then, if it resurfaced, these feelings would have to chip at the bone and that would take time. And if they did successfully find their way to every corner of Malice's being, he would completely break. Which was better than having fragments of his destroyed self he would meticulously have to put back together.

Difference
XLVIII

The Kings Summit, a place where rulers gathered to discuss the political state of their regions. Kiran read about it since Malice had never stayed long enough to tell him anything more than *it's boring. Trust me, you'd fall asleep.* When he was younger, he wanted to go simply because Malice was going. Now, as his advisor, Kiran almost felt he needed to go at least once. He would stand behind his king, jotting notes, perhaps whispering his opinions in Malice's ear, making a sly joke about a ruler, surely getting a snicker out of Malice.

Malice's bedchamber was neat, not a speck of dust to be seen. If Kiran were to run his fingers over every surface in the room, they would come back clean. Sitting on the edge of the bed, it was old or poorly made as the wood constantly creaked. The mattress wasn't much better with its lumps and bumps. An empty gold lamp sat on the short tables on either side of the frame. To Kiran's left, bookcases lined the wall, half of the shelves bare, the other half sorted with books he'd gifted Malice. A handful came from someone or somewhere else. As they got older, the size of the books grew. The thinnest stories, mostly fables and poems, were at the top, while newer, thick-spined books started on the middle shelf. Beyond the cases of mahogany brown, two chairs faced the open closet, the velvet cushions as orange as a pumpkin, furs draped over the back. A third of Malice's closet was designated to Kiran, and it had been that way since they were kids.

Eventually, when he had taken in enough of Malice's room, Kiran flopped backward, the bed screeching in protest as it always did. The clock on the desk ticked the silence away. It was evening, meaning Malice should have returned, seeing as how he flew to the summit. The carriage was a foolish idea, admittedly. Had Malice taken it, he would've been over a week late, missing both the summit and the Celebration of Peace three days afterward. Thinking about it now, Malice purposely waited until the last minute. Kiran sighed heavily. *I should have known.*

He lurched out of bed, strutted into the hallway, and headed downstairs. Since Malice took over, the windows were unbarred, the rugs changed, and flowers decorated the vast corridors. He had changed nothing else, yet it was enough to introduce a lightness to the castle, a breathability that was absent while Vendetta… was alive.

In the foyer, three royals burst through the doors, two on either side of a lolling, beaten third. Kiran rushed toward them, falling into their stride on the way to the infirmary.

"What happened?" he asked, noting the tears in the beaten royal's clothes, the bruises swelling his face, and the odd angle of his leg protruding from his pants.

"Took up his majesty's offer to spar," the one closest to Kiran said, a little breathless. "Got his ass handed to him."

"Mal—the king has returned?"

The royal eyed Kiran. "He returned hours ago, Advisor Kiran."

The eastern wing housed the infirmary and shared a wall with the ballroom underneath the staircase. Stepping into the sterile, white, well-lit space was blinding in a way. Beds were positioned against the walls, curtains on metal rods portioning each one, trays of medical supplies at the head. Most everyone had a royal lying or sitting injured, waiting for treatment.

Mother, skirts hoisted with leather straps over her shoulders, scurried from one patient to another at the furthest end, her assortment of bronze jewelry winking. Kiran directed the newest edition to one of four empty cots. He groaned, hissing back the pain as the other two gently laid him back. Tendai was closer, wearing a tunic and trousers of the same warm grey, a tanned apron tied around his waist, but he was preoccupied with suturing a stomach wound closed.

Kiran went to the tray adjacent to the royal's bed, grabbed the jar of milk of poppy, shook it, and unscrewed the eyedropper.

"Open your mouth," he said with a nod of his head. "For the pain."

Obediently, he opened his mouth for Kiran to administer the dropper full of milky liquid. It wouldn't take long for the pain to subside. Before it did: "Why is the king sparring so fiercely?"

Licking his lips and swallowing, the royal's eyelids relaxed. "Don't know," he said. "I guess the summit didn't go so well." An attempted laugh turned into a cough and brought tears to his eyes. He quickly settled himself, though, and sighed.

Anger. Kiran shifted around the bed toward the back, glancing at those laid up in beds, sleeping their injuries away. Sleep was the best remedy for magic recovery, allowing regeneration and healing to deal with the rest. In Hordes Kingdom, like most regions, however, if the wound was minor, doctors were taught not to use their magic as it was a waste of energy to heal something trivial.

Garments, sheets, cloths, and pillows stuffed cubicles. Shelves lined with jars, vials, and books divided them. Below it were drawers spanning the length of the back wall, storing needles, mallets, scalpels and more. Thanks to his parents, Kiran knew where everything was by heart, quickly gathering the supplies he needed, closing the drawers with his hip, and hurried back to the royal he brought in.

"What's your name?" Kiran asked as he ripped the man's pants and exposed bloodied bone poking out of his calf. He grimaced and looked at the royal.

"… Ash," he slurred, unfocused eyes blinking rapidly.

"Ash." Kiran grabbed the leather strip and held it in front of the royal's mouth. "Bite."

Leather in place, Kiran needed to reset the fracture, apply a salve, place the splint, then wrap it all up, and it was going to hurt like hell. He took occupancy at the foot of the bed, Ash's right leg beside Kiran's left knee. The break was a tricky one, but not bad enough to need an amputation.

"Need help?" Blodwen asked from somewhere behind him.

"Probably," Kiran said as he firmly gripped just below Ash's left kneecap.

Another group limped into the infirmary, bringing with them a fresh wave of iron and sweat, momentarily nulling the smell of herbs and ointments.

"I need you two to restrain him," Kiran told Ash's friends, gesturing with a jerk of his chin. They nodded, assumed their positions at Ash's sides, and anchored themselves, one arm wrapped around Ash's, the other pinning his shoulders down.

As Kiran steadied himself, a hand patted his back. He peeked, Tendai flashing a smile. With Father holding Ash's good leg down and two royals at Ash's head, Kiran pulled the lower leg, the bone slowly retreating beyond the skin. Ash jolted, skin pale and sweat soaked. Further Kiran guided the bone, Ash screamed and thrashed, throwing the shins alignment out of place.

Kiran, brows furrowed, waited for Ash to calm as much as possible, his aids giving reassuring nods. He'd repaired broken arms, but nothing as severe as this. A little voice whispered, *Hand it over to Father.* Kiran ignored it. He would never learn if he kept handing patients over when they got too tough. Once again, taking in a deep breath, he got into his prior stance, and began coaxing the fracture into the flesh, Ash struggling against the hold of two royals and his father, his screams filling the infirmary. Perspiration trickled down Kiran's forehead, slipped onto his cheek, followed the curve of his jaw and neck. He repressed a shiver. The tedious process required careful insertion into the correct position, else the leg wouldn't heal properly, and Ash would be stuck with a hobble for the rest of his life.

Tendai always described it as a suction and release, as if fitting two puzzle pieces or sliding a peg into the corresponding hole. Kiran maneuvered the lower leg with as much caution as a craftsman handling glass until he felt the slide and release of bone fitting to bone.

"Needle and thread," he said, snapping his fingers at the royal standing next to the tray.

"Yes, sir," they said, scrambling to get what Kiran asked for.

The moment they were in his hands, he sewed the puncture wound where the bone met the outside world. Ash's regeneration kept the bleeding at bay and once his leg was in a splint, daily healing sessions would mend the bone within a week.

Kiran released Ash, fell back onto the cot, and sighed. "Thank you."

"You did good, son," Tendai, alongside the royals, stepped away from Ash, whose breathing was haggard, body convulsing.

They smiled at one another, but there were more who required treatment, so Tendai didn't linger for long.

Resetting broken bones was the most time consuming: cleaning, salving, fitting a splint, and bandaging were the simple parts. Between the pain and poppy, Ash was affirmatively knocked out when Kiran finished. If he wasn't, he would've been dosed with a combination of valerian and chamomile.

Less than an hour since coming here, the infirmary was full despite a few having left while Kiran massaged a salve over Ash's injuries. All of it because of Malice. Supposedly. Kiran knew he had a temper. He had seen bits of it when Zephyrus was alive, and they'd sparred. More so when he'd trained with Odovacar. Since the Claymore's death, however, Kiran had seldom seen Malice go to the training grounds let alone actually train. He doubted Malice had let his anger get the better of him. There had to be another reason. And it better be good with all the damage he caused.

Hundreds surrounded the training grounds, voices loud the moment Kiran stepped out of the castle, which only grew in volume the closer he got. The evening sky was rapidly darkening, yet remained scorchingly hot and muggy. Grass swayed and rustled as Kiran marched through the plains.

He hated the training grounds. The noise, the stench, the pain, everything about it. When Malice and Zephyrus were here every day, it was tolerable, fun, even.

Racks of weapons at the edges of the beaten dirt kept the horde in an oval around the open center. Pushing into the mass of undulating bodies, Kiran was squished, pressed between one sweaty, stinky body and the next. The odor of onion and cumin burnt his nostrils. He tried to go faster, shoving at people who glared or snarled back at him. Realizing who he was, they either acted as if they had never seen him or dipped their heads in apology.

Kiran eventually broke beyond the front lines, and stumbled into the clearing, paused, and scurried backwards. The shouts were deafening. He could hardly make out his own thoughts. His clothes were damp with perspiration, most of it from dealing with Ash, clinging to his skin.

Malice was easy to spot with his head of white hair and his pale bare back facing Kiran. He was slightly hunched, daggers of darkness poised in his hands, scuffs of dirt tainting the purity of his skin. His trousers were the same midnight black as the ones he wore to the summit. He hadn't even changed. Standing off against him was Alkeim, whose olive-green skin glistened and Odovacar, his expression severe. Both had steel swords in hand. Neither preferred using magic unless they had to.

Kiran had wanted to step in and yank Malice elsewhere to talk some sense into him, but his legs were frozen in place. He didn't dare interrupt them, not when all three resembled starving predators staring down their meal. Each were heaving, Malice more so than the other two. It was clear Odovacar and Alkeim joined later, perhaps to let Malice tire himself out.

Odovacar moved first, a foot sliding across the gravel, the opposite following, sights trained on the king while Alkeim and Malice were as still as statues. Then Alkeim shifted, stalking toward Malice's flank. A sudden chill raked Kiran's spine as Malice shuffled to the right, a line of shiny ice leading back to Odovacar. It melted in an instant.

Malice sprinted for Alkeim. Kiran jolted. He was fast! Alkeim reeled and snarled, uncovering the fullness of his tusks. Malice swung left and right, ducked and swerved Alkeim's strikes. Odovacar was there in the blink of an eye, attacking Malice from behind. Malice dodged, and the blow connected with Alkeim's sword, sparks flying. Crouched, Malice swept Odovacar's feet from under him, sent him backward and took the chance to score a few slashes on Alkeim's legs, forcing his fall. Unlike Alkeim, Odovacar used the motion to flip himself, so he landed upright, a quick recovery.

Crimson dyed Alkeim's cream-colored pants and seeped into the dirt. Pain screwed his face as they regenerated, the slices in his pants showing pure skin where cuts had been seconds ago. Malice only needed a few heartbeats to put Odovacar on his back, earth spears fixing his shoulders and thighs to the ground, blood staining his garments. Odovacar knew his defeat and didn't fight against the restraints. It would only worsen the injuries and cause a significant amount of pain if he struggled, anyway.

"Concede," Malice hissed and held a blade of black at Alkeim's jugular.

Kiran's heart pounded violently. *Yield, Alkeim!* Now was not the time for Alkeim's retired knightly pride to come back to life.

Glaring, Alkeim said nothing for what felt like hours, the entire yard motionless. He averted his gaze. "I concede."

Relief made Kiran lightheaded for a moment. Faster, tension stiffened every muscle in his body as Malice turned to observe the crowd.

"Who's next?" he asked, arms held out at his sides, mockingly inviting the next adversary.

Eyes darting from person to person, Kiran hoped no one would take up the challenge. His parents would work well into the night, as was. They didn't need anything more on their plates. Seeing the pain and fear on the royal's faces curdled Kiran's stomach acid, introduced maggots to his veins writhing beneath the surface.

Kiran stepped into the circle, his shoes crunching the mix of dry soil and grit, and marched forward. Malice spun on his heels to meet his new opponent and immediately halted, daggers vanishing from his hardened grip.

"What are you doing?" Malice asked, the surprise shifting to annoyance as his brows furrowed. "Leave, this is no place for you."

"And it is for you?" Kiran shot back, stopping. He was close enough to see how the dirt sat in Malice pores, a subtle musk wafting from him. "Your place is to beat your own royals into the ground?"

"They could have said no."

"So you could demand it from them?" Sweat dripped down Malice's neck to his chest, streaking the dirt, his eyes blazing. Kiran refused to yield. "You're angry, I understand, but what did they do?"

"I'm not arguing with you," Malice said and made to step away when Kiran grabbed his arm.

"Well, I am!" he yelled, his head on fire. "First you reject company to the summit, and now this? I'm your advisor. I can help with whatever the issue is."

Malice ground his teeth, his jaw straining. "There is no problem." Yanking his arm from Kiran's grip, Malice put space between them.

Fury balled Kiran's fists, heat spreading to every fiber of his body. "You felt like pummeling a few poor royals. Was that it?"

Grounds quiet, heads craned to see the fuss at the center. Odovacar and Alkeim got to their feet—Kiran's interruption must have distracted Malice enough to release the magic restraining Odovacar— both standing awkwardly nearby. Kiran's blood boiled. They were looking at Malice as if he were an object to observe in a gallery. They were looking at Kiran as if he were crazy for touching said piece of fine art.

He and Malice hadn't had a conversation deeper than what to paint on the ceiling. Zephyrus died, and Malice wouldn't explain anything about what had happened between them or what had happened on his campaign. He tried to ask about Magnus, who Malice used to speak of so fondly, and said he wanted Kiran to meet Magnus repeatedly. Now, Malice hadn't so much as uttered a word about Magnus.

"Tell me, Malice," Kiran pleaded.

He'd been there all this time, watching Malice grow colder and colder, grow distant and unlike himself. It hurt, a wrenching within his ribcage, the ripping of organs from his abdomen.

"There," Malice squeezed his eyes, mouth a hard line, then lifted his gaze to Kiran's, "is nothing to tell. Get off the field."

A humorless grunt escaped Kiran as he shifted his weight and stepped back. He studied Malice for a time, searching for anything. Searching for his *brother*.

"I get it," Kiran finally said when his heart sank. "You came to show just how similar you are to your mother."

Malice's green orbs doubled in size as if he'd been shot with an arrow. The world turned sideways, and Kiran hit the dirt with a thud, pain blooming in his hip and cheek. Tears stung and blurred his vision, his cheek stinging worse. Dumbfounded, Kiran looked up at Malice, at his quivering bottom lip and knotted brow. Heartbeats went by, drawn-out, strained ones, till Malice rushed past Kiran. In a series of thumps, the crowd parted for the king. Silence descended.

Malice—he—he slapped me...

The Blood we Share
XLIX

Malice walked and walked and kept walking after the stars glinted, and the warmth of day finally receded.

He *hit* Kiran. *HIT* him. Of all people, Malice had never considered he'd be able to raise a hand against Kiran, but he had. Out of anger. Oh, the look; the expression of complete bafflement; Malice couldn't handle it, so he ran. How could he apologize? Could he apologize? Kiran had been there for Malice through thick and thin, had seen what Vendetta had been doing to him, watched as Vendetta's plans had ruined him, and had offered him a shoulder to cry on. Regardless of his hesitation, he accepted the role of advisor, so they could stay together.

Malice was frustrated. With himself and no one else. He didn't know what he wanted to say when he attended the summit, but what he had said wasn't it. Fear tore rationality from him, buried his ability to think or see clearly, and forced dribble from his lips so he could escape. So desperately had he wanted to leave, a need overwhelming all of his senses. He went to training grounds to relieve some of his frustration, aiming to spar with Eunice, Odovacar or Alkeim. He didn't expect the royals to approach him first. Not knowing how or when, what was meant to be a release turned into a one-sided competition Malice single-handedly won.

Malice stopped his ever-moving feet to wipe the tears from his face and look at where he ended up. Sulfur scented the air, wet soil and moss underlying it, a shimmering mass ahead of him. He was close to the Lake of Zephyrus. The day he named the body of water, he had simply written *Zephyrus* on a map, and that was that. It served as a constant reminder of the good times they shared and the mistakes Malice made afterward.

Estera's glowing silhouette sat on the horizon—specific light sources were too small to see at this distance. Malice went on, grass caressing his legs and torso, bugs chirping, comfortable warmth hugging his exposed chest and back. Fireflies danced lazily around him, their glowing bums reflected on the water's surface dotted with flowers. Malice practically tasted the mud and fish of the lake. It was too dark to see his mirrored self at the water's edge. He supposed he was thankful for it. He probably looked as miserable as he felt.

Kiran and Zephyrus had laughed endlessly the night Zephyrus turned thirteen, swimming out to the lake's center, coughing whenever they got a mouth full of water, throwing each other around in the shallows. Malice would go no deeper than his waist; he didn't know how to swim. Still didn't.

Malice bent down, unlaced his boots, and tugged them off, stuffing his socks inside. He set them near a cluster of milkweed. Grass cushioned his feet on the way to the bank, where he sank into the earth. The further he waded, the cooler the water became. He knew from watching Kiran and Zephyrus how quickly the shallows dropped off and let himself slip into the abyss. The fireflies were wiggling yellow dots above him, quickly dimming. Darkness swallowed him, the cold creeping to his bones.

The first release of breath came, and bubbles leaped to the surface. Malice found it oddly comforting. He couldn't see, hear, smell, or breathe, could only feel the water, the slight sway of his hair and pants, and the weightlessness of his body. When pressure built in his chest, he released another cluster of bubbles. Eventually, he had no air left to expel. That was fine. It was peaceful down here.

The pressure returned. Malice ignored it. Constriction spread beyond his chest, squeezing his shoulders a bit too tightly as his brain throbbed against the confines of his skull. He shook his head to dispel the feeling. Staying at the bottom of the Lake of Zephyrus was for the best.

Unable to keep his jaw clamped, he took in the water, earthiness coating his tongue, lungs filling. He spluttered and coughed, which only brought in more water. His arms and legs thrashed violently. *Stop,* he told them. *Let it happen.* They didn't listen.

Until cold tendrils snagged his feet like fingers belonging to corpses and he couldn't propel himself to the surface. Struggling against whatever trapped him, Malice's throat and chest were tearing, searing as more water entered his airway. Panic set in, and with it came a force so intense it hurt. Truly hurt like all the times Inyene drowned him in a basin of water. Darkness and specks of random disorienting color sparked the little vision he had.

Then dryness hit his hand like a wall. The surface. Had he been stuck at all? Malice pumped his straining limbs and his claws sank into the bank of mud as he hauled himself out of the water, hacking up lungfuls of it, choking on every breath he unconsciously tried to take.

He flung himself onto his back when he stopped coughing and sputtering, though he was winded and wheezing, his throat scratchy. The mud was uncomfortably wet and cold on his overheated skin, but he didn't have the energy to move. A shiver raked him, goose-bumping his flesh in a single wave. *That's one way to learn how to swim… albeit stupid.*

Constellations twinkling, Malice gradually settled and waited for his strength to revitalize his arms and legs. He wouldn't be returning to the kingdom tonight, so he would need it.

Morning came with its blinding light and intense heat, and Malice took to the sky. Snowy peaks cut the voluminous clouds in the north, a minor mountain range to the southwest in Cain's Region, a smaller one in Florence's. Forests were dark green clumps scattered across the continent like lily pads across a pond. He was flying leisurely, the wind gentle on his skin and refreshing.

When Malice neared the border of Zeldine's Region, he dipped lower, Bextierther's stone fortress coming into focus, but he was more interested in the section of cleared land with a single house outside the woods. As he descended, it dawned on him where he was and who lived in the cottage like a hammer to the head. Debris surrounded him for a moment, his wings whooshing as his feet settled into grass and wildflowers, the stench of swamps filling his nose—the smell was not dissimilar to that of the Lake of Zephyrus.

Draga's journals described Karlisle's and Nyx's home in great detail and wrote about their daily lives as if it were her only duty. The forest on the cottage's backside, stragglers to its sides, was a cluster of pine and cedar. Only slightly bigger than Kiran's, the house was old, wooden beams covered in moss, clay walls cracked at the foundation, its thatch roof as green as the weeds. No light emanated from the curtained windows on either side of the door, indicating a lack of life. Malice was half tempted to say this wasn't the same house Draga depicted and head back to the kingdom. Age and neglect were to blame for its poor condition, not Draga.

Away from any kingdom or stronghold, it was tranquil. Only the birds and bugs disturbed the quiet. Malice stayed put for a while, gathering the courage to go knock or leave. He'd only thought about his blood parents once or twice since learning about them. The curiosity was simply never there, was never an itch constantly distracting him. Nyx and Karlisle were a fact he accepted and didn't linger on. Partly because he didn't have the time to linger.

Would he rather face the sudden interest tickling his brain or face Kiran?

Greenery rustled as Malice approached the lone house and knocked on the rickety door. Though not too hard, it might fall off the hinges if he did. Silence greeted him at first, then cautious footfalls got closer to the entrance. He moved back a bit in case the door abruptly swung open.

The slab of wood creaked ajar, a sliver of a face peeking out. Malice's eyebrows rose as the door opened a hair more.

"You are?" Karlisle, Malice assumed, questioned.

"Malice Reap," he answered.

After a moment of consideration, Karlisle let the door swing inward, revealing his entire person. Malice's father resembled the current noble of Mondlesgrave with his inky black skin. His hair, however, was black as charcoal and his irises were as white as snow. He was gangly, his clothes ill fitted and stained. Malice couldn't tell if Karlisle's hair was usually unkempt or if the rat's nest on top of his head was due to poor hygiene. Based on the stubble masking his chin, upper lip, and cheeks, it was the latter.

Eyes narrowing, "What business does the king have with me?" he asked bitterly.

Malice caught a whiff of dust and something putrid like vomit from inside, nose crinkling. "I'm not sure," he said honestly.

"Vendetta's spawn are not welcomed here," Karlisle hissed.

"And your spawn? Are they not welcome?" Malice held his father's angry gaze, too tired to return the sentiment. Crying and nearly drowning took its toll on his energy.

Karlisle recoiled, brows furrowing, and his lip curled back in disgust. But then he stiffened, and his expression morphed into confusion, eyes searching Malice the whole time. Horror pulled his body taut, buckled his knees, and made him drop to the floor, surprising Malice.

"Berhane?" he shuddered, reaching for Malice with quaking hands. "My Berhane? My son?"

No man had ever called Malice *son*. It was a vile sound, centipedes crawling over his skin into his ears, chittering across his brain.

"I'm no more your son than I was Vendetta's," Malice said, his tone so poisonous Karlisle flinched, and his hands fell to his sides.

"Please." Karlisle fumbled to his feet. "Come in. I—I'll make us some tea."

Spinning inside, he left the door open for Malice. He stepped through the threshold, eyeing every inch of his blood parent's home. It was a mess. Clothes and toys littered the ground, dust particles floating in the air like miniature clouds. Dishes were piled in the kitchen to his right, where Karlisle was currently preparing tea. In front of him was a short hallway, two doors on either side, a third at the end. There was an abundance of things, yet it felt empty, like something was missing amid the clutter.

"Make yourself comfortable," Karlisle's voice snagged Malice's attention back to the kitchen. His father had a tray of treats, little porcelain bowls, and a teapot in hand when he placed it on the small table between the counter and the entrance. He gestured to the only other chair at the table.

Malice gingerly sat down while Karlisle poured them a cup of what looked and smelled like chamomile tea, steam swelling. Taking his own seat, Karlisle dropped four sugar cubes into his and swirled it, bringing the rim to his cracked lips for a long, savoring draught. With a deep exhale, he set the teacup down.

"Ask me anything," he implored, a controlled yet solemn excitement edging his voice.

If not for answers, why was Malice here? "Why did you abandon your nobility?" *Give me three years to become worthy of that throne.* Zephyrus's voice flooded Malice's ears, and his heart clenched. The three-year mark was rapidly approaching.

Hesitantly, Karlisle asked, "Is that what you are curious about?"

"Yvonne, the current noble of Mondlesgrave, banished the most profitable household ten years ago," Malice said, almost in a ramble. "Had she not been so insecure about her position, they'd be alive."

Genuine surprise widened Karlisle's eyes and parted his mouth. His fingers fiddled with his teacup's saucer. "As to not take on the burden, I fled."

White-hot anger robbed Malice of sight for a split second, hands tensing on his lap, nails digging into his thighs.

"Your mother, Nyx, had a similar opinion about the crown," Karlisle went on, seemingly oblivious to the change in Malice's demeanor. "But her father presented the choice to live normally. We met around four hundred years ago, traveled throughout Vinyamar." Grating on Malice's nerves, his father's voice softened, as did his expression when he glanced out of the window. "Eventually we returned to Hordes Region. The Claymore line had already taken over and replaced the Reaps."

"You did nothing?" Malice gritted out, staring at the golden liquid in his cup.

"Why would we?" Karlisle chuckled awkwardly. "The first generation of Claymores were not as ambitious nor as cruel as Vendetta. We felt the region was in capable hands."

Head spinning and pulsing as his veins went rigid, Malice blurted, "Tell me about Nyx." He couldn't listen to his father's drivel anymore.

A small fraction of him had hoped his blood parents were forced to give their kingdoms up. Instead, they did so *willingly*.

"Ah." Karlisle reclined and sank into himself. "I loved her as though she was life itself," Karlisle said, his voice quiet and brittle. "She was so much like her father, strong, tender, yet fierce. You would have gotten on well with her, Berhane—"

"She's dead." This was worse. Listening to the fondness in Karlisle's voice ripped at something deep inside Malice, tore the carefully placed plaster out of the cracks.

"… She… she is dead." His breath hitched. "She died giving birth to Juno, your little sister."

Malice's head shot up, gaze locking on Karlisle's. *I have other options to exercise.* Vendetta knew. She knew Nyx was pregnant. Nyx… *had* another child… while Malice was trapped.

"You." Malice's mind reeled. "You gave me up just to replace me?"

"What?" Karlisle jumped out of his chair. "No! Berhane, my sweet boy, no. Giving you up nearly killed us."

"You let them take me," Malice shot back. "You went on with your life, even had a daughter, as Vendetta tortured me." He rose, his breathing unsteady, as if his lungs were full of water again. As he shifted backward, he knocked the chair over with a clatter. Malice nearly tripped but caught himself.

"Tor—what do you mean, *tortured*?" Karlisle asked, his stance cautious, ready to do… something; Malice couldn't think straight anymore.

"What the hell do you think I mean?" he shouted. "Tortured! Every single day since I was four!"

Karlisle shook his head. "No," he uttered. "No. He said you'd have a better life. He promised."

"You'd believe a bird telling you it's safe to jump off a cliff because it had wings!" Into the living room, Malice tried to focus on anything else, on the worn, mahogany brown couch cushions. The hearth with freshly chopped wood stacked within. Dried bouquets tied to a string spanning the wall. The rug patterned with colorful geometric shapes underneath the furniture.

"Papa?" a high-pitched voice cut through everything, halting time.

Footsteps hurried toward the voice. "Juno," Karlisle said. "Did we wake you?"

Malice turned to see a little girl in Karlisle's arms, head resting on his shoulder, legs dangling. She mirrored the true self Malice saw when he died on the campaign—pressure returned to his chest, a trace of the misery when it was obliterated. Her braided hair was the color of the ocean at night, her skin a dull red, and her irises as vibrant as leaves in the spring. Her sclerae were orange and little knubs for horns protruded from her forehead.

"Who's that?" she asked and yawned as she rubbed her eyes.

Karlisle looked from Juno to Malice, then back to Juno. "He's," he started. "He is…"

"The king," Malice interjected. He could handle being her king, but he wasn't sure he could handle being her brother.

"Like grandfather?" She tilted her head to peer at Karlisle, who smiled warmly back at her.

"Like grandfather."

She said, "I'm hungry."

Malice turned on his heel and bolted outside. Karlisle called for him once before the sound became birdsong and screeching insects. He ran southward because he was good at it, had been running since he was a child. Back then, he could use his age and inexperience as an excuse to run, use his fear of Vendetta as a reason to hide. He had none of those things now. He ran anyhow and ran and ran.

He stopped in the middle of nowhere—the hills he died upon, he recognized. The land held remnants of what he had done to Vendetta's army. Earth pillars protruding out of the ground at random angles, and jagged lines like torn fabric of black from his darkness. Blood had been washed away long ago; there was still a subtle iron tang hanging in the air. Steel glinted in the grass, deserted weapons and armor too damaged for his warband to pillage. Despite the carnage that once ravaged these hills, a rabbit hopped carelessly through the flowers, ears twitching every time it came to a stop.

What am I doing? Malice knew Hordes Region like the back of his hand, yet he was lost.

Grass rustled behind him. He whipped around, a sword manifesting his hand. It vanished a heartbeat later. Hyacinthia stood there, hands clasped together, body wrapped in a dark cloak. The wind tugged at her silver hair and lured strands from her multitude of plaits.

"Do not put too much blame on Karlisle," she said to Malice's dismay. She'd stalked him? "Or Nyx. They did all they could."

He laughed because he couldn't help it. *They did all they could.* What a load of horseshit. Had they done all they could, Nyx would have carried on Hordes' legacy. "Did all they could to avoid raising me."

"They loved you, Malice," she said defensively. "To keep yours and their lives intact, they had no choice."

"Just as they had no choice but to stay here?" Malice countered. "Just like they had no choice but to give up their duties and never fight to get them back? Let me guess—"

"Enough, Malice."

"Vendetta imposed another child onto them because she knew I was a failure."

"They did what they thought right!" Hyacinthia shouted, throwing her hands to her sides, face scrunched.

"They were cowards!" Malice matched her tone, their voices resonating beyond the surrounding space. His skin was flushed as anger boiled beneath the surface and his chest rose and fell at the same rate his heart raced.

"They were cowards for abandoning their kingdoms and their child, and so are you. Face the truth." He had to. Time and time again, he had to accept how his own mother hated him to the point where she wanted him dead. Had to accept his blood parents bestowed Vendetta with their newborn in exchange for their peaceful little lives. He had to face the monster he had become, accept the corpses that built his throne, and live with the blood forever staining his hands.

The truth stared him down, no matter where he looked.

Hyacinthia visibly quaked, her jaw was tightly clamped, and her eyes were on the ground. "I know you blame us, that you hate us—"

"Hate," Malice repeated incredulously. "Do not flatter yourself with such kindness. What I feel for you cannot be put into words."

She slunk into herself, her rage defeated by grief and regret, agony sweeping her pride off the table and bringing a flood of tears Malice couldn't stand seeing.

She once said he was much like Hordes—Karlisle said the same about Nyx, but it couldn't have been further from the truth. If he knew what Karlisle and his daughter had done, he would be disgusted, and he would loathe their actions because Hordes was a better person, a better ruler, and a better parent than they ever were, than they ever could have been.

Point of Breaking or Repair
L

In the eastern wing of the first floor, across from the infirmary and ballroom, was the great chamber. Malice thought it was the same as the great hall where royals gained their promotion. Apparently not. The high-ceilinged room was smaller than the great hall, two bronze chandeliers shedding light over the long table at the center. The floors were surprisingly bright, the color of a sunset, while vertical lines of white swords and green vines decorated the walls. Whoever designed this room had not kept Vendetta's dark tastes in mind. Perhaps it was why Vendetta ignored the great chamber.

Empty vases sat in the corners and were spaced evenly along the walls, double doors leading to the corridor behind Malice at the head of the table. Thirty minutes had passed since the start of this so-called meeting. The five nobles of Hordes Region, with their elders and guards, sat with him alongside Eunice, Kiran, Odovacar, Nikanor and Alkeim. Odovacar had requested Nikanor take part in the meeting since he was so involved with Khuomouth. Malice wouldn't have minded whether there was a reason for him joining or not.

Alkeim was the only question. The orc, hair more grey than orange now, had gradually stepped back from the life of a first sword and royal. Malice only allowed him to sit in because of his experience serving the region.

Within the first ten minutes, Malice's presence was quickly disregarded. Conversation started at; *He's too young to be a monarch. How can a boy whose voice hasn't dropped be king? It's too much of a burden.* Then praise; *Look at all he's accomplished. He saved the region and established another kingdom in the span of two years!* Now; *Look at how he sits, so arrogant. Have you heard how he speaks? I'd never raise my children in such a way. He's too much like his mother.* Because comparing one to his mother was seen as the highest form of insult in Hordes Region. At one point, Malice would have agreed. But coming from these morons, it meant nothing. When it came from Kiran… the pain it brought had caught him by surprise.

He'd watched Eunice suppress a yawn five times. Although, for the sixth, she had to turn away, hand covering her mouth. Kiran had sat there, pen poised over his journal, ready to note down anything of significance. He'd yet to turn the page now full of doodles of plants and animals. The only three unaffected by the pointlessness of the conference were Odovacar, Nikanor, and Alkeim, having been used to the tediousness these councils created.

Malice, turning his head from the nobles, sighed and released every ounce of air his lungs held.

The voices ceased. When he glanced around the table, all eyes were on him.

"Have the squires finished their squabbling?" Regardless of his tone and choice of words, Malice was utterly serious.

Thutmose, Lord of Estera, scoffed, resting his hand on the table, palm flat. "You cannot speak to us in such a manner," he said. "Wait until you've reached our age, boy."

Sophronius had been the only one to converse quietly with his elder and guard. And he was the only one at the table who bowed their head after Thutmose's statement.

"Boy this, boy that." Malice further slouched as he rolled his eyes. "Have you any better insults?" Using his age against him was growing redundant and boring. "And wait till what? Till I've grown a beard and have my spawn running amuck?"

Thutmose nodded, mouth opening.

"I think you forget yourself," Malice cut him off. "Remind me of what you are."

"I am Lord of Estera," Thutmose answered proudly.

"Lord," Malice repeated. "Lord of a kingdom in which region, again?"

"… Hordes Region."

"Ah." Malice put his hand to his temple in an exaggerated display. "How could I forget? Now, one last thing—"

"Your point has been made clear," Lady Yvonne said, bitterness coating her voice.

"Who rules this region, hmm?" Malice ignored his aunt, despite having a basket full of things he would love to tell her as well.

Shoulders deflating, Thutmose's eyes fell to the table. "… You, your majesty."

"I am not below you or your equal because of my age," Malice said, a hardness in his voice making the nobles and their attendants sit straighter. "I am the King of Hordes Region. It would do you well to remember that in the future."

"Our apologies, your majesty," the noble of Bextierther said feebly, gaze averted. As Draga's journals wrote; Balios was cowardly.

Malice couldn't care less about apologies. He wanted to get on with this meeting, which should have ended within twenty minutes. He let them speak for pleasantries' sake, thought it would be nice to have a relaxed atmosphere rather than an overly somber one.

He sighed again. "We've lost the income from the slaves, weapons, poisons, and pits. Each of your kingdoms had revenue over one hundred and fifty years ago, prior to Vendetta's reign." The shelves and drawers of Vendetta and Draga's studies stored documents dating to the first of the Claymore line. For nearly four hundred years after Hordes' demise, the kingdoms prospered well, but, of course, it wasn't good enough for Vendetta.

Peeking over his shoulder, he motioned for Shevanti, who stood near the doors, to bring her tray of papers. She promptly handed out stacks to each noble and retook her place by the exit.

Malice tapped the parchment. "What is in front of you entails the history of your kingdom's greatest imports and exports. I want trading routes restored, partners made, and wares leaving this region as quickly as they come in."

Silence sank into the walls and floors, settling in the crevice of Malice's chest like lead, as everyone skimmed over the contents of their stacks. Besides the prior state of the economy, Malice wrote out a timeline for the nobles to adhere to, had listed old and potential trade cohorts, had also given an estimation of how much coin they'd have in three months' time if they did as they were told. All were stubborn— save for Sophronius—and used to being handed their wealth on a silver spoon in exchange for cooperation.

"You cannot expect us to accomplish so much in this short of a timeframe," Yvonne said, her wholly black orbs on him, brows furrowed, lip flared.

Her skin, mirroring Karlisle's, was as black as the ink on the papers in everyone's hands. Unlike Karlisle, Yvonne had long, silver hair, the braid resting on her shoulder and dipping below the table's edge. She was thin and bony, her cheekbones and the joints of her shoulders, elbows, and wrists coming to a point. Malice was surprised they didn't pierce skin. Scarlet painted her lips and nails, ruby's dangling from her ears and around her neck, matching her off the shoulder dress, deep green vines and leaves cascading to the dress's train.

Malice shifted his weight to one side and observed Yvonne with as much impassiveness as he could muster. And it wasn't a lot. "You did this to yourself."

"Excuse me?" Her snarl drew higher.

"Ten years ago, you exiled the most prominent household in Mondlesgrave." Zephyrus surged into his mind. Remembering the day he finally opened up to Malice in Mutuwa, wrenched his heart to the right side of his chest. "The Laska's were your biggest source of income, yet you destroyed their stronghold and banished them."

Yvonne reeled slightly. "They were threatening the kingdom. I had no choice!"

Kiran, surprising Malice, both hands on the table, hovered above his seat, shadows spilling over his expression. "You always have a choice. Why didn't you discuss—"

"The cow wasn't asked a question!" Yvonne snapped, her glare turning on Kiran. He reeled, utterly shocked.

"How dare you address my *advisor* with such disrespect!" Malice stood and his chair clattered backward. Blood thrummed so violently in his veins, he was sure Eunice could hear it, too. "Your choice or Vendetta's; it doesn't matter. You should be grateful I don't strip you of your nobility and banish you the way you banished them. For insulting my *brother*, you should be on your knees begging for forgiveness."

He refused to break eye contact with Yvonne. Had it not been for her selfishness, he and Zephyrus would have met as prince and noble. Their relationship would have formed a greater connection between Mondlesgrave and Hordes Kingdom. Together, they would never have let matters grow this concerning. Zephyrus, as a lesser noble, future head of his house, would have had a better standing to become king.

No. Had his *father* not been so goddamned spineless, Yvonne would've never become Lady of Mondlesgrave, and Zephyrus would still be alive.

A hand gripped his arm. Malice whipped toward Eunice. Their gazes locked on to each other. After a moment, he shook her off, sucked in a breath, and retrieved his chair, his body on fire. He threw himself down and glanced at Kiran. The beastman gave a wry smile, as if to say he was fine.

"The same can be said for all of you," Malice eventually gritted out. "For your incompetence and egotism, I can have you all replaced, and this region would be better off. Prove yourself worthy of the second chance I'm giving you."

Malice was sure a few, if not all, of them wanted nothing more than to curse him out right now, but they had some wisdom left in those hollow heads of theirs. Malice was no longer in the mood to facilitate their antics. He no longer had the patience for it, either.

"Leave," he said.

Chairs screeched across the floor as the nobles hurried out, their elders and guards on their heels. At least they somewhat knew when to keep their mouths shut and their heads down. Excluding one. Freya stayed behind a moment longer, staring at Malice, her expression distant yet contemplative. Her frown deepened. He couldn't read nor assume what the look had meant when she left with Heba at her side.

Malice's usual company remained, occupying the seats at his sides. Something about their presence irked him. Even Kiran's big eyes, brimming with concern, grated on Malice's nerves, nails shrieking down a chalkboard.

"I meant everyone," he snipped.

"What's wrong?" Eunice asked.

"What isn't wrong?"

Odovacar pushed his chair out and rose, Nikanor doing the same. "Your people are flourishing. Mother's influence will soon be forgotten," he said.

"My people are *flourishing* obliviously," Malice said. "This region is thriving more than ever since Hordes' rule, but never has the threat of it collapsing been so severe. Vendetta's influence won't disappear. She has engraved her ideology into the heart of the land." He wanted to stop talking, to swallow the anger and bury it, to never let it to the surface again.

"Three poor excuses for nobles belittled me, acted like toddlers whose toys were stolen instead of adults." Words poured from his mouth anyway, each one laced with the rage Malice had been desperately trying to keep contained. "They had become so used to laziness I have to force my hand. I have to use fear just like my mother. Somewhere along the line, I have to make up for the loss of ripping Hordes region most significant exports out."

"Malice," Kiran began.

"I am on a throne I never wanted because I killed my best friend." Malice was shouting at this point, chest buzzing as if bees were locked beyond his ribs. "The rulers view me as nothing more than a child to pity. My father is a coward if I have ever seen one and my mother is dead. Still, here I stand because the sun still rises every morning."

Out of breath, Malice wasn't looking at anyone in the room. His eyes were fixed on the wood of the table, thin cream lines where his nails ruined the grain. His vision suddenly blurred with tears, so he screwed his eyes shut.

It had only been two years since he killed Vendetta. He barely had the time to breathe, let alone absorb all that had happened. The expectations of the masses, of his nobles and royals, sat heavy on his shoulders. A weight impossible to escape. What made those expectations worse was there was nothing for Malice anymore. Nothing to make those expectations something he wanted to meet and carry. He'd come to the conclusion a while ago, but had refused to accept it. Odovacar was right. Hordes Region was doing fine, all things considered. Malice didn't want to admit he felt lost. That after spending every day fighting for his life, he didn't know what to do with himself anymore. What was his purpose now that Vendetta was gone?

Biting his lip, Malice lifted his head, righted his posture, and turned toward the exit. No one stopped him. No one pursued him as the doors slammed, and Malice was in the corridor.

"Odovacar"

Odovacar had constructed a training area in the southwest corner of the castle when he was an adolescent, a pavilion with a sword rack and sawdust on the ground. Simple and only meant for him. Everyone knew of it, however. It was not as if he could hide it, but no one dared tread here unless invited.

Eunice stood across from him, her cuirass dull, her boots muddied, and a well-maintained sword in her hands, the steel glinting. Her black hair was tied back, as was Odovacar's. They were anything but close, but he noticed her fuming anger, like the steam of a blade fresh out of a forge plunging into water. It was hard not to be curious about Malice's first sword. Odovacar had only observed her spars at the training grounds, never had the chance to experience her skill.

"He is lost," Odovacar said.

Eunice scowled. "I'm aware."

She shuffled forward, sword raised and brought it down as Odovacar swung his to meet the blow. Their blades rang, his arm tingling. For someone as small as her, she was strong. She attacked again, the steel a whistle from the right then left, both times Odovacar defended.

"It doesn't give him the right to take his vexations out on those around him," Eunice grunted as she deflected a feign and retreated a few steps. "I understand what he's been through. I do. But what right does that give him?"

Eunice twirled around Odovacar, scoring the low of his back, feet still moving when she faced him again, weapon ready. Odovacar clenched his jaw at the pain radiating from the slash, wetness soaking his shirt and trousers. It was superficial and regenerated quickly. He knew better than anyone what Malice was reeling from because he felt it, too. Which did not make Eunice any less right, it made him more biased.

Lunging, Odovacar swept his blade diagonally, catching Eunice's and drove her backward. Once, twice, thrice, he struck, and she countered, a rhythm of violence. In this moment, his heart did not speed as if to outrun a fox, and his blood did not pound against the confines of his veins. He'd grown used to danger. He'd relied on it. Missions only brought so much reprieve before anxiety settled in because the threat of his mother no longer loomed over him. He did not know how to live without fearing for his life.

"You did not know my mother," Odovacar said. Their swords slid together, sparks flew, and their shoulders slammed into each other. "Neither did I."

So close, he could see the ring of amber around Eunice's pupil, encased in the color of coffee. They flickered defiantly when she shoved him off with a grunt.

"I thought I did," he continued and turned defensive. "I had convinced myself she loved me. When she flogged me nearly to death, I wanted to believe she had left because she could not stand seeing me hurt." Anger, a sea storm inside his gut, swung his sword with enough power to sever a head. Eunice, one hand bracing the flat of her blade, took it head-on and dropped to her knees, pain scrunching her face.

"She was bored. She left me tied to a post because she was *bored*. It was then I stopped deluding myself, stopped pretending I knew the one who birthed me."

Eunice shifted, angling her sword to one side, forcing Odovacar's balance to falter with it. Freed, she sliced his calf and got to her feet, attacking him once more. Odovacar narrowly dodged, searing pain pulsing. Drops of red tainted the disturbed sawdust. Left, right, the sweep and whistle of her sword, the sudden impact of her fist to his solar plexus robbed him of breath as white sparked his vision. Refusing to relent, the beastman jabbed her pommel upward, clamping his jaw with a sickening clack, ears ringing, skull rattling.

Odovacar staggered backward as the metal tang of blood filled his mouth. He spat. Eunice's breathing was deeper, a slight sheen to her dark skin, the brown of wet soil, little coils of inky hair sticking to her forehead. He was winded and sweaty too, heart racing, focus trained on Malice's first sword. Odovacar had yet to put a scratch on her.

Disrupting the silence, Eunice said, "The danger you faced with Vendetta can't reach you. But the danger I present can."

They sparred into the evening hours when the sun turned the world to gold, the heat gradually cooling, the birds singing, and the salty spray of the sea rode the breeze.

"Malice chose well," Odovacar panted as he lay flat on the sawdust and Eunice leaned against one of the pavilion's support beams, swilling liquid from her waterskin.

"I was the only name he could remember," she remarked, a slight chuckle in her breathless words. "Aren't you angry with him?"

Odovacar lurched upright. "It is hard to be." Malice had given him a second chance. Because of it, he'd found love, realized he could laugh so hard he would start coughing, and slowly but surely, he was learning how to live.

"He has many faults," Odovacar admitted. "And he is no saint, but I know how it is to live without the purpose of survival."

Footfalls approaching, Eunice extended her hand. Odovacar took it, and he was standing.

"Be angry," he told Eunice. "What he is doing is of his own volition. He is not blameless."

Head shaking, a small smile on her lips, Eunice said, "Whenever you want a good spar, let me know." She turned and left, gone within seconds.

Nikanor replaced her in a matter of seconds, towel in hand. "Ready?" he asked.

Odovacar smiled at the one who taught him it was all right to love and to be happy, taught him *how* to do these things. "Yes."

Gods
LI

During the sleepless nights, if not staring at the mural Kiran painted on his bedchamber's ceiling, Malice found himself in the underground library of the Barren Circle. The place had a magnetic pull whenever Malice allowed his mind to wander. Nostalgia struck every time he glimpsed the book he stole, which started the spiraling of his thoughts. He ignored it for a while after meeting Karlisle months prior, ignored most everything outside his responsibilities as king. Since his outburst, he needed to do something, go somewhere, anywhere, that didn't remind him of his mother's castle.

Even now, sitting at his desk, claw tapping the leather-bound book of Archangels and Devils, Malice had to stop himself from leaving to seclude himself within the archive of history and the unknown. He'd read this book three times in all the years he had it, knew some pages by heart.

Malice sat back against his chair, the wood a bit chilled, and glanced at the clock. Hardly noon. Freya would join him for lunch to further discuss the future of Khuomouth. The other nobles of the region would join him throughout the week to report their progress. Alkeim wanted to go over the training regimens alongside Odovacar and Nikanor, Eunice most likely accompanying them. All the while, letters, statements, and requests would pile up on his desk about gods know what.

Malice glided the book to the edge of his desk. The library had to wait.

*

It had waited two months. Winter cooled the days and nights, leaving frost on the grass, and the new year was upon the land. His birthday had passed already. Malice was sixteen, not quite a boy, not quite a man. At least Kiran was right there with him at seventeen, both awkward ages when the weight of a region rested on someone's shoulders.

Today, there was nothing that couldn't be put off till tomorrow or the next day or the next week. Malice had every intention of taking advantage of it. First, he had to learn the limits of shadow travel. Room to room was one thing, easy both in execution and on his magical energy. From the highest, darkest point of the castle to the dungeons, was just as easy. The one time he'd traveled miles, it wasn't his magic at play, it was the voident's Lazarus. Whenever he had the time, Malice went further and further, sinking to Khuomouth, climbing into an alley at the edge of Hordes Kingdom, in the fringe of Kiran's Forest, Malice called it, to the closest kingdom.

The question was, could he get to the Barren Circle's underground library?

A part of shadow travel was knowing where you were and where you were going. Malice closed his eyes in his already pitch-black room. His smell—the freshness of clean linen, the sharp tang of ink and various herbs, eucalyptus underlying it in an attempt to mellow the strong scent of tonics—entered his lungs. The library was clear in his mind, the jade floors and pillars, the rows of wooden cases packed with books, the trinkets on the tables, the cavernous walls and ceiling, the cool air, the stairwell leading into the smaller, empty library of the castle above. He remembered everything; how he had practically claimed the third table from the door on the right side. Remembered the one time Magnus had sat with him—his chest tightened. Malice scowled at the surrounding void. Would he ever be able to think of Magnus and not feel miserable? They were friends who saw each other once a year, nothing more. Yet he acted as if he'd lost a piece of himself.

Clearing his mind, Malice stood, eyes closed once more, and stepped forward. Another step. He braced himself for the door he would surely slam into. Twenty paces his feet carried him, nothing in his path, nothing below him, nothing around him either. The sensation consuming his body was the same as it was at the bottom of the Lake of Zephyrus.

Then the heel of his boot hit marble and echoed—not marble, jade. Fire burst in his palm. Malice was in the archive. As he went to light the lamps, nothing was out of place. Maps of foreign lands were splayed across the tables, books and journals stacked on top of them. A wooden tube lay beside a collection of medical supplies, a stethoscope it was called, used to listen to another's heartbeat, so Malice had read. He'd thought about stealing the stethoscope and the other medical journals for Kiran. But he would ask questions and demand Malice return them to the library, anyway. He had also found designs for a thing called a 'piano,' a clunky-looking instrument with black and white keys that struck cords inside to create melodies.

With all the lamps bright, coloring the space auburn, giddiness welled in Malice's chest, rode his bloodstream so it reached the top of his head and tips of his toes. He smiled and felt like a kid again.

Up and down the aisles, plucking random books, scrolls, and journals from their place, Malice didn't care if they were in an alien language. He would decipher them. Didn't care if the pages were torn as he would put them back together or connect the information like connecting the stars in the night sky.

Setting his mountain of books on the third table from the entrance, the chair legs scraped the floor as he sat down and scanned the table. He slid a journal toward him. The inside was empty save for a stick of wood and graphite stuck in the centerfold. He scribbled on the page and the stick produced a squiggly line of dark grey. He opened the first book.

Twenty-four books were organized before Malice, each stack varying in size and tongue. So far, he'd found seven languages, one of which was his own. Five were composed of Vinyamar's common alphabet, except jumbled. Symbols and characters comprised two others, which were more outlandish. He had nowhere to start with them. The other five, he had a chance at deciphering.

Draga had given Malice prompts as a child, fictitious codes she said spies used to relay information with one another, a secret language. The key, she had said, was to find the similarities between their made-up tongue and Vinyamar's dialect. Years down the line, he hadn't the slightest clue as to why she had taught him that—he was an assassin, not a spymaster—but he was grateful.

From stack three, where the content was the most like his own tongue, Malice glided the top book toward him. In the journal to his left, he copied the title, seemingly four words. *The* was easy enough to figure out, so he wrote it below the third word. From there, he noted repeated letters, symbols echoing what he was familiar with, and compared them to the four books in the stack.

Gods of the continents. Once he got through a page, he had the entire alien script written next to him, a new journal below it so he could jot each word down and translate it. He was no scholar or linguist. Learning a new language—at least how to read it—was exciting all the same. One day, perhaps he would come to speak it as fluently as his own.

Time passed sweetly. Malice was completely absorbed in the book despite having gotten through very little. He reclined, head tilting toward the ceiling, an ache behind his eyes. He knew he wouldn't be able to do this often, but by the gods, did it feel good. For the world he'd grown so accustomed to disappear as he put his entire being into a task other than fighting or killing. Of all the things he'd suffered through during his childhood, Draga's lessons were the most tolerable and enjoyable at times, if he had forgotten Draga was in the room with him.

He pushed his chair out and stood, stretching his stiff limbs, joints popping and cracking like some old craftsman's. Now that he could shadow travel, be in the library within a few seconds instead of flying, Malice's nights were about to be occupied by the unknown hidden on the shelves. The wave of a hand snuffed out the candles and lamps, the smell of linseed oil and burnt wick spreading.

He strode into the wall, darkness reaching out to devour him, his shoes striking a nonexistent ground. It always disrupted his equilibrium and caused his stomach to twist for the first few heartbeats, then his nerves settled. When he reached his bedchamber, Malice flopped face first onto his bed, gathered the pillows and sheets to him as he toed his shoes off, and that was how he slept.

Till the nightmares forced him to light the lamp on the table. And when that wasn't enough, he downed one of the last bottles of nightshade he had. He needed to stop taking them so often. People were noticing the effects faster than Malice was. Without pain, it was difficult to tell when he'd drank too much as all he felt was blissful dreamless slumber and a lessened appetite the next day.

*

Earith is home to six gods, living on the six continents. It is said the land in which they reside is the land they created. Such is the way of folklore, hearsay over fact.

Ahrimeph is the youngest of the gods, born of humanity's ill deeds as warmongers, as deceivers and bastards, as cheaters and rapists. Relishing such negativity, Ahrimeph stole flames from the sun, and gave them to lesser beings so it may watch the fire incite more destruction. When given the tools, humanity has chosen violence first, peace always an afterthought.

Page two went on about the god Ahrimeph, who took precedence in a land called Guruhm. Malice couldn't refute the ease with which people fell into aggression and resulted in bloodshed. Not when he was the way he was.

He wondered if religion was as dead in foreign realms as it was in Vinyamar. Temples, churches, and cathedrals were nothing more than empty buildings for those without a roof. History books hinted the devotion to the god of life and death, the practice led by archangels before they went extinct some millennia ago. Malice assumed once they had, the worship of the god nearly vanished and had completely died with the founding ruler's generation. If it wasn't, what did those on Guruhm pray for if Ahrimeph was as hell bent on anarchy and devastation as it was? Mercy?

Another question arose: if the gods were so powerful, where were they?

*

In Strvey, Malice scribbled across the page in the low, warm light of the library, *the god of sea and rain is known as the bringer of life; what is life without water, after all? Hyhacdros' is much like the domain it controls, calm but easily enraged. Myth says Hyhacdros takes on a humanoid form to create storms strong enough to wipe mountains flat with a mighty swing of an axe or to summon endless rains, claiming land for its domain beneath the waves.*

Malice stopped there, staring at what he had written and the page he had read from. With the paper between his fingers, he flipped it back and forth. The handwriting was slightly different, as was the way of speech for Hyhacdros' section. It could very well be two people wrote the book together, or was passed from generation to generation. Something in the back of his mind told him otherwise. Closing the book, he set it across the table near the edge. He would find out if it were false by reading other sources. It was the only thing he could do unless Hyacinthia was willing to confirm the materials. Malice, however, didn't want to involve his grandmother, nor did he want to reveal the Barren Circle's second library. The archangels kept it hidden. Whoever had found it prior to Malice did as well, the reason clear. Information was dangerous in the hands of the ignorant and avaricious. Vendetta was the perfect example of that in Malice's mind.

Celebration
LII

"You should have a party," Kiran suggested.

They were walking around the castle's courtyard, enjoying the sun warming their cheeks and the breeze keeping the rest of them cool. Clouds floated northward, the trimmed shrubs and stout trees rustled as birds sang.

"What for?" Malice asked. He was barefoot, which was nothing unusual, a loose tunic waving against his frame, his black trousers doing the same.

"New year has passed," Kiran thought out loud. "Your sixteenth birthday has as well. It's been three years since you claimed the throne, two since your coronation. Those are all events worth celebrating."

Reasoning out there, Kiran expected a hard no. Malice didn't seem to be one for celebrations or much of anything. Except hauling himself away in the Barren Circle's library—it had been one of the few topics he had ever babbled about in their youth—or poisoning himself. Kiran knew it technically wasn't poisoning, not for him, but close to it.

"Why not?" Malice said with a shrug, putting his hands behind his back. "When?"

Kiran stared at Malice, slack-jawed, eyebrows high. With a quick shake of his head, he answered, "Two weeks should give everyone enough time."

Preparation would be extensive. When was the last the ballroom was used? Centuries ago? If Malice wasn't one for parties, Vendetta doubtlessly hated them. Musicians would have to be found, food and drink selected, outfits picked out or made, invitations sent, and the list went on.

"Two weeks it is," Malice said.

The celebration would be open to all within the city, the gates would bar no one. Ravens had been sent to the kingdoms, invitations for the nobles sealed with black wax and signed by Malice. Food would be light, sweetmeats, cut fruits and cheeses, honey cakes and tarts, served with various wines. The ballroom, thanks to the castle's servants, was spotless, bare and gloomy but clean, nonetheless.

Before he knew it, the night of the party came.

Kiran was given a room of his own in the castle, as his parents were, soon after Malice became king. The bedchamber on the third floor was as big as his cottage was. High vaulted ceilings stared down at him, a reflective bronze chandelier at its center providing ample light. His bed, low to the marble floor, sat at the heart of the room. Opposite the door was his desk. Above that, hanging on the wall, were his diagrams of animals and plants. Further down were his books, a chaise beside the shelves, so he could lounge and read. Behind his bed, curtains obscuring the mattress, was his closet.

He stared at his collection of garments hanging on the rod stretching the length of the wardrobe, shoes below, a good pile on the floor from him searching for the perfect outfit. He much preferred picking Malice's clothes than his own. Eventually, Kiran settled on the newest pieces of apparel. Although, most of what he had gone through was new because of his growth spurts over the last few years.

Dragging his clothes to his bed, Kiran stripped out of his daily robes, embroidered with colorful patterns, and changed.

Once he was finished, he strutted to the full-length mirror next to his vanity near the door, the mahogany fur rug silencing his knee-high boots. He wore a sage green slim-sleeved top, gold winding a serpent down his torso, a wide sash around his waist, his pants the color of a forest. Over the top of everything, his white tulle drape, sweeping the floor, should be enough to keep the chill from his bones.

As the advisor to the king, he needed to look the part. He snatched the thin copper chains hanging from the oak jewelry display and wrapped them around his horns. The chains fit along the grooves nicely, giving them a slight shimmer. In his nose was a slender hoop, a dainty chain extending to his earlobe. At eighteen, Mother said he would receive a thin bronze rod between his eyebrows, above the bridge of his nose. Blodwen would also wear bronze tonight, a tradition for witch doctors to show experience and age.

Kiran checked himself over one last time, smoothing the already smooth fabric of his shirt, fixing his sash, and brushing his hair back to uncover his pale-marked forehead. Now he needed to collect Malice from the fourth floor and trek down to the ballroom.

Knuckles gently rapping the door, Kiran waited till the hinges squeaked and Malice stood in front of him. The gold painting his cheeks, eyelids and lips caught Kiran's attention first as it brought the sharpness of his serpent-green eyes to life. Dangling from his ear was the blue tear-drop earring Magnus gifted him. Alongside it, in each ear, were the obsidian earrings Kiran gave him. The tooth of the onyimyth Malice hunted, dyed black, hung around his neck, a thick cord wrapping around it. Two years his hair had grown, which allowed Malice—Shevanti, actually—to braid one side of his head, his crown of blossoms resting atop his brow.

Malice smiled, held his hands out, and leisurely spun, giving Kiran the full view of his outfit. "What do you think?"

Kiran swallowed the lump forming in his throat. "I picked it out knowing you would look good," he said and meant it.

Despite the fairness of his skin, dark colors had always given Malice an intimidating yet regal aura—an air of power. Tonight, he wore no ill-fitting garments. Kiran made sure of it. Capping his shoulders were crow feathers, veiling the ground he treaded on, the vest underneath wine purple, edged with gold to match his painted face. Laces crossed the sides of his trousers and the front of his boots, while rings decorated his long fingers.

Pride swelled in Kiran's chest, a smile tugging at the corners of his mouth. Not only for his brilliant choice of outfit, but for the considerable lack of pungent smelling medicine leaking out of Malice's bedchamber and the cleared pace on his desk where vials once were. He bowed slightly. "Shall we go?"

"Wait!" a voice shouted from behind Malice.

They both whipped around when Shevanti emerged from beyond the door and attached something to Malice's chest with a click.

"Now you may go," she said with a satisfied huff and nod.

Malice turned. She'd pinned a sword through a horned skull brooch to his chest, an incomplete Hordes Region's sigil. They listened, though, and hurried into the corridor and down the stairwell.

Activity was already loud, music overlaying the echoing voices, feet clambering the floor. Food and wine, a sweet yet pungent smell, grew stronger the closer they got to the first floor.

People crowded the foyer and flowed into the courtyard. Kiran supposed the enormous ballroom wasn't big enough to fit thousands of bodies. Thrice as many people as expected had gathered to celebrate all the reasons Kiran had listed off to Malice two weeks ago. His birth and coronation, and the dethroning of Vendetta.

Entering the throng of people, the tang of sweat hit Kiran's nose, but what else had he expected when there was dancing and alcohol present? Together, arms linked, Malice and Kiran made their way into the ballroom where the melody of laments originated, and the tables of food never emptied.

Malice stopped, forcing Kiran to halt as well, and said, "Have fun." With that, Malice detached himself and vanished.

Awkwardly, Kiran briefly stood there, blinking after Malice. He'd never attended a party because there had been no parties to attend. What was he supposed to do without Malice? Immediately, he banished the thought. Malice was king. He needed to interact with his subjects and needed to have fun himself. Kiran was glad his mood had lightened since the summit. He was approachable again.

He, too, needed to interact with the people as Malice's advisor. Gingerly walking through the crowd, Kiran listened for any conversation he could insert himself into. A horse gave birth to twins, someone tattled on about, a rarity indeed. Good omen, they said as well. The harvest would be plentiful this year, another babbled. A cheating husband brought home another woman's babe—Kiran skirted away from that conversation. Business compared to Hordes Kingdom and the cities, which depended on what was being sold and to whom. How beautiful the waters were during winter, explained someone from Ryzion or Mondlesgrave, probably. Perhaps Estera with the Lake of Zephyrus at its edge.

Gossip. Kiran had little interest in idle chit-chat or economic affairs because he had helped get them in order. When he reached the back table of wine and food, he snatched a sweetmeat, the sugariness rich and the pastry center flaky. Then grabbed a silver goblet of wine to wash it down, the tartness perfectly combating the sweetmeat. He chose the refreshments well, if he said so himself.

This close to the stage, the music reverberated through his body. And it was warm, with as many bodies stuffed in the ballroom as there were.

"Never been to a party, Advisor Kiran?"

He spun to meet the curious gaze of a girl as she partook in the feast, picking, he assumed, her favorite treats to fill her plate. Her long, auburn hair was partially up, braids on the sides of her head twisting to create a bun, a hairpin of rubies made to look like butterflies holding it in place. Rose red painted her lips, burgundy sharpening the corners of her golden-brown eyes. Her floor-length dress was simple, high-collared, butterflies climbing her sides and down her sleeves.

Kiran shook his head. "I haven't. Have you?"

She giggled. "Of course not. Unless you consider a drunken fest at the tavern a party." She looked at him, and he averted his gaze.

Hesitantly, he peeked at her again, trying to figure out why she seemed familiar. "What do you do for a living?" he asked.

"Make sure the shelves and portraits don't get too dusty, Advisor Kiran," she said with a sly smile.

She's a maid. He must've seen her around in the hallways. "Are you enjoying yourself?"

She shrugged, and, once her plate was full, turned toward the crowded ballroom. "The food is good, so I suppose I am."

Satisfaction settled heavily on his shoulders to hear someone else delight in the fare he'd chosen. "I didn't catch your name," he realized.

"I never gave it." That sly grin again, only this time, powdered sugar smudged her scarlet lips.

"Since you already know mine, will you give me yours?" Strangers knowing his name was unusual. Kiran felt he would never get used to it.

"Rosalina," she said.

Kiran sucked in a breath. It was a beautiful name for a beautiful girl. His cheeks flushed. *By the gods, am I glad she can't read my mind.*

"Tell me, Advisor—"

"Just Kiran is fine," he interrupted, speaking a bit too fast. His blush spread to the rest of his face.

"Kiran," she amended, "how did you become his majesty's advisor? You hardly look old enough for the position."

He wasn't, truth be told, nor was he qualified, but he accepted the offer because his heart needed to learn what had truly happened with Zephyrus. There was more to the Laska's death than what Malice was willing to tell. Neither could Kiran say no to Malice's begging.

"I've known the king since he was four and I was five."

"He has a soft spot for you?" Rosalina inquired, bringing another sweet to her mouth.

"… I suppose you're not wrong." Heart sinking, Kiran eyes fell to the black marble floor ribboned with gold. Changing the topic; "Are you originally from Hordes?" It was a joyous night. Why ruin it with the negativity of the past? Malice was improving, the region prospering. When he was ready to talk, Kiran would learn about Zephyrus then.

"Born in Cain's, actually," she answered and offered her plate to Kiran, who gratefully took a cube of hard cheese. "Migrated here when I was a toddler."

"And," Kiran said, "how old are you?"

"Seventeen." Rosalina's eyes sliced to him, making him jolt. "Didn't your mother ever teach you it's rude to ask a woman's age?"

"Ruder still to guess," Kiran countered. "Did I offend you?"

Chuckling softly; "No."

He sighed as a smile crept onto his face.

"Care to dance?" she asked, her voice low and velvety.

"Me?" Kiran blinked at her. "Dance? I've never danced a day in my life."

"Neither have I. We'll learn together."

Faster than a heartbeat, her plate was on the table. She had stepped forward, turned, and was reaching for Kiran's hands. He let her drag him to the center of the ballroom where duos, trios, and groups were dancing. Smiles were bright, faces were red, the music was loud, yet the laughter was louder. Candles and lamps burned fiercely throughout the space and in the three chandeliers above.

Together, they bumped into other party goers, stepped on each other's toes, and twisted and swirled, one hand on her waist, her hand around his neck, the others clasped. Rosalina's copper skin glowed, her eyes alight when they were open—her smile often squinted them. He was dancing with a stranger on a night meant to celebrate his brother and king. Yet, everything but her diminished as if it never existed, as if this ballroom was theirs, as if the castle itself belonged to them.

Eventually, the night growing shorter as his feet grew sorer, they made their way back to the tables of wine, indulged a few cups, and talked with a lightheartedness that made Kiran's head float. Or perhaps it was the wine. No matter, he hadn't felt this good in years. For tonight, he could forget about the past and he did so blissfully.

*

Too many to count had shoved a goblet of wine in Malice's hands. He refused numerous, but he couldn't refuse them all. Now, his entire body was fuzzy, the world and ground spinning in opposite directions, warmth tickling every inch of his skin. He'd gotten drunk during the campaign too, felt exactly like this. It was pleasantly and strangely uncomfortable.

He had enough sense to make out the room, his vantage from a table close to the dancing horde at the ballroom's center. Though, if he didn't focus, it was like putting a puzzle together. He had watched Kiran and a girl dance clumsily before retreating to the wine. Eunice and Helle, wearing matching flowing dresses of cream white and pearls, also danced. Only they knew how. Hand in hand, they were slow and absorbed in one another. Which was very similar to how Blodwen and Tendai had danced earlier in the night. Age changed them, their skin and hair not as vibrant. Blodwen wore bronze bracelets, earrings, and necklaces—a display of her status as a witch doctor—shimmering against her pale spotted skin. Tendai's outfit was simpler, a light blue boubou robe, the front patterned with peach-colored diamonds.

Malice spotted Shevanti's emerald skin in the shadows behind the curtains of the stage, the flute player laughing beside her. Shifting his gaze toward the doors, Odovacar and Nikanor, arms linked, walked into the foyer and out of Malice's sight. Alkeim and his wife and daughter had made a brief appearance. Elder Priscilla was enjoying herself and her title to the fullest. Behind him in the corner, five young men tended to her every whim, it seemed. He cringed and deliberately did not look in that direction again.

"My king!" a voice shouted, startling Malice upright in his seat. A beastman with the lower half of a jaguar approached, two goblets in hand, both dripping purple liquid. "Another toast to uh… well, to you!"

"I can't," Malice shook his head. "I might retch if I have another." His stomach was so full, he seriously might.

"Come now." The beastman thrust the goblet into Malice's hands. "What's a party without a few drunks?" He bellowed out a laugh.

"I do believe he said no." A black hand reached down from over Malice's head and stole the goblet out of his hands. "I think you ought to leave."

Unsteady eyes narrowed on the man behind Malice, when his hands shot up, spilling more of his second drink. "All right. Heard loud 'n' clear, your majesty. Majesty's shadow," he said with two wobbly dips of his head and stalked away.

Malice's heart pounded, surprisingly drowning out the music and chatter. He didn't want to look, so he closed his eyes, a presence removing itself from his backside, shifting around the chair, and sitting across from him.

"Malice," Karlisle said softly, tenderly. "Please look at me."

Begrudgingly, Malice opened his eyes. Partially because if he didn't, he would fall asleep.

"We need to talk." Concern poised his father's eyebrows and glimmered in those stark white irises.

Malice gestured lazily to the table. "Then let us talk."

Knowledge is Power
LIII

Peace was difficult to get used to. Chaos, fear, anxiety; one learned to accept and live with such things rather quickly. Eunice had. Learned to ignore the constant budding and blooming of dread in her stomach. Five years of peace had steadily squandered the terror.

Being the only set of feet on the stairwell, Eunice's boots clumped to the fourth floor as servants and royals greeted her on the platforms. The early morning rush had passed. Noon would be in an hour, meaning Malice was in his bedchamber. He'd started visiting the Barren Circle three years ago after he learned he could shadow travel the distance and found the best use of his nights was there.

Eunice couldn't complain about his nightly routine. Why would she? Whatever was in the Barren Circle had given Malice an escape, making her life and everyone else's that much better. He was alive again, ambitious, content.

Knocking, she entered Malice's bedchamber. Candles lit and scented the room with wax and rosemary, the slight musk of sweat and tangy herbs mixed in. Every time she entered, she couldn't help but look up at Kiran's mural. Trees gathered near the opposite end of the ceiling, an abundance of flowers in the foreground, the sky shifting from evening to night in an array of reds, oranges, pinks and blues.

Clouds were pale yellow and voluminous, as if Kiran plucked them from the sky. On the other side, Eunice found the constellation of Heracles from Fae myth amongst others.

When her sights finally dropped, Malice's hands were beneath his chest, feet off the floor, the muscles in his back flexed and damp. Sweat dripped from the tip of his nose. Both impressed and confused, she half wondered how he could remain statuesque and quiet, the ticking clock being the only sound disrupting the solace. If it were her, she would grow annoyed with the sounds of her own wheezing and grunting.

Then he pushed himself up with one arm, tucking the right behind his back, feet in the air.

"I've come to share some information, my liege," Eunice said at last and pulled the seat away from his desk to sit.

"Share it," he breathed out, his voice low and raspy. It had dropped significantly in these past two years. At times, it startled her.

"Scouts from the northern border returned last night," she said. "Karlisle and Juno are fine, house still stands."

One of the most wicked storms she'd ever seen wreaked havoc on Hordes Region nearly two weeks past. Lightning struck trees, created brief wildfires, and left the land blackened. Winds tore roofs from homes, flung saplings like rag dolls, capsized boats, and so on. There were a few times she thought the thunder was an earthquake.

Eunice, picking the dirt from underneath her nails, went on, "There's a new resident on the small stretch of border between Dun Raik and Bextierther, though." Malice switched arms, exhaling. "The royals investigated and found a tent as large as your bedchamber, teeming with gold, jewels, and other trinkets."

"A thief?" Malice asked.

"Thieves are smart enough to run," Eunice remarked. "They said the tent belonged to a woman, an elf from a foreign land."

Bringing his legs down, Malice turned and grabbed the towel from his bed, wiped himself off, and threw on a shirt. "Which land?"

"Didn't say."

"And the royals knew what was in her tent?"

"They detoured and delayed their return."

"Leave their punishment to Odovacar," Malice said, motioning his black-clawed hand dismissively. "He's too strict to leave them be."

She raised a brow. "You're implying you'll be doing something else."

"This elf," he said. The bed creaked under his weight, screeched even louder when he leaned backward to support himself with his arms in an arrogant, relaxed position. "Hails from a *foreign* land. I want to know where. She has wealth. I want to know why and how. Perhaps she stole, and if she did, I want to know who she stole it from."

If she were a thief in Hordes, Malice would have to arrest her and restore the stolen goods or compensate the victims. "You also want to know, if she's none or all of those things, why she's here," Eunice assumed.

He nodded. "We'll head out this evening."

"We?"

"Not curious?"

She was, but it would take over a week to reach the border. And she would be damned if they flew. Malice taking her from the ledge in Khuomouth flooded her senses and she shuddered. "How do we get there?"

"By the shadows. It's the easiest and quickest."

That sounded worse.

"It doesn't hurt."

She wasn't worried about pain. "Fine. How long will we be gone?"

"A few hours at most," he said.

Surprised; "That's it?"

Malice smiled. "It'll take seconds to reach the northern border, not days. Talking won't take long either."

Dubiously, she stared at Malice, and sighed a defeated noise, knowing his way was for the best. "This evening then."

After dinner, Eunice knocked on Malice's door and entered the dark room. Light from the hallway illuminated the king sitting on his bed, legs crossed, before he rose. He wore a shirt of deep, brooding green, the high collar and sides laced, his black leather pants were as well. Eunice suddenly felt underdressed in her loose cream tunic tucked into brown trousers, her sword belted to her hip. She ignored the feeling; it was not as if they were meeting anyone of importance.

Malice extended his hand. "Close the door," he said.

The door clicked shut, but she didn't take his hand. "Why do I need to hold your hand?" It was pitch dark now, a void where only sound, smell, and touch were present.

"You'll fall or stumble," he said matter-of-factly. "Whether you do or don't, we need to be connected."

She clasped his chilly hand as he drew her closer, tucking her arm under his. Which wasn't hard now that he was over a head taller than her. His breathing was inaudible; Eunice felt the expansion and deflation of his chest instead.

"Walk," he mumbled, as if the darkness needed quiet.

In unison, they stepped forward. If they kept walking, they would crash into the wall. She tensed. There was no wall when the floor fell out from under her feet. Gasping, she clutched onto Malice's arm, heels striking solid something. Every pace brought the sensation of falling in your dream, only to jerk awake in the middle of the night. It was disorienting, Eunice couldn't grasp the concept, her mind and body battling for domination. *We're falling*, her brain said. *We're walking*, her feet argued. Sailing would've been better. At least she would've gained her sea legs. And with flying, she imagined the view would be worth clinging to Malice for dear life.

Malice's arm was the only thing aside from her own person Eunice was certain of. Blackness overwhelmed everything else, as if suspended in the water at the bottom of a chasm.

Then a wall of sulfur and pine hit her, evening light blinding, as true solid ground supported her weight again. She breathed it in, let the chill of the north wash over her. The sunset bathed the world in a vibrancy only artists could capture. Releasing Malice's arm, she turned toward the rolling hills behind her, flowers and trees dotting the land.

They had emerged from the shadow of a tree, hence the pine smell. In front of them lay forests of it, oak, cedar, and spruce scattered within. They were at the border, Bextierther's stone city south of them, a battlement with pin pricks of orange in the distance. Dun Raik was northwest, an ominous wall of black, growing blacker still as daylight receded. Closer—no more than a hundred meters out—and brighter was a glowing pitched canvas.

This far north, snow turned the dirt into mud and mostly white mounds were few and far between, the sun having melted winter's touch. Their shoes smacked against the sludge. Eunice's did anyhow. Malice was silent because of the thin layer of magic underneath his boots. Bugs clicked, birds whistled, a howl, too far to discern species, echoed, and the breeze rustled foliage.

She'd never been so close to Dun Raik or Zeldine's Region. When Malice went north to eradicate Vendetta's followers, he'd brought Odovacar, allowing Eunice to care for Helle while she was ill. If Hordes Region's winter could make her skin goosebump, she wondered how cold it was in Jared's or Wolfgang's.

Two horses with black coats and white underbellies grazed near the tent, a cart peeking around the backside. The closer they got, the more perfume scented the air, a rich, sweet fragrance. Eunice's nostrils flared. She was partial to Helle, who almost always smelled of lemongrass.

Inside was still, no shadows on the canvas, and quiet. Malice approached the flaps, back straight, Eunice a few paces behind.

"Enter," called a voice before either of them said anything.

Malice glanced at Eunice. She shrugged, and he lifted the flap, Eunice walking in first, then Malice. The royals were right. The inside of the tent reminded her of an extravagantly decorated bedchamber, brimming with junk to make the space feel plush. Gold shimmered wherever Eunice looked. Animal hides littered the ground and adorned the walls.

"What brings you here, your majesty?" a woman said as she tucked her long, raven black hair behind her pointed ear. Her accented voice was silky and alluring. Her eyelids were painted with a smoky darkness and her lips were blood red, opposing her ghostly complexion. Slicing from Malice to Eunice and back to Malice, her amethyst eyes glimmered.

Eunice didn't like the dark elf's expression, a look of hunger as if she found the perfect meal.

"I have reports of your lavishly decorated shelter," Malice spoke smoothly, matching the elf's tone.

"You believe me a thief?" she questioned, hand darting to her heart, expression appalled.

"Are you?"

"I bought what you see with coin I earned," she said. "You've no thief in your presence tonight, sweet king."

Eunice cringed as she rolled her shoulders. Sweet was not how she would describe Malice. Even on a good day. She didn't think he had ever been sweet, never had a chance to be.

"But," Malice trailed his hand up the tent's center collum, his nails catching the silk wound around it, "I have a foreigner in my region."

The elf shifted on her round bed, blankets spilling off the edges, pillows galore stuffed behind her, so she was fully supported. "I am a Gurhend."

Gurhend? Since when had dark elves called themselves that? Perhaps she was from Mani Bay in Maziar's Region or an islander.

"From the land of snow, Guruhm," Malice muttered, sights fixed as if he were a fox, and the elf were a rabbit, lips slightly parted. "You speak Vinmarian well."

She chuckled. "I speak many tongues, sweet king."

"Tell us about Guruhm," he said.

Eunice glanced between the two, still comprehending Malice knew of alien lands. Was that what he had been doing in the Barren Circle, learning about faraway realms most had never heard of? If he knew for certain they existed, would he have reacted in such a way? Still, if other realms were out there, far beyond the shores and cliffs of Vinyamar, what did Malice want with them? Whatever he wanted, he needed relevant information on other continents and their civilizations. Why else would they be here, speaking to a foreign elf?

A ringed finger waved back and forth. "I don't think so.

Knowledge is a powerful thing."

Eunice moved forward. "You dare put a price on your information? In the presence of a king?"

"He is no king of mine, little knight."

Little? Eunice clenched her jaw, hand reaching for her sword.

"Name it," Malice said, motioning for Eunice to stop.

"Your body."

Eunice jerked forward, but Malice's arm held her in place. "One night," he said.

"Till I am satisfied," she corrected, an unimpressed brow raised.

"As I said." He put his arm down and shot a glare at Eunice. "One night."

Eunice returned his glare. This was outrageous. To sell his body for information, which could very well be a lie. And then to be so confident on top of it all!

The elf's smoky eyes narrowed as she licked her full lips. "Let us hope that is not arrogance speaking," she said and gestured to the table near the foot of her bed. "Sit. I have much to tell."

More like ignorance and blind optimism. Malice had bedded no one if the trail of weeping suitors told her anything.

Before Malice sat, Eunice grabbed his arm and tugged him down. "Do you understand what you've gotten yourself into?" she whispered.

He whispered back, "I'll find out."

None too happily, she took her seat across from Malice at the quaint oak table.

Quinci Genkov, the dark elf revealed her name, spoke of all the continents she knew. Six in total, starting with her motherland. Guruhm was a cold, harsh continent, nothing but snow and ice as far as the eye could see. The people were set in their ways, embracing tradition rather than advancing their technologies.

Strvey, the land of deserts, after hearing Quinci's explanation, was much like Yeager's Region as Guruhm was like Wolfgang's. Forli was next, the land of mountain pillars where people lived at the peaks and chieftains ruled villages. Similar to how Vinyamar was prior to the war of species six hundred years ago. Ehime was said to be the birthplace of the extinct high elves, ancestors of elves, and dark elves. The realm's soil was rich and forgiving. Lastly, the land of mountains and valleys, Ragar. All four seasons were mild; it snowed lightly in winter, rained often in the spring, the sun warmed everything it touched in the summer, and the leaves changed colors in autumn. People dedicated songs to animals, to the earth, and to loved ones, the harmonies reproducing the qualities of the object. Quinci had smiled when she told of how a young man tried to woo her with a song centuries ago.

These continents mirrored the regions both in climate and culture. Was Vinyamar humanity's motherland? If someone confirmed Eunice's thoughts, she would believe it. Although, it was just as easy to believe other civilizations had found and settled on Vinyamar, creating its diversity. The biggest question raking Eunice's brain was what Malice wanted with this information. Was it purely for curiosity's sake after reading whatever the Barren Circle offered? Or was there something his twisted mind was devising?

"Each land has a god, sweet king," Quinci said as she reclined further into her heap of pillows.

Fascinating as her wealth of knowledge was, Eunice was a bit surprised she'd told them as much as she had. She must be expecting one hell of a night.

"Guruhm has Ahrimeph, god of war and destruction. Legend says the gods' wrath is to blame for Guruhm's harsh environment." Quinci drew a blanket over her legs when a shiver raked her body. "Shanvati resides in Ehime and is said to still provide bountiful harvests. On Forli, the god of love and fertility, Tushuni took the ability to bear children safely from immortals out of spite." Darkness spilled over her expression, thinned her mouth, and furrowed her brows.

She continued, "I have heard the god of sea and rain, Hyhacdros, revoked its blessing, thus turning Strvey into sand; a realm forever tormented by the blazing sun. The god of earth and wind Asaselil was enraged by humanity and created the mountains and valleys of Ragar." She shrugged, seemingly not entirely believing her words.

When Eunice peeked at Malice, his arms were crossed, his face deadpan. Eunice couldn't tell if he thought she was lying or was wholly invested in her tales. For someone who grew up with an open book like Kiran, one would think Malice would have adopted some of those qualities.

"Finally—"

"Coatliris," Malice interrupted. "The god of life and death here in Vinyamar."

Quinci, quirking a suspicious eyebrow, nodded. "You are well-informed?"

"I like to read."

Silence followed, Malice lost in thought, Quinci taking a moment to wet her throat, Eunice absorbing what had been shared. There were other lands. And they knew of Vinyamar, yet Vinyamar knew not of them. Eunice's mind went to the darkest side of humanity, the one she was familiar in dealing with. If any of the continents invaded, Vinyamar would be a sitting duck, clueless and defenseless until it was too late. How have they remained a secret? How long had

Malice known and chosen not to share anything about continents? She understood his reluctance to spread information about other continents without confirming their existence first.

They know about us… Why haven't they done anything? Eunice knew without an unequivocal doubt there were few like Quinci throughout the regions. People questioned things. They ventured beyond the known. They conquered and raided, ruled and fell. It was humanity's nature, as it was to evolve and persevere. Something kept them from coming to Vinyamar, but what and why? Was that what Malice wanted to find out?

"Eunice," Malice said, green eyes on her, bringing her back into reality. Quinci was looking at her too, keenly. "You should leave."

"What?" She blinked at him.

"Unless you want to watch us fuck."

She stood immediately. "That I don't, but how do you suppose I return home if you plan to stay here?"

"Take one of my horses," Quinci commented, which earned her a scowl.

Riding back to the kingdom was better than waiting for Malice to finish fucking his new friend. Or shadow traveling. "I didn't bring any coin." She needed to stop at a town to rest and get supplies for the week-long journey to Hordes Kingdom and doubted any villager would give her a second look without payment. There was, slight as it may be, hesitance about taking a horse she wouldn't be able to return.

"Does it appear I need coin?" Quinci asked, one hand pointing to her insufferable amount of gold.

"Be thankful your information was enough to keep you from the end of my sword." Eunice's tolerance for the elf's attitude was thinning by the second.

"Be thankful," Quinci returned with a devilish grin, "your king's cock was enough to buy said information."

Eunice jerked her head toward Malice. *And this is who you want to bed?* He stared for a moment, then nodded toward the exit, his face saying *I made a deal.* Scoffing, Eunice turned and stomped out of the tent.

Too Late to Understand
LIV

Horse hooves stamping through mud progressively faded into the night, and Malice was left with Quinci. He knew everything she spoke of; he was glad to have confirmed the books in the circle though. Despite the many inconsistencies in the handwriting, what he'd read was true, and that was what mattered.

"Let me tell you something with your little guard gone." Quinci slithered to the end of the bed, her silk robe trailing behind her. "Coatliris differs from the rest, sweet king. It craves death more than life and it will destroy till nothing remains."

Coatliris was the biggest mystery, and, conversely, the most known out of all the gods. Folklore depicted the mighty god of life and death throughout Vinyamar, and some regions still prayed to Coatliris. Interpreting what was truth from lie was the tricky part, and so far, Quinci was his only source of accurate, relevant information outside those books. They took time to read and decipher. Symbol-based languages were still utterly cryptic to Malice.

Choosing to ignore Coatliris to give his racing mind a break, Malice said, "Sweet? I believe I am anything but."

A smirk curved her mouth when she swung her legs over the edge and extended her hand toward Malice. "Have you not seen yourself?"

Malice stood and took her hand. She tugged him closer, so his shins almost brushed the mattress. "I don't make a habit out of ogling myself."

Her hands felt his torso, drove the fabric up, and slid back down. "You, sweet king, are gorgeous. From your waist—" That was where her hands landed and squeezed, revealing his slim figure. "To your legs and the plains of your chest. Your face could make the fairest of maidens' weep of envy, the brutish of warriors' swoon." Rising, Quinci's fingers worked to unlace the sides of his blouse, then carefully pull it over his head.

"With the purest of hair, cruelest of eyes, you have yet the fullest of lips, sweet king. Blind to them as you might be, you have suitors lining themselves up for the slightest of glimpses."

Head tilted, Quinci kissed him, her eyes closed, her red painted lips sticky against his. Of course, he knew of his suitors. His rejections sent as many home with tears as he had with curses under their breath. Right now, however, he needed to focus on Quinci. She would be entirely disappointed to know Malice had never thought of or brought anyone into his bed. Kissing or pleasing himself never crossed his mind, either. Platonically speaking, the only one who he had ever slept with was Kiran when they were children. Sexually, Malice knew the concept.

She deepened their kiss, her tongue slipping inside Malice's mouth. He had to stop himself from moving away, the sensation making his skin crawl. While she continued tugging laces from the eyelets on his pants, Malice copied her and untied the silk cord, keeping her robe closed. It slipped open, uncovering full, heavy breasts tipped with rosy pink. She was curvy, thighs squishing from the way she stood, belly soft and striped, with marks paler than her insipid complexion. When his pants were finally undone, they fell to the floor and Malice stepped out of them, thankful to have a reason to separate himself from Quinci.

Him straightening his posture became an invitation for her to wrap her hand around his exposed cock, bring it to her lips, and envelop him. He watched the deliberate rhythmic bobbing of her head, the swelling of her cheek as she moved him around as if a different angle would allow for a better taste. Subtle heat, the warmth of a winter day, bubbled to the surface, a dull ache in his veins.

One hand gripped his thigh, and the other tucked a strand of inky hair behind her low-pointed ear. Quinci's pace increased for a few short bursts. Withdrawn, she wiped her mouth with the back of her hand, looked up at Malice, and frowned.

"I see I am not to your liking," she said, gliding backward onto the bed until she was resting on her mountain of pillows, arms supported, knees bent to keep herself hidden. "Tonight, sweet king, is not about you, now is it?" Her low and seductive voice might've worked on another as her legs spread leisurely, enticingly.

Only the fur blankets rustled as Malice crawled onto the mattress, the smell of jasmine thick in the air, flames in the lamps shifting every so often. His stomach lay flat as he wrapped his arms around her legs and kissed the dark hair of her inguen. Further down he went, thinking both of Tendai's and Blodwen's anatomical lessons, and what she had done to him. The slightest hitch of her breath reached his ears.

Malice licked and teased and sucked, her clitoris stiff and throbbing, her juices and his saliva mixing into one. Moans gradually infused the tent, soft and matching his movements, then intense and drawn-out. He focused on it, forcing his thoughts to be glued to what he was doing and Quinci. Accidentally scraping his teeth against her made her spasm and her legs tremble in his grip. Releasing one of her legs, Malice broke his nails and circled her entrance, a finger slipping in.

Quinci jerked her pelvis, a small movement, and moaned. Her hips sped up, her hands bunched the bedsheets as Malice continued pestering her with his tongue and added another finger. Drool dribbled down his chin, soaking the blankets. Her fluids and sweat overwhelmed his nose with the tang of arousal.

She grunted a phrase in what Malice assumed was her native tongue. Voice cut into breathy gasps, her hips stopped thrusting, and her legs quivered, body twitching.

Malice dragged his tongue along her clit one last time, sending a wave of shivers through her, and put her leg down.

"How many have you brought into your bed?" she panted, her chest rising and falling rapidly, her pale skin flushed.

"None," Malice said. Perhaps, he realized, he should have said it a bit more abashedly.

"You," she eyed him suspiciously, "are a virgin?"

"Yes."

"Liar."

"I'm a quick study," he said.

She stayed quiet until her sights fell to Malice's nether regions. "Have you no one to fancy? To lust for?"

Malice followed her gaze and sighed. "I thought I was here to pleasure you, not for you to pleasure me."

"What am I to do with that?" She gestured toward his placidness. His brows furrowed. "Go on, sweet king, touch yourself. Surely, you've done—you haven't pleasured yourself, have you?" she gasped.

No, but he was about to. "Not a word," he said, disregarding her snarky little grin.

He sat back on his knees and leaned into his right arm. The hair above his groin was as white as the ones on top of his head, and everywhere else, for that matter. He glided his hand across his torso, his fingers following the curve of his cock, when he grasped it softly and started stroking. He had never done this, had never felt the urge or want to. If anything, he was more clueless about pleasuring himself than he was about pleasuring another.

Blodwen and Tendai had given a lecture about sex after Kiran mentioned his interest in a few girls around the castle. Kiran's entire body had flushed, his head buried in his hands, mumbling regrets to himself. Malice, on the other hand, had listened half-heartedly. He didn't think it applied to him if he hadn't seen anyone the way Kiran had.

Eyes closed, he continued to stroke, yet nothing came to mind. No one appeared behind his eyelids. The tent was silent, awkwardly so. He let out a breath and quickened his pace, hoping stimulation would be enough to end things soon. He felt himself stiffen somewhat, but there was no excitement.

"Think," Quinci said, disrupting the quiet, "about the one you love, sweet king."

Letting his head fall back, Malice didn't love anyone in that way. He was probably incapable of such feelings if his cock had anything to prove.

I could teach you if you want, a familiar voice suggested, a tickle in Malice's ears. His hand slowed. The voice was deep and smooth like honey. He'd last heard it a year ago, addressing the crowd during the Games of Retribution. It'd been seven years since Malice last talked face-to-face with him. *Go on, Malice, faster.* He'd never said that to him, but his hand listened, the muscles in his arm tensing all over again.

I know the feelings you have, and they're wrong. On both ends. Malice's eyes flung open, head lurching upright. Everything, his breathing, too, had stopped. In his hand, his cock was hard, hot, veins twitching. Horror washed over him like thousands of wriggling maggots. Was this what Magnus meant? Malice had been and was attracted to him? *On both ends.* And he had been attracted to Malice?

"Everyone has an object of affection," Quinci mused, not noticing the strife within Malice. "Even you, sweet king."

She prowled toward him. Closer, her breath tickled his stomach and chest as she moved her lips to Malice's ear. She lifted herself to her knees and straddled Malice's lap. He looked into her eyes, saw the desire burning brightly, and averted his gaze, sick to his stomach.

Quinci reached behind her, her breasts in his face, and, grabbing Malice's cock, sank down until their skin touched and she let out a breath. Heat instantly rushed through Malice, a wave from a smoldering forge. He scowled to himself while Quinci started moving, her hips rotating and bouncing simultaneously, her breasts following the cadence, wet skin slapping.

Grinding his teeth, Malice pushed Magnus out of his mind. Mere glimpses of Magnus shouldn't be enough to get him primed, nor should his voice—a tone his imagination created no less. After so long, it didn't make sense. Yet, his mind had other intentions. Closing his eyes meant Magnus painted his eyelids, his dark, freckled skin, his brick red hair and lilac eyes, his muscular body straining the buttons of his shirts. The noises pouring out of Quinci's mouth were misconstrued in Malice's ears, her high-pitched, mellifluous voice replaced by Magnus's soothingly low and angelic one.

Malice grabbed Quinci, arm supporting her back, and laid her down as he shifted his feet out from underneath him. Gliding back in, he thrust at the pace they'd left off on. Consistent, lazily increasing in speed. Hands on her knees, Malice could see all of her and so perfectly could he picture Magnus. He admitted what he felt as a child differed than what he felt toward Zephyrus or Kiran, the ones he saw as brothers, their connection not the same. It was warmer, frantic, the wild bursts of excitement at the thought of him, the way he dreamed of a future where they were always together, the distance between their realms gone. How no one compared to the beauty that robbed him of intelligence.

Oh gods.

He wanted Magnus.

He wanted to be in Magnus's presence again, listen to the rambles only meant for him. He wanted to lose himself in Magnus's soft, down-turned eyes, and attempt to count his freckles. Hear Magnus's voice infect him like poison, taint his head, and ruin his senses. Feel Magnus's touch, small insignificant contacts leaving traces of life on his skin. Anything he'd ever wanted was nothing compared to how much he craved Magnus. He tasted Magnus in Quinci's sweat as he kissed her stomach, all the way to her perked nipples and flushed neck. Felt her moans vibrate her chest and could imagine it was Magnus, the vibrations more intense, the escape of a low growl as Malice thrust faster. Moisture clumped and curled Quinci's midnight hair to her forehead, temples, cheeks and sides of her neck; Magnus's would curl and darken, too. Her nails dug into his back while foreign words slipped from her smudged lips.

Suddenly, ripping Malice from the madness, Quinci squeaked, pain pinching her expression.

"Your nails," she panted.

He'd changed positions. When? Her legs were around him, and his hands gripped her hips, her lower back elevated.

One hand at a time, "Sorry," he broke his long nails.

Back to himself, heat clung to him as if summer had made itself at home in Quinci's tent. Droplets slid down his abdomen, tickling his overstimulated skin, making him quiver. He didn't need a mirror to know he was as red as Quinci right now. Pleasure snaked through him, rushed beneath his flesh whenever her insides spasmed.

Malice, Magnus said, appearing beside Quinci in a blurry afterimage. In the next moment, he disappeared. *Go ahead.* A hand caressed his face, Magnus pressing against his spine.

Quinci's mouth gaped, body trembling, her voice gone. Instead, Malice's raspy breaths turned into groans, filling the void she had left. Heat pulsed violently, his mind growing fuzzy. He slid out, let himself experience every twitch and jerk of his orgasm till only embers remained.

Breathless, sweaty, and reeling, neither moved for a time. Malice was revolted with himself. He bedded someone with a man he couldn't have, obscuring his thoughts.

Malice was the first to move, crawling to the foot of the bed, and shook out his pile of clothes.

"Piece of advice from an old woman." The sheets rustled as Quinci sat up. "Learn to give into your desires more often," she said tenderly, her voice a bit hoarse. "How long do you plan to deny what you want? How far will you destroy yourself? How much will you drown in your regrets?"

"Got all that from fucking me, huh?" Malice chuckled humorlessly, feeling exposed and foolish, and stood, struggling to yank his leather pants over his damp skin.

"Your majesty—"

"Regret," Malice cut her off, "is not something I was taught. That was a bold piece of advice from the likes of you." If she wanted to pry deeper, she was not the only one who could twist the knife.

"Must you rub salt in my wounds?"

"Must you?"

She laughed grimly, an echo of Malice.

Malice left the laces of his attire be. They were too much of a fuss. "Tell me something."

"You've earned a bit more, I suppose," she said.

"The gods." He turned to face her. "Anything else I should know about them?"

She considered him, a certain invigorated look to her. "They have visages, messengers, warriors; in Guruhm they're called—"

"Voidents," he interrupted, a smile curving the corners of his mouth. "Thank you, Quinci."

"The more often they appear, the closer genocide becomes," she added.

He froze, recalling the first time he'd eaten at the dining hall with his kin. Yoon Woo had mentioned something about disappearances, of which had annoyed Draga. At the time, it was seen as irrelevant, but was it truly? Without a response, bending to grab his shoes, Malice headed toward the tent's exit.

"Should you ever feel lonely, sweet king," she said solemnly. "Come find me."

If I'm lonely, I'd much prefer to indulge in Magnus. He knew better than to believe said dream would ever come true. He knew better yet not to say it out loud. Quinci was a beautiful woman. Heartbroken and lonesome. After her tale of the man who serenaded her, Malice guessed he died before Quinci ran to Vinyamar. Or perhaps he had an affair. Either way, filling the hole in her heart was proving more difficult than filling her bed for a night.

The cool night air bit his skin like frost biting the grass. Clouds drifted in front of the half-moon. Serenity embraced Malice but was quickly dispelled by the truth: Magnus had been right all those years ago and Malice simply hadn't known. Yet again, maybe the feeling was different, a puppy love. Six continents lie between the seas. The gods lived. And Malice was no longer a virgin.

Devil's Release
LV

Malice walked through the night to cool himself down and by dawn, he stood at Karlisle's front door. Frost glinted on the browned grass and the ridges of frozen dirt. Birdsong never ceased, a symphony of rattles from wrens, melancholy whistles from blackbirds, and the chirps of sparrows. The cold muted the smell of wet soil and swamp, leaving the refreshing scent of pine.

Karlisle's cottage had been repaired, the roof no longer in shambles, the doors newly stained, the clay walls a pale orange. He supposed a thanks to the storm that passed a few weeks ago was in order. Light painted the kitchen's curtained window. Malice knocked. Footsteps approached, the knob squeaked, and the door opened.

"I don't suppose you have any wine?" Malice asked quietly. Juno was probably asleep.

Dazed, Karlisle glanced behind him and shook his head. "At five in the morning?"

"Tea?"

He nodded. "I'm brewing some now."

Malice had come more often since the celebration. Karlisle was at the furthest edge of his life, someone he could share as much or as little as he'd like without repercussions. Karlisle refusing to acknowledge their first meeting, or the past made it easier.

The small table against the wall below the window hadn't changed. It was always meant for two people. First Nyx and Karlisle, Karlisle and Juno, and now, though rarely, Malice and Karlisle. A plum tablecloth ran down its center, trimmed with frilly laces. Two cedar chairs sat across from one another, Malice occupying the one closest to the door, a cloak on both back rests. The floor was cleared, the rug in the living room was actually visible, and the sink was usable. Instead of dust and molding food, it smelled of burnt timber and honeysuckle.

Karlisle carefully set the tray of tea on the table and passed Malice his cup. It was tan clay rather than porcelain. The storm must've broken the previous set. Steam floated upward as Karlisle poured rooibos tea, a naturally sweeter drink, a tad nutty and earthy. Karlisle added a spoonful of honey to his cup.

"You look like him, you know," he said, voice soft as he brought his tea to his lips.

How many others would comment on his looks today? "Like whom?"

"Hordes. His brother took after your great-grandfather, while Hordes took after your great-grandmother." The cup clinked on the saucer. "Or so Hyacinthia told me."

"Save for the white hair and pale skin?" Malice questioned, eyebrow peaked.

Karlisle chuckled, "Aside from your white hair and pale skin, yes." Still lighthearted, finger twisting the silver band on his left hand, he asked, "Why ask for wine so early?"

To Malice, it wasn't early. He hadn't slept in… when was the last he slept? Whether he had or not, coming to the revelations he had just hours before, he felt a drink would be nice. "A celebration for an insignificant victory."

"What kind of victory is insignificant?"

"I confirmed the validity of my source of information," Malice said. Karlisle's forehead wrinkled. "How many in your generation know about the continents and the gods?"

Rigidity took over, his black eyes going wide. Karlisle swallowed his surprise, and his shoulders slumped. "Only a handful. Most who had known no longer live. In Hordes generation more knew, but during those times, the clans were far too focused on themselves." He shifted uncomfortably and went on, "When the war of species ended, the attention moved toward healing. Vinmarians remained too absorbed to rediscover lost knowledge."

Known but not cared about. "What of the gods?"

"Gods were always folktales, bedtime stories, legends and myths," Karlisle said. "Religion is obsolete and has been for millennia. When archangels roamed the lands, gods were actively worshipped, and faith was prized above all else."

How true was it? Evidence of religion lay throughout the continent, chapels, temples, and holy scripts, the biggest being the castle in the Barren Circle. Myth had it the castle belonged to archangels tens of thousands of years ago who prayed to their god; Coatliris, Malice imagined. If it was so outdated, why were these places of belief as unsullied by time and nature as they were? Strongholds from the war of species were in worse condition, crumbling heaps of vine and moss infested stone. The books in the archive depicted the god's genocide as abrupt, a plague where all were dead within a day, villages slaughtered under the veil of night, untamable wildfires so humanity might feel an ounce of the god's rage. Perhaps it *had* happened, which explained all the out-of-place trinkets down there.

Excluding the last mass genocide, Malice had the feeling it was tedious, archangels dying an agonizing, forlorn death beneath unsuspecting eyes. And if that was the case, the last archangel died centuries past, not a millennium. One might have escaped the odds, spending their time wandering as the last of their race. So, where were they?

Malice dropped his head into his hand, slipped his fingers through his hair, and looked out of the window, the sky blue and cloudy. *How to find the truth and who to get it from.*

"Malice?"

Thoughts disrupted, Malice turned toward the short hallway leading to the bathroom and bedrooms. Juno, sleepily rubbing her eyes, stood at the cusp of the kitchen. Her night gown was crinkled, her deep ocean blue hair a snarled rat's nest. Malice felt bad for Karlisle. He was the one who had to brush it out. Yawning, Juno shuffled closer, tapped Malice's leg and waited until he scooted away from the table to climb into his lap. One arm wrapped around his neck, so she'd stay put.

When Malice looked at Karlisle, he got up and headed into the kitchen, a smirk on his face. He grabbed a whicker bowl of bread slices and hurried back to the table. Juno immediately reached for one and chomped away, crumbs falling onto Malice's lap. She was as messy as Kiran was at her age.

"I can use dark magic now," she said in between bites.

"That so," Malice said, grateful to give his mind a break.

She nodded. "Only a little." With big, sparkling eyes, she asked, "Want to see?"

"Why not."

Stuffing the rest of her bread into her mouth, chewing, and swallowing, Juno lifted her hands like there was water in her palms. Darkness flickered, an ember of it floating away. Her brows knotted and more black flowed from her hands like fire smoke, shifting and contorting. The semblance of a rabbit formed and a fox chasing it around in ascending circles.

Malice's breath caught. He understood Magnus's reaction back when they were children. The awe was so unlike when witnessing his own magic. Her darkness dimmed the space at the table. He checked to make sure Karlisle didn't curtain the window; he didn't. Tendrils followed the rabbit and fox, residuals shooting from the fox's bushy tail. In an exasperated huff, Juno could do no more and released her little show.

Before her hands fell to her lap, Malice scooped them up, fueling her magic with his. The rabbit ran as the fox gave way to the hunt over the table, fled past Karlisle, swerved the counter, ducked under the faucet, climbed the ceiling's rafters, and jumped on the couch cushions. Eventually, the fox of night caught the inky rabbit beside the teapot on the table. It all vanished in a plume of black.

Juno smiled, baring all her teeth and gums, eyes nearly closed. "Again!" she exclaimed and raised her hands higher.

So Malice did. This time, they were fish of all sizes swimming through the cottage, mirroring the ones he often watched in Mutuwa. He created a pack of howlers stalking a deer, making Juno jump when they pounced. An onyimyth skittered across the table, took to the— Juno winced.

Blackness crept from her nails to the first knuckle of each finger. It was consuming her? Whatever magic in the room died. Malice gripped her hands and swiped his thumbs over her fingers. He didn't know how or why, but he absorbed the darkness, and watched her hands revert, the nails their dull red color again. Everything was motionless and silent for a while. Malice stared at the back of her hands. Glad whatever he did worked, it shouldn't have happened to begin with. He fueled her energy, taking all the strain off her magical core.

Was his magic different from hers?

Malice slowly lifted his gaze. "Never let her use her magic to that extent," he told Karlisle. "Always watch her." Malice couldn't be here all the time to make sure she didn't, to teach her about her magic. Nor could they reach each other fast enough should this happen again.

Frantically, Karlisle nodded.

"Why?" Juno asked, concern pulling her rounded features.

"It will corrupt you," Malice explained carefully, as to process the information himself. Albeit, he was talking more to Karlisle than Juno despite who his sights were on. "The pain will be unbearable and it's hard to stop when it gets here." He tapped the middle of her forearm. "Understand?" He gently placed her on the ground.

"I understand," she said dejectedly while Karlisle nodded out of the corner of Malice's eye.

"I should get going." Malice had drank less than half of his tea, he noticed. He quickly downed the rest of it, stepped around the chair, and made for the door.

"I hope you get your glass of wine," Karlisle commented.

"So do I."

"Kiran"

It was mid-morning, the hallway blissfully silent outside Rosalina's bedchamber. She lay alongside Kiran, curled in the sheets, which left little more than a corner for him. Her head of auburn hair poked out from beneath the blankets, where his fingers gently twirled a lock. They were both naked, the night's *adventures* sticky on their skin. Memories tickled his mind, and he smiled and flushed, butterflies dancing in his stomach.

Alas, he needed to start his day. Rosalina could rest a while longer. He would come up with some excuse or another if anyone asked where she was.

As carefully as he could, Kiran slipped out of bed, the cold floor shocking his system. As to not wake Rosalina, he blindly shuffled to find at least his pants. He thought they were close to the bed; he was wrong. They were closer to the door. He used the wall for support as he put them on, waking her up by falling on his bum or face would be mortifying.

The door creaked open and Kiran peeked into the corridor. Coast was clear. With only pants, he needed to stop by Malice's room to grab a shirt and a pair of shoes, so the king's advisor wouldn't walk around the castle half naked. He slinked out of Rosalina's room, made sure her door clicked shut, and rushed toward the eastern wing, passing the stairwell. Then he was there, hand reaching for the knob.

"Looks like someone had as much fun as me," a deep voice said behind him. One Kiran would recognize anywhere. He whipped around. Malice wore a sly grin on his face, his eyes bright.

"This—this is not what it looks like—I—" Kiran stammered. How could he explain where he came from? Who he was with to be in this situation—practically naked in front of the king's bedchamber. Heat flared through his body, his eyes on the ground.

Malice's bare feet snatched Kiran's attention. The laces of his leather pants and shirt dangled. Eyes trailing further up, there were red stains on his neck and exposed clavicle, his long white hair wind-blown, lips tinted a few shades darker.

Just then had Malice's words processed in Kiran's head.

"You… laid… with someone," Kiran said warily.

Malice's smirk simply grew. "And I wasn't the only one, it seems. You reek of it." He crossed the hall swiftly, his strides long and quiet. Kiran had to look up a bit when they were face to face. He frowned at the difference between them. Not long ago, Kiran was taller and broader. Malice had a few inches on him now. His muscles were sculpted, and his shoulders were hardly wider than his hips.

Kiran swallowed. Malice was different. Maybe Kiran only realized in this moment, but Malice was beautiful in a way Rosalina and Nikanor weren't. He couldn't describe it or understand it, really.

"Reek of what?" Kiran asked, his tone hushed.

"Sex."

Startled, Kiran shot back, "So do you!"

Chuckling, Malice opened his door and gestured for Kiran to enter. He instantly flicked flames to the candles on his nightstands and desk. In his closet, there was still a small section where he kept Kiran's clothes. *In case you ever need them*, Malice had said when he asked. He was glad Malice kept them, not that he ever thought it would be under these circumstances. His cheeks burst with heat again.

Despite how much, well, everything had changed, Malice's bedchamber was essentially untouched. The ceiling was the biggest difference from when they were children. The bed was the same, vines carving the wooden canopy frame—he never had drapes to complete the canopy, though. There were more books on the shelf across from the bed. The armoire near his closet, however, was new. Jewelry decorated the brass hooks on the open doors. Resting on the single, topmost shelf was his crown, and below, leaning in the corner, was a sheathed sword. A tunic, trousers, and boots were displayed in the armoires heart, all scuffed and torn, sun-bleached and dirt-stained.

It had been a while since Kiran last visited Malice's room. He didn't grasp how much he was soaking it all in until Malice presented him with an outfit, shoes in the opposite hand, with a look on his face that said, *Did you hear me?*

"Were you talking?" Kiran asked and took his attire from Malice's hands.

"Was it Rosalina?" he repeated himself, turning back to his closet of mostly black.

Kiran turned as well. "Yes," he mumbled.

"You followed your parents' lesson, didn't you?" Malice said mockingly.

With a roll of his eyes, he said, "Yes. I expect you did the same."

"I found their lecture rather helpful."

Kiran cringed, audibly gagging to emphasize his point of thinking about his parents whilst bedding someone. Malice chortled, a genuine laugh making him sound boyish. Unconsciously, he snickered too, and an ache started behind his ribcage. He missed moments like these where the past died, and they were brothers again.

Ebbing his joy, Kiran's eyes latched onto Malice's desk. It was old, a few more scratches tainting the wood from how often Malice sat at it. But there were vials, jars, bottles, and mortars arranged on the surface again. A book of herbal remedies sat beside them, small pouches on top of and alongside it. Kiran thought Malice had stopped taking the tonics.

"When will I meet this lover of yours?" he asked, letting the tonics go, when he spun and sat on Malice's bed.

"She's not my lover," Malice said lightheartedly. "Not by any means."

Kiran's brows twitched. "Why'd you sleep with her then?"

"I needed to confirm a few things. Her information came at a cost." He shrugged while Kiran stared dumbfounded.

"You can't be implying what I think you are."

Pausing, Malice's hands halted at the third bottom from the top, smile dying. Green eyes sliced to Kiran's. "That I sold my body to get what I wanted? Why deny the truth?"

"You are the king." Kiran rose. "You are *the* king. To sell yourself is a—"

"Is a what?" Malice's voice hardened, his expression suddenly distant. "An embarrassment? A tarnish to my reputation? A disgrace?"

"Yes," Kiran said. "It is." What if word got out? Already, Malice had admirers begging for a chance to get in his pants. Kiran worried about what Malice's royals might try to do and how many would wind up in an early grave. The nobles would give him hell and the rulers would be worse, Kiran was sure. How could someone in Malice's position not think of consequences such as those? Rumors spread fast and far. All it took was one loose pair of lips for the entire region to look at Malice with disdain.

"Did she force you? We will find her and throw her in a cell to rot!" Surprise had melted into a rage Kiran didn't know he had until it was flowing out of his mouth. "Think about your status. You sold yourself like some common brothel whore!"

"Kiran," Malice said with a fatal calmness, a slight growl at the back of his throat. Kiran flinched and fell silent, an involuntary reaction. "Knowledge, in the right hands, is a powerful thing. I never expected her to give it free of charge." He sighed, and scowled, and looked at the floor and, finally, regarded Kiran, eyes much softer and earnest. "How can one enjoy sex when they have to imagine someone else to feel anything? I enjoyed the release it provided, nothing else."

Disgust coiled in Kiran's gut for a split second as the question of who Malice had envisioned sprang into his mind. More than that, the idea of laying someone for a reason other than love was something Kiran couldn't fathom.

"I had sex because I needed information," Malice said, distress no longer darkening his features. Anger thinned his mouth instead, made those bright green eyes glow and his arched brows knit. "You had sex because you're in love."

The truth felt like an insult coming from him, as if love were worse. Kiran hated how he could do that. He scoffed, gathered his discarded pants, and stomped to the door. *Release*, Malice said. Anger dispelled as Kiran recalled the release he had experienced, the first kiss they had shared, the little grazes and caresses they'd allowed themselves to indulge in, the first time his and Rosalina's bodies became one. He shivered.

The circumstances were different. Far more different from selling one's body. The heat of fury returned as Kiran's hand wrapped around the knob. Kiran loved Rosalina. It was what made their intimacy so sweet, so exhilarating.

He stopped before he yanked the door open, sights fixed on his brown-skinned hand, black hair steadily creeping onto the back of it.

Looking over his shoulder, Kiran said, "I hope it was worth it."

A Poison Worth Drinking
LVI

Malice wanted to see what would happen if he gave Freya trust and power over Khuomouth.

In front of his desk in an armchair, Eunice sat relaxed, legs crossed, fingers drumming the arms. Her black hair was thickly braided with string cascading past her shoulders, her jaw set.

"Factions one through seven remain peaceful," she said bitterly. "Freya introduced five more to replace what you took away. She's bringing more and more non-criminals into the pits, thinking if she does so gradually, you won't notice or bother to look."

He had placed royals down there the moment he returned to the surface after his first visit. They practically lived underground. Reports were to be made weekly, and they had been. Defection was easy to understand. Malice was not Vendetta. Whatever deal they had was, apparently, far better than the one Malice had offered. Or Malice hadn't established himself as a proper threat, someone you needed to fear like Vendetta had.

"We need to get rid of her." She muttered, "I never liked the wretched bitch, anyhow."

It wasn't a bad idea. Using Freya as an example could work to keep the other nobles in line. And yet, it was a double-edged blade that gave them an excuse for mutiny.

"If it came to war," Malice said, his tone easy. "Who do you think would stand with me and who would stand with Freya?"

"Thutmose and Yvonne hate you, my liege," she answered instantly. "Give them a reason to disobey or rebel, and they'll take it."

Sophronius was a good nobleman, young and loyal. He'd also taken a liking to Malice. Since he… understood a bit more, he knew Sophronius felt more than friendship toward Malice. Malice could use that. Personal feelings aside, Ryzion belonged to the Valor bloodline. By right, the kingdom was Malice's before it was Hyacinthia's since she'd abandoned her nobility for a lost cause.

Eunice added, "The one I'm unsure about is Balios."

"He would haul himself behind his fortification and wait it out," Malice said indifferently. "Two on two are good odds, if you ask me."

Eunice nodded. "You think it'll come to that?"

"Not right now, but eventually." If he kept them in power.

Khuomouth took precedence. There were roughly one hundred thousand citizens in Hordes, double below. He'd chosen not to collapse the city because of the population. Would dismissing Freya be enough to send a message? Would it be enough to keep Khuomouth safe? It was something he needed to discuss with Kiran as well, the notion causing dread to nestle in his intestines. They'd done nothing more than exchange brief pleasantries since they fought.

"I'll pay Freya a visit soon," Malice said after a time. The underground city was the last remnant of Vendetta Malice knew of, and it was proving difficult to cleanse. "What if I—"

The door opened as Kiran stepped into Malice's study with a tray of tea. "Apologies for the interruption," he said.

"You've good timing." Eunice turned slightly, smiled, and dipped her head, Kiran doing the same.

His heels clicked against the marble floor as he passed Eunice. She stiffened, eyes flitting to the teapot painted with little birds on branches, Kiran, and finally to Malice. The tray clunked on top of the desk and Kiran poured the tea. Malice caught a whiff.

"We'll talk more later, Eunice," Malice said.

For a heartbeat, she lingered on him, and stood. "Of course, my liege," she said naturally, turning to leave.

"I'm glad you're here," Malice mentioned as the door closed. "I've been wanting to ask you a question." Not the one he sought for Khuomouth.

Kiran dropped five sugar cubes into his cup, stirring it tentatively with a miniature spoon. "I'll help however I can. Lay it on me."

Malice hated that tone, one of false lightheartedness, as if their last quarrel didn't weigh on his mind like it did Malice's. Taking the offered cup, he sniffed, brought it to lips and drank it in two swallows, inclining it for a refill.

"Am I good king?"

He answered, "You are the best since Hordes, and it's not an understatement. Your people believe the same." Steam rose once more and Malice sipped this time, listening to his brother's praise. "Mother and Father once said what made you great was your determination to fix the damage Vendetta left behind."

Despite knowing who Malice was in conference with, there was a single teacup. It was black tea; Kiran wasn't a fan of it, Eunice didn't drink tea at all, and Malice never altered his drinks, never cared to.

Kiran went on, the slight quake in his hands making the teapot's lid clink. He set it down and clasped his hands. "I believe what makes you great is you don't put yourself above your subjects."

"But I'm not a great person, am I?" Malice questioned, deliberately gulping his third cup of tea, sights locked on Kiran's big brown eyes.

"I'm not sure—"

"Did you think I wouldn't recognize the smell of poison?" The mildness of his voice hadn't changed. Matter of fact, it grew lighter, as if they were back in Malice's bedchamber joking about Blodwen's and Tendai's sex lecture. "No matter how much sugar you add, the bitterness never leaves."

"If it's bitter, I must've over-brewed it," Kiran said, despite the obvious tension in his posture and the slight sheen to his complexion.

Malice reached for the teapot and leisurely placed the lid on the metal tray. "Do you know what Inyene did to me the month after my campaign?"

Confused, Kiran glanced at Malice, hands twisting into themselves as if his skin were a towel needing to be wrung. "She… tortured you."

"I could no longer feel pain," Malice explained. "Every day she tried something new, something deadlier. Then I took over. I thought tonics of nightshade and henbane would help rid me of the nightmares."

He hadn't entirely stopped. Just tried new mixtures he kept in his nightstands, more like bottles of death for the average person, for the occasions the nightmares were too much to handle. He slipped his fingers into the pot, nails clinking against the porcelain. Anxiety sparked behind the deep umber of Kiran's iris, struggling to stay contained. Malice chugged, and the tea spilled from the corners of his mouth, soaked his shirt. Tart bitterness, as if he had taken a swill of vinegar, coated every inch of his mouth and throat. Kiran's hand snapped upward, but he forced them to his sides and averted his gaze.

Gently setting the teapot where it belonged, Malice rose from his chair and stepped around the side of his desk. He leaned against the front, so he and Kiran were side by side.

"What did you use?"

Kiran turned his head away, brows furrowed, chin trembling.

"Answer me."

"… Hemlock roots, oleander, and rosary peas," Kiran breathed.

Malice whistled. Quite the fatal combination. One he never thought of. Blodwen's signature. It was why Vendetta kept her around, or so Draga wrote. The victim only needed a mouthful for her poisons to kill; one taste would not lead to a second due to the vile flavor, hence the potency.

The liquid hit his stomach like a boulder, instantly curdling the bile. Room fogging, Kiran doubled and grew hazy. It must've been especially potent if the symptoms had an immediate effect. "Who made it? You or your mother?"

"Do not patronize me," Kiran hissed, shoulders bunched as his fists were pale knuckled.

"To you, when was I ever so terrible?" Malice asked, voice cracking.

"I," Kiran's didn't though, "am tired of living in fear."

Malice grunted. "Fear of what?"

"That one day you'll remember how much my parents aided Vendetta and decide to kill them. That you'll conclude they weren't enough and kill me, too."

"You're my brother, I would—"

"Sok and Rayen were your siblings," Kiran shouted, stumbling backward. "Draga and Inyene were your sisters, Vendetta and Emil, your parents. How am I supposed to feel safe when I serve a kin-slayer?"

Kin-slayer. Malice hadn't heard the phrase since Ko Wolfgang used it against him five years ago. "You know why it had to be done."

"You *relished* in their death," Kiran spat, hatred dancing in his eyes like embers from a bonfire. "You delighted in their pain and suffering. Instead of killing them with mercy, you tortured them."

"As they tortured me," Malice shot back, the room spinning when he whipped his head toward Kiran.

"Had Zephyrus tortured you too?"

"*He* challenged *me*!"

The room fell silent. Malice never explained what led to the Laska's death, subsequently, what happened between him and Zephyrus. The timing was never right. Kiran never asked and Malice; he just couldn't spit it out. He closed his eyes because if he looked at Kiran, he would forgive him. How couldn't he? After everything Kiran had done, had allowed Malice to do, to forgive his brother would be as easy as breathing. As it would have been for Zephyrus, had he said something.

Malice spoke softly, "If I wanted to kill you, I would've done so six years ago alongside my *loving* family."

At last, Malice let his sight glide over to Kiran. His horns had fully come in, angled around his ears like a bison's. Adulthood made him lean and handsome, his jawline slightly squared, nose hooked and somewhat flat, shoulders wider than his hips, legs long. And Malice always came back to his eyes, the softness of them so unlike the harsh sharpness of the glares he'd received all his life.

He'd given Kiran everything. Wealth, status, protection. Malice would have given more—his crown, kingdom, region, heart and soul—had he said the word. Without Kiran, Malice would've gladly died in Mutuwa when he was seven. Or during his first mission. When Inyene had full intentions of torturing him to death, he wouldn't have fought, yet he did every time.

Sighing, Malice kicked off the desk and approached Kiran, who stood awkwardly hunched as he convulsed from his repressed shaking. He guided Kiran's chin, slipped his hand to cup the beastman's oddly cold face.

"Tell me what I am to you," Malice said, forcing his limbs to be still and locking his knees so they didn't buckle, and he didn't stumble. Heat bashed him in waves of blistering needles as his organs knotted.

"The monster I hate most," Kiran whispered. Tears reddened his eyes and spilled.

"Then allow me to play the role you've so generously given me." Thumb sweeping across the plain of Kiran's cheek, Malice knew betrayal was an expectation waiting to be met. Nyx and Karlisle created the expectation by killing Berhane to bring about Malice. Vendetta was the first to embrace it; died for it. Zephyrus met it too and lost his honor. Magnus offered it through a letter and left Malice broken all the same.

Now Kiran felt the need to join them.

He opened his mouth. Blood gurgled out, splattering Kiran's face. Ears ringing as Kiran's lips moved hastily, Malice grabbed and squeezed Kiran's shoulders, nails biting deep into his robe.

"Kiran Pretorius, advisor to the king, doctor of the castle," Malice strained, his vision pulsating. "I, King of Hordes Region, strip you of your titles, wealth, and land."

Kiran ignored him, and suddenly his knees were on the ground. His voice reached Malice as muted murmurs, then horrific screams. "I can fix this," he sobbed, a hand shooting to Malice's abdomen. "I can, I'm sorry! I—"

Malice caught his hand and gazed into the eyes he never dreamed would look at him as if he were his *mother*. "The practice of medicine will be forbidden for you and your kin from this day forth," he said, though it sounded vile, phlegmy, the sloshing of organs as they spilled onto the earth. "Should you heal so much as a fly, it'll be seen as an act of treason, and you'll be executed."

"Fine," Kiran spat. "I'll face my punishment, but *let me heal you.*"

Of course, he would gladly take rotting in a cell or execution over watching his childhood friend, the one he declared as his brother, succumb to the poison he specifically curated for Malice. It was funny. And it was exactly why Kiran *would* watch Malice writhe in agony. Wetness streaked Kiran's mahogany brown skin, snot dripping from his nose. What a pathetic sight. Malice almost said he was in a poorer state than he, but the poison reached his core. A sound was ripped out of him then, guttural and primal.

The door burst open, and feet clambered closer alongside a raging voice. Blood trickled down Malice's face and the sides of neck, the streams like fire. Kiran's touch was fleeting, the caress of a feather, and staggering, the score of a knife. Such a funny thing his body had become. Most of the time, pain eluded him. Although headaches were harrowing. And now, his core brought the sense back tenfold. Six long years since the last he'd felt such excruciating pain. His mind was nothing but static.

Dully, he realized more than Eunice had entered the room, their presences surrounding him. Eunice's voice reached him, however, broke through the haze enough for him to register that she had mentioned Kiran.

"Kiran stays," Malice spluttered, clutching his brother's shoulders as if his life depended on it.

Choking on ichor became vomiting. He was sure he was going to upchuck his entire stomach with how violently he retched. It took everything in him to stop his spasming muscles from faltering any further or hurting Kiran more than he already had. Had his nails sunk past fabric into flesh? Were the bones of his hand shattering under Malice's grip? Kiran did well in either choosing or concocting the perfect poison for Malice. He wanted to congratulate him for it, too. Even if it didn't kill him, Kiran knew it would send him through a whirlwind of pain, and he was right. Which hurt worse. Fifteen years wiped from history, destroyed by poison, and one day, buried. If it was what Kiran wanted, Malice had little choice.

On the floor, surrounded by unknown and known faces, Malice waited for the worse of it to pass. There were always highs and lows, the build, the climax, and the comedown. The entire process would have been a hell of a lot worse if he had average regeneration skills.

When Malice released Kiran's shoulder, he glided his hand up to the back of his head, hoping his touch was tender. He fought against his poisoned muscles, lifting his head as he tugged Kiran down, their foreheads tapping. "I will display your heads on spikes in my courtyard if you're not out of my castle by nightfall."

The study was a swirling mass color behind Kiran, the only anchor Malice had, the only source of reality tethering him to consciousness. He wondered what he looked like to Kiran right now for him to be weeping as he was. If not for the misery coursing through him, Malice's heart would have ached at the sight. Some part of him, his entire soul, he guessed, wanted to wrap Kiran in his embrace like all the times he'd done for Malice and whisper a litany of apologies, lies that everything would be all right.

But Kiran brought this on himself. Malice wasn't a child anymore. In the same tone, he added, "Unless the spikes on the gate are too appetizing to resist, stay." The same part that wanted to coddle Kiran meant the word stay, as well.

His hands loosened their hold on Kiran. He rose, wobbled, staring at Malice, though now that he was on his feet, Malice couldn't read his expression. Then he darted out of the room. No one went after him. The worst punishment was not giving one at all. Kiran would live with what he did to Malice hanging over him for the rest of his mortal life. There would be no repentance in a cell or retribution via beheading. Malice would truly become Kiran's nightmare, as Kiran would become Malice's.

Eventually, he motioned for Eunice to help him up. Using her as a crutch, Malice stood, legs weak, numb, pulsing with needles. His vision wasn't much better, the study doused in whitewash, the walls undulating. Just wanting to be upright, he stood there for a time and sucked in strained wheezes. Eventually, he let go of Eunice when strength returned to his limbs, little as it was, and his eyes steadied some. He turned. Odovacar, Nikanor, and five other royals were staring back at him. He supposed they all wanted an explanation. One he didn't feel like giving.

"Remember what we discussed earlier," Malice said, his voice rough like he had swallowed nails.

"Yes," Eunice answered hesitantly.

"I know the solution." Kiran had walked in as he was about to propose the idea. "I want this kingdom destroyed."

Death of a Kingdom
LVII

Part I

It had been over a year since Malice last visited Khuomouth. The reports were accurate. The limestone streets were cleaned in factions one through seven, lanterns containing blue fire hanging from metal lamp posts, houses newly built of smoothed stone much like those in Estera, the people wearing proper garments rather than stained and torn rags. The stench of feces and death had also dissipated.

Both Malice and Eunice were known down here, as they were on the surface. Citizens smiled and waved at them, bowing or dipping their heads in respect.

Faction seven held the fighting pits and Freya's conference *house*. Hut was the better name for it. Crossing the distance between faction six and the caged pits surrounded by hollering bodies, echoing screams, and clashing metal, Malice and Eunice approached the rounded building, a curtain acting as a door. The smell of excrement and blood was sharp and foul, enough to make a person unused to the stench retch on the spot. Like Kiran and his royals almost had five years ago.

They entered without warning. Heba jumped to her feet, knocking her chair over. Freya whipped around, eyes a bit frantic.

Inside was nothing special. Maps of Vinyamar, the regions, Hordes Kingdom, and Khuomouth adorned the walls. A wolf's pelt covered the ground beneath the single square table at the center of the room. Two torches lit the space, one by the entrance, the other directly across from it.

"Your majesty," Freya said with a false smile. "To what do we owe the pleasure?"

"Questions," Malice replied evenly. He dragged out one of four chairs and sat down while Eunice remained standing at his backside.

Heba's golden brown eyes moved from Freya to Malice. Stiffly, she righted her chair and joined them.

"Have you heard of the voidents?" he asked.

Inky orbs flickering, Freya maintained eye-contact as her tongue darted across her wine-colored lips. "I haven't."

"What do you know about the voidents?"

"I know nothing, as I—"

"What do you know about the voidents?" he repeated, his tone neutral. "I'd like the truth this time."

Freya licked her lips again. "I'm as ignorant as the sky is blue."

There was plenty of time in those dungeons as a child. Aside from injecting his magic into another like poison, he learned to condense formless energy. Imagining a string, he coaxed a line of magic from his core, everything outside of Freya blurring. The string connected to her chest. Heba stiffened, confusion striking her tanned features, while Eunice didn't react. This amount of residual intimidation wasn't enough to affect his first sword.

Freya, on the other hand, reached for her neck, her shoulders bunching as her breaths turned into rasps. Her grape-colored skin darkened and her sclerae reddened.

Malice said, "I won't ask for honesty a third time. What do you know about the voidents?"

"Not much," she strained. "I swear."

He cut the stream off. Heba's posture loosened, and Freya gasped, gulping lungfuls of air as if she'd been suffocating for minutes. It'd hardly been thirty seconds.

The dark elf said after a moment, "The last known disappearance was in Maziar's region, outside the capital. Voidents haven't expanded beyond rural areas yet."

"I'm glad you'll go to the grave having told the truth." Malice smiled. Looking over his shoulder at Eunice, he nodded toward Heba. "Would you do the honors?"

From plain to delighted, a grin twisted Eunice's mouth, her sights coming to rest on Heba. "Absolutely."

"You're betraying us?" Heba shouted and stood, her chair clattering into the wall for the second time—she must not like it.

Eunice indolently drew her sword from its scabbard, the metal ringing. Heba ripped her bronze sickle from her wrap in response, face scrunched, teeth bared.

"How could *we* betray *you* when it was you who created an additional five factions and started throwing innocents into the pits? Again," Malice countered, Eunice and Heba's swords clashing at his side. "You went behind my back, disobeyed our agreement, and recommitted yourself to my mother's cause."

"I've done no such thing," Freya hissed. Hands flat on the table, her brows were knotted, and her lips were curled back.

Flippantly, Malice gestured to the hut. "If you thought, after working with my mother for decades, I would trust you completely; it makes me wonder if you ever truly met Vendetta." Those who played her game knew better than to believe her words held the weight she promised. "I've had eyes on you the moment I gave you control."

Freya paled. Metal clanged, feet shuffled, and Heba grunted.

"You can't kill me," Freya spat, smirking. "Or you won't leave here alive."

"And what will kill me? Your army of four hundred currently being dispatched by my warband?"

Out of the corner of Malice's eye, Eunice rushed behind Heba, impaled her core, and, for good measure, slit her throat, the actions swift and precise. Blood sprayed, warmth splattering the side of Malice's face at the same time it painted Freya's. Neither flinched. The ichor dripped, quickly cooling and drying. Heba's body thudded to the floor. Eunice bent down, wiped her sword on the guard's shirt, and returned her blade to its scabbard, inserting herself at Malice's backside.

"I expect one of my royals to arrive and give me an update any moment now."

Freya huffed, her fists trembling on the table, her eyes fleeting to the corpse staining her rug, jaw spasming. Her rage was palpable, radiating from her body like steam.

"My liege," Odovacar announced as he moved the curtain aside, the fabric rustling. Malice's smile was of genuine satisfaction. "Four hundred soldiers have been rounded, healers have been killed, the criminals put to death, and the bystanders released. What would you like done with Freya's... *army*?"

Gaze locked on Freya's, Malice said, "Strip them bare, stab their cores, and toss them in the pits. Let them rot."

Damage to one's core required healing soon, if not immediately after the damage was made, as well as nourishment and sleep. Without it, the core could not regenerate, meaning death was a guarantee.

Inyene was smart about attacking Malice's core. She always had healers on standby.

There were no longer healers amongst Freya's men.

"Yes, my liege." Odovacar promptly left.

"Didn't notice how quiet it became?" Malice questioned, his voice rich with sarcasm. "Did you think I wouldn't come prepared?"

To his feet, Malice walked along the edge of the table till he was next to Freya. Hand slipping underneath her chin, Malice guided her head upward when she jerked away. He caught her jaw again and wrenched her out of the chair, his claws biting her cheeks, red running over his fingers. Her own nails dug into his forearms, her grip surprisingly strong.

"Freya Venczel," he breathed. "The perfect example of how I respond to treachery, a warning to the other nobles."

Kiran wasn't here to stay Malice's hand anymore, to whisper softness into her ear, to be his voice of reason and kindness. If he were, he would've advised against something as bloody as what Malice was about to do, and he would've listened like a good dog.

In his hold, she shuddered. Malice added more pressure and snapped her mandible. The scream she let out was gut-wrenching, her fingers ripping his sleeves and gouging skin. Tears bubbled and flowed. Now that she was slack-jawed, Malice opened her mouth, thumb holding her lip up. With his opposite hand, he glided his black nail underneath her gums. Her eyes bulged, pleas escaping the back of her throat as he ripped one golden canine out. Then the other.

Blood overflowed from her mouth when Malice dropped her, Freya stumbling but not collapsing, and placed her teeth on the table.

"You lost a few teeth, not a limb," Malice remarked, receiving a glare in return. He turned and headed for Eunice, but stopped a few paces away. As words tumbled from Freya's tongue, he whipped around, arm following, and a blade formed in his grip.

Malice met Freya's shadowy eyes, her expression frozen in anger and confusion. Red pricked a line across her neck and her body toppled, her head falling with a wet thud, rolling away. A head and two teeth should be more than enough for Balios, Thutmose, and Yvonne to get the message.

"I want her body thrown in the pits with the rest of the shit," Malice said. "Send her head to Thutmose, her teeth to my aunt and the shut-in."

*

Maziar's Region was dry. The summer heat was as intense as days in Hordes Region, the nights bitingly cold. Inside the tavern, however, it was comfortably warm. The mead Malice was sipping on might have been to blame for his temperature.

Wood encased him from the vaulted ceiling to the planks beneath his feet and the round table he sat at in the corner, the booth cushioned with dark red cotton. Lanterns hung from the beams and sat on the bar to Malice's right, columns spaced evenly throughout the tavern. Beer and the savory smell of pig over a spitfire sat heavy in the air—he couldn't tell whether his stomach was knotting because the scent of pork was enticing or horrible. Barmaids raced from table to table. Fur swathed patrons and kept their feet warm. To blend in better, he wore the same and felt as though he would melt into a puddle at any moment. The room was relatively loud, bouts of laughter drowning any conversation Malice could make out.

Quinci mentioned the visages of the gods months ago, reminding Malice of the voident who taught him to shadow travel. Lazarus spoke mighty words back then and had yet to pay Malice a visit. Killing Vendetta's army of six thousand was probably enough to pay off the debt he owed the creature anyhow.

Taking what Freya said, he asked the townsfolk if they'd heard anything about the random disappearances. Someone had. So here he was, in a tavern about fifty miles away from Maziar's Kingdom, further west. Sighing, Malice took a long draught of honey mead, called honey-wine in the realm of dark elves.

He'd arrived in town earlier that evening and had been waiting ever since. At this point, he was wasting his time. He didn't know what he was supposed to be looking for after confirming the last disappearance was in this village. From Hyacinthia's explanation, apparently, he would sense the darkness of a voident because Hordes had been able to. As if it truly explained why or what he would feel. Six hours later, he hadn't sensed a damned thing besides annoyance quickly growing into irritation.

New customers entered the tavern as Malice rested his head in his hand, closing his eyes. It was a risk coming out here, one he thought was worth taking. Kiran probably would have presented this outcome, along with how Malice's plan could come back to bite him in the ass, but Malice would've taken the risk, nonetheless.

When the door slammed shut, Malice's skin tightened, a tingle racing up his spine, forcing him upright. A group of seven walked in and picked out a table a few from Malice's booth. One was a fishman with silver scales, piercing blue eyes, and grey hair brushing the tops of his shoulders. Underneath the black fur cloak, he was broad, not much shorter than Malice. More importantly, the longer he stared at the fishman, the stronger the sensation of thorns caressing his back became. Darkness had somehow attached itself to him, and Malice had finally found his target.

Drinking till he was red-faced and bleary-eyed, the fishman eventually stood from his table, glanced at Malice, and made his way to him. The remaining six snickered to one another. With his cloak off, the fishman was indeed muscular from chest to biceps to thighs. Dingy brown trousers tucked into fur boots at his calves, a belt around his waist, his tunic too tight for someone of his build.

"Pardon me, miss," the fishman said as he approached the edge of Malice's table. "I just wanted to say you're—you are—you," he stuttered, cheeks flushing as the four gills on either side of his neck flared. "You're very attractive!" His accent had a different quality than King Thorn's, less formal and stiff, with a slight rolling of the *r*'s and some of his *o*'s sounded like *aw*.

Lifting his head, tucking his hair behind his ear—he hadn't cut it since his coronation—Malice met the shy glances of the fishman. Up close, the thorns morphed into daggers, raking his spine, the tug and separation of tissue.

"Miss doesn't quite fit," Malice said. The fishman's blush deepened and his bushy brows curved upwards. "Call me Berhane instead." He smiled sweetly.

"I-I'm so sorry! You're j-j-ju-u-just so beautiful."

Malice, chuckling, gestured to the open space at his side while waving down a barmaid with the other hand. "Won't you tell me your name?"

As if the seat would bite, the fishman carefully sat next to Malice. "Name's Erik."

Goblets thudded on the table. Malice found some silver coins from his pocket and once she had her money, the barmaid left. Grabbing his own, Malice slid the second toward Erik.

"So," he started, voice low, a hum at the back of his throat, "what does one have to do to get muscles like those?"

Erik twirled the contents of the goblet, scales twinkling in the soft light. "Oh, I w-w-ork on the family's farm, help our neighbors t-t-to-to—as well." He peeked at Malice, grinning bashfully. "What about you?"

Malice's brow quirked. "Me? What muscles are you referring to?"

Flustered; "No! I-I me-mean-me-mean what do y-you do for l-l-liv-liv-liv-living?"

The fishman's drunken spluttering was endearing, Malice had to admit as he laughed, his hand coming to rest on Erik's shoulder. He'd seen the expression often between couples in the kingdom, and figured it was the natural thing to do.

"I'm a botanist," Malice said at last, mouth curved into a smile yet.

Thoughtfully, Erik nodded, guiding Malice's hand off his shoulder, studying it as if the back of his hand were sacred. "I can see that," the fishman muttered.

Malice snatched Erik's hand and held it. "Tell me about yourself."

Back and forth they went, speaking about their professions, Erik telling stories of his childhood, Malice lying about his own. Patrons dwindled as time slipped by. Eventually, he and Erik left too. Light trimmed closed windows and doorways, the moon bathing everything else in grey. The streets were cobblestone, resounding every footstep.

Together, Erik and Malice walked southward, turned into an alley, and stopped. The fishman spun on his heels to face Malice, opened his mouth to speak, but his shadow blackened, darker than the midnight sky on a stormy night. Long, jagged fingers reached up. Malice got to Erik first and yanked him by the front of his shirt, simultaneously grabbing the voident's hand, pulling the creature from the ground. Its screech rang against the stone walls of the alley.

Erik stumbled behind Malice. "The hell—" He gasped. Measured footsteps retreated, then fled, the sound of boots on cobblestone growing distant.

"Can you speak?" Malice asked.

He had no way of finding Lazarus and couldn't think of anything better.

"Who are you?" it sneered.

Patience having dissipated a while ago, Malice wrapped his fingers around the voident's neck, squeezed, and kicked its legs out from underneath it, forcing the thing to its knees.

"Bring me to Lazarus," he demanded.

"No," it choked.

Perhaps he wasn't kind enough. Stiffening his fingers, Malice stared into the void of the creature's face as he sluggishly punctured its midsection. It tried to scream but Malice tightened his grip around its throat, cutting the gargled noise it made short.

He repeated, "Bring me to Lazarus and this—" His hand twisted. The voident jerked violently—"will stop."

When it nodded, Malice released the inky creature, watching the cluster of black collapse to the ground and choke and cough for air. One very important thing was learned: Voidents felt pain, they needed air, and they had a magical core. All of which meant a voident could be killed.

They were underground, wet stone and moss filling Malice's nostrils with a pungently stale, earthy aroma. Above him were stalactites longer than a house was tall, the peaks like spearheads ready to drop at any moment. They walked along an edge overlooking a sea of darkness, the truest of blacks against the grey backdrop of the cavern.

Malice expected silence but was met with teeth clatter, strange releases of breath that weren't quite grunts or wheezes, and incomprehensible babble. Like the voident he was following, Malice's footfalls were nonexistent. His boots would make far too much noise.

Glancing beyond his new friend, light pricked the slate landscape, growing larger and brighter, voices increasing in volume. At this distance, he could make out bits and pieces. *Can't*, one voice said. *Thought better,* another chimed in. Later; *Zephyrus.*

Ever so gently, his chest constricted. *Anyone can name their child Zephyrus*, Malice told himself. *The Zephyrus I know is dead.*

Nearing the light source, the voices hushed and the voident escorting Malice stopped outside a chamber, harshly carved archways acting as entrances.

"The child of darkness wishes to speak with you, Commander Lazarus," it announced.

Holding a council and being addressed by titles was rather civilized for blood thirsty creatures.

"Malice," Lazarus drawled. "Come, join me."

He rounded the corner of an archway, a single bowl of flames at the center of the long table, the walls marginally smoother, curving inward to the dome ceiling. Whoever Lazarus was speaking with took their leave. Only Malice and the vaguely faced, lanky shadow he met as a child remained.

"What brings the King of Hordes Region to my place of operations?" he asked, orbs reminiscent of eyes following Malice across the room.

Malice leaned his lower back against the same edge of the table Lazarus stood beside. "My debt," he said.

"Was paid the moment you slaughtered your poor mother's army."

"Onto more pressing matters," Malice amended. "Since my debt is clear, allow me to propose a deal."

"A deal," Lazarus crooned, falling back onto a chair of darkness that spit embers of black like a bonfire. "Do tell."

Copying the voident, Malice stepped away from the table and gingerly sat on a seat of air, crossing his legs. "I've recently been betrayed, and I believe now is the time to set an example."

Lazarus twirled his gnarly fingers, beseeching more.

"Vendetta ruined the kingdom my grandfather created. It's too damaged to be repaired anymore."

"You want it gone?" the voident guessed.

"I can't destroy my own kingdom." He would be damned if nine years of building a decent reputation in Hordes Region went up in smoke.

A wide, vicious grin split Lazarus's mouth. "Explain the benefits for both you and I as I am failing to see them."

He's cautious. "I get a clean start. You get to kill to your heart's content."

"What?"

"Nearly three hundred thousand, ripe for the butcher," Malice said conversationally, hands out as if he were a merchant showcasing his stock of goods. "It's a win-win."

Lazarus was tight-lipped for a while, contemplating Malice's offer with more seriousness than Malice would have thought possible. But what was there to refuse? There were no clauses, no loans. It was an equal exchange of labor and payment.

"I have no trust in you," the voident finally said.

"Neither I in you," Malice returned. "I'm hiring you to get a job done and your payment will be in blood. Nothing more, nothing less."

"When?"

"Autumn."

Thin brows jumping, Lazarus gave Malice an apprehensive look.

"I need time to prepare, inform my nobles, and find a new dwelling for myself," he partially lied.

"If," Lazarus leered, "I refuse?"

Malice smiled. "You've no reason to refuse."

The creature's chuckle expanded into a cackle, reverberating off the walls. "Before the new year, your kingdom shall fall, King Malice!"

"Good." He rose, swiftly turned, and strutted the way he came, Lazarus laughing manically behind him.

Walking along the ledge, Malice caught movement in his periphery. A voident as large as Lazarus moved down the aisles of idle shadows, a slightly smaller one behind it. It seemed they were taking inventory. Malice paused. There was a hierarchy at play. Perhaps Lazarus was the highest ranking, but he couldn't be the sole commander in the cave. Even if he was, there had to be more like the one who escorted Malice with enough intelligence to spew information if he hit the right buttons.

As he moved backward, the wall absorbed Malice, and he climbed out of the floor a row down from the big voident jabbering to its servant. It was as a good of a time as ever to see if voidents *could* be killed.

Malice slipped behind the smaller of the two, hand covering its mouth while the other stabbed through its core and tore out whatever substance he could grab. The voident evaporated in a plume of darkness, the last tendril of smoke from a snuffed-out candle. Malice pushed down the fluttering of excitement in his chest.

"Make note," the big voident said and pointed to its left. "Platoons fifteen through twenty are—"

He wrapped his arms around the voident and sank, giving the creature no time to react. Without a clue as to where he was, Malice took a chance. They resurfaced in a shroud of darkness, the air much warmer than in the cavern. He recognized the smell of paper and ink, of old wood and earth.

Malice slammed the voident into the archive's wall, the creature hissing from the impact. He needed more information about the voidents, about Coatliris, how they functioned and coincided. How did they choose their victims and why? How long till the next genocide? Were they connected to the other continents?

Who better to answer these questions than a commander?

Death of a Kingdom
LVIII

Part II

A kingdom is nothing without its people.

Evacuation went smoothly. Sixty thousand retreated to Khuomouth and now that Freya was gone, it was safe for them. Forty thousand were split between the kingdoms in Hordes Region, including Malice's royals.

Generously, he predicted Lazarus would have enough patience to wait till the dead of summer, cutting the agreed timeline in half. For the past week, he'd returned to an empty castle, waiting for any sign of the voidents, and at night, he occupied Karlisle's couch. During the evacuation, Malice transferred all important documents to the Barren Circle's underground library, where they were safest.

He stared at Karlisle's ceiling. Bugs outside chirped relentlessly as the wind whistled. Already, he missed the mural in his bedchamber, missed studying every aspect, tracing the brush strokes, and finding little details Kiran hadn't told him about like the crow he painted on the branch of a tree. Between its small size and the leaves obstructing it, Malice hadn't seen it at first.

The blanket Karlisle offered was thrown over the back of the couch, his shirt over the top of it. Malice's head rested on the arm, his feet propped on the other, his boots on the floor. He would stay like this till dawn too, with nothing better to do than wait for Lazarus to strike. This time of year, the Lake of Zephyrus had water as warm as baths. He could go for a swim. But he knew himself. The temptation to stop swimming, especially after he banished Kiran, would be too strong to fight. The beach would be better. Sophronius would likely enjoy Malice's company, and Ryzion was a beautiful fishing city. The Kings Summit would take place in a few days, he could prepare to head to the Barren Circle. He could very well go to Alucard's Kingdom, declare himself the adult he was, and rekindle his and Magnus's relationship.

His mind went through all the possibilities of what he could do and yet, lying on his father's couch, watching a spider weave its web between the beams, wasn't so bad. Though he knew he'd go mad before long. If he were stagnant, he would wither into oblivion.

Dawn finally came. Malice stepped into his boots, shrugged his shirt on and left, sinking into the shadow of a tree a little ways from the cottage.

The voident's had struck.

Hordes Kingdom had been reduced to a pile of smoldering rubble overnight. Pillars of dark grey smoke rose, each column curving with the moaning wind. The acrid smell was enough to send Malice into a coughing fit, eyes stinging and watering. Even Kiran's Forest was nothing more than a collection of burnt skeletal trunks. He had a handful of good memories to make the sight of his fallen kingdom bittersweet.

Climbing over debris, ducking under beams supported by partially collapsed buildings, Malice explored the wreckage. Granite streets were torn from the earth and shattered like glass. The carnage left in the voidents' wake showed pure chaos. It was as if Lazarus had unleashed thousands of rabid howlers. Malice allowed those close to death to remain if it was what they wished, and now their corpses were like stomped bugs on the ground, hardly anything Malice could recognize as once human, elf, orc or any other race. He planned to select a group to stay in Hordes, feigning life so the voidents wouldn't get suspicious. He was glad there had been a choice involved at all. Save for the criminals.

Outside a destroyed wooden inn on the northeastern side, charred splinters and planks dispersed about the street, a body lay against a chunk of concrete. Malice stopped inches from what he assumed were once legs but were instead red, brown and white sludge and chunks splattered across the ground. Following the glob of flesh, his eyes trailed up worn trousers, a tunic, and landed on a face.

Birds got to him, the blistered and bubbled skin of his face picked apart and hanging, in some places revealing the pinkish gore of bone. The eyes, however, were untouched, which was uncommon. They were soft and easy to pluck out, so birds usually went for those first. Malice knew those eyes better than he knew his own. Crouching, he brushed aside locks of copper brown hair, singed together and coiled. Based on what was left, it was like he'd starved himself, his figure all sharp angles instead of the soft handsomeness Malice was used to.

Malice swept his hand over Kiran's eyes, closing them. He wished he could ask why he stayed when his parents found sanctuary in Florence's Region. They were some of the few who had fled to neighboring realms when presented with the option. Malice stared at the answer, forced himself to look at, *to see* Kiran, and feel something. Anything. He wanted to hurt for this, to be sorry and regret stripping Kiran of his titles. He wanted to weep and beg for the forgiveness he would never get. The moment he drank the poison, let it fester and seep into his veins was the moment he'd abandoned those emotions. He hadn't realized it till now.

"Eye for an eye," Lazarus said, his voice the equivalent of disorder in paradise. "Life for a life."

Malice caressed the side of Kiran's face one last time and rose. "I killed your commander of no relation." He faced Lazarus. "You killed my brother."

"As per our agreement," Lazarus said. "But when did we agree you would murder one of my own? Admittedly, I'm more curious as to why you did it."

"I needed information of which Amarjeet willingly gave." He met Lazarus's gaze with a snide grin. "After I cut off a few unnecessary appendages." The voident squealed like a hog, too.

Hands behind his back, the mass of shadows stalked around Malice, stopping beside Kiran's body. "So not only did you kill him, you tortured him?"

"Say the word, and I can tell you exactly what he thought of you," Malice said. "He had much to say."

"You had no right!" Lazarus snarled as he made his way back to Malice's front.

"Camaraderie doesn't suit you."

"You think I fear you?" Lazarus asked, body tense with anger. "Boy-king. Kin-slayer. It is you who ought to fear me."

"The one I feared, I killed." And there was no one Malice feared more than his mother. She was the standard of terror, the typical in nightmares. The people Malice slaughtered hadn't haunted his dreams the way Vendetta's black eyes had.

One long, jagged finger jabbed Malice's chest. "You came to me. One would think you'd be a little nicer," Lazarus chided.

"I am the son of Vendetta," Malice said, flicking the voident's finger away. "I was not raised to be kind. I was raised to hunt."

Lazarus took a step backward. "You are not hunting me today, boy."

"You're right, I'm not." Malice put a few more paces between them. "Why hunt a single sheep when I can feast upon the whole herd?"

He could feel them, a non-stop tingle in his nape. Lazarus's army was close, a few thousand strong, idle. Bones broke through the flesh of his back, the tissue morphing into wings, wet tearing noises filling Malice's ears as Lazarus reeled, turned and crawled into the nearest shadow, darkness swallowing him.

With a single flap of his wings, Malice took off, leaving a cloud of dust and debris in his wake. To the north, a little before the Lake of Zephyrus, thousands of voidents swarmed the plains and meadows like flies on a fresh pile of dung, turning the green land into a sea of black. The army was much larger than Malice anticipated. Closer to eight thousand. A hulking figure emerged at the furthest end of the cluster of darkness and started shouting, Lazarus attempting to warn his disregarding, mindless band of servants.

"Don't do this!" Lazarus pleaded. "Would you dishonor your name by fighting one whom cannot fight back?"

If he thought Malice would do anything else because of some moral he didn't have, well, that wasn't Malice's fault, now was it? He slowed to hover above the army, his wings a constant whoosh at his sides.

"Leave or stay, Lazarus," Malice said. "Die with your puppets or flee to see another day." Preferably, Malice wanted Lazarus to leave.

There was a chance if he killed Lazarus, the one ranked above him would take it as an act of war. Malice was confident in his abilities, but he knew his limit. One day, Malice would test the waters, see what it took to drive the voidents out of their holes.

Lazarus thoroughly considered based on his hesitance to flee. Malice knew how to kill a voident now. He knew how to draw it out and if Amarjeet had as much information as he had, how much was Lazarus sealing within that skull of his? How well would he hold up in comparison to his so-called comrade?

The commander vanished into the sea of shadows, gone in a heartbeat. *Wise decision.*

Closing his eyes, Malice lifted his arms. The sensation was as if his own skin was eating itself, a searing, spiking throb over every inch of flesh as darkness consumed his fingers, his wrists and forearms up to his shoulders. He inhaled, and the world seemed to freeze as the scent of blossoms, grass, earth, and salt entered his lungs. Unhurriedly, he flicked his wrists skyward.

All went still. The calm before the storm. The floating before the fall.

Sound reached him first, a slight rumble, then a strange, hollowed lament, wind hitting his feet and rushing through the rest of his body. When he opened his eyes, darkness cascaded beyond Malice's place in the sky and tore through the clouds. In the mountain of night, every single one of Lazarus's army was engulfed, became one with Malice's magic, and ceased to exist while the weight suffocating him was stolen.

Wings relaxed, Malice tilted back and plummeted, the release of his magic euphoric. Laying with Quinci was the discovery of what he'd always felt. This, free-falling from tens of miles in the air, using the full extent of his powers, was something else entirely. It was every burden and worry, all the blood on his hands, and his history being left behind for the clouds to absorb and rain upon him another day. It was the high mugwort delivered, the daze of alcohol, the thrill of running a sword through someone's person, the heat of passion. Yet, it was nothing at all; it was freedom.

As the ground grew nearer, the darkness sank with Malice. In no time, his feet touched soft grass, flowers and stalks grazing his legs, and the black wall he summoned was no more. In its place was a scar, starting at his toes and stretching beyond the border into Zeldine's region. There was nothing in front of him. For miles, the land was barren, any life shriveled and grey, the breeze turning husks to dust. Behind him, his kingdom was dead.

Acknowledgements

Compared to *The Black Throne*, *A Tale of Origins* was much tricker to write, forcing me to start over again, which created draft four (I usually stick to three). Writing from the head of a child under the age of ten, I feel, was the hardest part. Second, I struggled with figuring out what relevant information to add and where to put it. How far can I delve into this topic or character? Where can I do so? Will it be beneficial? The list of questions and doubts goes on.

There were two saving graces who kept me from yanking my hair out in frustration.

Dominique Whiton was one beta reader I invited to read book two, since she helped with book one. With her expert advice, she truly shed light on my writing errors, allowing me to better represent a child and to better get my intentions across to readers. Not only did she give honest and accurate critiques, she stuck it out despite all my tedious requests.

The second beta to read book two was Mew Clawfur. She, too, was a trooper, I must say. Like Dominique, she started from the beginning when I rewrote the entire story, highlighting where I had improved and where I still needed to improve. Her support and kind words extended to The Black Throne, being the first to review it!

Without their support, honesty, and kindness, I can confidently say *A Tale of Origins* would not be as refined as it is, nor as good. To help and give me the wonderful opportunities to read their stories is something I don't think I can ever express my gratitude enough for. Still, I want to thank these two inspiring authors, and I wish them all the luck—even more luck, actually, than they had wished me.

4. As a preteen, I wanted to become an astronomer and marine biologist solely because of my interest in deep sea life, sharks, and the abstract properties of space. I would say that it turned out just swell, wouldn't you agree? 5. Like my taste in architecture, my taste in 'fashion' is a mix of gothic Victorian, fantastical medieval, and modern cottage core. Think slutty vampire, if you will. At least, that's my *dream* wardrobe, of which I am steadily working to create. Buying from good quality stores and small businesses, however, is expensive. As is buying quality material to sew my own clothes, and it is also something I have intentions to do. 6. My favorite part of writing, besides writing itself, of course, is research. I love diving into real world cultures so I can dissect them, stitch them with the ideas from my twisted mind, creating the tapestry of my stories. Since writing this trilogy, my love for learning has been reinvigorated. I am most excited to jump head-long into Norse, African, Aztec, Greek, Japanese, and so many more mythologies so I can spice my stories with them.

I suppose my nerdy tendencies have only shifted through the years.

www.ingramcontent.com/pod-product-compliance
Lightning Source LLC
Chambersburg PA
CBHW010555310726
48969CB00009B/2433